Psyaint David:

A Concise but Reliable Narrative
of Six Months of Fun and Mayhem
in The City of the Gods

BY

WAYNE LANTER

Psyaint David

Wayne Lanter

Twiss Hill Press
Freeburg, Illinois

ISBN 13: 978-0-9838412-3-4
ISBN 10: 0983841233
LCCN: 2014941402
Twiss Hill Press
P. O. Box 122
Freeburg, Illinois 62243

Acknowledgements: Thanks to so many people who helped me with this book. Among them were Donna Biffar, Leslie Lanter, Nathan Lanter, Bobbi Page, Mary Ann Speno, and Barnett Weiss.

Cover by Donna Biffar and Bobbi Page.

For Bobbi

to those who suffered
to those who died
and
for those who grieve

Man . . . is a tame or civilized animal; nevertheless, he requires proper instruction and a fortunate nature, and then of all animals he becomes the most divine and most civilized; but if he be insufficiently or ill-educated he is the most savage of earthly creatures.
— Plato, *The Republic*

"Charles, you so smart."
"Un huh. I know what's in every book in the world."
"What's that?"
"Words."
— Brother Dave Gardner, "The Motorcycle Story."

"What does it add up to, anyway? Newspapers have sold more papers. Politicians will make more speeches. Police… will get more blame. More laws will be passed. Everybody will pass the buck. And then, next month, next year... the same thing will happen again."
"Well, maybe this will help to stop it."
"Never has."
— Truman Capote, *In Cold Blood*

Capitalism is a purely cultic religion, perhaps the most extreme that ever existed.
— Walter Benjamin

Psyaint David

A concise but reliable narrative
of six months of fun and mayhem
in the City of the Gods

Psyaint David

a killer prepares
for a fun filled night
in the Big Apple

Richard Falco pulls on his Berkowitz mask, a wig borrowed from the Wasp, takes his .44 and goes to the door. He pauses, glances over the room: crumpled potato chip bags, Coke cans, liquor bottles, news clippings — the yellowed reviews of shootings.

He thinks this may be the last night — but he's thought that before — and wonders at how simple it is.

The seventh floor of 35 Pine Street, Pineview Towers, is not the Hall of the Mountain King, and he is by no means a highland troll (Dovregubben), at least not yet, although as a creature of his own fantasy, he may now have several heads, an extra personality or two, and end up mated to the Green Lady. And had he the intelligence beyond that needed to find a victim, crouch, aim, and squeeze the trigger, he might be whistling nervously along with Peter Lorre (actually Thea von Harbou), a few bars from Grieg's *Peer Gynt Suite No. 1.*

He seems, however, mostly unaware of the stir he's caused, of the terror and madness of which he is both cause and effect, now seeping from the unconscious of The City, and basks in a warm effusive self-possession, until he comes out to the street and feels the initial assault of a bitter wind on his face.

The night is cold, the air sharp. He shrinks back, as if struck by an invisible hand, a silent blow, rubs his mouth, glances over his shoulder to the corner of the streetlight-night. He fingers the brown paper-bag with the .44, smiles weakly, excited with the possibilities of the frigid night. Encouraged, hopeful of a sign, a command, an opportunity, and filled with promise he returns to the apartment for his Peter-(Kürten)-Lorre-Hans-

Psyaint David

David-Beckert-Berk-O-Witz-Black-Belt-Epaulet-Notchcollar-Midnight-Meant-For-Murder-Brown-Imitation-Burberry.

a relatively minor attraction
   sets the theme
and tempo for the evening

Earlier, near the Williamsburg Bridge at Clymer and Division, undeterred by the chilly weather, in the failing light of late afternoon a small arena is set up, roped off. Just in from the *Divine Comedy*, and sundry venues, the boys and girls — Acedia, Avaritia, Gula, Invidia, Ira, Luxuria, and Superbia — supported by randomly selected local merchants and male-factors prepare for a bit of street theater.

A morality play evolves. Tickets are sold to passersby, quickly gathering a curious crowd seeking a causal connection of act and spirit. Heather "Bad Weather" Whitman of 65-21 Cromwell Crescent in Rego Park, Queens, dressed for success in comfortable low-heeled shoes and a classic pantsuit, made from top-quality fabric in sober, business-like colors (for that polished look), and a grey wolf faux fur coat asks, "What's happening?"

"Wait and see," she's told. "Five bucks for a ticket."

"Well," she agrees, "I suppose it's worth a chance. God knows I lost fifty on the numbers last week."

"It's an ambush," she hears from a thin, nervous man in a parka and blue Dickies.

"An ambush?"

"Yeah."

"Six tickets remain. Now only three."

"You, sir, have the last two."

At the outer edge of the sidewalk-stage, vendors appear with beer and hotdogs, Italian sweet sausages. A crap game, sheep knuckles for the sheep, erupts, spontaneously, on the sidewalk. Pickpockets and purse-snatchers move into the crowd. An organ grinder, his monkey on a rusted chain, cranks out an old tune. A fat lady, Olivia Brockmeyer, with a large feather in her Afro, and her two-headed pet dog, Orthrus Demikhov II, takes over a vacant storefront across the street.

A van of prostitutes crawls into an adjacent playground and unloads a finely fleshed cargo of camp followers in time to add a bit of pandering sauce to the elemental pudding of assault and violent death — and to make a few bucks to boot.

Bartering breaks out, trades made, deals struck, and customers go off arm-in-arm with the girls to doorways, into an alley among garbage cans and cardboard boxes. One fearsome twosome scrambles into a trash bin, and the delirious dusk pulses with the ecstasy of soft animal sounds, the impatient groans and sighs drifting street ward.

At 5:37, with the crowd primed and roiling restlessly in the frigid late day, preliminaries give way to the main event. The chorus files onto the proscenium.

Then, according to the laws of natural selection, a sacrifice to the God of Infinite Variables, an ambush develops. A no-name Everyman happens along, selected for an end already chosen for him.

Enter stage left, the next person along, later identified by police as Melvin K. Jung of 777 Washington Avenue, peddling home from work on his 26' heavy duty flamboyant red Schwinn with an electro-forged cantilever style frame, is dragged screaming from his bicycle by a trio of see-no-, speak-no-, and hear-no-evil thespians.

For ninety minutes the performance endures amid taunts and cheers from the audience, with the assailants pausing between felonious acts to quaff refreshing swills of rum and eulogize their victim in lengthy soliloquies, praising him for having the courage to ride a bicycle on a Brooklyn street.

They resurrect the historical influences of Aristotle on tragedy and while calling for good to triumph over evil, speculate on the origins in human psychology of the need for sacrifice.

Through a classical five-act structure (kidnapping, assault, battery, sodomy, and murder) they torture and violate Melvin, in the tradition of the best of urbane entertainment, hold him face down to the cold concrete, stuff his large mittens in his mouth to stifle his screams, until participants and spectators alike have exhausted their esprit malfeasant.

And then the denouement, the climax breached, they conclude the performance, offer a tribute to the state of the arts — a spate of action for five dollars, a fair price, and a decent show.

"Did you see his eyes? The way they popped when the knife went in?"

"I actually heard his dying gasp — the air leaking out of his lungs."

"Goddamn, that was better than a dozen O. J. Simpsons. Did you see him in *The Diamond Mercenaries?*"

"Poor bastard didn't know what hit him."

"Just like the rest of us."

"What'd he say?"

"Something like, 'Who are you? Why me? What did I do?'"

Well-thought-out answers, too.

"Nothing."

And, "You were just the next one along — somebody to entertain the crowd."

Souvenirs are taken: a watch and ring, his wallet with thirty-one dollars, pictures of his family, another of a girlfriend, his Social Security card, a shoelace. Apologies are made, forgiveness begged for oversights.

"We could have had an orchestra, maybe a brass sextet, an MC. Next time we'll do better."

Psyaint David

Predictably, with the exhalation of last breath, the cooling of flesh, excitement dwindles and the crowd retreats, disassembles, and drifts away homeward breathing grey-ghost puffs on the air, with the utterings of "hubris," "tragedy," the bone-bare sounds and sighs of "goat song" hung in the murk replacing the expended day.

Still, the performance is enough to whet the appetite for the evening to come, foreshadowing a better show, a rollicking romp on the town; done with savior faire, inspired, with impeccable Eustace Tilly taste; top hat, spats and cane elegance.

for the less adventurous
  a compendium of delights
on evening teevee

Along 7th Avenue, Village apartments light up. Curtains drop on the pale-blue of teevee campfires, the wizardry of elec-tech. Following the news with Bob Schieffer, the evening's fare features an all-star cast. Channel 4 serves up *The Magnificent Seven* and Yul Brynner, expressionless bald-headed badorado, wheeling about the vacuum tube of rebellion and mayhem in an Americanization of *Seven Samurai.* After *All In The Family,* the possibility for abolition is on the air; *Roots (Part VI)* with Ben Vereen, George Sanford Brown, and Lloyd Bridges. When the Civil War begins, Tom is recruited and cruelly treated. Adaption of Alex Haley's book. (Network cautions that the program deals with a mature theme.)

Channel 7 carries Evel Knievel's *Death Defiers*, with Telly Savalas (Αριστοτέλης "Τέλλυ" Σαβάλας) and Jill St. John (Magic, 36-22-35) as host and hostess. Knievel is booked to jump the world's largest saltwater pool stocked with thirteen sharks.

Experts claim the sharks are not man-eaters, although jumping thirteen of anything that resembles sharks and might possess habits even remotely similar to those of sharks, is enough to draw a crowd. Not entirely in jest, someone notes that if Evel ends up in the soup, the sharks will be mightily disappointed. Knievel is 68.3 percent stainless steel; ball joints, plates and pins.

However, bashing his head on concrete is old-flat-hat and Evel cancels and spends the evening in a Chicago hospital, banged up and suffering from a midafternoon spill. And since the show must, will go on, a pyrotechnic phenom named Orval Kisselburg (Orval the Daredevil Clown), who, instead of cars or planes or embassies, blows up chairs (The Russian Dynamite Death Chair), on which he is seated at the time, takes center stage.

Following the explosion, Orval's thirty foot tumbling blast off, and a Sealy commercial, CBS airs a syndicated live-talk, *Topics of Interests to The City.* Tonight it's Dr. Henry Armbruster, professor of Medieval History at

Columbia and First Counsel to Mayor Beame on The Metropolitan Planning Commission, discussing the "Sources of Evil in Western Society."

As town crier, court jester, the good Doctor offers a pastiche of suggestions, a tripping triptych of tripe theories. There have been historical epochs, other places, he believes (Sodom, Carthage, Salem) when, where "Conditions of social decay and corruption were sufficient to produce the embodiment, the personification of evil, and people reported seeing and conversing with a creature with horns and a tail who cannot be described as anything but the Black One, Old Scratch — yes, the Devil himself.

"Of course," Dr. Armbruster continues, tongue not altogether in cheek, but pleased with his twaddle, "we have no way to explain the source of these sightings or hallucinations, if, indeed, they are hallucinations. Obviously, these folks saw something."

Nonsense or not, the Doctor's humor is not lost on the sanguine, phlegmatic, choleric, and melancholic nightly patrol of marauding Gray Panther hostiles who have gathered outside the studio. The 10:00 news reports the Panthers, too, have intimations of serious evil in their midst, and show up in support of Dr. Armbruster with a placard and banner demonstration of *comportement de mauvais parent*. Armed with ice picks, hatpins, and pepper spray, the Panthers are preparing a search-and-destroy mission against the Black Spades, Savage Skulls, Glory Stompers, Blue Diamonds, Black Cats, and Westies gangs.

"We're launching our midwinter offensive," grizzled Panther Prince Harvey Leer tells reporters. "We've been taking too many casualties. For years, the streets have been littered with the elderly dead and wounded, the maimed. Today, that's changing. We intend to engage the enemy. Them sprouts may be younger and stronger, but we got more experience."

Harvey is especially annoyed by a row of jars behind the bar of the 596 Club (596 10th Avenue) in Hell's Kitchen of pickled and shriveled fingers of guys (over sixty-five) who crossed the Westies. Rumor has it the proprietors keep several severed hands beneath the bar to imprint weapons with fingerprints — the fingerprints of dead men — for police entertainment.

"We got a long and vicious history in the fine arts of filial warfare. No more of this bleep (bullshit) notion of the elderly as kind, gentle, wise, etc. We put young flesh on notice that if it wants its collective ass kicked, The City is the place to come, and we're the people to do it. We're prepared for a long, gory campaign."

Not to be outdone, attempting to hold its place in the ratings, the late evening Channel 31 news carries a series of local interest stories. A Queens' fruit vendor takes unexceptionally comforted from a CCTC assistant professor's observation that the environment has not changed appreciably in the Western World in a thousand years and is unlikely to change in another thousand or two. In a special interview, Carl Sagan amplifies the horror with an astronomical contention that the sun can make it another million or so years.

Clearly, relief still lies somewhat out of sight. The Cult for Organizing Paradise, on its way to a better place than this world ever was, invites teevee camera crews to the Brooklyn Bridge for exclusive coverage of its seven charter members, arranged by color — black, red, yellow, beige, white, white, and very white — going off the bridge — a plummeting daisy-chain of rainbow expiry — a row of multi-colored dominoes, inventive and failsafe, bound by leg irons and chains, just to be certain no one backs out.

Before the weather, an on-the-scene crew with handheld cameras to further accentuate documentation breaks in with a report from the Bronx. A man in his mid-thirties, tentatively identified as Harold Wiesenberger, an accountant with the national firm of Findly, Findly, Findly, Finch and Belsen, police believe, has executed his wife and two children.

At the moment, details are sketchy, but police say Mr. Wiesenberger, who has long suffered from city-trauma, reportedly spent the late afternoon and early evening with one of his bosses drinking in various bars. Sometime after 9:00, he returned home in a nasty, agitated humor. At 9:30, the neighbors report loud voices, screams, and three or four shots sounded in the apartment.

Police found Mrs. Wiesenberger in the bathroom. She has been shot in the chest with a .38 caliber revolver. The children, Mara, two, and William, four, were shot once each in the head.

The neighbors, those willing to talk to reporters (and some will not answer their doors) say they do (did) not know much about Wiesenberger, and did not know the wife. They say the kids were noisy — made too much racket. Some think the noise may have caused the trouble.

for those who wish to venture out
offerings
in the City of the Gods are limitless

By 7:00, pleasure seekers are out in droves on a live Saturday night for the time of their lives. Despite the bitterly cold night, discos fill up, the Minnesota Strip working, Times Square meccas packed with revelers. Crowds push along briskly in a turbulent, prodigious migration. Steam-phantoms rise from manholes. Reflected in rhomboids on shop windows abstract faces blowing into hands raise ghosts on the air.

Theatres abound with pop-theme plays giving the world the latest word on what's in, what's not. The MET features *Lucia Di Lammermoor.* The Bleaker Street Cinema proffers Visconti's twin bill of *The Damned,* the Von Essenbeck Nazi saga, and *Death in Venice*, a Mahler song of Mann's heart-throbbing, soul-worn tracking of the Apollonian-Dionysian presence in the choleric and death-torn city of the Rialto.

Quad Cinema offers *The Erotic Adventures of Pinocchio,* the wooden wonder snooping about for an unprotected orifice, poking his nose into nearly everybody's business.

Eve Merriam's musical entertainment, *The Club,* set in a gentleman's club in 1903, is at Circle in the Square Downtown. The company consists of seven women lightly disguised in top hats, white tie and tails, singing and dancing to authentic, indelicate songs of the period. As feminist projects go, this is unusually good-humored, and the performance — the singing, and especially the dancing — under Tommy Tune's direction, is proficient and exhilarating.

It's *The Brownsville Raid,* at Theatre de Lys, Charles Fuller's tragic drama (with considerable comedy and mystery as well) based on an actual event — the dishonorable discharge, by President Theodore Roosevelt in 1906, of three companies of crack, experienced black troops for purportedly shooting up the town of Brownsville, Texas. The production celebrates the tenth birthday of the Negro Ensemble Company, and artistic director, Douglas Turner Ward, appears in the leading role.

here the author offers
  a brief speculation
  on the sordid tale's
variegated possibilities

However, in spite of the entertainment glut, the Big Apple is unsettled, grimacing with a collective angst. The City is besieged by crime. Homicide is advancing at an alarming rate — upwards of four a day — mostly young women. Rumor has it the ghost of the Saturnalia (Saturn in opposition on February 2 on the borders of Cancer and Leo, and in conjunction on August 13) has infiltrated the subways, alleys, sulks in darkened obscure places. Sightings are reported in Queens, several in Brooklyn.

The crowds that crowd the streets, Broadway, Times Square, the individuals moving through Central Park and the boroughs, drift, uneasily, silently, always on edge.

Is it the lunatic fringe? Aliens inhabiting the moon? Could it be the heralding of the Jupiter Effect? It is said good things come from Jupiter. However, this is more like a virus, a parasite, an energy force, magnetic fields in conflict. What does the Man in the Moon say? What or who is it?

A cadre of spiritual misanthropes?
The Genesee River Killer?
The Backstreet Butcher?
The Jolly Black Widow?
Mad Dog Taborsky?
The Moon Maniac?
Blue Jaw Magoon?

Psyaint David

Aaron Kosminski?
George Metesky?
The Mad Hatter?
The Black Hand?
Fritz Haarmann?
Carl Grobmann?
White Handers?
Lupo the Wolf?
Mad Dog Coll?
Peter Kürten?
Hostileman?
Karl Denke?
The Joker?

Peter Lorre
prepares
for his role in *M*

Still, the show will open on schedule off Broadway. László Lowenstein, aka Peter Lorre, paces his dressing room, scowls, pages through the script, contorts his face, his bug-eyes larger now, mouth agape, jaw slack. His costume dangles like a ghostly corpse from a hook on the back of door; brown overcoat, wig, a Charter Arms Bulldog Special .44 in a paper bag in the coat pocket.

He drifts in and out of character, his history, marking milestones of comic selfishness and madness in *The Recruits of Ingolstadt, The Lost Ones.* He explores old-role personages, created, lived, short-lived then abandoned, tumbling through the thickets of twisted minds and knotted hearts. He imitates Cairo's cunning whine, among the emotional nuances, behind the mask, sheathed in the voice of villainy and perdition that drifts into the deep space blackhole beneath the arch. He searches patiently, thumbs through the insinuations of impulse, the responses to the doppelganger of *Mörder Unter Uns, M — Eine Stadt sucht einen Mörder.*

What will he have for this role? An insidious little man with bulging eyes? Or maybe a con artist posing as a detective to gain access to victims.

and David,
or someone
who might be David,
speaks for himself

I park at Greenway Terrace and begin walking. A wall clock inside a pizza shop shows 11:35, and by 12:15
I am near the Long Island Railroad tracks. It is extremely cold and my

Burberry, which
    I pretend is a thin jacket, is not much protection.
    I am about to return to my car when
    I see them for the first time coming toward me. As we pass our shoulders almost touch.
    I gaze into her eyes, her face, and know immediately she is the one.
    I breathe a lover's sigh. The voice of love whispers to me, "Get her. Get her."
    I am ready.
    I follow at a distance through the Long Island Railroad underpass and step sleuth-like behind a small Norway Maple which is not large enough to hide me.
    I am an illusion.
    I remember Kitty Genovese and Kew Gardens. No one wants to see me.
    I see them get into their blue car and the demons begin again.
    I know they are impatient. "Get her. Get her."
    I hear the engine running and
    I walk up from behind.
    I want her.
    I have not been told to kill him.
    I don't like males.
    I love pretty girls.
    I stand in front of the car and crouch.
    I bring the gun up with two hands.
    I aim for her head, quick and effective.
    I know practice makes perfect.
    I fire three shots. All
    I need.
    I am able to control the gun.
    I see the glass fly into the car.
    I hit her.
    I know
    I hit her.
    I just want her, nothing more.
    I only use three of the five rounds.
    I have no reason to use more.
    I have to save my ammunition.
    I run to my car.
    I am far away.
    I have a long run.
    I pass the Long Island Railroad station.
    I hear a car horn blowing.
    I hear a man screaming.
    I am far away.

Psyaint David

I know she is dead.
I hear voices:
>"Slay him.
>Sam's son has killed
>The King's daughter!
>Slay him!
>Slay him!
>Cut off his fingers.
>Pull out his hair.
>Boil him in oil.
>Roast him on a spit.
>Slay him" (Ibsen).

Then the voices abate.
"I wait five minutes before starting the car. After the shooting, I think I might weep for some of the people killed. But I can't. It is all puzzling, you know."

**the inspector hears of mayhem
and commits his magnificent
deductive mind to the enigmatic**

So flames fly, screams fill the air. The hollow haunting of a car horn, a clarion of malevolence, trumpets the frigid night. The great cloak-wings of fear spread wide, ride the cold, diablerie, an inky cloud shrouding the crumbling tenements, the lower confines of metropolis, elevating the metaphor of The City of the Gods to a common, senseless horror. Indeed, *Eine Stadt sucht einen Mörder.*

A 5:00 dawn flickers in on a 19" black-and-white, the picture drifting with horizontal distortion. The sirens have faded, lights dimmed, the furor subsided. Over the East River, over the city, a pale sun rises in the mist, carrying intimations of Florey's *Murder in the Rue Morgue.*

A camera dollies down to a medium-shot along the corridor of Elmhurst Hospital in Queens, then focuses on the regal, refined persona of the nocturnal Inspector with his *Chinatown* nose. Smoke from his exalted Calabash circles slowly in the will-o'-the-wisp glow of the gaping red-gray eye of a sooted window facing the latest dawn.

A sidekick waves to his comrade and chief, aka Zadig ou la Destinée, Wolfe, Wimsey, Telly (Τέλλυ), Spade, Poirot, Marlowe, LoKoJakMan, LoKo, Lohmann, Lestrade, Lecoq, Vidocq, Kojack, Holmes, Hammer, Dupin, Dalgliesh, Charles (Charalambides), Carella, et al. — as well as a mix of many of the above. Nothing of West, Bane or Peel here — at least not yet.

"Over here, Inspector," the sidekick calls.

"What have we today?" the Inspector inquires, his well-trained elegant and seasoned voice caressing the corridor's deep silence.

"Another shooting. Just after midnight. She was in the front seat with her boyfriend."

Super Sleuth removes his Calabash and studies it pensively, wondering about the quality of the tobacco, if it is tobacco.

"Out on lover's lane, no doubt."

"No. Not this time."

"That is a pity. You know, lovers' lane mysteries are the best. Ah. Yes, indeed.

"Is it autumn?"

"No, Inspector. It's January. The end of January."

"Autumn would be better. Ah, autumn, she is magnifique, and autumn in Paris in my memory is a match made in heaven, as lovers sometimes are."

"Paris? Why Paris. This is The City. It's January."

"It has to do with my French nature. You know, we French are incurable romantics. As Alexander Sergeyevich Pushkin tells in *The Captain's Daughter,* 'The Captain's daughter was reading French novels and, therefore, was always in love.'"

He pauses wistfully.

"Ah, but yes. I have it. It comes to me now. Memory taunts us. We forget, then remember, and the heart grows sad with melancholy. When someone leaves us, it is as if they have condemned us to invisibility in their life. If we should hear about them or see their picture, even if they are alive, it is no better than memory. Mnemosyne, mother of the muses, will not forgive us, but hold them deep in the night of our longing."

He pauses, drifting down center stage with Monsieur Lecoq, mumbling.

the inspector
  (as an historical type)
  reminisces with melancholy
on a very special affair

"Fool that I was!

"Said to myself, thousand times a fool to have hoped, to have believed, that she would ever love me. Madman! How could I have dared to dream of possessing so much grace, nobleness, and beauty? How charming she was that evening! Could anything be more angelic? What a sublime expression her eyes had in speaking of . . .! How she must have loved . . .! And I? She loves me as a father. She told me so — as a father! And could it be otherwise? Could she see a lover in a somber and severe looking constable, as sad as his black coat? Was it not a crime to dream of uniting that virginal simplicity to my detestable knowledge of the world? For her, life is yet the land of smiling chimeras; and long experience had dissipated my illusions. She is as young as innocence, and I am as old as vice (Emile Gaboriau).

"You see, one autumn, my most memorable, involved just such a case as this. I had been dejected for some months over a small but salient financial misfortune, the type of irritant that lingers at the edge of the mind and dulls, ever so slightly, even the most enjoyable moments. I had gone to Montmartre to inquire of a friend about the exact location of the offices of her broker, a certain Monsieur L' Amount, the foremost financial wizard in all of France.

"The ride over had been intoxicating, the sun painting a brilliant hue on the crisp afternoon, and I was lost in thought as I climbed the stairs to her apartment. I rang not once, but twice, without thinking, and suddenly imagined myself in the wrong place, having chosen and entered a building only similar to the one I sought, when a woman I had never before seen answered the door. I was surprised, not only by the appearance of an unexpected face, but by a most beautiful and enchanting countenance. She was, as we say, exquisite. Ah, yes, and fashionable red hair and sultry green eyes that were raised ever so slightly at the corners.

— Excuse me, I said, fully aware by then that I had blundered but had no reason to regret my error or to seek hurriedly to correct it. I am inquiring for Madam R___. I was sure she resided at this residence, although I must admit, if I am mistaken, I would prefer not to know where the mistake came.

— You have come to the right place, but at the wrong time, she said and smiled warmly. Madam R___ left yesterday by rail for Nice. I am Mademoiselle C___.

"If my misfortune had mounted in seeking escape and solace from troubled finances, I could not but take hope in the playful tone of her greeting. Her voice as Helen's own, a fully mature blend of experience and confidence that so taunts the male mind in remembrance and dream to add ambiguity and fascination to even the most casual encounter."

— My misfortune in not finding Madam R___ has been meliorated, I am pleased to say, ever so much, by your presence.

— You are, no doubt, the renowned Inspector Lecoq-Dupin.

— Indeed, you are correct.

— Madam R___ has told me a great deal about you. Would you care to step in?

"She led me to the parlor where I had spent many afternoons with my friend Madam R___ and her paramour Monsieur Q___. The memory of those meetings was hardly with me now, so utterly did my lovely companion brighten that musty, dim, sad room.

"For the next hours we conversed at length on art, music, and philosophy — taking great care not to touch upon the indelicate opinions of religion and politics. Later in the conversation, she queried me about the methods and processes of police acuity.

— I have always been interested, Monsieur, in how the police conduct investigations. Their methods for solving crimes seem to me truly ingenious.

— The police, Mademoiselle, are merely an extension of the populace and use methods not unlike those most use to conduct their daily affairs.

— Inspector, you are too modest. I should think a man of your acumen would know a great deal more about the criminal mind than would someone with a mind no better than mine.

— Ah, ha. Just so. But the criminal lurks within each of us, waiting for the proper moment to spring loose, to be set free. It is a part of our psyche to which most pay no particular heed. I have learned to listen to its advice.

— But would you not say that to solve a crime you would have to think not like the criminal, going from one foul part of his hideous deeds to another, but as a man tripping through a forest following a trail that seems to be vanishing behind him as he goes?

"Before I knew it, the afternoon had escaped and dusk shaded the day. I tried to excuse myself, but she insisted I join her for dinner. We dined at seven, sipped an aromatic Bordeaux until shortly after midnight and then retired.

"The following morning I returned to my quarters, certainly not a richer man, having failed to discover the information after which my mission had taken me, but now a bit wiser, and, for the first time, thoroughly entangled in the intemperate thicket of amour.

"We met regularly after that, three or four times a week and on weekends. We met mostly at the Les Deux Magots and then Café Belnoir in mid-afternoon. I would arrive by carriage and take a table at the corner of the terrace, nearest the arbor and order whisky à l'eau. Minutes later, punctually, she would appear. I would see her first through the arbor and lattice of those truly intoxicating autumnal days. She possessed such grace I imagined the breeze guided her steps, giving a gentle, lilting elegance to her footfalls.

"She would see me and smile a most charming, welcome smile, and as she made her way through the tables, would sometimes pause to greet an acquaintance, and not forgetting for a moment that I was waiting — quickly, she'd excuse herself and make straight away for my table.

— Bonjour, Monsieur Inspector.

"She had learned that I preferred, in public, to be addressed by my proper title."

— Bonjour, Madam.

— You have been waiting long?

— Non. Not so long except as it was without you.

"In the warm afternoons, each day her beauty was even more intoxicating than I remembered. As if some detail had been added, or was now just brought to my attention, I found my eyes unwilling to leave her.

"That day she had paused to converse with a gentleman I had not seen before. He had silver-grey hair and a fine salted moustache and was dressed quite well, as you might say, in the fashion of the times. I had to assume he was a distinguished Parisian."

— You have friends here? I said.

"She had only just been seated and the question, as unexpected as it was, seemed to annoy her.

— Not exactly, she said with a note of irritation. An acquaintance, certainly. Jean and I met in Marseilles in 19_.

"My question marked clearly the point at which our liaison entered onto a different path. The hollow echo of her voice filled my head with what I had long ago learned to identify as a sure sign the speaker wishes to avoid the truth. I knew nothing about her, but assumed the best because of her friendship with Madame R___.

"I deduced later, after bitter contemplation, that my words had awakened a lingering disappointment, stirred an improvident memory or admission, and understood finally that she could not ignore my blunder.

— Yes, he is handsome. I suppose I . . ., she paused, then continued.

— But it is sometimes better to leave certain matters untouched.

— Indeed, memory may be dangerous, I chided.

"She did not respond, and moments later excused herself and without ordering left immediately the precincts of Café Belnoir, leaving me alone and deeply troubled with my flippant prodding.

"That week I attempted to contact her repeatedly but did not succeed until Friday afternoon."

— It is necessary, I told her, that I beg your forgiveness for the indelicacy of my remarks. Little did I know my natural curiosity, although touched with a bit of envy, would offend you.

"She granted the forgiveness I sought and consented to a rendezvous the following evening at Diabolique, a secluded brasserie on La Rive Gauche.

"The night was alive with the first chill of winter and we passed the evening chatting quietly, renewing our affections. As enchanted as I was with the soft vitality of her presence, I sensed, now, an aloof, distant intonation to her words, which I assumed emanated from deep within and reflected the true puissance of her sensitive nature.

— Monsieur Inspector, she said, addressing me in the most formal of all formal manners, I must on the morrow journey to London on an important matter, and cannot say with certitude when I will return or if we will meet again.

"I heard her words but did not fully understand their import. And though I feigned indifference and unaffected acceptance, as one might surmise, I was wounded grievously by her pronouncement.

"Ah. But how insightful she was. True to her word, and my dismay, we did not meet again. Even today, I find I cannot easily revisit the details of our parting. But that night, a most terrible night of storms and ill-fortune, a most wicked villain stole into her apartment and committed her to the hideous annuals of unsolved crimes.

"Yes. She was murdered in her bed, and two days later I was assigned the case, not because I desired it, but, again, by misfortune — because another inspector had to attend to his invalid mother.

"However it was, I took the case with vigor. I lost myself in the facts, in the investigation, as intoxicated with her absence as I had been with her presence, maddened with the hunt for the tueur of this most lovely woman. But without success. Times too often over the next years, I would be certain I had the fou in sight, and needed only to reach out and grasp him by the collar, when he would turn a corner and disappear — into a mist, the recherché — vanish as if a ghost.

"My diligence notwithstanding, the case remained unsolved, in the cold file. It preyed on my mind for years. Even today, tonight, I can feel the deep wound of her absence. The mystery of her going."

"Okay, Inspector, but what does that have to do with this case?"

"Romance. Intrigue. Deceit. All matters of the heart. The clandestine and evil. Yes, a four-pipe problem."

"Then you suspect a love triangle? A jealous lover killed your friend?"

"Ah, ha. A triangle within a triangle."

"That would make a six-pointed star."

"Oui. Just so. And it has to do with what has transpired tonight."

"You know something about the case."

"Certainement! Are people not the same the world over? Do we not know them in the depths of our minds as we know the elements of spring?

"But do not mistake the obvious for the obscure. This is a lover's triangle. I have it well in mind. But as you shall see, although Mademoiselle F___ did write a letter to M. D___'s German lover Frauline G___, telling her to, how do you say, to 'Knock it off, sweetheart,' as with most lovers' lane slayings this will not be explained by such intrigue. We will find that Frauline G___ is guiltless. She could not have gotten to Forest Hills and returned to Germany so quickly, where she is at this moment preparing to attend a symphony."

"Germany? Inspector, this wasn't on lovers' lane or in Germany. Nothing about Germany."

"Non, non, my impetuous friend. It is most unlikely that a young woman of her education and background would conceive or devise such a plan."

He gazes out into the new dawn, a faraway cast to his eyes.

"Then I should refer you to the case of Monsieur G___ in the year 19___ when I was called upon, as you might imagine, instructed by the reputed rigors of my powerful deductive reasoning to investigate and expose a misanthrope in a case thoroughly similar to this one. The case of M. G___ was not on lover's lane either, though I imagined, for the sake, not of argument and idle speculation, but for the romance of mystery alone, that it was. I reconstructed the sordid affair, down to the murder scene with the villain holding his victim by the throat and slashing her with most indelicate strokes, as if it were on lovers' lane — a rather brilliant innovation on my part that led straight away to the perpetrator."

"This was in Forest Hills. They were waiting for the car to warm up in front of the Forest Hills Inn."

"Ah, yes. So you've said. A pity Forest Hills does not have a lovers' lane."

The Inspector wags wisely, an irrepressible glint of sagacity in his eyes, a not-so-perfect example of Le Chevalier C. Auguste Dupin's *ratiocination,* using the method of Zadig in his quest. Nevertheless, for a moment he is the epitome of Dupin, emphasizing forensics not so much in the validity of the inference, as in the quality of the observation, extoling the power of the spoken word.

Of course, he has read Poe and knows that when Dupin questions a man about a murder, the man's ". . . face flushes up as if he is struggling with suffocation . . . the next moment he falls back into his seat, trembling violently, and with the countenance of death itself."

More than that, he is master of the media. Media accounts of crime pique his curiosity and allow viewers, who follow his adventures, to discover the clues for themselves.

"Yes, you see, murder is so horrible it will be easy enough to see and hear the killer," the Inspector says.

"Abductive, not deductive, Inspector. The perp is merely an assailant. The girl isn't dead yet."

"Ah, yes. I see. Well, let us suppose, for speculation purposes, that the lovely young woman is dead. You'd have to agree that an assailant would not shoot someone that enticing unless he intended to murder her."

"Maybe he wanted to wound her."

"Ah, ha. You are observant. He did just that. But isn't it true in your experience that even when an assailant intends to kill, wounding occurs more often than killing? And isn't it true that many times someone is killed with no intent to wound?"

"Yes, I suppose so."

"Then, would you not agree that if the girl is merely wounded the assailant is, no doubt, un tueur?"

"I'd have to agree with that."

"Of course logic would suggest the boyfriend M. D__ had nothing to do with it. Since he was in the front seat and the fusillade came from outside the car, he did not see anything or anyone. Indeed, it is quite mysterious, but understandable, and fairly obvious that he did not see le stalker de nuit because of amour — and because the car windows were frosted up."

"Can you be certain?"

"Certainement. For a very long time now forensic psychology has understood the phenomena of selective perception. Experiments have shown, to an intelligent observer's satisfaction, that when witnesses are involved in a crime, victimized by it, they see less than if they are merely standing by. Standersby see even less, since most are involved with some other inconsequential thought at the time they witness what they do not see of the crime."

"And this will expose the killer?"

"Yes. It is the perceptions we select that will make the tueur appear."

"Have you ever dreamed of killing someone?

"What more did M. D___ report?"

"He had the shit scared out of him. And I don't mind telling you that if someone smokes three big ones into the front seat where I'm sitting, I'm gonna be shitless, too. He says he couldn't get anybody to help. Ran his car out into the intersection at 71st Avenue and Burns Street and sat there blowing the horn."

The Inspector concurs.

"Have you informed Santucci of this?"

"No."

"Well, it would be best not to involve the District Attorney. For although we have not seen the assassin, he is readily identifiable. That which first in thought is next in sight. We don't know what he might dream up. This is a three-point-three-four pipe problem, maybe four."

"Inspector, do you not think it preposterous to claim that a creature, a miscreant no one has seen is readily identifiable?"

"Ah, yes. Possibly. But I did not say he (notice I said 'he') had never before been seen. You see, the times of the attacks indicate that the villain prefers nocturnal sorties and is nocturnal by nature and is therefore accustomed to the night. For even though most attacks occur in isolated areas, away from direct light, he has demonstrated remarkable accuracy."

"He can see in the dark?"

"He is a creature that prowls invisibly in the night."

"A Werewolf. Lycanthropy?"

"Just so. The lack of light and frosted windows in M. D___'s car do not explain why the predator was not seen or, once his sordid deed done, how he disappeared so effortlessly."

"So the antagonist could be a shapeshifter?"

"Therianthropy. The assailant takes on an animal form, which explains why those first to arrive on the scene report hearing a dog or some other such canine whine or snarl, and seeing a black form with red eyes shining in the depths of an alley, wooded area or other concealed, secluded spots. He did not drop his ears or wag his tail. At times, the grisly animal in him turns out, and when he is finished with his reprehensible deed, it turns again inward, making him invisible.

"Indeed, he seeks the spirits of young women, preferring the delicacy of blushing female flesh to that of any other variety. Such taste must of necessity be acquired or cultivated. Where else than in the age-old ancient ritual of sacrificing virgins and taking on their life-sustaining sustenance?

"The annals of crime document the need for man to enhance his spirit, inflate his courage, and generally placate fear by consuming the flesh of fierce, respected enemies. This inverted hero-worship has been noted throughout the world in savages who debase themselves by eating humans. In one well-known case the Countess Bathory of the Imperial Court of Vienna, to enhance her beauty and preserve her youth, daily bathed in the blood of slain virgins.

"The durations between the predator's appearance (even though he is not seen), indicates he kills only when his yearnings weaken his resistance to temptation and excite him to a homicidal, famished frenzy.

"This can only be explained by lycanthropy. This is indeed the hour of the wolf. But do not despair."

The Inspector clicks his teeth.

"Quiet minds cannot be perplexed or frightened but go on in fortune or misfortune at their own private pace, like a clock during a thunderstorm."

Detective Bobby Crocker is amazed.

"Ah, c'mon Lou. You're guessing, again. You haven't got a clue."

"Reason will save us," the Inspector says. "The human mind is a wonderful thing — a tool capable of unlimited applications and manifestations."

"But it's not in the script. At least not those I've seen. So what are you saying? I mean, you're Greek, not French, just an American-Greek actor." Crocker shakes his head. "You're not French. And what's with the Pollok name? You're a lot closer to László Inke than you think."

"Ahh! But you see, it is possible that ma grand-tante on my mother's side was married to a Frenchman from Toulouse. As I was saying, we French, in the power of our most vigorous minds, love, I dare say, respect, nothing more than fabrication. We expect man to act as the supreme creature he is. We romantics love nothing if we do not love the enigmatic. Yes, romance and murder are enigmatic.

"Is it not true that love, jealously, anger, not to mention lust, and the vagaries of carnal desire, can lead to uncontrollable impulses, freeing the vile, and the fascinating and depraved side of man's nature? The best way to find uncontrollable impulses is through the imagination.

"My observant friend, we have to begin somewhere. It doesn't hurt to pretend. Why I know thousands of people who pretend all the time. And most of them do all right with it. That's all we do, anyway. Why, Wall Street is 90 percent pretense."

At the end of the hall the blimp-like Stavros, frizzy headed Demosthenes, Heathcliff, Fatso, Brother George, bumbling, comes on camera.

"Murder, now, Inspector," he says. "She's dead."

the disciple returns
  to his
seven-storied mountain

After a stop at an all-night diner in Queens for a cheeseburger and a
Coke, Lykaon's nocturnal protégé returns to his Pineview Home of the
Mountain King. At 4:33 he rides the elevator to the seventh floor, pads
along the hall, carrying the .44 in a brown paper bag, and turns the key in
the lock. Inside he drops the bag on the chair and bolts the door. The edges
of the blankets over the windows are stained with the first light of day.

He snaps on the teevee, clicks over to *Kojak* and waits with the electronic
guns humming full-force for the light to form in the cathode-ray tube. He
relaxes, relieved from the tension of search and kill. His leg aches
pleasantly where he banged it on a fireplug while sprinting back to the car.

Satisfied that he has made it in time, with nothing to do but watch and
wait for the reviews in the papers, the news on the radio, he peels off his
Hans Beckert mask and yellow wig, falls into a chair, feet up, takes the .44
Charter Arms Bulldog Special from the brown bag, fondles it, holds it up,
then removes the spent cartridges.

This is his magic, his wand. He reads the stamp on the barrel. "Charter
Arms Corp. Stratford. Conn." He holds it out, likes the weight, the feel and
balance. It has a wild-west Boot Hill aura about it. He bought the weapon
in Houston, which makes it special, gives it a special appeal. The 1876
Merwin Hulbert 1st model pocket-army revolvers, with the skullcrusher
butt, and the Colt SAA Peacemaker were both .44s.

> Here lies the body of Lester Moore
> Shot with five slugs from a .44
> No Les(s)   No Mo[o]re
>   (Boothill Graveyard)

Designed by Doug McClenahan, founder of Charter Arms Corp., the Bulldog is an inexpensive, serviceable, no-frills, snub-nosed revolver known
for its rugged reliability and stopping power, a versatile weapon for
personal or home protection.

A solid framed double-action revolver with a five-round cylinder, it can
be opened by pushing a release slide on the left of the weapon, or in the
original model, by pulling the ejector rod. The trigger pressure required
to discharge the Bulldog, in both single and double-action modes, is
minimal. If residue accumulates inside the revolver because of heavy
usage, the cylinder cranes axle screw can be removed and the cylinder
pulled out of the gun for cleaning. This is a convenient time-saver for
modern day users on the run or who do not have time to waste.

The Bulldog can be concealed easily because of its small size, and has no sharp edges to impinge access when carrying the weapon in a holster or a pocket (or a bag). With a barrel length of 3" the .44 Special is one of the larger, more manageable revolvers used for concealed carry.

Most critics believe the Bulldog is best employed for self-defense. This safe, reliable revolver is powerful enough for serious home protection, but has the size and weight for effective concealed carry. This is an outstanding double-duty weapon, designed to kill and maim.

The teevee warms up and after ten minutes of commercials — Chicken Lickin', Salvo, Crisco, Serta, Ford and Chevrolet — *Kojak* opens at St. John's Hospital in Elmhurst with a medium shot of a victim being wheeled in on a gurney, the motionless form wrapped in a white blanket. Several plain-clothes detectives huddle at the far end of the hall.

Now he is humming. He made it back in time for the beginning. He's fascinated with the bright lights, sirens wailing, police cars, ambulances — the wonders of technology. He fingers the blue steel barrel, the rosewood grip, and slips in three new cartridges.

"I am literally singing to myself," he reminds the police later. "The tension, the desire to kill a woman had built up in such explosive proportions that when I finally pulled the trigger, all the pressures, all the tensions, all the hatred vanishes, dissipates — but only for a short time."

What's he singing?

"It's a Barnum and Bailey world . . .."

After *Kojak*, he drifts into *Bugs Bunny* and *Roadrunner,* but dozes off in the middle of a Mattel Big Wheels' ad.

a killer reflects on his ride
  through the dreams
of the valley of death

> A bold young man from The City
> Thought his sexual life was quite shitty.
> So he conjured up Sam,
> Took a gun in his hand,
> And went looking for girls that were pretty.

I'm driving, gazing at the lights, counting and multiplying by four hundred and ninety, which is the average number of bulbs in a sign, watching the marauders walk stiff-legged, staring at the night. Red stoplights blink at me — they know — they know

I know — and two blocks from Times Square

I roll up the window to keep out the smells — especially the prostitutes. It is dangerous to breathe the night air. You learn about The City — the stench. No matter where you are — the time of day, it smells like a sick dog on a manure pile. It comes up slowly, though strangers never notice. They concentrate on the bright lights. It takes an educated nose to appreciate what is beneath the perfumes and other stuff. It's the prostitutes. That's why

I roll up the windows. You tell yourself it will go away or that you will get used to it. But that does not happen. Sometimes

I lose track of where

I am — forget to remember and then right in the middle of thinking or crying or wanting something, it comes back — in my throat and before

I can think it away.

I'm sick. That's what happens tonight. Coming up Broadway at West 40th Street

I count the lights, making up for the ones

I missed last time, when

I see the first fiend of the night. The light at 7th Avenue is bright red and a woman with white hair and a dog — a large black, slick-haired dog — is standing on the corner. They are dressed in matching outfits — identical colors.

I do not want to get sick again — then

I smell the old woman and her mongrel. She signals for a taxi and gets in with her dog. On 43rd Street a tall, thin light-skinned nigger with a large hat, lipstick, a tight skirt and platform heels shakes his/her derrière across the green light. A taxi driver almost runs over the him/her, and hammers on the horn

I roll down the window to let out the stench.

I pretend the outside air is fresh, but

I know it is fouled and poisoned. It is fouled by the fires — pools of sulfur burning on the corners. Steam from sewers — the underworld under the underworld. Bursting veins, sinews snapping, bones burned black in fires.

I remember something no one else knows and my stomach feels better. It is 1:10 Times Square time and night-stalkers are filling up the porn shops. Whores in hallways, in cars, are turning tricks — people screwing and drinking, pretending they are happy. How many copulations a day? A woman with torn clothes crawls from an alley. A crowd gathers to watch and cheer as she tries to get to her feet. They make filthy remarks, point out that her act is definitely "Off Broadway." A man asks who is in charge of her wardrobe. She mutters something about needing help. They laugh and agree that if she is going to make it big she needs a great deal of help. She is bleeding, her thighs splattered, and falls again. The crowd takes pity on her. Several toss coins on the sidewalk. An old woman in a brown coat and red hat bends down, touches her hand. On the street, the crazies wander about in groups of two and three bumming cigarettes and money for wine.

I watch them and wish my eyes were a machine gun.

I could wipe them out. Fatality gives meaning to life. Are you washed in

— in what? Dying is bad if you think you will live forever. Or if you're a miser, wanting to hoard life and pleasure, wanting more. It has to do with the lights and stench, the sirens and horns, screeching sirens and horns yelling for attention with the flashing lights. Red means stop, green means go, but no one stops for red. Sometimes the lights stay yellow all night like campfires or a long line of suns coming up in the fog.

I pretend to be happy.

I smile at those watching me and they frown, wondering what trick

I have played on them. Two heavy men with long overcoats, hulking like large specters on the corner approach me.

I smile at them and they pull up their collars to hide their eyes. But

I can see through the coats.

I can see the red spots of their eyes. Before

I can roll up the window,

I hear a voice next to me. "Guided tours. Times Square. Five dollars. See girls. Good pussy. Good fucking. What you say, friend?"

I turn to a little man. He is dressed in a black leather coat and a gaucho hat with fringe on the brim.

I cannot see his eyes, but his lips curve back over his teeth. "Good price. Ten dolla' piece ah ass."

I shake my head. It is 10 degrees. The wind blowing. The tip of my nose is cold and he turns to another car, then makes it to the curb as the light changes.

I am pushed along by the flood. The street is a river. It is flooded with cars bobbing and weaving. They are caught on a current. My car is a capsule and

I am a space traveler on a foreign planet.

I keep a close watch on the aliens, ready in a moment to protect my crew, to save them. A crowd waits at the curb. Fires burn on corners, in barrels, against the curb — old mattresses, rags left on the street. Newsvendors warm their hands and stamp their feet. They don't know. Do they read the papers? Then before

I can yell, my right arm is numb and

I can feel a sharp pain in my side. Then it comes to me and

I know why they are here. It says, Welcome to The City, one of the most exciting cities in the world! Its 319.8 square miles include five boroughs — Queens, the largest — Brooklyn, the best-known — the Bronx (nothing exceptional about the Bronx), Richmond, and Manhattan. More than eight million people live here, in this, the world's most popular vacation spot. Small wonder it has become a year-round vacation center, for no other city anywhere offers so much. Here is headquarters for the best in Theatre, Music, The Dance, Museums, Fabulous Hotels and Motels, Shopping, Restaurants and practically everything else. The City is also the financial and business capital of the United States and the nerve center of American progress. Over three and a half million are gainfully employed in manufacturing plants, banking and finance.

I have seen the map. They bought the book and came here with cameras and tote bags to search for souvenirs. Tomorrow they will go to the Guggenheim or Lincoln Center to avoid the dog shit and garbage piled in the streets. They are moving, talking with their hands — walking as if they are not touching the sidewalk. But

I am prepared. My bulletproof chamber will not admit a sound. The temperature inside my spaceship is 397 degrees centigrade.

I am ready — my eyes straight ahead so they won't notice that

I have seen them. That is how they do things. You have to pretend not to notice them and when they think you are not watching they sneak up. Jesus! Three of them are women, foul-smelling hags, with bats' wings and coal-black skin. Their faces and lips are painted red, their eyes dripping — one, small, with a long neck and a bird-beak nose. But

I float away and watch in the rearview mirror and they stop at the curb with their great round eyes and pointed ears, moving their mouths, baring their teeth. They are trying to steal what

I know. To throw them off

I wave to a cop.

I smile to let him know that he can trust me. His eyes are two white slits shining like stars. When they see the cop, they start screaming and hissing and prowl back and forth along the sidewalk. They are trapped by the river. They do not know why they are here or why they are screaming at me or why the steam from the sewers bubbles in the street. They are howling demons of night. The cop smiles. He knows.

I hear sirens. A thousand at a time.

I have faith in god.

I trust him and have asked him to make me strong and to protect me from evil. It is written god shall protect his children from evil.

I have written

I prowl like a roaring lion, seeking someone to devour. The streets are rivers leading to swamps and

I ask god to part the rivers, to carry me through the swamps. But the lights come on in a single flash. It is important to think you are happy. Someday

I will walk across the rivers and the lights will go off and

I'll be able to see what's behind the bulbs, the secrets hidden in the lights and how to understand. Point number two to remember from King Wicker's Book of Foul Deeds. Light penetrates the brain and brings in sin. The thief comes only to kill and destroy. This is the plan.

I laugh at the plan.

I have been sent to collect the sins and show everyone how light brings it in.

Psyaint David

I read eyes.
I get my signs from eyes.
I peer into eyes and get my signs from them.
I can tell by their color, by the way they are shaped.
I know the drug-peddlers are out tonight.
I can tell who they are.

I see their wide wings and necks and beaks. They have claws, and feathers on their large bellies to keep them warm. They are not dope peddlers but cops, pretending to sell dope as a cover for what they are really doing. They are testing us, searching for communists or foreigners who plan to destroy The City.

I guard Manhattan. It is a giant pinball machine, lights blinking, flippers flapping. It will tilt and slide into the East River and sink like the great ship Titanic on a video-game with the Trade Towers sparking and smoking as they go under. They are angry because of the cold, and flap their wings. When they screech it sounds like sirens. That is why

I live in Yonkers and hunt in Queens. In The City jungle
I hunt only for big game.
I am Jim Corbett.
I'm no fool.
I am no maniac.
I am a hunter.
I do not run through alleys to get away. The police don't know me. My mother doesn't know me.
I do not know her. She says 'Who are you?' and
I say 'Who are you?'
I am the giver and taker. The soul of the wasp with the stinger. The King Wicker with his flashing sticker.
I am the heart that Theodopolous Kapsalis Kojak seeks, the Son of Dis, and he is just a schmuck with a teevee show.
I watch him and guess how he is going to solve the case. Usually, he is wrong. He is still chasing Ricky Robles. Most of the time he gets the wrong person.
I am also looking for the killer.
I know how killers think.
I come from a long line of killers.
I am King David.
I am the King of Diamonds
I will find the killer.
I've called Kojak with advice, and his answering service says he is out on a case — and
I can leave my name and number and he will be glad to return my call if
I can help.
I say, "What is his case now?"

the lieutenant manages to adjust
his image to more modern personae

On the waterfront, the American Dream smolders in Hell's fire-barrels. Perplexed, chagrined, the Lou is taking heat from the critics and his Nielsen ratings have slipped. Even before anyone knows a serial killer is loose, word has it the trouble comes out of Manhattan South, his beat, his nightmare, possibly the 11th or 9th precinct. The City murder rate is running randomly at five a day. Whispers in the hall, gossip, hearsay imply that as a derivative of Baretta (You can take dat to da bank, cuz dat's the name of dat tune), "Dirty" Callahan, Lestrade (a little sallow rat-faced, sallow-eyed, fellow — a lean ferret-like man, furtive, and sly-looking), J. J. "Jake" Gittes (average height, with straw-colored hair, a beaked nose, and a vaguely foolish face), Mannix, Rockford, Tibbs, Vargas, he should have collared a cell full of perps by now, and stuck it on someone.

However, he hasn't made a collar in two weeks. In an early afternoon meeting, the boss wants to know what he is going to do about it. His supervisor, Captain Keener-O'Neil, threatens to turn him back to a flatfooted, bald- headed on-the-beat-boy-in-blue.

Straight-arrow cop is irascible, angry, contempt bubbling in the depths of his macho, short-fused soul. The dagos, he suspects, cause all the trouble, along with the spics. What chance does a classic Greek have with the barbarians? Even his title, Lieutenant, is French. What's wrong with υπαρχηγός? Or לוטענאַנט. Or ملازم. Damned foreigners — should never been allowed in the country.

But in the end, it's a private affair, a matter of personal pride, and he's heard to say he intends to straighten it out, to purge The City, excise the demon and get the Big Apple polished up, before someone reminds him that as a teevee cop, an actor, a fictional bozo, between shows, he would do well to wipe off the paint and get the mustard out of his ears. He's heard it before, but still he doesn't like it.

Otherwise, temperatures hover in the low teens, the morning is clear to partly cloudy and windy. The faces of Janus show east and west, the gates open. The sun floats in from the lower latitudes to a higher course. In a two-hour made-for-teevee special, dapper darling super-sleuth and clever-cop, in electronic full-color, the very best of Dupin, metamorphosed, *An American Werewolf in London*, the traditionally assembled mag- nificence of many popular parts of gumshoe, shifty, glaze-eyed, square- jawed best, commits his eccentric, deductive mind to the hunt.

Tonight he's Marlowe, Spade, Carella, maybe Mike Hammer, a smart-ass, quick-quip menace in love with nothing, prepared to go two-out-of-three falls with the Angel of Death (though he may be named Jacob and not yet know his nemesis).

It's hard to tell. The old film stock is not very good with grays — simply blacks and whites. So he wears white suits, to appear thinner and younger. He's laid-back, virility in a white shirt, vest and tie — draped clothes, wide lapel, peaked or notched. Nothing here of Pierre Cardin or Yves Saint Laurent. He shows up as a not-so-well-stitched rebuttal to Hart Schaffner & Marx chairman John D. Gray's observation, projection that, "There is a tremendous new interest in dressing up."

He comes on in varying attires of déjà vu, Corning Ware glasses that change from dim to light or darken in the light, thin cigarillos, and lollipops — once he resorts to bubble gum.

He noses onto Channel 2, gives orders, dispatches Crocker and Stavros to the action. Instinct, some say — confined to a storied world that depends on plot, sleight-of-hand, leaps in logic, coincidence — a stereotype or two and cheap dialogue — but always upon words. He's been sleuthing a long time, back to Zadig, Dupin (though not blessed with Sherlock's logic or Vidocq's acumen), believes in the vital link theory, finds connections, knows he's on to something.

Tonight a red glow paints the East River from Beekman Street to Catherine Slip, broken only by the beaded, dipping, concave light stings of the Brooklyn Bridge cables. A deep brown fog drifts slowly beneath the Manhattan Bridge. A late run East River 34th Street Ferry glides into Pier 11. Somewhere in the distance, the drone of a ship's horn buffets the fog.

Yes, something is afloat. Some ominous why and what the hero has not encountered before. He muses, whines quizzically — could it be?

He's not sure, decides to continue the hunt, glares into the camera, faces south and puts his ninety-dollar Bunga Ballys to the beat. He pads off dragging his magnificent nose over the pavement, a hare-hound sniffing cobblestones, manholes, analyzing the odors, the street clues.

Of course, clues are plentiful. Near Pier 11 he turns up a snorkel skin — missing a body — probably a female — the handle of a zip gun, a dead pigeon, a box of fish bones and several broken Old Grand Dad and Ancient Age bottles. Indeed, the neighborhood is bountiful, abundant with clues.

A short time later, he's running in circles, patiently, methodically. Then just before midnight, the scent clear, the trail narrowing, tripping over the wharf (Ware House at River Front) near the Brooklyn Bridge, prophetically, with a tedious twist of providence, the investigation takes a hit. He picks up a splinter in his nose and snorts off whining, trying to paw it out.

shaytan al mephitis
(homo-capra aegagrus hircus)
rides the evening tide and slips
into the Big Apple, unnoticed - almost

Midnight.
The night is still clear when the spectral ship *Goddam* emerges from a

fog bank and appears, as if painted on the night, at anchorage, motionless in the East River. Slowly the fog dissipates and her visage intensifies in the red-light glow of the river.

A moment ago, she wasn't there, but now she is. And she's a beauty. A standard seventeenth century galleon, at 65 meters she features a triangular overhanging forecastle, a square-ended forecastle set back under the foremast and a long raised beak of a galley projecting beyond the stern.

In the night, her fore-, main-, and mizzenmasts, draped with giant webs, tilt against the deep black like a triptych of unused crosses. She rides low in the water, deathly still, as if set on a stone base, and for several hundred yards around, supporting the vision, the water is flat and smooth as a weathered rock.

The *Goddam* is the flagship of Captain Shaytan al Mephitis, better known as Sam — a 64 gun menace he picked up working with Barbary Christian corsairs (providing aid and comfort to the enemy) during the 1618-1626 campaign, collecting over 6,000 slaves, property worth over 15 million livres, and some 2,600-2,700 ducats of merchandize. As always, the Captain has numerous other means of transport, but for sorties with easy access to a bays or rivers, he prefers the *Goddam.*

Recently he's had her re-outfitted with long-range culverins, sakers and falcons — all for show today. The latest in SAMs, chaff guns, and armor penetrating cannons are camouflaged in the antique layers of decks and bulkheads. Three mini nuclear ICBMs and seven nuclear torpedoes sulk beneath her waterline.

Tonight a black fire flares on the poop deck, silhouetting the gaunt shapes of the First Mate and the Watch keepers. They hover in pointed hats, the notched collars of greatcoats pulled up so only their hooked noses, Mr. Spock ears, and hollow white-eye sockets show.

Motionless as the sea they ride, the Max Schreck crew gazes empty-eyed into the penumbra of the sea, the only sound the groaning of the yardarms and the great masts creaking in their mores as if lashed in place and held to the deck and hold by the accumulated suffering of the tortured and maimed the *Goddam* has left in her wake.

Large midnight-black rats (imported to give the Goddam charisma and style) nose over the crew's hands, their curved claw-nails hooked to the rails and glinting in the moonlight. Behind them, against the forecastle bulkhead, a stack of coffins with names from the future: Freund (with the lid up), Voskerichian, Saurani, Esau.

The hour is early.

The scythe-striker on the bell, swung by a skeletal hooded bell-ringer, rings six bells of the Middle watch, the echo slithering on to the infected water, crawling portentously in a small toxic cloud toward shore. The representation is as yet indistinct, blurred, a face in a garish dream, mythic, and medieval — human, but not yet fully conscious.

The night is fierce, the water in the bay black and cold, thick with garbage, sewage, the souvenirs, the spinoff of Homo sapiens' clever but lopsided intellect holding him hostage on the march from wilderness to oblivion. The bell's knell falling on the water echoes Dr. Armbruster's words. Between a bag of trash and a headless mongrel (which may or may not be a portent) a chuckle bobs to the surface, ripples toward the dock, disappears then breaks above the water.

Sam surfaces, backstroking, floating, keeping a patient pace, his face contorted but content, for the moment. He's in from the Baltic by way of the North Atlantic, a long trip, with time out to see the sights, frolic, poking up a storm, lollygagging with a school of misplaced scoundrel sharks.

Coming across he guided a couple of globally warmed liberated icebergs into shipping lanes (something for the future) and to keep a promise, pay an old debt and even a score, induces a situation awareness failure for a 747 and guides three hundred thirty-three passengers and a crew of ten, into a sea of thirty-foot waves. The FAA reports the mishap as "unfortunate — an act of god and pilot error" — but the fine print has Sam's scratch on it.

Sam smirks, a twitch on his lip, content with his pranks, and blows a spout of fouled water into the chilled air. Then he's at the dock, a landing party of one, one hand up, another, lifts himself out of the river, long knobby fingers, claws, mini-horns, pointed head and ears, bristled wire-hair over small-flame eyes, a flat nose, broken black and decayed teeth, a thin wispy beard. His skin glows with a putrid green phosphorescent over a man's torso and the crooked goat legs of hock, saggy fetlock, dewclaw, pastern, and hoof. The plethora of imperfections of nature's meandering in the alliance of the élan vital with matter.

Wet and soiled, he pauses, sits cross-legged on the end of the pier, shakes a small spray on the air, pulls a cigarette from the ether and puffs it up to a bright mini-star. He stares out over the water to Babylon ruminating, plotting, a festering furuncle of treachery.

He's been here before, a misty mirage in a Platonic mirror, exhorting chaos, humming to himself.

"I form the light and create sight; I make weal and create woe; I am Lord, who does all these things."

He cackles, mocking. Misokalos, accuser, master-of-matter, tormentor. Iblis, ash-Shaytan.

He rubs a scaly hand across the knob of his horned cock.

"Good to be back," he says. "All is as it should be. Yes, indeed, it is good to be back."

Minutes later dockside at South Street and Catherine Slip he insinuates himself into the Post Mortem bar. The customers at the bar squint through the smoke watching *Kojak* on Channel 2, the Lieutenant stumbling along the pier holding his nose. At the far end a customer has passed out, snoring, mouth open, eyes rolled back. Another sits in a corner rolling a joint. Two more are lethargically arm wrestling, as if it is the only thing left to do. They have been motionless, in a stalemate, for twenty minutes, watching the teevee and sipping small glasses of rum. As long as the bottle lasts, holding hands appears to be more desirable than winning. The company and the rum are good, and if someone wins, they will have to start again — so why bother?

Otherwise, the entry is unremarkable. One customer raises his head, lifts his nose to the stench stirring at the door, along the floor. But no hand-shakes, no back-slaps. The dim of the barroom shades him with a Mr. Hyde mien of coarse animal hair, carbuncles and boils, broken, dripping pustules, scabs of old wounds festering on feculent scaled sea-green skin. He secures a bottle of rum — something to attenuate the aftertaste of polluted, brackish water, to warm up and celebrate the end of a journey.

Then, transposed over the room, front to back, bottle and glass in hand, his black cape fluttering, beating the stale air in the deviltry of film noir best, he finds a table, concealed in part, his slant eyes flaring in the haze of the dim, red neon mist rising from the pool of water around his chair.

Sam and the Lou
come very nearly
eye to eyeball
at the Post Mortem

When the door swings open, baldheaded Super Sleuth comes on screen in close-up, holding his nose, and asks the barmaid for a tweezers.

She regards his round knob and asks, "How did that happen?"

The relaxed level of the announcer's patter and the comfortable conversation distance over the imaginary extension of the bar are transformed by the barroom noises broken by a total blackout on the teevee screen. However, the blackout is quickly replaced with an extreme close-up of the Lou's head, shot in profile from the left. Kojak is uncomfortably close, at a distance most viewers might find themselves when kissing, embracing or whispering. Super Sleuth comes on from an angle slightly below his eye level so the viewer must look up to him, via the camera, both literally and metaphorically. He has a stern, severe expression on his face.

Now he glances down, slightly to the right. A light emanating from the right of the picture, possibly from a beer sign in the window, exaggerates the contours of his profile, the shadows creating a silhouette effect of mystery, intangibility and the inaccessible. This is an introverted man: he is not involved in conversation or physical action; he is thinking. His profile is elucidated by intimation and innuendo. What is he thinking? What does he look like head-on in daylight?

Of course, the most obvious peculiarity of the Lou, as the waitress observed, is his baldhead. This leads everyone in the bar to a suspicion of archetypes. Shadowed, silhouetted profiles and figures, as mysterious as executioners, are inevitably bare-headed and bald, hooded or both, maybe malicious hairless devils or serpents in the Garden of Eden or xenophobic archetypes of Orientals, such as Genghis Khan, or the implacably brutal Japanese in western war films such as *Camp on Blood Island* and the 'yellow peril' stereotypes symbolized by Fu Man Chu.

The exaggerated silhouetting and shading of his baldheaded profile is reminiscent of the stylized head-profile portraits on coins and medals and the portrayal of 'strong men' used in Renaissance paintings and sculptures of the condottieri. These hairless, helmeted misanthropes, usually depicted on horseback (again requiring the viewer to look up), were employed by the monarchs of mini-states to command their private armies of mercenaries.

Baldheaded, helmeted, hooded or hairless archetypes share the common denominator of brute force. The majority are associated with some kind of threat: devils, dragons and serpents, maybe not physically strong, but brainy, wily, dangerous figures, not to be trusted.

Tonight in the dim barroom Kojak's muscular, masculine physiognomy and his physical features associate him with the bald bull's head of the Minotaur and with the broad-shouldered baldness of the condottieri who were renowned for their brute force and severity (Tagg).

However, it is likely that this is not the case.

"We're all born bald, baby," he says.

"Not true," the waitress says. "My nephew came out with black hair a foot long. His picture was in all the papers. Looked like a Persian cat."

She eyes him suspiciously.

"A tweezers? What you been smoking?"

"I got a splinter in my nose."

"That's what you get for sniffing wood dildos. You'd stayed with lollipops that wouldn't happened."

"Look, sweetheart, you got a tweezers or not?"

"You been messing around on Bayard Street again? How about a pliers or ice pick? This ain't no operating room."

"You always change the customer's order?"

The customers laugh.

Sam watches from the corner, the bottle nearly emptied, his eyes brightened to a red-white flame.

"What I should have expected," he says. "Someone to keep the fires, provide a touch of invention for hard times. Predestination."

Sam smirks.

"When conditions are right, the right disposition appears."

The Lieutenant hunches his shoulders, shivers.

"It's cold," he says.

Black-fire eyes burn at his back. He eases around to survey the red glow, the faint haze of the room, the rising wisps of steam.

"Have you seen anybody strange tonight?"

"Everybody is strange every night," the barmaid says. "How'd you get that splinter? Sure you don't want an ice pick? Here, let me help you with that."

"Who's your friend in the back?"

"In the back? Oh. Just a rummy. Get a couple dozen a day."

"They all come in wet in the middle of winter?"

"Look, Bozo, I should know from what. So he took a shower with his clothes on. Maybe he fell off the dock. Some do things a lot worse than that. I don't know. Says he's on his way to Yonkers to visit a friend. Maybe we'd all be better off if we had a friend in Yonkers."

"Yeah, it makes your heart thump, don't it? You got a tweezers or not?"

"Here, let me see your nose."

The barmaid frowns, squints, extracts the splinter with her fingernails, holds it up to the light, turns it carefully.

Super Sleuth massages his proboscis, takes a deep breath.

"Okay. I gotta go. I appreciate the extraction. Maybe I can do something for you sometime?"

He pauses at the door, for affect, before making a swift but plausible exit.

The barmaid examines the splinter. She jiggles up to the camera, her eyes wide with the sincerity audiences have a right to expect from tarts. She drops the sliver into her pocket.

"He thinks he's on to something," she says, speaking confidentially to the camera. "Comes in here two, three nights a week. Says he's on the trail of evil. Always wants to know why. Why this, why that? Never met some-body who could ask so many questions. Like he was born to do that. Had a neighbor once always wanted to know what I'd done the night before — who I was with, when it all started. Same thing here. But it ain't about me. I can't tell him nothing. Looks like he's lost the scent, though. I'm not surprised. With a nose like that, what can you do?"

She takes the empty bottle from the table.

"That may be the best thing. Hell, who knows what kind of trouble a crazy bastard like that might cause. A splinter in his nose. How did that happen? Next, he'll say he got his dick caught in the pickle slicer. Makes you wonder who she is?"

She stares at the water beneath the table, looks back to the bottle.

"Jesus!" she says, her voice rising. "The poor bastard. Jeeeesus!" she says again, somewhat more slowly. "He's gone. Just melted down to a puddle like Little Black Sambo's tigers. Hey! Wait a minute."

She turns to the bar.

"Charlie, come here. How in the hell? Charlie! This S.O.B just disap-peared, like . . .."

Psyaint David

"You remember that night, I mean it's like . . . the guy who comes in here one night, yeah, you remember, what's his name, like Sutaner something from over on Saint Germaine in the Bronx, and I ask him if he wants a beer or whatever and he says, 'I think not,' and then just disappears. I mean, puufff, he vanishes, just left me standing. What you gonna do with a bastard like that?

"And now. WOW! Again. Like in a circus. Holy shit! An' the cops are gonna be in here wanting to know about . . . what . . . I seen? I mean they'll be on me like pissants on a toad. Charlie come here! And I gotta tell 'em I wasn't watching. I ain't seen a thing. I mean, I was . . . Charlie! Goddammit, Charlie?"

Sam joins Times Square revelers
  in a frivolous frolic,
    then integrates himself
into an apartment in Yonkers

No simple thing is simple. In spite of Super Sleuth's dogged regimen Sam is out and about, undetected, makes it up from the shattered burnt-out WWIII lower East Side, quickly, easily, rubbing elbows on the subway, pushing through.

Tipsy from the rum, he stretches, yawns, bleary eyed and wheezing — too much smoke and fiery depths, nights of discontent, anxiety, resentment eating at his liver, his spleen already halved.

Otherwise, the mien is vintage Sam. He speaks with a lisp, a harelip, appears at angles cross-eyed. A swirl of thin hair hangs around one broken horn, his arms and legs boney, a torn hoof, one leg shorter than the other.

He could use a new costume, a wardrobe. The saltwater, he thinks, and the shit floating in the East River. No Angora or mohair, no cashmere or pashmina here.

"Shit," he says, "one of these days I'll find material that can bear up under stress, time, resist fire and mold, wear well."

Want to go back and come out again? Disguise the shaggy wild beast semblance? Say, top hat, tails, and spats? Maybe an uptown uniform: Prada loafers, Calvin Klein black socks, a swart Hickey Freeman suit, or a Navy Brooks Brothers blazer in traditional worsted flannel — a three-button model with patch pockets, welted edges and embossed gold-plated Golden Fleece buttons — a white shirt and French cuffs with skull and crossbones cufflinks.

"No, no," he says, dour, uneasy, annoyed. "There'll be time for that."

Yeah, the old bones creak, muscles ache, but he has a few hours until doomsday, time to strike a pose, mastermind a plot or two. More than that, he's up for an argument, cantankerous, bellicose, rum-courage, gets off at Times Square, slides into the crowd in the 42nd Street IRT West Side labyrinthine underground with mischief in mind.

He grins, mingling in the reflection of man's true soul, man as mole, he thinks, rushing along the narrow passages pretending progress.

The small coals of his eyes play with the torn signs, green and red decorations, limericks spray-painted on raw concrete walls.

> There once was a woman from Algorz,
> Whose cunt was full of sores,
> And the dogs in the street
> Would eat the green meat
> That hung in hemorrhoids from her drawers.
>   (Anonymous)

"Lascaux, Pech Merle," Sam says.

The impulse to share, shock, please, to capture for a moment a vision. As with horror, art lies in the flesh, festers near the perimeter of act, and Sam can cradle a palette and lay on strokes with the best.

The possibilities are pleasing. Today the IRT West Side, tomorrow buses, Dondi and Futura 5000, 11 West 53rd and the MAM. Easy success. An accidental discovery, popularity assured by a dowager patroness to carry the silver-cross torch for enlightenment (according to her word), the flares of her conceit licking the black cavern walls. Big bucks, clout, intrigue, the excitement of deceit and double-dealing.

Sam's crotch aches. He's pleased to be back in The City. His horned-cock bulges prominently beneath tightly stretched goatskin breeches. Goatskin sheathing a goat's skin. Soft strains of a fugue for voices drifts down from the street, rides the air about him, marking the dimensions of Pan's parts, his intentions.

Two drunks stumble onto the landing, arm in arm at the top of the stairs, singing, slip, grab for the handrail, and, embracing, tumble down, together, yelping, laughing, the frivolity of good times rolled into a pile of overcoats and hats.

Before they can recover, Sam steps in, gracefully, with a quick hand and comes away with wallets and gold watches, a diamond money-clip of twenties. Easy pickings. Clean work. No fuss. No complaints. Just another service Sam provides.

On the way out, he hands the plunder to a not-too-surprised twelve-year-old, Claude Sitton of 11-36 Newton Street. Coming down the stairs, Sitton was eying the possibilities. He's thrilled with Sam's generosity — the benefaction. He grins and waves as Sam lifts to street level prepared to mix with the night.

Along Broadway, a stiff wind presses carousers against storefronts, pushing them into the peep shows and topless bars. For a block Sam drifts with the traffic, the warmth of the rum wearing off, his throat parched, his stomach queasy, bubbling bile. He scrutinizes the faces floating in the bright of neon lights, the eyes, the grim expressions, lips pursed, muscles set against the cold, certain now the hunt will be made easier by the hour and temperature.

A block on, walking in a shadow, a walking shadow, indeed, a poor player, he steps up the pace, overtakes thirty-one-year-old Helen McCarter on her way home from her job at the Public Library, and slips his arm in hers. When she resists, screams, with a lover's embrace and the affection of malice, he loops his free arm about her shoulders, digs his curved canine-teeth fingernails into her throat, muting her cries, and preparing for the dance and a cold night of terror, drags her into an unlit alley.

A night on the town, the possibilities of entertainment, Sam's private version of Select a Sexmate at Random.

ABSOLUTELY BETTER THAN ANY OTHER MATE

Don't confuse HELEN our female mate with any
other. She is not just another sex-mate — she's the
original, now made with a new scientific
process that guarantees her to be puncture proof.
No need to have those noisy, bothersome sex-mates
hanging around when not in use. HELEN is the
best at the price.

EXCITING EXPERIENCE

You can do anything you want and she will never
complain. She's receptive to your most wicked
advances. HELEN gives you her personal attention
and guarantees satisfaction – every time.

COMES COMPLETE . . . DOWN TO THE LAST INTIMATE DETAIL!

Caress this lovely lady's curly light brown hair.
Explore her perfectly proportioned 5'2" body.
Then fondle her 34-C breasts with throbbing
nipples — and when you are ready — plunge
into her perfectly formed pulsating vagina.
If you desire the unusual, HELEN owns a pair
of engulfing lips. Or maybe you'd like some
Greek style fun with her firm, tight ass. Her
body simulates actual movements and she yields
to anything you may try. She comes to you
complete and ready for action.

(Sexmate ad)

Holding her in the shallow depth of a doorway, he shreds Helen's clothing, exposes her pale, shocked flesh to the bitter air, her buttocks pinioned to the frozen steel of the door, his throbbing member piercing, ripping into her. He takes her with a vicious demon sigh of pained, ecstatic grumbling snorts and prolonged bleats that swell into a final grunt. With sated animal rumbles, he disengages, his limp horned-cock dripping, and drops her to the pavement, leaving her torn and bleeding, slumped against the building, dazed, numb with pain, and crying, her arms wrapped tightly about her.

Sam titters, smirks.

"The best we have to offer. It doesn't get any better. Assault with a friendly weapon."

Indeed, it is good to be back.

Her bloodied torn dress trailing Helen crawls from the alley to the center of the sidewalk and with half-crazed pleas begs a passerby for help. A crowd gathers to watch as she tries to stand, clutching her dress, but cannot. Again, she tries and a round of applause goes up.

"Bravissimo," someone yells as she falls again.

A man steps forward and nudges her with his toe, makes an obscene remark, points out that her act is tedious, but not that far "off Broadway."

Another man wants to know who is in charge of her wardrobe.

She mutters something about needing help and they laugh and agree that if she is going to make it she needs a great deal of help.

The crowd takes pity. Several toss coins on the sidewalk. An old woman in a brown coat and red hat bends down, slips a ten-dollar bill in her hand, and takes Helen's gold watch.

Across the street Sam puffs on a cigarette, regards his reflection in the plate glass of *GIRLS GIRLS GIRLS,* the neon sign announcing Live Sex, Private Booths, two shows nightly with Adam Alwise in his "sinuous, pointed and snakelike dances."

Not only is Adam Alwise in matters of sexual titillation, but claims ancestry to Henry Cyril Paget, 5th Marquis of Anglesey, nicknamed "Toppy," who was noted during his short (mostly nineteenth century) life as "the dancing marquis" for his habit of performing "sinuous, sexy, snake-like dances," and who, as Sir Thomas Browne says, in a not too Baconian remark, ". . . seems only to have existed for the purpose of giving a melancholy and unneeded illustration of the truth that a man with the finest prospects, may, by the wildest folly and extravagance, foully miscarry in the advantage of humanity, play away an unutterable life, and have lived in vain." However, limited as Adam's "finest prospects" might be, the passage does have an authentic ring.

But Sam's cantankerous, bored with the sideshow and the rhetoric. He abandons the street, takes north-wing, and drifts into Yonkers near dawn, hangs in the eaves, on the façade of apartment 7E, 35 Pine Street, a soot-stained vestige, an ill wind, a seepage around the window, buffeting the soiled blanket-curtain.

Psyaint David

David dreams of Sam
  and speaks plainly
of the powers of Sam's voice

I am the circle in the fire. What
I do is for Sam. For love, the sake of Sam, this anointed King, David — how
is it?
I have been given a mission to impose violent ruin upon my enemies. But
I am a very sensitive person.
I am aware of things about me.
I concern myself with something alive, like a bird or a plant.
I love birds and plants.
I love nature. People, too. That leads to my downfall.
I have these howling thoughts and they make me do wild things, and
I shoot people. It scares me. After the shootings
I hear so much news about victims, the sob stories. In the United States,
they show sob stories on teevee so much. Women in tears. After a while
I don't feel anything at all. Then
I see in the papers that they are out to get me. It is in the papers and on
teevee — Borrelli, Cavanaugh, and Coffey maybe even Kojak. So
I follow them from that day on. Whenever anything is written
I read it.
I know they will get me someday. The only question is how . . . and when.
But they do not know about Sam. Sam has been around since the
beginning. People should take me seriously.
I know Sam. They should try to look into it. Sam and his demons have
been responsible for a lot of trouble. The people should try to destroy Sam.
It would be hard because they'll continue till the end, until god destroys
them in the last heroic final battle. Sam's a speck of evil cosmic dust that
has fallen to earth and flourished.
I am the Son of Sam. Sam works through me. We are one body, but are
not the same.
I am Sam's tool. People really don't know anything. They don't know
what's happening in the world. Some think it's the rich like the Rockefellers
or the Kennedys. But it's not. The forces of god and Satan. They have their
hands in the world. One day, god will bring peace to the world and hope
for mankind. It is Satan's will for me to kill the innocent. It happens. Why?
I don't know why. It just happens. But god will want to help and in the
end peace will win. People are dying every day in the most horrible ways.
There's nothing
I can do about it. Without Sam,
I'm nothing.
I am the Son of Sam
I believe in god.

Sam annotates the dream

· "Nicely put, nicely put. He dreams a child's dream of remaining a child, living the warrior king metaphor, lawgiver, his swollen member dripping fire, women weighted with fertile seed, the sting of life — the piercing steel-tipped shaft of generation.

"So he is sacrificed that others might live, will give his life to spurious justice. For it is by the strength of the rod that life is given and kept. He feeds the angry gods — the thirsty gods that threaten to destroy the world. His is the monk's chant, the bulldog's bark. He gives them what they ask, keeps them happy so the world may be safe for dreams.

"So much for the nonsense."

Sam's covenants
are signed in sunlight,
song, and blood

The footlights dim, the curtain falls. Day breaks over Yonkers and the Palisades. The apartment is overheated, stifling, oppressive. Hans-Peter wakes in a sweat, breathless, heart throbbing. His mouth is dry. His eyes burn. He has voices in mind. Voices. What? Who was it speaking to him? Sam. Yes, Sam filling the dream. The void.

He rises slowly, inspects the room, the apartment, circumspect, hesitant. Spends the next minutes on the edge of the bed wondering, what?

He fumbles a razor blade from the bathroom cabinet, slices his right index finger, and collects the dripping fluid in a coffee cup. He sucks the wound for a few minutes, carefully wraps it in a paper towel, and holds it in the air as if it were a prize.

With a toothpick dipped in crimson ink, in awkward, broken letters he scrawls out a brief message of salvation. The paper is soiled, the blood leaking through. He holds it up to the light.

It is for Sam we live.
Sam gives meaning to life.
Sam is our father.
Sam is a thirsty lad.
Sam's will be done.

The covenant renewed, signed, the humors once again in balance, his agony ameliorated. He relaxes, calm, no longer melancholic.

Then it is morning, sunlight at the window, soft clouds in the far sky over the Hudson. His finger hurts, his trigger finger, but his visions cleansed, and he basks in a pensive, almost reflective pose at the crossroads with Theophilus. He folds the message and lays it on the windowsill. He chants a few lines from "The Court of King Caractacus." It is morning. Yes, the ladies are just passing by.

Psyaint David

in the hall of the Mountain King
Mathias, Marcelo, Lukema, and Juan
plot the *Kojak* show   •

Good morning!
As expected, with Christine Freund's death, the hows and whys of whodunit have finally attracted the interest of the paters familias.
Orlando Cervantes of 737 Park Avenue with the obituary column from the *Daily News* in hand stops at St. Bartholomew's Episcopal Church to pray for the dead.
Marcia Bergenstein of 53-91 71st Avenue in Forest Hills launches a "Catch the Killer" campaign.
"It's enough," she says. "Young women getting killed. I will have no more of it."
She solicits neighborhood woman to go door-to-door, block-by-block, knocking, asking, hunting for the killer.
"Have you seen him? What does he look like? You will tell me when you see him."
Several days later handbills appear with Christine Freund's photo and name, offering a reward.

$10,000 REWARD
WHO IS THE MURDERER?

The fliers are stuck to trees, lampposts, shop windows.
The initiative, however well intended and furious, is short-lived. The impulse languishes and the images and prayers, the spirit of the hunt subsides. The handbills wilt and are torn from the trees and posts and pushed along the street by the wind. Chris Freund's likeness fades, even in memory of sudden, random death, giving way to time and the torpor of human lassitude.
Yet, lest all be dismissed and loss in the swamp of antiquity, there does seem to be a remaining tinge of interest and hope. While it appears no one cares, or cares much about the dead, the possibilities of making money off an anonymous serial killer roaming the streets is enough to titillate even the most benign latency of greed. Speculation, conjecture, ripples into the narrows of The City's newspapers, radio, the teevee Bs and Cs. What value is a killer if death and dying are not symbolized, molded and cast into words and images? For a very long time now, we have made a profit reporting crime. What if? Yes, what if we . . . ?
The phone rings in The Universe Studio Executive Producer Mathias Teivel's office.
Yes, he reads the news.
Well, why not develop a format (aka as a plan, strategy, proposal) he is

told, take advantage of the platform, the public interest?

Are you available?

It's late Friday. He's going over the final preps for a new show — he could use another.

Teivel (Showrunner) scratches his crotch, tips a glass of Old Pulteney.

"Well, yes," he says.

He will see what he can do. He replaces the phone, thinks for a moment. Takes another sip. Who? Well, yeah. Okay.

Teivel at best resembles an R Crumb oddity out of the *Motley News* or *Snatch Comic.* Possibly a teevee addict, mesmerized with the tube, a beer type drink in one hand, a sack of cheesy chips in the other, his head soaked with the residue of variety shows, cheap dramas, and commercials.

Then again the question.

"Are you interested?" for three-finger colleagues: Juan Lamiae, Casting and Production, Lukema Kesil, Photography, Marcelo Aigilas, Director.

Can you make it?

"What?"

"A séance.

"Where?"

"Monday, my office."

Again, "Yes, yes, and yes."

So it is.

Monday, off Park Row, early, near Theater Alley at 5 Beekman Street, out of the ooze of a brown fog blowing down from the Bronx shrouding the concrete and steel canyons, they materialize. By subway and bus, they trek forth in circuitous migration, a temporary inhibition of station keeping responses to promote their eventual disinhibition and recurrence. Nearly somnambulistic, as they have from the beginning in camps, encampments, towns, boroughs, wherever people gather, they emerge. When summoned, they appear, by an anomalous impulse or metaphor of as-not-yet-other appreciated insistence of nature. In a disjointed, herky-jerky, Marx Brothers' reminiscence, an anamorphic aura of a wavering holographic stereogram, with thousands of other morning denizens of The City, they show up on Beekman Street. They show up by instinct, hunting the buck, a break, an elixir, poking their way through the fog.

Up the street in City Hall Park, a Pace University troupe is planning a Sunrise Mime of the 1776 execution of Nathan Hale. The mimes are scattered around the Hale statue, sipping coffee, exchanging small words for crème, powder, and paint. The gist of the skit is bravado and patriotism. However, getting hanged and inspiring statues does little for your net worth. The mime message in the fog will suggest rolling with the flow, staying silent, and getting your hand in the till in whatever way, whenever you can.

Metro Transit driver Rodgilio Rieso of 17-55 Orlando Street, Bronx, stands in the door of his disabled bus, waiting assistance, smoking a cigarette, watching the mimes. This morning, he too, is wordless, silent, but not for the same reason. He's contemplating icing his wife who he suspects of stealing from him. He has already decided to do it. The question now, is how?

A homeless man at the corner approaches Rodgilio panhandling a cigarette, then walks away wondering why he asked.

Up the block, in front of 5 Beekman, fifties something pudgy, grey-eyed Martha Farnsworth of 3324 Chapel Hill Drive, Brentwood, on a click-pic safari (certain she is destined to become one of the world's great photographers), mingles with the crowd recording the activities — for posterity.

This morning Martha uses a Canon AE-1, a 35 mm single-lens reflex, with an electronically controlled, electromagnet horizontal cloth focal plane shutter, and a speed range of 2 to 1/1000 second, plus bulb and flash X-sync of 1/60th second.

Peering through the lens into the fog, watching the mimes, the driver, the homeless man, she spots the gnomes, one, then another, and another. She pauses. What is this? Who are these people? She, too, is reminded of the Marx Brothers, or at least that's what she says. Though frightened by what she sees, the driver and the gnomes, ". . . the hidden, evil possibilities of The City," Martha admits she savors the feeling.

Indeed, this is what she loves about photography.

"So many things can develop in the unseen," she says.

Today she is just as disturbed by what she doesn't see, what seems not to be. Her lens fogs up, and despite her attempts to clean it, the images remain blurred. Exasperated, she decides that the warped figures of her vision are part of a plot to discredit her talent. Prepared for such occasions she has a number of presumptions with which to fashion a theory — that may not be a theory at all. She abandons the shoot and shows up at Police Plaza One to report her lack of vision, as well as her imaginings.

She tells the desk sergeant that she was on Beekman Street, that she left her children alone (though she did prepare breakfast for them) and elaborates on her connections with her extended family — three brothers, a very old mother — and how she still communes with her dead father. He died in 1972. He fell off a third floor fire escape (there was no fire) into a dumpster. She confesses that she intends to be the next Diane Arbus. Oh, and yes, she did see something strange in the fog while taking pictures with her Canon AE-1, 35 mm single-lens . . . .

The sergeant, a grizzled veteran of street warfare and internecine squad room squabbles, is circumspect. He understands, suggests she not believe everything she thinks or dreams, and asks if her phantasms resemble dogs. He suspects the apparitions are Gabriel Hounds (Luke or Asta or Old Shuck?) hunting for something (or someone), you know, collecting lost souls.

"We've had a number of sightings," the sergeant tells Martha.

She says, "No. You don't understand. Not exactly dogs."

Later in the day, she processes the film and finds that nothing beyond conjecture develops. Fingering the blank film, dreaming whimsically of what might have been, she is left with little more than a significantly warped memory with which to support her visions.

For their part, the shapeshifters navigating the fog, negotiate the crowd (languidly) and elude the photographer's eye. They make their way to 5 Beekman and Mathias Teivel's office — a couple of rooms in the abandoned late nineteenth century ten story Temple Court palace.

The Court is an amalgamation of red Philadelphia brick, tan Dorchester stone and terra cotta of new-Grec, Queen Anne, and Renaissance architecture. Conceived in 1891 as an office building, in its heyday home to suits of lawyers. It's only paying tenants of the moment are restoration architect Joseph Pell Lombardi and Mathias Teivel. Otherwise, it has fallen into legal limbo and disrepair. Today the lobby is a minefield of broken glass, exposed wires, pipes, and rubble.

Deftly, the gnomes traverse the debris and ride the service elevator to the seventh floor where they are greeted by Teivel's secretary Vivian Blasberg. Blasberg is a fifties something, not-too-recent divorcee with red hair and sad eyes. Already at her makeshift desk, she nods and as they pass grunts something like "Good morning."

The office itself is sequestered in the northwest front of the building, a corner two-room complex with small pyramids of debris stacked along the walls and an extensive peeled-and-peeling-paint motif complimented by a ceiling of dangling twisted water pipes and bare wires.

Along the far end outside walls, a collection of dilapidated furniture fronts a spread of grimed, almost floor-to-ceiling windows. Worn and dusty eighteenth century Met-discard drapes frame windows that would, if not for the Beekman (Panhellenic) Tower and sundry buildings, offer a view of the East River. The vista, though neither helpful nor pleasant, does on occasion provide reflected sunlight. However, not today.

The far-end office furniture includes a highly functional desk, with minor concessions to style — the plastic top advertised as "attractive walnut-grained plastic-over-chipboard" (Sears, Roebuck and Co., 1971) offering the appearance of wood for the price of plastic. Its enameled metal surface, originally green, was, after a season or two (something like a Tom cat backing up to a curtain and lifting his leg) spray-painted black. The desk is surrounded by an Eames Soft Pad and three Task chairs.

In a corner a defunct Culligan watercooler, its yellow-stained bottle displaying a *Jaws* decal (a piece of the fish eaten away), tilts precariously on its plinth. A six-foot tattered Younger Sam Sofa with a boxy profile, tufted cushions, thin track arms, a sink-in comfort, and a worn goatskin slipcover, rests against a windowed, but otherwise blank wall. The couch appears to be original to the room, and depending on the season, and the availability of the service elevator, provides a nest for a pack of enterprizing rats.

Across the room, the interior wall opposite the couch backs a row of flickering and flashing, but soundless teevees — this morning a 25" Admiral Color Console bubbling a *Happy Days* rerun, a 25" Muntz Color Console with *The Price is Right*, and an 18" Color Tabletop Emerson spinning the *Wheel of Fortune.* A 12" B & W Tabletop Sony displays the lurching widgets of the Fairchild VES, the world's first CPU video game console — the cartridge-based game code storage format for *Desert Fox/Shooting Gallery.*

As arranged, this morning Teivel is at his desk. After a brief greeting, the usual hellos, while the Watchers locate their assigned seats, he fiddles with the remote on his desk.

He's a small stereotypical fifty, going bald with white hair in a Caesar-cut (absent the laurel crown), an otherwise paunchy, nearsighted (with glasses) exec-type. This morning he wears a grey sweater, Khaki Chinos, and tan quarter brogue oxford shoes.

He punches the remote to light up the tri-pod Plumbicon set between the teevees. The Plumbicon has an active-pixel sensor and complementary metal-oxide semiconductors to capture light. It dumps its images on to a ¾-inch Broadcast Video U-matic tape.

"Otherwise," Teivel says, "a hundred years from now no one will remember us or even know we were in this room."

"So?" Aigilas says. "And twenty thousand years from now?"

He chuckles at the thought of oblivion.

"And who cares, anyway?"

A hunchback with a large head of thick red hair and beady eyes, Aigilas chain-smokes Cleopatra cigarettes. How long does it take to smoke a cigarette? A Cleopatra? He is nearing the end of his first pack for the day.

"Do you know what today is?" Teivel asks.

"Hell, I don't even know why we're here," Marcelo says. "What time is it?"

As a leading director for The Universe Studios, he may be the muscle of the story. Nonchalantly he redirects, poker-faced, to Teivel.

"Today is Valentine's Day. The fourteenth of February," Lamiae reminds him. "The day Fat Freddy is scheduled to shoot-up Neptune Moving in New Rochelle."

A frail, thin little man (but no Nick Charles), Juan Lamiae is well on his way to anorexia. He has deep, narrow-set silver eyes and jaundiced hair. He has an ashen countenance, his pale-yellow hair combed over an invading bald spot.

As he speaks, he alternately files his nails, and cleanses his throat with an herbal spray of marshmallow root, echinacea angustifolia root, sage, calendula, myrrh, and clove bud. He seldom eats, but brushes and flosses three times a day, and sprays relentlessly, a habit he picked up in prison (three states — fifteen years) for child pornography, and numerous other, as he claims, "occasions of a colorful past."

In the big one, he did nine years. He copped a plea for buying and selling eight-year-olds (on a Saturday night at Washington Square — where you can buy anything, anything — if you have the cash). In 1967, he produced and directed an ahead-of-the-curve porn series, *The Dispensable Child.* From appearances, even beyond doing time, life seems not to have treated him well.

"Do you know we're headed to the middle-ages?" he says. "People just sit and watch — somebody else provides the program. All they do is point and grunt, and go back to the last picture. Masturbation. It may be satisfying and fun, but you're not getting much done."

Today he wears a cheap deep blue blazer with a two-button lapel front, two lower patch pockets, one chest pocket, one inside breast pocket, and a two-piece back with two side vents. The blazer has slightly padded shoulders for a better fit and shape with lining sleeves and yoke over a five-button vest with two lower patch pockets. His slacks are pleated in front, have slightly flared legs and two slant front pockets; one set-in back pocket, belt loops and hook-and-eye closure with a nylon zipper and hemmed bottoms — mostly navy. He sports alligator shoes and a snake-skin belt. He has a small snake tattooed on his right arm that is not visible at the moment.

"So what do we get out of it?" Marcelo says.

Mathias shrugs.

"Don't know. I haven't seen the contract. Maybe a dead cop. Four or five workers. A dead perp. Not much. But some interest to the public, I'm sure. It'll sell a lot of soap and mattresses."

"Don't forget the parade," Juan says. "Every time a badgy gets killed they have a parade. With bagpipes."

"But Cowan? What's that?"

"Oh, another revenge shoot. Something about a disgruntled Nazi fired by his Jewish boss returning to the warehouse with genocide in mind," Juan tells him.

Aigilas is puzzled.

"Who did it? We didn't do that, did we?"

"No, no. Dear Marcelo," Lamiae says. "No doubt an independent from the Bronx."

"I don't know who wrote it," Mathias says. "Or who's rolling it. But I'd not be surprised if it came out of the Bronx.

"Revenge is old hat. Not the kind of thing we do these days. It's what you do when you don't have a good story. I mean, Americans, Christians, love killing. Hell, it's fun. So anything with blood in it sells. I don't know, maybe it's the adventure. But the best is definitely beyond revenge.

"We're after new angles, stuff with mystery."

"Like what?" Aigilas says. "What do you have in mind?"

"I don't know. How about Acronology? Bottle up whatever you got, entertainment, news and info—one package. Put it all in the same box. Then everything looks the same. Like staring into the universe. The farther you go, the more you see, the less you see and understand — which is very little."

"Let me count thy names," Juan says. "*Point Blank, The Last House on the Left, Lady Snowblood, Sex and Fury, The Great Silence.* How can I do this? There are so many.

"Oh, my god!

"Did you see Sylvester Stallone in *Rocky*? It was marvelous — just superior. He's such a grandiose, parading around with that wonderful chest."

Aigilas waves his hand in the air.

"The *Rocky* horror show was not revenge."

He turns to Teivel.

"So what are we doing? Not revenge?"

"No, no," Mathias says. "This is beyond that. Have you read the papers in the last couple weeks?"

Everybody agrees. They haven't.

"Well, we have to do is what the people are doing. Feed it back to them."

Mathias explains
the ins and outs
of the new *Kojak*

"So. Here's the latest. Right now, a looney, a creep, is walking the streets. He's already wasted a couple people. It could be a serial — not exactly every Tuesday prime time, but close. In the last few months, he has banked enough publicity to sell fifty shows. That's big bucks. And as you might imagine The Universe wants in on it."

He pauses reflectively.

"Our job is to find this nut and work him into *Kojak*. For four or five shows. Four shows — and Kojak collars him in the fifth. All to air in the fall. However, we have to get the foundation before summer. The opening is scheduled for October 2nd."

"Another October Horse," Juan says.

"The schedule called for the queen of hearts is wild to open the fall campaign. We'll push it back until November 6.

"Then, too, others will want in. Solaria and Galaxy are already poking around."

"So who's the publicity phenom?" Aigilas wants to know.

"Son of Sam," Teivel says.

"Son of Sam? Who's Sam?"

"I don't know. Maybe a grandfather, an uncle, a member of an organization. Who knows?"

"But definitely good stuff," Aigilas says.

"Yeah. Some of it real, some not. This is high-class stuff. The count in The City is five a day. In raw numbers that's thirty-five a week, a hundred fifty a month. Most of it sloppy and amateurish."

"Maybe it's time for an Elimination Cult," Lamiae says. "My goodness, would that be fun. Why wait for Cris Korda? We can start now. Suicide, abortion, cannibalism. Oh, I could go for that. How about, 'Save the Planet, Kill Yourself.' Or 'Eat a Queer Fetus for Jesus?' Or euthanasia. Assisted suicide.

"'Was it assisted?'

"'Certainly. The sucker just didn't have sense enough ask for help.'"

Everyone nods.

"There's precedent," Teivel says. "Remember, Dutch Schulz showed up at a Bronx police station and offered a free house in Westchester to anyone who could find and kill Mad Dog Coll. They made movies out of it. Hell, the enduring legacy of cinema and teevee is the technology of eradication.

"It worked in the U.K. *I, Claudius.* This is just a little more of Caligula's and Drusilla. Even if Milne put his foot down on *Brimstone and Treacle,* this is what people want. If the BBC can do it, we can do it.

"And it's going to get better. Rupert Murdoch is in town. When the *Post* unfurls its flags, things can only get better."

"It's up to the audience," Aigilas says. "The audience controls the on and off switch."

"This will keep the academic turd-snappers busy for years."

Mathias pushes a memo across the desk.

"Okay," he says, "here it is. This came to me in a miasma."

They laugh.

Lukema frowns.

"A dream. You see, I have these . . . what . . .? Visions? At night I see ghosts," Mathias says with a straight face.

"What kind of ghosts?" Aigilas inquires. "Round or tall or green?"

"Well, not like Hamlet's old man — nothing that dramatic. Ghosts in sheets. Sometimes I see them at the beach. Especially at sunset. Like walking on air, a spirit. A different one each time. Ghosts in sheets or in a cloud, a white cloud. Nothing definite. No arms or legs or faces."

He laughs.

"It hurts my eyes to think about it. Maybe Blue Lady or The Maid of the Mist or The Gay Street Phantom. Maybe Christmas Present or Casper. I don't know what they are.

"But the next day I can feel the persona."

He is still sober faced. No one is laughing.

"I suppose you hear voices, too."

"I do. Lots of voices. Groups. Crowds, choruses."

"All telling you what to do?"

"They're real. I mean, they could be real."

"Yeah. But how do you know?"

"It's like everything else. A matter of faith. You have to take it on faith.

"Anyway, I've been told to find this spook and get him under contract for five shows."

He pauses.

"Otherwise, it's going to get ugly. Like an ugly spirit. I mean, the spirit is loose. In fact, it's already ugly.

"You know how it is when people don't make the money they think they should have made."

Kesil squirms.

He stares at Juan.

Juan is shaking his head.

"No, no, silly. What Mathias means by find, is locate, not apprehend. To discover, not grasp."

Kesil seems satisfied with the explanation. He nods and goes back to eating.

A short, blue-eyed, once-upon-a-time pubescent math savant with greasy black hair and thick glasses in a grey stone frame, he's the youngest and most obese of the gnomes. MIT offered a scholarships , and Cal State, but he turned them down, gave up the xs and ys of quadratic equations for bags and boxes of calories, where x (potato chips) plus y (custard-filled, chocolate glazed Eclairs) equals ninety pounds overweight.

If the project gets off the ground, he will be the director of photography (head cinematographer). He already has a substantial résumé on both sides of the camera. Once an aspired actor, he actually landed a part in Fellini's *The Satyricon,* though he never made it on camera. He was in the chewing scene of Eumolpo's testament that stipulates, "All those who are left legacies in my will, with the exception of my freedmen, will obtain my bequest only on one condition, that they cut up my body in pieces and eat it before the eyes of the citizens . . .."

Kesil showed up on time with his knife and fork, but the cameraman that day was drunk, supporting Federico's observation about the "vulgarity" of the film industry, and did not include Kesil at his best, cutting and chewing — and grinning.

The least articulate of the gnomes; he is also the most introspective (though how would anyone know?). During his savant days he cultivated a habit (among others), a pleasant routine, he thought, of talking to himself (answering voices he often heard), as many people do — and not just occasionally in the shower or when leaving a party embarrassed by mistaking the host for the hostess, but habitually, even at small times, about small matters. In the beginning the ideas, the words he volunteered to the dialogue, like most pubescent notions, were pretty much pro forma, clichéd and innocuous.

Then one day the discourses, as he thought of them, morphed into what he referred to as wit-fits. These included responses to his mumbled observations that provided details with which he was unfamiliar — facts and descriptions of events that were unknown to the self he called self, or were in the least unrecognized.

At first, the peculiarities pleased him, though he found the anonymity of their source both frightening and confusing. Clearly, the figures the lens regarded were different from those displayed. Maybe the limitation of light was skewing the image. Whatever, it was a different vision — possibly akin to Kekulé's Ouroboros dream of the snake finding its tail — possibly a tall tale or a tell-tail-tale.

Eventually, to stave off the fits, he determined to shun all discourse. He recused conversation with himself, and finally with others. So today, he doesn't have much to say. He accepts Juan's words and goes back to masticating a Marshmallow Peep (chick) from Just Born, Inc., while taking inventory of the fat, salt, and caffeine contents of his Orange Salesman Sample Case.

At first glance, it's encouraging. In addition to three boxes of Peeps, he has five packets of Moon Pies from Chattanooga Bakery, three Little Debbie Oatmeal Crème Pies by McKee, and seven bags of Wise, Lays and Blue Star (imported from Rockford, Illinois) potato chips.

"It makes sense," Mathias says. "Theatre of human disorder. A nut-fuck loose, like a meteor or volcano or tornado. No rhyme, no reason. Random acts. Illusion and metaphor.

"They're already talking about guest spots on the Johnny Carson and Tom Snyder shows — or Joe Franklin."

He pauses dramatically.

"If the shoe fits, wear it. I mean, we need this. We really need this. Next time you get ready to lay a twenty on the bar, take a close look at it. Ask yourself if that's the last one you will ever see.

"We have to be sure that doesn't happen. See the 'In God We Trust' and Jackson's stare? It's called 'hard currency.' Hard and current."

He rocks back in his Eames Soft Pad, opens the desk drawer to retrieve a tumbler and what's left of a bottle of Jura Prophecy. He pauses for a moment, peruses the label.

In the early 1700's the Campbells of Jura Island, Scotland evicted a wise old seeress. Bristling with resentment, she prophesied that the last Campbell to leave the island would be one-eyed with his belongings carried in a cart drawn by a lone white horse. In 1938 it came true when Charles Campbell, blind in one eye from the Great War, led his white horse to the old pier for the last time. Just like Jura, Prophecy is a dram that's steeped in stories, and every drop has a different tale to tell.

Mathias pours half a glass. The light from the window paints a golden glow on his plain face and white hair. He turns to gaze out over the fog.

"Anyway, I saw a ghost last night," he says, "a bad-ass white-sheet spook. It came out of a mist. The kind of thing that sneaks up and wraps its fingers around your throat. You know, like you lose all your money or maybe the awesome babe with the big tits sitting next to you at the bar is more interested in the dude on the other side than she is in you."

"Oh, most unkind of him," Juan says.

Mathias nips a bit of Jura. Ah. The first tip of the morning with a strong iodine, sea air and some smoke on the nose, burnt caramel on the palate, and smoky, soft caramel on the finish. This opens up with much more peat and less iodine on the nose, with brown sugar and toffee on the palate, and a long, peaty finish. A "profound" peatiness, surrounded by a strong oak presence — an American/bourbon oak residue with a hint of sherry cask scent. The A/b/o gives way to other oak-related flavors — first vanilla, then a full-on butterscotch. Later some grass or barley, and a hint of citrus — and maybe a little ashy smoke.

Mathias continues.

"We need to get on with this *Network* thing."

Aigilas acquiesces. He too has nightmares.

He says, "I know what you mean about bad dreams. Twenty years ago I said 'I do' to a nightmare. So I gotta sleep with it every night. Well, most nights, anyway. What's new?"

They've been in the business a long time, too long, he thinks, (maybe three hundred shows — he hasn't counted) and has given up trying to make the best of a bad situation. He puts his Flic Your Bic to another Cleopatra and blows a cloud of gray smoke across the desk.

He has a severe spine condition (Kyphosis) and has trouble sitting erect for any length of time. He averts his eyes, his large head jerking to the left, back and upward until his thin chin is in the air, his eyes scanning the ceiling. When he's not blowing smoke or scanning the ceiling, he fiddles with the legal pad on his lap. It is important that he does this. Why? No one's sure. But he thinks it is important. He shifts in his chair.

He listens intently to Teivel.

Mathias turns to Kesil.

"Tomorrow monkey on a string airs. Kiss it all goodbye next week, and Abroms tells me lady in the squad room will be completed early next week. Look, *Police Woman* is soaking up the ratings. We need to do more. So.

"A couple years ago Gertrude Schimmel was appointed as the first female PD Inspector. Then last year Vittoria Renzullo made Captain and was appointed 1st Precinct Commander. We need to take advantage of this. We need to get women into the scripts. More women. We need a leg-over."

Kesil turns to Aigilas.

"Okay. Five shows," Aigilas says. "How many writers do we have?"

"I don't know," Mathias says. "Boretz, Crawford, Oliansky — how many do you need? How much time?"

"Two weeks, maybe."

Aigilas focuses on Juan.

"You have any influence with these people?"

"Oh, Marcelo, I wish."

Juan raises his arms and waves off the bird women with a hand of Phineas fingers.

"'At my commands substantial darkness soon o'erspreads the skies and hides the silver moon; my skills as great, my power no less extends, the Serville World to my enchantment bends,' (Petronius)."

He pauses.

"You know I haven't."

"Then our baldheaded wonder has to go over the scripts," Marcelo says.

He leans back.

"I know, I know. It's in his contract. Shit. Even I have to have his imprimatur."

He points to his forehead.

"See the stamp? It says 'Telly Approved.' He has the right to choose the director. Fortunately, he thinks we're friends. So it should be okay. Though you never know."

"Oh, he's still peeohed about *Cape Fear,*" *Juan* says. "He thinks he should have had a better part. Too many lawyers and not enough detectives."

"That was fifteen years ago," Mathias says. "You got to forget sometime."

"Why? Some never do," Juan says. "I never did think his Charlie Sievers was all that good. Paul Newman could have done better.

"I have things I will never forgive people for."

Mathias shakes his head.

"We need two scripts by next week. Then we can heat up the story-board."

He takes another sip, smacks his lips, and lifts the glass to the light to admire the amber haze. The Jura is holding up. He turns to Aigilas.

"I want copy on my desk by early next week."

Kesil chews and peers through the smoke at his watch.

"Seven days," Aigilas says. "That's not much time. Why the rush? Do we have any spec-scripts?"

"Too much time," Lamiae says. "Just too much time. Darling Marcelo, if we have to sit here not doing a thing for seven whole days, I will surely go mad."

Breaking from filing and spraying, he takes up the joystick/paddle controllers of the Fairchild Channel F — a primitive game with one plane of graphics, one of four background colors per line, and three plot-colors (red, green and blue) that turn white if the background is set to black. Impertinently he points the controller at the screen, blasts a few rounds, then sits back in his chair. Seemingly satisfied he resumes filing his nails.

Mathias regards him skeptically.

"Juan, you look fucking terrible, like you crawled out of a milk bottle. Are you eating enough?"

Everybody stares at Juan.

"Too many nights at The Mineshaft," Aigilas says.

The Mineshaft?

"You only wish," Juan says.

The Mineshaft?

A three bars hangout with a roof, several playrooms, a (bath) tub room, and various pieces of equipment (slings, bondage equipment) located in a half-block long building at 835 Washington Street in the middle of The City Meat Market — all to be used and shared to enhance the wildest sexual fantasy, and more.

"Or was it The Anvil? D'ya get hammered at The Anvil?" Mathias says. "You been slam dancing again?"

"You mean skanking," Juan says. "Sisyphus skanking."

"I don't know," Aigilas says. "Don't worry about the scripts. You have the shooting dates?"

"Five," Mathias says. "Here's the list.

March 8 — a student walking home from school.

April 23 — a young woman and her boyfriend on lovers' lane. The police find a note signed, "Son of Sam.

June 26 — a couple siting in a car outside a disco.

July 31 — a couple in the car parked on lover's lane. The girl dies and her boyfriend loses vision in one eye and partial vision in the other eye."

"How did that happen? Why can't he see?"

"I don't know."

"What about the fifth? There are only four here."

"Yeah. We're not sure about that one yet."

"All on lovers' lane."

"Well, the lover's lane locales have been selected to placate our hero and his French fag fetish."

"I do like French fags," Juan says.

Lukema pops another Marshmallow Peep.

Marcelo wonders why
the show cannot reflect nature

Marcelo's skeptical.

"Does every show have to be bloody? Doesn't anybody die of natural causes anymore? Like typhoid or cholera. I don't know anybody that's had small pox or Asian flu?"

"Natural causes?"

"Who said that?" Juan asks.

"Said what?"

"Natural causes."

"I don't know."

"It doesn't make any difference," Mathias tells them.

"Natural causes?"

"You mean other than those dreadful dead chickens and pigs they feed you at restaurants?" Juan says. "Well, if we are part of nature, and I'm sure we are, whatever happens is natural. Whatever we do is part of nature. Old age — heaven forbid — even poison. Do you realize how much poison there is in nature?

"Remember, 'Sanguinaries are not good people. I am good. Therefore, I am not a sanguinary. But I am a part of nature.'"

"How about 'Malignity is not good. I am not malignant. Therefore, I am good?'" Aigilas says.

"My dear Marcelo," Juan inveighs, "life is a crapshoot in a natural-selection casino. And you only crap out once. So why worry?"

"What's AWRT say about this?" Aigilas wants to know.

"Oh, they'll howl. They always do," Mathias says. "They'll be pissed. But that's what they want — something to bitch about — a bigger footprint in the business. Well, now they got it."

"Okay. So we know the dates and the story. We know the story — the structure. Revenge or no, it's the same. Why not film the shooting later and cut in around it? We have enough footage of muggings and rapes in the park for a two-year series. I mean. The dope-sheet's extensive."

Juan prophesizes
on the future
of humankind and unkind

Aigilas pushes back his chair and stands. He stretches, walks hump-shouldered to the couch, hesitates, then kicks it. A puff of dust clouds his foot. Two rats scurry from a tear in the fabric and disappear into a hole in the floor near the water cooler.

"I wouldn't do that," Juan says. "You know, rats are very sensitive and are scheduled to take over the world. Like they did Easter Island. You're going to annoy them and then they'll come looking for you."

"They need exercise," Marcelo says.

He's bent over the rat hole.

"They're getting fat. Life's too easy. I mean, after all, this is the home of the trinity. I know they're good at fucking. That's why there's so many of them. But they need to feed themselves. So cross yourself."

The phone buzzes. Mathias pushes a button.

A scratchy disembodied voice announces, "Mr. Aegean Zeus is here for his appointment."

"He'll have to wait," Mathias says.

"Do the prelim people have this lined up?" Marcelo says. "What's his name? Beckert? Peter Beckert? Is that the same one?"

He's still gazing down the rat hole.

"What the fuck do they do down there all day?"

He turns to Mathias.

"Sam Beckett? I thought he was in France. You mean Berkowitz."

"Beckert-O-Witz. Hans-Peter-David-Beckert-O-Witz," Mathias says. "How did you know that?"

"The people over at casting were talking. If it's the same one, they're not sure he'll go along with it."

"Oh, he'll go along with it," Lamiae says. "Believe me. We've already had monstrous discussions with his agent. Such a lovely man. He reminds me of an uncle I once had who thought he was a supreme devil. But he wasn't."

"Mr. Berkowitz will do it. He would just love an opportunity to eradicate more natives."

He smiles, pleased with the prospect.

"It will be so exciting."

"Jesus," Mathias says. "So casting has been talking to this dude's agent. The fucking world without me. Why wasn't I told? Everybody knows about this but me."

"Yeah, but why worry?" Aigilas says. "We have time on our side. Time to create and murder."

"Oh goodness," Lamiae says. "Here we go again with Eliot. Marcelo, you are such an imaginative person."

Aigilas stares at Juan.

"Where'd you get that about the rats? About rats taking over the world?"

"Oh, everybody knows that. Haven't you seen Gordon's *Food of the Gods*?"

"Again, I shouldn't have to tell you. These are not the usual shows," Mathias says. "People are already queued up from Nantucket to Boca Raton. It's our task to get them in the can before our guest star is apprehended or gets himself wasted by the police. There's what you might call 'a certain urgency' here."

"And yes, the PR gurus have been on it for weeks."

"How about budget support? Do we get the Shackleton?" Marcelo says. "The bogus news reports and all that? With teevee guide?"

"All news reports are bogus," Mathias says. "They never get it right."

"So which gurus?"

"I don't have a list. What difference does it make? I mean, the friggin species is already on its way out. So what?"

"On this first one," Aigilas says, "who's the girl?"

Mathias turns to Lamiae.

"Well?"

"Oh, just a twit off the street. Another inconsequential vagi."

"Limiting the competition?" Aigilas says to Juan. "Why not Fenech or Nicolodi? Somebody with class and a decent rep? Did you see *Strip Nude for Your Killer* or *Deep Red?* That would add appeal."

"Oh, my," Juan says. "I certainly did. Absolutely scrumptious. But they are so overpriced. You know, both your testicles and mine — and any number of other people's. And this is just a walk-on-carry-off part."

Mathias shifts in his chair.

"Okay. Look. We have to get on it. The Mafia and Wall Street are already nibbling at the prospects."

Juan puts his finger to his lips.

"Shhhhh! Naughty, naughty man. You can't say that anymore."

"Say what?"

"M-a-f-i-a. It is no longer in season. We are required to address them by a kind name. Dear Mathias, we must watch what we say and how we say it."

"Well, whoever they are, they have noses like bloodhounds. They'll want in. I mean, this will pin the Nielsen for months — a real Easter egg. The reiterations will go on forever. More than that, we'll be in line for doing the blackout and the Bronx fire this fall. Listen. The friggin City is burning. Especially the Bronx. All that shit in the air this morning blew down from the Bronx. We should be able to make something off that. But we have to do it now," he warns.

"By the way," Aigilas says, "do you have anything to say about the writers?"

Mathias screws up his face.

"I'm not sure."

"I mean, maybe we could add some graphics."

Mathias goes back to the Jura Prophecy.

"Maybe they could work in a stringer or two with a few Weegees for historical authenticity," Marcelo says. "This has been going on a long time. We could add a verse or two to an old song."

"Yeah. Something like that."

"But you know the rap on our heuristic-super-sleuth-hero," Marcelo says. "What he's like without words. Pictures are good, well-set scenes — but did you ever hear him adlib? He needs words, our words. Where they come from — where, matters as much as when. We'll need scripts as soon as possible."

They've had this conversation before. However, with or without the adlib, it comes back to words.

Out of the clear blue one day, Aigilas asks Mathias, "Where do the words go? I mean, when I do something, it's done. I can see it. But what happens to words? You paint words into a script, then somebody recites them. Then where do they go?"

Mathias stares at him quizzically.

"But they're still on the page."

"Not if they're spoken."

"Then there is two of them. One setting and one flapping."

"Maybe in somebody's ear?"

"You mean like *Horton Hears a Who!?* But what if they miss somebody's ear. Where else? When you pray, where do the words go?"

"Why to god, of course. Where else?"

"But what if you don't believe in god?"

Mathias grunts.

"Then I don't know. Maybe they bounce off the moon or burn up in the sun. Yeah, the sun burns up everything around it. Or maybe they just loop out into space and then come back to haunt you when you're old. You know, what goes around, comes around. Maybe you're praying to yourself. You just have to wait a while to hear what you asked for."

Aigilas does not doubt Mathias. He regards him carefully, as if, indeed, this is likely.

"Why? You thinking of praying?"

"Well, I might," Aigilas says.

"Why would you do that? You want something? That's the only reason to pray. If you want something."

"You mean asking god for it."

"Yeah. Or someone else. I hear people pray to the saints. Hell, some of them even pray to dead friends or picture postcards."

Aigilas frowns.

"What do you want that god can give you?" Mathias asks. "He doesn't have anything you need."

"I don't believe in god," Aigilas says.

"Yeah," Mathias says. "I know. You said that."

"Christ. I'm still worried about this — about that stamp on your forehead."

Mathias nods to Aigilas.

"You're right. We need to get the writers on this. Our sleuthing-wonder just directed kiss it all goodbye. And he'll want more. He's going auteur — and lobbying for adlib time. We'll need strong stories to protect the integrity of the project.

"He's been reading about cops like Horan, Friedman, Biller — maybe Louie Eppolito or Paul Rangonese. Who's the most decorated cop in The City?"

"Which one?"

"Depends on which one you ask.

"He's trying to get in touch with Eppolito's machismo. Calls his family. Wants to be a crime-buster. I don't know what he wants. He's been working nights looking for the Mad Dog Veterans in the Park. Spends a lot of time in Astoria.

"I don't know what he wants. Hell, he's already in the movies. Shows up on the set wearing an Eppolito mask. I mean, what more is there?"

Aigilas turns to Lamiae.

"You speak Greek, don't you?"

"Yes," Lamiae says. "I can also write Greek. Dear Marcelo, I have tried to talk to him. I cannot understand a thing the man says. I mean, it's some other kind of Greek to me."

Mathias' face hardens.

"You look like a stone man," Aigilas says. "How are we gonna shoot this?"

"Oh, I think he's superb," Lamiae says. "Just like Teddy on mount Rushmore. Mathias, I do hope you have a big shtick?"

"Okay. Three cameras," Mathias says. "A pedestal, a crane, and a Steadcam. Credibility. The handheld will give it a doc effect. We can say somebody was taking pictures and accidently got the footage, etc., etc. You know, some schmuck just dropped it off at the door. That always makes good ad copy."

Mathias stares at Kesil.

"Lukema you got the camera crew and the pedestal."

He pushes a paper across the desk.

"They're writing letters. To the neighbors, the police. The police will put together a composite. Images are easy to communicate, easy to grasp, and easy to remember. We don't want to end up on The Flop Wall at Allen's.

"They'll be sending a letter to Breslin sometime near the end of May — to keep interest up. We should have two episodes in the can by then. It's a rendition of the letter Hans Beckert sent to the Berlin police, which is similar to the letter Peter Kürten sent to the Düsseldorf police. They expect Breslin to run it, or part of it at least. It should get the interest ball rolling."

Aigilas gives up on the rats.

"He'll run it. He'll drool over it," Juan says. "He's such a goy."

"Wait a fuckin minute," Marcelo says. "Who's sending this to Breslin? Why wasn't I told about this?"

"The PR people."

"Who gave them the to do that?"

Mathias shrugs.

"I don't know," he says.

He takes another sip. The Jura is fine.

"But I'm with you."

"It doesn't hurt to advertise," Juan says. "As Mathias says, we can't expect much until the word gets out. In the beginning was the word, and the word was good PR, and the word sells. Remember, word is logos and logo is what we're all about. It's called product affection or brand loyalty. Call it the creator of The Universe.

"Dear, Marcelo, haven't you heard of ambiguous capitalism?"

Now he's singing.

"I see a Blood Moon arising. Oh, do go out tonight, it will surely be alright, when an eye is taken for an eye."

"Entertainment capitalism?"

"Why of course. That or something else. Everything we do is entertain-mint. The ninnies watch and applaud. It doesn't matter, as long as they get devastation. They're fascinated with corpses. Especially dismembered corpses. Then they want more. Haven't you ever heard of bloodlust? My goodness, the Romans had a field day with it. The Coliseum day and night.

"Surely you've heard of the contest of Amazones and Pygmy men, when those horrid, beastly monstrous women impaled the lovely little men on spears, then walked around the floor of the Coliseum showing off, holding the wriggling bodies in the air so everyone could cheer."

"Juan, that's bullshit. Myth."

"Yes it is. I would never cheer for something like that. Nor would the Romans. They were not barbarians."

"Anyway," Mathias says, "they've located the splinter from the Loo's nose. I don't know how in the hell they found it, but they did. Bought it for a song from a waitress at some waterfront dive. It'll be auctioned off at Sotheby's. Soon as the first Sam show hits the waves. Opening bid fifty thousand dollars."

"Auctioning a splinter at Sotheby's?" Marcelo says.

"Yeah. It's art."

"A splinter from a fictional police Lieutenant's nose is art?"

"Well, this is from the nose of an icon. The best loved member of The City's Finest," Mathias says. "You could have one of them blow his nose on canvas and it would sell for art — for big bucks. Art resides in the pocket-book of the buyer."

"I suppose that makes sense."

"Believe me, dear Marcelo," Juan says, "they know what they are doing. The more they pay, the more intrinsic the beauty. That's art.

"Have you seen the latest of Mapplethorpe? He is so with it. He is working on a new urophagia series — the ceremonial, medicinal, and cosmetic as well as sexual. But I'd still rather have a pot of gold.

"'Whoe'er his magic gold, secure may sail, where'er he please, he's lord of Fortune's gale. In short — when of the money you're possessed, you need but wish — you've Jove within your chest' (Petronius)."

"I'm glad you told me," Marcelo says. "I never would have figured it out."

"Whatever they want to call it — it behooves us to agree," Mathias says.

In spite of the Anglo-Saxon "behōfian," which he sometimes uses in careless moments to soften the hard sell, he's serious. Nothing as yet to put his finger on, no clearly definable scent or pattern, but he is leery, uneasy, suspects someone could have him in the crosshairs, or at least by the shorthairs. Otherwise, it is too easy — the assignment, the support. He thinks there's got to be more to it than he is getting. He takes another sip of Jura Prophecy and sits back to think.

By now Sam's bored with the gnomes. Having done what he can for the moment, he slithers away, relocates to Broadway and Wall Street, barely discernable in the acid-fog of churning, stock bashing, and bear raiding. He ambles goat-gaited along the predatory tunnel from Trinity Place to South Street, then to Bowling Green Park, 26 Broadway.

Indeed. This morning the juice is flowing. He tips a flask of Sam Thompson (Rye Whiskey) Old Monongahela, 1791, mixes with the crowd.

"What do we have here?" fabled passerby Senior Federico Lorca of 4-18340, Fuente Vaqueros, Granada, Spain, says to a companion, lifting and sweeping his arm in a gesture wide enough to encompass the Street.

"Rivers of gold run here from all over the earth," he says, "and death comes with it. Here, as nowhere else, you feel a total absence of the spirit: herds of men who cannot count past three, herds more who cannot get past seven, scorn for pure science and demoniacal respect for the present. And the terrible thing is, the crowd that fills the street believes the world will always be the same and that it is their duty to keep the machine running day and night, forever."

Where is Sammy the Bull when you need him? The chorus, echoing a kiddies' rhyme, chants,

> Why, having most indelicately killed a man,
> Sammy the Bull is in the slam.
> (Child's Rhyme)

Ten years ahead of Arturo Di Modica's whimsical gift, Sam has his hand on the bull's ass, tickling the old guy's light-brown testicles — hoping for a little generative potential.

"The goodfather greed," Sam mumbles, chuckles, evangelizing the obvious. "The best of Protestant morality. WASPs love animals but hate people."

He reaches over, pinches the Golden Calf's balls. This bovine is cast in bronze. His head comes up. He roars.

Lukema lifts his eyes as if from a dream, regards the phone.

"Who is Zeus?" Marcelo says. "What's he waiting for? I mean, why is Zeus waiting?"

Who, indeed?

"Hey, Zeus, by Jove! Taurus and Zeus . . .." Mathias laughs and holds up two fingers, together. "Zeus took on the shape of a bull to kill Agenor's daughter Europa. He joined the king's herd and was the toughest stud in the pack. That got Europa's attention. She wanted to ride him — so he gave her a ride, if you know what I mean. Still, it took him all the way to Crete to get his rod into her burning bush. For her to get her hand on his horn."

Lamiae says, "Yes. I heard something about that in college. Yes. But what about the fifth show?"

again Sam finds substance
  with which to paint
himself into the fabric of The City

From behind the tormentor-right, Sam emerges basked in a dim purple memory, glares into the depth of audience, the lines of The City's streets running out behind him to infinity.

"So we find ourselves once again begot of the word, a lightwave spawned by idea, energy forced into matter," he says and hacks up a yellow putrefied effluence.

"The story unfolds with nothing to guide us but wit and guile and menace. Suffering is both sacred and damnable — the cloth out of which life is rent."

He's rhapsodizing man, not as fallen from the fantasy of the gods, but wallowing in a groveling helplessness that may be changed (by a modicum of solace) only in revising judgments of the other and the designs and intentions of seeking — the Golden Fleece, the Holy Grail, the Perfect Pearl.

"That numinous martinet of heaven, the grand and glorious monarch, wizard of the spheres, damned his creation, his feeble failures, an amateur sculptor attempting to smash the form, the vision his mallet and chisel did not find. He cast us out and down as we struggle against the form that binds, to what was imagined grievous ruin, not because he is right, but because he is unwilling to admit that it is already glorious in heinous, shameful ruin."

In a typical ungulate Flehman response, Sam curls an upper lip. He stretches his neck and breathes in as over a fetid curiosity, pausing to savor the scent. He gloats. A goat laugh. The shrill reverberation bravado of arrogance.

"He will wash his hands of his failures."

Behind him the streets are replaced by a bed-stack of two mattresses floating above a clutter of newspapers surrounded by the trash of a twentieth century campsite — a Zenith 19" tabletop Chromacolor II atop a small wooden packing crate, a Westclox Solid State Clock Radio and a carton of Ronzoni Ziti 2 on the floor near the bed, and a Sharp Carousel microwave on the kitchen counter.

In a far corner, on the bed-stack, Peter-David, Sam's cherubic protégé breathes softly the exhilaration, the peace-of-mind of a completed hunt.

Sam circles, drops to one knee and takes David's white hand in his.

David stirs. Sam stands.

"Innocence, a fine and delightful child, a fiend. Already in his confusion, striking out he has manufactured a profound and magnificent revulsion. And while the true test is yet to come, the sting of slander, defamation, denunciation, the encompassing full scope of hatred and vengeance, the covenant is sealed."

He watches David.

"We will be delivered into the hands of our enemies — ridiculed, maligned, tortured. Even now, they are gathering in the hall, at the door. Do you hear that? That woman. What does she say?"

Child-David stirs, restless. Sam chuckles, his voice deepens, spreads over the room.

"Picture yourself the brute, groveling, grunting, misshapen, dirty and diseased. Oh, how easy to forget. Forgive and forget and you lie awake, exhausted, watching, seeing yourself finally as others see you.

"You agree, consent — plead guilty and beg her to leave. Her stare, her glare, tells you she'd dance and sing an end to you as brutal and savage as anything you could devise. She'd have your head on a platter.

"Then you consent, you admit to what she has wanted from the beginning, you confess that you are a freak, a warped and deranged, seven-headed drooling fiend festering with abscesses and boils. You are the underside of life. You are death.

Sam sneers.

"'I am become a reproach among my enemies, and very much to my neighbors; and a fear to my acquaintances. They that see me flee from me. I am forgotten as one dead from the heart. I am a vessel that is destroyed' (Psalm 31 :11-12).

"The impasse between aura and act," Sam says, "one on the horizon taunting, inviting but unattainable, the other here and hard, painful and exact — the sand blowing in your face, the end of the desert nowhere in sight."

He's humming softly, the melodious but seared harmony of insult and mockery.

The song fades and David wakes, roused by the panting in a grey mist of a dog nuzzling the window, paws on the sill, teeth bared, a white froth on its tongue.

"Revenge," Hans-David says. "For all the suffering they cause."

The mournful piping of Sam's voice a small, duplicitous whine.

it's Valentine's Day (again)
and the Big Apple blushes
with hearts and flowers

As a prelude to the festivities of candy, cards, and flowers, a settling of affection on not always willing subjects, a reasonable fair price to pay for a consortium of concupiscence, Richard Malestri of 33-45 Altmond Street, Bronx, takes his paramour of two weeks to a Freilich Jewelers at 312 E. 204th Street. She is to choose her Valentine's Day present. Anything you want. Money's not a problem. And while she gazes in lustful rapture over the pickings, he drops a thousand dollar diamond necklace into her coat pocket.

"Listen," he tells her, "I've got to feed the meter. Give me a minute or two, then meet me outside. We'll go to another store. Shop a bit."

She does not ask, "If we are leaving, why the meter?"

He waits across the street. When store security detains her at the door, he drives away.

Hell. Works two out of three times.

Anyway, his name isn't Malestri, and he doesn't live 33-45 Altmond.

Still, another day of love and passion, bliss and plotting in the Big Apple, and everyone's ready for action. *The Times* reports:

> Margaret Watt has sold Valentine candy at the Li-Lac Shop on Christopher Street for thirty years, and her tidy knot of white hair and stacks of creams are a constant in a changing Village.
> "It's a big day," she says. "Easter is bigger because the children can get in on it, too. But Valentine's Day is big. That's odd, isn't it? I guess there's still a lot of love in the air."

At 6:25 on the feast of St. Valentine, in the deep smog of a not-so-brightly dawning day, prompted by shafts flung from Cupid's Eros with constricted visibility and a poorly slung bow, even without the aid of aphrodisiacs, philters or charms, it seems those afflicted with the rising passions of the morn can hardly contain themselves.

A man, in the West 4th Street Station of the IND, it is later reported, rapes a woman and robs her of two hundred dollars.

An hour later, another woman is hit on the head, à la Neanderthal, and dragged off, déjà vu, to the somewhat less than sanitary or romantic murky recesses of an unlocked toilet of the West 86th Street Station of the IND 8th Avenue line. She, too, is raped, then robbed of one dollar and thirteen subway tokens.

In customary brevity, resigned to nature's impulses and double-dealings, a detective with the specialized obscenity squad wanders into the restroom to relieve himself followed by a reporter and notes, without consideration for the guy in the next stall who has to listen to the whole thing, that, "Any place where there aren't other people around is a rape hazard."

Thus, while it appears somewhat undesirable to be loved indiscrimi-nately, sex beneath the loins of ardent barbarity may still be the best The

City has to offer.

As Sam is quick to note, even in the best of times some things just do not work out.

"We need to let go of the life we have planned," Sam says, "so we can accept the one waiting for us."

How about, "The hour of departure has arrived, and we go our separate ways, I to die, and you to live. Which of these two is better only god knows" (Socrates).

as promised the Chief of Detectives
seeks diligently in the round-abouts
and discovers a clairvoyant
to aid the investigation

Hit in the whump by shrapnel of a stalled manhunt, Captain Keener goes off limping, trying to lick his wounds, again resigned to the hazards of trench warfare, life at the bottom, the vulnerability in mortality, etc.

"We're expanding," he declares. "We've hired a forensic-extrasensory expert to assist the taskforce, give it direction, charm, fortitude. We will no longer endure these belittling attacks, or tolerate the insufferable harangues of press-core harlequins."

Yes, the word is out. But just who is the seer the CD has in mind? No one knows. Speculation and uncomplimentary guesses abound.

That afternoon, in a squad room hastily arranged for a gathering of select members of the press, she appears at the Captain's side dressed in a lust red pullover tunic with a round neckline, barrel-cuffed raglan-style long sleeves, two patch pockets and side slits at the waist with Trapunto stitch-trim. Today she has chosen a self-tie belt and pull-on style pants with elasticized waistband and wide straight legs.

Her raiment is completed with burgundy fourteen-and-a-quarter-inch pull-on shiny patent-look vinyl backed — cotton fabric for comfort — boots with molded sole — deeply lugged for traction — and a two-inch wedge heel of Kraton polymer.

She has shoulder length hair, topped by a slouch hat, and wears a white cotton blindfold. The eyes, it is said, indicate the antiquity of the soul, and rumor has it what remains of Our Lady's are transparent pods of green luster. This, however, has yet to be verified.

So who is the lady?

A Bellevue reject.
A Hoboken refugee.
A deaf mute with psychic powers.
A weirdo in a town of freaks.
She can hear the sound of color.

Psyaint David

She hums, chatters, buzzes —electrical storms bother her.
She operates on radio waves — a baby white dwarf, a pulsar.
She runs on a couple dozen Eveready s.
She's an advertisement for Electric corsets.

All right, but who is she?

A badge bunny.
A holster humper.
A sibyl.
A sybarite.
A sylph.

Brigid O'Shaughnessy.
Cathy Wood
Irma Grese
Mary of Magdala tickling Christ's toes.
Mata Hari with her bangles, beads, and small boobs.
Nancy Drew with jaded, kinky, swinging pastimes.
Vivian Rutledge.

Some think she's a survivor of Fat Sammy (Mayor of the Bowery) Fuchs' alcoholic haven, Sammy's Bowery (Foolish) Follies — maybe the Queen of the Bowery or

Coney Island Mae,
Goldie Shaw.
Juke Box Katie.
Madame May.
Prune Juice Jenny.
Tug Boat Ethel.
Skid Row Molly.
Broadway Betty

After all this is show biz.

> Oh, Sammy's Bowery follies is
> The only place today.
> Life of the old time Bowery
> That once was wild and gay.
> Stop in an' Sammy'll tell you 'bout
> That gay and hectic whirl
> When – "The Bowery, The Bowery"
> Was the song of all the world.
> (Sammy Fuchs)

The papers are full of it — opinions, guesses — no one knows for sure; intrigue compounded by the cryptic. His Honor, the Lord Mayor, is asking questions.

"What is this about?"

"We're grabbing at straws," Police Commissioner Michael "Soft Fin" Garfield (named after an ancient order of "primitive" ray-finned fish known from the late Cretaceous onwards of two genera that still inhabit fresh, brackish, and occasionally, marine waters of eastern North America) says.

Beame shakes his head.

"This is bad for The City, using vaudevillian has-beens in a police investigation. The City won't stand for it."

Garfield thinks otherwise.

"Oh, they'll go along with it. Superstitious, unscientific bastards. They'll believe anything we tell them. Tell them it's art. It's spiritual. That she will cost a lot of money. What else have they got? They'll buy it."

"And what about the press?"

"They like her. They understand a good scam. This is show biz. They need something to fill up the spaces between ads."

"You'd better be right."

"Who knows, she may stumble onto something."

Then more speculation.

Rumors gain credence.

The little lady is said (and claims) to be an unconfirmed victim of Son of Sam, lives with a .44 slug in her head. Her eyesight destroyed by the projectile, doctors fear an operation may cause further damage. However, Queen's District Attorney John Santucci wants the evidence, has asked for a court order to retrieve the bullet.

Santucci is a highly visible D.A with a mobile office, a van emblazoned with his name, to take complaints from citizens on street corners. And he will appear personally in court, especially if the case is newsworthy, as in the recent bail hearing for the youths who firebombed two subway clerks.

"Evidence," he claims. "We need the bullet to continue the investigation."

Still, she refuses to consent to the operation. Of course. It's her head, her body, her private property. Someday it will be worth a fortune. She plans to auction it off at Sotheby's with Kojak's splinter. So why mess with it?

Of course, there's the practical. With the projectile in place she conjures likenesses, depictions, has visions in full colored of uncharted realms. Already she has become the mystic muse of Wall Street — led an assault on securities, engineered a merger that left ITT with its fingers in the door, and collected a pay check in seven figures for her services.

She has a .44 GB memory and has been heard at times to thank her attacker — the single stroke of the hammer falling on the firing pin of a . . ..

Psyaint David

"That blow raised my consciousness," Our Lady (Notre Dame des Sept Questions) says. "Elevated me from the ignominious pastimes of a hapless little frivolous snatch with no prospect beyond the hope of someday finding a pointless, dull-minded, sappy weasel to marry and to live forever-after in the endless cycle of getting screwed a couple times a week, tending a house full of screaming, soiled brats, and cultivating the paths of a rather substantial inability to think into major arteries of ignorance. Now, that is done."

Along with her eyesight, she might add.

When asked to make a comment for the press, she steps forward and smiles.

> She will turn fate's misfortune to nothing.
> She will inundate the earth with magic.
> She will bring humanity beneath her wing.
>
> Life is a moving vaudeville production.
> All is a play, the ending is tragic.
> The denouement of an eternal production.
>
> The performance ends on Walpurgisnacht
> When earth gives up its fantastic
> Story, engraved on water-washed rocks.
> (Kriemhild Gretchen)

The press is dumbfounded, amused.

"Riddles and bad poetry. Doggerel. What is this leading to?"

But intrigue, nonetheless. She features a radiant Ultra Brite cover girl smile meant to convey receptiveness, arousal, mirth, as well as contempt, disapproval, disgust — all directed by an insatiable appetite for money — cold hard cash — as much of it as possible.

"Why does she wear a blindfold?" a reporter asks.

"Everybody's got something," Garfield says. "That's hers."

"Who recommended her?"

"Well, no one exactly."

The Mayor questions what she's done lately, her experience in police work.

"She has a stellar record," he is told. "She's been instrumental in a number of criminal all-star cases."

"Yeah?"

"Yeah. Names like Countess Elizabeth Bathory, Myra Hindley, Valerie Salanes, Ulkire Meinhof. She's a psychic chameleon, shifts along the affective spectrum with incredible rapidity, can change affectations on the fly, and that makes her especially valuable for police work. In her youth she was lily-white (which is no color at all), then she turned red. Now she is decidedly green, headed for gray — and black (which is all colors). She aided and abetted Queenie St. Clair and The Forty Thieves. Gave them their start. Lent them seed money. Remember, what FDR said of putting Joe Kennedy in charge of the SEC — "It takes a thief to catch a thief."

"Oh yeah? That's right."

She is made an honorary member of the Major Case Squad, given a key to The City, which isn't worth much these days — with The City bankrupt and facing foreclosure. However, if need be, at least she can unlock the metaphorical door to get out. She's to be paid two hundred thousand dollars The City doesn't have, for whatever she does or doesn't provide.

the Lou attempts to improve
  his image and discovers
  he too is being tailed
by a shapeshifter

Despite his tender-nosed skepticism, the Lieutenant has mellowed, thinks it might not be a bad idea to have the little woman on The Job. He already has his lines down for the lady in the squad room and shimmers in at medium close-up on a 9" Sony. He takes the afternoon off to go shopping, strolls The Avenue of the Americas, buys Telly Apparel, dude-dandied up, Peter Wimsey at his best, finely dressed, the master of the obvious — matures into a dapper little Charlie Chaplin dandy with a hand-carved mahogany cane — waddle and all — hooking the skirts of young women, rolling his eyes.

"Who loves ya, baby?"

He moves quickly on the black-and-white screen, jerks off into the night.

Otherwise, he's on the job, prepping himself for the investigation. He monitors the squad rooms on teevee, takes notes, sucks lollipops and scratches his crotch. Clues accompany crimes as surely as madmen find murder, and he knows that small details, in the end, make the difference. He's certain the night-stalker can be found somewhere in the electrical impulses cavorting in the vacuum tube. He knows if he waits long enough it will come together.

The third day the action picks up a step from the monotony of ethnic jokes, cops picking their noses and trying to appear dignified.

"What's a Greek funeral look like?"

"Three garbage trucks in a row with their lights on."

"Daddy, everybody says I have the biggest dick in the fourth grade. Is that because I'm black?"

"No, no, son, that's because you're nineteen."

And just when all seems to be lost, Heathcliff bumbles in.

"Aigilas is on the line. Says he wants to talk to you."

"All he has to do is tune in. What's he want?"

"Didn't say."

"Well, well, a nickel for the newsboy. I'll take it off-screen. Keep an eye on this."

Two weeks have passed since the last shooting. Time progresses even in silence, inactivity. Expectantly, the Lieutenant takes the phone and Marcelo comes to the point.

"Something you'll be glad to hear," he says. "We're moving the show to The City. Everyone agrees, it's the best thing to do. It doesn't make sense to have the first-unit on Colonial Street or in Century City when we have ready-made street scenes here. Anyway, they're having trouble finding enough mongrels to keep the sets supplied with shit. It has to have some verisimilitude.

"Thought you'd want to know. And I'll need to see you as soon as possible."

"Who decided this?"

"Well, it was a corporate action. We made it. Someone made it. But I'm not sure about the others. I don't know. Why?"

The Inspector is intrigued.

"Anything you say, sweetheart. Listen, I gotta get back to work. Tune me in at two. Channel 2. It's about teenage heroin addicts. There's a couple slow spots near the middle. We should be able to talk."

Then a pause on the line.

"Death takes a lover? Who did that?" Marcelo says. "We didn't make that."

"It's a rerun from a spook studio in Queens. Hey, baby, you ain't in the world alone."

The camera pulls back, the tableau dissolves, fades in on the Captain's office as the Lieutenant returns. Fatso is watching the monitor, reading the latest *Detective Comics,* Vol. 1, #455, "The Heart of the Vampire," his feet propped up on the desk. He's finishing a mid-morning Wimpy snack of hamburgers, French fries and matzah with peanut butter. Some think he is more closely related to Kesil than to Kojak.

Otherwise, the office is empty. Earlier, Rizzo (not Ernie) was in the outer office looking for new lines, a place to step in, when a woman showed up to report a purse snatching. After a brief "Hello" he left with her — ostensibly to take a report that a person or persons unknown snatched her purse. Now he's on a photo shoot of the crime scene — and of the victim. He's expected to resurface later in the story, with or without pictures.

On the other hand, Detective Percy Saperstein, a perennial face of the 9th or 11th is noticeably absent. He would have been part of the story and included in this scene had he not suffered a serious injury in a gunfight.

During lunch hour January 15, he stumbled on an armed robbery at a Deli a few blocks from Manhattan South. After confronting the gunman, who shot at the Detective three times (all three shots going astray) Saperstein drew his service revolver and was about to fire on the perp when Anna Marcella of 256 Schenk Avenue in Brooklyn, screaming obscenities and alleging police brutality, grabbed the Detective's arm and pulled him to the ground. The robber then shot Saperstein and fled.

At this time, details of Detective Saperstein's wounds are not clear. It seems a round lodged uncomfortably close to his spinal cord, resulting in nerve damage and extensive trauma that has not yet subsided. He is currently in Einstein healing and congealing. If his wounds are not serious, after a few weeks of rest and therapy he is expected to be back at work.

It is easy to say Saperstein deserved better. Certainly, he deserved to be a bigger part of the story. As information about his condition becomes available, it will be passed along.

Just now, however, without consideration for those watching, or parental warning, the theatrics on the squad room teevee take a sudden *cet obscur objet du désir* twist. Demosthenes chokes on his peanut butter-matzah, coughs red-faced.

"Will you look at that?" he wheezes, blowing bits of food on the screen.

The Lieutenant turns to his Chief.

"Who's the lady in the squad room?"

"The lady in the squad room?"

"Well, it seems the men, or at least one of the men, is enjoying himself."

Indeed. A swarm of flies in the ointment, a complication, a hellhound loosed, prowling, howling at the moon, the yellow dog-devil of discontent. This is not supposed to happen in a police station in The City.

Did your mother dream a pale dog leapt from her womb carrying a torch with which to set the world ablaze? Ahh! Domini canes?

A howl goes up from the Captain.

"What in the name of god's hell is going on here?"

"It's just teevee," Heathcliff says. "Hell, this is better than cable."

"And it's coming from one of our squad rooms."

"I know squad rooms are for officers to get together," Aristotelis says in his best macho Kojak-Spade intonation, "but this is a new one."

"Who's the woman? How did she get in the squad room? Who's the cop? Where's this coming from? Do we have to go back to knock over?" the Captain queries.

Fatso snickers, blushes.

"Can't tell, Captain. Matter of privacy. Got serious Third, Fourth, Fifth and Ninth Amendment overtones. Requires you to see things you would rather not. Could be from anyone of ten or fifteen precincts."

"But it's not. Clearly, that is coming from one room some place, from one precinct station in this city."

"Don't worry," Theo says, "we're the only ones in town watching. I mean, this is closed circuit."

"What about the spies?" the Captain warns. "There are spies every-where. Eyes and ears with equipment so advanced they can see everything. And you know they're watching us, trying to break our code to know what we know. What if they see this? It could foul up the investigation. What if the press gets wind of this? I don't like it."

"Dan, it ain't the first time a lady got hopped by a cop in a station house. You ever hear of a Holster Harlot?"

He uses "holster" here for alliterative purposes. The most obvious other possibility for an "h" reference to a cop's equipment would be "handcuff," though he could have use "Holmes Harlot" or "HBO Harlot." Otherwise, "strumpet" — "S/H Strumpet" would have sufficed.

"And you can bet your cookies it won't be the last," he says. "Hell, the precincts are full of hopping cops. Their little black books have more numbers than π."

"But who's the cop?"

"Captain, what you are beholding is the upright and honorable Bobby Crocker, with his pants around his ankles, pursuing with fervor and enthu-siasm one of the few pleasures a man has in life."

"But that woman works for me," the Captain says.

"So you hired her to turn the squad rooms into Topless Go Go? She always wear a blindfold?"

"I've never seen her without it."

"How many precincts do we have in The City?"

"I don't know, Captain."

"Well, goddam, give me a number. Take a guess."

"Seventy-seven. But I can tell you it ain't coming from none of them."

Keener picks up the phone.

"Give me the 109th," he says.

"It's no use," Stavros says. "It's the same at the 58th."

"Try the 111th," the Lou suggests. "It's not exactly what you would call family entertainment."

Demosthenes is confused.

"Lieutenant, I don't understand this."

The Loo smirks knowingly.

"Heathcliff, you amaze me. What you see is obviously our friend and fellow officer, Bobby Crocker, somewhat out of uniform, on a couch some-where in a room in this city. And on that couch with our unfrocked friend is a woman who may or may not be in the uniform of the day, and they are, and have been for some time now, humping like a couple of stray curs in a weed patch. And you ask me what is going on. Didn't momma ever tell you about the snakes and the clams?"

Well, okay. Patting a hooker's derrière while conversing with her in street lingo about the existential significance of crime is one thing. This, however, appears to be another.

Moreover, important questions remain. When did it begin? What has happened to the in-house teevee system? When will it end? Is it eternal? Will the lovers be joined quomodo canis and left to whirl forever in a series of hellacious unending reverberations? And more. Who wrote it? Will advertisers pay for this kind of programing? Maybe some things cannot be undone.

Dapper Dandy Dick
decides to make some
points for the good guys

Dapper Dandy Detective-inspector is scheduled late tonight in kiss it all goodbye — Channel 2, 10:00. For fifteen minutes he drifts about, lollipop in place, in an unimaginative plot, without direction, waiting for the call that will send him on his once a night — most often — high-speed-Keystone-Cops' chase.

He's at the wheel of the bronze beast Buick Century Regal 455 cruising, the lights of The City bobbing outside, a glare on the glass, with Under-inspector Kevin Crocker Dobson riding koala-shotgun.

"I don't know how it got on the in-house set, but I don't want to see it again," Dapper Dick says.

"It's everywhere," Crocker replies somewhat sheepishly.

"We're cops — can you dig that? The public expects more from us."

Crocker is dejected, his face obscured by the gloom of the bleak, deep, cold city night, and the seriousness of what it means to be a cop in the Big Apple.

"Lieutenant, the lady didn't complain. I mean, what more could I do?"

"No, no, dummy. People. I mean people watching. Where do you think we are? Studio City?"

Crocker hangs his head, clearly unaccustomed to rebukes.

"You don't have to talk to me that way. I grew up here too. That's why I was hired. I have what they call 'street quality.' A 'certain street quality.' I grew up in Jackson Heights in Queens."

"Do me a favor. Remember you're a cop and this is a tough beat. We got yo-yos all over The City planning twists for us. So keep your head on The Job — and stay away from Our Lady of the Transcendent Tuch. Stay out of her fur. You get hung up in that theatrical agent bullshit and you'll forget you're a cop."

Crocker mumbles. "It's not my fault her buns transmit radio wave pixels. What she does on her time is her business. If her pants fit as tight as that goddam fur-lined blindfold this wouldn't have happened."

He slides down in the seat, pouting, when a call crackles on the two-way.

Crocker's eyes light up.

Dispatcher: 723, 10-20.

Kojak fingers the mic, clicks in.

Kojak: Centre, 723, East 7th Street — 1st Avenue, 10-4.

Dispatcher: 723, proceed to 267 Bowery. Shots fired. Officer down. Suspects with gun running toward Broadway.

"Let's go," Crocker says.

Kojak: Centre, 723, 267 Bowery, suspect with gun running toward Broadway, will intercept, 10-4.

Dispatcher: 723, suspect last name, Beckert — B-Boy, E-Edward, C-Charles, K-King, E-Edward, R-Robert, T-Tom. First name, Hans-David, H-Henry, A-Adam, N-Nora, S-Sam, D-David, A-Adam, V-Victor, I-Ida, D-David.

Donnely: Centre, 359, 10-20.

Dispatcher: 359, go ahead.

"Let's go," Crocker says.

Donnely: Centre, 359, Rivington Street — Clinton Street. Will back-up.

Dispatcher: 359, Rivington Street — Clinton Street, 10-4, affirmative, back-up.

Kojak: Centre, 723, what's going on? Do not need back-up, 10-4?

Repeat, do not need back-up.

Dispatcher: 723, back-up is proceeding to 267 Bowery, 10-4.

"Let's go," Crocker says.

They're spinning through The City the Federal Signal Fireball rotating emergency light atop the beast ([as mentioned earlier] a 1975 Buick Century 455 with a stage 1 package and Gran1Sport trim, 455-4, headers, performance cam and intake, 73 stage 1 engine, turbo 350 transmission, bucket seats, full console, power steering, power disc brakes, and radio), their otherwise unmarked cruiser, the picture jumping, rolling.

Telly breathes deeply, shoulders thrown back in his masculine, author-itative, snarling best.

"Hold it," he says, and slows at the corner. "We don't have to do this. I have script-rights and rewrites. He snaps off the radio. Pulls the light from the roof.

"It ain't gonna work. This is a rewrite. This has to be a rewrite. Déjà vu. An Adams and Laird redo. We've been through this. It's a requiem for a cop redo."

"That the one where Donnely gets killed?"

"Yeah. But we did that. I'm not going through that again. We'll stay out of it."

"Maybe it's Barnes' 'Money Back Guarantee?'"

"Either way, it'll work."

He takes out a lollipop and unwraps it. It's a Life Saver Swirl Flavor Fruit that has just hit the market. Taste tests prove seven out of ten kids prefer new Swirl Flavors Life Savers Lollipops to the two leading competitors. And nine out of ten kids wanted to buy them! Rumor has it they went wild over the three exciting new taste combinations: Orange & Vanilla, Cherry

& Bananas, and Strawberry & Cream. They've never tasted anything like 'em.

And like most kids, once the lollipop is in place, his mind is free to wander, to explore. He excogitates for a moment.

"We can do better," he says.

"Beneath this hardened exterior, I'm feeling compassionate — right now. This is not the time for a shoot-out. Donnely's going to get killed either way. So why bother? We'll ignore the call. We have better things to do. I want to interview Olga Freund one more time — the virtuous woman who lost her daughter to the mad clutches of violent and vicious mortality on the cold and brutal morning of January 30th."

"You're not going to start that again."

"What?"

"That French fag routine."

"Alright. Do you know what day this is?"

Crocker shakes his head.

"February 14th. Does that mean anything?"

"When we get paid? What did the Dispatcher mean, 'Have a nice Valentine's Day?'"

"C'mon, dummy. Lupercalia. It's Lupercalia, an ancient Roman pastoral festival to avert evil spirits and purify The City. That's when the dudes in charge run around in goatskins. It goes back to 44 BC. Haven't you ever had a girlfriend?"

"I got a wife."

"Valentine's Day. The day birds begin mating. The day Christine Freund was to announce her engagement."

Crocker is surprised.

"We met on July 18th, 1972 at my brother's wedding and have been together and . . .."

"I know. I know. But by the way, what did your squeeze think of your in-house teevee debut?"

"Is Valentine's Day police business?"

So Super Sleuth is at it again — manufacturing connections, finding significance in an unrelated scramble of circumstances, dipping into his vast pool of insights.

"What does it mean?"

"It means we will talk to the woman. A little macho empathy, pat her ass, pinch a cheek or two, and make some points for the good guys. We can do the chase scene later."

"But what about Donnely?"

"A dozen cars'll answer that one. The perps are gone by now, anyway. They can always hire someone else."

He regards Crocker with a fatherly, baldheaded, moist-eyed gaze. This is one of his better poses, in profile.

"Trust me. Teivel and Aigilas are plotting. Times are changing A week from now they'll have us jumping. We won't have time to tweak cheeks or pat asses."

meanwhile a mini revolt
forms outside City Hall

The NBC evening news lashes the police and the Commissioner. Garfield is accused of poor choreography, little technical merit, and no artistic expression. Rumor has it that he might not be a gar at all, but a catfish.

He shrugs off the attack. After all he is the Commissioner of the police in The City — a horde of some twenty thousand or so. And the Mayor likes him.

Still, there's more to it. As Garfield simmers in the warmth of private sun, clouds gather outside City Hall with a grey day in mind. A thousand citizen-taxpayers who have been gerrymandered to the dark side of The City lunacy want the territory of light and heat redistricted. The Crime's Victim's Rights organization lurches toward City Hall — pulls up a block away (without a permit for a parade or rally) to avoid for the moment at least, creating more victims.

The demonstration kicks off a campaign to end plea bargaining and lenient sentences for criminals. Speakers parade to the fore in the sub-freezing weather to raise hell. They trot out hackneyed, moralistic Old Testament saws, take potshots at the muscle at the top. It is crime they want to emphasis, clearly, since the week before, at their first annual convention, when given the chance, the delegates rejected, overwhelmingly, a proposal sponsored by the group's right-wing, to declare an aborted fetus, one anonymously chosen from the thousand trucked out of The City hospitals and clinics each day, honorary chair non-person-victim of CVR.

It seems dead people do not yell. Victims yell. Therefore, dead people are not victims. Victims are those who yell, and live to yell again.

Representative Mario Bioggi, a former cop and now a Democrat out of the Bronx, claims that, "The justice system has broken down and the people of The City are unprotected."

Bob Grant, a radio station WMCA talk show host wonders, "Are we going to take this lying down? Do we have to surrender to the forces of lawlessness?"

The crowd responds with a resounding "No," and Grant waves a menacing finger at City Hall.

"One of the smallest reasons, which is also one of the biggest reasons why there is increasing crime, is working in that building there."

In a vignette for comic relief, another ex-cop regales the crowd with a moral tale from his life on The Job.

"I was just a couple months or so out of the Academy," Shamus "Shameless" O'Connell recalls, "when I got this call that a robbery was underway at a small grocery store on Sheffield Avenue in the Bronx. So I bust my buns getting to the address, thinking who in the hell would rob a grocery store? Steal food and go home. But robbery? Hell with food stamps and all that, nobody keeps cash in the register. So I suspect it must be some kid on his way to music lessons or something.

"Anyway, I get to the store and the perp comes running out with a plastic grocery bag and a gun. I tell him to stop, this is the police, and he whirls around, faces me and shoots himself in the foot. I goddam nearly died laughing. This simple shit shoots himself in the foot. It's like he pissed his pants.

"Then he decides to run. Only problem is, he can't run. He can't get his left foot off the ground. He's stuck to the pavement, and every time he tries to run he goes in a circle. He tries this three or four times, but goes nowhere — just hops around in a circle.

"Did ya ever hear that kid thing? 'Mommy, mommy, I'm tired of running in circles.' And the mother says, 'Shut up, or I'll nail your other foot to the floor.'

"Well the perp has his foot stuck to the concrete and can't lift his leg to run, and every second circle or so the gun goes off again and bits of concrete from the sidewalk are flying in the air like snowflakes. He's running in circles and shooting the sidewalk like he's got his foot in the monster's mouth.

"So I just watch. I guess a nerve in his leg was traumatized or something from the bullet in his foot. So I wait until he wears out and sits down in the blood.

"But not to waste tax-payer money on a misfit like that, when he sits down I walk over and disposed of him."

A cheer goes up from the crowd.

"And that's about as much justice as you can ask for."

Another cheer and a chant in the crowd.

"Kill! Kill! Kill!"

"He points the gun at me. It's empty by then. I don't take chances. Anyway, everybody's better off.

"No one says anything. I mean, what can they say? The grocer's glad to get the sack of food back. It comes to a little over four dollars. Yeah, he's glad for justice."

In a pincer move, another attempt to rejuvenate the spirit of protest, Salvador Reale leads a parade to the Manhattan Criminal Court building at 100 Centre Street, his right leg and hand encased in casts. He watches Pablo Gonzales (the man Reale claims caused his injuries) walk away, and, as a man truly aggrieved and outraged, Reale announces doom, ruin and damnation. In a dulling diatribe of cackling clichés, he states the obvious, the now overriding maxim of business and life in The City of the Gods, that, "Crime does pay, if you're a criminal."

It's very Reale.

But no matter the pleasantries of innumerable eye-gouging, the indignity of getting rapped in the teeth with a steel pipe, or the sheer joy of tales inflicting revenge-justice on perps, it is clear that the interests of the crowd huddled in the cold and wind lie somewhat beyond an eye-for-an-eye. It's the eye of Providence. Novus ordo seclorum for the illuminati.

Speakers quickly turn to money — pledging to work to obtain better compensation for crime victims. Money. They want greenbacks, and sentimentality, as well as a claim to the small fame or celebrity, a quest for recognition as victim, that might be transposed into a best-seller, maybe a movie — and more money.

Within the hour the rally fades. Hoping to be heard and not forgotten, in a graphic display of maternal grief, Doris Masi produces the photo of her daughter that she has cradled reverently to her bosom. The girl was attacked and strangled a month earlier on her way home in a Brooklyn neighborhood one night deep in the bewitching hours of trolls and wolves.

"She wasn't even recognizable later," Mrs. Masi says. "She wasn't even recognizable."

But no one's interested. Without additional ado the demonstration breaks up, drifts into Ash Wednesday Eve as The City prepares for a forty-day penitential posturing of chest thumping, sackcloth and ashes. Fasting is the main bill-of-fare, and a general assumption that the human soul is not only contaminated, but down right corrupt, and must be purged, corporally, if it is to have even the slightest hope of gaining the improbable but fantastic fantasy-bliss of life everlasting.

in the season of denial
  and flagellation
  Mathias consults
with the gods' representative

A dull chill rides the late penitential season's winter air, threatening the idea of rebirth and spring. Rising somewhat weakly to the challenge, The City's waning ecumenisms musters its forces, tightens ranks, and prepares for battle. Episcopalian Bishop John Maury Allen initiates a Lenten dial-a-prayer service for those who wish to solicit divine approval from the misfortune, debauchery, and turpitude of home.

Not to be outdone, Terence Cardinal Cooke provides a bizarre twist of Kwakiutl patshati logic and one-ups the Bishop suggesting that those who, because of self-denial have treasures to give, be given to. He suggests camp followers and religious groups "Pray more intensely to deny one's self more effectively and as a result of that self-denial to be able to receive more generously."

Almost as a knee-jerk reaction, to encourage his cartel of devotion and mischief, in the late afternoon Sam sponsors a celestial concomitance at a lower East Side rectory. Just to keep his fingers in the penitential swill, as much in jest as malice, he dispatches two associates to St. Stanislaus Church at 101 East 7th Street, where, with a cosmopolitan touch of class, hauteur, and a rather respectable presence of mind for the irony of the jest, and heist, they ask the Rev. Stanislaus Koral for the blessing of ashes. Thus received, with the aid of a bowie knife, they usher the old man and his pet Shakhi, Rocco, into an ante-room and make off with thirty-eight hundred dollars in cash, jewelry and merchandise. Sam's stretched out in the Sacristy, chin on his paws, watching Rocco closely, pleased, and not about to lick anybody's wounds or hands. *But against any of the children of Israel shall not a dog move his tongue, against man or beast* (*Exodus* 11:7).

But there is still time for an evening on the town. And that the season, of which it heralds the beginning, not recede in face of the affront, keeping the spirits of religion and art in the same basket, Sam shows up at The City Opera's Spring Season opening at the State Theatre for Rossini's *Barber of Seville*. It is a performance inspired by the improbable, especially in Act II when Figaro and Almaviva climb the ladder to Rosina's balcony and a thirty-foot section of scenery pitches forward and crashes to the floor. No one is injured, and the show goes on to its usual "and they lived happily ever after" — for everyone except Bartolo.

Sam is in the back row, feet up, hands behind his head, amused with the comedy. The deep flagrant guffaw of mischievous spring floats over the heads of the audience.

And with the springing renewal of hope, Mathias dreams of warmer weather. He revisits the previous year, ambling up a beach in the Bahamas, the warm sand on his feet, frolicking with a blonde he ran across on the plane. Still, he is plotting, as always, even in his dreams, returning finally to his conversation with the Insipid Inspector.

Sometimes, he thinks, people are a pain-in-the-ass. Make that most of the time — all people. The nonsense about doing the right thing. The cops' persona — what will the kids think? Let them think what they will. Kojak's a neat stud — they'll get off on it — just like everybody else — and who cares anyway?

Mathias shakes his white, wizened head.

"The ninnies act as if they can buy big cars and mansions without dollars. What does a penthouse on Central Park cost?"

He's talking to Lamiae and wonders about the unions. The blue-collar hysteria with death.

"How many unions are there?" he asks. "Needing something to do, to get their hands in your pocket. Like the Police Benevolent Association — which long ago ceased to be benevolent. Graft, bribery, extortion. Out and out thievery and murder.

"What did they do last year during contract negotiations? They threatened The City with a pamphleteer campaign. The called it the Council for Public Safety. The police and fire tagged us 'Fear city.' The Sanitation workers use 'Stink City,' and the teachers 'Stupid City.'

"The hypocritical bastards. Liars, laze around, especially on the job, cheat, steal from one another, drunk most of the time, beat the shit out of their kids, malign their women, and then come in moralizing like a bunch of Sunday School teachers. The moral fiber, the backbone of the nation, the conscience of the political corpus. No wonder the friggin animal is dying."

The intercom's hiss snaps his reverie.

"Your two-o'clock is here. Mr. Drake from the Justice Department."

Lamiae stands, stretches.

"Okay, send him in," Mathias says. "Oh, by the way, has Kesil decided on the cameramen for the Sam project?"

The voice comes back, "No, not yet."

"Well, I want that as soon as you get it."

He pauses. Juan's choices, Aigilas' lists.

"We need bohunks with guts," he says, glancing over his desk, pushes a pile of papers to one side, and reaches for a fresh cigar.

"Oh, I concur," Juan says. "The bigger the better."

When the door opens a small man with silk black hair, a flat nose and protruding lips waddles in. He's wearing a finely feathered coat (for a chilled spring day) and carrying a small brown portmanteau.

Mathias, struck by the waddle's resemblance to a duck's, smiles and watches intently as the man crosses the room. It's spring, he thinks. Time to return from winter habitats, to fly north.

"My name is Donald Drake," he says perfunctorily and extends a vaned hand across the desk for Mathias to shake or pluck. "You are M. Teivel, no doubt. The showrunner Exec-pro of the *Coke Joke* show."

Mathias points to the chair, shakes his head, stares at the floor. Jesus Christ, he thinks, Disneyland again.

"This is Juan Lamiae," Mathias says. "Have a seat, Mr. Drake."

"You can call me Donald," Drake the duck says. "I've been assigned to work with you as a producer of these shows."

Mathias picks up the cigar box and holds it out to the duck. Drake takes a Cohiba Robusto and plops down in the chair in a splash of plumage. He swings his case across his short legs. Drake has unusually large, flat, wide shoes.

He pops the latch and removes a legal size folder and a handful of ground corn he stacks on the desk.

"I suppose you know why I'm here," he says, nibbling at the corn.

"Is that Trail Mix?" Mathias asks.

"Maze," the duck says. "Every time I eat it I'm a mazed. Quack, quack."

"No," Mathias says. "As a matter of fact I don't. May be you should enlighten me?"

"This is a Preliminary Interrogatory Security Session, Drake duck quakles. "Did you get that? I'm here for a PISS.

"Mr. Teivel," ducky Drake says, flapping his arms (wings) and nesting more firmly in the chair. "As you know this is covert business, but one that is not without precedent."

Drake tilts his head slowly, turning for a bird's-eye view of the room.

"Are there bugs or butterflies in this room?"

"Not that I know of."

"Why not?"

"Why not?"

"When was the exterminator last in here?"

"We've never had problems with insects."

Drake leans forward, furrows his brow and whispers.

"You mean to tell me, Donald Drake duck, that with ABC and NBC — not to mention the KGB, CIA, FBI, KKK, DAR, BSA, USAF, USMC, and god knows what else — you do not now, nor have you ever worried about," he snaps his head quickly to the left and whispers even more softly, "bugs?"

"Anything they'd hear coming out of this room, they'd already know," Mathias says.

Drake draws back.

"I see. Hmmmmm. Thought thieves. What you're saying is that someone somewhere knows what you are thinking before you think it?"

He nibbles at the corn.

"Which makes you guilty of larceny for having your own thoughts."

"Something like that," Mathias says.

The duck shakes his head, fluffs up, and begins jotting on his legal pad to give an impression of legality.

"This is bad," he says. "What else can you tell me?"

"About what?"

"The thought thieves. We'll put the best men in the department on this. We have means. We have systems you have not yet thought of. We have Input, Output, Processer, Control, Feedback, Boundary, Interface, and Environment."

"First, I'd like to know why you're here?"

Donald's beady bird-eyes light up.

"Ah, ha. Yes. There has to be a reason."

He glances at his legal pad.

"We've heard rumors. Some of them came from this room, and to tell the truth, the whole truth and something reasonably close to the truth, so help me, the Attorney General — the man — the big man, is not happy with what he is hearing. His thoughts bother him, too."

"The Attorney General?"

"That's the Honorable Griffin Bell — affectionately known as our Southern Freedom Bell. Not of the ball, but, you know how it is. He's a little cracked.

"Of course we have plenty of peanuts. We have Snoopy and the peanut farmer."

Drake quacks, then glares at Lamiae.

"Who else knows about this?"

"About what?"

"About why I'm here."

"Dear Duck, why are you here?" Lamiae wants to know.

"To be certain that the shows are in line with studio values. And to inform you that the Attorney General is not pleased with his thoughts."

"Those he stole from someone?"

"No. No," Drake says. "Those he hasn't yet had."

"I see," Mathias says. "The thought thieves are after him. He's worried about them stealing his thoughts, so he has decided not to have any — just to worry."

"Worse than that."

Drake drops another pile of corn on the desk.

"Care to nibble with me?"

Mathias declines.

"What has he heard?"

"Let me ring in with Mr. Ding Dong's sounding on the matter."

"Oh, my. He has ringing in his ears?" Lamiae says. "I know a superb doctor who can cure that."

Drake shuffles through his case.

"Now, Mr. Teivel, I don't want to cause a flap, but I don't suppose it comes to you as a surprise that in this country, those with means, prestige, and power are treated differently by the law than are those at the bottom of the pecking order.

"Polls indicate that the poor, the underprivileged, the disenfranchised, those without a vested interest in Dow Chemical or McDonalds, go to jail twice as often and are sentenced to 50 percent more time. It's the same with medicine and education. Only those with means can afford first-class medical care and meaningful education.

"Of course, we suspected this.

"Over the centuries we listened to accusations, rumors, guesses, what have you, of inequality and injustice, and suspected that they were probably true. But we didn't have any way to measure the extent of the gap between the haves and the have-nots. Now we have. The Attorney General believes that we have not progressed nearly fast enough or far enough.

"As you know, the poor shall always be with us. In a free enterprise system, to control inflation and keep markets growing, it is necessary to have a flock of unemployed and starving. It is also psychologically sound. People feel better when they know others are worse off than they are. And that is our mission. To make people feel worse off than they are. All the people.

"I'm sure you head the old phrase 'We the people?'"

Duck rubs his head.

"Well, maybe not."

He rocks in his seat as if he might suddenly bob head down into the water — if he was on water.

"It is now, I'm proud to say, administration policy that the privileged shall be treated differently: granted favors, monetary favors, excused for their mistakes and passions — their malice and treachery, if it comes to that — and given every opportunity to disapprove of their lives. If in god we trust, and we do, and do not take care of the respectable, god-fearing, landed and titled partisans, then god will not bless us. I mean, with the power he has, and having created the great wealth of the earth for our use, he must be sympathetic with our cause. Despite what you might have heard about that unfortunate row with Adam and Eve — that has more to it than CNN ever reported — god is on our side. We are his creation, doing what he wants us to do."

"What if you don't believe in god?" Mathias says.

Drake lights the cigar and puffs it, raising a cloud of smoke.

"Well, we'll just pretend that we do. That's easy enough.

"Now, rumor has it, and hearsay, that you are planning to clean up *The Coke Joke Show.*"

"*Kojak*, Mr. Duck, as in 'Notary Sojac.'"

"I have it on reliable authority that the hero of all the people has had an unfortunate twist of heart and that the work and planning that's gone into this project is on its way to the muck at the bottom of the lake.

"Of course, we don't believe the rumors. We know these malicious accusations are unfounded — but you need to understand that the plans were formulated a long time before our eggs were laid or hatched. And in the big nests, at the top of the aviary, I dare say, are many feathered, two-legged, egg-laying vertebrates with sizable wing-spans and matching influence, who are tied to this."

"We've had a few, small problems," Mathias says, "but nothing major."

Drake quacks confidently with the enthusiasm of a pleased duck.

"I'm glad you understand," he says.

Over the years, flapping south in the autumn he has feathered-up in the vee. Diligence and hard work — and duplicity. And while he may never make it to the point, to feel the glory of fresh wind in his face, the sense of power and prestige of the more famous quackers, his hopes remain intact, and he intends to protect the way of life of the American Mallard, his birthright and heritage.

"There are risks," he tells Mathias. "Hazards that cannot be totally fore-seen."

He sniffs the air, apprehensively, a frown creasing his fowl brow.

"Feathers," Lamiae says. "You smell burning feathers. My dear Mr. Duck, you have set yourself on fire."

Duck flaps furiously, rising out of the chair in a small cloud of white smoke, quacking wildly, scattering his pile of chipped corn.

The cigar tumbles to the floor and Mathias douses it with water from the small pitcher on his desk.

Drake scurries and bounces about the room trying to flap out the fire and when he goes by the desk a second time Mathias dumps what remains of the water on him.

"You have to be careful with cigars." Mathias says. "If I had to wear feathers, I'd give up smoking."

Moments later, Duck regains his composure, and with the smell of singed feathers still on the air, resumes the discussion.

"Hazards, I was saying," he says, "are there, but if we are eternally vigilant we can keep our casualties to a minimum. Right now our adversaries are restricted to the first Tuesday in November, every four years. With our natural enemies in confinement or extinct, and food preserves expanded along migration routes. Well, Mr. Teivel, I need not tell you that if this project fails, a flock of preened plumages will be ruffled with number-six shot and we'll have a sky full of hissing, flapping, and quacking.

"As it stands, Son of Sam and Syndie keep the hunting-schmucks away (quack, quack, while the ducks play) and give direction to our enterprise.

"We have to believe in fiction. The country's hopes rest with the Fat Man, The Thin Man, The Continental Op. Yes, and with Spade and Marlowe. If Mr. and Mrs. North fail, America fails, and confidence in the system erodes.

"'Good evening, Mr. and Mrs. North America from border to border and coast to coast and all the ships at sea. Let's go to press.'

"On Wall Street that translates into many piles of corn and many, many loaves of stale bread. We fail and the shotguns going off in Central Park will sound like World War III.

"On the other hand, if we can keep the schmucks running, everything will be just ducky. If you succeed, the entire aviary will be at your feet. Turkeys, chickens and pigeons are as welcome as buzzards and vultures. We have room on the wagon."

Drake picks through his case and pulls out a piece of paper.

"This," he says, waving it in the air, "this is the security agreement. You will be protected, given immunity from hunters. Everything has been ar ranged. We don't want anyone falling out of the nest or off the wagon."

"What about the PD?" Mathias proposes.

"What about them?"

"Did it ever cross your birdbrain that on dumb luck or chance they might stumble on to us? The authorities are taking a lot of heat on this one. How many cops do you have? And the Major Case Squad. They never catch anybody. They just find someone who looks like he might have been there or acts like he might do it, and stick him with it. Hell, death row's littered with these people. They could just as well go after us."

"No, no," the duck says. "The blue dabblers are good people. We have Hornick Brothers Stoney Point Decorative Mallard Decoys, widgeon drakes by Joseph Whiting Lincoln, and many, many others. Dozens. Every blue feather within a hundred blocks belongs to us. A brace of Whio per block.

"Otherwise the CIA is still involved with Pinochet in Chile and the FBI dwarfs are up to their Blicks and Whicks in Operation Snow White.

"The TCPD is a diverse organization. We also have moles. The Commissioner has agreed to help us — to provide camouflage. We're in the blind on this one."

"You're sure about that? I mean, ducks with dwarfs and moles?"

"Quack, quack. Get paddling. And don't worry about publicity. Whiners want to hear bad things about cops. It's what they expect. You can't save them from themselves.

"The anas platyrhynchos at the DOJ want to normalize its posture. We've not been as clear about this as we should be. Right now we're moving to extend the policy begun by the greatest foul of them all, the former, great Attorney General John (Jailbird) Mitchell. From this day forward, words like "Mafia" and "Cosa Nostra" are no longer operative."

Juan nods.

"As you know, once the words are gone the idea of crime will dry up. Then it will be business as usual. High-quality PR, Mr. Teivel. Meaningful PR is the quickest and cheapest way to get rid of crime and turn questionable activities to profitable free enterprise and respectability.

"This is not an of, by, and for matter, but over, beyond and without."

"It would be nice to know who's behind this," Lamiae says. "Little Duck, who's pulling our strings?"

Drake muffles a quack with a mouthful of cracked corn.

"Strings? String theory. Vibrating strings. Yes, that is important. But it will get done. Predestination. Just like having flatfeet or kidney stones."

Super Sleuth
and his nemesis
stand toe to toe

And that's pretty much the sense of it. The noon temperature hovers in the mid-twenties, pollution at a tolerable level for asthmatics, the wind out of the northwest at 5 mph. Mathias signs out The Universe Studio's staff car, and on an astral riff, an OBE, with a 5" Panasonic Solid State B & W

Psyaint David

Model TR-555 Portable Battery teevee riding shotgun, heads off through the midtown (Queens) tunnel, beneath the East River, northeast past LaGuardia into the Bronx.

He snaps on the set, Channel 2, waits for it to warm up, then interrupts the Lieutenant in a hunt for a serial killer. The screen is washed over. Too much light, glare from the windshield.

"We want to wrap it up by 3:00," Mathias says. "A couple drinks, a quick lunch, chit-chat, and the deed done by 3:00."

He pulls the address from his pocket and reads the numbers again. He's suddenly aware that he is talking to the teevee. Well, people talk to their teevees all the time. Why not?

Forensic Fop is dispatching his troops for the manhunt. It's the girl in the river (1973) an episode of a serial killer named Excalibur who strangles young females with a purple cord and a silk stocking with a quarter in in it, then leaves an Excalibur mark on the victim's forehead. A "momma told me to do it" adventure.

Forensic fop: *For those of you who are less familiar with this case than others, I'm not gonna waste time going over the tons of paperwork: autopsy report, forensic data, et cetera, dead ends that we've accumulated during the course of this investigation. You do that on your own time. I just don't want you to familiarize yourself with this case. I want you to commit it to memory. Because this time, we're gonna nail the creep.*

For reasons we can only guess at, Excalibur has signed off for two years. And now, out of the blue, he's decided to make a comeback with a very interesting touch for us to consider — a quarter, put into the stocking with which he garroted his victims. Does that ring anybody's chimes? Crocker?

Crocker: *It's a Vietnamese torture gimmick. It's the tourniquet principle. The quarter means a more gradual death.*

"This may be alright," Mathias says. "A couple places along here might have class. Lamiae set it up. He's gonna meet us. He usually knows what he is doing."

Forensic Fop: *Interesting. Very interesting. Okay. We haven't heard anything from the big Ex in two years. Maybe he was in the military. Maybe Vietnam. Off in the legal killing fields. Now he's back to his old habitat and habits. Maybe.*

Crocker, you check up on veterans' hospitals, outpatients, anyone with mental disturbances, violent behavior patterns. You know this creep's makeup. Oh, and concentrate on Vietnam returnees. Uh, that house where Edna Bell was staying — you speak to the owners yet? You stay with it.

Stavros, you stay on top of that autopsy all the way. Watch everything. Ask questions. If she's been sexually assaulted, look for blood underneath her fingernails, have it typed. Look for the presence of foreign saliva. Have that typed too. One thing we know from these past murders: whatever else

Excalibur may or may not be, he's definitely type O-positive.

Oh, yes. We struck out with that last time. Run it down. You may get lucky.

He sighs, held in large closeup sweaty profile, reminiscing.

Forensic Fop: (whisper) *Five girls.*

Indeed, he is suffering. This is more than any dick should have to endure. Young, lovely, lovable females getting wasted.

"We're scheduled to meet with the guest star," Mathias says, "or his image or symbol or whatever you want to call it."

But more to the point the Lou has found a witness. The dead girl's roommate. She works at a message parlor. Has a story to tell.

Eloise: *That was a bona fide death threat! You could say he technically threatened me, but actually, he's a very gentle man, a vegetarian.*

Her Boss: (in a squeaky voice). *You're too trusting, Eloise. She's too trusting.*

He's, a balding little man with a large moustache and small mouth in a white turtleneck. He's excited.

Her Boss: *A vegetarian, okay, but so is a gorilla! If you'd seen the way he looked at her.*

Forensic Fop: *You've known him before?*

Eloise: *He used to be my guru. And then I got into Tibetan Buddhism so that I wouldn't see him, but he keeps coming around for a massage. Actually, it's just an excuse to see me (chuckles). See, like, he was this intense spiritualist, but then he fell in love with me physically. And it was, like, my fault that he lost his spiritual integrity. So, since he couldn't have me physically, he needed to kill me, because it was due to me that he lost his spiritual integrity. But killing me would be a violation of his religious principles, so it's really got him in a bind, you know?"*

Back at the office Stavros is bored with sexual assault and looking for bloody fingernails. He decides to run his own investigation, munching a hamburger and listening to the radio.

"This is the Radio 2 Answer Man. What's your question?"

"I'd like to talk to the Answer Man."

"This is the Answer Man."

"Oh. I'm trying to settle an argument with my wife."

"Oh, yeah? Go on."

"Oh! She claims Humphrey Bogart played the original Sam Spade in the movies. I told her she's crazy."

"Half crazy. Bogart did play Spade in *The Maltese Falcon.*"

"Forensic, right?"

Forensic Fop: *And let's do a number on the tags and pins. Outline the total area they cover, and then run off a dozen copies of Excalibur's victims. And then cover every singles bar within the area of those tags and pins.*

"Drake's idea," Mathias says. "He's got connections. Somebody. We could do it by proxy — even by mail, I suppose. Anyway, one place is as good as another."

Forensic Fop: *His art. You know, any man that can put so much violence and sex into a piece of stone, he doesn't have to violate flesh. He gets his kicks with his hammer and chisel. You know something? I love art. Bad, good, I love it. This is good. Very good. Powerful. Kind of loves ya and kills ya at the same time.*

"And how do you sign up a symbol, anyway? What's the deal?"

"Again, Duck's idea. He likes symbols. Thinks they have meaning. He wants you to be aware of what's going on.

"Look, Swinging Super Dick, they expect a screwup. That's fact. They expect us to come apart at the seams. Otherwise, why send Dynamic Duck up here? I know it's spring, and all that crap, but this is off his migration route."

Eloise: *You know, when I got to The City, I didn't know what girl I was. Then I went to Columbia, and I got into Buddhism, and I flipped.*

I still keep up my chanting. I mean, it really gets me through hard times, you know? (Chanting) Wow! Are you into Buddhism too? I'm the reincarnation of the goddess Shiva.

Wow! Hey, listen, everybody. Let's all say it, okay? (Chanting–all chanting) *Come on, Gus. You too.* (Chanting continues).

Voice at the far end of the bar: *I'll have a Soft Stinger, please.*

Mathias adjusts the fine tuning, balances the picture. Talking to a teevee is not easy.

"Take it easy, we're okay. I mean, this is a big name guest star. We have to be careful."

Forensic Fop: *Yeah. I'm okay, you're okay.*

The Lou is worried.

Forensic Fop: *But what about the rest of the asylum? We don't even have a make on this monkey. And that's not all. We're not likely to get one.*

"Why not?"

"What if he's an imposter? What if he is one of the composites?"

"You mean, come to life? Why shouldn't there be an imposter? A dozen or so? So what? Everyone's an imposter."

"What's an imposter?"

"Did you ever see a poster?"

"You mean a bad portrait."

"A false likeness — a sad representation. There are no good composites, no good pictures, no good metaphors. Only weak and useful metaphors."

"And then what?"

"It doesn't make any difference."

"So there's nothing authentic in this."

"That's right. Neither good nor bad, safe nor sorry. No beginning — no end."

"So where are we?"

"The other night I had a call from a woman I met thirty years ago. She remembered me. She remembered that I was not a churchee. Says she has been praying for me for thirty years. Paying for my soul. Determined to convert me. That I might 'see the light.' She's probably got a deal with god. Gets extra points. A bounty hunter. Maybe ten points for every vagrant she brings in. Dead or alive. Points count in the afterlife — like Wall Street."

"She put the collar on you."

"No, but she wanted to check if she was making progress — to see if god had spoken to me. She wanted to know if I had found god. I told her I wasn't looking. Didn't know where to look. She said she had a vision of me holding god's hand.

"By the way. When Dipshit Duck showed up in my office, Lamiae asked him, 'Who is pulling our strings?' Duck says it's like a contract for flatfeet or kidney stones. And that's it.

"When I was a kid I knew a dude who killed his mother. Of course, she'd been asking for it for a long time. And one day while she was at the market he waited behind the kitchen door with a .22. When she came in he put her away. He was fourteen.

"He divided the rest of his life into 'before I killed Mother' and 'after I killed Mother.' As far as I could tell, he was always better in the 'afterlife' — much more together — had a history and psychology to lean on. One he didn't have in the 'before.'

"He knew who he was. He wasn't a motherfucker, he was a motherkiller. After that, when he got out, we called him Mama-K. He liked that. Always had a maniacal smile.

"We are what we do. That's integrity — becoming what we do.

"Anyway, I thought I'd check, ask about the contract Duck mentioned. Who wrote it — who signed it. Like a 'Why me?'

"I came across a clause containing a scheme for an infinite regression of options — most of them damned near accidental. I mean none of us ordered or negotiated this dance. We got into it in accordance and compliance with an infinite progression of options — when our mothers got fucked and where they happened to be when we were born."

"Sometimes you don't make sense," the Telly says. "We have to believe we'll find the degenerate — that we'll get a yellow-sheet on him. Otherwise, how can we continue in our never ending quest?"

"Well, he'll be easy to spot. How many Hans-Peter-Davids are there?"

"Jesus. You serious?"

"That's what I mean. Tuchus oyfn tisch."

"What about the woman praying for your soul? What did you tell her?"

"I thanked her. It's always nice to have someone pray for you — especially when you're ass-deep in snakes and goats — even if you don't know where the words are going."

Psyaint David

A block later, the neighborhood shifts to rundown tenements and abandoned shops. A platoon of Gray Panthers, watched by a troupe of unattended kids among uncollected garbage, are holding maneuvers in a trash-strewn lot. Two twisted canines are humping in an alley.

Mathias is less optimistic.

"It's the lead in the air," he reminds himself. "Gets to the mutts first. Dogcatchers? Where are the dogcatchers? How many are abandoned or escape each year? Hell, the harvest could be substantial."

What happened to the good old days when maverick canids were captured and impoundment, and, unless redeemed within twenty-four hours, dipped in the East River's 26th Street canine bathtub?

Execution day, the curs were dropped through a sliding top door into a crate (7 x 4 x 5) made of steel bars set three inches apart. When filled, caine-executioners wheeled the the cage to the water's edge, attached it to a crane that swung it out and dropped it into the river. Ten minutes later they pulled the crate from the water, emptied and refilled it.

On a good day, they dipped seven or eight hundred full-grown dogs and puppies. A rendering establishment near the foot of 28th Street handled the carcasses — the hides sold for $1 apiece.

Waiting at a light, the Lieutenant stares into the camera, spitting and rubbing his nose.

"Where the fuck are we?"

"Pelham Park. We're almost there."

"This is a wild goose chase. A waste of time. I should be working on the Excalibur case."

"Maybe."

Mathias's well-seasoned, confident face shows signs of strain.

"Relax," he says. "Take it from St. Mathias, we're in capable hands. Think of it as the mythic spirit of high theatrics. The spirit of the drama leading us. Simple as an image in a mirror. Eye to eye you shall know them."

He chuckles and LoKoJakMan scowls and glares into the opaque glass.

"This could be Montmartre in the nineteenth century," Loco says. "But I'm still wondering what's under that pier in Hoboken."

They wheel into a side street parking spot watched over by a ten-year-old wearing a cheap yellow wig, propped against a lamppost, cleaning its sexually indistinct fingernails with a jackknife.

"You got the serial number on the motor?" the Lieutenant asks.

"Listen, Bogie, your personality's coming apart. Where's Marlowe's nerves of high-test steel?"

But that's the Lieutenant, the bare-bone of the American Dream, still pissed at Mathias for casting him in a New Year's Eve special in which he was seriously upstaged and nearly eradicated. He claims he will never forget. He suspects Teivel may be at it again. Leading him into something new, certainly unexpected.

"You're going in first," he says.

"You still don't believe that wasn't planned."

"It was a cheap stunt. The women had the shit scared out of them. Sally can't watch that show, even to this day, without crying. I almost disappeared. Nada, zilch, nothing. Not a wisp or scent on the air. Nothing."

"We'll go in together," Mathias says. "Side by side. A doppelgänger. Remember, this is an OBE."

It's a small Colombian restaurant, Tio Asesino, with a bright red sign, three steps down, dimly lit, a bar, stools, square tables, red and white checkered clothes, and wine bottles with candles poked in the mouths.

Mathias envisions Lamiae waving wickedly (how else?) from a table across the room.

"In the corner," Mathias says.

"The old man?"

"Old man? Look again."

Fosdick does a slow, round-eyed gaze and agrees.

"I see what you mean. What's with him?"

"Probably an agent or lawyer."

"A hood? A lawyer."

"Why not? Maybe he's a judge on recess. Didn't have time to take off his costume. We're still just an outline on a glass screen."

"Why are they sitting so close?"

"Don't know. Maybe they like each other."

"Matt, something's wrong with that dude."

"Which one?"

"The one with the glass eyes and shiny face. The white male with the MOD hair style, maybe 5'8", 210 lbs., well-groomed, clean-shaven, tan complexion."

"Yeah. See what you mean. The rest is an awareness."

"Doesn't resemble any composite I've seen. More like a hard-headed knee figure, maybe fiber-reinforced resin."

"But that's not Edgar Bergen."

"Then who is it?"

"Pythia? Eurykles? I don't know. You watched *Sesame Street* lately? You're not automatonophobic are you?"

**in a scene that may or may not
   make prime time, the Lou
and Son of Sam face off**

Mathias sets the Sony on the table facing the hood. Juan introduces everything.

"We don't need introductions," une personne non-dits says. "We've met. You're on teevee."

"Yes," Runyon says, reluctantly. "I've heard a great deal about you, too."
David flinches.

"You have? Who? What are they saying?"

"Mostly psychiatrists. A bunch of hard-nosed Marxist — Freudians up at Columbia. Pulp fiction novelists — come to think of it, a couple anthropologists and a sociologist or two. Maybe ontogeny recapitulates phylogeny."

"Gentlemen," Mathias says, "do the fan-club routine later. Right now we've got business."

Karl peers into the camera, trying to see into Beckert's eyes, to the end of the tunnel. They are frowning.

Of course, H-P-D's personality is elusive. It waxes then fades. The historic significance of the meeting is finally melting into Fosdick's fibrous consciousness. He has traveled nearly to the ends of the earth seeking the Form in the Mist, the Stone Louse, the Jackalope.

And now, Jesus H Fucking Christ, the real Charlie, the real McCarthy.

The thought tickles his toys, makes him giddy. He giggles. Lifts his arms in the air. A dyed-in-the-wool white male with the MOD hair style, maybe 5'8", 210 lbs., well-groomed, clean-shaved, tan complexion with glass eyes and a shiny face. A wooden psycho without a plan.

He turns to Mathias, just the slightest scent of soiled water, tart fumes on the air, then the sweet aroma of fat burning in the kitchen.

"Something's wrong," Fearless mumbles. "I'm having trouble with my eyes."

Mathias ignores the mumble, opens his brief case and withdraws a folder. He, too, is having trouble with his eyes.

"Have you seen the waiter?"

The Duke of Death's head bobs mechanically. The haze hanging over the table thickens and Mandrake the Magician steps out of the brume. He's waiting tables, trying to survive until he can find a movie of his own.

"Would you like to order?"

Lohmann wants coffee, black. He's on a diet. Lamiae scribbles a note to himself on a napkin, then goes back to filing his nails. He passes on this one — maybe a glass of water. It is thought Hans-David wants a coke. Mathias orders sopa de lentejas, with ajiaco, avocado and white rice.

Sam declines. At least it seems so. He doesn't break bread with just anyone.

"Let's get started," a voice grunts from the tube.

"We will," he is assured, by the politest of conventions. While they wait, Mathias turns to another image, Peter Kürten, with small talk and queries. How old is he? Where does he live? What kind of a town is Yonkers? How far did he go in school? Did he like school? Does he like the Bronx? Where does he work? Does he like women? What has he learned from previous performances? How did he get into the business?

However, these are pointless questions. All of the information is in the backstory.

The answer is nothing, nothing at all.

Mathias sits back.

"Christ. I feel like I'm talking to myself."

He is.

Lamiae the Ghoul leans forward, speaks intimately to the suspect, hoping to locate the source of the voice (which may or may not still reside in the stomach), to solidify an H-P-D persona.

"Dear David, you don't have to talk to us if you don't want to. It's up to you. But if you want to talk, I expect you to tell me the truth. I want the truth, Hans. I don't like lies."

He nods. There appears to be some agreement here.

"Now. Someone saw you running from the scene of the shooting. Why did you do it?"

"It's not true. I never even heard of her."

Juan frowns, pats Hans-David's arm. There is no arm.

"It will do no good to lie. Remember, only the truth will set you free. The truth, the whole truth and nothing but the whole truth."

"Do you want to talk to me about it?" Mathias says. "We need to know who we will have on that tape. Is it you?"

"What will happen if I talk?"

"If you cooperate we will take care of you."

"You mean? How? You will turn me into kindling?"

"No kindling. Not this time. We'll run a full-scale campaign. Press conferences. Lucrative sponsor's contracts. A bottle of Old English."

Wicked Wicker frowns, thinks. He turns to Mathias.

"I'd rather talk to you about it."

"You don't have to, but if you talk to me, I want the truth."

The aspect of hood and robe waivers. Everyone wants the truth. But no one knows what it is. Lamiae bends over the table peering into the hood. He wants to see into his eyes, suspects they have a great deal in common.

"Okay."

"Now, on March 8, 1977, which is several weeks from now, you are out hunting, for someone, preferably a young female."

"Yes. Yes. A young woman."

"You are carrying a Charter Arms Bulldog Special .44 in a paper bag."

"Yes."

"You get into your Galaxie and drive from Yonkers to Forest Hills Gardens. You have had hunter's luck in Forest Hills. A month earlier you successfully engineered the stalking and execution of Christine Freund and decided that lightning might as well strike twice in the same place."

"Yes. Un huh."

"So it's about 7:15, maybe 7:30, and you're walking along Dartmouth

Street toward Continental Avenue. Having failed for nearly six weeks, you are anxious and a little bit careless."

"Yes," Sam's protégé discloses, "I am anxious and nervous which makes me careless. But how do you know this?"

"We know. Anyway, you see a girl, a young woman, coming at the corner, and you step into the cover of a large row of bushes so she can't see you."

"No, no. That is not the way. I'm not in the bushes."

He lets the words die, sorry then that he has spoken.

Mandrake appears with their order.

Lohman's having coffee — black. Lamiae has passed on this one — only a glass of water. Hans-David has a coke. Mathias regards his sopa de lentejas, with ajiaco, avocado and white rice with skepticism.

Mandrake bows.

"Will there be anything more?"

Mathias pokes at the white rice. "Nobody else eating? I should have brought Lukema with me."

The Lieutenant grumbles.

"Stick to the story. You're hiding in the bushes. You've been hiding for an hour or more in the cold waiting for someone — anyone — you are cold and pissed and . . .."

Between bites, Mathias intervenes.

"You are hiding in the bushes."

"Yes. Aladdin the Destroyer is secluded in the bushes."

"Sam is with you."

"Yes," Hans-Peter says, watching the teevee. "I am praying that . . .."

"Praying? Jesus Christ."

Marlowe turns away from the camera.

"He's sincere. He means it. Praying for what?"

"Okay," Mathias says, "we didn't come here to get a confession — just to set down the particulars and get a few of the details straight."

He shuffles through the folder and pulls out a photograph of a girl he has clipped from *Ms.*

"Have you ever seen this girl before?"

"Is it?"

"Yes. A girl just like the one on March eighth."

"Yes. That's her. I'd remember the face anywhere."

"You're sure about that?"

"I'm sure. I wouldn't lie to you."

Spade holds up a .44 as the camera dollies in.

"That must be the gun," David says.

"No. It's a twin to the one you use. It's not the gun."

"Oh, yeah," David says. "It's like the gun I use."

"As the girl comes around the corner you are hiding in the bushes. You step out, walk toward the girl, and when you are face to face you bring the gun up and fire one shot."

"Yes."

"Then what happens?"

"She hits me with her book."

"No."

"I miss."

"No. You're right on target."

"I shoot her?"

"Yes. She brings the books she is carrying up to protect her face, but the bullet goes through the books."

"The bullet goes through the books."

"Yes."

"Oh, yeah, that's right. She falls in the street."

"Into the bushes, and you run away. You brush against a man. You think he has seen your face."

"Oh, Jesus!"

"That's right. Then you say, 'Oh, Jesus!'"

Mathias finishes his notes.

"You say, 'Hi, mister.'"

"Okay. That's all we need for now."

He focuses on Hans-David.

"Boy you have the gift, the knack, a sense of the nasty" — though it is not clear why he says this.

Mathias takes a document from his briefcase and hands it across the table to Hans-David.

"Read this?" Mathias says. "Do you have any objections? Does he need to read it?"

As it stands he doesn't, he hasn't, and he wouldn't know the difference. He fades into a sylvan trance, lips moving mechanically over the words, eyes rolled into his head. A cackle curls out of the hood. The robe and hood stand — a hoof clicking gently on the tiled floor. The hooded bows graciously.

"Allow me."

A genteel gesture, and a hand of emaciated scabby fingers with a certain grotesque charm, a hard-nosed flair for the pretentious, slips a pen into David's hand. Still, this is no deadhead nervous-Nellie. whispering behind the skirts of money. This is an out in the open American transaction — a deal made, a dollar bet.

"You will be absolutely magnificent," Lamiae says, patting Hans-Peters arm that isn't there.

"March eighth. Late afternoon, early evening. That's the date. We'll be in touch before then," Mathias says.

He closes his briefcase, turns to finish the sopa de lentejas, with ajiaco, avocado and white rice (brown rice has higher levels of arsenic).

He's dined alone before. In fact, he prefers it.

Twenty minutes later, he pays the check and prepares to go.

He picks up the teevee. Today he is the keeper of the Lou.

"Lieutenant?"

The Lou is back at the office of the 11th or 9th, feet up on his desk sipping black coffee.

On the street again Mathias tells the telly, "Pretend we've never seen him. Remember to forget. Imagine the restaurant as a vacant lot, a burnt-off spot in your mind, a cave in a park somewhere."

"That face," the Lou says, despairingly, obviously feeling dishonored by the vision. "That SOB looks real, as if he could breath."

"He's real," Mathias says. "As real as any actor I know. You just have to let your imagination work. Well, maybe Henson could have done better. But not much."

"Just no way to encounter that face," Marlowe says, "and still feel the peace in your heart you need to live a sensible life. I mean, where is life, liberty, and the pursuit of happiness? I've seen the face a thousand times. I have this grinding in my chest. I've seen it, and I've never seen it."

"You have," Mathias says. "It's like an acid trip. But you know, in the end, he'll become a prophet. Hell, he already is. The icon is selling like wildfire. People are already writing to him — asking for spiritual advice?"

"But we got two dead. Four wounded. We need to catch this madman, whoever he is."

"Will you remember the face?"

"You said to remember to forget."

"Yes I did."

A pause in the action.

The Loo smells something amiss — temporary difficulty on the network. He studies his coffee cup.

"Remember?" he says. "How can you remember a wraith?"

"You have to imagine it, forget."

"A dream?"

So, it's not clear what he's seen. But then it never is. We only see what we believe. So? What does he believe?

"First we want him on tape," Mathias says, fumbling with the car keys. "That will be his undoing. If we can get him in the can, it'll be our coup. Like getting a demon in a box."

"There's gotta be more than we saw today."

"Okay. Something like screwing your mother. No matter what is said, it didn't happen. No one needs to know."

Mathias unlocks the door. The ten-year-old has relocated to the far side of the street with two others — look-a-likes, dressed exactly the same — cleaning their nails with 9" Italian Stiletto switchblades.

"Jesus," he says to himself, "they're multiplying."

Hurrying to get in he drops the teevee. It bangs on the bricks. The CRT shatters, the batteries roll away.

"Shit," he says, and sensing a growing disorder glances over his shoulder again, alert, prepared . . . for what?

The trinity has vanished. He stares at the broken teevee, the Lou's scattered representation and words, the sprinkled foreshadowing glistening among the stones like shattered glass.

"Just as well," he says.

He remembers hearing that god knows when you eat of it your eyes will be opened, and you will be like god, knowing good and evil and have life everlasting.

Why does he remember this just then? Why didn't he forget to remember? He doesn't know.

Okay, so knowledge will set you free. At least that is what he heard in grammar school. So Adam got his buns tossed out of Paradise. And what happened to the rest of us? God's a greedy bastard. Wanting to keep everything for himself, after giving man barely enough to survive — and sometimes less. You have to suspect that would have happened anyway — as part of the master's master plan.

His reverie broken by footfalls, he jerks around, convulsively, prepared for . . . hand-to-hand . . . what? Combat? Wombat? Nothing. A rusted streetlamp — slum tenements, The City in the background, a mirage.

Yeah, he thinks, god's a silly bastard. Incompetent, too. Has trouble with damned near everything. The universe blowing up: novae, supernovae, pulsars, and quasars. Humans going around seriously fucking with one another. It's a mess. And that's just to get the story going.

So, where is Sam? No one seen him in the last couple of days.

unaccountably the lethargies
  and boredoms of dies irae,
dies februatus multiply and expand

The days mount, collect. Hans-David waits placidly, stupefied, the first stirrings, an uneasy tumbling of enzymes and tensions bubbling, nudging him. He prowls the night, unobtrusively, seeking . . . what? A sign, a divination, providence, a fiery sword flung from the gray firmament?

> Day of wrath and doom impending,
> David's word with a lady's blending.
> Heaven and earthe in ashes ending!
>
> Oh, what fear man's bosom rendeth,
> When from heaven death descendeth,
> On whose absence all dependeth.
>   (Thomas of Celano)

Psyaint David

Mostly Sam is along for the ride, the hunt, tonight a bobblehead St. Bernard (Thanjavur Thalayatti Bommai) in the back window, eyes narrowed, head rocking gently through traffic, onto the freeway, sixty, seventy, crossing, tailgating a car chosen by the proximity of entry and exit ramps, speed. Drivers glare at him, swear to themselves as he mimes a Frankenstein monster's face, sticks out his tongue, flips them the fish, pretends his index finger is a gun, and silently, with his lips, forms Bang! Bang!

License plates portend messages. YAN 792. You are next. $7+9+2 = 18/3 = 6$. Well, close enough.

The ghost of the Whiteside Expressway.

The sprite of the Whitesboro Bridge.

Then the traffic slows. The hunt falters. They wander, meander, visit sites of previous encounters. Take a break from the action. Sam disembarks, sniffs the black as-yet-not-washed blotches on the sidewalk, lifts his leg to a lamppost, posting his approval.

Hans-David slides down in the seat, masturbates, and stains himself.

It is a pleasant pastime — a smug satisfaction. An unknown in the lives of the unknown. Touch and run, alter existence at whim, and disappear, quickly, quietly, the strings of taillights streaming into another unknown.

Well, words are fine, but Sam's restless, ticking off the days on the calendar (a red X for bad, black for good), gnaws at his nails, chain smokes Old Gold. He's never bothered with dope: weed, hashish, opium, a bit of crack — doesn't care much for amateurs.

Otherwise, he plays solitaire — games of limited chance — rearranges old arguments, perfidies — shaves the deck, counts cards and wins with monotonous regularity.

The King falls three times, the Queen of Hearts, skirts flying, bares her rump and taunts the Jack of Diamonds. No mere omens, signs — the order of things, the mirror of spirits who walk and talk. Babysitting is a pointless pain in the ass — downright dull.

In a fortnight, the moon will slide into the last quarter. Hans-Peter returns, eyes glazed, distant, his head jerking with a newly developed tic. Sam lays the cards away. The room warms. He spreads a silhouette on the morning light and fades into the dirty, gray grime of the Yonkers late February sky.

The Universe Studio now hiring
walk-on parts for *Kojak*

Casting calls. Lamiae takes it.

"Okay. Got the perfect fit. Sent the specs over this morning. A natural. A student at Columbia. Dean's list, hard-working, quiet kid, loves her mother, a real doll. Think of the sympathy she'll generate. She's the ideal sister, daughter, hell, little girl. She's the best America has to offer.

"Pretty, too, yeah. Brown eyes, long brown hair. Met her agent on the subway a couple days ago. Told him I could get her a part in the movies.

"He brought her to the office for an interview. Well, actually, she couldn't make it. But we're good to go, anyway. He said she was more than willing to do a walk-on. So I signed her. Basic fee. Nothing extravagant. Worked with this guy before. She's a perfect fit. You'll like her."

"So you promised her the part?" Juan wants to know.

"You ain't never told a chick you could get her into the business? Yeah, I know. The women you hang around with would be better off playing puppets."

"Do you have a snapshot?"

"For what? Listen, you'll like her. You won't need a callback on this one. Her agent comes well recommended. He knows what he is doing. Has been at it for years."

Juan hangs up the phone and takes the folder from Mathias.

The specs:

NAME:	Virginia Voskerichian
ADDRESS:	69-11 Exeter
SEX:	Female
AGE:	19
HEIGHT:	5'6"
WEIGHT:	125
HAIR:	Brown
EYES:	Brown
OCCUPATION:	Student
EXPERIENCE:	None
AVAILABILITY:	Immediately

"Here." Lamiae opens a map on the desk. "She's a student at Columbia."

"Where's she live?"

"69-11 Exeter."

"Forest Hills?"

Aigilas places a finger on the map. He turns to Mathias.

"We should do this in a studio backlot."

"Nah. We don't have a Forest Hills. We'll do it dans la nature," Mathias says. "That's the best way."

Lamiae concurs.

"Void of expensive art, the reverent shrine with natural modest ornaments doth shine. Her bounteous heart a grateful praise shall crown, and Muses make immortal her renown" (Petronius).

"Okay," Aigilas says. "Usually she rides the IND. Takes the bus from the Continental Station. It drops her across the street from her house. Tonight she won't take the bus. She has a late class and plans to stop at the

Psyaint David

Armenian Club.

"It's six blocks, Continental to Dartmouth. She'll be on time. We'll do some tracking shots. When she turns the corner, it's a right turn, here" he fingers the map, "a lamp's out and a row of large bushes. We'll have three cameras — track with the Steadicam. When she turns the corner . . .."

Mathias picks up a flier from his desk.

Marcelo is still talking.

"The whole thing should take, oh . . . no more than ten or twelve minutes. We've hired witnesses to give the police sufficiently imprecise descriptions — for the police artists — a passerby to discover the stiff and tell the family."

He laughs.

"Eyewitnesses are icing on the cake. After the centuries of the 'If you've seen it, you know it,' the word has it that eyewitnesses are 90 percent unreliable. People have psychic cataracts, macular degeneration of the occipital lobe.

"Even the courts are getting savvy. Not that it makes any difference. They still use people. To cloud up the case. It's nice to have a few on hand.

"Also, it gives snoops something to work with — the media something to to chew on. Helps the conspiracy people. Remember, imprints on the mind can't be undone — maybe altered with a little propaganda, suggestion. But not undone. We'll have them believing and saying the opposite of what they said in the first place — and then the opposite of that."

"We'll do the two-shot stuff with Fearless and his sidekicks in the studio," Mathias says.

He opens a box of cigars and passes it around.

"I'm feeling better about this. Anybody care for a drink?"

He crumples the flier and drops it in the wastebasket. The phone rings.

"It's always a relief when the first one is done. I'll breathe easier then. Too many things can go wrong."

The phone rings again.

An hour later all is quiet. He takes the service elevator down and exits the Court to the bleak of Beekman Street. Ten-year-old busker Ezra Jagel of 1416 Madison Drive in Brooklyn, and lately of the Alworth Academy of Music and Art, is outside the door with his violin, his hat on the sidewalk. He's fingering a well bowed version of Sarasate's *Carmen Fantasy.* Mathias pauses, listens, nods, drops a five in the hat, and turns, looking for a cab.

here are sketched the agonies
of László Lowenstein

László's having a tough time becoming Peter Lorre who is having a tough time becoming the killer. The elusive Hans-David Beckert-O-Wisp slips away, vanishes, without a trace, sometimes for days. LL/PL wanders into unfamiliar psychic locales, bugs his eyes, practices drooling, exposing himself to passersby, visitors on the set. Some things will not work, even for genius, talent, for actors who sometimes come in character.

To relieve the tension, he takes to other divertissements, entices a script girl into his dressing room, peals away her few layers of veils, nibbles her, tickles her, and screws her a couple of times during the afternoon. He mumbles the sacred lines. "But I can't remember . . .. Who knows what it is like to be me . . .. How I am forced to act . . .. Don't want to . . . must . . .."

March eighth 1977 (morning)

The sun also rises, pinpointed at 6:17, casting light into an atmosphere of 33-F, the wind out of the N.W. at 8 mph. Mars is already up and working and will be followed shortly by Venus.

The day, new life, begins somewhat convulsively on Channel 11. In a parade of mayhem and cunning at 7:00, Popeye and Brutus slug it out over the emaciated, forever desirable extra virgin Olive Oil played by Shelley Duvall.

In recent weeks Lamiae has developed a fascination for redundancy. Yesterday it was Mike Hammer — the day before Peter Gunn and Lord Whimsy. This morning he's in Mathias' office with Aigilas viewing old *Kojaks.*

Today the Lieutenant locks horns with a street gang running a protection racket on small neighborhood grocers. The food peddlers do not want to give in to intimidation and corruption, but both have teenage sons for whom they fear.

"Nothing's the same," Juan tells Marcelo. "Even if we remember it. Stories change so much."

He pauses as the beleaguered grocer relates his tale of woe.

And it is a tale of woe. An immigrant food peddler made good in the American wasteland through hard work, diligence, and savvy now taken for a ride by predators.

Lamiae is near tears.

"Oh, Marcelo, has the FCC or FDA no heart?"

Aigilas doesn't know.

"You familiar with the parable 'The Seeds and Stones?'"

"No."

"Well, somebody figured out that planting stones and throwing seeds is better than planting seeds and throwing stones."

Lamiae frowns.

"What if you plant seeds and throw seeds?"

Aigilas frowns, shakes his head. Clearly, he doesn't get it.

"Why would you do that? I mean, what about the stones? Then you'd have stones all over the place. That would take us back to the stone age."

Lamiae agrees.

"Even when you know the story, it's not the same. We cannot assume actors do not know what is happening just because they are involved in an earlier program. And it is difficult to tell what the sequence is or what the individual will do. Oh, it is so disturbing."

"You think we'll have trouble with Beckert-O-Witz?"

"No, no. He's not the one I that worries me. I'm still worried about the seeds."

While they're talking, Kesil appears stage center-right, partially hidden. He pokes his head out from behind the tormentor.

"Everything ready?" Aigilas asks.

Kesil is affirmative.

Aigilas is directive.

"We'll do a couple quick runs-through about 6:00 to 6:30. Then the final shooting at 7:15-7:30. We should have it wiped up by 8:00."

They return to the teevee, LoKo on stakeout, waiting for the gang leader, a surly Puerto Rican with a limp and a withered left hand, to return to the store for payment. The hand is a souvenir from sitting on the right hand of god — the heat is intense.

Loco faces the camera mounted on the passenger side of the car so he can keep an eye on the store and talk at the same time.

"What about the girl?" he whines, as if he already knows the answer.

"She'll be there," Aigilas says. "Don't worry about her. It's in the script — says, 'She appears innocent, gentle and friendly, with a homey trust-worthiness.' But you never know. Life seldom follows the written word. Anyway, no one loses a life other than the one he lives, nor lives a life other than the one he loses.

"This is real time. All is present — a present of bad memory and fantasy. No different from any other crime. The past is made evil only by the retribution which follows."

"I've always been sensitive about young women," the Lou says. "Did you see girl in the river? In the beginning, just thinking about the girls, I got moist-eyed. Damned near cried."

"Oh, it's not so bad," Lamiae says. "She'll get a great deal of publicity. Be a celebrity. Do you know how many sightings there are each year of John Kennedy and Jim Morrison and Hitler and Anastasia? If it hadn't been for photography and the media, no one would recognize them. In spite of Cerberus, people slip out of Hades — they become famous.

"Then there's Saint Winnie. I'm sure you've heard of Winifred. Every-body knows about her — if they attended one of those horrid Catholic schools. It's so exciting. My favorite fairy tale.

"Winnie is a pretty, but pious prude. Well, Prince Caradoc wants to get in her panties, but she has made up her mind to devote her life to god. Such a wretched decision. So Caradoc cuts off her head. And why not? Well, her head rolls down a hill and where it stops a spring springs up. This is called

Saint Winifred's Holywell. It's in Wales. I've been there.

"Everybody says 'Oh, goodness, she's dead.' However, even without her head, Win is not lost. Her uncle, Saint Beuno, a real hunk, appears gallantly on the scene and replaces her head. As if waking from a deep sleep, Winnie rises, and with no sign of decapitation, other than a faint white circle around her neck, and a bit light-headed, goes on to live a happy life."

Aigilas nods. He's enjoying this.

"Hell, Rasputin had more lives than a house of cats. They stabbed him, poisoned him, shot him, and threw him in a frozen river in the middle of a Russian winter. They're still not sure he's dead. There's been sightings for years.

"And Lazarus. How about Lazarus?" Aigilas says. "And his mother, Lady Lazarus? The act ran in the family. The old woman could shut off her vitals. And when your vitals are off — I mean, you're dead. Unless you're a two-thousand-year-old Buddhist monk they just dug up. Then you're said to be in 'deep meditation.'

"But Lazarus' old lady could bring herself back. She'd just turn on the vitals again. Course it got to her finally. People were used to her coming back in an hour or so, late in the afternoon, so when she went for the record — maybe two days — they must have had something like the Guinness Book of Records — ancient records — after two days, her skin clammy and pale, they thought she had definitely gone over the edge. They covered her up with a couple tons of rocks.

"Later some of the townsfolk said they could hear her under the rocks grunting and puffing, coming back to life — but that was just a rumor.

"Then last fall some guy named Luigi Bonnicelli, from some place in Queens was in an accident on the Cross Bronx Expressway. Luigi got banged up pretty good — head injuries, internals — and a doctor at the scene declared him dead. The doc told the ambulance driver to take Luigi to the Bronx morgue at Jacobi Medical Center.

"Okay? Okay.

"So far, so good.

"Halfway to the morgue, Luigi sits up and asks the driver for a cigarette. The driver don't know what from snot, thinks he has seen Caesar's ghost, gives him a cigarette, then deposits Luigi at the Emergency Room at Jacobi, instead of at the morgue.

"As it turns out, Luigi doesn't smoke the cigarette, but croaks for real this time. After an ER exam by two doctors, who do not find anything even close to a vital, Luigi is once again certified as totally dead and wheeled into the corridor to wait for the morgue to collect him. An hour later, when a morgue attendant arrives, Luigi is sitting on the edge of the gurney with the cigarette he bummed from the ambulance driver. He asks the attendant for a light.

"When he finishes the cigarette, Luigi stretches out on the gurney and the morgue attendant notifies the ER people that they tried to rout a living soul to the morgue. So Luigi goes to the ER for a second (third) examination. Only this time, when there are no vitals, instead of declaring him deceased, and definitely on the other side, the docs put him in a private room for observation. For three days, without life support, he's unresponsive to all forms of human communication.

"Then they call his wife and she comes to claim the body. She says, 'Not because I want it, but because it is the right thing to do.'

"Anyway, she claims, 'Luigi's always pulling stunts like this. I'll take him home and see if he comes out of it. You never know.'

"By then there wasn't a doctor in The City who'd declare Luigi dead. I mean, you know what that would do to a MD's rep — declaring the living dead?

"That's why they drive silver stakes in vampires' hearts. To be sure they stay dead. They keep coming back to life. If you put them in the coffin without the stake, they'll just dig their way out, get up, and take off again.

"Anyway, there's a Luigi society now in Queens to keep count of the Luigi sightings.

"Yeah. There's been a number of people who have come back from the other side."

The Lou is silent. Not necessarily thinking — just silent.

"I'm sure Juan has friends," Aigilas says, "people with magic wankies who could use the work. Remember, she who is no partner to the act bears the heavier punishment of the two. That's the way of it.

"Did you ever watch an NFL game? Two players get into it and when you see the replay, the dude that is hit first is always the one stuck with the penalty. Well, our job is to film it."

Aigilas paces away, turns to Mathias who has come in during the conversation.

"I'm a director, not a moral theologian."

He points to the teevee.

"The ethics of survival in twentieth century America?"

"He's into magic mushrooms again," Mathias says. "Unity, sacredness, ineffability — that sort of stuff. His noetic sense. Our hero wants to be transcendent."

"I don't know," Aigilas says. "He looks the same to me. Hey, no sacrifice is too great for a chance at immortality. If you know what mortality is?"

"It's fate," Mathias says.

He's picked up the thread, the pattern in the rug.

"Do you know where the writers got the idea? The plot? Well, I don't. I suspect it's just the way the words came out. They've had the killer in chains for weeks now. Watching him. No telling how many we've already saved by doing this. Sometimes it's necessary to sacrifice one or two to save many.

"Be on the scene at 7:45," Mathias tells Theo. "That's all you need to do. And remember, this is no different than any other show."

The camera pulls away from the Lieutenant and focuses on the store as a man with a black leather jacket and black hair staggers in through the door.

It's soon discovered the leather jacket and limp belong to the wrong man. At least that's what the grocer says. Not much to do but trust him and wait. The Lou unscrews a fifth of Lagavulin 16 Year Old, takes a nip and wipes his mouth with the back of his hand.

Whoa! He regards the bottle. This is Cask Strength — it kicks like a kangaroo, and a feisty one at that. Very spicy, pepper-fiery with clove and cinnamon, burnt-oak and smoked-elm and scorched-hickory and smoldered-maple and a touch of lemon. This could set the woods on fire. Yeah! A bonfire in a bottle.

Mathias snaps off the teevee.

"Will the girl be on time?" he asks Aigilas.

"Oh, yeah. She knows we're doing a teevee series. Like most, it'll be a piece of life. And she's got a small part. She knows we've already filmed the sequence at her house. With her mother and brother."

He picks up his briefcase.

"We don't need Beckert-O-Witz until 6:30 or so. No point him hanging around like a rat in a cheese shop. No telling when he'll get a sign and start on his own."

"Where is the shoot?"

"Two possible locations," Aigilas says. "One is Forest Hill Gardens."

Mathias is dubious.

"Your idea, right?"

"Yes it is," Aigilas says.

"That's where he shot the Freund girl."

"Yep."

"Why go back?"

"One morning I'm on the IRT Broadway coming down from Times Square sitting next to this kid. His mother is across the aisle. He's working a *Times* crossword puzzle. I don't know how old he is — maybe nine or ten — and he's writing in the words like he's got a crib sheet or something and doesn't need the answers. Without even thinking, one word after another, filling up the spaces.

"When they got off he leaves the paper on the seat and I pick it up. I'm off at the same stop and follow them. When we're out of the crowd, I tap the woman on the shoulder and hand her the paper.

"'Your son left this on the seat,' I tell her.

"She glances at it. 'He's not my son,' she says.

"She's — I don't know, sixty or sixty-five — I'm not very good at women's ages. Has a tired face. Possibly the grandmother.

"'But it's amazing he can work puzzles like that', I tell her. 'I mean, that quickly.'

"'Oh, he does it all the time.'

"'Are they correct? Does he get them right?'

"'Perfect,' she says. 'He never makes a mistake. The letters are all in the alphabet.'

"'What is he? Nine? Ten?'

"'More than that.'

"When I look again, it's like he's changed. He still appears to be nine or ten, but something in his face says he's, as she says, older — really older. I still don't know.

"I hand the woman the paper. 'He's not your son?' I think she's shitting me."

"'No,' she says.

"'Then who is he?'

"'I don't know.'

"'Does he have a name?'

"'We haven't given him one.'

"'What does he say about that?'

"'Nothing. He can't talk.'

"I mean this dude, or whatever it is, lives in a world by himself. Maybe a parallel universe or something? A consciousness that just popped up — like the rest of us, but different, sort of free floating. Maybe an alien or a savant. Maybe she keeps him in a cage in her kitchen. Maybe we're all parallel parking. Maybe this is a case of cryptesthesia or, hell, I don't know."

"How was he dressed?"

"You know, I'm gawking at his face. I don't remember."

"Well that doesn't help."

But that's the way of it. A twist to further heighten the drama.

They go back to the mise en scène. Is it a coincidence that the girl lives in Forest Hills? Does she have to be on her way home from school — or is she?

"Authenticity," Aigilas says. "Verisimilitude. In the real world, everything is smoke and mirrors. You know, you do a puzzle, then hang it on the wall. Somebody says, 'That's a very nice piece of art.' And you say 'That's not art, that's a puzzle.' This'll give the scene a realistic touch. Something of continuity. I mean, what's life? A metaphor? Maybe we're all just pictures, composites hanging in somebody's flat. We'll put her face on the wall, her personal emblem like Batman's moon over Gotham."

March eighth 1977 (noon)

Sam's into mint juleps, his Epicurean best, the Pleasant Life, an unkempt garden of mind populated with old friends: Disease, Dysfunction, Poverty,

Crime — the perennial defrauds of the mind-matter dilemma tossing about in a modicum of casuist reality.

He has a theory about advantageous adventurous psychos. Psychic confidence, he believes, makes the difference. A smattering of animosity. Of course. But deep down, when the accounting is done, it's still frustration, frustration padded with scars of having been disparaged, ridiculed, that make for a mind both facile and vicious enough in its own self-aggrandizement to kill at random.

Today's the day and mint's the perfect saveur for an accomplished formateur on a chilled March morning. By noon he's sloppy-ass drunk, into nostalgia, conjuring friends, fiends, depleted spirits, the refuse of terrors and grotesques. He'll ruminate on "old reliables," call them up for a bow, another round of shrieks and gasps. Spirits with spirit. Do spirits have spirits? What are they called? Esprit, Geist, spirit, and, Duch, szellem, πνεῦμα?

Meanwhile, enfant terrible hovers on the edge of his seventh-level gloom, psychic shadowboxing. His eyes are bright, his lips pressed.

"Action," Sam says. "Only act cannot be undone or redone, has meaning. All else is idiots babbling about their genitals."

The newspapers are full of it. The old woman, the Cassaras, are only the beginning, the tip of the iceberg. Blessed are the Peacemakers. They are the children of god.

As if words might win the day. David feels it.

"They're out to get me."

"So what will you do?" Sam says. "Are you up to the task?"

"Tonight," he's sure. "If the signs are fair."

Sam's thinking. A fait accompli? Fate?

"Yep. It's in the bag."

Still, there's a modicum of time. Hans-David watches a Rin Tin Tin rerun, "The Southern Colonel."

The Colonel is played by Robert Lowery, the dog Rinty (Rin Tin Tin) by Golden Boy (aka Flame, Jr. and J.R.).

The black and white copy will be tinted and refitted with a colored beginning and ending.

He's always liked dogs. He's humming the "Rin Tin Tin Theme," then singing along,

> So brave is Corporal Rusty.
> Though he is just a boy.
> How true as Private Rin Tin Tin
> They are the Army's pride and joy.
> Yo Rinny, Yo Rinny
> Pals through thick and thin.
> (Stanley Keyana)

Psyaint David

Sam's into his own fantasies, hunkered down in the corner conjuring old times. He drifts back to the Corriganville Movie Ranch, Northwest of Los Angeles in Simi Valley and the Fort Apache set — then again, among the sandstone boulders of the Iverson Ranch in Catsworth.

Back stage rummaging a chest of old costumes, wanting to get into the act, he comes up with a white suit and Panama hat. Crusty, mindless old fart. He's still drunk, parades around chuckling, leering, scratching his balls.

Clearly, this is not the Wild West. He's on the front porch, framed in wisteria, fluted colonnades, spinning his yarn as a wagon train of seven wagons of cotton driven by his plantation Negroes rumbles off, out of the yard headed for the gin.

"And Ah says to that boy, 'So you splat the girl. Then what will you do when Ah whip you for it?' Well, he's been around white men enough to have learned some civilization. He says, 'Ah will turn the other cheek.'

"Nauw, Ah'll tell you, Ah says, 'Boy, how many can you kill before they whip you silly? Five? Six? Seven? Why would you take a whipping when you could avoid it?'

"An' he says, 'Ah'll kill me four hundred and ninety.' You can see he's been readin' and listenin' to them preachers again.

"Now what can you do with a buck like that? Told him Ah'd put the other niggers under him. But there are rules you got to follow and can't expect to turn water to wine.

"He says 'Ah drive out spirits. Ah will drive out spirits. Why deal in wine when you can trade in turbulence and mayhem?'

"You see, she was a pretty little thing. Played too much on that. But not as bad as some here. She got it in for him and not a day's gone by but that boy was in a fever. Then she ignores him, pretends she ain't done nothing to encourage him.

"Ah can tell you that was some sight to behold. Then he caught her with his brother and he come to me saying, 'A'm gonna kill her and end my misery,' and Ah said, 'but donu harm your brother. We got us a shortage of agreeable hands.' But he killed both. A reincarnated Cain. And Ah had him whipped three times for that. Once for each killing and once for not doing what Ah told him."

Sam's tongue is thick, speech slurred. "King David." He raises his glass, "Salute."

> And David said on that day. Whosoever
> getteth up to the gutter, and smiteth the
> Jebusite, and the lame and the blind,
> that are hated of David's soul, he shall
> be Chief and Captain.
> David returned from killing the Philistine,

and the women came out of all the cities
singing and dancing, to meet King Saul,
with tambourines, with joy and with musical
instruments. The women sang as they played,
and said, "Saul has slain his thousands,
and David his ten thousands."

(2 Samuel 5:8)

March eighth 1977 (afternoon)

At 2:30, HD settles into watch *As the World Yearns*, a six-thousand-year-old dialogue: a man and woman, distraught lovers, the distant echo, a recitation of patterned and printed memories. The woman poises on the edge of the couch near the back of the cave, knees together, hands folded, head bowed (an averted gaze — pious humility). The man paces, posturing, silhouetted on the cave's gapping mouth, the setting sun, a fire flames between them. Both are sorry, sad, but unwilling to an undoing without a quota of screams, scratches, and scars.

> SHE: I shouldn't have trusted you. Mary told me in the beginning it wouldn't work. I don't know why. I didn't listen to her.
> HE: Because you loved me.
> SHE: Yes. Because I loved you. I loved you and look what I have to show for it.
> HE: That's always been your trouble, Betty. You can never think of anyone but yourself.
> SHE: And who do you think of? Me? I've given you everything I have. Tony, I was a virgin when we met. Now what do I have? That's all I had and I gave it to you.
> HE: I wasn't the only man in your life. My god. The one child you had wasn't even mine. You led me on all these years.
> SHE: But how could I tell you I had an affair with your brother? Until he died, it just didn't seem right.
> HE: You mean until you killed him. You murdered my brother.
> SHE: It was an accident. The Coroner's report said it was an accident and that's why I gave my son away. I couldn't face him knowing I had killed his father.

So nothing is left to chance, nothing to break the spell before Act I. Small waves rising, rolling, and breaking, nerves stretched out, clouds pushing in. Rain, thunder threatens, a heavier storm on the horizon.

Lorre is incredulous.

"Did you see that?" he whines and slides down in his chair.

Sam burps up a gray vapor.

"I know," he says, toying with another idea, willing now, to take on what-ever will aid the cause.

Sam knows his boy. Before the hour's up, he takes her back, apologizes, confesses yet another infidelity, beats his breast, begs forgiveness with a plausible mea culpa. She returns to her lover of the moment, assures him that, "Yes, it works. He's such a fool. Such a helpless and lovable fool."

So only one detail in Sam's plan remains which needs attention and direction. He turns to the teevee screen of the grime staining the Palisades. Lightning flashes illuminate the dark day.

March eighth 1977 (night)

Fade In

IND Continental Station. It is early, shortly after the evening rush. A number of commuters wait for the subway which can be heard approaching in the distance. As the train creeps in the camera travels closer to the tracks and stops at eye level, with a long shot of the train.

A clock on the wall shows 7:05.

The train grinds to a jerky stop and the doors slide open. Passengers disembark, others board, and as the train pulls away the camera slides in at an oblique angle on a young woman walking out of the station.

Another Angle

The camera comes in for a medium closeup and reveals that she is about nineteen, and has a round face, with large, warm pleasant eyes. She appears innocent, gentle and friendly, with a homey trustworthiness. She is dressed in a Paris styled winter jacket, a peasant skirt, knee high, high-heeled beige boots, and is carrying several books.

Exterior IND Station (night)

It is a cold, blustering night. Outside the station, she pauses momentarily near the bus stop. She turns up the collar on her coat, braces herself against the wind, undecided, and checks her watch. She stands with her feet together and turning, views the street, both ways. Finally, she steps into the opacity of Continental Avenue toward Dartmouth Street.

Another Angle (night)

In the distance, a block away, we see Virginia approaching the camera. A few people are bundled and hurrying in the cold on the sidewalk. At the corner, which is well lit, a middle-aged man with a full beard and a suit and topcoat passes out handbills. Virginia sidesteps him. He turns, follows her and hands her one. Their eyes meet. She smiles. He smiles.

Another Angle (night)

She tucks her books under her arm, turns her back to the wind and holds the flapping pieces of paper in both hands. A storm is blowing in.

Another Angle
As she reads, the camera shifts to her POV.

$10,000 REWARD
WHO IS THE MURDERER?

On Sunday, January 30, 1977, Christine
Freund was shot and killed. Various
evidence leads us to believe that she
was murdered by the same person who
killed Donna Lauria and wounded Jody
Valenti, Joanne Lomino and Donna DeMasi.

HELP US GET THE KILLER.

Closeup of Virginia
As she reads, her face takes on a deep, concerned frown. If she was unaware of the danger, she is now worried. She glances over her shoulder for the man who gave her the handbill.

Virginia's POV
The man has disappeared. She stares after him for a long moment, as if expecting him to reappear. He does not. Where the man should be, scrapes of paper are pushed along the street by a gust of wind.

Another Angle
Now, she is frightened. She looks at the handbill again as if to confirm the danger, folds the paper, and pushes it into her pocket. As she continues toward Dartmouth Street, there's a noticeable urgency in her steps. Here, the first sounds of a guitar play off camera, one note, then another, one more, in a slow plaintive progression.

Voskerichian House–Living Room (night)
The Voskerichian living room is a relatively large room with an overstuffed couch, several chairs, end tables, a large television, a coffee table, lamps, etc. It has a soft, old-world flavor of lace, rugs, and polished wood. In one corner on an ornate desk are photos of Virginia, her sister Alice, and their Brother Dikran. The camera picks up the photos, holds the shot for a moment, then pans the room to the chair where the bearded Dikran Voskerichian is playing the guitar and singing.

Dikran

Down in the willow garden

Psyaint David

Where me and my love did meet
As we sat a-courtin'
My love fell off to sleep
I had a bottle of Burgundy wine
My love, she did not know
So I poisoned that dear little girl
On the banks below
I drew a saber through her
It was a deadly knife
(Traditional)

Another Angle
The camera cuts to the doorway of the dining room. A small, middle-aged woman enters the room. Her gray hair is tied back. She wears a simple housedress and an apron.

Mrs. Voskerichian
(With an Armenian accent)

Dikran, I wish you do not sing those horrible songs.

Dikran

It's an old American love song, Momma.

Mrs. Voskerichian

They sound not of love to me. But it is time to eat. Your sister will be home. So put away your songs.

She goes to the front window and pulls away the curtain. The clock on the table shows 7:08. She glances at the clock, then to Virginia's picture, and stands for a moment with her head tilted slightly as if she's listening for something. She turns back toward the kitchen.

Mrs. Voskerichian

I don't like your sister by herself at night. She should go to school in day and home at night. If you meet her at the station.

Dikran

Momma, you worry too much. People are out tonight. There's not a chance of anything happening to Virginia.
The woman shakes her head as if she knows too well. She wipes her hands on her apron and stops to listen again, then returns to the kitchen, speaking

softly to herself in Armenian.

Continental Avenue (night)

As Virginia approaches Dartmouth Street the camera swings slowly around. She stops a moment to consider a display at a leather shop — purses, boots, jackets, then continues on.

A well-dressed trim figure leans against a lamppost, smoking a cigarette. His eyes are glowing.

She sees the figure and walks quickly, but not running, hoping to get past the figure.

The camera closes on the figure. Beneath the rim of the hat, the glint of two small-fire eyes. The figure flips the cigarette away, smiles, bows, touches the brim of his hat. The girl freezes, as if she has seen something terrible, horrified, and steps back. It appears she might run, but she does not.

Shadowed Figure

Lovely evening, my dear.

Another Angle

Watching him closely she takes several steps to one side, attempts to pass him and finds she cannot. When he straightens up, she retreats another step.

Virginia

What do you want?

Shadowed Figure
(All we can see are broken black teeth smiling)

You.

Virginia
(She is squinting, trying to see beneath the hat)

Stay away — just stay away.

Again, she surveys the deserted street and seems not sure what to do. It is as if she has been preparing for this all her life — but is not sure what to do, and may actually challenge or attack the shadowed figure. She hesitates. Looks away.

When she turns, the figure has disappeared and a yellow-white Golden Retriever has his leg lifted at the lamppost.

Quickly she turns down Dartmouth Street.

Voskerichian House — Kitchen (night)
Mrs. Voskerichian is at the stove stirring a pan. She looks up from the stove
to the wall clock — 7:15. She goes out of the kitchen.

Voskerichian House — Living Room (night)
Mrs. Voskerichian returns to the living room. In the background, on the
sofa a Golden Retriever — like the one in the previous scene — is resting,
watching. She pulls back the curtain and stares into the night.

POV — From Voskerichian Living Room Window (night)
A city bus pulls up to the curb opposite the house.

Voskerichian House — Living Room (night)
The camera catches a closeup of Mrs. Voskerichian's relieved face. She
mumbles a prayer and turns back to the window with a smile.

POV — From Voskerichian Living Room Window (night)
Slowly, the bus pulls away with five or six passengers seated in its well-lit
interior. Beneath the streetlight at the bus stop two young women, dressed
in jackets, skirts and high-heeled boots, chat for a few moments. One
gestures and backs away, holding an arm full of books — then they part,
going in opposite directions.

Voskerichian House — Living Room (night)
Mrs. Voskerichian's face is strained. She sees the dog on the couch and puts
both hands over her mouth, as if to stifle a scream. Dikran, who has
continued to play softly in the background, sees this and stops. The music
ceases. This will be a freeze frame.

Dartmouth Street (night)
Shot of Dartmouth Street facing Continental Avenue. It is a fashionable,
well-kept street with ornate, old time electric lights that resemble
gaslamps. The lights are extremely dim, one is out. A large row of black-
green bushes borders one side of the street.

Another Angle
A man walks along Dartmouth toward Continental. He comes on behind
the camera. He sees someone at the corner and steps into the bushes.

Another Angle
In the dim light, the camera closes and catches the outline of the man's face.
Then, more light. We see it is one of the police composites of the specter.
    The composite crouches in the bushes. The head features a sipple cap
and a confident, sinister Peter Lorre expression. The camera focuses on his
right hand as he reaches into his coat and withdraws a brown bag. With

his eyes fixed on the girl, he pulls a gun from the bag and holds it at his side.

In the bushes behind him, we see the Shadowed Figure. A leer on his face. He leans down and whispers into David's ear.

Shadowed Figure

A few more feet — step out casually. Now!

Angle Facing David
With a slight swinging motion, Hans-David is out of the bushes walking toward the girl. Four strides, six.

Two-shot
Then she sees him. As they come together, he brings the gun up over his head in a looping motion toward her face. She falls away and pulls her head down behind the books she has held up to ward off the attack.

Another Angle
The Shadowed Figure steps out of the bushes, his eyes dancing brightly.

Shadowed Figure

Virginia, meet King David.

Another Angle (slow motion):
An exaggerated replay of the body movements of the girl and the man as they come together; a slow, beautiful, tempestuous dance, with him moving forward in several hesitating steps, while she leans away prepared to fall beneath him. He brings his right hand up with the gun high over his head. The gun drops to her face and goes off. A dog whines, then barks.

Another Angle (slow motion):
The sound of the barking continues in an unbroken report as the bullet flashes out of the gun into the books in a splash of paper as it tears its way through, and Virginia, pulling back, propelled by the force of the impact, spins, head back, mouth open wide, and falls into the bushes face down.

Another Angle:
David runs down Dartmouth Street with a yellow-white dog (a Golden Retriever?) trotting at his side. He comes upon a man who might have seen the shooting. Still running, David pulls the knitted stocking cap down over his face to obscure the concept of the composite.

David

Oh! Jesus! Hi, mister!

"Cut," Aigilas orders, his face relaxed, pleased.

A spattering of applauses echoes in from the small playground across the street where spectators have gathered to watch the action. Oddly enough, there are no flash-pops from cameras. No one had the foresight to bring a camera. Where is Martha Farnsworth when you need her?

"Alright, roll it up."

A swirl of bodies. Indwellers along the block stare out into the night as camera operators and gaffers move about unplugging the spotlights, dissembling the cameras and booms, collecting cables and battery packs, and loading them into The Universe vans.

What had been focused, choreographed motion and quiet voices, punctuated only by the sound of a single gunshot, a dog barking, becomes a beehive of activity and voices.

"All right," Aigilas says, "Let's do it. Quickly."

He turns to Lukema.

"Jesus! That was some shot. If that's not the best chunk of realism ever put on film, I'll kiss your fanny. It couldn't have been done better. I mean, it gets you right here.

"Hemingway's 'moment of truth.' The 'mot jus.' The white bone shining in the sunlight. This was some idea."

He watches the crews break down the equipment.

"We got three rolls."

He grabs an assistant.

"Get everything."

He returns to the body. It lies twisted, face down in the bushes, feet on the sidewalk.

"What about her?" a grip says.

"She's dead," someone yells.

"Just as well," a cameraman interjects. "She'd been messed up something awful. Messed up for life."

"What about notification of next of kin?"

Aigilas shakes his head.

"They can read about it in the paper — like everyone else."

However, even before they have the gear packed and stowed — before Loco's appearance, two men come out of the crowd and want to see the body. The taller of the two tells Aigilas that he is a friend and neighbor and has brought the girl's brother to identify the body.

"Yeah. If you want to. Why not?" Marcelo says.

He takes one last look at the body. He walks away.

Just the faintest melody floats on the night air someone whistling the tune from "The Banks of the Ohio" or "The Knoxville (Wexford) Girl."

The scene goes to freeze frame, the sound over of a woman crying and a dog barking in the distance. The shot fades, but the dog continues to bark, for a moment.

(pro/an?)tagonist celebrity
  reflects on his
role in the drama

today no one to tell this story the details of the haze to say i am here alone
in the city on continental avenue alone unknown disjointed assembled by
the magic of the baron of bits and pieces he has stolen from the rubbish of
cheap apartments the shabby infested rooms of the city i am walking alone
when my legs turn the corner and take me down the street scraps of grimy
gutter paper cling to my ankles and shins and i kick them off downwind
spin trying to get them off leech like they cling to my stalking legs and then
flap away and i cower in the bushes beneath two lampposts where lights
no longer shine and my legs know when to make a patient retreat to cross
the street and how to stop and circle back toward the small playground the
swings swaying in the winter wind the voices on the wind waiting for me
so they can cheer and be free and live again waiting on the swings the
chains clanking with hell's cold fire hanging on a pipe frame creaking with
the agony of tormented souls to pause in the tall hedgerow blackness of
dart mouth street when the thin hipped swift booted gazelle breaks stride
to gaze on the glass of leather coats and purses waiting my legs designed
for night patrols in enemy territory swamps twenty three missions to the
commissary in korea search and destroy then retreat swiftly surefooted
into the black cloud of night of no light failed vision oh i am the righteous
king lion wicker my brain in the froth the baron keeps beneath his bed
without seeing or hearing i know he snores and what he dreams and the
gentle fair maidens the fake virgins stoned squealing and screaming with
delight at the sight of the size of the baron's great magic shaft and his sharp
sure scalpel cutting the night dissecting them for the parts he will use for
his next creation the baron asks if i will give him new bodies and my brain
says yes a bubble floating in the barons vat with two teevee cameras as
eyes in color and black and white to show me what it is necessary to see
for me to please sam and the baron who is sam my brain shines through
large fisheye lenses seeing all telling nothing since I am the barons creation
the myth of life constructed from parts he has gathered to create a heart to
manufacture fear and i have a left hand from herkatonkheires which he
gave me with a thousand stitches to replace the hand that would not kill
and I could see in his eyes when he realized his mistake and had to give me
another hand or see his plans spoiled even when none other was available
so he cut off his left hand with his right and stitched it to my right arm the
thumb where the tiny finger should be a hand of ghostly gray skin
twitching impatient for action capable of anything not wanting my teevee
eyes to tell it what to do a hand with eyes to guide us to afterlife so my
brain must now ask whose hand is this and i say whose hand indeed and
do not want to see the deep scars between the fingers the small craters

burned into the skin with the bright fires of cigarettes as uncle mengele smiles amid screams and pleas for mercy that are answered by blank stares and yawns so my right arm seems not to know what to do with its newest tool the arm an affectionate limb developed a friendship with the first hand the kind of guarded affection and respect partners thrown together drawn and stitched together sometimes get from their joint ventures but mostly my brain burns with insinuation innuendo says who are you sarcastically asks who are you and i say i am john wheaties breakfast of champions and where have you lived and i say in the bowels of typhon the bunghole of the city of the gods where i have pieced together legs brain heart and hand from remains of the gods creations nourished by the fear and greed and kept in a great house of horror to stalk the halls to provide pleasure for the klaus barbie residents and tourists taking indecent and vicious liberties for their sake to join the multitude of desperados who have struck out at whatever whomever they find in the formlessness of self expression making a claim to verify the self myself warrior tribesman shaman to follow the unthinkable in the unconscious to testify to the roots of power of life thwarting the belief in rebirth and life eternal casting the self before others my loyal upside down right hand twitching with something foreign to repentance expressionless faceless nameless in the crowd with no one to tell these tales to say how my pieces have been molded by the baron in babylon and how the pieces must be obedient to the barons wishes or be dissected unstitched lost forever in the empty space and fire of an endless desert left to wander the concrete streets pulling hope screaming and thrashing gasping from the womb of safety and confidence false assumptions assertions striking into the night an ultimate reality swiftly unscrambling the order one man celebrating the absurd the vile the hopeless made flesh and bone admitting to an entire lifetime of solitude enforced loneliness the focus the purpose of christian crusades heathen pagan infidel barbarian to be shown neither compassion nor mercy burned with bruno at the stake pinioned pinned to the wall of a wrathful gods edicts chided and mocked fool and animal in a billy the kid daze walking into a saloon unknown a drifter at the end of the bar lifting his whiskey blurred eyes saying william bonny how the hell did you get here set down between skyscraper and sewer outcast the renegade degenerate by nature lost somewhere between genius and idiocy a hybrid of missionary and savage schizoid and clairvoyant knowing this withered hand its shattered lifeline will not be healed and then and then taking heart insolent arrogant to wear the red badge to salvage what can be redeemed in a bargain struck with uncompromising laws of the legions of the vanished smiling less than confident a smile of resignation and resolve never again to admit to intimacy forever in the moment of impressions printed on memory hammering out electrical messages racing along the paths of a national geographic photo display of some hidden inner world of electron microscope investigation of parts reduced finally to this the thin hipped gazelle turning toward dartmouth street and the baron pulling the strings of my parts whispering in my large left ear now one two ready go and my stalking legs swing out goat gaited does not each son learn from his father onto the sidewalk and teevee lenses zoom in on the black gazelle eyes and lovely nose the dainty pointed ears beneath the camouflage puff of fur on a moroccan desert oasis watching me mournfully my baleful large eye holes absorbing the weak light of her beauty as we move together close enough for me to hear her breathing the now soft deep sounds of fear purring in her throat as we come together stitched to one another hooves clicking on the concrete her fine musk filling my flaring nostrils and then a voice the barons voice virginia meet david only one bullet flying out of my sore finger on the trigger to pull quickly the hammer trips and leaps forward in one ten hundred thousandth of a second to send to send a messenger out of the cave into the world beneath the iridescent light display of the hunter lover a flash my stalking legs carry me away my twitching hand reaching and my brain saying whose hand is that oh jesus whose hand is that and I can relax and enjoy the bright lights of night and sing again on my way home some old song about love and

once again the Big Apple
    returns to some thing
approaching life as usual

It's a pleasant evening, temperatures in the mid-forties, wind out of the southwest at 6 mph. David returns home, a small bruise beneath his nose where he bumped the car door. Inside, he sets the bolt, draws a deep breath, and is suddenly aware that he hasn't eaten for three days.

Fasting, he thinks, on his way to the refrigerator, fasting in Gethsemane, the agony of the trek still to come. He opens the door and removes a pack of month old hotdogs. Moments later, the rancid meat hung in his throat, he vomits into the kitchen sink, and, face flushed, eyes watering, decides he is not hungry. He snaps on the teevee, Channel 2, and slides down in his chair to watch *Kojak.*

Tonight Sherlock Super Sleuth, the phantom of forensic finesse, plays opposite George Maharis, tagged by the ever lovable Crocker and a couple of actors dressed up as cops.

They're on route to an assignment in Forest Hills, Queens. A young woman has been shot near the IND Continental Station. The interior of the Beast is dim and grim. At the scene lights flash and photographers leap about, squatting, contorting to get an improbable angle, a Weegee of the corpse for the morning paper — for ad-copy, press releases.

Lamiae, who has accompanied Aigilas, another participant in the melo-drama, reaches down and slips a gold friendship ring from the second finger on the left hand of the body. He dips a finger in the blood pooled on the sidewalk, touches it to his tongue, crosses himself. He holds the ring up to whatever light there is, examines it, glances about, furtively, and pockets the ring.

The chorus in the park across the street breaks into a chant.

> The means to self-fulfillment
> understanding and divinity
> within without to pass the abyss
> the ecstasy existence
> to rejoice while others sleep and cry
> the cowardly and weak trapped
> in failing deeds revered
> by the cosmic balance
> of passion and arrogance
> mindful of what cannot be seen
> defy the matrix of the mediocre
> the submissive in the realm
> of the forbidden and hostile
> the power to carry on in the image
> the pride of Sam
> defiance through magic
> in an age of fire to reach the stars
> (The Dark Forces)

"Did you know nuns wear wedding rings?" Lamiae tells Aigilas.

"For all the good it will do them," Marcelo says.

"Married to an illusion. But then, dear Marcelo, maybe we are all an illusion — a few variables in a mathematical formula."

Marcelo doesn't know.

"We are breathing metaphors, two as one. If we begin on one side, how long before we cross and become the other? Is it possible we are both sides — from the beginning?"

The Steadicam is still churning when the Loo arrives — additional newsreel footage — the image blinks and rolls. A *Post* photographer steps past the Loo and brushes against the bushes, which partially conceal the remains of Virgo Vestalis Maxima Virginia.

"Don't touch that," Kojak yells.

"Bushes ain't evidence," the reporter, retorts.

"Everything is evidence," the Loo tells him. "You can get a year for messing with evidence."

"You're generous," the reporter says. "Always something to give away. Last week it was VD. Tonight it's time."

Loading the body into the ambulance, a snit erupts between an interested bystander and the EMS crew.

John Merrick of 20-18 Boyne in Forest Hills (later identified by a *Times* article) thinks the crew should be more delicate with the body.

"You're a bunch of cruel bastards. Don't you respect anything?"

"Fuck you, asshole," the driver responds. "Dead is dead. She ain't gonna come to life by better handling. We ain't hurt her by it either."

Merrick swings first, but the driver ducks, spits in Merrick's face and tries to kick him in the balls. Reporters turn their attention to the fight, though it ends as quickly as it began, in time for a Chevrolet commercial.

But so it goes. Snarling and bickering over the carrion.

The news follows at 11:00 with a brief blurb about a mysterious shooting in Queens, a girl on her way home from school. Four other young women have been murdered that day — so what else is new?

David watches attentively, humming, then singing softly.

> We went for a little walk
> About a mile outside of town
> I took my gun from its sack
> And I shot that poor girl down
>   (Traditional)

"At this point I imagine I didn't care much anymore, for I finally convinced myself that it was good to do it . . ., and that the public wanted me to do it."

Before the end of the show, he drifts off, dozing, safe, warm, listening to Sam's soft approvals. Indeed, the first show is in the can, with time for a respite, a little entertainment, a return to ritual's fine fantasy.

Meanwhile, Sam is suffering from gastroesophageal reflux. Not a Judas Goat, but a scapegoat — a goat all the same, and the goat shall bear upon him their iniquities. He has a fashionable scarlet ribbon tied to one horn.

He waves a crooked finger at the teevee. It quiets, sputters, and clicks off. He's had enough of detectives, even those with split-hooves and broken horns, pretending to save the world. He regards the Palisades, the tree-line, thinking ahead to the festival of rebirth and the Feast of Fools, yes, and his confab with Czarmine Galante.

the media berates the misogynist
and suggests the police
may not be up to the task
of ending this latest reign of terror

The morning papers carry reviews of the engagement. *The Times, Daily News*, "Woman Dies in Mystery Shooting."

A face in the night plucked out of the crowd, named, assigned a history, a residence, an occupation.

"We are checking into the possibility that cases with similar circum-stances may have occurred in this borough and other boroughs," says Queens District Attorney John J. Santucci, ". . . the mysterious shooting death of Christina Freund."

The *Post, The Times* carry editorials, and teevee and radio spots, condemn the police for failing to apprehend the anti-hero.

"It is perfectly understandable," an editorial states, "that most carnage in Sophocles' plays occurs offstage. But we're in the latter part of the twentieth century and it is time for the PD, the citizens of The City, Americans, someone, anyone, to bring the scoundrel into the sightlines. The audience deserves a chance to see into the rogue's eyes and enjoy the full benefits of the drama. We have come to expect as much from the quality of life The City provides."

Reflexively Garfield provides an explanation, a spiny announcement. The police would like to move more quickly, he says, however the First Amendment is in jeopardy. But then so are jobs, lives, and a lot of currency. He regrets the inconvenience of danger in the streets, feels the snarl on The City's lips, but does not see how irresponsible reporting of what is going on in the streets can possibly help the situation.

By 9:00, Garfield has his Chief of Detectives, Captain Keener-O'Neil, on the phone.

"Did you see the NBC editorial tonight?"

The Chief is a wise old boy. He hesitates, but admits he did not.

A heavyset man with white hair, large ears and glasses, his face is marked with the scars and traumata of years of worthless intrigue.

A career city employee, as a returning undistinguished WWII vet, in 1946, he began on a garbage truck on the lower east side. Those days he could not read or write very well, but made it through CCTC (in ten years). In another year, he collected an MBA from SUTC where he discovered the risk factors in Pastel's Gamble. After that he read something about Frederick Winslow Taylor's scientific management principles of replacing rule of thumb work procedures with methods based on the scientific study of the tasks to select, train, and develop employees rather than leaving them to train themselves, while providing instruction and supervision of workers, and dividing work, somewhat equally, between managers and workers so managers can apply scientific management principles to planning the work and the workers can actually perform the tasks. Of course, none of it made sense to the capable Captain at the time — and it still doesn't. Truth is, the process has little more to offer than keeping management occupied and convinced they are up to speed with latest business doctrine.

After SUTC, he picked up a criminology degree at Columbia, then worked his way up through the ranks to Chief of Detectives. For ten years he's been directing and coordinating activities of the various detective squads for auto theft, armed robbery, missing persons, homicide, vice, narcotics, fraud, and crimes involving youths, and assigning detectives to other posts or criminal cases.

Additionally, he submits reports of reports of cases to superiors; ensures that apprehended criminals are fingerprinted; directs crime scene and suspect photographing. He submits records of suspicions (his) along with statements of witnesses and informants to the office of the District Attorney for submission to a Magistrate to obtain warrants required to search premises suspected of illegal activities. He conducts late night raids upon suspected gambling or prostitution establishments. He assigns officers to public gatherings to protect against pickpockets and other criminals. Sometimes he personally investigates criminal cases and is occasionally designated, according to the nature of the crime to be investigated, as Commanding Officer, Automobile Section; or according to rank as Detective Captain; Detective Lieutenant; Detective Sergeant I. Today, however, he is just the Captain, a captain who has seen enough to know what not to say.

Garfield asks again, "Did you see the news tonight?" then rambles on into a silent phone. "Well, it wasn't very flattering. These clowns are out to cause trouble unless we can come up with something substantial. I want action," he barks.

The Chief's stumble through the system includes a decade of ass kissing. He puckers up.

"You mean you want a miracle," the Chief says.

"You goddam right. I want somebody to walk on water, cast out a few spirits. It wouldn't hurt to raise a couple souls from the dead. I've got a discarded voters' list you could use."

The line is silent.

"Do you understand?"

The Captain thinks he does.

"I'll get on it with personnel in the morning."

"Morning is too late. I want something done now. I want somebody with a little vision."

The Captain agrees.

Besides puckering he has, on occasion, grabbed at straws and remembers reading about someone, who, when others fail, with an inner-eye, Wimsey without a monocle (as the Chinese say, hoping not to see more than he can understand), sequestered as it might be, can see the source of deviltry.

"Have you talked to Lieutenant Kojak?"

"The Lieutenant?" The Commissioner is impatient. "And what about our blindfolded wonder?"

"Yes. It just came to me that he has a reputation for solving mysteries. Do you know him? He can walk on water."

"Kojak's a suction feeder, a water strider.

"I know him. But crimes are solved on the street, not in some French fag's living room. All we need now, to get our asses nailed to the wall, is a limp-wristed wimp with an accent, smelling like he just came from a cathouse, parading around in the middle of the night babbling manifestos and giving press releases."

"We have possibilities," the Captain says.

"I'll expect results in a few days," Garfield says. "Keep me informed."

The Chief is circumspect.

As bad folks go, Garfield is probably not the worst. Now he'll just have to get with the program, step on toes, juice up the graft, get the sap flowing — something uncommon, out of the ordinary, an attention getter to give the public faith — collect a few handshakes, hoorahs for the Commissioner.

However, the next day, before he can move, Garfield calls a press conference. A full-page ad for the police appears in *The Times*.

"We are here to protect The City," it reads. "We have trained men and women and Rottweiler's and Dobermans and Tibetan Mastiffs and Pit Bulls (all kinds) on the job twenty-four hours a day, regardless of weather or circumstances."

In the same issue, *The Times* carries the first of a four-part series by Pulitzer Prize winning crime reporter Winslow Bennett, examining the variation coefficient of organization and efficiency of the Syndie and the TCPD. By the second column, the Syndicate has the upper hand.

It is a bad day for the good guys.

When asked about the report, Czarmine Galante (currently attempting to muscle in on the Bonnano Family), is justifiably proud.

"We have an effective system," Galante says. "It's what Stoics call, 'the premeditation.' We have a lot to gain in not thinking about how bad things can get. All you gotta do is what matters.

"And we have excellent retirement facilities — the cemetery, open fields with scenic views, the slam (both state and federal), the East River, the concrete placements on new construction.

"Nobody keeps count. The bridges over the East River are monuments for hundreds of our associates. Even if we don't like 'em, we give 'em immortality. I mean, they are dead forever. That's about as immortal as you can get.

"Sometimes our associates retire or disappear to mystical or exotic locales. We have a very reliable system. No need for Social Security or government pensions or Medicare. No misery in old age. Aging is a painful waste of time and money. We save the government money. Take associates off the welfare rolls, keep them out of rest homes. They are happy with the plan. We have not had a complaint yet. One hundred percent effective. Our people go all the way for us, so we go all the way for them — we take care of our friends."

with uncharacteristic courage
  and guile
the commissioner strikes back

Along with Martha Farnsworth, the Commissioner smells a conspiracy. There are those who do not like The City, who do not share his love and belief in the kindness and compassion of the light green malus domestica with rough cheeks and the Orange Pippin Cultivar ID: 1203.

"Shizuka," he mutters.

He knows apples, thinks The City is misunderstood, as, say, an unexceptional but seriously maligned child.

"Call a cabinet meeting," he tells his secretary. "I want everyone there."

She does, and they appear, sheepish, baffled, whispering, but brave.

"Ladies and gentlemen," Garfield begins. "I am sure you heard the rumors and read the editorials. Well, we are required by law and duty bound to see that our side of the story gets out. However, that will not get done unless we do it. We are about to launch the largest advertising campaign ever undertaken by the TCPD.

"How are we spending on this?" one administrative assistant asks.

"By last account there's 1.2 million in the PR box."

"But The City is bankrupt and crime ridden. Shouldn't we be putting that into hiring more police?"

"We've added men, stepped up the investigation. We are spending taxpayers' money as fast as we can. We are honorable public servants and the public will believe whatever we want them to believe.

"Naturally the discontents disagree and question what we say, and we will (out of the flimsy fabrics of fantasy) manufacture a success story — a manhunt and, of course, apprehension.

"I want news leaks plugged. The inside line is that we have identified the fiend, have him under surreptitious surveillance, but because of his accomplices, who we have yet to identify, locate, appropriate, and interrogate, we are not ready to make an arrest."

"He has accomplices?"

"Criminals always have accomplices."

Sam grunts. Accomplices. Mayhem, chaos, mendacity. Garfield is inventive. He will no doubt pull the sword from the stone — or at least manufacture a plausible story for why he failed. Deceit is still at the heart of government. Sleight of hand, a shaved deck.

When an aid says, ". . . we have identified the fiend?" Garfield shrugs.

"We know he is a lawbreaker — and that's good enough for now."

Sam is hunched over the watercooler, adding his presence to the duplicity.

"Maybe next time," he says

Does he have a plan?

"I'll handle this personally," Garfield tells the Mayor and the Chief of Detectives. "We can't afford some Mad Ave hotshot screwing it up. I've done enough public speaking and radio. I have a journalism degree from Columbia. I don't want anyone giving out releases. We got our hands full of trouble."

"Censorship?" the Chief says. "We've got real trouble here."

"It's been a long time coming," Telly tells him. "Look at this."

He points to his red, swollen nose.

"This was no accident. Some S.O.B left that splinter on the dock."

The Chief has a quizzical twist to his face.

Mayor Beame seeks
to alleviate the notion
of Big Apple rot

Washed by the sacrificial juice of the lamb, a virginal spirit loosed to the spheres, the metro-psyche of the Big Apple takes on new life. Not to be outdone by the cops, Mayor Beame arrives at a mid-morning press conference of his own wearing a jester's hat with bells. City Comptroller, Harrison J. Goldwin, in a comic attempt to upstage Beame, pulls up a chair, which, in a graphic metaphor of the bankrupt City and the times, collapses, dropping Goldwin on his ass.

Exhibiting an excess of élan, undaunted, the effervescent Beame takes the mic to read from a newly prepared list of the famous Americans and American things that have gotten their start in The City. Today he wants to honor a buffalo from the Bronx Zoo that helped impregnate a western animal and thus preserve the species. The announcement brings a brisk round of applause. Beame bows, savors the moment, but reluctantly turns to less significant matters, the mundane, the inevitable. He announces that instead of two days, The City actually has four days until default. A murmur runs through the crowd.

Reporters are disgruntled. They want to know why, and claim they have been deceived, deprived of a first rate catastrophe, their prepared copy of The City's demise made untimely and irrelevant.

"This creates a new deadline," they complain. "We need more news."

"That's the way it works," the Mayor says, and refuses to discuss it further. "The City will not be repossessed and sold at auction to the highest bidder," he tells them. "At least not until Monday, and at this very moment The City Attorney is in Federal Court filing a motion to have all Monday's proceedings cancelled."

After the question session the reporters clamber about Beame. They want to know the western buffalo's name, address, and pedigree. They want to know the span of his horns (do Buffalo have horns?) and the weight of his testicles.

Robert W. Cox

Officer Robert W. Cox responds to a burglary in progress. When he arrives, he spots the suspect, who flees. After a foot pursuit Officer Cox overtakes the suspect, who puts up a violent struggle, striking Officer Cox in the chest, before being taken into custody. Officer Cox then returns to the station house and collapses. He remains in a coma for almost three months and dies as a result. Officer Cox is survived by his wife and three children.

others join the Mayor's crusade

In a mid-afternoon matinee, something less than a command perform-ance, beneath the proscenium of Plato's Cave, the Act Two curtain goes up on John Shelly's *Peer Gynt.*

> I'll come into your life at midnight tonight.
> If you should hear someone hiss and spat,
> do not imagine it is the cat.
> It's me, little girl! I'll drain your blood into a cup,
> and your little sister, I'll eat her up;
> ay, you must know I'm a werewolf at night.

Late afternoon at 204 West 55ᵗʰ Street, an unknown disguised as an art critic spins through the revolving door, slide in among a gathering of moss-grown trolls, stumbling about their stairs-mountain.

Blinded by the glare of spotlights, fuming with discontent, the trolls' grotesque figures are cast large on the backcloth. Ignoring them, the executioner provides a definitive, permanent critique by way of two .38 slugs to Ernest Lubin, a sixty-year-old pianist, composer, and artist, who has just returned from the deli with a carton of milk. We are not sure why he does this.

Nor are the noobs.

The noise of the shots rankles the trolls. They leap several feet to one side, scramble into huddled bunches, then wait, heads cocked. When they are sure the squall has subsided, they resume bickering.

At 8:00 sharp, Paul Dooley takes to the boards at the American Place Theatre in *Jules Feiffer's Hold Me!* in which he is the paradigm of paranoia as a baseball pitcher determined to outstare not only opposing batters, but also the entire threatening universe. He is the utterly defeated victim of a voracious washing machine hungry for its weekly tribute of socks. He is the eternal outsider doomed to loneliness by the wrong deodorant. He is the embodiment of private fantasy, as with top hat and cane, he becomes the Fred Astaire of his dreams, "tap-dancing through life's crises, sensational but isolated."

Of course, other possibilities arise.

Was he a god — the Devil — or something even more terrifying? We may all be victims of *Demon Seed* — starts today at Blue Ribbon Theaters.

Glenda Jackson gets it on as Sister Alexandra in the Watergate of high Christian fashion, *Nasty Habits,* and Lily Tomlin brings her gallery of zanies to Broadway. She admits she doesn't separate the serious from the funny.

"To me it's mixed together, like in life. Look," she says, "I'd like to answer you frankly about my private life, but — let's say that the culture has advised me not to."

Later in the evening, under the influence of "cultural advice," adding mayhem to the misery of Act III, twenty-five-year-old Deborah Williams and her three-year-old daughter Karen are slashed to death in a South Bronx tenement. A second daughter, Michele, five, is left in critical condition. The month has been a barrel of bad apples for the females of the species.

The City of the Gods
launches a full-scale hunt
for the soul of the killer

Of course, despite the variants of entertainment, terror grips The City. Cries (hysterical — as well as historical) rise from the tenements, the crumpled brick-strewn canyons, for the police to apprehend the villain and set the collective unconscious of The City of the Gods back on its narcissistic track.

In a move to placate the masses with a bowing mea culpa, Garfield announces that the police have placed twelve men under suspicion. All twelve are cops, priests of the holy-order-of-blue, trained to kill, to shoot straight from a crouch, two-handed, and to kill.

Louie Eppolito, later convicted as a Syndie hitman cop, claims he is one of the suspects. But then, so is every cop writing a book about policing The City — and at the moment there are dozens. An old story, reporters are told, Judas at the table, betrayal in mind, a hand in the proverbial bowl — the seeds of aggression, bearing fruit in the orchards of a New Jerusalem.

Someone asks, "Are these apostles or jurors?"

The public is skeptical, but frightened, and seizing the opportunity to further pad Police Plaza coffers, the Commissioner calls for an increase in law enforcement funding.

"We need more funding, more honest men," he says. "The fiscal fiasco of '75 thinned our ranks. We have crime inflation and need to keep up with it."

Opportunism and viciousness translate into crime and cops linked in a spiraling dependency.

Still, no one's silly enough to imagine that cash and surveillance will do away with crime. No one except the Commissioner, who, taking a cue from the malignancy of the malfunctioning in-house teevees and the Crocker episode, calls in his wizard of cop-snoop, elec-tech, and okays a plan to have new high-resolution teevee cameras installed in all precinct squad rooms.

"We have video-recorders attached to the cameras," Captain Keener-O'Neil explains to Dapper Dandy Detective. "No one knows about the cameras or the instant replay. Push a button and whatever is in front of the camera goes on tape — even if the monitor here at headquarters is not on. There's a button for every station. Here. That's the 109th in Flushing."

The idea pleases the Lieutenant who also suspects one or two of the boys-in-blue might be the perp.

"I've been waiting for something like this. It's only a matter of time until we catch this ding-dong," he says. "Cops on the beat have also been on the take. Some are even working for the Syndie. I knew one who thought he was a CIA agent."

The camera dollies in for a medium closeup.

"If the guy's a cop, we'll know who it is in a few days. You can tell by his long nose, the pointed chin, and all that."

Sam does a bit of fine tuning
adjusting
the contrast and tracking

On the wall, a stain — pulsating — horns, tail, bright eyes circle the room, the bed. A voice rises over Hans-Peter's heavy breathing.

And Sam's promise.

"Yours," he tells David. "The virgin of your dreams."

"'Verily, for the Muttaqûn, there will be Paradise; gardens and grape yards; and young full-breasted maidens of equal age; and a full cup of wine' (*Surat An-Naba*: 31-34).

"Yes, a vessel of flesh, your Princess of the conjugal bed, the cerise-stained wedding lace, trumpets sounding against the warm night, pressing the walls of your bedroom crypt."

Hyperbole, but Sam likes it. His promise to Don Juan. An old story that never fails. They buy it every time.

The climax of the dream is a Technicolor rerun in VistaVision, accentuating a warm night flashing in the fury of gunfire, screams, Donna Lauria toppling, slow motion, light pouring through the celluloid, toppling as she must, could not but otherwise, with a small twist, slumping, finally motionless in the spotlight.

"He sleeps, now," Sam says, "sleeps, dreaming a half-realized hope of salvation, the mutterings, as it is, given to sorcery, children marching about chests puffed believing they will live to see their dreams come true."

Psyaint David

Sam waves his hand, a leaden glint reflected from his curved and brown broken nails.

"We will have it now, Παιδί-Θαύμα — the infant mind struggling in the ramifications act tosses into the moral order. To believe, to act."

Sam coughs.

"A peculiar sleight-of-hand not to segregate homicide from whim — power from pleasure. A monastic mind of single purpose in its pursuits."

The lord of the flies speaks, speaks of many flies in the ointment.

lust sated for the moment
the wanderer
is consumed with longing

Beneath Sam's gaze, Son-David languishes in a melancholy of lover's torment. He spends the morning leafing through newspapers. His stories. His narrative. The image he creates. He reads intently, listens to the intonations of print, wheezing, whispering, the breathing of the beast.

"Dangerous," he tells himself with a wry, playful grin, enjoying the encounter. "Dangerous and hungry."

Again, he returns to Donna Lauria. Chosen at random, anonymous until her name and photo appeared in the paper. He has wrapped her in the visceral enthusiastics of eroticism. Her name, her likeness infuses his reverie — the illusion of skin and hair, her soft, wide brown fawn-like eyes.

She haunts him as he is haunted by a tapping hoofed-thing, the painted tracings of soot on glass, her cropped brown hair and face shaded from the light, hands folded, eyes closed, sleeping beauty, waiting as Juliet waits.

He touches the soft-fall of hair, his palms moist, and bends to her with a fair heart-felt Romeo sob, a lover's-mask anguish, as if to raise her, Lady Lazarus-like, with a Frog-prince kiss. The delicate bow of her lips parts slightly, her lids flutter and open, her eyes larger and softer than he imagined.

"David," she whispers.

"The story," he tells her, "doesn't say that. You know, this wasn't supposed to happen."

How can you believe and disbelieve in something at the same time? She would have preferred another fate, another choice, says, "No," the pleasant warming flow of acquiescence rising in the pliant ambiance of her voice. "No," she says, caught in the tantalizing, erotic, sky-blue, demon-hollow of his eyes.

Sam says,

I mean, people don't ever really die. Juliet is always alive at the beginning of the play. She even makes a curtain call. Sam says we will be together," he says, "and

I know we will." He takes her hand. "You see, it's like this. Every four

months or so, on Sunday mornings
   I go to the cemetery.
   I have the urge. Just to hang around. Talk.
   I visit the graves.
   I know a couple.
   I don't remember the names.
   I have paper and mark down people
   I want to visit. Mostly young girls — a lot of young girls and some young
kids, young guys.
   I, you know,
   I talk to them. They can't hear me,
   I don't think. They are teenagers. Young twenties.
   I don't know how they died.
   I want to find out.
   I'm curious. Was it a car accident? A disease? It intrigues me. The
graves are near where my mother is.
   I feel like I know the people. People
   I have never seen. Girls, whether they were pretty or not.
   I want to know. It's like the people in the cemetery. Their spirits.
   I feel akin to them.
   I can't see them. But they are alive. Their spirits. Their voices all over the
place. And
   I hear their names. When they were born and died.
   I mean the spirit is alive.
   I can feel them talking to me," Hans-David says.
   She regards him with a suspicious fascination, the way the girls in high
school watched him, as if they sensed something unpleasant and alluring
in his laugh, the quiet, unassuming self-effacing manners.
   "That's how you feel about me?"

hoping to preserve his good name
the commissioner
announces a late spring offensive

   The following morning at 10:00 the Commissioner's limo snakes into the
Police Plaza parking garage and Garfield disembarks on the first leg of his
PR itinerary. He stumbles into the outer office and instructs Deputy
Commissioner Frank McLaughlin to "Schedule a press conference for 2:00.
Make certain everybody's there."
   "Everybody? Teevee, too?" McLaughlin asks.
   "The whole package. I have a script. I rehearsed far into the morning
hours for this. I will be my absolute debonair, dashing and irresistible best.
What better way to win the public's confidence than to have the
Commissioner, the Mayor's General in the field, come to them with the

facts?"

McLaughlin's face shows nothing.

"I guess you know what you're doing."

"I have what we need. I'll give them a real scoop, one that will set the wires and airwaves humming."

By 1:30 the room is roiling with technicians stringing cables and setting up mics — Porta Pac cameras, their large dull glass eyes focused on the lectern, perch precariously on tripods, ready to spin into action.

"Son of Sam. Rumor has it they've caught Sam. He's going to announce the capture of Son of Sam. Otherwise, there's no reason for this."

"It's been in the wind. A couple of hours. He has a prepared statement."

Reporters, cameramen mill about, a blue haze of cigarette smoke clouds the room. At his appointed hour, Garfield appears, trailing McLaughlin through the crowd to the battery of mics, and in his best Ronald Coleman, raises his hand for order. The nodding cabal of Inspector Lieutenant LoKo and Captain Keener-Frazer (on a 20' Sony) along with Our Lady of the Mystical Booty, are at his side, giving a sacred weight to his words.

Today Our Lady is at her bubbly best, with a black silk blindfold and a cover girl smile. For the occasion she wears a knee-length long sleeve beige wrap dress, a clinging jersey, and grey suede mid-calf zipper boots with three-inch heels. She is aware that all is appearance, or as Françoise Sagan says, "A dress makes no sense unless it inspires a man to want to take it off you." She wears a large Bonwit Teller Mood Ring on the second finger of her left hand.

The only thing missing is the replica of the illuminated giant *Codex Gigas,* the *Devil's Bible,* Garfield keeps on his desk as a reminder that over the millennium whoring, thieving and killing have been a constant of human activity.

Garfield takes the mic. A strange shuffling silence pervades the room as reporters stretch to capture his words, jostling for position.

"We will not abide wit," he says, "that portrays the police department as a babbling batch of baboons and makes a mockery of the principles of Justice, Courage, Temperance and Prudence — not to mention Wisdom. At this moment we have a plan underway. We have implemented a course of action which will expose the monster — capture the perpetrator.

"I have it on reliable authority," Garfield says, "from a confidential but trustworthy source, that Kojak (here he turns to the teevee to acknowledge the idol of the TCPD), with his magnetically mounted Federal Signal Fireball rotating emergency light atop his unmarked police vehicle, while carrying a Smith & Wesson Model 15 or a .38 Special snub-nosed Smith & Wesson Bodyguard revolver (the kind The City Police Department detectives usually carry [in the front right pocket of his overcoat or suit jacket, or in his hand as he approaches a scene where he is expecting danger]), will be permanently transferred to The City to rewrite the law enforcement idiolect for The Big Apple. No longer will the best The City has to offer spend most of his time in the Hollywood of Adam and Eve. And while this, in-and-of-itself, does not solve The City's crime problem, it is a step in the right direction. The relocation provides additional support for our attempts to clarify our vision, to isolate the villain, and in plain police jargon, get a lineup and provide a yellow-sheet on this dement."

Reporters in the back of the room come up from their pads, stretch to see over the crowd to hear what Garfield is saying.

"You'll have to speak a little louder," a technician says. "We're having trouble picking you up."

Garfield, unaware that he is mute, carries on in mime, lip-synching his thoughts. The lights dim, then brighten. A buzz spreads over the room.

Video difficulty compounds the audio failure. A Channel 2 cameraman lifts his head and stares at Garfield. Behind his machine again, he turns to his assistant, hunches his shoulders, taps the eyepiece with his finger.

"What is it?"

"I don't know. A synergy failure."

"What about the elevators?"

"I know Garfield is in descending mode, but this is something else."

"How do we get out of here? Exterminating angel? What floor are we on?"

Garfield grimaces.

Whatever else they do, the press, the media magnates of The City oppose him. It's an on-going struggle. Dissatisfaction with the way the Beame Administration dispenses City Hall news, the press responds with semi plausible fictions of fatuous factional rivalries surrounding the Mayor.

They object to Garfield as Commissioner and refuse to report, with anything approaching journalistic accuracy, his attempts to bring the unwieldy pack, a.k.a. the PD, under control. *Post* reporters track him, create links with the Syndie's prostitution operations. They accuse him of everything from petty-cash thievery to maligning neighborhood children. And though he's kept a Schnauzer and Lab in his white-glove 5th Avenue apartment for the last ten years, some claim he is anti-dog. The *Post* is the worst. Murdoch's sheet runs cartoons of Garfield as a catfish — the all mouth and no brains variety.

It's the politics of revenge in an election year escalation of hostilities. As with most election years, the trolls are out and burping, and the good Mayor Beame is under siege. Bella Abzug refers to him in *The Times* as a strawman (with a reference to the Wizard of Oz) that she could easily turn into a large floppy, without a logical argument. Ed Koch grins and clings a bit more tightly to Bess Myerson's arm. Bess has not yet run afoul of the law. But Sam has plans — and Robert Edwards waits in the wings.

Moreover, the police strike the previous fall, and the growing concern with corruption in The City, provided an opportunity for additional scribe-scribbling invective and lunacy.

They are at it again, he thinks, conspiring to further embarrass him and erode public confidence in the ability of the Department to do its job. Media at its best: mendacity, keywords to fan bigotry, stigmatize, assassinate his character. Garfield's persona has lost its efficacy, gone two dimensional.

the malady of malignant
   media mutates
to a magnificent magnitude

Indeed, a major media glitch infects the major broadcast centers. CBS, first struck and most seriously ailing, is already in a perilously weakened condition.

"We lost our aerometric rhythm," an executive announces. "The control-room is occupied by an unknown, but definitely, alien force. It's a vector field. A mass of highway signs pointing into, around, over, and above The City. We have been permeated by the magnitude of our indifference and insignificance.

"We did manage to get up Video Trouble on The Network. But no telling how long it will last. We've notified the proper authorities in Washington — the Pentagon, the FCC. Some kind of geometric current is surrounding The City. Someone or something is tampering with the synthetic synchron-ization level. We are anemic."

Six hours later, unobtrusively as it began, the malignancy lifts. At eight the transmission refocuses, crystal clear with *The Mary Tyler Moore Show*. Top brass at CBS breathe a sigh of relief, light cigars, and watch in open-mouthed distress as two heavies drag a kicking and screaming Mary into an unlocked toilet at the West 86th Street Station of the IND 8th Avenue line and rape her. After the attack they make childish faces at the surveillance cameras and vanish into the gloom of the tunnel haze. Is this a Warhol prophecy?

"That was taped two weeks ago," Allan Burns says. "If it can happen to WCBS, think what it might do to WJM-TV."

However, with a true heroine show-biz spirit, Mary disregards the indecencies of time, and carries on, teeth flashing, her composure only slightly rumpled. She stumbles around the West 86th Street Station for the next twenty minutes looking for her hat. Suffering the mental anguish of not knowing why, only vaguely understanding how, she endures the remainder of the hour beset by a baffling ailment, apparently precipitated by the attack. As a reward, she ages a year for every minute of airtime exposure. By 9:00 she's a withered, lame, bouncing, grinning, nearly bald hag.

"Lucky it wasn't a two-hour special," an assistant director says.

"Brave girl," Lou Grant says. "But, then, we knew she had it in her."

An hour later, *Death in a Change Booth* on Channel 11, features Oscar E. Williams as the change booth clerk in BMT Station of the Carnarsie line at Sutter and Van Sindern Avenue. After being robbed Williams is doused with gasoline and set on fire by five youths of The Watchful Dogs Underground gang. The camera dollies in for a closeup, then locks on Williams' charred, smoking remains for the remainder of the hour. Indeed, it is a Warhol evening.

"Fascinating program," claims Norman Glim of 2792 West Octane Avenue. "You don't realize what staring at a charred cadaver for an hour can do for your psychic comfort."

Forthwith, the FCC releases a memo condemning evil in broadcasting, praising the virtues of wholesome family entertainment, and dispatches a troop of electronic troubleshooters, a photon SWAT team of trained radio wave assassins to The City. They, too, are annoyed by what they see, surprised by the arrogance of the invader, but mill about Police Plaza One, unsure of what weapons to use or how to otherwise explain it all.

"We'll figure it out," their leader says.

He's an inconspicuous, evanescent, maharishi, electronic sage. An Echo Resolution Imaging Expert named E.Erie™.

E.Erie™ is a new breed of technologically astute, intelligent, playful wizards recently acquired by the FCC — Information Specialists, that participated in Project Shamrock, the government's collaboration with RCA Global, ITT World Communications and Western Union International to bug the world — and to eventually spy on US citizens. It was one of the masterminds behind the creation of the "blue box," and has developed an advanced line of FishersOfMen, V — 4:19 stalker-software. It hums with a buzzing renaissance optimism.

At the Mayor's request E.Erie™ takes up residence in the annex of Garfield's office, prepared to direct the automata through the rigors of what is believed will be a hard and long campaign.

E.Erie™ is accompanied by a fog bank of high-tech gumshoes carrying patented iSolitonEMP weapons capable of generating a solitonic EMP that will destroy or disrupt any electro-magnetic wave target of choice.

Superior to the previous generation EMP devices which emitted non-localized EMPs creating both excessive target damage and unintended collateral damage, the new device emanates a highly encapsulated soliton EMP in a variety of size and power settings, based on targeting needs.

The iSolitonEMP_rifle is designed to emulate a standard sniper rifle for ease of transition from traditional weaponry. Using one of several preset power and size settings similar to drink and food settings found on a standard microwave, the weapon can be simply aimed, using the iScope, a patented advanced targeting scope, and engaged.

The iSolitonic EMP travels up to 2700 horizontal yards without the wind and elevation limitations of traditional weaponry. The iSolitonEMP_drone is designed to fit nearly all standard model drones and can be used for distances up to one 5,280 feet in altitude. (Want to anonymously disrupt a pacemaker installed in the target? Use the pre-set pacemaker setting [small pulse, low power], aim and fire. Want to disrupt the function of a moving motor vehicle? The automobile setting [medium pulse, low power] will disrupt all vehicle computer systems. Want to destroy the electronics in an entire building? Use one of several building settings [large pulse, high power] to eliminate all electronics).

The iSolitonic comes with a one-year or 500 Target Money back guarantee on every device* and a five-year mechanical warranty.

*Note: This guarantee does not include missed or collateral damage targets due to user error.

"This is where the story begins," someone observes. "January 31, Christine Freund's death. That's when the police became conscious of a serial killer."

"People were killed before that."

"But that's another story."

"So we're back to the parallel universe rap?"

"Well, a lot of things do happen simultaneously. I mean, how many avenues do we have to walk before we discover what The City is about? The street's pretty much the same. But some say sex. Some say sadism. Others want money.

"But wherever you go, there are other things — art, music, architecture — to transcend the destruction of pleasure seeking and entertainment, the manifestations that seep out of consciousness.

"How many shops must we pass before we find one where we can get our fingers into the sticky goo of significance?

"It will be simple when we discover the causes. The clues are here. We just have to find them. And it is in our nature to find them — though human personality is evasive."

The following morning the Cs' and Bs' mailbags are stuffed. Complaints, observations, suggestions on how to encourage even more prurient, salacious offerings.

"We need better censors," Agnes Grossman of the See Nothing Amiss Group protests. "These people are far too censorious."

Robin French, an executive of Tits & Tuch Productions, which distributes material produced by Norman Lear, says his company is staunchly against laundering and will not permit deletion of scenes or dialogue.

"Our shows are not immoral. There is no nudity, obscenity, indecency or violence in them. They are provocative and done with impeccable taste," Mr. French says. "They have passed the test of the industry code and the even more stringent standards of the networks. What happens to them once they take to air, is not our concern."

Throughout The City, committees form. The polemics of virtue and sin develop into meandering theologies. An Age of Aquarius sect, hoping to make room for the new values of *love, brotherhood, unity, and integrity,* points to an evolution in consciousness of happiness and peace, with Piscean values to be exposed and taken down (this includes governments, corporations, individuals, and personal relationships), appears along Broadway, on one side of the street. The Nuwaubians gather on the other.

"We must realize that when a people is trying to make themselves look bigger than others, they must take the main characters and heroes of a false or true story in religion and/or mythology and build their own story around heroes and characters, and this means that the story may be greatly changed to suit the purposes of those rewriting it," (Amunubi Rakhptah [Malachi York]).

Within the hour the warriors are clouding up the screens of a couple 15" Sonys, trading tasteless (as opposed to subtle and humorous) insults, and a bit later flood into the street to participate in ecumenical hand to hand, black and white combat.

In the aftermath, a woman combatant of the A of A on West 42nd Street claims to have seen god. Another with dripping mascara and swollen lips checks into the Emergency Ward at Mount Sinai, holds up scorched fingers, swears she got her hand in Sam's pants.

The old Devil grins, shakes his head.

"She ain't but halfway there," he says.

in search of copy and hoping
to enhance its good-citizen standing
The Times engages the commissioner
in desultory dialogue

Taunting, mocking The City's idiosyncrasies and vagaries, *The Times* carries the story on the front page and adds an editorial.

"It seems," *The Times* chimes and chides, "that in face of waning political popularity brought by the growing crime rate and the double-dealing of party rhetoric of the Beame regime, the person of Police Commissioner and patron of TCPD, Michael Garfield, last week suffered a severe embarrassment. At an ill-conceived and hastily assembled press conference, contrived to further enhance the Commissioner's (the Police) and, therefore, the Mayor's image, an electronic glitch caused a malfunction of video and audio equipment. It is not the first time the Commissioner has had difficulty conveying a favorable impression to a disbelieving public, but it did indicate how far the forces of evil have advanced in The City, and how powerful they are. The Commissioner, however, promises to return, via radio, newspaper, or whatever means necessity might allow, to get his massage-image through to the public. Knowing fully well his difficulties with faceless, fading identity, we wish him well."

Garfield points to the editorial.

"Did you read this crap? Glitch, my ass."

"A microelectronic maelstrom," E.Erie™ intones.

So, an E.Erie™/Sam confrontation looms.

Only once did E.Erie™ and Sam come eye to eye. That was in the late Nineteenth century and ended in a staring contest — neither had anything to say, and both came away knowing less than nothing about the other.

"Sunspots. The Zeeman effect," E.Erie™ whirrs. "We've reconnoitered and found traces, a couple of warm campfires, footprints leading into the bush. Trouble is, the damned thing knows where we're going. Inquiries just push it further into obscurity. I've never seen anything quite like this. It's got the acumen and cognition of a couple Einsteins. We know it's communicable, reproduces easily, possibly on sight, that it rides the airwaves, can infect a host channel in a few hours and will metastasize and grow more virulent with time. It has a lot of the quirks of human consciousness."

"A mask," Garfield says, aware for the first time of the size of the problem. "An electron mask controlled by . . . ."

True to E.Erie™'s prognostications the infection reappears and spreads to NBC and ABC. An afternoon science program of Dr. Ignaz Semmelivier of the Biological Sciences Department ate Columbia University, *Microbes and Men: The Deadly Enemy*, a buggy exposé uncovering the contagious principles of diseases, is commandeered.

Invisible, but powerful hands usher Semmelivier to the wings, to the door, and firmly set him out.

"An outrage," Garfield complains. My god, if you don't respect MDs, who will you?"

E.Erie™, the true warrior, sees the humor in it all.

"If you're going to be infected, it may as well be with humor. Remember, it is better to fail your VDRL than not to have loved at all."

"What about the radio?" Garfield wants to know.

"Sounds okay," E.Erie™ bleeps. "At least for the time being. But you can't tell."

"Then we'll try it," Garfield says.

He leans over the intercom. It buzzes rudely.

"Jesus, even this dime-store toy's picked it up."

"Carrier pigeons," E.Erie™ offers. "We could use carrier pigeons. We could get the mumblers in on this."

Three stations, WXLO, WEVD, and WYTC agree to sell Garfield twenty-minute drive time slots, and late Thursday he goes on with his message.

"The insurgents of mal-tech reflections are upon us," he tells the creeping canyon chariots. "They have invaded The City. All we know is that we think we know some young people have been killed. It appears, and I must emphasis, it appears that once projectiles pass through the skin, into what appears to be organs, which appear to be functioning, appear to cease functioning. Sometimes, and I should restate, sometimes, for reasons we do not fully understand, the person becomes immobile, at least to our perception, and after a time we think we can trace a movement of the elements of which it is assumed the corpse is composed, from complication, a complexity of order, to what is thought by most humans to be a natural state."

"Disorder? That's called entropy, Commissioner."

"Precisely! And now the forces of evil are evilly forcing more entropy upon us. They have attacked our integrity, our sense of fair play, the very attributes of which just and honorable men are comprised. For this reason, we have resolved to fight back, to recreate ourselves in an icon and likeness of what the public demands of its servants."

the Loo determines
(sort of) to take matters
(sort of) in his own hands

In truth, however, the streets are littered with bodies and the only reliable fact is that the police have nothing to go on. Inspired by the Commissioner's speech, the Lieutenant storms out of the office, intent now on search and destroy, in zealous pursuit of the Chubby Behemoth that holds The City by the throat.

Mathias turns to Channel 2 on his office Muntz Color Console (25") and conjures up his shooting star in Death Takes a Lover, a contrived bit of tripe about a teenage hooker who stumbles toward the deep end when one of her marks, a thirty-five-year-old deaf heroin addict, erases himself because he loves her but cannot love her profession.

"This is a tough one," Mathias tells the Lieutenant, "a serious matter. As you know, the situation at CBS could not be worse. I'm not exaggerating when I say that if we don't come up with a new idea, we'll be off the air. I mean, what does it profit a man if he . . .?"

"Every time I turn a trick," the girl says, "no matter how much I make, I think of him. I see his face. It's just terrible. I know god hates me."

The Lieutenant's eyes are moist. He's saddened by the girl's anguish.

"I'd rather not talk about it right now," he tells Mathias. "I'm having trouble with this part. Sometimes I'm just not the hardboiled cop I'm supposed to be. Know what I mean?"

"Well, okay. But get your act together. This is the real thing. No longer fun and games. Our collective video ass is on the line."

Theo watches Mathias's face where it is written in Aramaic or maybe Greek, clearly, that someone has already made a decision.

"You have suggestions," he says wiping his eyes.

"Several," Mathias says.

"So?"

"I'm not here to destroy anything."

The girl peers into the camera and breaks into tears.

"Now see what you've done."

"Well, as you know, the decision has been made. If we don't produce a killer, they will terminate the show. And I understand that. What's a cop show if the nasty runs wild and undetected? Where's the suspense? We have an obligation to our fans. What will our sponsors say if we don't catch the killer?

the Syndie, feeling left out,
demands a piece of the action

Word of the CBS dilemma twists along the grapevine, settles in the underground. Capo Czarmine Galante wants a piece of the action. He has a daughter, the rumor goes, in fact two daughters, to protect, knows murder is a lucrative business, and may be this time as well. Presently, too many cops populate the street — dope traffic detoured, slowed, and while the coffers are not empty, exactly, sales are off.

Of course, the police have a theory, several in fact, since theories are for those without clues. The crystal ball says the perp finds victims in discos. Ninety percent of the young females in The City spend at least one night a week in a disco, so extra cops are showing up to supplement those already on the take and make.

And things could get worse. Czarmine envisions a pandemic of police kicking in doors (which they already do), searching houses and apartments without warrants, of snipers on rooftops watching Syndie social clubs, of helicopters with spotlights circling overhead.

For his part, Czarmine has an organization to rebuild, wants to return to the old days, the honorable, lethal traditions of his youth, and finds the police are only an echo away. He conducts business from phone booths, in cheap restaurants, scuttles away, harassed, and trying to avoid the FBI's Miami investigation.

Still, he is the man, gives the orders, passes word to the enemy camp, Police Plaza One, a smoke signal from a chewed cigar, a torched Cadillac of a small-time hood who welched on a bet.

"Who knows the thugs better? The coppers or . . .?"

The answer is obvious. In the realm of hits, Czarmine may have as many as eighty notches on his belt. And though no one has kept score, exactly, bodies have been numerous. Assuming he started with "hits" for Vito Genovese in 1940, at sixty-seven in '77, he would have racked up an unhealthy (even for a homicidal maniac) 2.1621 killings a year for thirty-seven years — with time out for twenty years in jail.

Is there a serial killer in the house? In The City?

Galante puts out an A.P.B. *Kill the killer.*

Still, the question hangs on the air.

"Keep your fuzzy blue-boys away from my men and we'll get this gavone in a week or two."

Garfield listens, puzzles over the message. He knows that tracking the Syndie's trail can be a complex, touchy business. Most often the connections are subtle or hidden.

"Few hoods are in power themselves," Syndie investigator, Harvey Coldstoking says, "They are behind the people in power. The real connections seem to come between the pols, business associates, and certain union support. Almost every politician needs business and union support. The pols need money, phone banks, lawyers, manpower to get petitions signed, buses to take people to the polls, flatbed trucks with loudspeakers to get the word out."

"So what does the encryption mean?" Garfield wants to know.

Whatever it is, he decides finally to take it at face value. After the teevee debacle his skin is tissue thin. He's been hit from all sides — welcomes a kind voice. A strange sea where sharks and lion fish swim side by side, their schemes enhanced and jeopardized by a crazy.

Who are we? What have we encouraged? Bickering. The hateful struggling of Siamese twins, of one body, two minds, dependent but divided. What energy gives strength, what provides direction, and who has written the rules?

He sees dollars flying out the door. He will take advantage of the offer while he can. He sends Czarmine a note via a numbers carrier.

"We must get together for a drink."

Czarmine gallantly concurs.

The City falls silent, the rumblings of an ancient prophecy stirring.

the extended case and putrefaction
of Child-David's multiple afflictions

It is a pleasant morning, time for reflection, introspection. Soon Hans-David will make another entrance into The City. It's nice to know the multitudes are thinking about him, fondly, though with apprehension. The morning offers possibilities. Will Agamemnon accept Clytemnestra's invitation? Of course he will. He always does.

Ensconced in his hole-in-the-wall dressing room, Peter-David pulls back the blanket and peers out from the seven-story mountain to Wicker Street, the river, the New Jersey Palisades. He watches Sam Carr's house.

Child-David, enfant prodigy, the metaphorical Messiah, eyes shining, steps into therianthropy, lycanthropy. Today he crawls, laughs, and plays with ghosts, the nimble, tumbling spirits of the chase. He will be assaulted, loved and brutalized according to the custom. Children should be seen, not heard. The child is father to the man. He is invisible, heralded in the echo of a canine's bark.

> Higher than a house,
> higher than a tree,
> underneath the water,
> underneath the sea;
> oh, whatever can it be?
> (Mother Goose)

He is to be encouraged, scolded, fondled, beaten — sensation and perception molded, coaxed, and cast by invisible hands.

A poltergeist shatters the china, a phantom rattles wall hangings. It is in his eyes. Still he recites his letters and numbers, creates stories, sagas of brigands and ladies, cannons booming.

Son, why hast thou thus dealt with us?

At age twelve, about his father's business, he captures a neighbor's blind miniature poodle, binds the animal, front paws and back, and amid the screeches and howls, eviscerates the creature with a pocket knife.

"He has friends," his mother says. "Dr. Pollowitz believes it is all right. Small boys have fantasy lives. He's well-behaved. No worse than others."

Friends. Creatures with penetrating eyes. And urges. Life among the Philistines. All things are inspected, explained, but nothing matters.

"He talks to himself. That is a sign of a very sensitive, intelligent child."

Indeed, a child in the temple instructing his elders. About his father's business. But what is his father's business? And who is this son's father?

"There is no doubt
I am a demon and
I have had a demon living in me since birth. All my life
I've been violent,
I am mean and cruel.
I've been irrational, angry — and destructive. When
I was a child
I had very real and wicked nightmares. In fact, they were so bad
I had to sleep with a light on, or with my father in the room, or
I had to sleep with my parents.
I saw monsters often and
I heard them and would scream hysterically.
I would say that they, the bad dreams, were very severe.
I know, that they were real — just like now.
I am a bad dream.
I am living a bad dream.
I've been tormented all my life by them — never having peace."

in abbreviated consultation
   Mathias instructs the Lou
in the realities of The City

Returning to death takes a lover, Mathias settles into his Eames Soft Pad
Executive swivel-throne and gazes intently at the Admiral 25L-911 Color
CRT.

"Here's what I have," he says.

The Lieutenant fondly fondles the young hooker's buns. His Sister Maria
therapeutic stroking works wonders. The girl expiates the vision of her
dead lover, and, on several brief hustling sorties to West 42nd Street,
performs with something akin to orgasmic regularity.

"If the bread's decent, I go off like popcorn," she says. "It's the old days.
I've been born again."

"I know you've been concerned about your image," Mathias says, "about
not yet apprehending the maniac — the bona fide, full-fledged, dyed-in-the-
wool malcontent. Someone who is not interested in profit, vengeance,
anger, hatred, or patriotic causes. Simply, someone who wastes people
because that is what he is does. Because that is what he *is*, say, in the same
way some people are blind or stupid. Someone perfectly suited to blowing
people away."

The Lieutenant is skeptical.

The young hooker watches his face, mirrors his concern.

"He won't do it unless it's cash up front," she says, the confidence,
authority of experience in her voice."

"I know, I know. You have been on a talent hunt," Fabulous Flatfoot says.

It's obvious the Lou is stoned. He got into some good shit in the
afternoon. The girl probably supplied it.

"Yeah. We got the right actor, and it's a tough story, so you'll have to be
at your best, utilize brilliant forensic acumen," Mathias says.

"And if I don't?"

"I know three or four who would be willing to take the job," the lovely
harlot tells them. "Provided the change is right."

Of course she trusts the Lieutenant. He is described as a "basically honest
dude, tough but with feelings — the kind of guy who might kick a hooker in
the tail if he had to, but they'd understand each other because they grew
up on the same kind of block."

"For Christ sake," The Mathias says, aware of the inherent difficulties
involved in mass communications. "You have never failed before. Why
now?

"Okay, let me explain. When you find this person, or whatever you want
to call him, and I'm sure you will, our troubles are over. The guy will be an
instant celebrity. We'll jump the shark. I mean, that should be worth some
effort."

The irresolute cop is skeptical.

"I don't know."

"Jesus H. Christ, you know how little it takes to become a celebrity (if you have a bit of luck) and how eager the groundlings are for new, slightly off-beat talent? This guy'll be an immediate superstar. We'd have the entire market to ourselves. It'll make the Super Bowl look like drop the handkerchief. I mean, it's a once in a lifetime shot, and you will be the hero, the savior. Talk about bringing someone back to life.

"Have you read the papers lately? In case you haven't, you might like to know that Fred Prinze is dead. He shot himself. Nothing dramatic. And that's the problem. Just sitting around with his agent in a hotel room. Put a .32 to his head and wham! And for what?"

A wail goes up from the steamy strumpet. A wail and then an anguished moan.

"Yes," she cries, "Oh, I can see it as if it happened only yesterday."

"That's enough," the Lieutenant says. "You've set her off again."

Mathias tries to ignore the high theatrics of cheap weekly productions, knows that when the budget becomes a whip you aren't going to get much. For a few dollars extra they could have a pro — any one of the experienced hookers on the list.

"That kind of thing has to be controlled. If Fred Prinze wants to blow his brains out, why in hell's name didn't they have him do it on an episode of *Chico and the Man*? Entirely too much talent going to waste. I'm just sorry we didn't get to Gary Gilmore in time. He had a natural flare for publicity. If we're going to get in on this stuff, we have to be ready. Jesus, with a little help from promotions we could have made a billion. If you can't stop it, and you may not want to, you have, even in the most primitive ethical sense, an obligation to get the most out of it. Man, that's the business of life. You know what you're doing and you make it. Otherwise, you're out on the street."

The Mathias turns up the volume, corrects the contrast and tint. He glances at the 18" Emerson Tabletop Color CP40WR "Champion." Thinks maybe it would provide better reception.

Unavoidably, his words have comforted Kojak's consort. Always one to see the merit in hustling a buck, she finds a strange sort of sense in his logic. Aren't diamonds, furs and penthouses the center of the American girl's dream? She gazes wide-eyed on her companion, a revelation dawning on her soft, peaches-and-cream brow.

"He left me with nothing," she says in a nearly inaudible whisper. "That's it. He left me with nothing."

"Look," Mathias says, "here's the story. Serials are dead. From now on mini-series or long movies. Four to six hours a week, then something else next week. That's what we're doing.

"We got the antagonist under contract for five episodes. Four times he goes out to perpetrate and four times we tag along with cameras, sound, support actors. Each time, he gives you, our gumshoe gladiator, the slip. The fifth time, the last show — bang, the long arm of an expended budget gets him. The hero makes the collar. Hell, we already have one show in the can."

"This is better than anything I expected," the girl says, unbuckling the Lieutenant's belt. Her fingers are red and sore from recalcitrant rusted belt-buckles.

She slips out of her bra — she has already discarded her panties — and turns the firm, full rounds of her breasts with their rose-tipped nipples toward her now distracted/interested therapist.

"This may be your greatest case, the moment of your immortality," Mathias says. "A hunt to end all hunts, in which the personality of your nemesis and your detective heart coalesce to punctuate the legitimacy of film noir. The reviews are beyond your finest dreams, a festschrift for the modern inquisitive, searching, probing mind."

"And all you need to do is catch one instinctive, compulsive homicidal maniac?"

"Or something like that."

"At this moment the goddam City is half an inch from going off its nut."

Mathias stands and walks to the window. The vista stretching out to a wall of bricks blocking the view of the East River is fogged up with the collected pollutants of ozone, sulphur dioxide, nitrogen dioxide, carbon monoxide, and lead particulates. A parallel universe.

"Right now we have a lunatic the world wants to know about."

The youthful hooker's gotten into the Lieutenant's pants, with one hand, but turns her attention to Mathias.

"Does he mean that?" she says.

"Every last simple-minded twit in this city is about to shit his pants," Mathias tells them.

Theo pulls away from the girl, hobbles across the stage trying to pull up his pants.

"It won't work," he says, shaking his head, sidling up to the camera. "I've seen that nut. You've seen him. Or at least we saw what appeared to be his aspects and configurations. In the first show he didn't leave a clue. We got a bit of a bullet frag. That's all. I mean, how do we know who this is?"

"Well, okay," Mathias says. "But take my word for it. It will work."

"The other day in the Bronx when you dropped the teevee, I blanked out. Just gave it up. It was like I wasn't there. I don't like it."

"You weren't there. But that's showbiz. You're nothing without an audience. Whatever song and dance you do — no audience, no review. Who's to know?"

"He's a respectable cop," the hooker says, pouting over the sudden turn of events, no one paying attention to her, hoping to get back in the act.

"He's not like them others. They just want one thing. They don't care about us."

"I don't know what happened after that. Anyway, I already got an audience."

"But this is bigger."

"Okay. So I go along with it. Then the next time it gets a little easier — the time after that easier still. Others agree and join the club. A cult develops, a way of life, a culture."

"Hey! We're already at the bottom of the slippery slope. The Job is a magic show of stealing imitation pearls from the swine. Do you know how far down you have to go to keep people happy?"

"Yeah, I'm a hero. And heroes, true heroes, function within the constraints of their persona. They live according to what their followers think is heroic," the Lieutenant says, surprised by the erudition of his own words, though perplexed by their import.

"Jesus. Where do you get that? You at the library Saturdays reading?"

"My fans expect great things."

"You still got to get them to watch the Sealy commercials. You'd do better to go along with the story."

"I know, I know. But I don't like it."

"Look, you have three daughters already, and may have more. I mean what's their names? Christina, Candace, Penelope? What would they say? What would Penelope say if Odysseus hadn't come home to fuck with the suitors? Have you asked the girls? What would they say about a father who passes over an opportunity to cash in on a lucrative gig and solidify his immortality and their lives at the same time? I mean, after this you'll be forever listed in the annuals of teevee superstars? What would they say if you gave that away?"

The girl loses interest in the conversation, sits on the bed, unclothed, picking paint off her toenails. She wonders, now, what love is, and why the memory of a man who left her with nothing should haunt her.

"It makes cash," Mathias says. "First-class cash. We've already got the crews in Central Park running up footage. You wanted your gig in The City. Okay. We're in town for this one."

"What if I try to collar him and he starts shooting? What then?"

"Look, three people drowned filming *Noah's Ark.* Curtiz dumped six hundred gallons of water in the studio and drowned three extras. Another ended with a broken leg and several dozen others were hospitalized. There's always a small risk.

"When moviegoers heard about it they came out in droves."

"But perps might shoot at Kojak with real guns."

"Well, all the better. You can shoot back. If you kill him, good. Yeah. The audience will love it. And love you.

"There is nothing to say killing is wrong. Only the people who don't want

Wayne Lanter

to be killed, and some of them are okay with it. Otherwise, humanity supports it. It's good for business. People love it. Especially when they can sit and watch it at home. It's good family entertainment. It's good for the country. From the top down.

"That's why the Feds don't have laws against murder. Hell, the best laws we have say just the opposite. Create a principle, 'Thou Shalt Not Kill,' then figure out how many ways you can get around it. Self-defense, executions, abortions, war — not to mention hits that are ignored, overlooked, as well as operating tables and highways and starvation. You know how many kids are done in each year by their parents?

"And most of them before they are a year old."

He laughs.

"The old man comes home drunk — the baby cries — wham, a fractured skull, convulsions — a dead kid.

"Hell, the future is kids killing their parents in self-defense. Haven't you ever wondered about that? Where it came from?"

The Loo is skeptical. Shakes his head.

"The society tells you to do away with people. For love, for money, for convenience, for whatever you want. Do what you will, but by all means kill. That's the Judeo Christian story. That's the NRA story. They're the future of this country. A kid four or five — give him a gun. He doesn't like his mother — Bham! — get a new one.

"Okay, so it's coming down or up or over. It has to be done this way."

Mathias chuckles blithely.

"Here I am, talking to the most revered teevee cop in the history of the tube. A cop with a larger following worldwide than any known gumshoe. The demand for Kojak is overwhelming. Man, when I talk about the people, I'm not talking about a couple dudes with a pocket full of loose change at Blackrock. You know what the Blackrock is?"

> The CBS building [1961-1964] is one of the country's great examples of modern architecture. It was the last completed work designed by master architect Eero Saarinen, whose goal was to build "The simplest skyscraper in The City." Unlike the steel-cage office buildings typical at the time, the CB building was the first postwar reinforced concrete skyscraper sheathed in Canadian black granite with gray-tinted vison glass. The 38 story tower, nicknamed Black-rock, rises 490 feet without setbacks. Constructed as the headquarters of one of America's legendary radio and tele-vision networks, the CBS building was commissioned by William S. Paley, Founder and Chairman of CBS.

"Nothing. Nothing at all. Remember moirai controls the gods and man.

Psyaint David

Have you ever asked yourself what this is all about? Why people watch detective shows?

"But I'm just a neighborhood kid."

The hooker agrees. Nods. She's puzzled by the clap-trap. Doesn't understand the part about killing. All she knows is life and death (that's what the script says). She's stepped over a few dozen bodies on the sidewalks. She figures that's the way of it. Some just don't make it.

"You're the Golden Geek — or rather Greek," Mathias says. "Have you ever seen the FCC do a rain dance? They go around shaking bones and chanting, but nobody at that table will touch this one. For a couple years Eisenhower (who signed the execution order) and Kennedy put the skids to the Slovik thing. Why? To maintain the superstition that Americans don't do things like that. But no one's gonna mess with us. This is people based. The great unseen hand of the market. The herd. Lowing. The soft rumble of hooves in the dust pushing toward the cliff.

"Fearless Fosdick, you're at the top of the food chain. How many people does *Kojak* feed? Don't be selfish. How many people? Not just The Universe Studios hired hands. Think of the network and affiliates and the people who depend on the ads for your shows. It's your obligation to take care of these people. The hard working schmucks all the way down the line."

"So, how do we find him?"

"We start with a description. A collection of parts. We have a drift. A vision, a bit hazy, but a vision of how he might appear. And that's a beginning — where we begin. Then we follow the yellow brick road."

The girl with the petulant pout matures quickly, brought to life by the import of their words, aware now, not only of the politics, but also of the lesser possibilities the double-dealing offers. Her face shows signs of enlightenment (although this may be a pretense). She pulls the sheet up to cover her thighs, her breasts, waits for the camera to swing away and dresses quickly, in an elevated taste-consciously-chosen dipped-in-tea-beige blouse, ivory-linen vest and silky-beige skirt with the finest of brown stripes.

Her gestures take on a studied grace, an almost imperceptible affectation. She speaks softly with a well-schooled, stylish French accent, and while she still regrets the misfortune, the unseemly end of her deaf-mute lover, she now knows well the advantage it could provide. She realizes adversity builds strength.

Moist eyed, in a rather unimaginative two-shot, the Lieutenant discovers the woman in the child, as beautiful as ever, the hue of her lovely skin heightened ever so lightly with makeup. He gazes into her eyes, finding there the languid, liquid, limpid anguish of a heart too many times broken.

Could this be the lady with green eyes and red hair, Madame _____?

"So how do we find the Master of Mayhem?" he says, his voice distracted, his mind clearly now on something beyond the hunt, attempting to understand the transformation he has just witnessed, the child-woman, tart-lady as shapeshifter.

"That will come later in the story," Mathias says. "Some things you just have to take on foreshadowing and faith."

"So you've had a vision. You just came down from the mountain. Or gone to the mountain. What's next? Walking across the Hudson?"

"Something like that.

"Look at it this way. We can maim two birds with one rock. Get shows that have a real audience appeal and apprehend the night-stalker at the same time."

He pauses reflexively.

"And that's how business is supposed to work. We are mankind's liberator—lifting people from the doldrums, giving them courage, hope, if not life and fear."

"And it's only a small matter that we don't know why?"

"Hey, the Sixth Extinction is upon us. Why not make a few bucks off it? It's gonna happen anyway."

Anyway, in a final gesture, the Lou's ingénue strumpet with a heart of gold regresses rapidly, cannot maintain her newly acquired elegance, and tries to kill herself, to join her lover. Of course she fails, but still has time in the closing minutes to rediscover compassion and tenderness in the assurances of her detective hero. She takes his words to heart and, along with a firm pat on the ass, goes back to the street, eventually, and by the end of the hour, is again turning tricks with something akin to born again verve and vitality. Now, however, lest the presentation be without merit or redeeming graces, social as well as personal, she is no longer a thoughtless, inconsiderate strumpet, but because of the Lou's intervention, a sadder and wiser whore. And there's supposed to be something socially redeeming in that.

The truth is, of course, a cliché. But that's the way of it, and about all anyone has a right to expect.

Still, Sam's fingerprints are on the knob. You can smell the putrefaction from both ends of the hall. Rumors drip off the grapevine at Blackrock, at ABC and NBC. The prophets demand attention. Intent on assimilating the murmuring, the hum become allusion, allegory, a metaphor of mayhem, the prophets demand consultation. The word is out, about to become act — celluloid and magnetic tape. Meetings are called, tables thumped, careers threatened, and decisions made. Plans are formulated for a kindergarten *Peyton Place* to compete with the forth coming pre-pubescent *Lady Chatterley's Daughter, Maladolescenza,* and *The Other Cinderella*.

What else? A mass suicide (à la Jonestown which is yet to come?) is suggested, with prizes for the most inventive method? There are any number of misanthropes The City could do without — and this is only the later part of the twentieth century.

Why not be capricious? Stonings? There are Muslims available. A witch-hunt, a public flogging and burning at the stake — headhunters.

And there's more.

A bloke in a Lincoln green tunic, hood and velvet tights, wearing leather vambraces, (starring in "The Crossbow Incident") is reported in the 41st South Bronx. He's carrying a crossbow and a quiver of aluminum quarrels with Plastiflech vanes. An hour after the sighting anorexic/pot-bellied Sabastian Boitel of 784 Hewitt Pl is discovered in an alley with three arrows in his abdomen. It seems Irene of Rome who was supposed to be looking after Sabastian was playing shuffleboard in a local bar and did not get word in time. When told of his demise, Sabastian's wife claims that, "Christ is loosing arrows on the world."

Later in the afternoon two members of the Seven Immortals street gang are found in an abandoned playground off Intervale Avenue, pinioned like a pair of tattered butterflies in a grammar school cigar box display to a wooden light pole, each with an arrow through her throat.

Word on the street claims the Lincoln green Hood is not a bloke at all, but Maid Marian in drag out looking for Robin's cheating ass intent upon adding a bit of equality to the forest saga. Of course she has given up the longbow for a small conceal-carry crossbow (easier to handle and still powerful) which offers the novice improved accuracy with little or no training.

No one knows for certain the whereabouts of Little John, Will Scarlet or Friar Tuck. Rumor has it, however, they are off wenching in another part of the forest, stealing from the rich (or at least from those who have a few quid) to fill their moleskin pouches.

the mass-com virus spreads
leaving media experts
and divine providence miffed

The following evening provides a new twist, part two in the continuing tale of video-viral deceit. Maverick programs from ghost studios intercalate themselves into Bs' and Cs' prime time slots. Players take on episodes of raw sex and violence evolve into anti-social oddballs. Children are kidnapped and disappear. The dead and wounded are everywhere.

The mass-com gurus are still guessing. More here than mere radio wave interference. No one knows how to explain it — least of all E.Erie™, who takes it circumspectly. He's propped up at a desk, in the aroma of coffee, Old Gold smoke, and a miasma of the morning *Times.*

"The Josephson effect," E.Erie™ reports. "Josephson's macroscopic quantum-interference phenomena."

But what to do?

CBS mogul Paley considers interrupting his current romp in Rome. Then a third level underling takes a fling. Maybe man was not meant to take dominion after all. She suggests it might be wise to ride the crest, roll with the flow, confess that this was planned. Paley likes the suggestion, cancels his flight, and goes back to playing. Maybe this is the new Jerusalem, the new media.

However, smart capital is skeptical. Will it last? The Nielsen has been bouncing like a rubber ball. There are intimations of an unlimited revenue bonanza, but only time, not guess, will tell. It will most likely last at least until the March sales meetings convene at the Hilton — though even there the fishbowl may be spiked with puffers.

To sell air time, à la lottery, the names of programs and their probable aberrations, plots (schemes) penned in red on yellow paper strips are dropped into a large fishbowl. A delegate from each network assigned to handle scheduling draws out scraps from the fungal file designating the season's newest fare, as well as extensions and resurrections of worn and beaten sitcoms, westerns, and cop shows. The free enterprise of choice becomes chance — the past to be replicated by the past. The present limps in. There is no future.

The new CBS fare includes *Gunsmoke* reruns (after a two-year hiatus). The show is slated to be canceled in 1967, due to low ratings, before Paley intervenes. He moves the show from Saturdays to Mondays (cancelling Gilligan's Island), placing sad Matt back in the Nielsen Top Ten (Paley and his wife are both big fans of the show). In 1972 Paley again intervenes in programing. He orders the shortening of a second installment of a two-part CBS Evening News series on the Watergate investigation. Based on a complaint from Charles Colson, an aide to President Richard M. Nixon, Paley orders the suspension of negatively critical comments and analyses by CBS news commentators and pundits, which follow Presidential addresses.

For the recapitulation, as with Paley, Dillon ripens. He keeps a bottle of cheap booze in his desk. His hands shake, his voice trembles. He throws tantrums that suggest a compulsive homicidal predisposition. Not even his horse can live with him or love him. It shits at embarrassing times, comes up with an improbable erection — farts a lot and screams unexpectedly — as slow-witted and ill-natured as its master.

Before the month ends, to get away from it all, a disillusioned Kitty packs her bags into *Hot L Baltimore*, another hustler in from Kansas, gone east to make a new name and her fortune as a protégé of Our Lady of the Licentious Libido.

Innovation echoes invention. Private eye mountaineer Jed Clampett, newly knighted, frolics with nymphets, solves crimes with backwoods' guile — the cunning of a true hillbilly — offers to help hunt for the Evil One.

The national spelling bee of *Hollywood Squares*, *Name that Tune* and *What's My Line* are stuck with unanswerable questions.

Psyaint David

> Little Nancy Endicott
> In a white petticoat
> And a red nose
> The longer she stands
> The less she knows.
> (Traditional)

The guests are stumped. It seems not to be a light matter. They wonder, why? Does the cow go over the hill? To the mill?

> There is a mill with seven circles
> In each circle stands seven bags
> Upon each bag sits seven cats
> Each cat has seven kittens
> Then the Miller and his wife come in
> How much wheat is now in the mill?
> (Traditional)

Two paramedics on prime time *Emergency* take sexual liberties with unconscious female patients. What are her vital statistics?
"I don't know."
"Take a guess."
"How about 24-36-36?"
"That's a beer bottle."
"Okay. What are we checking for?"
Heartbeat?
Breathing?
"Christ, I don't know. Talk about a dead . . .."
"Anyway, the oxygen tanks are empty and we couldn't have saved her."
"Saved her? From what?"
"Oh, poverty, ignominy, ignorance, heartbreak, fear, etc."

> The man who needs it doesn't want it.
> The man who invented it doesn't need it.
> The man who bought it doesn't know it.
> What is it?
> (Traditional)

"But who was she?"
"One of Charlie's angels. A Charlie's Angels' doll?"
Technology, law, politics, nested in a patch of damp matted pelt between the archetypical thighs. Long-legged, skinny sacks of skin and bone leaping about, setting the world straight with karate chops and magic. Carrie Nation, Elsie Borden? How about Calamity Jane?
"Yeah. A piece of quality meat for sale. Bionic, police, and wonder. That

kind of thing."

"But ya' know it's just a job — bring home the bacon, another way of making dough, selling your ass — or someone's."

"Yeah. Another part of the women's' movement. Expand the market, open cash procurement avenues. A way to get an out of control environment under control."

and then, again,
as of one mind,
Son of Sam speaks

I am alone with Sam, his son, condemned to my secret.
I do not confide in them. Everything after the truth is a lie.
I cannot say
I am sorry. They do not want sorrow. They want revenge.
I am the avenger.
I must pretend to be like them.
I pretend they are like me.
I cannot say
I have howling thoughts, and they make me do wild things.
I've been shooting people.
I am scared. Be my friend.
I won't shoot you.
I am the demon from the bottomless pit, here to create terror. "Where there is terror, there is salvation" (Augustine).
I am war. There can be no enlightenment without mutilating flesh.
I am destruction! Oh, cruel clemency (Louis Antoine Saint-Just).
I am devastation.
I know who has whored and pimped.
I know who has committed grievous sins.
I know the great one who can cast me away.
I suppose he likes me — David the shit, the filth.
I am the wretch.
I am to "Provide love with perfect hatred" (Jacques Clément).
I am Son of Sam who fears nothing and destroys!
I stomp on the dwellers of earth in the name of the wretched.
I am king.
I am hell.
I am heaven.
I am degeneration, and Nyssa the harlot shall not escape my curse.
I shall kill her children.
I am a fallen angel.
I have come to avenge and to establish the kingdom of misery. ". . . and he that hath no sword, let him sell his garment and buy one (*Luke* 22: 36)."

Psyaint David

I am Son of Sam.
I am the Prince of Darkness who fears neither mortality nor hell.
I am Sam's son and where
I live is nobody's business. Don't listen to David the fool, for
I am the king, the powerful and my father is Abaddon!
I rule the world.
I work for Sam, or Sam works through me.
I pick Queens because of the pretty women.
I like pretty women.
I create destiny.

inspired by the spirit of Sam
Peter Lorre revives
the presence of Hans Beckert or . . .

Even before the script girl (Claire Carleton?) is out the door he feels a surge, flush-faced, the grip of the personae of frenetic Kürten, Speck, etc., a psychotic, a fractured personality of the abominable at his throat.

He shuffles on, hands in the pockets of his greatcoat, his eyes wide, a torment-scorched heart seeking release, cessation, prepared, now, nearly, for mayhem and carnage.

Mephistopheles, Steppenwolf, the nuances of Sam's selves are up, stretching, whining, a mournful baying in the night, a serenade at a campsite of Huns, circling the fire, casting bones (Shagai, Sangoma), low man loser out, a dirk each in his heart in turn severing the temporal bonds of servile limitations, spirit loosed to its journey, until one, alone, remains, breathing, staring into the coals, embers glowing brightly, a white fire with no flame.

Sam is no whimsical fool of a Satan to be outwitted by the toothless guile of peasant maliciousness. In his sundry selves, slick, deceitful, at ease and agile within the sandbox, schoolyard theology of his adversaries, he's prepared to mount the Christian battlements, to rout the sanctified heroes with his cunning.

The Duke of Death smiles. A charm to compliment the predator, he's familiar with Sam's stains on the glass, the sweet scent of brimstone. The signs are for him, he knows, and wonders if possibly . . .? The following day he discovers a note on the street near the Galaxie, the scrawled scratch, the hieroglyphs of arrows, twisted lines on a piece of white paper edged in red. A map, directions, he assumes, believes — a portent, a summons, a calling to orders.

Guiding the Galaxie along River Parkway to Baychester, he shadows the floating goat heads on the windshield, the horizontal eye slits and pointed, sharp ears painted in the dusk.

Below Fleming Park, he edges the Galaxie into a parking space and sits a full five minutes with his hands wrapped to the steering wheel. Opaque clouds of blowing snow swirl around the car. Briefly, he thinks of turning back.

Then with the diagram in hand he sets out through the park, navigating, translating the lines and circles, the arrows, into directions, landmarks.

"Too big," he grumbles, tracking the inner walk into the trees, pausing, facing the wind, his eyes tearing.

If the bench is beneath the tree at the bend in the walk, the large red X could be in the bushes just beyond the water fountain. But the fountain is on the wrong side of the bench — it's the wrong bench — possibly the right fountain — which is today no fountain at all.

He can make no sense of it, and is about to turn away when a black dog appears at the end of the bench. David backs away several steps before he realizes the animal is watching him.

The dog walks slowly toward the Emerald Green Arborvitae, then turns slowly and breaks into a trot. David runs, legs numbed, into a small clearing, a grid of stones — another Homo sapiens attempt to placate the gods by the laying the unknown beneath the ground.

As quickly as it appeared, the dog disappears in a swirl of snow and David stands, hands in pockets, petting the Bulldog's snubbed nose with his thumb, hunched against the wind, staring into the fissure. The opening is well concealed in an outcropping of rock, but large enough for all but the tallest to enter. Truly, "It is easier for a camel to go through the eye of a needle, than for a rich man to enter the kingdom of god" (*Matthew* 19: 24).

Is that true?

He approaches wearily, carrying the Bulldog Kojak Style, at the ready, prepared, then hears Sam's hollow whine in the wind gusting through the rocks.

"I form the light and create darkness: I make peace, and create evil." (Isaiah 45: 7).

Another angle, dollying in, medium closeup, top and left, to a goat head on the grotto wall.

He pauses, goes no farther, then returns, blowing into his hands, rubbing his sore finger, waiting for the engine to warm. He wonders. What kind of car does Kojak drive?

A copper 1975 Buick Century Regal 455.

Yes, that sounds right.

Sam reflects on human folly
and
the delicious prospect of it all

Sam grins, malocclusion, rotted yellow teeth glinting in the pale of a weak winter-sun metal-halide gas-discharge medium arc-length lamp.

Psyaint David

"Look at me," he says, "beat up, tattered, torn, ridiculed, berated, damned and condemned. I haven't had a new suit in two hundred years — friendless, without family or home."

Actually, he was asked.

Would you like to disguise the shaggy, wild beast semblance? Say top hat and tails and spats? Maybe an uptown uniform: Prada loafers, Calvin Klein black socks, a swart Hickey Freeman suit, or a Navy Brooks Brothers blazer in traditional worsted flannel — a three button model with patch pockets, welted edges and embossed gold-plated Golden Fleece buttons — a white shirt and French cuffs with skull and crossbones cuff links?

And what did he say?

He shuffles down-center stage, his face shadowed.

"And the insolence of kicking me around. The fool. The clown."

He waves a crooked finger in the air.

"I have served him well, the wrath side of his person. The father, the son, the ghost. The Fourth Lateran Council (November 11, 1215) and I was there, declared, 'It is the Father who spawns, the Son who is produced, and the Spirit who advances, co-equal, co-eternal, and consubstantial, and each a whole and entire person, expression, or hypostases — in other words tricephalic.

"Theological gobbledygook," Sam says. "Three persons distinct and of one nature (nature is what, while person is who). And creation a single oeuvre common to all, in which each shows forth what is proper to him so that all things appear 'from the Father,' 'through the Son,' and 'in the Holy Spirit.' More gibberish. Divine drivel. Indeed, a dog with three heads. One growling, one barking, and one whining a melody into the symphony.

"They take up one side of the deific coin, but I alone am imprinted on this side forming conjoined twins, a theological corpus callosum binding us as one in war and peace, love and hate, cruelty and kindness. 'Oh, merciful cruelty' (Augustine).

"Yet some things can't be undone. Not even they can undo the laws without becoming what they are not. The problem of creation in an abhorrent imagination."

Sam's face is red. He sucks a Havana cigar.

"And what do I do? What do I provide? Spirit, freedom, a mindful insensitivity beyond personal whim."

> Speech full of hate and bold presuming boast,
> Refused god suit, said that his own form beamed
> With radiance of light, shone right of hue,
> And in his mind he found service not due
> To the lord god, for to himself he seemed
> In force and skill greater than all god's host . . ..
> (Caedmon)

"This is a true American religion, consecrated by every sect in the land.

"I'm no beatific toadstool sitter, basking in the glory of luck. Hell's strewn with cosmic edicts, the red tape of chaos, the fantasies of a wholesome life. And I've burned for them, for every one. My ass is scorched and scarred from stem to stern with the hot irons of conflict and wrath.

> And there was a quarrel in the firmament:
> Sam and his angels opposed the wizard
> of double-speak and certitude. And the
> sorcerer fought as did his angels, but did not
> prevail. And heaven was shattered into
> a thousand pieces. And Sam and his angels
> earned their freedom from great beast,
> that old liar called divinity and icon,
> which deceiveth the ether into the far
> reaches of oblivion.
>
> (*Sam* 7: 77)

"Well, now I'll have my turn. Times to pay for that. The chuckle of eternal bliss, the smoke of holy fire — twisted in the malcontent of praises which are never enough, even when well sung."

Sam's been in this part of the cave before.

Within the week *The Times* reports additional sightings — the Palo Mayombe, Mithraism, on the western inclines of the park preparing a sacrifice — a goat and a dog.

"A goat?" Sam says. "You gotta be shitting me."

He rubs his ass.

"A fucking goat?"

The thespians gather in the street. Tomorrow a feast, candidate anointed, forehead star-scarred, women waiting below the hill in the streets to be lashed and chastened, cleansed and made fertile.

Hans-Peter returns from his snow-blown odyssey, pacified for the moment with a modicum of time to digress, to ruminate, to wait on what Sam has in mind.

the meandering of Mathias' deadly affair whereby he loses someone he never had

Twice within the year, even before the Son of Sam project, Mathias smelled the stench of the hyena's breath — convinced by the incongruity of chance that it was not chance. Otherwise how to explain the tumblers falling to the numbers of a fifty-year-old, balding, paunchy, sight failing, bland exec-type in a bar — without intent or design, other than for a quick pick-me-up — a neighborhood tavern at 77-08 164th Street called Artoru's, a not unusual Queens drink-too-much-stumble-home-to-yell-at-the-old-lady place — in the area by mistake, the bar by chance, seated next to a pleasant, blue-eyed, shaggy nymphet, who he decides, after an exchange of two or three smiles, he has seen before.

Her eyes have a southern European cast — one slightly higher and larger than the other. The curve of her lips, her sculpted mouth (a thin upper and full lower lip) moves in ways he at first thinks it might, and then knows it will. And had conscious memory served half as well as the unconscious, he would have known her immediately. He would not have waited until she mentioned something to him about the bartender's long nose and red hair.

"I'm Mathias," Teivel says, "and you?"

"Suzan, Suzan Kemphill," the young woman, says.

"I'm not surprised," he tells her. "You have your mother's mouth and eyes. Your mother's name is Kate, correct?"

Her eyes fix him, the slightest tinge of curiosity lifting at the corners.

"Yeah," she says in a whisper. "But how did you know?"

Pleased with being not quite clairvoyant, he says "I'm supposed to know things like that. It's a long story."

"You've been following me."

"Not exactly, although now that you suggest it, why not?"

The girl smiles.

"But how did you know my name? Am I that easy to identify? Why?

"Ah. Now I know."

She hesitates.

"You know momma."

"That's right."

"When? I mean, recently? You're not one of her present entourage. Long ago? How many years?"

"Oh, maybe thirty years. At least thirty."

The girl is pleased, a first delight of the illicit in her eyes.

"That had to be before she was married?"

"Yes. I believe so."

"Was it nice? It must have been. You remembered."

"Yes. She disappeared."

"She left you. That sounds right. But she should have stayed with you," she says. "Tell me about it, I'm curious."

"Oh, it's not much. We were young and unsettled, not as willing to accommodate each other as we might have been. Finally, she wanted out."

"And you?"

"I didn't know what I wanted. I was awfully young."

"She was younger."

"Yeah, but females handle inexperience better than males. They're usually better prepared for whatever it is they're up against. I could have been in love with her and not even known it."

They sit in silence, sipping their drinks.

"I like that," she says. "It's nice to have memories."

"You could be my daughter."

"Oh god, wouldn't that be luscious. I meet my long lost father in a bar and immediately, because of our harmonious biology, fall madly in love with him. And only after a torrid affair that takes us from one end of the Continent to the other, to the Riviera, do I discover the truth."

"How do you find out?"

"His wife. She hires a detective. You have a wife, don't you?"

"Yes. I have a wife."

"And the detective, for the sake of a few bucks, produces a birth certificate. Of course, I'm broken hearted. My dream world is shattered. I contemplate suicide. Do you think I should?"

"That does seem extreme."

"I could cut out my eyes. A blind Electra, a female Oedipus."

An hour later they are outside the bar.

"Well," he says.

She takes his hand.

"C'mon. Let's go."

For the next two months, three, four times a week, on weekends, they lounge about her apartment, eat out, spend evenings in bed.

She works at the Stock Exchange, although he is never quite clear about what she does, or how she spends her time when he is not around.

He makes excuses, changes his work/play schedule, and finds himself adrift on a pleasant breeze, somewhere between failing resolve and the scent of female sensuousness. He, too, falls to the pleasing fantasy, entertains a half-thought-out wish to take her on an extended trip to . . . where?

Then one evening in the same bar in Queens, while she is in the john, a young man Mathias has not seen before slips into the seat next to him.

"What are you going to do with her?" he intones, as unobtrusively as if he were asking for the time of day.

"What?" Mathias whimpers.

"What are you going to do with her? You can't take her home with you."

"No," he says. "I don't think my wife would go for that. But, then, I'm not sure I need to do anything with her."

"Well," the boy says, "there's a reason for most things. You have plans?"

The Mathias catches himself about to say, "Who cares what you think?" but decides not to, and will forget the episode — if he can.

Two days later she doesn't answer the phone. Three days later the phone is disconnected. The following morning, he reads in *The Times* that she is dead. Found in the trunk of a car in Brooklyn.

He is shaken, wonders what she was into — thinks it was a mistake — goes to her apartment and finds it has been let to a couple in their mid-thirties who are having it painted.

"What happened to the girl who lived here?" he implores.

"I don't know," the woman says. "We rented it three days ago. I didn't know anyone lived here recently."

A mistake? Three months later, to the day, another young woman he has known intimately, though all too briefly, is discover in the trunk of a car of identical year and model as the first, on the same street in Brooklyn, hands bound, shot twice in the back of the head.

Someone is watching, he believes, must believe, as he replays their meeting, their endings. The girls were hired to track him, to seduce him, their killings served up as a warning — a man-made providence of sorts.

But who's watching, who's conducting the vendetta? And is it a vendetta? What is chance? Happenstance? A fluke? Are the details, like words, burned up by the sun?

The Mathias waxes
on the economics
of the Sam scam

As expected, Teivel carries on.

"I must admit, I've never seen a show come together as quickly as this one," he says. "If you never believed in the Graces guiding hand, you may soon. CBS has been contacted by a number of major sponsors. They're interested, and I mean *very interested.*"

"That's strange," Aigilas says. "Usually the agencies want to see the product and at least query their clients."

"Not this time. There has been significant demand for *Kojak* and inventory for the fall is moving. Ad-buyers suggest the network is finalizing details with sponsors who have multi-year deals, rather than selling to the less invested. We can only guess. It has something to do with . . .."

Lukema takes out a sack of potato chips, then closes his briefcase.

"It doesn't make a hell of a lot of sense," Aigilas says. "I realize these shows are profitable — but on a national scale, we're getting even bigger."

"That depends," Mathias says. "The economy is, as you know, definitely on a slide — which means business is now, or will soon be, taking a beating. This has to do with needing another war. That's Wall Street's line. One of the few markets that can be easily expanded, very nearly expanded indefinitely, is the military. When the military shuts down — and right now nobody wants to try to justify another war — at least not for another few years. So, where do you go? And how do you get it done? Well, why not funnel funds into building an army on this side of the pond? The police are military, and in cost alone, across the country, have a budget nearly as large as the Pentagon's.

"After Nam people fell asleep. Just like they did after Korea — lulled into a sense of safety. It isn't likely that the ghettos will go off by spontaneous combustion, so the country needs something to let the denizens know they are not safe, to convince them they need to spend greenbacks, many greenbacks. Something to scare the shit out of them. Someone to say 'This could happen to you if . . ..' That's where we come in. Here. This editorial in *The Wall Street Journal* covers it all pretty well. Why not spend it on police equipment? We're part of a larger project to get the country going again.

"Of course the project is a calculated risk. It is small scale compared to war — even a little war. But that's part of its attraction — a cheap way to get something done. And easily controllable. Hell, who knows, it might just work.

"Here."

He unfurls a large poster and tacks it to the office wall.

"This is from the Wells Agency."

"What is it?"

"An artist's conception of one of the themes they'd like to push in advertising the series. I love these things. Tells you a little bit about what people actually think about what you're doing."

"What is it?"

"Well, I'm not sure when or where they've set it. Maybe a foreign country, though? Maybe a little sci-fi. Some place off in the desert, A-rabs wrapped in sheets.

"But what they want to illustrate, the unspoken idea, is that sometimes sacrifice is necessary for the financial welfare of the country. I mean, how else is Wall Street gonna get its hands on government money, taxpayers' money?"

"What's the backstory?"

"I'm not sure. It's not important. The scene suggests more than it says. That's what's important. To touch the mercantile-social paranoid psychic of the viewer. I mean, it is clean. Only a little matte-red makeup on the guy's arms. A little more around his head. Just enough to be convincing."

He pauses, points to the bottom of the poster, to the figures kneeling, hunched over in the sand.

"This is genius. The subtle, cleverest part of the whole thing. The hucksters tossing bones for the dude's clothes, even before he's dead. It's a nice message."

"Who are they?"

"Hell, I don't know. Could be anyone. What's important is that they've seized the opportunity, got a grip on the future. With a little luck, the day will be ours."

Freeze frame.

That's the rap. The gnomes of The Universe in a daily tête-à-tête, the sound moving over the blurred faces. And in the haze of mass-com executive babble it is no longer possible to tell who is talking.

"It seems someone from the Justice is coming in to vet the operation."
A soft whistle cuts the air.

"And ABC thought they were pushing it with *Abortion Clinic.*"

"What's Justice got to do with it?"

"Just an assurance they won't get in our way, that they'll keep their bureaucratic noses out of it."

"Where is this coming from?"

"I'd say the bottom of the pile. Where everything comes from. The trash heap, the lowest denominator."

"The White House?"

"The White House? No luck. Jesus. No, the White House doesn't have anything to say about this. It's beyond that. Though Carter is fond of the rabble. What do you expect from a peanut farmer?

"Anyway, people are worried. Our boy's been on the loose for over a year now, doing his thing.

"They're worried that he might get picked up on a traffic violation or for vagrancy, loitering, hanging his dong out on a cold night — for something like that. What if the cops nail some hapless little prick and hang it on him? Then where are we? Remember Whitmore? It wouldn't be the end of the road, but it would complicate things.

"To keep him occupied until we get the series completed, we found a job for him at the GPO in the Bronx. The Postmaster says he can start sometime around the end of March."

"Don't you have to take a test? I mean for a job like that."

"It's all taken care of. They'll give him an eighty plus and five points for military service, which should be enough to get him in."

as in all things there is hostility
and hatefulness in Sam's benefaction

Indeed, in the second millennium of his reign Sam maintains a firm grip on the rudder. And while Hans-Peter in two weeks manages only a handful of fitful midnight sorties, Sam will not for long tolerate this whimsical meandering. His misshapen name, the authority of his presence demands more. He comes up out of his chair, prepares to spice the meat pie with a touch of thyme, garlic, and a Ghost pepper — 1,569,300 Scoville Heat Units.

Red-eyed and tired at 3:30 David calls off the hunt and stumbles into a diner in Queens for a hamburger and fries. Half an hour later he is on the street again, facing the cold, Sam waiting in a pack of wild curs circling a vacant lot across the street. They, too, are hunting, eyes fixed, noses on the scent, snarls laced with accusations.

They circle slowly onto the walk, baring their teeth, and David stands behind the Galaxie, his hands flat on the cold metal, then frozen, fixed, held by Sam's stare, Sam's smile twisted, demented, the sting of derision curling his lips. The dogs lower their heads and turn away, whimpering, tails curled between their legs.

"Tomorrow," Sam proffers prophetically, "tomorrow there will be others. Old women, children, infants, the newly born, ripped from the womb, eyes plucked out, brains dashed on the sidewalk."

Sam's chortle buffets the cold night.

David drives back to Yonkers, heart pounding, the words heavy on him, the threat hanging. The echo of laugher pulses on the new morning, a goat head, eyes blazing, shaded on the door.

He tries to sleep. Needs sleep. But the voices continue.

"Ungrateful."

A swarm of black flies.

"Failure, failure."

At 9:00 he gives up, goes to the kitchenette for a glass of milk and remembers the refrigerator is empty.

The flies swarm, insistent, unrelenting, pressing as he paces the apartment, circles from door to bed, watches Sam Carr's yard.

Sam waits at the edge of the room, eyes orange-white, the tip of a cigarette glowing brightly. His promises will be kept, his pledges honored.

"Yes they will," Sam says. "I can help you."

The flies collect on the open sores on his face.

Our Lady takes up the hunt
and
comforts the C of Ds

In a design inherited from Valentine's Day, as a matter of whim and personal preference, Our Lady of Pouting Pleasures, upgrading her part in the drama, returns to ply her ancient trade. She dreams complex, baroque sagas in high resolution upon which she will willingly elaborate, if asked.

Tonight, for her séance with the Captain, she wears a see-through peignoir tied snuggly at the waist and above and below the breasts. Her only concession to modesty is a Hanky Panky low-rise thong. She has a red rose in her hair.

"I'm communing with the real world," she tells Keener. "I'm intercepting his sphere, cracking the code. Why just yesterday I found myself in a park in The City, an enchanted, magic land of giant flowers with stems like trees and birds that talked — small, elfin creatures with huge heads. And a lot of snow. It was cold."

"But this is still winter," the Chief says.

"Oh, don't worry about that. The flowers were brilliant black, and the two suns that stood on either end of the park were great yellow eyes watching over the elves. And right in the middle of it all, I found him. At least I was sure he was nearby. I could hear a heavy buzzing as the elf-folk flew from flower to flower."

"You sure those weren't flies?"

At this point the lady appears (sounds) to be bonkers. Maybe she's advertising Keebler cookies. Is his name Ernie? Is he dressed in a green jacket, a white shirt with a yellow tie, a red vest, and floppy shoes? Have you visited The Hollow Tree Factory?

"Truly, a matter of discipline — mind over matter or maybe the impulse of matter over mind," Our Lady asserts.

"I have an exceptional body (the Chief agrees) and a superior mind (the Chief is skeptical). For years I've been trying to decide which is which and if one truly might be better than the other. But it is like comparing cathedrals and igloos — it comes down to your point of view — where you are standing on the sidewalk or on the ice flow, how hard the wind is blowing — and how good your eyes are.

"If the mind is matter, what's the matter? And how can it become mind? You know the final word isn't yet in. So we'll just have to live with it."

"I don't know. We're grabbing at straws," Keener says, "but does he . . . can you see where he lives, his face, the name of a street, numbers of any kind?"

"Well, yesterday, just after the snow, I picked up a debate about angels."

Anselm of Canterbury, Denis the pseudo-Areopagite, Alexander of Hales? It could have been Heloise and Abelard and the angel of love or the marriage prostitute.

"I saw several angels. And there will likely be more. But dreams don't always coalesce. Later I saw a rather beat up, shabby old turd. Maybe Apollyon. But I am definitely on his wave length. It's only a matter of time and mind."

"We don't have time. Right now, he's getting ready to kill again."

"Nothing I see indicates further carnage. And remember, ". . . men of action are active just because they are stupid and limited" (Dostoevsky), mistaking a secondary cause for a primary one."

She smiles.

"The regression of justification," she says. "Though I do love fools. What would a girl's life be without a fool or two? Know what I mean?"

"The present is enough," Keener reminds her.

"Yes," she says nostalgically. "Yes it is — for some."

Her response puzzles the Chief. What the hell does she mean?

"This thing is heating up," he says. "People are scared. And when they get scared, no telling what they'll do. They might even have a vote, a referendum, or something like that. Maybe a lynch mob. This goddam city's about to have a nervous breakdown. Anything is possible."

His eyes reflect the strain.

"We don't have a clue. Not even a footprint."

Our Lady's face lights up. Even with the Purple Satin Eye Mask she shows a beautiful smile, perfect teeth, wonderful skin and bone structure. And as most often when he visits her, with pulchritude in mind, even under duress the Chief has trouble minding business, although it is his own. His attention wanders over the tight stretch of her shear peignoir, the gentle fare of well-formed breasts, thin waist and svelte hips, the smooth expanse of an inner thigh leading heavenward.

Moreover, she's tuned in on several telephonic transmissions. A lengthy conversation concerning a merger, a business venture. Where? Possibly the lower East Side, the Fulton Street Fish Market. Another at PP One. The caller claims to have information on the shootings.

"I don't give a shit about random phone calls," Keener tells her. "Every nut in The City is calling with a personal fantasy about the gunman's identity."

At saner moments he suspects more. I mean, no one's this flakey.

"You know how much we're paying you for information leading to the arrest and conviction of this mad Monster of Mayhem?"

"Indeed I do," she says, purring seditiously. "But remember, no matter how frustrated you may be, I am your only hope. And once I apprehend the story's theme and plot, I'll have the temperament. I'll know how and where to find him."

Keener leans closer and stares at the angelic face, at the Purple Mask shielding her Hiddenite eyes.

"Do you know what happened to me last night? Do you?"

He pauses dramatically, then reconsiders.

"Of course, you don't. Then again, maybe you do. The goddam Fifth Division of the Second Auxiliary of the Women for the Return of Christ to this Continent in this Century came banging on my door waving a petition. You know what they did? Seven thousand signatures. I didn't know there were seven thousand pilgrims anywhere who would agree to something, much less sign for it. For Christ sake, only five thousand thirteen made it to the Sermon on the Mount.

"But even that wouldn't have been so bad, but those bleating Christian maniacs actually threatened my life. Me! The Chief of all the Detectives in The City — for Christ sake. Some things even a detective should not have to endure. I don't mind telling you, for the first time in my life, I'm scared. Oh, they never came out and said it, not in so many words, but their meaning was clear.

"They suggest that Son of Sam is a male establishment plot to intimidate the women's movement, and said further, that if I didn't find this woman-destroyer and bring it — Christ, him, her, it — they were outraged when I said we expected to have *him* — they started waving guns and knives and fists — butcher knives, large and very sharp butcher knives — and shouting 'What do you mean? Are you implying that a woman couldn't do what the Denizen of Darkness has done? That women are inferior?'

"'It,' I said, 'We expect to bring it in soon.' And they suggested that if we didn't, they intended to take out a contract on me. And not just a contract, but a castration contract. Lady, they are out to cut off my balls, to emasculate the police force. Next they'll want our night sticks and guns and expect us to go mano a mano with every nigger, queer and pimp in town."

"Oh, my," Our Lady of the O-cult tells him. "You make it sound so exciting. Did you poke them with your billy? Does it glow in the dark and have spurs on it?"

The Captain is skeptical. It is clear the woman has no intention of sharing her secrets, now or later. He suspects in the fluttering, flimsy, gauze wrappings of her seductive wiles she is determined to keep for herself whatever she has of advantage.

She avoids violence (unless it is unavoidable), but encouraged by Sam's successes, hopes to take her place at the corporate table. Just now she's toying with the possibilities. With posterity in mind, as well as for the hell of it, à la Hitchcock, she has already written herself into a number of prurient plots. In a few short weeks Hardon Inc stock, she prophesizes, will make a potent rise, shooting above less virulent competitors to a full .44 a share.

Just yesterday she rented space on East 54th Street, a front for new business — a variation on an ancient theme. By mid-morning the painters had the plate glass splashed with a red and passionate-purple foot-high, chilling but apropos symbol and appellation of Hardon Inc. She has gathered a stable of suitable (or unsuitable, as it may be) bikini beauties, models and iron-built muscle pumpers, and signed a lucrative contract with four city theatres for a series of first line, top drawer, "A" quality skin and splatter flicks.

She plans to incorporate Vibrant Veritas, a subsidiary of Hardon Inc, to develop and market a wide, long line of tawdry orgasmic accessories and lingerie for women who are willing, but do, too often, without. The VIP line will be merchandised in a pyramid scam her floating-visual research pre-dicts will infect The City like a virus.

A less than benign Morticia Addams, she convenes the Seismic O Sorority of BDSM cutters, slashers, and flayers, women for whom the mere sight of maimed or severed male appendages inspires an earth shaking Big-O.

She has contracted and refurbished an abandoned warehouse on the East River into three floors of advanced Pain Chambers outfitted with chains, whips and racks — Judas Cradles and Crocodile Tubes — and has cadged an ample supply of pliant, incoherent males purloined from the numb-dumb of The City's homeless.

She named the chambers in honor of historical celebrities: Barbie, Torquemada, de Rais, Vlad, etc. In a not-so-high-tech innovation, a chute and conveyor belt beneath the FDR Expressway will (for convenience) dispense severed appendages (fingers, hands, arms, toes, feet, legs, ears, noses, and genitalia), as well as the occasional stripped body, into the East

River for Gulf Stream marine life to feed on as the warming waters push beyond The City into the North Atlantic. She has already received three nominations for The Nature Conservatory's 1977 award honoring those who support endangered marine life. She is marketing organs acquired from the dispatched or depleted.

"Nothing," she has been heard to say, "will go to waste. The Wall Street wonders will not believe their eyes — or the bags of loot we haul off to the vault. Anyway, it's better than leaving the pieces lying around in an abandoned warehouse for the homeless to chew on.

"Not only will we rake in a ton of cash," she claims with a petulant, well-endowed Marilyn Monroe squeal, "but the novelty and timeliness of the artistic message will give the series a collectability. My name shall be Anais."

The Chief checks his Timex, taps the crystal.

"It's late," he says, certain the big hand has given up.

"I have to speak to the Policemen's Benevolent Association at 8:00. If anything comes up, anything at all, be sure to let me know."

"Yes I will," she purrs. "But, you know Captain, even when I have a lead, sometimes it slips away, and then I think maybe it's impossible to know anything at all. I mean, how do we know?"

snow angels

Child Peter is happiest playing with the neighborhood children (especially the girls) and numbers among them some odd friends and possible victims. Already several remember his name and at least one climbs to the seventh floor to knock at his door. Marie is nine. Joey, her brother, doesn't know his age. Together they vault down the stairs, clumping in large boots, bulky coats, and burst into the winter day, shouting, singing, leaping through the small drifts of a new seven-inch snow.

Today The City is quiet, peaceful and crisp beneath their thin voices.

"Can you make a snow angel?" Marie wants to know.

"I am a snow angel," Hans tells her.

"My mom says angels come from heaven," Joey insists.

"Not those kind," Marie tells him.

"What kind then?"

She hurls a white ball at a passing car, the projectile thumping the metal, punctuating the theological rift. Marie affects a Madonna pose, but no one is fooled.

Peter Lorre in his angel pose, lies, for a moment, motionless, on his back, watching the expanse of grey sky over the Hudson. White birds swoop low to the water, a 727 lifts into the thin clouds and drones away in the cold distance.

"Good morning, Angel," Joey shouts, waving to the plane.

Psyaint David

Can angels fly? Yes, they can. Angels generally appear as god's messengers to mankind. They are instruments by whom god communicates with man. They are depicted as ascending and descending the ladder from earth to heaven while god gazes upon the earth. God made guardian and warrior angels, angels to sing and avenging angels. And, of course, the demon angel of death.

> And David lifts up his eyes,
> and sees the angel of the lord
> hovering between the earth and the heaven,
> with a .44 in his hand. Bang! Bang!

Anselm's ontological
argument morphs
into a public stoning

The discourse dwindles, fades.

"A snowman," Hans-David says, "then a castle. This will be the kingdom of the Great Snow Troll."

He waves his hand over his head.

Angels aren't important. They rumble up the block to the playground, rolling large balls of snow into the walls of a miniature fortress. "Have you ever seen a snow troll?"

Joey hasn't. Marie is skeptical.

"I'll be the Lord, His Excellency and Highness of the Snow Trolls. This will be my castle."

"Will the Snow Troll have a carrot nose?" Joey asks.

"Trolls have two heads. One head sleeps while the other watches."

"We can use this for his heart," Marie says.

Moments later, a boy and girl who have been watching from a short distance, cross the street and join them. The boy is eight-year-old J. Edward Hooker, the girl his ten-year-old sister, Huberta. J. Edward bears a striking resemblance to an English pit bull and paws the ground (snow) while deep-throated guttural vibrations emanate from between his clenched teeth.

Huberta is the toughest kid on the block with a propensity for assault with intent (preferably against five-year-olds), bending back fingers, pinching and pulling hair. She spits like a truck driver and announces periodically, without prompting, that she mostly hates wops, spics, and kikes, and likes to bite niggers. She eyes Peter-David suspiciously, then wants to know about the snow castle.

"Who built that?"

"I did," Hans-David says.

"No you didn't. Not by yourself," Marie says.

Then silence and a clattering of cars in chains along the street.

"I'm King Hans-Peter-David of the snow trolls."

Huberta circles the castle, examines the rough walls.

"What's that?"

"A snow troll. It will have eyes and a mouth. It is the wisest of all trolls."

Huberta frowns.

"You're a nut."

"I'm a king."

"You're a flake," Huberta says.

J. Edward has dropped his pants and is urinating on the snow troll.

"Hey, you can't do that."

"Yes he can," Marie says. "It's a free country."

"But you don't understand about trolls."

"I don't care about trolls," Marie says, casting him off with a definitive wave of her fist. "Anyway, it's my turn to sit in the castle. I don't want to make angels anymore."

Joey shrugs his shoulders and turns away.

During the night he had an earache and wanted to stay indoors and play with his new Tinker Toy set. But his father chased him out of the apartment.

"You need the fresh air," the old man said.

Joey hadn't asked where he was supposed to find fresh air and thinks now that he would prefer making a Ferris wheel with wooden sticks, a lumber wheel.

"The angels we made yesterday are gone," Hans-Peter says. "We'll have to make more."

"They are trampled into the snow and pushed down through the ground," Marie says.

"No, they flew away," Hans-David yells. "They flew away. Up to the sky to troll heaven."

Joey makes a swooping motion with his hand.

"It's a 747. My dad says 747s are the fastest airplanes ever, ever, ever made."

"It was a troll-angel with wings and a red eye, and big teeth."

"You're a nut," Huberta says.

"Angels don't have teeth," Marie says. "And angels and trolls ain't real."

Tears fill David's eyes.

"They are real."

"And you're a fat-ass nut," Huberta says, kicking at the snowman. "What would a fat-ass Kike know about angels?"

"I'm not a Kike. I'm a Baptist. I believe in Christ."

"Well, he don't believe in you."

Huberta makes a snowball, spits on it several times and launches it stiff armed in David's direction. It shatters against his brown coat and they are chanting, "Nut. Nut. Nut."

A stoning at Mt. Olive, more snowballs, and Hans-David, shoulders hunched, turns away, slips and falls in retreat. The cries of their laugh sharpen as they advance. All four pursue him. The air is filled with missiles. One strikes his cheek, another his ear. Inside, again, safely behind his apartment door, red-faced, breathing heavily, he can hear their chants, "Nut. Nut. Nut."

On behalf of the fool, it seems Snow Angels and Trolls, but not killers, are merely defined into existence.

A profile on the wall, a face in the cold, a dim March dusk falls over the Hudson. David watches, puzzled by the events of the afternoon. He had not suspected they would hate him and cannot remember what he did to precipitate the attack — then he hears Sam's voice and Sam's laugh. Sam chanting.

> Lo! the book, exactly worded,
> wherein all hath been recorded:
> thence shall judgment be awarded.
>
> When the Judge his seat attaineth,
> and each hidden deed arraigneth,
> nothing unavenged remaineth.
>
> What shall I, frail man, be pleading?
> Who for me be interceding,
> when the just are mercy needing?
> (Thomas of Celano)

in the love affair of Big Apple
   crime and politics
   the commissioner
offers a public relation's pitch

The next afternoon, in a sparsely attended press conference, Borough President Percy E. Sutton of Manhattan declares his mayoral candidacy to "Help The City" off its knees. He admits, freely, however, that, "If [he] embodied all the attributes of Jesus Christ, Moses and Allah, [he] would still need three and a half billion dollars to accomplish that."

However, lacking the attributes of heroes, as well as ready money, Sutton does the next best thing and calls on local hero Rocco Barbella of Paul Newman's *Somebody Up There Likes Me* fame to help him "KO Crime."

Rebuffed by the media in his attempts to reach the public with a message from the Police Department, Garfield wonders, now, if Sutton plans to part the waters of the East River (the Hudson might be too difficult) or better yet, instead of wine at Canaan, suspend nature's laws altogether, along with other tedious and tiresome realities, and ride the subway across Brooklyn without getting mugged. Truly. The Broadway and 42nd Street Station gauntlet of rapists, muggers, and purse snatchers makes The Way of the Cross seem like a stroll on a sunny day.

The implications are clear.

Something must be done.

That same afternoon two skyscrapers in mid-Manhattan are bombed. Then subway passenger, sixty-two-year-old Catalina Salazar Maldonado of 125 E 113th Street in East Harlem (El Barrio) is beaten and stabbed by eight members of the Devil Rebels Gang. She is taken to the Mt. Sinai Hospital. Catalina is not available for comment, but requires seventy stiches to close her wounds that are not considered life-threatening.

To counteract further attacks, Metropolitan Transportation Authority Chief of Police, Sanford D. Carpclick, orders one hundred eight extra transit cops onto the trains.

Faced with the size and malignancy of the opposition, Garfield decides to follow Carpclick's example. Since the trouble the previous fall he has been accused of running a wimpy department. He considers he has, for too long, been a gentleman. What The City needs at the moment is aggressive, outspoken leadership, a tough, no nonsense S.O.B, someone to put the fear of god into the cops and crooks.

He flashes on himself as an SS officer, goose-stepping along in New Rochelle with General Jack Cosmos' boy, fatty Fritz Cowan. Poor, miserable Cowan. He should have been a cop. Garfield has always had a deep admiration for the Gestapo. Could never understand what all the fuss was. Just cops taking orders from superiors, what any soldier would do.

A little more nightstick justice, he thinks. Whip the perps into line — then use the media, with whatever yelp they will give, to applaud, encourage the image of a well-educated, -trained, enlightened, and humane department. And though it seems certain that as of January one of '78, Beame's light will be out, Garfield thinks with a little luck he may have time to make a respectable appearance.

"Okay, let's get on with it."

But where to begin?

"It's easy," the wise Commissioner says. "People still believe nice things about cops. When a man, any man, a dummy, a retard, a dement, puts on a uniform, straps on a pistol, and we hang a badge on his chest, he becomes a symbol of everything this country thinks is worthwhile but has never had the time to try. It's the moral-order-of-blue. Gives them hope, something to believe in.

"As part of our advanced PR campaign," he tells his executive assistant, "I'll need someone to stick a medal on."

Psyaint David

"Who?"

"Hell, I don't care. Give me a detective who has gone out of his way to empty an old lady's garbage, saved a drowning kid, I don't care. One who's rescued a cat from a tree."

"That's not going to be easy," they tell him.

For just a moment, the illusion wavers, belief falters. A round of nervous laughter circles the room.

"Commissioner, nobody's going to believe that. That kind of thing isn't done anymore. Not in The City. Not by cops. Not by doctors. Nobody will believe that.

"I've seen bodies in the streets, the injured, the diseased, maimed and dying, the deranged writhing in agony, and watched doctors, medical doctors, slip out of their Hippocratic Oath faster than a snake out of his skin. I've seen them step over or around bodies (alive and dead) simply because there wasn't a two-hundred-dollar check pinned to the vest. No one's going to believe a story about some cop spending his time and bucks to solve a case."

"Find me some forgotten, ignored schmuck," Garfield says, "some misfit who hasn't done anything for the last twenty years. It doesn't have to be that hotshot teevee super-cop crap. We'll make a case for him — and a ceremony. We can say he used his own money and time to investigate a case that no one wanted. Say he spent three months tracking down a young woman who most thought did not exist, to testify against a couple of thugs who had beaten her. My god. That'll make those vengeance seeking little hearts palpitate with ecstasy."

"Commissioner," Deputy Commissioner Barret J. Scourby says. "I didn't think much of this at first, but I might have what you want. The other day a file came across my desk. One of our detectives who was last seen years ago. I mean, nobody even knew the guy existed. He dropped out of sight when he realized that no matter what he did or didn't do, he got paid all the same. He's been gone so long that only two secretaries in the office even remember him — and one of them is damned near deaf and blind."

A roar of laughter. His assistants smirk, wipe their eyes.

"Jesus," one gasps, "that is priceless. You know, somewhere in The City there's more than one who has done that."

"We could use him as detective of the week," Scourby says. "Say he's been off on his own, doing his job. Like you say. He's done as much as anyone else around here."

Garfield agrees.

"That's what I'm talking about. We'll say he acted on his own, took what thin information was available and did that little bit extra — that little extra that didn't have to be done.

"That's the kind of thinking that keeps the department alive. We need people like that. A phantom detective, a bit out of focus, hanging out at the end of the street ready to help. I mean, he doesn't have to be a neighborhood protector or pulling kids out of the path of a speeding taxi."

He spins in his giant leather chair embossed with large gold letter PCMC, turns to survey the Manhattan skyline. Refracted through the thick gray air, the thermopane, the sunlight lays a dull glow on the day.

"Like I say," Garfield says confidently. "People will believe anything we tell them. We can sell this. If we do it right, they'll buy it."

"Or we could start with Walker?" Robert Bennet says, the PC's Executive Assistant in Charge of Lawsuits. "Killing is always better than pulling cats out of trees."

"Walker? Walker what? Who?" Garfield wants to know.

"William Walker, the cop who killed the nigger. Brabham. John Barbham. It's been in all the papers."

"So?"

"Well, the jury's probably gonna turn him loose."

Garfield nods.

"Wasting niggers never has been much of a crime. Spics, Wops either."

"Word has it Walker carried a toy gun. When he felt like wasting somebody, he'd toss the toy gun on the ground next to the deceased. He did it a number of times, but this is the first time anyone called attention to it."

"That's the idea. We'll investigate Walker. If we bust him after the trial, we can get some real press. If he walks, we kick him off the force. Hell, we'll be better than the jury."

"That's what I thought."

"By the way," Garfield says, "does anyone know if *Kojak* is on tonight?"

"I think he's on at 10:00, Channel 2."

"I'm out of town tonight," Scourby says. "Gonna watch *Police Story.*"

"Anything else?"

Garfield shimmers in an orange, luminescent glow. He's feeling good. It's the kind of thinking that makes Solicitors And Martial Intervention Enterprises successful.

"Yeah. And on your way out tell Maggie to make an appointment for me with Czarmine Galante — at his convenience."

Broadway Sam mingles
with the natives
and welcomes
old friends to the Big Apple

Sam's in a mood for something special. Vultures seldom have sense enough to choose attractive feathers — though Sam may be the exception. The Big Apple's a kinky kick-in-the-ass and he's decked out in the latest from Christian Dior: gray flannel pants, teamed with a matching battle jacket for sports, velvet or corduroy blazers for leisure and single-breasted jackets with matching vests for business. He's wrapped in pongee over shirts in blue, black and red, drawstring waistlines, casual layerings, reversible raincoats and bloused jackets.

Still, he's partial to the top of the line from Telly Apparel. Sam knows people like Telly because they know Telly likes people. Telly fashions for the man are real, because Telly wouldn't have it any other way. And although Telly's not a model or designer, customers are not models or designers either.

Today his teeth are capped and he's added an uptown strut to his walk, which is difficult with goat legs. He's making it to the best restaurants — fashionable dives. Tonight he's at "21", tomorrow the Broadhurst Theater with George C. Scott and Trish Van Devere in *Sly Fox*.

Then there's a whiff of sulfurs. The slightest scent of double-dealing attracts disciples, a coterie of the aberrant. Tonight the Cornet features a stock company directed by a middle-aged, finely tailored miscreant of medieval vintage, the sinister, sniveling Brother Blaxton.

The Brother has worked with Sam at other places, other times — the summer of 921 in Turkey, 1253 in England, and for three years from 1469 to 1472 in Damarionas on Naxos, Greece when he terrorized the village with an experimental program (designed with Sam's aid and approval) for collecting pre-pubescent male sex organs from living donors. His successes numbered in the twenties before the storm of outrage and superstition drove the town into a frenzied vendetta of murder and mayhem. The carnage in the village, the animosity and hatred, led to six decades of feuding that killed or ruined thousands.

Today, he works out of retirement, directing rapes, child molestations and beatings, sends woman screaming for revenge after their children. Word has it he is in town to help Czarmine Galante round up a troop of ten-year-olds to smuggle drugs into The City. He grins a lascivious welcome, squeezes Sam's hand.

"It's good to be back."

"Nice to have a specialist on the job," Sam says. "For the time being, we'll be working the Times Square area."

Hans-David is visited by the anima
of his trembling and fear
unto the passing of others

Firmly ensconced in his job at the GPO, Peter-David broods with mild complaints, the first stirring—the pigeons have his voice, the sun his breath.

"I can't breathe," he tells Sam.

It's no wonder. The Air Quality Index (The AQI provides information on pollutant concentrations for ground-level ozone, particulate matter, carbon monoxide, sulfur dioxide, and nitrogen dioxide) for The City has been in the 287-293 range for two weeks.

Sam listens.

Protégé David has been taken on as a Mail Processor, which requires 20/40 [Snellen] vision in one eye and the ability to read without strain, printed material and to distinguish basic colors and shades.

He's required to stand for prolonged periods of time loading and unloading mail from a variety of automated mail processing equipment.

"It's killing me," he complains.

Moreover, he's assigned irregular hours. This throws off his hunting schedule.

Sam's seen it before. When aerobic metabolism is slowed, visions fail. But the time is near. He snaps his fingers, lights the fire, encouraging the pot to boil.

A tapping at the door, light but insistent, brings David's head up from the teevee figure of Fatty Karl Lohmann shuffling along a Berlin street.

"Who is it?" he inquires, in a muffled voice, the answer distant and unintelligible.

"Who is it?"

He rises, slowly, hesitates, then trips the lock and pulls off the chain and is greeted by the bright hall light, brighter than he remembers, and a small girl, frail, scarlet lipstick and rouge, eyes blotched with blue-mascara bruises, standing with her coat open, her right arm akimbo.

David's face blanches, and Sam slips through the crack, into the wall.

"Well, you gonna invite me in?" the girl says. "I mean, this hall ain't exactly a private club."

"I . . . I can't," Peter says, his voice breaking, trailing off.

The girl stretches up on her toes to see into the room.

"What'd ya' mean, you can't."

"Who are you?"

"Who am I? The Virgin Mary. How's that sound? Now, do I come in or not?"

He backs away, one step, surprised by the demand, and she pushes into the room and circles the bed.

"Jesus," she says. "You live here? This is some dump. I mean do you live here? Who else lives here?""

"Who?" he says, his throat dry. "I live here — and sometimes . . . you know who lives here."

"Yeah I'm an ESP freak."

She considers the mistake, her eyes playful, mocking, and throws her coat on the bed.

"Well, one place is as good as another. You wouldn't have a coke, would you?"

"No," he says. "Who are you?"

"Man, you already asked that. I'm Carol. Now, how many Carols do you know?"

"People have two names, or more."

"Carol's enough," the girl says, cautiously. "If you're that curious, make it Carol Q. By the way, I ain't got all day. Now what kind of a party you want?"

"You're Donna," he says. "They didn't kill you."

"Who?"

She regards him, carefully.

"Man, you okay? I mean, you strung out? You call me — leave a message — send Carol over right away and I bust my toenails getting here and you go into this dumb act. I'm not — what's her name? Whatever it is. C'mon, John, what you take me for?"

She pauses at the window, traces a line through the grime on the glass with her finger.

"Oh, Christ. Jesus. I'm sorry."

She turns to face him. The camera dollies in for an over-the-shoulder of boy-wonder's face.

"Really stupid," she says softly. "Okay. I get the message. If that's what you want. That's what gets you off. It's just I ain't had nobody who wanted to play-pretend in a long time. Most johns I get, got their heads up their ass. They come over from Jersey. Don't want to get caught. A quickie in the back seat on their lunch hour. One john — one? Shit, a dozen a day. Always in such a goddam hurry. You don't know. Such a damned fool rush he didn't get it out of his pants. Messed himself something awful. Then started whimpering. 'How can I go back to the office like this? What will they say in the office?' It was a mess. I only charged him half, since I influenced it, and he was thankful for that."

"That scar on your forehead. You have a scar?"

"I got shot with Cupid's little arrow. What's this about?"

"I know a girl with a scar like that."

"So do a third of the people in the world."

"Here."

He sorts through a stack of newspapers piled on the floor near the door.

"Here's the story."

He hands her the paper and points to an article at the bottom of the page. The girl examines the paper.

"You think that was me. That I'm dead."

"Yes," he says. "And I didn't call you. People shouldn't use the phone for things like that."

"Look. Nothing personal. Okay? I don't care about your rap on the phone company. I got a call, says, '35 Pine' with apartment 7E on it. Says, this john called, wants Carol, and he wants her fast. Well, here I am, fast. Now you think I'm somebody else you know. You got it for some dead chick. Okay. So's okay. I'll play dead. But I gotta have the bread first. It's called overhead. Expenses."

"But that's not it."

"You mean, now that I'm here we might as well make a deal?"

She lays her hand on his chest.

"What'd you do to the phone company? What kind of a ball you want?"

His face is flushed.

"I didn't call you."

His stomach hurts.

"Sam," he says. "Sam."

The girl follows him into the kitchen.

"I seen some strange acts," she says, "but Sam ain't got nothing to do with this. It was Jeremy who gave me the message. Jeremy McCoy, and if he thinks you are mistaking him for Sam, he's gonna be pissed. You better say it right now. Say 'Jeremy McCoy ain't Sam.' That way both of us will be better off."

David turns away, abruptly, his hands above his head.

"I know who you are. You got out of the cemetery. You're not dead. I'll show you. Take off your pants. Let me see your legs."

"Honey, my legs ain't in my pants. That's not where I keep them. But thanks for asking, anyway. If that's the way you want to do it."

The softness fades from her face, and for a moment she's hoary, the intimation, shade of old woman beneath the smooth, pale skin.

"But you put up the cash before I do anything."

"Your legs are scarred. Like with scratches."

"Scratches?"

"On the inside of your thighs."

A small gurgle crawls from the girl's throat, then a soft whistle.

"Who you been talking to?"

She stares at him as if she should recognize his face.

"You're not a muff-diver, are you? I mean, we done business before?"

"Show me the scars."

"You can't know that. I mean, you can't even see them that much anymore. Since the doc patched me up."

She backs toward the door.

"That's enough. You called, I need bread. We can call it even. Jeremy is gonna be into what-for and if the bread ain't in my pocket I'm gonna get the snot slapped out of me. You get off calling girls to tell them they look like somebody you know who's dead, that's your shtick. But I need the dollars. I don't know nothing, except I need twenty-five for a house call. Cab fare, time lost getting back to the street. Twenty-five and I'll walk out of your life forever."

"Sam sent you."

The girl smiles, a reflection in the mirror, her frail features on a handbill, a poster, a picture in *The Times*, a name, the hollow sound of memory.

"Okay," she says. "So I remind you of some dead chick you want to ball. Maybe she reminds you of your mother. A sister. It happens all the time. Men want to screw their mothers and sisters. It makes the world go round."

Hans-Peter's eyes open — large blue orbs.

"I didn't call you."

"You're still gonna pay me. I'm not leaving without the cash. And if you call the cops — go on. Call the cops. I'll go out of here yelling and screaming and calling you every name under the sun. I'll tell them you iced that girl you were talking about. An hour later you'll be at the police station getting a nightstick shoved up your ass. And when they're done with you, I'll be back at work and you'll have a landlord in here telling you to find another hole in the wall. Believe me sweetie, it's easier to pay me — and if you want the action, you can have that too. I'm not such a bad deal."

She laughs, her voice playful again.

"Dead or alive. Hell, even dead I'd be the best you ever had."

"You don't know who I am?"

"I don't care who you are. That's not part of the deal. What am I supposed to do, investigate every john that wants business? I'd starve. 'Why honey, got a letter of recommendation?'"

Cybil Shepherd at the end of the diving board, Alice wraps her hands around the Wasp's stinger, tightly, taunting. His eyes are clouded, his voice shaking. He opens the drawer, his back to the girl, and pokes through the papers. He fingers the .44, lifts it, turns the cylinder, listens to the click, click, one second at a time. Five rounds, lipstick painted for a crimson kiss.

He hands her a twenty.

"That's all I have."

"This Jackson don't make it right. But since you lost your nerve, I'll let it go. Next time it'll be thirty-five."

She stops at the door and stares at him.

"Do I know you? I got this idea I should know you."

She pushes the twenty into her bra.

His eyes are moist.

"Jesus," she says, "don't cry. Hey, nothing personal. This is just business. I ain't meant to hurt your feelings."

She steps toward him and touches his cheek.

"I guess some people cry a lot. Life is like that. I mean, we'd have met someplace else this wouldn't have happened. Listen, you find yourself a nice girl. Don't go calling girls you don't know."

"Get out," he whines, in his best Peter Lorre whine. "Get out . . .."

"I'm going," she says. "It's been nice seeing you."

An astral light glows on the wall brightly, red, black, Sam's aura shrouding the girl, the child-woman, newly blossomed. No Cordelia, he's sure, in the honor of love for a sovereign father. No. No Cordelia, no Lady Macbeth courting disaster. But perhaps, yes, perhaps a budding Kate, to shout, to mock, even in a whisper, her words ringing in his ears, abbey bells announcing a spirit entirely possessed of itself. Yes, a plotting, scowling Kate, he thinks, with a heart bent upon setting a course freed from convention, from limiting opinions. An HPD-Kate, waffling — raging and buoyant, dagger raised.

"I'll call on her again," he says, "give her a hand whenever I can."

And Hans-David falls on the bed, eyes closed, the girl's face, her gestures, her walk, the seductive, insidious impertinence of the undeniable female figure — his spirit burned with her impression, the thought of . . ..

"He's ready," Sam says, "as ready as he'll ever be."

He snickers, wheezes.

"'The mind is its own place, and in itself can make a Heaven of Hell, a Hell of Heaven,' (Milton)."

Yes, all is well. Sam puffs up an Old Gold, shakes a ticket from his hat for *Network* and muses over what other invitations he might wrangle. This could be an interesting week. Yes, it could be.

Our Lady as prophet prophesizes

Garfield arrives at the office early, a copy of *The Times* under his arm. The 1976 The City Crime Index on page one reveals a 13.2 percent increase over 1975. On the Big Board Manslaughter and Murder are off 1.4, Rape down 12.1, Assaults off 1.2. In a record volume of trading Robbery makes a 3.6 gain, Burglary up 10.3, Larceny/Theft growing 22.9. Auto Theft races to a substantial, bullish 16.2.

When the press responds with "What the hell?" Garfield describes the increase as "minimal" and turns it over to Assistant Chief Henry R. Moore who states that the "relatively small rise in violent crime reflects the concentration of the police toward reducing robberies and assaults."

"Each time we have a downturn in the economy, we get an increase in property crimes," Deputy Chief Joseph C. Hoffman says.

Well, that's one way to explain it. Sam has others.

"By the multitude of their merchandise they have filled their midst with viciousness" (*Ezekiel* 28:16).

What did Hume say?

"This avidity alone, of acquiring goods and possessions for ourselves and our nearest friends, is insatiable, perpetual, universal, and directly destructive of society."

But the mild Captain still has needs and therefore . . ..

His sixth sense tells him the dreck is in the tube headed his way. Tonight he'd appreciate some motherly warmth, hopes to find a bit of solace in Ma Bell's illusory technology. He touch-tones Our Lady of Prodigious Pride, a new urge, an old surge tingling in his loins.

"I have a strong feeling we're onto something," he tells her.

"I have something for you," she purrs.

The Chief is not exactly thrilled. He resents having to depend on a retard, a cripple — remembers seeing Pete Gray, a one-armed outfielder for the St. Louis Browns in 1945 — a baseball oddity (except for the Browns) even during the war.

On a blistering afternoon in St. Louis, swinging the bat with one arm, Gray rifled a shot off the right field screen for a game winning double. That was during the war. A satisfactory excuse. The real ballplayers were in the military using their superior eyes and reflexes behind anti-aircraft guns. Well, some of them were.

What would Gray have done with Feller's fastball? He'd got the other arm sawed off. Of course, Bill Veeck and Eddie Gaedel were yet to come. But the good guys won the war. Pete Gray filled in where he could. Thank god for the circus and Pete Gray.

"Listen to this," she says. "In the glass-eye of your mind's ball imagine a snowman with an apple heart."

Here it comes. He wonders where the moon is. In the light of the full-moon. The pull of the tides. The lady's receptors are buzzing.

"A snowman in The City? What kind of an apple?"

"A Hanbury."

"What is that?"

"Medium-sized, roundish-conic with a thick, greenish-yellow skin covered almost entirely with a deep red blush, red stripes, and russet dots."

Well, almost. She was never good at descriptions. Try gold. Three?

"I see a woman," she says, "a girl, the Blessed Virgin — a small boy."

"With an Idared?"

"Is that an apple?"

"I think so."

"Yes. And when the weather breaks, the snow will melt," she tells Keener. "The apple rots. Down will come . . . then . . . and then . . . ."

It's Dorian Gray at the core. She's reclining on her red velvet couch nibbling a Malus domestica — Orange Pippin Cultivar ID: 1750 — UK National Fruit Collection accession number: 1971-015. She replaces the receiver and runs her full lips, her ample tongue over the slick, red skin, the juicy pulp.

donning a mythic guise
  Mayor Beame
becomes Don Quixote

During the evening, a week before the official opening of the Feast of Fools, mayoral candidates gather in the Harvard Club to recite the litany, their remedies for The City's ills. Barry Farber, a radio talk personality states that "We need Joan of Arc, a General Pershing, a Patton" — as if The

City was not already plagued with ample disorder and destruction — a mystic psychotic and a couple of homicidal megalomaniacs.

Of course, the honorable Mayor will not concede without a fight. He is out being personable, takes a cue from the PC's PR posturing. Hoping for a connection with The Little Flower, Beame calls down the spirit of LaGuardia, to bless him with a stellar reputation and good will.

The following day, in a display of strength, bluff, and bravado, shining with the light of the LaGuardian angel, the Mayor ambles into the Times Square, looking for a windmill. His small beam focuses on midtown porn establishments (a topless bar and a peep show parlor). He levels an assault on Show World.

Five performers are arrested and charged with performing live sex acts. Waving a copy of his newly developed Beamish Manifesto, in a latter day Martin Luther ruse, he tapes a "peremptory vacate order" to the front door of Jax 3-Ring Circus on 53rd Street east of Lexington Avenue, then reads to the crowd from the prologue of the Manifesto.

"Do unto others as they do unto you. Pleasure and pain are in the eyes of the beholder. Idols are not sacred. They are the work of human hands, and what man has made, man can destroy."

As might be anticipated, the demonstration of mayoral courage and fortitude draws critical fire. Adam Lamour, of the Adam and Eve act, who collects seven hundred dollars a week when booked into Show World for performing live (as opposed to?) and simulated sex acts, complains that, "The manager of this theatre doesn't want us to go all the way. Maybe he's afraid of getting busted. Ha — that's ironic. Who are we mugging? Who are we maiming? What's the crime? The joy of sex — that's what I say. The joy of sex. I want to work."

A few hours later, responding to Adam's complaint, a court vacates the vacate order and everyone goes back to work.

The same afternoon, in the Bronx, in a relentless pursuit of justice, fair play, and the seminal authority of the parental and elderly, a battalion of Gray Panthers is spontaneously outraged by a youth gang's multi-block offensive to eliminate another vestige of the evil of old age. The Panthers claim the gang has systematically stolen, purloined or otherwise removed 90 percent of the canes, 80 percent of the crutches and walkers (rolling and standard) from stores and private residences in Brooklyn — as well as two dozen Rolling Swivel Walkers with twin ten-shot .32 ACP semi-automatic pistols mounted in the frames.

The Panthers call in reinforcements, prepare for battle, and organize a "case watch" in Bronx court rooms.

"Once we get those snot-nosed little pricks inside, we've got 'em one up," a Panther spokesman says. "Just remember, there are a helluva lot more of us on the benches of this city than there are of them."

Still, it appears the odds favor youth. Bucking the first principle of natural law by which the young and healthy prey on the sick and infirm is not easy. No easy matter justifying excessive age, to attempt to hold off nature's decay or to excuse the foibles of withered dreams. The Panthers invoke old-age clichés, common place inanities, pleas for dignity, and respect. They claim their rights have been violated. By nature? Time?

When he hears of their plans, Carlos Nickonovich, leader of The Pyramid street gang faces off the Panthers.

"Let them foul smelling, broke-down-has-beens say what they want. We here now, and we gonna stay. They ain't had enough abortions to shrink our ranks. So now theys have to live with it. Them old peoples don't lock theyselves up all the time with them big padlocks on they doors jus cause of us. It's shame got 'em. Ah says they ways theys look and smells, shame ain near a nough. When theys was tough and gung we din go on no hunts lookin fer thems."

Nevertheless, the contest intensifies.

Panthers move about in platoons and/or larger units. They crowd court-rooms, crones and cronies, hovering ominously in blocks of seats, remin-iscent of a Sophoclean chorus, to monitor the proceedings, chanting, with a nod of the head (with many heads nodding) or a wag of the finger, the slow motion of eyes circling the defendant, providing prejudicial suggestions to the (wo)man on the bench.

the PC talks about the case

At One Police Plaza, Garfield calls a cocktail party conference for select voices of the press corps. He announces that a positive link now exists between the Lauria and Voskerichian murders.

"We have evidence that the same .44 Charter Arms revolver was used."

"Commissioner Garfield, how can you be so certain a single gun was used in all the attacks?"

"The Police Lab, our Ballistics Unit in particular, has positively linked the ballistics in the Lauria and Voskerichian cases to one another. Through an exhaustive process of weighing the fragments for comparison of the striations peculiar to the weapon used, a .44 Charter Bulldog, we have concluded that the same weapon was involved in both previously mentioned homicides. Armed with this conclusion, not shooting from the hip, we made comparisons and can say for certain the same .44 was used in other attacks."

"Commissioner, I believe everyone would like to know what the police are doing to catch the individual or individuals responsible for the attacks."

"Well, first," the esteemed Commissioner says, "we believe that the shootings have been the work of a single individual. Second, this morning a warrant was issued based upon the statements of available witnesses and surviving victims. It names a white male, twenty-five to thirty years, six feet tall, medium build, with black hair. We have increased our patrols in those areas we feel have been targeted and hope the public will cooperate in our unflagging, perennial efforts to apprehend the gunman."

A stir buzzes the room.

If the vision is more distinct, tell-tale features of hair, eyebrows, a chin sketched in, the Commissioner's doodle still lacks definition.

"Commissioner, isn't that profiling?"

"We'll have him within a week," Garfield says.

"Why wait a week?" they ask. "You already know who he is."

"We're close to an arrest," he tells them.

A roar goes up.

"In other words, this crazy could be anyone. A neighbor. A friend."

"No," Garfield says angrily. "We have evidence that the perp is male, between the ages of twenty-five and thirty, of medium height, has yellow hair, and can speak English. We have a sighting. A witness saw his face in a storefront glass, heard him say, 'Oh, Jesus!' We don't think it is a prayer."

"Then this is a real person."

"That is correct. At least for now we assume so. And, as I said, we think he uses a real gun with real ammunition."

"Commissioner, did you ever doubt that he was real? I mean, The City is full of phantoms — artifacts and pretense. This is the entertainment capital of the world. Isn't it unusual that something like this turns out to be real?"

The noble commissioner of all twenty-five thousand City cops seems not to be puzzled by the question. Indeed, he often deals with the ambiguity of facts, the smoke and haze of reason.

"Of course, art is always real."

"But what if this is not art? Not even art for art's sake?"

"We had a problem at first," Garfield admits. "A time when we weren't sure if this was just another extravaganza. We didn't want to move too quickly. That's how mistakes are made. We didn't want to arrest Othello. As you know, Lear has done some strange things. All the same, we were pretty sure it would turn out to be somebody. Forensic evidence tells us the perp is probably human — though some think otherwise."

"Commissioner, what is the color of the perp's hair?"

meanwhile the Loo
looks forward
to The Feast of Fools

So the police have their work cut out for them. And at the center of it all, the Lou, the phenom of forensic fastidiousness, goes tooling along knee deep in the sins and miseries of The City street scene. Tonight he is on Channel 30, 8:00, at The Excelsior pool hall with Captain Frank McNeil. They've run a couple games of Spots and Stripes, had a few drinks, passing time, bonding.

"This is going to be tough," he tells McNeil. "It has all the makings of a whodunit.

"So, what's the latest?"

"We're checking all the melting snowmen in The City. The place where snowmen might have been. If the heart of this case is in a vacant lot or on somebody's front lawn, we'll find it."

They've been at the bar for several hours. The Excelsior crowd is light tonight. Four players at two tables circle, scrutinizing the offerings, trying to line up the perfect shot, to make the most of a bad situation.

Tony "Flaco" Rodriguez is off in a corner in a workman's black baseball hat, blue work shirt and Levis. His partner hovers in a corner, waiting, sulking, his face hidden in a large brown hood.

The Excelsior dates back several years to the days following the trade off when McNeil's wife Lillian was kidnapped by drug dealers and Frank and the Lou engineered a sweet bit of sleuthing to get her back — unharmed. It was a touching story, with a shotgun blast administered by McNeil (after all it was his wife and he was in charge) as well as loving hugs and kisses at the end.

The problem was, McNeil wasn't sure he wanted her back. Weeks following the episode he developed the habit of trailing LoKo to The Excelsior after work to drink and complain about Lillian's penchant for weird adventures, hoping maybe one of them would lead to another kidnapping, this time without her leaving any clues about where to find her.

Tonight McNeil sips gin and tonic, the Lou works on Rob Roys with cheap scotch perfect.

"Did they get the in-house teevee fixed?" the Lou wants to know.

"Apparently it's okay. The PC had E.Erie™ check it, and he says that's just the way the damn thing works. Has a mind of its own. Picks up whatever happens to catch its attention or interest. Seems to be suffering from Hyperactive Electronic Attention Deficit Disorder."

"You don't say?"

"Yeah. An insatiable appetite for sex. Accomplished sex, that is. Sex without a moral, a theme. Know what I mean?"

"I still have a couple nice numbers, if you're interested," the Loo says.

The Captain grimaces.

"Damn. It's been a long dry spell."

"Marriage always is. Tell you what. I could make a phone call. It might wet your whistle to have somebody blow on it."

The Lou sips his Rob Roy. How many tonight? Who's counting? Why bother?

"Theo, I have a question for you."

"Have at it."

"You've been married. What? You have had two wives?"

"Three. But not at the same time."

"Three wives? Bad choices?"

"No, no. Good choices. I like bad women. It was all dysfunction and chaos — as if all three marriages were one. And I had one helluva time trying to discover who did it. Never did. There was more wild-eyed madness than a psyche ward during a full moon. Sometimes I was the patient, sometimes the victim.

"You gonna have another one?"

"Yeah, another one."

Kojak raises his hand.

"Charlie, two more.

"So what's the maverick tube into now?"

"Into? What?"

"Who?"

"Oh, it's monitoring some schmucks in Brooklyn. Something about the inability of a family of four to find love and happiness through incest and other taboo and prurient pursuits. Sort of a roving buzzard's eye searching for primal carnage and corporeal gratification."

Kojak eyes him suspiciously.

"Hmmmmmmmm."

The loyal Captain agrees.

"Yes," he says. "I sometimes follow my more poetic impulses."

The Chief shoves a folder into the Lou's hand.

"A new policy from The Commissioner's Office, for the manhunt."

Keener pages through the detective directive, a detailed outline for the cop on the street to follow. Under initial police action, point one boldly set out in black and white — Arrest the perpetrator(s) of the crime if possible.

The Captain knows the difficulties. Crime is often not what it appears to be. A couple months back one of his investigators responded to a burglar alarm at a liquor store just before dawn and shot a couple teenagers. He wasted one, wounded the other, then discovered that Sam had his finger on the alarm — ha, ha, a devilish malfunction — and the kids were on their way home from an early breakfast at a local diner.

"That'll give you something to think about," the Chief Inspector says.

Point Two — Secure the area, give first aid (only if required) question witnesses (at the scene) transmit alarm properly.

Point Three — Make a preliminary search for, recording and preserving of, and delivery of pertinent physical evidence to the laboratory.

"This was Our Lady's idea. She wants to tighten up the investigation. Cross all the "Is" and dot the "Ts."

The Lou's had a good bit to drink. Doesn't want to think. It was bound to come out. He doesn't like having a woman on The Job.

"I could have handled this case alone," he tells Frank. "Regardless of what I said before, I don't need a blind seeing eye dog. Or in this case a bitch that can't see."

"Well, we got her," McNeil says, "like it or not."

"You know how many cases I've solved, alone? At present, "The Marcus-Nelson Murders" pilot and ninety-five cases. I've been a cop for four years, four years and counting, and have not failed to solve even one case. And some of them required genius. A question of answers, Kojak's days, and the Chinatown murders took me two hours. The rest I got done in record time. A couple were real heart-thumpers. Gets you right here."

He thumps his chest with his fist.

"When I think about it, I have a hard time realizing how successful I've been. Can you name another cop with a record like mine? I'm the shamus."

"You may be the shamus, but she's the shaman," McNeil says.

He's about to recite the list, but thinks better of it. They order another.

"But I got another question. You're on the street a lot more than I am. You must meet all kinds of good-looking women. Did you ever give it up?"

"You don't expect me to answer that."

"From a cop's perspective you already have."

"Okay. Listen to this. There's a new pitch out by Joe Gores, an ex-private-eye and a Hammett aficionado. A case without a file. A lot of Sam Spade stuff from the *Maltese Falcon*. Will most likely run next season. But there's a female in it, Jocelyn Mayfair, Angel Tompkins, Jocelyn Brean — whatever you want to call her. A true blue-eyed vamp. Yeah, yeah. I walk away from it, from her. But just between you and me it was damned close. If Gores hadn't been loyal to Hammett and Spade handing in Brigid O'Shaughnessy, Mary Astor, Lucile Vasconcellos Langhanke, or if I had been writing the story, it would have ended different."

He laughs.

"A 'Here's the microfilm, the atomic plans, just open your purse, baby, they're all yours. Now where's the nearest hotel?'"

Fearless Fosdick lays his hand on McNeil's shoulder.

"Hey," he says, "let's forget about The Job. Tomorrow is Friday. You know what that means."

They are pensive. Indeed, the Captain does. The Feast of Fools, the annual celebration of contraries when the principles and rules of normalcy, the laws governing the cause and effect of reason and logic, dissolve — as if they haven't already. For a week, civilized conventions and behavior, law and order, are suspended. In keeping with the spirit of the aberration, it is a RDO for SAMIE, with only a perfunctory contingent on duty to man the precincts.

Frazer's appreciative. It comes at a perfect time, will give him a break from the routine of his unyielding, pertinacious pose, of staring down Our Lady of Serpentine Superbia, and oblivion. He's still trying to shake the slicing sensation of the Fifth Division of the SAWRCCC's butcher knife on his scrotum. It is time to forget SAMIE, to relax and enjoy the festivities. Well, forget if he can.

"Listen," the Loo says, "I got a couple tickets for The City Opera — a SAMIE perk. Why don't you take Lillian?"

"That's not much of an idea for a good time," Frazer says. "Why don't you take her? Take her off my back. It might do her some good.

"But then again, ya' know, it might be okay. I haven't seen a decent musical in a long time."

He smiles wearily, listens to the tidings of the times, "The Feast of Fools, Mephistopheles," whispered, whistling, wheezing beneath the door of the Excelsior. He wonders what Our Lady of Awesome Avaritia is doing tonight, what she has on her mind.

The Feast of Fools (a prologue)

By 8:00 an eager audience assembles at the Met for *Mefistofele,* the auspicious advent, prelude, foreshadowing of the high holy days. A magnificent prologue, a fanfare of trumpets lifts to the heavens, to the right, left and center, followed by a hymn like theme and an invisible chorus singing a paean to the lord of creation.

Called forth with a melodious mocking scherzo, enter Sam, (Lucifer, El Diablo, Duivel, Solfernus, etc. — played by Stig Järrel, Enrique Larratelli, Emil Van Horn, Ivan Rassimov, James Harris, etc.) elegant, arrogant and scornful, eyes febrile.

> Ave Signor.
> Perdona se il mio gergo
> Si lascia un po' da tergo
> Le supreme teodfe del paradiso;
> Perdona se il mio viso
> Non porta il raggio
> Che inghirlanda i crini
> Degli alti cherubini;
> Perdona se dicendo.
> (Arrigo Boito)

Posturing contemptuously, he continues.

"I haven't much to say today — only that man is a fool, if you wish, an ass, a creature for whom brutality serves as reason, animosity as virtue. An insect groveling in the mire while singing his own praises, he is hardly worth tempting. But then, what else is?

"I should have been content to stay in Hell these centuries and let the universe spin on into oblivion. And I would have, had the arrogance and foolhardiness not swung down from the trees, hand over hand.

So it's been for a long time. Sam's taunting presence, encouraging, offering clues to a larger scheme. Tonight an intimation of Faust's struggle, the impulse awakened, shaken free on All Fool's Eve.

Yes, better pay attention to Sam. Without him the story loses efficacy.

The Procession
of
Glorious Migration

In Central Park, just after midnight, by torchlight, Beame opens festivities, officially ushering in a week of celebration.

"Of all the festivals and feasts on The City's liturgical calendar, this one is closest to our hearts. The Feast of All Fool's Day belongs to The City."

To celebrate the festival countless of The City's low-life gather in the park to hear the Mayor. Fools from the five boroughs, in full costume and festival regalia come together for the wandering Procession of Glorious Migration.

Fools from every walk of life, spread across the spectrum of mental and physical and spiritual fault and failing — the lame and halt, retarded (to be later designated as mentally challenged), deformed and aged — fools of every ilk, shape, size, color, and sex mingle in the park. Many are refugees forced from mental hospitals and psych wards two years earlier by The City's fiscal failure. Others are on loan from City Hall and the Beame administration. Some, in keeping with the custom of contraries, celebrating the archaic, regressive nuances of human inclination, are dressed in ancient costumes. A few are draped with more contemporary styles, the latest ragged fashions feathering their twisted and bent frames. Some have no clothes at all.

"Many are called, few chosen, and the best shall enter last," Beame says.

The request has been

> Give me your tired, your poor,
> Your huddled masses yearning to breathe free,
> The wretched refuse of your teeming shore.
> Send these, the homeless, tempest-tossed, to me:
> (Emma Lazarus)

And the City has not been reluctant to accept them and to keep them that way. The streets leading to Central Park are a mass of humanity. *The Times* will estimate the crowd in tens of thousands — multitudes, throngs.

An occasional police car wheels in and out, lights flashing, commands barked over bullhorns, directing the fools to The Pond end of the park, were crowds of more fortunate quasi-fools gather beyond cordons of ropes and sandbags to watch the proceedings.

A blue and white radio-unit from SAMIE leads the procession. As part of Garfield's intensified PR campaign, forty-four officers (only forty-four?)

will join the parade, ambling and sauntering fatuously and fool-like shoulder to shoulder with the demented, the deranged, and diseased. First estimates suggest a need for a bit more, if anything, than five loaves and two fishes for this one.

By dawn the roiling throng, excited, hyped, made nervous in the turmoil, with anticipation of the gaiety to come, is all but unmanageable. Two withered, and what appear to be female, fools lock hooks over some imagined or pretended insult. In the torchlight of the hanging gloom, they go rolling in the dust and dog shit, screaming and clawing, tooth and nail.

The crowd cheers, bets are laid. When they separate, finally, breathless, exhausted, clothes torn, eyes flaming, one has lost an ear, the other a finger. Moments later another fool collapses with a seizure (grand mal?) and is kicked about the head into unconsciousness by four companions.

Fun for all.

In the early morning chill a near record crowd is on hand along the procession route. Stimulated by first light, madness mounted to a frenzied pitch, at 6:00, the slouching, bedraggled, bashing mass, moans forward drooling from the park into the streets. The crowd shouts scathing approval and hurls pieces of mud and rocks at the marchers who grimace, smile, and recoil, snarl and scowl, pleased with the cheers and accolades. Celebrity at its best. The sun only shines on a dog's ass once.

At 6:51 a batch of fools wanders onto Central Park South, W. 59th Street, and is scattered by a bus. The impact decapitates two. Several others lose arms and legs. All are left unattended, the dead and dying in the street.

Later in the morning, as an extra attraction, four skinny-dipping fools go off the Queensboro Bridge, arms and legs and dongs and boobs flying.

At Pulitzer Fountain, Grand Army Plaza (with a horde of rats watching) a squad of Gray Panther commandoes on a search and destroy, ambushes a troupe of skinheads.

Just people beating the hell out of other people.

But Harvey Leer is right. The skins are humiliated. The Panthers give a post skirmish body count of seven enemy-dead, sixteen severely wounded, ten disabled and ten routed or rerouted. The Panthers tally one injured and one missing (wandering in a parking lot trying to find his car).

"We accounted well for ourselves," Panther leaders say. "We will push forward with our campaign until The City is safe for the elderly to die. That, after all, is our mission. To provide our followers with a safe death."

By noon, beaten by the unyielding torture of banging into fireplugs and brick walls, the procession grinds down, nearly spent, a trail of bodies stretched through the streets.

As sanitation crews move to clean up the remains, Douglas Dogger of 768 5th Avenue, Edwardian Suite 21, a veteran observer of years of migrations notes that, "The Procession of Glorious Migration is a leading program in cleansing the TC welfare rolls. It is truly inspirational."

For the remainder of the day officials and imported dignitaries give speeches about Golden Apple psychology and philosophy.

Polly Holiday tells the crowd that, "It is only a short step from believing in what is not there to not believing what is there — and City dwellers have shown the world how to take the next step." She adds, "And if you don't like it, you can kiss my grits."

Travis Bickle reminds listeners that "City folk are fearless (which suggests that they do not understand the real world) and have demonstrated that the line between courage and stupidity does not exist."

In an hour long speech, Thomas Babington "Babe" Levy reiterates the obvious, that, "City denizens are reasonable people who have proven that reason is whatever you want it to be, whatever you can sell."

To highlight the celebration Mayor Beame issues a proclamation declaring April 1ˢᵗ as The City's birthday. It is still the Big Apple to the little man. He has grown up with The City, tells a record crowd at Gracie Mansion about his City youth. He's reminded of growing up on Stanton Street with his boyhood chum, Nervo. He is a man who recalls street fights with the nostalgic, moist-eyed sentimentality with which others recall a dead mother's kiss. He points to his head.

"Right here on my brow," Beame says.

"That's where she kissed you?"

"No. That's where I was hit with a brick. We used to have block fights. People back then thought that was the ultimate in street crime and disruption. We'd throw bottles and milk cans from the roofs. I got hit and knocked down and cut my head — here. I remember going to Kohler's drugstore and standing on a chair as the druggist sewed it up."

The City holds promise. That is the Mayor's message this festival day.

"We are promise," Beame says, "or why would the fools take to the streets? We open our arms to those who want to build a better life. We invite the world to The City."

The Tournament
of
Ethnic Dominance

To be sure, the world does watch and listen. Crowds pour into midtown, line the streets, spectators jostling for position and a better view of festival competition. The evening features The Tournament of Ethnic Dominance. This year the rules committee has expanded the games to include groups who, while not ethnically pure, are in their struggle for power and, thus, for wealth, making themselves heard. The struggle is no longer merely black and white and red and yellow and beige, but now a very green affair. Sex, age, and profession, along with a few of nature's more grotesque misadventures, are considered sufficient for qualification. But when all is said and done and then said, it is sex and dope, mostly, since pleasure spells dollars, and dollars is what The City of the Gods is all about.

The first contest pits 46th Street of Times Square neighborhood residents against a battalion of prostitutes and pimps who work the area. A company of riled residents in full battle gear, armed and prepared to do mortal combat, form along one side of the street. Signs are raised, banners and pennants waved to ward off evil spirits, to intimidate the sex peddlers.

I'M MAD, I'M SORE
DOESN'T ANYONE
CARE ANY MORE?

10,000 DECENT
PEOPLE LIVE HERE.
BUZZ OFF FILTH.

Hostilities erupt at 6:37 when Mrs. Paula VerLinda takes her Miniature Schnauzer for a walk on the wrong side of the street. A prostitute with blonde hair and an excess of mascara follows her home, into her apartment building. In a flash of righteous indignation, defense of property, territory, Paula turns on the harlot.

"You ain't coming in you pig."

It's not much of a contest. A second later Paula finds herself ass-down on the floor for a ten count, the first casualty of the games, and unable to come out of her apartment for two days.

Later she tells sports reporters, "She took me down on the floor so hard I saw stars. And you know, it wasn't even a woman," she adds, with disbelief. "It was a transvestite dressed like a woman. He had long blonde hair and breasts and everything."

Two blocks to the west on the left flank, Marcia Gonzales catches a prostitute defecating in the front hall of her building. Using her broom as a truncheon, she puts the strumpet to flight and scratches out a few points for righteousness.

An hour later the prostitute's pimp evens the score. He sidles up to Marcia and whispers in her ear, "Don't be surprised if you find your four-year-old daughter dead."

Quickly the decent folk, all ten thousand, regroup. Marcia begins carrying an unlicensed gun (even though she is not sure how to use it) and Carmin Ramirez drives a pleasure of pussy and pimps from the sidewalk in front of her building with a seasonally symbolic dropping of dyed red, raw eggs onto their heads from the window of her third floor apartment.

Since the Romans offered them to Ceres, eggs have provided a symbol for rebirth, fertility, and luck, a symbol of the silent universe exploding into activity and chaos. And the settling (splattering) of a couple raw, red agates, by a woman who believes the delectable spreading of legs (and eggs) is for breeding, and breeding alone, onto the crowns of 46th Street whores who collect indiscriminately and for cash the seeds of many men that not one shall fertilize their eggs, is enough to hump up the Richter scale a point or two.

At other venues, in a renaissance, a celebration, a revival of gaiety and joy, versions of Help This Fool Drool are played throughout The City.

> No sooner does St. All-Fool's main approach
> But wags, ere Phoebus mounts his gilded coach,
> In shoals assemble to employ their sense,
> In sending fools to get intelligence.
> And to reward them for their harmless toil,
> The cobler 'noints their limbs with stirrup oil.
> Thus by contriver's inadvertent jest,
> One fool exposed makes pastime for the rest.
> (Poor Robin's Almanac for 1738)

in a featured event
   Sam shakes out a deal
   with capo di tutti capi -
well, almost

The following afternoon, taking a break from Tournament activities, diva Maxine Jarret of 72-93 Lexington Avenue, Brooklyn, and recently of the MET, spends several hours in Maria Hernandez Park with her two-year-old Minnie, watching while the toddler empties the sandbox onto the sidewalk. To entertain herself Maxine exercises her lyric-soprano voice, lifting the careful notes of "Joyce the Librarian" and "The Diva's Lament," into the trees.

> I've been offstage for far too long
> It's ages since I had a song
> This is one unhappy Diva
> The producers have deceived her
> There is nothing I can sing from my heart
> Whatever happened to my part?
> (Monty Python)

A small crowd gathers for the performance.

Sam comes in the far end of the park to join the crowd, for a moment.

Having skipped a midtown fête, now biding his time, he's headed around the corner to a business lunch with Capo di Tutti Cape, Czarmine Galante. It's an afternoon follow-up. The old goat's interested in the Syndie's plan to find the killer — wants to see what they have, what they plan to do, what additional havoc he can promote.

He admires Maxine, the possibilities for her voice, what he might encourage.

Then he moves on, his cogitation shifted to Galante. Of course, Galante is special — a stone-killer, Sam's favorite type, encouraged by the confusion about who Galante might be or exactly what it is he does. The old boss has more names than the quasi-protagonist of this saga — a long list of aliases, over the years associated with a variety of businesses and activities.

By any account Czarmine is a gang of one. His known names (listed alphabetically) include: Carl Acquevella, Charles Bruno, Joe Dello, DCI #137561Y, Camille Galante, Carmine Galante, Carmone Galante, Carmine Galanti, Carmine Galanto, Carmine Galente, Carmine Galento, Carmine Galicino, Joe Gagalino, Joe Gagliano, Joe Galicino, Ch. Garrey, Joe Leio, Joe Lelo, Joe Lilo, Joe Nelo, Joseph Russel, Bruno Russo, Charles Russo, Joe Russo, The City PD #B66994, USFBI #1194-95, and Louis Volpe.

At one time or another he is named as a participant in: Rosina Costume Company, Abco Vending, Bonfire Restaurant (Montreal), Union Siciliano, American Gambling Syndicate (Canada).

Beyond name, profession, relationships, and those looking for them, humans generally have a difficult time identifying themselves. As means of identification, Czarmine's RAP Sheet lists: Assault, Assault second degree, Attempted robbery, Counterfeiting, Grand larceny, Homicide, Loan sharking, Making and selling illegal alcohol, Narcotics trafficking, Parole violation, Petit larceny, Violation of the internal revenue Code (in other words, anything that might make money).

Old stuff, for the most part, though Czarmine added a few distinguishing oddities to the mélange. Psychiatrists at Sing Sing list him as a neuropathic and psychopathic personality with the mental age of a fourteen-year-old and a 90 IQ, who is shy with strangers and has no knowledge of current events, routine holidays or other items of common knowledge. Appropriately, FBI reports to agents identify him with the following warning.

> *IN VIEW OF SUBJECT'S CRIMINAL RECORD, THAT HE CARRIES FIREARMS AND IS KNOWN TO HAVE SHOT A LAW ENFORCEMENT OFFICER, HE IS CONSIDERED ARMED AND EXTREMELY DANGEROUS.*

Of course, even within the billowing veil of Galante's ghosting practices, his record, and habits, he's not hard to find. His drug imports have flooded the streets with addicts, sellers — and cash — as well as small turf wars. Today heroin's the hit of choice, sustained by CG's latest innovation, the "nigger test," which he claims is a foolproof way to determine the purity of the heroin his confrères peddle.

The test involves shanghaiing an addict (actually, any homeless dude will do) and injecting him with a "double bag." If the specimen goes comatose and dies within a specific time the heroin is deduced to be of proper purity.

Sam loiters on the avenue, perusing the Bonanno family hangouts: Café Del Viale, Café Dello Sport, Café Bella Palermo — and finally to Joe and Mary's, a small two-room American Italian joint at 205 Knickerbocker operated by Galante's cousin — profitably fortified with hijacked meat.

This late noon he comes on in a gray suit, open shirt, a stylish paunch, baggy pants to cover his crooked goat legs, an El Presidente cigar casting a heavy cloud on a cloudy day. He drifts among the Hart Street and Knickerbocker Avenue granita peddlers pushing carts of shaved ice, old men playing bocce or sitting on cane chairs listening to radios and lifting bottles of beer in brown paper bags. In the last few years the neighborhood has gone to hell, a bit of a Sam urban fragmentation project — one of his favorites.

Outside Joe and Mary's he steps over a spent body, slides in among the fragrance of garlic, old yeast, and stale coffee. Yellow curtains cover the front glass — the walls decorated with Gold & Gold Matte velvet flocked paper, the tables draped in yellow oilcloth.

Sam permeates the air inside the small room, takes up time, peruses the art-hangings — a worn photo of Fernando Lamas (signed), a faded print of a soiled copy of Giampiertrino's copy of da Vinci's *The Last Supper*. Judas' hand, while not reaching for the proverbial bowl, does clutch a bag of silver. Pleased with the concept, the prospect of a Judas Goat, he waits — taps a nervous split hoof on the linoleum floor, leaves a sticky splotch on the flocked wall. He simpers and lurks, hovers at a small corner table — the acrid effluvium of a not-too-well-cooked contraband fallen and left (unswept) to rot — or maybe a drunk pissing his pants while slavering on his plate — flies welcome.

As usual Sam has art at heart — finds the Giampiertrino print pleasing — slides in behind a corner table and takes out a stack of twenties. He peels one off and holds it up to the light, now doubly pleased.

"Perfecto," he mumbles, or almost, anyway.

He checks the ink, the spacing, the clarity. Yes, this is art and first class art at that, a fresh run off the 2 color, 19 x 25.5" Heidelberg SORKZ he scammed from a dealer in Boston when the owner, Basilia Ariadna, got sent up for printing Franklins. Not that there was anything wrong with the prints — just too many of them floated too quickly.

But the machine is a beauty, with standard damping, 75 MM original imps, chrome cylinders, square buttons, dual re-circulators, an IR dryer, and sheet de-curlers.

Indeed, counterfeiting is close to the old devil's heart.

"Lisbon," he breaths — in a moment of silence reminiscing, Alves Reyes and Adolph Hennies — the good old days.

He's still musing when Galante comes in sandwiched between two Zips (fast talking Sicilians). Today he's a Curly Howard look-alike — short, heavy-set with a round head and a knit shirt that might be a sack stretched over a barrel of hijacked pork. The Zips are a recent innovation in protocol Galante, with Sam as consigliere, has implemented — imported from Sicily to set up The City drug network for Syndie business — and to provide muscle and authority in the intimidation and removal of opponents, be they men, women or children. As planned, the practice has been successful for Czarmine — but not without critics. The Zips foment mumbling on the street, and agita (a small rumble in the belly) among family bosses that will, eventually, as part of Sam's pleasantries and double-dealing, require a meeting in the spring of 1979 at Gerry Cantena's place in Boca Raton, Florida — to organize a piece of work or gata? And though whacking Lilo is a case of evil overcoming evil, on the order of two negatives making a positive, Sam knows better. He's doubling down, getting two birds (betrayal and murder) with one stone. Then, too, in an evil plus evil world, one evil plus one evil still equals two — as one whack requires another — the old making way for a newer edition. That's Sam's logic, the way Sam's world works.

So he's counting his fingers. He's into previews, a dress rehearsal. Two years down the road. July 1979? Yes, he will encourage the rumors, a last supper, or at least a last lunch.

Owner Giuseppe "Joe" Turano greets Czarmine and the goons as they walk to the courtyard at the back. Lilo sniffs about suspiciously, before taking a seat beneath a yellow and turquoise patio umbrella.

"These are friends," he says, "family," to no one in particular, talking to himself. "I'm come here all the time."

With nothing else to do the goons snoop about the small garden surrounding the patio, sniffing for headhunters and stooges, among the tomatoes, behind the potted plants. One lifts the lid off the garbage can. Peers in. Well, hell, why not? The search is fruitless, however, echoing Galante's own beliefs that, "Nobody's got the guts to oppose me."

Sam slips into the chair, amused with the padre's conceit. With a wave of a hand (always willing to serve a compatriot) he brings up a bottle of Marsala Superiore Riserva 1923 and two glasses.

Czarmine glares.

Sam chuckles.

Superiore Riserva (often simply "Riserva") by Florio Winery is a vintage wine aged in wood for four years, and sometimes as long as six. Unlike the mass-production companies, Florio relies on estate-grown grapes — high-quality grillo, aromatic inzolia, and catarratto, and keeps yields down in order to heighten fruit quality. The hot Mediterranean sun generates a high level of grape sugar, which ferments into alcohol, so the wines are powerful, ranging from 14 to 18 percent. Florio wines mature into gold and amber hues.

Furthermore, Florio has departed from standard practices in the complex method of making Marsala. Many of them are not vintage-dated, because they are made under the solera system (also the basis of making sherry in Spain), in which fractions of barrel-aged young and old wines are blended to preserve consistency of style and quality. These wines are dry, with a lot of wood and the taste of the sun of Sicily in them.

Sam's seen it before.

"Joey, won't like you bring your own stuff."

"From his cellar," Sam tells him. "A respectable Sicilian wine. He got it off that truck in Hoboken in '69. Twenty-three cases. Your dago old man would have appreciated that."

Lilo chews on his cigar.

"What do you know? You a wise guy?"

"Yeah," Sam says. "An original. With your family in Sicily."

Sam places his cigar in the ashtray, the gray smoke rising in a thin column forming the stem of a single, pink rose with two green leaves. Galante watches the flower for a moment, teeth clenched, turns to Sam, then to the flower again. He removes the cigar and lifts his half-filled glass to drink before he realizes no one has poured the wine.

"What you?" he says, staring at the glass. "Un illusionista? Un mago? Who sent you? Funzi Tiere send you?"

Sam opens his cloak a little wider, filters the scene into soft focus.

"Business," he confides, "I raise the dead. Good business for the family business."

Czarmine motions to his bodyguards stationed at the bar. They haven't seen anything.

"Un demenza," he says.

"Quite the contrary," Sam assures him, lifts his glass. "Realisimo. Salute!"

"Un mago," Lilo whispers. "Un mago amichevole?"

"A family friend. Your grandfather and I worked together. In Castell-ammarese. Un servo fedele."

"Essere completamente independente."

"Independente. Essere alla testa di."

"You want business."

Lilo turns his cigar over in his fingers as if he suspects it might explode. He regards Sam, peering intently into the small fires of Sam's eyes.

"Cumpà," Sam says, "Last century. A bad storm. He lost most of his nets. The small ones he saves were torn and unusable. I helped him — where — how — to arrange replacements. Arranged a . . . business."

Sam places an amulet on the table — a small gold goat's horn.

"Regalo," Sam says.

Lilo examines the figure, his face contorted, an involuntary gurgle in his throat. "Malocchio," he mutters and pushes the table away, spills the wine and stands quickly, faces Sam.

"Bugiardo. Di mentire per la gola."

Sam gestures for him to be seated.

"Glad you still have a sense of honor. That's mostly missing now."

"Compare. He is a great man. Noble man," Lilo says, recalling his lineage, his birth (initiation May 24, 1940) in the Tenebrosi Sodalizi, blood dripped onto a Holy Card of Our Lady, Help of Christians, the print crumpled and burned, the Virgin's ashes scattered. Then the oath.

"This blood and fire symbolize my entry into the new world. Death to those who defy the family. Long live the family."

"Amico," Sam says. "Never go beyond the ring of the village bell, except to sea. The sea is your mother and mother will feed you. A man of steel — of principle — to the end — he respected his wife and honored his country."

"Men like him make Rome great," Lilo says, and sets the charm on the table between them. "The world is a bad place. Mal. We protect our family. Guardia. Communista, they kill my grandfather. Communists from Balestrate. They take his nets and boat."

Castellammarese del Golfo

Sam's agreeable. Revels in the story. It was an impressive vendetta, carefully planned, arranged, executed.

The grandfather, Don Gennero Galante, named for the patron Saint Januarius of Naples, is already an old man, grizzled and skin-burned from years at sea. He is retired, made wealthy by the tribute he extorted from other fishermen for violating his fishing waters or for selling to his customers.

He is old and has not worked for many years, which coupled with excessive eating and drinking has weakened him and diminished his powers. What is not diminished, however, is the rancor engendered by his years of intimidation, extortion, and drinking at the taverna at the expense of others.

One hot afternoon he is drinking and playing Passatella with the town's mayor, two fishermen, Sam, and a young man, Vito Indelicato from Guarrato, whose father not long before lost his boat to Don Gennero, and his health to ill-fortune.

Sam narrates.

"In those days Passatella is a favorite taverna recreation. In it players find ways of assigning winners and losers — a card game or a roll of the dice. The winner is in charge of liquor, drinks for free, appoints a sub-boss, and chooses an idiot. The idiot must place his hands on the table (to show he is without a weapon) and is subject to the law of the others. The law consists of "the telling of truths" to one's face and those at the table ask questions to humiliate the idiot. So, if you're the idiot of the drinking game, why submit to the rules? Well, play enough and you will become the boss.

Then it is your turn to belittle the others.

"That night Indelicato wins at cards, and is made King of the Passatella with control over the wine and who will drink. He fills the glasses of others at the table, but ignores Don Gennero. This is proper and within the rules, but no one before has ever confronted the Don this way.

"Educated by the communists in Rome, Indelicato won contests for public speaking, showed great promise in politics, but left the Party and returned home to care for his ailing parents.

"When he makes answer to why he does not fill Don Gennero's glass, which the rules require him to do, he speaks elegantly, drawing out his answers with irony and humorous metaphors and fables, stories of a feeble old man (who everyone knows is Don Gennero) trying to prove he's still a man by taking a young girl to bed and failing with great effort to satisfy her burning passion. In the end, like Don Juan in Hell, the old man grows donkey ears, and whenever he speaks, he brays.

"The Don listens for a time, amused by the wit of the young man's affront, and, at last, when the attack persists, becomes annoyed and then enraged at the length and viciousness of the oratory. Maddened in the heat, by the stories and the Indelicato's refusal, even at cards in a game, to pay him homage, Gennero slams his fist on the table, this, too, symbolizing what is left of him as a man, shattering his empty wine glass, and hurls vile insults at the youth. The King of the Passatella answers the challenge, and in a moment they are on the floor, locked in combat."

Sam chortles.

"One thing to be said for inviting trouble. As a rule, it generally accepts the invitation.

"Gennero is no match for the younger man and is soon beaten, and breathing heavily, face flushed with the strain of the fight and his humiliation.

"He falls to the tavern floor, head down, crazed to rage at having been shamed by the youth standing over him.

"No one wants to stop the fight. The players take bets, not on who wins, but how long it is until Indelicato kills Don Gennero. This is the best part.

"Gennero takes a knife from his boot (what else could a friend do?) — it was the only thing to do — he needs assistance — and with a weak, awkward sweeping motion strikes out, slashing Indelicato's leg, leaving a large gash across the thigh above the left knee. Indelicato responds with the swiftness of a leopard, draws a knife from his waist band, and plunges it into Don Gennero's heart.

"The village is shocked, but gloats over the circumstances of the Don's demise and the mayor, who the dead man often paid for favors, announces that after the funeral which will last three days, Indelicato will be tried for murder.

"The night following the burial fishermen carrying torches gather at the mayor's house and demand he drop charges and set the young man free."

Sam pauses pensively.

"I didn't get that one right. A little bile on either side, a bit more plotting to the tale and the mayor could shoot a couple of the fishermen before they burn his house.

"The mayor does not come out to meet the fishermen, but they see him at the parlor window, the strained, worried, the pale face of his wife hanging behind him like a tortured, waning moon. A frail woman whose father was mayor before this one, she has been ill for years, and to save her further hardship, the mayor consents to the fishermen's demands.

"Justice has a sweet ring," Sam says, his eyes damp and smoking.

"'Justice for our troubles,' the crowd shouts. 'Regardless who pays.'

"The following day your father, Vincenzo, kills Indelicato. Now a marked man, he goes to another village. Unable to find a boat to work on, a year later he comes to America.

"It is a matter of the heart. Truth comes from the heart," Lilo says.

"As Indelicato avenges the village, your father avenges his father, then comes to The City."

"Loyalty," Lilo says, a glare in his eyes. "It is faith that we know. We have faith to kill. He was communistia sent to kill my grandfather. Everywhere. Communista. Carlo Tresca? He ruins the world. All that is honorable. Tresca and Carlo Gambino. Slime. That's what I say. Filth. What is one Carlo Gambino compared Richard Nixon and Gerald Ford. La Duce. He is a great man. He is a friend for Joe Bannano, saved Italy from the communists. Kept Stalin out of Sicily."

"Amittere, quibus natura corporis salva et incolumi habetur, quam illa committere," Sam says.

Lilo lifts his glass.

"Seguire i vostri desideri e interessi. Dio è ciò che si crede in."

"Another matter," Sam tells him, the bottle again filled, the tablecloth crisp and clean except for a few stains. The Shroud of Turin — maybe, maybe not. Maybe Mary hasn't heard of the salt or ammonia method.

"The Stoic phantasiae," Sam says. "Impressions on the mind can create fear."

"Ah," Lilo says. "The brave become cowards. Fear is easy to make. Stupidity, fear, greed.

"Is great way to make bucks." Lilo leans back without a smile. "You want business?"

Well, why not. The statute of limitations has run on The French Connection. Vincent Papa is in the pen in Atlanta. Who knows what happened to Louis Cirillo? Yeah. Who knows? Nasty Louie. During a fight he once bit out a man's Adam's apple. With Louis' attitude and gifts, it's anybody's guess. The rap was that "when Louis does a number on some-body, even the hitmen and sadists left the room."

Where is he now? He's probably still chewing on the Adam's apple.

But Sam's pleased. The air carries a pleasant fragrance — the company's convivial, the conversation upbeat.

He tilts his glass.

"What have we — a little porn, baccarat, pump-and-dump, hijacking, gambling, prostitution, loan-sharking, extortion, assassinations, drug traffic?" He pauses, offers a flash or two of subliminal ads.

"Did I miss anything?"

He hands Czarmine a roll of twenties. Cackles. Hisses. Rasps.

"How do you know a good man?" Carmine says.

He grunts.

"He is the one with all the money."

Sam knows the story, knows his man.

Having evolved semiconsciously, afloat in the ensuing conditions of vicious fantasy and demented illusion, Czarmine set out to flay life, The City, for profit. He blinks, squirms, his itch for deceit and mayhem tickled.

Sam chortles, and with a Lucigraph (camera obscura?) or maybe a hologram, configures a day several years down the road, Czarmine fixed as he is at the moment, after a fish sandwich and salad, finishing a carafe of red wine, a Cuban Presidente clamped between his teeth. Classic Syndieoso.

The Zip, Baldo Amato, is seated to his left. Baldo's cousin Cesare Bonventre (who in the gauze-like haze of a second mirage a decade later will end up in pieces in three barrels of glue in a deserted warehouse) sits at the right hand of god the goodfather.

Joe Turano, sweating, strips down to his undershirt, and takes a seat facing Galante. Nardo Coppola lazes across from Bonventre in a corner between a wire fence that borders the cramped courtyard and a row of potted plants against the restaurant's outer wall.

This is a sit-down to discuss Turano's complaint that Coppola has been messing with Turano's wife Mary. Lilo is the moderator.

However, before the discussion heats up, a tall, thin man trots into the restaurant, then on to the dining patio. He's wearing dark clothes, an olive-gray ski mask, and carrying a pump-action shotgun. He is followed by another man with a double-barreled shotgun — he, too, wears a ski mask. A third masked man carries a pistol.

Turano turns to face the gunmen, then screams, "What are you doing?"

The first man blasts Galante.

Again Turano screams, "What are you doing?"

The second gunman unloads one barrel on Galante.

The first racks another shell, pokes Turano in the chest with the shotgun, and pulls the trigger.

As the do up proceeds, Coppola attempts to stand and is shot twice in the face, then five times in the chest by Baldo.

Sam smirks.

Obviously Czarmine does not anticipate death in the afternoon, of his consciousness vaporizing, the universe going blank. Within the deception of failing vision, staring into a black hole, Czarmine becomes oblivion, along with Turano and Coppola, while the Zips, for the moment, avoid the void. That day they walk away dry to collect their reward — though it appears in the smoke of burnt gunpowder and the scatter of blood, bone, and brains across the patio, that Bonventre has pissed his pants.

"Here's to a formidable and alarming external cause," Sam says. "Fantasy does the rest."

He tips his glass, taps the table top with a cracked, festered fingernail (Onychoschizia?).

"The dark of night shades fear, every sound an unknown footfall," he says to the vanishing man.

"What you propose?" Lilo wants to know.

"A new twist," Sam explains. "Bigger and better. More territory. Better organization. Bigger projects. No police. No prosecutors."

The vista spreads, a mirage in the smoke from Sam's eyes, a city in the noble seizure of terminal discomfort. Sam lays his hand on Czarmine's arm, pats him on the back.

"Generalissimo, this will be The City of Sam."

"Dio non interferisce con quello che faccio, così egli deve accettare."

So it is, deals are made, another contract, Sam marking up a little grief, the Syndie taking another step into the gratuities of its nightmare.

"They need help managing the Son of Sam icon," Sam says. "Promoting and selling the design. They'll want a deal."

"Who is this?"

"City Hall. They want to expand the agreement you have with them, add a few paragraphs to the contract. They know you have the expertise to give the symbol substance.

"The only way to do that is to get your men inside, as close to the top as possible."

"They are inside," Lilo says. "We have men at the Puzzle Palace to talk with."

"Ahh, but remember," Sam says, "Son of Sam is a phantom, a fantasy of fear, and what the police don't know, can be used to improve the image. Dio aiuta chi si aiuta."

Czarmine assents.

"Gli esseri umani sono corrotti."

He knows the need for phantoms. Especially serial killers. He, himself, may be the most productive serial killer in City history. He reminisces. How many? Sixty, seventy? Well, some estimate over eighty. Maybe as many as eighty-five. He's lost count — doesn't have a very good memory about these things. Ah, may their souls rest in peace.

But so it is. Son of Sam as Divine Providence, a cog in god's wheel of fortune, lifting and pulling the chains of destiny."
"We do not kill young women."
"Is that so?" Sam says, drains his glass.
"How about Carensi's daughter?"
"Angelo Carensi. He deserve to have his family killed."
"I know," Sam says. "So he does, so he did."
Sam smirks, lifts his nose, savoring the putrescence.

the spreading of palms
heralds the election
of Festum Papa Fatuorum

From 11:18 until 12:06 the night features a partial eclipse of the moon, but remains rather typical otherwise, with packs of feral canines roaming Brooklyn, Manhattan, whining in the disquiet of lost light.

The morning dawns gloriously, however, Palm Sunday, Passover, the Stuyvesant Oval on Wall Street with small boys in white robes and false beards astride donkeys. An ecumenical procession.

Twelve-year-old Warren Valensky rides in from Marine Midland Bank's plaza, 140 Broadway, among many of the district's major financial institutions, to Our Lady of Victory Roman Catholic Church at 60 William Street.

While a chorus sings "Hosanna! Blessed is the one who comes in the name of the lord! Hosanna," the donkey approaches on a carpet of palm fronds, climbs the church steps (attollite portas principes vestras: et elevamini) and proceeds down the center aisle to the altar for a special blessing.

Moments later, its serape-draped handler leads the balking, braying beast away. The congregation breaks into song.

> Orientis partibus
> Adventavit Asinus
> Pulcher et fortissimus
> Sarcinis aptissimus.
> Hez, Sire Asnes, car chantez,
> Belle bouche rechignez,
> Vous aurez du foin assez
> Et de l'avoine a plantez
> (Anonymous)

Completing the Mass, the priest turns to the parishioners, brays three times, "Hinham, Hinham, Hinham," twitching and flipping his rag tail and large plastic donkey ears to keep the flies at bay.

As a ceremonial of the Festum Asinorum a Papa Fatuorum is to be chosen. Terrance Cardinal Cooke steps forward to moderate the selection of a candidate from among the several dozen priests the Archdiocese keeps in an East Side cloister, the shells of men whose minds have run amuck in pursuit of their vows, the self-mutilation of flagellation and fasting.

It is a noisy, babbling throng, excited by the announcement that this year CBS and The Universe Studios has offered a contract to the winner for the lead in a new series, *The Finest Fool*, and that the Church has recently created the Order of Only Fools, over which the Papa Fatuorum will reign in perpetuity.

On the third ballot, amid a spat of spitting and breast beating, a champion, The Right Reverend Raymondo Siginatori, emerges to wear the miter and carry the crosier of fooldom. Reverend Siginatori is renown throughout The City as a pederast and co-founder of the Order of Flagellants General, an organization dedicated to the proposition that "corporeal punishment is god's caress," for "by the pains of contusions shall you know him or her."

"Only when you have parted or bruised flesh, can you hear god breathing," Father Siginatori says. "It is like looking over god's shoulder at creation."

This is the same Pater Siginatori who, on two occasions, to repent his errant and sinful ways, chained himself to a pillar at Our Lady of Vacuous Victory church and with a stack of Easyburn self-igniting faggots at his feet attempted to fry himself for Christ. Another time, packaged in a large black garbage bag, he set himself on the curb in front of the rectory, hoping to be committed to the refuse of The City dump.

"It is where I belong as a sinner," he reported to astonished workers at a Brooklyn waste incinerator when they discovered him seconds before he was consumed by the not-quite fires of hell.

Today he comes contrite and blind, accepting the chasuble of office, wearing spectacles of orange peels, his clothes turned inside out. The clamoring army of god's soldiers shouts approval and bursts into song.

> Oh, if a virgin is such a great lay,
> So what was Joseph doing in the hay?
> Yes, what did Joseph use for luck,
> If he went a lifetime without a fuck?
> Oh, flagellation has its ups and downs,
> As Joseph found beating his gown.

In the first official act of his new office, Father Siginatori, as Precentor Stultorum sings, "Deposuit Potentes de sede" and proceeds to the altar to celebrate the Massa Dementia. Those who have been passed over, but nonetheless elevated to the Profane College of Disorder, assist at the mass, some dressed as women, masked in paint and powder, some with no clothing at all, dancing and singing in true apostolic fashion, while feasting on bits of raw meat and sour wine or playing at dice on the altar.

The celebration closes with the Benedicto Calceamentis, a burning of leather in the censer and the Exit Aeterni Ignomania, out the back door of the church where Papa Siginatori mounts a Muck Master dung wagon and is drawn off up William Street to the cheers of fools and festival spectators.

However, quite unexpectedly the noon bear-baiting is canceled. On second thought, organizers did not think it appropriate to draw people away from their Sunday religious services with a pagan ritual.

Still, the afternoon offers a round-robin of rat and cock fights. Rumor claims, and Mayor Beame reiterates that The City has something like four million rats, including one of the two largest varieties extant — animals that respond viciously to captivity, are large enough to knock the balls off a nice-sized pit bull, and can, with some small effort, be trained to do it on cue.

To supplement the illusion, an early afternoon cock fight breaks out in the El Santuci Social Club, 785 Webster Avenue, Bronx, and breaks up when a street gang dressed and masquerading as police sets three hundred patrons and twenty-five birds to flight through the rear wall of the building. Five men and two birds (one dead) are arrested and cockfighting paraphernalia, drugs, and weapons confiscated.

The imitation cops repair the rear wall of the building, the cock-ring, and with a somewhat reduced cartel, set to betting on the next fight. Odds on champion "Little Red," a Red Quill, are set at seven-to-one.

The drugs and weapons seized have a street value of forty thousand dollars, which divvies out to around three thousand per invader.

Child-David
in
the Garden

Temperatures creep into the upper 60s, with wind out of the northwest at 12 mph. A balmy day, indeed, much like that of our misty-eyed somewhat mythic subject's seventh birthday when his father took him to the Festival of Fools. In an event singularly etched in his memory, they walk along 5ᵗʰ Avenue to Central Park North to a gathering at The Pond to watch the Procession of Glorious Migration. He does not know what to expect and asks repeatedly why they are there.

"A circus," Nathan says. "Mostly like a circus. A freak show."

Already three fools have fallen into The Pond and drowned, their bodies stacked against a tree like sacks of sand.

Hundreds of others are scattered about, or sitting in pools of water, mumbling incoherently, the air rife with the effluvium of those who have soiled themselves and are now playing in the excrement. Vendors move through the crowd hawking small sacks of dried dung, vials of 20 percent sulfuric acid, and baskets of rotten eggs and spoiled fruit.

Waiting for the procession, David notices a fool who seems to have set herself apart from the others. The woman, if indeed it is a woman, has a massive head, pointed nose, thick lips, and broken teeth. David will remember nothing about the face beyond the eyes — the vacuous eyes.

"That woman," David says in his small voice, "is that woman a fool?"

"Yes," his father says. "Everyone here is a fool. This is the bottom of the pile, the accidents of nature — of life, what everyone wants to avoid. That's the reason for the Procession."

By then they are nearly abreast the woman, standing at the barricade the police have erected to assure a safe separation of fools and spectators. His seven-year-old's curiosity whetted, David breaks away, skirts the barricade, and approaches the fool. The fool seizes him.

Attempting to retrieve the child, Nathan falls over the barricade and yells for assistance. The police respond with customary brutality, extract David from the fool's clutches, and club the misanthrope into insensibility.

At home, shaken and mystified, David examines the scratches on his throat where the claws dug in, the cuts around his eyes. He runs his hand over the abrasions, his heart stung, and in the mirror, for the first time, imagines the depths of sorrow.

"We cannot forget," his father tells him. "It is necessary to see life."

Years later he recalls the madness of the creature's gripping him by the throat and biting at his eyes.

"The world is getting darker now. I can feel it more and more . . .. The girls call me ugly and they bother me the most."

the greatest
story
ever to unfold

Hans-David is at home for the day with Peter Lorre, waiting for the full moon, ruminating on the Vampire of Dusseldorf. He can, he has noticed, these days with an appropriate ease, capture and sustain the elusive nature of Hans Beckert. He peers into the reflection, stares at the face in the mirror, eyes circling the room, the clutter of wigs, paints and powders, masks, a closet hung with the rags, hairs, and sequins of the stage. Their eyes lock, and Hans reaches for another mask, another visage, focused on Peter-David, stealthy high priests, brothers.

In a far corner, out of sight, Sam hunkers down, shuffling through a stack of offers — requests for service — keeping an eye on the teevee.

"We're not running a hit service," he says. "Most are interested in re-venge. Nothing wrong with revenge, but it's usually just a one-time thing."

A new confidence reigns. He has neatly laid to rest Augustine's premise that evil merely enhances the admiration for good. He suspects it will prove a matter of taste, education, the resilience of minds tempered in different fires.

Already there's a proposal for a new police detachment, akin to the Special Investigating Unit for the PD Narcotic Division of the early 70s. An operation Sam got his fingers and claws into rather easily.

The SIU battalion of cops assigned to investigate The French Connection theft, left unsupervised, ran quietly for several years blackmailing and jack-rolling drug dealers and taking bribes until nearly every cop in the Unit was worthy of serious prison time. It is worth remembering. He'd like to see it again. Maybe SAMIE this time. He shuffles through the requests, turns to the teevee.

In keeping with the season, Channel 4 carries the first of two three-hour segments of *Jesus of Nazareth*, a recreation of the biographical myth of drinking and whoring from Jerusalem.

"NBC," Sam says. "Never hurts to keep tabs on old friends."

He switches the channel.

"You'll enjoy this," he tells his protégé. "A little something for everyone. He goes around staring at the sun, giving his money away."

The greatest story ever told?

Well, that depends.

As expected, the Christ cults send up flack. A plethora of objections. Too much fantasy, too real — the idea of teevee tampering with god's image. The debate heats up and GM pulls out (mōtus interruptus) withdraws sponsorship. The production morphs into a slick Proctor and Gamble splash, featuring Robert Powell as the ever popular son of god, with Olivia Hussey, undone of Zeffirelli's Juliet and draped in the deprivation of virginity, as the lovely, innocent Virgin Mary. For three hours the all-star cast thrusts and heaves across the screen, through a relatively unimaginative story of political double-dealing and hopped up piety.

"Hell, it was better than that," Sam says. "So many stories.

"One time we went off into the desert, and it wasn't for fasting. And it wasn't exactly a desert. He went back to visit one of the groups he had lived with a few years before. The visit turned into a month of wine, women and brawling. And that's easy to appreciate. But then he comes back saying, 'Not by bread alone does man live, but by every word that comes forth from the mouth of god.'

"But even that wasn't as bad as the time outside Gadarenes. He was holed up in a woods with that pack of losers he had collected. Jesus, that was something else. Simon Peter. Simple Simon the mindless wonder. Below the woods on the slope leading to the sea, swine herders moved their pigs into the meadow for a couple days. Christ and his crew were in the woods drunked-up and raising hell. You could see it coming. You knew there was going to be trouble."

Sam pulls a cigarillo from the air, takes a long drag.

"Anyway, they found two old men living up in the rocks, a couple of deranged half-wits who'd been run out of town a couple years before for hassling the townsfolk and generally making a nuisance of themselves. They'd been living in the tombs, generally ding-batting it up, so the countryside was crawling with stories about how crazy and violent they were. Of course, they had invented most of the stories — and after a while the silly old farts had gone to believing their own tales.

"By now they can't tell fact from fantasy and they got the whole bunch believing they are possessed by evil spirits. And honest to . . .. Well, I didn't have anything to do with it. Some things people make themselves. They get these characters on a self-examination confessional bender, a sort of laying bare of the private parts, and after a day or two, with a little encourage-ment and wine, the stories get better and better and they're convinced the cave dwellers are plagued by the crazies, fits, demons — that they have been chained up — the whole routine.

"Finally, Christ decides evil spirits are causing the trouble. For the next day or two they sit around arguing about evil spirits and what to do about them. They had a little of that right. Especially the history, my name, etc. Then, when the argument is about to burn down, Christ says he's going to chase the spirits out of the old men and into the pigs. Again, you could see it coming. He had dozens of stunts. One inventive S.O.B. A little crazier than most. Mean, too. Of course they were Semites and didn't like pigs. I mean, if you can't eat a pig what do you do with it?

"So they're running around with sticks, shouting and stomping, raising dust and three kinds of hell, chasing the pigs. They were all drunk or stoned, and the herders couldn't stop them and finally went off to town for help. There were only three herders and what could they do against thirteen crazies?

"Anyway, it was too late. By the time they got back the pigs had been run off the slope into the water and drowned. Hell, a couple hundred dead pigs were floating along the shore.

> Down the river did glide, with wind and with tide,
> A pig with vast celerity;
> And the Devil looked wise as he saw how the while
> It cut its own throat. "There!" quoth he, with a smile,
> "Goes England's commercial prosperity.
>
> (Coleridge)

"Yeah, even Coleridge got it wrong. I knew better. He didn't. They could swim, but they couldn't find a place to come ashore.

"The best part, however, was Christ sitting there pronouncing on the loonies, claiming they were now cleansed.

"The pig farmers returned with a posse. And were they pissed. They came damned near tossing Christ into the soup with the pigs, which would have been a little less dramatic than getting nailed up. But I don't know. I wasn't in on that one. It probably never happened. The nailing up, I mean.

"The dimwits who started the whole thing were at least smart enough to know they weren't going to be safe if left alone. The pig herders had brought most of the town back with them and weren't going to give the crazies a hearing. So when Christ and his misfits get into the boat to leave, the newly cleansed want to go with them. Then what does Christ say? Well, he says, 'Go home to thy relatives and tell them all what the lord has done for thee, and how he has had mercy on thee.' These poor demented bastards don't have relative one and are within a hair of getting shit knocked out of them by the pig people — and the lord has shown them mercy?

"Driving out evil spirits, my ass. If there had been anything or anyone like that around I would have known about it."

Immediately following the *Jesus* special, Billy Graham takes to the airwaves on Channel 2 delineating what Christ could not say, did not know about his message.

Still, the story gets bad reviews. Christ's mission, Billy claims, seems unclear, his countenance weak, faded, his disposition poor.

The faulty reception, some think, has to do with the weather. Possibly the networks have not fully recovered from their near fatal bout with the video-tech ghost, have developed complications, side effects, a palsy.

Peter-David's not surprised. Some more of Sam's bullshit, the voice arrogant, belittling, greasing the skids — from either side, belief reduced to absurdity. He turns to the wall, pulls the cover over his head and listens to the soft rhythms of his own breathing.

Hans-David reveals
a brief
religious history

I begin searching for a kind of religion at Fort Knox in 1974. There is an emptiness, you know, with god.

I read a lot. Soul searching, you know. They have guys in the barracks, like real Christians. They go to church all the time. One of them, John Almond, asks if

I want to go along.

I do.

I go to church. The service is really uplifting. Men, women, children, singing, holding hands.

I never felt anything like that before.

I consider converting,

I want to go to church.
I go quite a bit of the time. But not to lose my Jewishness.
I still want to be a Jew. But
I do not want to miss church either.
I finally convert.
I go through the thing. They want to dunk you in water. Yeah.
I go through it because you're supposed to, if you want to get in.
I want to join.
I do not want to lose my Jewishness. But again,
I want to be with them.
I tell them
I am Jewish. It does not matter. What they want me to say, is like the minister he is the lord. You say,
"I do." It is a very warm feeling. They accept you. They crowd around.
I want to accept them.
I know that if
I accept Jesus,
I am giving up my Jewish religion.
I do not think it is related.
I am still Jewish. Then this girl. She is standing next to me in church.
I hold her hand while we are singing.
I want her to take me home with her.
I do not know what I will do with her.
I want to meet a minister she knows. He is from another church, which is also Christian. He like talks to god all the time. She says he can see the cosmos. He knows how we think.
I want to believe in him. She is a very nice girl. Very pretty, if you know what
I mean. But the minister does not like me.
I think that god does not know who
I am or does not like me. "God has told me you are evil," he says. He says it is evil to be a Jew but
I can do nothing to change that. "Jews are Christ killers," he says. What about the Romans
I ask? "Blaming others won't change the facts," he says. "Every man is born with the sin of Adam on his soul. Jews have the sin of Christ's crucifixion on them. That cannot be washed away with water." He tells the girl, "It is a great sin for you to see this man. He does not respect god's word." The girl says she is sorry, that she would have been more careful if she had known. Later,
I find out that the girl is pregnant. The minister, he . . . well, it is his. Towards the end of my tour at Fort Knox,
I begin to lose interest in Christian stuff.
I think, maybe Sam's right, maybe Christ is crazy. But

Psyaint David

I can never stay with anything long.
I do not know what to believe.

Sam picks up the beat
and encourages the dancers

Anyway, it's a first-rate story, an argument for the cause, for a convert, and Sam holds out the contract with The Universe.

"The twenty-seventh," he says. "They've edited the first show. That's two weeks from Wednesday."

A melody on the air, someone in the street, in the hall, whistling the suite from *Peer Gynt*, (with a chord or two from Mischa Bakaleinikoff interposed) and Hans-Peter poses at the mirror pasting on the wistful white face of Frost on the beach, cannons booming. The bright star of surprise and joy are painted on one eye, his opposite cheek scarred with a tear. Retrieving Alma, he steps sure-footed over the sharp stones, into the sawdust circle of the circus.

Koko, an august, peaked cap and bells, the spotlight, beneath a drum-roll, unassuming, awaits the herd-like fury to be rained upon him. He flees their pursuit, hesitant, unbelieving, to the far extremes, the confines of the ring, protests with his surprised eye, complains that there must be a mistake, as they descend, toy guns, a soft cloth cat-of-nine, and elicit laughter, innocence betrayed, the first stirrings of sadness, disappointment, and rage scaring his broken-hearted face.

Then it is done.

The drum-roll crescendo, the alter ego face, a murderous indignation held in triumphant élan, he turns defiantly, offering a tear-stained visage to the crowd. Posturing, mocking his pursuers, fearsome, enduring, delighted in the pretense, the applause, he shakes two white ghost-gloved hands above his head.

But even now, signs are that Sam's latest appearance will be short — gruesome and brutal, but brief. He has seen small messages, the warnings of the campaign now under way to Stamp Out Smut.

Our Lady takes on
a cardinal virtue

In another noteworthy festival event, making the rounds, Our Lady of the O-Clit sidles up to Terrance Cardinal Cooke to tweak his cheek. It is justice after all, Divine Justice, he calls for and of which she approves. Just as long as it is *divine*. She is, however, not certain how he got on her wavelength, although she does like clerics — there seems to be no problem about that. All she has to say about it is, "God. OH! Do I!"

As a novice, an ingénue in an eastern region of thirteenth century France, for the hell of it, just to see if she can get away with it, she wangles admission to the Benedictine Cluny Abbey at Saône-et-Loire. Hair cropped and tonsured, her ample bosom strapped down and hidden by the loose draping of an overly large robe, she slinks in among the monks undetected, free for nearly a year to ply her magic within the confines of celibate habits.

During the day she keeps a monk's routine of Canonical hours and as a helper in the kitchen. At night, however, she sets her own agenda. She traffics the hermit cells, entering the sultry struggle of the brethren with their wrathful god, the torment of reconciling body and soul, succubus, dreamlike on the straw pallets of black-night secrecy, unspeaking, taunting, teasing, her lovely soft, delicate lips on swollen parts, taken finally into the moist, accepting depths of throb, thrusting, and profluent relief.

For a year she's the best kept of the abbey's secrets. The monks are reluctant to confess the nature of their nighttime phantasms and dreams, unwilling to betray the nocturnal visitor who flits about their half-sleep to provide a peace even devote prayer does not provide.

Eventually, however, as she must, she ventures farther afield, to the gated quarters of the abbot, a worldly, case-hardened profligate named Perceval LePeneus, who claims, among other inventions, a confessional with upper and lower sliding grates so while father confessor listens to the sins of his female flock, his hands might roam about gently exploring the nether regions of loosely wrapped garments and venture among the inviting contours of soft, warm but not-too-penitent flesh. Indeed, it is understood by all that man is a sinful creature and there is little to be done about it beyond accepting what god has given you, and confessing.

Abbot LePeneus gains a rather substantial reputation for lengthily inter-rogating his penitents, who are quick to discover the size and leniency of his forgiving nature, and of his dispensation of penance, if, instead of fingering their beads, they repentantly reciprocate with the laying on of hands to massage the holy abbot's forever hardened rod.

However, Our Lady of Penile Pursuit, in the bloom of young womanhood, already experienced in the ways of love, of bodily pleasures, is by no means prepared for the brutal, animal lust of the incontinent rutting pursuits of father-abbot. He keeps her abed for days, dresses her as a nun, undresses her on the altar and has her in an organ duet, filling her chalice, in sessions of instruction and guidance which change her profession, as well as the nature and focus of her habits.

In the end, Abbot Father LePeneus is reported to his superior by his jealous monastics, and Our Lady of Loquacious Luxuria is cast out, driven from the abbey walls to work her wonders else-wherever, but not before she extracts two-thirds of Cluny's treasury and secures an appointment at court of the French throne — on the reputation of her abbey activities.

Base urges, they are called. Base urges, and she giggles. Truly, the urge lies at the base, at the animal's root. Debauchery, she knows, as beauty, resides within the thighs and sighs of the bolder.

"My gentile man," she tells the Cardinal (is it genial or genital? She wonders. The difference is a single consonant — which fits Terrance to a "T") "you were simply born in the wrong century, at an unfortunate time when your parishioners actually believe in evil. Such a shame. Tsk, tsk."

She has an enchanting smile, her hair coiffed to appear as if she did it herself, a flower placed just perfectly, slightly to one side, giving her a feminine but not frilly presence.

In the mood of the new spring fashion romanticism, sexy and soft and gay and pretty and happy and confident, instead of blazers, kilts and anoraks, she wears dirndl skirts, a big over blouse (loose), and an unlined shirt jacket.

She takes the Cardinal's hand and presses it to her lips, nibbling at his gold and amethyst ring. He is well trained in the discipline of denial, withdraws politely, (digitus interruptus) and turns away. A small tremor ripples along his skin, but nothing more. Another continence callus on his spiritual epidermis.

The idea is to keep talking. He motors off in his limousine, Our Lady of Glamorous Greed at his side, to the Holy Cross Elementary School, 332 West 42nd Street, to meet with a congregation of parents and inject a little church into state.

The school rec room is packed with anticipation as Cooke of the red yarmulke and flowing robes enters left onto the small stage, the King of Life, shorn of his companions Sanitas and Fortitude, ready to do moral combat.

"From this time on," he states, further scrambling the fantasies of religion and politics, "no mayor, commissioner, district attorney or judge should feel safe in office, or in running for office, if he or she does not declare in favor of supporting law enforcing actions against these destroyers of our city."

His words carry an intimation, a suggestion, a small message for Our Lady of the Calculated Climax, that she might do as well in legitimate pursuits.

"Do you think so?" she purrs.

"We're dealing with a sex industry that brutally degrades the god-given act of sex, and men's and women's bodies; it uses children in ways that would shock and sicken any human being, and dwells on perversions so sick that we fear for the emotional health of those who are exposed in their formative years to such traumatizing materials and activities.

"The Constitution isn't really in the way," Cooke pontificates, whittling away. "It has been misinterpreted. The First Amendment isn't intended to be interpreted so that the rights of our citizens are abused."

This is pretty much what Our Lady of Apathetic Acedia expected — the bedfellows of wraparound politics and religion. She wanders off, slips into the crowd, a twinge at the back of her head. She listens to the hum, and would settle for a game of hide-and-seek — blind (wo)man's bluff.

An hour later, in a round of "Confessional Chairs," Lillian Fable of 731 8th Avenue takes the floor to confess.

"My fifteen-year-old son can't walk on 8th Avenue because he's always given those 'check it out' brochures for massage parlors," she says angrily. "I've been approached and asked to join a stable," she brags, "and my seven-year-old son is beginning to be impressed by pimpmobiles."

"Some things cannot be undone," someone says. You can bet on that."

Fond memories for Our Lady of Tawdry Times. She's been taken for a ride a time or two. Maybe this is another.

Of course she's willing. She hasn't had an orgasm in two weeks. Her head's ringing with the distortions of a rock-station in Jersey. She pushes out of the crowd, goes backstage. Definitely, something is wrong. Her pulse is up — she was sure, nearly certain this was the place — and the time. It's all here — clerics, righteous indignation, sexual repression, deceit — Cooke hawking his Castrati illusions, giving direction to the crowd, according to god's word — for a price. Easter envelopes are passed out, the crowd asked to be "generous" when giving to god, especially to Cooke's god for whom Cooke is the sole accountant — at least in this time, in this place.

"He should be here," Our Lady of Irascible Ira says.

Generally, stalkers leave similar tracks — maybe a whiff or drift of air over the skin. Circles in the sand. She hoped to narrow the circle, find a better definition, but seems to have missed. She thinks maybe the clerical atmosphere has muddled her perceptions.

A baby cries in a far corner and a man speaks to it apologetically. Then the audience is silent, motionless, transfixed, faceless, anonymous, a miniature fresco of the masses. Agnolo di Cosimo?

St Mathias and Aigilas discuss
the Lou or what has not yet
been exposed of the Lou's character

Mathias is at his desk, sipping Jura when Aigilas stumbles in.

"You always make entries like that?" he asks the disgruntled director.

"It's part of my savoir-faire," Aigilas says. "Have you talked to Super Cop recently?"

Mathias refills his glass, takes another from the drawer, fills it and hands it to Marcelo.

"No, can't say I have. What happened?"

"Honest to god, Matt, the S.O.B is crazy. He's been crazy from day one. Now he's out to prevent crime. He not only wants to solve crimes, he wants to prevent crime."

"Well, maybe he wants to influence what he thinks will happen not to happen."

"How do you stop something before it happens? This is crazy. The only way to stop what has not yet happened is to make sure it happens so you can stop it before it happens. Then you have failed to make it happen. I know, it's a modern American belief that you can both do something and not do it at the same time.

"I mean, I'm fucking losing my mind."

"What's he doing?"

"Okay! You ready for this? He's decided we should tell the actors working on the show that The Universe Studios productions could be hazardous to their health. I mean, a truth in hiring, of sorts. Put the label on the bottle. He thinks it will improve the conflict. I got it from a very reliable source. He's already spilled the beans to the Tamiko and Bellina kids. Goddam Matt, if the word gets around, we'll be back to making promises. And you know how clumsy and expensive that is."

"Yeah. Sounds like natural progression to me. When people start believing, just no telling what they will get into or where it will end."

Aigilas is staring down the rat hole again.

"What do those fucking rats do down there?"

He pours a slug of Jura into the hole. They listen. Nothing.

Freeze frame.

Of course, the hero's failure to comprehend the importance of the project did not escaped Mathias. Just last week he phoned Abby Mann to discuss the possibility of Mann doing a new cloak-and-dagger when the difficulties with the Kojak persona came up.

"Something's missing," Mathias says. "Do you have any suggestions for correcting the situation?"

"Not for something like that," Mann says. "His acumen lies in areas other than comprehension. I envisioned the composite as an old detective type with a special City-tough-guy crust. The problem, as I see it, is that with this approach the original is insincere and has a tendency to drift, unless the writing is very tight.

"If it's a matter of brutality, you know, obliterating the bad guys, or helping a friend in trouble, the personality will hold up pretty well. Otherwise, it's impressionable and floats with almost any suggestion.

"Also, it's difficult to know when an actor becomes the character or the character becomes the person. How many times do actors have to recite lines before reality becomes pretend, before they are the ghost?

"Keep in mind," Mann says, "you only see him in two dimensions at 4 : 3. In closeup. The closer you get the more the personality tends to blur.

"Of course there's the 'fifty-four' minute thing. At best he only gets fifty-four minutes, if that much, on each show to be himself."

"Another thing," Aigilas says, after Mathias further explains the problem, "he's playing LoKo again. He wants to resolve major historical crimes. He wants to find out who wasted Elsie Beckmann. He's collected the old clippings and photos, a piece of rope he claims belong to Peter Kürten, and says he intends to turn them over to the DA and the Grand Jury in Düsseldorf. He's even learning German."

"I'll take care of it," Mathias says, speaking with the customary cultivated executive presence of mind and the authority of experience. "I'll tell him we're going to use cascadeurs."

"Vampires," Aigilas says. "He was friends with José Marco. I'm not sure."

"You go back and work with him. He thinks you're his friend. See what you can do. We'll postpone the shooting for a couple days — redo the script.

"Should we erase Rizzo?"

"Rizzo? What's he have to do with it?"

"Last night he was talking about building a bigger and better department. Wants more time for Rizzo. Since Saperstein is out of it, he wants Rizzo."

"What do you think?"

"Rizzo always had a hard time finding something to do. His parts are small. He only has two lines. I'd scratch him."

Mathis consults the script. He uncaps a Sanrio Teddy Bear Trinket Green Felt Tip Pen Ex Cond and redacts Rizzo.

"What's going on with Saperstein?"

"Pretty much the usual. Scuttlebutt has it his wife left him. Seems the injury left him with a limp dick. She's not happy. Hooked up with the neighbor man. They're in Peru. He's going through therapy. Don't expect him back soon."

"Okay. You get together with u and Tramiko and do the location scenes of parked cars, the lovers' lane stuff. I'll take care of Lord Wimsey. Be ready to go by the twenty-seventh."

in which Goldfuss
attempts to put the skids
to the vanishing
visage of culture

However, other programs go off pretty much as planned. John Someone guns down William Rowland at 8 East 126th Street, then helps Richard Someone-else stab Edward Lupinski to death in his apartment on East 25th. As usual, it is easier to identify the dead than to ascertain the who-did-it.

In a mini-series pilot set for ABC in the fall, *Goldfuss and the Law*, attempting somewhat feebly to balance the books, mumbling through a symbolic plot for the worthy, State Supreme Court Jester Howard Goldfuss (played by Regis Toomey), sentences sixteen-year-old vandals Albertos Rios and George Ramirez to three years in Elmira for a Christmas Eve assault on the West Farm Public Library on Honeywell Avenue in the Bronx.

The boys are contrite but unrepentant.

"This is a crime not only against an individual, but to all society," Goldfuss says. "We have run on bad economic times and despite this we strive to hold on to every bit of culture we have."

But the story is sufficiently vague and Judge Goldfuss doesn't define which elements of the culture he would like to preserve. Nor do Rios and Ramirez indicate that they understand what the judge is talking about. All they were interested in taking out (after hours and without a library card) were several volumes on safe safe-cracking methods.

Easter egg hunters
go mano a mano

Tilled fields under siege. Cling to, embrace, enlarge, and hoping to further stimulate Holy Week cultural heritage, fulfilling the prophecy of Margaret Watt that Easter will be bigger (than Valentine's Day) because the children can get in on it, the All Fools Festival spreads to the Flushing Meadows, Corona Park Easter egg hunt.

Sam trots over from the Bronx, doggy style, for the fest — pausing to baptize a fireplug, sprinkle a little holy water on a garbage can. He makes a harrowing narrow escape in Bayside when he stops, scruff up in the street to nuzzle an asshole, and an oddball in a pickup, with menace in mind, runs a red light and knocks him tailbone and twisted testicles scudding into the gutter. He rights matters, however, extricates himself from the twitching corpse, catches a new skin, a Lassie look-alike, and gets back on his way.

The bane of Sam's manifestation is that he owes his existence, his popularity, to Christian fantasy. He is a feculent dream, the essence of malevolent intention and misaligned act. His ability to shift shapes, take on new forms — his countenance — to find substance in pain and fantasy — are at the heart of a depraved imagination. He winces — though the discomfort has often been alleviated by small triumphs. He has a definitive history of achievements, some small, but successes nonetheless.

In the late seventh century he provided the cover for *St. Cuthbert Gospels*, the oldest known intact surviving Western binding of decorative insular leatherwork — tooled red goatskin.

"A piece of my ass," Sam says.

He grimaces.

"Got nicked in a fight with the Picts, the Moor of Nechtansmere, 685 AD (approximate date). Some S.O.B took a patch of hide off my ass and it has never grown back."

He backs up to the mirror, examines the scarred contour.

But then, he's given up skin (they call it Morocco leather) for other projects as well — for rugs, Coptic Tracery bindings, gloves, boots. A little quid pro quo, if the price is right.

Of course, the 685 AD price was right. King Ecsfirth died in the battle and for the next twenty years Northumbria thrived on sedition, usurpation, and murder.

So why complain?

Then, too, though canine capering, trotting with the lobo pack, can be dodgy for a goat, he has a long history with canids: domestic, wild, hybrids and curs — dogs, wolves, jackals, coyotes, and foxes. Sometimes he runs feral, sometimes he's man's best friend — willing to suffer abuse, ape tricks, degrade himself for small rewards, food and shelter, a whimper or whine for the trouble. But he prefers it to cats, though he sometimes does show up as a bull (Vistahermosa) or serpent.

Today he's a medium-sized (50 lb.) Collie, stocky, short, flat fur and bushy tail carried low with an upward swirl or twist over the back. His overcoat is sable with white and tan under the belly and chest, over the shoulders, and on parts of the face and legs.

It's Maundy Thursday, 12:45. He stretches out, chin on his paws, on a small patch of grass near the swings in Corona Park. A Department of Parks and Recreation's Easter egg hunt (a child-developmental activity to enhance normally mushrooming cupidity), is scheduled for 1:00. To stimulate interest, draw participants and give activities a touch of class, Abraham & Straus has donated 360 pounds of chocolate Easter eggs. The park has been roped off and a large crowd is roiling about, waiting for authorities to give the signal.

Ten minutes before the hour, however, prodded by existential anxiety and avarice, without the protection or the restraints pseudo-civilization might temporarily in cooler times provide, the crowd breaks through the ropes. Unable to control the scavengers, and satisfied at not having assumed they might, park officials withdraw to the safety of the Unisphere Fountain.

The egg-picker throng swarms out over the grounds, trampling whatever happens to be in the way. Everyone's in on it — toddlers, pre-teens, teens, adults, and woddlers — intent upon getting his/her fair share (which in this case means more than whatever anyone else gets). The emissary from Abraham & Strauss, decorator Marcus Madden, is knocked down and his box picked clean of its chocolate eggs. Trees, three inches and under, are splintered, bushes flattened, and statues knocked off their plinths.

With first discovery the contest takes on revolutionary proportions. Friendships are forsaken, treaties abandoned, new alliances formed. Small kids mug smaller kids. Mothers knock the hell out of bigger kids.

Eight-year-old Carolyn Ufano is hammered by a couple of ten-year-old

Sumo wrestlers, her glasses broken, her eggs taken. Dazed, incoherent, she falls beneath a large damaged bush, tries to recover her senses, and is jumped twice more and frisked before she can find her basket and get back to the hunt.

Meanwhile, thirty-year-old Meta Canevari takes down a twelve-year-old boy from behind with a flying tackle, slips an open four-inch jackknife into the hand of her waiting three-year-old son Gus, and shouts, "Stick him, Gus. Stick 'em fore he gets loose."

The twelve-year-old smacks Meta in the snout. She loses the knife and crawls away, blood dripping from her broken nose.

To the spoils go the victors, and among the victors is Peter Carcido, another three-year-old who manages to collect an unusually substantial horde of chocolate eggs.

"He's not afraid of anything," his mother Wendy Carcido of 61-38 Madison Street, Ridgewood says. "They push him and he pushes back. He's a very strong little boy."

Peter grins and holds up a basket of smashed chocolate eggs.

Good Friday breaks
   with
splendor and aplomb

Good Friday awakens and saunters in with mourning and contemplation, a full nineteen days before the next scheduled shooting. David-Peter prays, hums to himself, meditates on the souls of the liberated, those stripped of matter, bon vivants, packed up and sent on their eternal voyage. Ivan the Terrible with no cause or policy to justify, he recites the runic beatitudes.

> Blessed are those who die for our sins.
> Blessed are those who suffer our whims.
> Blessed is Sam, who provides ill-health.
> Blessed are the men of wit and stealth.
> Blessed are they who create desire.
> Blessed are they who live by fire.
> Blessed are the cruel, for they shall be famous.
> Blessed are the killers, for they shall be shameless.

Even as he waits, rumblings, ripples snake along the wall, the beginnings again of a contest set and shaped in antiquity, in the spirit of the raven and fox. Distant voices. A long story of people nailed to crosses, told convince-ingly enough to be believed. Bubble Yum has spider eggs in it and causes cancer. After chewing Yum, a girl woke the following morning with webs on her face. Nine people have died after swallowing chewed Bubble Yum.

And that's the gospel.

Sam's voice blends with the rest, as usual, a consul to believe, to follow. The door opens, closes, latch dropped silently, a nearly invisible outline on the white-on-white misty wall, a long robe and two small, penetrating flames.

The Duke lifts the .44 gently from the drawer, snaps open the cylinder, slips in three rounds with red paint-splattered soft lead tips. He listens to the breathing, cradles the iron weight in one hand.

"We're being followed," he hears. "For a couple days. Someone is there."

"Who?" Hans-David mutters, sighting down the short barrel to a hole in the living room wall.

It's Sam again, anxious, looking for something to relieve boredom. He's in the corner near the window, fingers a few pages of Anton LaVey's *Satanic Bible.* An eyebrow raised in an ogee arch.

"Not bad," Sam says. "Not bad enough, but good. What's it worth if we don't occupy the mist of myth to foment a little rancor and bitterness?"

Mr. Teivel
lives
in the wall

I think his name is Teivel. Mr. Teivel torments me. He makes loud and weird sounds.

I think he lives next door in apartment 7D.

I never see Mr. Teivel. He just makes a lot of noise. Nothing
I can understand.

I think he lives next door, or maybe in the wall. Mr. Teivel torments me.

I have not slept all night and by 5:30
I am tense. Mr. Teivel is hiding in the wall making noises, when
I charge up to the wall and leap into the air to deliver a flying kick sending my foot through the wall and almost into my neighbor's apartment.

I kick the wall.

I jump and kick.

I try to kick his face in. Nothing happens. It does not have any effect.

I can hear sounds deep in the wall. A lot of sounds. Voices, thousands of them. Funny sounds.

I hear music like drums. It is all foolishness.

I cannot stop Mr. Teivel and the torment.

I wind up destroying my own property. My apartment is what
I call it.

I don't own it.

I pay the rent.

I hate it so much because of the demons.

Psyaint David

I am even thinking of setting it on fire.
I will need Rosebud matches.
I pay the rent.
I sign the lease.

I move in seeking quiet and rest only to find noise. No, this isn't my apartment. It has been reserved for me in hopes of trapping me, leaving me weak and unable to escape. Sam Carr, a six thousand-year-old man. What does a six thousand-year-old man look like? Sam Carr, who is but isn't Sam. Who is dead but lives to torment the earth. This is a puzzle.

I know my apartment is a setup, planned long ago.

He settles in the chair near the window, pencil in hand.

the first epistle
of Psyaint David
to Sam Carr

David, an apostle of Sam, to Sam Carr,
the reincarnation of a spirit 6,000 years old.
2 We give thanks to Sam for his direction
and instructions and faith in our labors.
3 For he is come to us in body and
spirit and power and in much fullness.
4 Indeed you know what manner of life
we have led without him.
5 For he has filled the void or our nights
when we are delivered from our enemies.
6 I urge, therefore, that you be more diligent
and resourceful in your ministrations and duty.
7 Allowing those under your care to speak
only at night as they have been commanded.
8 And I encourage you to keep the faith against
those who act ignorantly and in unbelief.
9 In like manner I will watch for a sign
in a time coming from you.
10 Be true, then, to our plan, and be not deceived,
but exercise control over sights and sounds
11 The spirits create, and rebuke yourself
for not doing your duty.
12 I write this hoping the voices will be quieted.
13 Use the power given to you for peace,
to quell the howling dogs with which we live.
14 I am your servant, waiting for your command.

He folds the paper and drops it to the floor next to the .44, then switches on the teevee, Channel 2 and *Kojak.* Stupendous slick-dick stands silently, staring at him with a curled lip and menacing scowl.

Twice he tries to call Kojak, receives a recorded request to leave his name and number.

"The Lieutenant will return your call as soon as possible," he hears, a plan, he believes, to throw him off, to confuse him.

Prince David finds
himself adrift
in the City of the Gods

So all is night in The City, all glorious gloom, and Sam's creation is up and about, listless, padding, circling the apartment, at the door, the wind at the windows, six of the Seven Whistlers. Again a dog howls, Gabriel Hounds, longing for . . . what? Voices emanate from the magazines on the floor. The dog howls.

They want credit for the success of the project. During the night he hears them discussing whether or not they should change the shooting dates — then the improbable, ecstatic moaning of a woman he has never seen and does not know. He creeps to the door, gun in hand, eases off the latch and springs into the hall, ready, now, to shoot it out with Serpico, Petrosino, etc., the hordes of blue. If Pabst is impressed with the action on Dartmouth, he'd lose his mind over this.

For two days he stays in, trying to remember what he's supposed to do.

"The demons," he tells himself. "The demons are protecting me. I have nothing to fear from the police."

He sorts through the usual debris of fantasy, magic, that strange alchemy of mind. He decides to satisfy their demands, their thirst, he will offer up whatever thoughts he can collect, saving important ideas for other times.

He will provide what they want, and for the next several hours lies on the bed playing with himself, drifting over the layouts in *Penthouse* and *Playboy*, the exotic-erotic photos of Betsy Harris and Susan Kiger, the rising and falling, the thrust and heave of a wild painted-paper frenzy.

And then the quiet and early evening, again flipping through the magazines he discovers the photos are shriveled, the finely airbrushed soft, pink skin shriveled, the sensuous forms reduced to bleached white skeletons. Dorian Gray. Yes, he's heard of that.

Quickly, they close their legs, sliding the sheets over their thighs.

He does not trust his eyes.

"The demons," he says, and hurriedly closes the magazines.

But still the bone women giggle.

"They act human. But they aren't. They howl. They want to get at children, to tear them up."

When he goes out to eat they follow him. He sees them in diners, on the street corners, painted with ironic smiles. They know he is not protected, no longer poltergeist, but el lobo, the scent unclear.

Then he is in the Bronx, circling, tongue out, panting, trotting along the throughway in heavy traffic, prowling streets he does not recognize. He realizes that the signs have been changed, the road moved, unfamiliar. He angles off at the first cloverleaf, spins down, around and up, intending to return to Yonkers. It's enough to forget, a moment's lapse, dreaming, driving, losing his way, only mildly annoyed at the loss of memory, the fading sense of direction. He can no longer find his way back to Yonkers, and circles in the tight knot of the concrete configuration for ten minutes, before he realizes he is thoroughly lost.

The terrible slant — the lost light of dusk is difficult to comprehend. The voices want smut, demand smut, and the SOS is out to stop him. Do they know? He isn't sure. Now he will tell them about Sam. After all, he has done what they asked him to do.

When he returns, Holmes is in the hall. Agents are everywhere. He pauses, waits instructions, tongue out, his nose lifted to the air.

He snaps on the set and turns on his bed, face to the wall.

In the background, a voice over, backstage, Mathias chats with Crocker.

"By the way, how's Margarita doing?"

"Not well," Crocker tells him, "not well at all."

"Did you ever find out what's wrong? I remember you said she was sick."

"Oh, yeah. They did explorative surgery last week. Found a tumor the size of a baseball in her stomach."

"Oh, Jesus. Really? Is that right?"

"Yeah. We had no idea. We knew she was having trouble. But not something like that."

"What's the prognosis? Is it malignant?"

"The pathology report said it couldn't be worse. Adenocarcinomas. It is usually caused by pollution."

"So what are you going to do?"

"There's nothing we can do. Absolutely nothing."

"Did you get a second opinion?"

"A second opinion isn't going to change the facts. All we can do is wait it out, like everyone else."

"We never expect things like this. How is your wife taking it?"

"Gloria? She's devastated. Spends most of her time crying. Keeps saying 'Why me? Why me?' Some mornings I don't feel like I can leave her.

"The neighbors have been kind. Mary Olenberger, who lives on the right, has brought over food — a cake, a couple pies, lasagna once — so Gloria doesn't have to cook. I try to help out whenever I can. You know, do some of the housework. Things like that."

"And Margarita? How old is she now?"

"She'll be six in November. She's still getting around. Seems pretty energetic. She tries to play. But you can see it in her eyes. She's not well. Gloria carries her around a lot. She has vomiting spells, tries to eat, but even that's a chore. No appetite. She's been losing weight."

"It's a shame. To think of all the years and fun she should have ahead of her. All of that cut short. Life is cruel. There's no other way to explain it."

"How long have you had her?"

"Five years. Five and a half. We got her as a pup."

when the driving in
of nails
leaves bullet holes

Six thousand gather with eighty-two-year-old Archbishop Fulton J. Sheen at St. Agnes Roman Catholic Church on East 43rd Street. The three-hour celebration of the crucifixion of Christ, a saga of anguish, suffering and death — the march to Jerusalem, the Last Supper, a thumping in of nails — provides an auspicious occasion for Sheen's garish performance. The steely-eyed posturing and pointing is roundly applauded.

> 17 And they clothed him with purple and plaited a
> crown of thorns, and put it about his head,
> 18 And began to salute him, "Hail, King of the Jews!"
> 19 And they smote him on the head with a reed, and
> spit upon him, and bowing their knees worshiped him.
> (*Mark* 15:17-19)

And among them is great wonder and rejoicing that he suffers so elegantly that they might live forever with remembrance.

Sam listens as the Lou
philosophizes
on the law and the lawless

Later in the day, at 256 Schenk Avenue in Brooklyn, in another Good Friday celebration, the Festival of Fools leapfrogs into a second week of carnage. Eight months pregnant Marcella Calderon, Anna Marcella and Digna Calazar are efficiently, if somewhat sloppily, dispatched by a hidden hand, wielding a knife, slashing the three women and one fetus to death.

For the occasion Sam appears in SAMIE best: black leather jacket, badge and all, enlivened by the spontaneity and enthusiasm of the celebrants. He's frolicked with the mad, deranged, the near human, inhuman. He has sanctioned great spectacles of madness and sorrow, whole centuries of torture, injustice, hatred — inquisitions and purges — pillage, rape and plunder, all catalogued efficiently in the small twists of nostalgia. Still, he envisions a new scheme, another plot to promote a scene, concoct a theme.

Psyaint David

He's at the 9th or 11th Precinct Station, monitoring Festival proceedings on the in-house teevee. Of course, he's not alone. The dazzling darling dandy of the detective division, Kojak, is in the second hour of a two-hour special made for teevee, pontificating yet another theory on night-stalkers, streetwalkers, the murderous marauders who occupy The City.

They are on location at the Fulton Fish Market, the set of the Lou's office, two semitrailers parked together, three sides removed, three cameras recording the action.

Actually, it's a shabby little cubicle, behind a one-way mirrored door, a grimy glass porthole with bars and a security screen overlooking the East River. A radiator in the corner hisses and clangs irreverently eight months of the year. A metal desk, beat-up typewriter, and two four-drawer file cabinets crowd another corner. The walls are papered with artists' sketches of Son of Sam, photos in cheap frames of great crime busters, and a calendar of pertinent police proverbs printed below each date.

The week of April 17th carries a particularly insightful batch of wisdoms.

> There is no such thing as an innocent man.
> The law is what you make it.
> Better to be tried by twelve than by six.
> Wear any hat you can get.
> A hand holding green is a hand without a gun.
> A hump with a broken leg won't stand to fight.
> Three behind the ear will cure a headache.
> (The City Police Proverbs)

The desktop blotter-assignment-sheet, scrawled with whimsical doo-dles and phone numbers for quick action, is surrounded with an assort-ment of pictures of gynecological phenoms clipped from *Hustler.*

The right-bottom desk drawer, as a hedge against an occasional likelihood, secrets an unopened, dust covered package of Knight Rider, two glass tumblers, and a bottle of cheap scotch.

"Good scotch," the Loo says, "is an insult to a man's intelligence. Course nothing is ever what it's cracked up to be. But bad booze, is bad booze. It makes no claim to fame and does the job just the same.

"Yeah," Telly says from the telly, "even the crazies I've played I've tried to give some dimension to their insanity."

He's reading from a teleprompter, attempting to establish verbal cred-ibility for his as yet unsubstantiated discoveries.

"Hippies and communists," he says, "cause all the trouble. (Earlier it was the Dagos and Spics.) We're having a breakdown in morals. The American way of life is threatened. We need less fucking and more fighting. Fucking drains away our strength, makes us weak. Then we can't fight.

"Look around The City. Our beloved city has become a swamp of dope and dog shit, populated by dudes in drag."

The soft strains of a violin support his voice. Ludwig the dog who snores symphonies is at it again. He pauses dramatically, locks eyes with Sam.

Then a new theory.

"There's at least two of them, maybe three or four. That's why we have composites. Each one is of a different killer. They could be brothers.

"Twenty-five years ago, maybe 1952, a woman in the Bronx had quadruplets, all males, and they just disappeared? After the hospital nobody ever saw em' again."

"What woman?"

"Nobody could find what she did with the kids.

"Well, this is it. She's had them in seclusion, training them to kill. Now is the time. Twenty-five is the best time for a killer.

"If we want to catch these shades, we'll have to turn The City into an armed camp. There's too many of them. Every man, woman and child should carry a gun and be prepared to use it."

Sam's in a chair in the corner, feet up, sipping from a flask of rum, recalls the Post Mortem, his prophecies—sooner or later, it had to come to this.

"Get a gun and in the best America spirit use it on anyone who breaks the law, looks like he is breaking the law, looks like he might break the law. We gotta stop this thing before it happens

"Then we won't need capital punishment. Why spend tax dollars on housing and trying and convicting criminals?"

He pauses for a long, wide-tongued lick on his lollipop as a voice off camera informs him that this is what The City is doing.

"I know. But it's not enough. The American people have not yet dedicated themselves to their wild-west MGM heritage. We need a hunt and run spirit. This country is unfinished. We still have work to do."

beneath a well-oiled lamp,
   quill in hand,
Sam pens a few scenes

Here's the libretto, with several new pages, Sam scratching in the City Rifle and Pistol Association. Heeding the Lou's suggestion, within a fortnight the RPA offers two hundred dollars to victims of robbery or assault who shoot and kill their attackers.

Sam cackles. It's too easy. He's set the misfits on each other's tails, fangs bared, circling, waiting for an opening.

On schedule, Jerry Preiser, the forty-two-year-old president of the Federation of Greater State Rifle and Pistol Clubs announces that "The object, obviously, is to encourage citizens who are properly licensed to carry firearms to defend themselves because of the complete breakdown of the criminal justice system in The City."

So the hunt is on. Hue and cry raised. Neighbors called in, relatives and friends take hot pursuit and The City drops back a few centuries into the iron grip of street law.

The first week three businessmen kill assailants and are sent checks along with scrolls of commendation. Several others shoot passersby and drag them into their shops. Pass Go and collect two hundred dollars.

The Inspector contemplates the developments. He wants more, would like a bigger bag of lollipops. He's examining the map hung over a large painting he had made of himself after he broke the Marcus-Nelson case — before he changed his name — or at least the spelling — a high camera angle, running the lines, the streets of The City through the paths of his brain sketched in the details of the map.

He calls Dobson in, points to the map, "Here's what I want. Get the ground-pounders out, remind them of their duties, obligations, the nitty-gritty of police work. Find a candy store in Brooklyn and sit on it. Maybe the Midnight Rose. The old Murder Inc hangout."

"Where's that? You have an address?"

"So who needs addresses? Okay. Try Saratoga and Livonia in Brownsville. But any candy store will do. Perverts need candy to seduce little girls.

"Heathcliff, contact The City's mental hospitals and see if they've come across any male patients in, say, the last ten years, who have demonstrated a dislike for women. I want every male fifteen or over, in the entire city, on notice that he stands a fair chance of being arrested if he is caught on the street talking to a young woman. We're gonna throw everything in to this. Helicopters, decoys, police, the K-nine people. I've personally requested thirty-five unspecified search warrants. I want everybody in SAMIE in the spirit. One way or another we're going to get this yo-yo."

Sam's at the window, scrapes a bent fingernail along the cold glass.

"There are other possibilities," he says.

LoKoJakMan glares at the camera.

"We'll consider them later," he says, his voice off mic and weak.

Sam's certain he will — break-ins, illegal search and seizures, wiretaps, goon squads, nightstick persuasions, and other small encouragements in pursuit of . . . justice?

"All right," Aigilas barks, "cut."

666 - the man of perdition is among you

Veronica Lueken the Bayside seer of P.O. Box 52, Flushing Meadows, or somewhere near 213th Street and 58th Avenue in Queens, is smelling roses again. Several years earlier while praying for Bobby Kennedy she smells roses and has an apparition of the BV and her son during which she (Veronica) passes into a state of ecstasy. When again revived or returned (to a normal state of mind?), Veronica appoints herself the "voice box" for the apparition, providing a detailed transcript of the celestial conversations for anyone interested.

During the intervening years Veronica's (to later be name Veronica of the Cross) numerous re-encounters and the volume of her recorded extraterrestrial experiences with the BV & J are known as "The Bayside Prophecies."

On All Easter's Eve (visions are to occur on the eve of religious holidays), as planned, gazing out over the Holy Mary statue in her backyard, Veronica acquiesces to her latest illumination of the BV & J — and transcribes the event, or non-event, as the case may be, for posterity.

Veronica - ... over our lady's statue. The left beam is so very strong that it seems to be piercing and penetrating the area all about the rear of the exedra.

High up in the sky — the darkness of the sky is disappearing — our lady is coming forward. The beams of light, I can see now, are coming from her hands. Our lady has her hands extended in front of her. I can see our lady's face now; she's very sad. Our lady is removing her rosary from her waist and she's holding the crucifix of her rosary in front of her. Now she raises the crucifix to her lips.

Our Lady of the Roses - My child, I weep tears of great sorrow because of the desecration, because of the lack of piety, holiness, and respect of the priesthood to my son. As your earth years' progress, my children, our clergy are going faster into darkness and taking many with them — children of light becoming children of darkness.

My children, what manner of abomination is being committed in my son's house? Can you not cry with him, suffer with him on his way to the cross? No! Demons have entered my son's house. They claim the human body to use them to defile my son's house until evil men of the cross are setting a church up now, a church of man with no angels guiding them, with no supernatural intervention from heaven guiding them. This church of man shall be built on naturalism, modernism, and humanism.

O, my children, there are doctrines of demons being given throughout your world now. The teaching of the prophets of old are being cast aside as being too old for a modern world.

My child, the father of all liars is satan. Satan has many faces, my child.

Veronica - Now our lady is going over to our left side. She's standing directly above the first tree, and she leaning over now. It's growing quite windy because her skirt is blowing now.

And now I notice a very large throng of people coming out of the sky, and now over on our right side. They're all dressed in long flowing gowns. They cover very loosely their arms and legs. They have no sandals or anything on their feet. They're standing there, and they're all holding green palms —

you know, the palm is very green and yellow like, but very long, like pieces of palm — over their right shoulders.

Now coming directly from the center of this very hazy looking sky, I can see J. Now J has nothing on his feet. And he's holding his cloak — you know, the outer garment he has — over his left arm. Now J is touching his lips with his first finger, which means to listen carefully. He's like floating forward. I can't explain the way he moves. It's, he's like carried on the wind.

J - Romans, awaken now! 666 has entered among you. The forces of evil are intent upon vanquishing the Eternal City of Rome. Satan has entered into the hearts of those who hold high places in my church.

My children, you must exercise great care in accepting what comes to you in print and through your news media. The master of all deceit is in your world now. Remain in the light, the knowledge given to you through your prophets. Do not join those who bring doctrines of devils into my house.

Warnings have been given and gone unnoticed. Man continues upon his way of evil. Many are selling their souls to get to the head.

Veronica - Now J is gathering his cloak, the burgundy robe that he has about his shoulders, about him, and he's going across the sky to our left side. And our lady is now going over to him. She's like floating across the sky. Oh, and she's standing now, looking up at J, and he's nodding his head. They must be saying something. I can't hear any voices, but I do know that they're talking in some manner to each other.

Easter Sunday
   beneath the Big Top
at center-ring

The barker raises his megaphone.

"And ladies and gentlemen, in the center ring, returning from a historic run in Nazareth where he played to Jew, Arab and Gentile alike, the Houdini of religious sects, the only man to be nailed to a cross, escape from a sepulcher, make a death-defying descent into hell, and then, within three days, to rebound on the ascendency to heaven. The one, the only, the fabulous and much imitated genius of double-talk and ambiguity, a man forever in command of his soul, the living myth, the legendary and the ever popular, Jesus Christ!"

Spotlights circle the vaulting of the big top. The band blasts out a march, echoing Alleluia-Hosannas on the highest to bring in the dawn, the new light, the day of rebirth. Easter Sunday blossoms, and searching for a pulpit sufficiently above the grime and disease of the streets, to symbolize the elevation of mankind from its sinful normalcy to an abode of grace, Reverend Frank Rafter and forty-four followers from the Richmond Hill

Baptist Church (belonging to the Lord) in Queens, rise to the top of the Empire State Building, and with an aubade of "When Morning Gilds the Skies," watch the sun burn the fog off the Carpathian canyons. Along the byways and side streets of the brick and stone forest, celebrations erupt, heralding the final day of the Festival of All Fools.

Police have 5th Avenue between 44th and 57th Streets blocked off. Crowds gather to watch the Easter Parade and when puzzled viewers ask, "Where's the parade?" they are informed in a circular metaphor of the conscious and unconscious spying on one another, that the crowd is the parade.

Then, again, it's show time.

Outside, on the steps of the Cathedral of St. Patrick, the choir from Odyssey House, a drug treatment center sings, "In Your Easter Bonnet."

Inside, in the center aisle first ring, direct your attention to the wizard in the red cape, the flaming robes, Terrance Cardinal Cooke.

At the Cathedral of St. John the Divine, Paul Moore, Jr., Episcopalian Bishop of The City, states in a sermon that "I believe City residents are beginning to wake from the paralysis of a year ago."

Of course, there's little to support his claim, nothing from recognized authority, little of intuition or common sense.

And, no doubt, meant to provide an otherwise somber melancholic morning with comic relief, the infamous, impotent castrato Marcus Christ, one of the top ten, two or three best known, and least trusted pimps in The City, splendidly arrayed, in a purple frilled and laced parade of his own, rambles down Broadway at 42nd Street, among the prostitutes already on their Times Square beats, gripping his crotch with both hands, chanting the improbable "Christus Resurrexit! Christus Resurrexit!"

David the anointed
laments his condition

Spirits crowd the morning, along the hall, seep through the wall, beneath the door. Peter-David does not sleep well, now, night or day, and knows he cannot avoid them indefinitely. He has not heard from Sam in three days and suspects, harbors, again the suspicion that he has shifted shapes—maybe a black dog, maybe holed up at 316 Warburton, under the alias of Sam Carr.

Then the inevitable. The demons creep into my apartment and go through everything and examine things. They read what

I am writing on the walls. It's like, loyalty. You know. And admiration.

I try to do what they say, but they are never satisfied. Sometimes

I argue with them, ask why they are making me do these things. But they never answer. They just laugh.

I am not a bad person, but they make me do bad things.

Psyaint David

I do everything they say to do, and still they are not satisfied. They keep needing spirits and if

I don't give them more Sam will do something real bad. Like mass destruction, maiming multitudes. Once

I remember his demons were howling all night and

I didn't do anything. The next day we had an earthquake. Where? Turkey, I think! And people died. A lot of people.

I want to enlighten the world about the conspiracy of evil and about Sam, and that wretched building on Wicker Street which is a Holiday Inn for demons who travel around the world.

Hans-David
confronts the agony
of his odyssey

Memories of torn bodies linger, enlivened by the crowd's cheers, the excitement, anticipation of festival activities. At Duffy Square Hans-David drifts with the crowd, the sidewalk packed wall to curb with humanity and trash. Fumbling for change, he buys a *Post*, his last seventy-five cents — counts out the nickels and dimes, his paycheck from the post office at the apartment, lying on the table.

The headlines are brief, "Will Easter Pass Peacefully?" with a picture of Beame carrying a large lightweight (Styrofoam) cross through Central Park. On page two, another bold headline, a black flag waving for him. "Hunt for Killer Continues."

Little doubt about it. They've caught on. He stops in the crowd, pushed along a few steps, then backs into a doorway.

What does it say? What do they know? He smiles, pleased. Nothing to go on. Going the wrong way.

He reads slowly, savoring the words, the small print, names addresses, guesses, Christine Freund, Virginia Voskerichian—the observations of Queens Homicide Chief Joseph Borrelli.

"What we have here is someone who doesn't like women."

A woman hater? He scans the words twice more, then moves into the crowd, slowly, mesmerized, as if someone has spoken his name, has called his name. Woman hater? So that's it. Isn't that what he wanted?

He folds the paper, scans the faces to see if anyone has noticed him, then hurries back to his car.

Two blocks up 7th Avenue, headed north, the first tentative stirrings, a wan smile, the words instructive, and for clarification, of an epistle already arranging themselves.

At home again atop the seven-storied mountain, with great care not to disturb the air, he stretches out on the bed and with the .44 near at hand takes up a pen.

the epistle of Psyaint David
  to Queens homicide chief
Captain Joseph Borrelli

David, Apostle of Sam, by the order of His
Majesty of Discontent, and of Sammael Malkira,
2 To Joseph of Queens, beloved son in search
and pursuit: greetings, salutations from Sam
the Father and his festering hoard.
3 As you know, it has been reported that you
have spoken to the newspapers about Son of Sam.
4 I am deeply distressed by you calling me a
woman hater.
5 For I am not, although I am a monster.
6 And I wish that men everywhere, lifting up hands,
with wrath and contention would keep women
in their place.
7 In like manner, I wish women to be decently
dressed, adorning themselves with modesty and
dignity, not with braided hair or gold or pearls
or expensive clothing,
8 But with tasks such as become women professing
sincerity and willingness to die for their masters.
9 I am the Son of Sam. I am a little brat
who serves his father.
10 When Father Sam gets drunk he gets mean.
He beats his family.
11 Sometimes he ties me to the back of the
house and I spend the night howling.
12 Other times he locks me in the garage.
13 And it is the first commandment of Father
Sam that "Thou shalt go forth and kill."
14 Let women learn in silence
with all submission.
15 Behind our house many women rest.
Mostly young — raped and slaughtered —
just bones now.
16 Father Sam keeps me locked in the attic, too.
17 I can't get out but I look out the attic
skylight and watch the world go by.
18 I feel like an outsider. I am on a different
wavelength — programmed to kill.
19 I do not allow women to teach or to exercise
authority over men; but she is to keep quiet.

20 For Adam was formed first. Then Eve.
21 And Adam was not deceived, but the woman
was deceived and was in sin.
22 Therefore it is written, to stop me you must kill
me since man did not come from woman
but woman from man.
23 Attention all police: shoot me first — shoot to
kill or else keep out of my way or you will
suffer Satan's wrath.
24 Father Sam has instructed us so. He is an old
man and needs fresh meat to preserve his youth.
25 He has had too many heart attacks. Too many
heart attacks.
26 "Ugh, me hoot it hurts, sonny boy."
27 For as though one man's sins entered into
the world and through sin and then death
has passed unto all men because all have sinned.
28 I miss my pretty princess most of all. She is
resting.
29 But I shall see her soon.
30 For I am the Monster — Beelzebub — the Chubby
Behemoth.
31 I love to hunt. Prowling the streets looking
for fair game — tasty meat.
32 The women of Queens are prettiest of all.
It must be the water they drink.
33 I live for the hunt — my life — for Father Sam.
34 Joseph of Queens, sir, I don't want to kill
anymore.
35 No sir, no more, but I must, since it
is written, "Honor thy father."
36 Remember in your heart that I want to make
love to the world. I love people.
37 I do not belong to this world.
Return me to Yahoos.
38 To the people of Queens, I love you.
And I want to wish all of you a happy Easter.
39 May Sam bless you in this life and in the next.
40 And for now, I say goodbye and goodnight.
41 Police: Let me haunt you with these words:
42 I'll be back!
43 To be interpreted as — bang, bang, bang, bang — ugh!
44 To be interpreted as Sam says hi.

as a true thespian,
   Sam returns
to play it again

At The City Opera it's Frankfort-on-the-Main, Easter Sunday, bells ringing, crowds streaming through The City gates on their way to a holiday in the country. Sam mingles with the crowd — same plot, repeat performance, posturing.

Then he steps forward, flings off his friar's cape, and proclaims in a splendid aria "Son spirito che nega."

He strides across the apron as he strides through the universe shouting an insolent, "No."

But these are mere words. And it is impossible to report act accurately with symbols. One is art, the other life, though the bargain is struck. David feels the scalding touch.

"Fin da stanotte."

Yes, the void is filled, the voices quieted — for the moment.

An early crimson moon hangs over the Hudson, over Pineview Towers. Peter-David drifts, sleeps soundly, wakened at midnight by a storm in the Palisades. Thunder hammers the trees; sheets of rain lash the windows. To the northwest, lightning splits the sky. Bolts from heaven, blue-white and yellow, a harmony of voices, a consort of winds.

"Listen," Sam says, "do you hear that?"

He chuckles and steps forward, towers over the footlights.

"If you are wondering now as he is, about his sanity — as with most of humanity it has always been borderline."

He turns to gaze on David's restive, tormented form.

"Yes, the wind blows in him that blows in all of us."

His hooves scrap the hard floor, a malodor of goat urine on the air.

Somebody is playing Mozart, then something from Gounod's *Faust.*

"Ah, yes. Trite, you say. Well, maybe. But consider this. Consider a desolate moor, a perilous, treacherous night, and a severe wind. Yes. And all without family or friends — not only separate in distance and time, but parted by an abyss of cognition so deep and wide that the voice not only will not carry to the other side, but drops swiftly and silently into the abyss."

Sam's gazing out into the night, the river lying far below, ebbing slowly southward like a sullen serpent.

Hans-Peter raises his head. His eyes are clouded. He feels Sam's weight on his arms — Sam's voice, the invitation. For a moment he is suspended, then a shrill laugh, and the skies quiet. The rain ceases.

He has seen it before. Riding over the town, above the river, swiftly on Sam's command, luminosities on the air.

"You will see," Sam says. "You will see all."

Psyaint David

He will see all, the ladies in waiting, the nameless, as yet, those already marked for a harem of carnage, the souls he must free. He will see the wisps of Donna Lauria, Christina Freund, Virginia Voskerichian in shrouds. He will see the ladies waiting, the coryphées, the danseuses, visionaries, seers, and psychics deep in the forest, a gathering in the trees, withered-skinned, bent-limbed, circling in a dance, eyes shining. He will envisage Sam's figure against the fires of the sun, a strident song on the wind, the robe of despondency, the mantle of misfortune swathing Sam's shoulders.

"You will see the world as it is," Sam says, and David waits.

"Here," Sam says, holding up a glass globe, his fingertips small fires. "This is the magnificent sphere that has entranced fools for centuries. And for what? It circles aimlessly, provided with plenty, more often scourged with want. Its surface crawls with a hapless creature bent on ruin and destruction, flaunting god, scorning the devil."

Sam cackles, coughs.

"What would you like to see?"

David's eyes are reflected in the globe. He looks away.

"What do you see?" Sam says. "Sanctus David. Here."

Sam slams the globe down spraying the sky with a sparkling shower of fragments of glass and light. It is Sam who gives grandeur to the light. Behind him a red hue caresses David, lying on the bed, facing the wall.

"More here than an ill-wind," Sam says. "The plot twists, now, turns more fully on the visions of the Psyaint."

He steps into the shadows, the sense of a scheme more potent than any he has contrived thus far.

Sam is singing (in a nasal operatic baritone, tremulous from an eternity of misuse).

> Guard yourself from women's tricks;
> this is the first duty of our Order.
> Many a wise man has been deceived,
> has failed and never seen his error;
> finding himself at last abandoned,
> his loyalty repaid with scorn! –
> In vain were all his efforts;
> death and despair were his reward.
> (Mozart)

St Mathias alerts the Lou
to difficult times - tells him
a thing or two in the process

And where better to construe Sam's scheme than in Mathias Teivel's office? The Showrunner isn't receiving visitors. He has indigestion, palpitations, struggling with crutches, and a painful case of podagra.

"Cancel my afternoon appointments," he tells his secretary. "I don't want to be disturbed."

He closes the door and stands for a moment, a painful moment on one foot, hands in pockets, head back, then reaches over to the teevee, hits the "on" button and watches the shades stain the glass.

He can hear the rats in the couch. They're bored, he thinks, trying to keep busy. More of instinct than anything else, he throws the remains of a Katz Deli Knoblewurst into the corner.

That should create some interest, he tells himself.

Immediately two entrepreneurs (scavengers) appear — squeaking and hissing, circling the find. There is a great deal of bruxing and chattering. A fight erupts in a series of eeeeps and prolonged hisses.

Rats, like sharks, will eat almost anything — even rat poison. Sometimes, after a few days of digestive adaption, they return for another feeding.

Mathias watches, choses a favorite, roots for his hero and boos the villain. When the villain is victorious and carries away the prize, Mathias cheers for him.

Today Telly is on a traditional laid-back detective gig, hat cocked over his eyes (occasionally he wears a fedora), feet up on one corner of the desk, a blonde in a tight dress with a slit up the side seated on the other corner. She has her legs crossed, a cigarette in hand, a tumbler with three-fingers of scotch. Her endowments rest firmly at the center of the assignment-sheet. The Loo has a hand on her thigh.

"Have you seen Kesil?" Mathias barks.

Telly sulks.

"Not today, if that's what you mean."

His voice carries a note of irritation, no doubt at Mathias for interrupting his mediations.

"That's not what I mean. Has he said anything to you about the next shoot?"

"No. As a matter of fact, he seldom says anything at all."

"Theo, come closer to the camera. The saturation is weak. It's time to get together on this."

The camera does a slow zoom. Mathias stares at the blonde, as if he's seen her before but can't remember where or when. He eyes her carefully. Maybe she's the problem. The Lou has turned morose of late. Maybe she's messing with him.

"Who's the skirt? And by the way, what is this? I don't remember any-thing with a blonde dressed in a forties' get-up perched on a desk."

"Listen, don't worry about her. We go back a long way. Anyway, I don't want any of this sob-sister crap. If Aigilas has a hardon, let him handle it."

"Bogie, you gotta understand. If Marcelo has a problem, the project has a problem. Then I've got a headache. And right now, you are it."

"Oh ho!" he says, or maybe "Ho, oh!"

He pushes his hat back.

"I see. Well, let's get this straight. It is you who do not understand, baby. I'm tired of playing games. I want this hump. I want that yo-yo locked up before he creates more bodies."

He takes a card from the drawer and hands it to the blonde. She's straightening her stocking, resettling a garter.

"Listen, sweetheart, give me a call when you have a little more time. I'm sure we can think of something to do."

She agrees and smiles, drains the last of the scotch, and slides off the desk.

"Should I know her?" Mathias wonders.

"She has a lot of connections."

"Okay, but stay away from the other actors."

"Just trying to do my job," moralistic Marlowe says.

Mathias's rises slowly, prepared to pace, his large toe extended, pained.

"We've got a contract for three more programs, and nothing in the fine-print says you won't catch the antag, or that you have an option to go screwing around with police work. You can't change the storyline simply because you've got a bleeping heart. Actors have been trying to do that for centuries. It doesn't work. The best bet is to go along with it."

"When I took this beat, I was just another teevee cop. I know it won't last forever, but I have the trust of my fans and I'm not going to blow that."

Indeed, it would seem the Loo has had a shift in spirit, a personality drift. According to Roget's he is, bad-tempered, cantankerous, churlish, crabby, cranky, crotchety, crusty, dejected, depressed, despondent, doleful, dour, down, downcast, gloomy, glum, grouchy, grumpy, ill-humored, ill-tempered, irritable, low, miserable, moody, peevish, snappish, sour, sulky, sullen, surly, testy, and unhappy. But at the moment he is not melancholy or broody.

"You may not have to. It may already be gone — even without . . . we're relocating to California next year. And if the ratings don't pick up — that's not all that will be relocated. You'll be an ex-cop with no tale to tell. In other words, a crime instead of a crime to solve."

"Who set that up?"

"Just another way to save quid. CBS is transferring programming and business news headquarters to the West Coast. The Universe has 333 sound stages on the West Coast."

The Loo is now in a serious ill-humor. Maybe melancholic and brooding.

"Well, we ain't heard the end of it, baby. We can fight fire with fire. I wanted the production in The City and I got it. I want to keep it here, and I'll find a way."

"Lieutenant, I know what you mean to this city. You've given it a respectable name nationwide. I know you love The City. But I also know that the people upstairs do not give one small shit for what you or I want or think."

Clearly, the exec-pro's patience is wearing thin.

"Do you remember, several months ago when that goddam silly duck from Washington came up here? What's his name? Donald Mallard? Drake? That's it. Donald "Duck" Drake. Well, I sat one entire afternoon and listened to him quack and hiss. Not only that, but I watched that feathered freak eat crushed corn and waddle around the room — he even set himself on fire, smelled up the place something terrible. He shat on my office floor — and I don't mind telling you I'm not about to do anything contrary to what he asks.

"Let me level with you."

His voice is soft and pliant.

"In the last six months two people I have been associated with have been whacked with the same M.O., after we met, in exactly the same way. It was mentioned — only mentioned — in the papers, and I have it from reliable sources that SAMIE has not and will not, I repeat, will not open an investigation. The question may be why not? Although that is not the right question. They were cold-case before they were a case. But the answer, nevertheless, is simple. People do not want an investigation. The only thing to do, the proper thing to do, is stay alive as long as you can, in whatever way you can."

"James Drought said it. The secret of American life is to stay alive and live well, as long and as well as you can, by whatever means available — whatever means."

"So we're supposed to roll over and play dead."

"Which is one homicide up from rolled over and dead."

"Un huh! And you expect me to go along with it?"

"Do you have a choice?"

"SAMIE has a lot of power — both on and off the street. I can drum up support all over The City."

"And all it will get you is an early grave. You'll deep-six the whole thing."

"As long as the spook is loose, this city will need cops. According to the latest crime index? Crime is up throughout The City by 13.2 percent. The whole place is turning into Fort Apache."

"C'mon, Lou, you don't believe that."

"Sure I believe it. The City will always need cops, another cop show."

"But it will be cops who get along with the town criers and their mundane mores. Man, you know what happened to Serpico."

"He was a dumb dago."

"Dago or Greek, it doesn't matter. His act was cancelled. More than that, I don't want Drake coming in here asking me why the program isn't going as planned. I've got this old fashioned belief in survival — mine. Right now you're screwing with it."

"So that's the way it is?"

"Well, I wasn't going to spring this, but you might as well know. See this? This is a memo from Blackrock, a stone tablet that came down off the mountain for the folks at *Hawaii Five-0.*"

"What's *Five-0* got to do with it?"

"Jack Lord wants to film *Five-0* here in The City next season. He wants to bring *his* pitch to town. He thinks they can handle carnage and mayhem and mystery better than we do. Maybe, maybe not. I don't know what he'll do for beaches and waves. I suppose he could use Coney Island. Maybe one day everybody will be saying 'Book him, Danno!' But one thing I do know, we can't afford any more screwups. We've rescheduled the next shoot. We're not going to use the Tramiko and Bellina kids. We'll pick up a couple others to take their place. Otherwise, everything is still on go."

"Why the change?"

"Well, people put two and two together. I suspect that's what happened. But, anyway, they're out of it. We'll use a couple cascadeurs.

"The first show's ready for airing — the sponsors are enthusiastic — at least at present. It will air early in the season. That's what you have to keep in mind. On the street or on the screen."

"Yeah, I know, but I'm still looking for the Why. Every series has a Why," LoKo says.

Marlowe reminisces

She was a good looking dame. Just like Chandler said. And tough too. She was worth a stare. Her hair was black, out of a bottle and not so wiry as it looked. Her hot coal-black eyes weren't so hot either, after you got to know her. They were glazed black and steady when she wasn't talking. Steady like she was thinking about what she was going to do to you next. Besides her fancy clothes, she mostly paraded around in sheer nylons. I think she slept in her stockings. Nothing else. I never saw her without stockings. Stockings and spike-heels. She was good in bed. Had a couple maneuvers I hadn't come across before.

When she wasn't pee-oed about something, she could be very nice. Very nice. I think that's why it worked for a while. That, and me trying to figure out who she was. Mrs. Regan. Mrs. Rutledge. Miss Strenwood. Lauren Bacall. They were all named Vivian. But she started off as Sternwood. Vivian Sternwood.

I had come across the name twice. Once when I was a kid. My mother read me a story about King Arthur. I liked Morgan le Fay. She reminded me of my mother. Then on a bus one night going from Chicago to San Francisco, at a bus station in Laramie I picked up a copy of a book. I don't remember the writer. The book was called *The Final Days.* I only remember a little about that Vivien. She wasn't much like this one. More like Vivian's sister Carmine. But nobody could figure out who she was, either.

But it didn't last. I think that had to do with the screenwriters not staying with Chandler's story. How I got mixed up with her in the first place. It was the thing to do. They probably wanted a romantic ending. From what I've seen, Dixon could have done better.

So we ended up together. Me doing my Bogie part. That was thirty years ago. I'd do better now.

I closed the office and we took time off for The City. With the money the General paid me, and her money. It was an easy trip. I figured we could hang out for a few months, maybe a year. I could get some kind of sleuthing work. By then I though Chandler would have another story ready. Maybe an adventure this time.

But I was wrong. I was wrong about almost everything. Including Vivian, or whoever she was. I should've taken Spade's advice.

In the end, I think it was the Regan thing. She wasn't exactly truthful about that. Not that she ever was. At least not to herself.

She said he didn't mean much to her, one way or the other, dead or alive. But there are always more ways than two. Sometimes the dead are not as dead as we think.

After a month or so she was restless. Drifted back to old habits. Got into some high-stakes gambling. Lost a lot of the money she inherited from the General. Drinking heavy, too. More than likely met somebody she could work her charms on.

I took a hookup with a detective agency in Brooklyn. Mostly tailing work. It wasn't a bad gig. Keeping track of rich ladies for their very rich husbands. Fitzgerald's right. The rich are different from other people. They got no sense at all. They parade around at night spending money going to fashionable watering holes so everybody can see them, then the next day they run around in broad daylight doing strange things thinking nobody will know who they are.

Six months after we reached The City I took an assignment from a Gloria Werlinger Lupé-Bouchard. The rich ladies in The City are all named Gloria. By then I was working out of a joint on 4th Avenue South called The Wounded Bear that catered to the upper crowd and specialized in no see, no tell parties for people who could afford the price. I'm not sure how she found me, but Gloria Lupé-Bouchard was some grand dame. Small, maybe ninety pounds. Sixty or so and looked it. A dirty blond, wrinkled and sun baked. Walked around barefooted in a sequined chemise waving a pearl cigarette holder. Said she suspected her husband for years. Thought it was time to find out who he was mixing with. She figured he might die in the near future. Was sure he'd leave his money to a chippy or whatever they called them. She offered a good fee, so I took it.

It turned out Henri Lupé-Bouchard was a wine importer that imported more than wine. He was a slick, always grinning and talking a mile a minute, spent a lot of time at the track and in cat houses. He was busy. I tracked him through the plate glass mirrors of half dozen import-export joints in Brooklyn. Some of it was import, most of it was sales. Crystal meth. Heroin, cocaine, as far as I could figure, imported from Brooklyn. A good bit of it going to Mott Street.

But there the trail died. I hit a dead end. It was like running in circles, lost in the woods. You come across a set of tracks and they're your size. You were here earlier, maybe a day or several hours ago.

I had all I needed for Gloria. There were other women in Henri's life, but none I could finger important enough for him to give it up. I told her so, and she seemed satisfied. Even if I wasn't. I had the doughnut, but there was still the hole. Something, someone missing. Maybe more like a whirlpool.

Then it blew up in my face. They found Gloria hanging from a fire escape of a tenement on West 44th Street. It looked like suicide. A pair of nylons knotted together, one end tied to the iron rod on the fire escape, the other end around her neck. She was still barefooted in her sequined chemise — without the pearl cigarette holder.

I got there about the time they were cutting her down. Talked the Captain into letting me go through the apartment. But like everything else in the case, there wasn't much there. Like I said, a dead end. The landlord said the place had been vacant for two months. He didn't how she got in. Or why. The police wanted to know what I knew. They knew she had hired me. But what was she doing on 44th Street in a vacant apartment?

Henri didn't seem overly perplexed by his old lady's demise. Almost as if people hanging themselves from fire escapes was a daily business. Then I figured he had someone else. Gloria's going was convenient. And that was that.

I told Vivian about Henri. She had run across him several times in the lofts and basements on Canal Street. A couple of her gambling sorties, she said, run by Nicky Louie and the Shadows. But that didn't help.

So a couple days later I was still trying to figure out where to go when I found that Eddie Mars was in town. It made sense. I suspect he was working off Chandler's version. Did he know Vivian was there? Was he following her? Us? Where was Mona? Silver-Wig? Margaret "Peggy" Knudsen? Deidre?

Then I got a call from a Detective McCormic of the 13th to meet him at Bellevue. It seems they had a body they thought I would know something about. And they were right. It was Vivian. It is hard to tell what she got into, but it didn't turn out very nice. She had a couple .44 slugs in her head. I hadn't seen her in three days, and she looked a lot better then than she did this time.

But that ended The City adventure. I suspect Vivian had something to do with the Lupé-Bouchards and the Shadows or Flying Dragons or White Eagles. But what? Was she in with them? Was Gloria's money meant to keep me off what she was doing? Had Vivian put her up to it? Vivian lost a lot of money. Maybe she thought I'd find out. Maybe she was paying off a debt. And what about Mars and Silver-Wig?

Who hung Gloria out to dry? Was it suicide like the cops said?

What about Henri Lupé-Bouchard? He was rid of both of them. Or maybe not.

I thought I'd stick around a while to unravel the strings, to see what Henri had to do with it. Then I decided to go back to San Francisco. I didn't care much for The City anyway. It was none of my business. Sometimes it's better to leave questions. I'd reopen the office. There'd be other cases. Other clients.

Of course, there will always be other clients, wanting to hire you, for you to straighten out their lives — or for them to mess up yours. They sit on the desk, expose a little leg, and more than that. Later they talk it up. Want to be a companion, a colleague, carrying in stories and clues. Think they are the shamus. When the stories unravel and the facts don't fit, you figure they just got out of the booby hatch. Trying to explain something they don't know much about or stuck together from guesses.

In the end she comes down to a cold case.

That's the way it is. All you have to do is wait for the next one. But the money's good. And maybe Silver-Wig is still in San Francisco, after all.

the commissioner gets caught
with his pants down and proposes
scrapping the First Amendment

Well, anyway, almost everything is on schedule. In boisterous battle, Garfield engages the media once again. He is accused of favoring The City's prostitution combine, tries to dodge the charge, turns his back to the camera, buries his head beneath his coat, and hopes it will go away — or at least that he can get away without being seen.

Finally, however, the smoke of his deceit becomes coughable and he comes out from behind his no-comment, red-eyed and wheezing, nearly asphyxiated, waving a *Daily News* in a screaming (hacking) snit about the allegations.

"Irresponsible journalism," he calls it. "It is time to get beyond that First Amendment nonsense of a free press having access to police files and pris-ons. The press is no different from other citizens and one day the courts will understand this," he whines prophetically.

"Then public officials will have the freedom to get on with their jobs without intimidation from yellow journalists and other low-life that feed off the polity.

"It's not crime that has ruined The City — it's that the media insists upon reporting it and maligning those involved."

He brandishes the latest edition of *The Times*.

"You'd think The City was nothing but murder and theft and robbery and arson and rape and assault and burglary and, and . . .." he pauses to catch his breath.

"Here, this article. 'Thefts Lead Factories in Queens to Say They'll Leave.' But we know better. This is fun city. The Big Gravenstein. Maybe at times a little tart, but if it's not happening here, it's not happening. I mean, we've got Wall Street, the Twin Towers, and The Great White Way" — where historically most plays are formula contrivances of morality with young maidens, Dapper Dan heroes, and the required shady villain who must be hissed and booed.

"What the clods in Chicago think of The City depends on the media. What the media offers is mostly okay. But it doesn't get to the nitty-gritty of what we do. Just the surface. The media doesn't tell anything about the planning and hard work.

"Now, I'm not condemning those who live in Chicago, because they don't know better, or because they believe the lies. Chicago has a few worthwhile attractions. People I know who have visited tell me the Golden Gate Bridge and the Mississippi are worth seeing. But those people don't know The City. They know only what the media tells them."

E.Erie™ finds refuge
in the cluster
of the First Amendment

As it stands, le nouveau prodige E.Erie™ isn't providing much in the way of assistance. With cash appropriated from an emergency fund for "Unusual Opportunities" he has knocked out the back wall of his ante-room office, taken over the women's restroom, and installed a bank of telephones, computers, and technicians.

Meanwhile, his So What Assassin Team hangs about playing *Destruction Derby* and *Death Race* — when not menacing each other.

This year Exidy's *Death Race* is the game of choice, notable in that its release last year triggered the first U.S. video gaming panic and made Exidy a household name. *Death Race 2000* competitors, in the "Annual Transcontinental Road Race," mow down pedestrians for points. The chase-and-crash game invites players to strike stick-figure "gremlins" with on-screen cars. *Death Race* forges a strong tie between video gaming and fighting (as well as homicidal driving), in narrative, theme and reception.

Of course, as a leader, E.Erie™ ignores the pranks and projects of his hackers and phishers, and hopes eventually to lead them into action. For the last two weeks he has been deep into a statistical analysis of the frequency and the vehemence of the use of four-letter words on the three major networks since they were struck with the video virus. He has suggested that, "We're waiting for cable and digital."

Is anyone listening?

"The report will be available within the month and should give us an idea of what we are dealing with," he says, and adds a reminder that action will be slow in coming since the FCC is reluctant to impose an outright ban on teevee sex and brutality.

"We realize the anti-gore and -smut crowd has a point, and that one man's meat may be another man (or more likely, a woman), but we don't want to hassle the First Amendment. The First Amendment is a godsend. Although it is an enormous pain-in-the-ass, it also provides protection for our most ridiculous stunts. It is our duty to exploit that. To take advantage of the gap between individual freedom and harm done to the public. Remember, sex, cruelty, and greed are god given rights — naturelle à l'homme. They are linked in the DNA daisy chain of the human psyche."

one of our heroes
  dreams
Son of Sam into action

Loko growls, flips to another channel, The Young Lions, at 1:00. Tracking three story lines the film follows the activities of Christian Diestl (Marlon Brando) — a German soldier bothered by the rise of Nazism in his country and his association via the war with Noah Ackerman (Montgomery Clift) a Jewish American soldier and Michael Whiteacre (Dean Martin) a pop-singer who is coerced by a loved one (trying to get rid of him) to join up and fight for his country.

The American soldiers Ackerman and Whiteacre go through training and are eventually sent to fight. Their story is balanced by the German soldiers Diestl and Capt. Hardenberg (Maximilian Schell) attempting to reconcile the German defeat and their own unfounded beliefs in a national phil-osophy. Ultimately the forces at work are reduced to the personal as the humane qualities of Man supersede the ravages of war.

By 1:30 Loko is asleep, breathing deeply, Hans-David's flaccid aspect pasted in the byways of his dreams, spinning off the Hutchinson Parkway, the locale the Psyaint frequented (July 29, 1976) the evening he found Donna Lauria and Jody Valenti.

Tonight — this morning — he turns up the service road, docks the Galaxie and mingles with the dark along the fence on Parkway Drive. He has the name, the street, the girl, the number.

The Lieutenant stirs, rubs his nose, yawns, stretches, the number blurred. Hans-Peter blinks, sight dimmed, and then 1750 Hutchinson River Parkway, one more block, the Lieutenant in REM, the car where Sam said it would be, a scene from an earlier shoot, a maroon '69 Mercury Montego with the girl and her boyfriend in the front seat.

Psyaint David

"Both," Sam says, "both," and for just a second Hans is sorry he is not on camera, the technicians, supporting actors, aware that this may yet be his best performance. How do you know when you are doing something right? Well, you feel it. Deep down inside you feel it.

If the Lieutenant sleeps as The Prince sleeps, his dreams of a villain schooled in sadism, wielding the sword of retribution, may soon come to fruition — the full-blown child of the American delusion.

At the corner a white Lab with yellow eyes whines and lifts his leg to a wilted sapling. Relieved, he canters into the park, orange-yellow eyes, black nose, nostrils lifted, mouth opened, smoke lifting from his tongue.

Peter Lorre corrects his posture, sets his profile to the available light and whistles a few bars from *Peer Gynt.* He waits, patiently, watching, ready to shake the seas, to flood the streets, set The City on fire.

"Failure," Sam whines, "will fold down in a festival finale. A new order."

Then cries, and the watchful gaze focuses on the car. The cackle of a laugh in the night splits the moon, *Un Chien Andalou,* with indifference.

He stands on the parapet, the Star of David, the six points of destiny stamped on the buttocks of Jewish women, their German keepers stripping them, capitulating to instinct.

Sam's hand caresses the condemned breasts. On the hard, small beds and rough woolen blankets of camp shacks the women are taken with nothing to excite the copulating senses, the intimate, beyond the horror of possibly incubating incubus progeny.

The ideology of race and genetics blur, if only for a moment, and imagining they will be spared, the women submit as they must. Condemned in an attempt to preserve the spirit, their dreams, they succumb to one more violation, the Moon Maniac unbridled and hardened in a final insult.

The men, spent, send away the capitulating vessels, the loam of their stunted husbandry to the chambers from which they (the women) were momentarily called, the flesh that reminds the spirit to intercept the death march, any death march, to promote the silent distress at the source of life.

And then a broken-toothed visage, the rattle of Sam's incessant, maniacal laugh, and the sharp knifing in of fingernail-claws, the air rank with a foul breath, a bitter almond stench, the odor of incinerated hair and flesh.

The night-stalker, street-walker, behind the second car, steps into the open traffic lane, levels the .44 reflected in the bent glass window, pointed at the man on the mirror in a bullet-shaped coat and hood. One, two, three, four. The mirror shatters, the façade fractures in an opaque, gray mesh.

Then, the sound of Sam's foul breathing, followed by the click of tumblers falling over the last finely milled edge and the lock snaps open to release again, brother death's grim countenance.

Devilish deed done, Peter-David flips his epistle to Captain Borelli into the street and turns away, hearing the Lieutenant's deep breathing, the sirens in the distance and someone, a woman, he thinks, shouting "Oh, my god! Oh, my god! You animal," and a chorus on the sidewalk, swaying in the night, picking up the chant, "Kill! Kill! Kill!"

But that is the way of it. Other voices, other wor(l)ds. The Lieutenant wakes, slumped over the arm of the couch, his head throbbing. Robert Stack and Virginia Mayo are the ghosts of *Great Day in the Morning.*

The Times reports "Murder by 'Strangers' Drops in The City," and a Manhattan homicide detective notes that "The City is probably the easiest city in America to commit murder in and then get lost in the crowd."

and again the dawn
of a spring day

Sam's primed. He's had a hard night — the usual anxiety, prodding lethargy, stirring the moment into action — meritorious service, the bark of the .44 in his ears, slugs tearing in, shattering bone. He smiles, congratulates himself as David guides the Galaxie through the sprinkling of early Sunday traffic over from the Bronx to Central Park.

At 8:30 the Park glows with a heavy dew, clean, fresh temperatures in the low 50s; spring's green titillating ritual budding beneath a blue cool sky. Hans-Peter finds a bench, leans back, stretches. His eyes burn. His arms ache. His hand is bruised where the .44 kicked against his thumb.

Park walks and paths are studded with people, strolling, lounging in the sun: lovers, loners, losers, Tai Chi practitioners, a smattering of crazies, madmen, lost in unkempt gardens, searching for a rose, a violet, alone within the pleasures of insular worlds.

It's a perfect setting, the peace and tranquility of Eden, nature in a playful mood, self-indulgent, the morning rife with shouts, joggers jogging, a small circle of chimps excitedly jumping up and down, beating their fists on the ground, announcing an odyssey. Sam trots off, finds a tree, whimpers as two lighthearted gays pause near the Lock to embrace.

Predictably, the wind shifts, a cloud shrouds the nubile sun and drops a chill on the morning. A couple of Puerto Rican heavies emerge with sawed-off pool cues, on a "Never fear/Beat a queer" excursion, and rain a shower of blows on the lovers, beating them into a sprawled, motionless mass of torn flesh and blood.

A discarded copy of *The Times* lying on a bench, page 67, carries an article on the Winchester County Dartgun Sniper. In six months twenty-two women have been hit by steel darts shot through open windows. Sheriff Thomas Delany is puzzled. Experts say it points to a man in deep conflict with his mother. A woman hater. Of course we've heard this before. David listens to the click of the gun, the frantic, panicked screams.

By early afternoon Sam's Son is again in the hall of the Mountain King, ensconced in his Pineview haven, with a horde of bickering trolls. Three of them are fighting over the single eye they are condemned to share, must pass around, in a never ending cycle of button, button, it's my turn with the eye. Of course, both sight and insight are limited.

Still, it's not a single vision they hope for, not even a privileged vision, but the small power of who can control what is seen — or to be seen.

A little later the long-nosed Troll hags and their quarreling brats join the fray. But otherwise, nothing serious here.

Mayor Beame
  dons a beany
to stamp out smut

At the annual luncheon of the Chamber of Commerce and Industry, Tex James, president and publisher of *The Daily News*, revisits the Commissioner's sentiments about the Big Apple. Tex entreats those gathered at the Waldorf Astoria for lunch to lobby the Chamber's seventeen hundred member companies to stay in The City for the next five years.

"When a company leaves The City it opens another wound drawing our vital juices. This hemorrhaging must cease."

Very nearly as an answer to James' treatise, in support of and in response to Garfield, determined to get his thumb in the publicity pudding, Beame shuffles on to 7th Avenue between 42nd and 43rd Streets, dons a whirlybird hat given to him by a cast member of *Godspell*, and joins the actors of twenty-five Broadway productions for an anti-smut rally. They're marching, protesting pornography. Even the cast of the nude review *Oh! Calcutta* joins in — dressed. One wears a yellow Lord Fauntleroy costume.

With hustling-a-buck scenery dissolving in the distance behind him the Mayor cavorts into the street and recites a soliloquy, a dramatic monologue of cold hard cash.

> Today and today and today
> seeps into Times Square
> until at last we reclaim
> the streets for the citizens
> of The City of the Gods.
> We reclaim it for the men
> and women who legitimately
> in their hearts and with their bodies
> do business here, who pay
> their taxes and contribute
> to The City's economy,
> and who will help Times Square
> in its petty march into the shadows
> of safe days and wealthy nights.
> (The New York Times – sort of)

Gerald Shoenfeld, chairman of Stamp Out Smut, says, "I think the public is finally understanding pornography in all its forms."

Sam chuckles. That should keep a few businesses in town.

In the afternoon, Beame and Garfield visit the besieged Mack-Allied Corporation in Queens to assuage, with promises and other political balms, the anguish of a business which is about to be aborted by repeated attacks from youth gangs. Garfield points out, in deference to his uninformed boys in blue, that businessmen tend to "overdramatize" (usually in three acts, with an excessive budgets and agreeable reviews) the extent of the crime by youth gangs, and adds that the police have no evidence of gangs directed by adults.

Business leaders reply, however, that reconnoitering employees have reported atavistic gatherings and numerous and distant campfires with dancers flashing among the flames.

Marcia Dismeten of 1621 Holbeck Avenue, a driver for Mack, reports hearing drumbeats punctuated by sporadic gunfire, and seeing painted symbols of half-human, -serpent creatures on brick walls. Her neighbor Reinia Glotto of 1623, who does not work for Mack, confides that she has found druidic stone configurations among the muck and debris of the vacant lot near her house. Chance alone will not explain this. Marcia thinks god had something to do with it.

The next night three Mack-Allied Schäferhunds, caged in the company compound's ten-foot barbed-razor-wire fence to protect the property are speared and excoriated, their hides stretched on the fence to dry — the head and legs and entrails of one found in a nearby campsite, its remainder of bones baked black in the ashes.

Marvin Wolfe of the Mack-Allied Corporation adds his cry-in-the-desert with a letter to the Editor of *The Times* in which, as a corporate right-to-lifer he claims, "Our company has a right to live."

Our Lady gets
a new set
of Wi-Fi vibes

Keener winces.

"Things are going to get a lot worse before they get better," he tells Our Lady of the Classy Chassis.

She agrees and admits that she is still without revealing insights. This job is tougher than she thought. Her visions have fallen on hard times, and while she didn't expect to locate the Son immediately, she imagined, envisioned she might by now have a path leading to the edge of the wilderness. Then, too, her sensors are misbehaving, malfunctioning, intercepting strange and unrelated ramblings and events.

"I'm off-channel right now. Shortwave from some place called Yankee

Stadium.

"Does this have to do with Yankee Doodle Dandy?

"Mostly mumbling and shouts. Nothing distinct — just motherfucker this and motherfucker that. Somebody always threatening to kick somebody's ass. Idiots flaunting their egos. I don't know why, if they're not serious, why they don't give it up. But they're probably no better at fucking than they are at fighting. So who cares?

"Then the Cooke thing. For three days," she tells Keener, "I tailed around with that senile celibate, that finial fop, for three days, not even waiting for a resurrection or re-erection, thinking I was on to something. For all the good it did.

"Then several days ago, between an old *Lucy Show* and a couple of gunfights from *The High Chaparral*, I hooked in on a death leap on West End Avenue. Some turkey named Oric Bovar."

She pauses reflectively.

"I met him last year. I mean, he was not without credentials. A mystic, an astrologer — had a friend Alexandros Hatzitheodorou who died. They were sitting around smoking — apparently they had some good stuff — and Hatzitheodorou decides to fly around the block. He went out the window flapping his arms."

"On the tenth floor, and Bovar didn't try to stop him?"

"No. Bovar said, 'Hell, I thought he could make it.'

"Bovar also thought he (Bovar) was Jesus Christ and could resurrect Hatzitheodorou. He hauled the body back up to the tenth floor and worked on it for a week, trying to get Lazarus on his feet, before they took the cadaver away. By then it had decomposed and the neighbors were threatening action."

"That's not much," Frazer says. "What else?"

"I don't know. Death leaps and more old *Lucy* shows. The other day I broke in on a Sabbath in Yonkers."

She frowns. The weakness of her vision seems to be outdone only by the failings of her erotic evocations. She's mildly distressed.

The noble and dull Crocker has tried to palm her off on Kojak, who in turn, and not without a customary smart-ass retort, suggested she find a place where her talents might be appreciated — that he never did have much for the handicapped, for cripples, and, anyway, she needs to clean up her act, improve her connections, find something better to do than stroking cops. Heard this before?

"Who is this creature, anyway?" she prods Keener.

"Oh, that's a long story. Right now I wouldn't pay any attention to him. He's been under a lot of pressure lately."

But that's only the beginning. She is having real trouble imagining the killer. Questions mount.

"Is the killer a killer when he does not have the means or desire to kill?"

she asks. "Is he a killer when he is not killing? If someone was to take away his gun, would he still be a killer? What if he lost a hand, or both hands?

"What if there is no body? Missing people are not always dead, even when we think they are. And what about those we think are still alive who are dead? What does it mean to be dead? When are we dead?"

Keener doesn't know.

"Eventually this will make sense," he tells her. "Your visions will make sense."

Still, she's lovely. Parades around in a black Fishnet Merrywidow and a low-rise Chantilly lace thong. As much as anyone, the Captain has enjoyed Our Lady of Flagrant Favors, takes delight in her kinky lines, now stretches the thong a bit, slips his hand in, hoping for another clue, a riddle or two.

Of course, she's petulant, feeling unloved and warms to his touch.

"Nothing works out," she says, her hand exploring his possibilities. "There's more than I'm seeing."

"Maybe we're not reading it correctly," Keener suggests, pressing his face to the soft mounds of her sweetly scented offerings.

"I seldom have a vision of place, of specific place. Just a green mountain-side. But it could be anywhere. Germany, Norway — even here on the island. Just trees and clouds, a river far below."

She unzips the captain's fly with nimble, well-practiced fingers.

"Does it resemble Central Park?"

"No, no," she tells the Chief. She pauses — tries to think. "The sound-track is off. I'm definitely out of synch."

the chief has serious reservations

Keener nods appreciatively. The lady befriended him, took him in, be-came his confidant when no one else would. He has, however, of late, come to suspect there is more to it.

The City carries 648 licensed detectives on the register and boasts another five thousand or so more who operate without benefit of City Hall's imprimatur — not to mention the tens of thousands of specifically suspicious, and the countless generally distrusting stalkers skulking about the streets and alleys following each other in an eternal carousel of paranoia. It is no wonder Our Lady of Audacious Activities is having difficulties — considering the competition. Getting a piece of the sleuthing action can be tough.

Then too, of late, her habits have become increasingly affected. The Chief has noticed her despondency, aware only that it is accompanied by a collection of what he believes to be tell-tale artifacts, the bits and pieces of herself that she seems intent upon rearranging.

She's taken a new apartment with a strange hoary decor, a plush arrangement of four rooms of Egyptian tapestries, ancient vases; a dim and lovely chamber devoid of the accouterments of modern technology and gadgetry — dim and dusty and damp, quietly haunting and tomblike.

She has been more reclusive, content to isolate herself to the company of a foul-smelling one hundred ten pound Alaskan Grey Wolf named Lupanar that nervously prowls the five rooms. She remains reluctant to talk about the changes, or the animal, and says only that she is "hoping for something to tell her she is still alive." Beyond this, she admits nothing, will not say, even, where she got the animal, although Keener suspects she lifted it from the Bronx Zoo.

But tonight, still petulant, she has the Chief in hand, her tongue teasing him, a soft rumbling deep in her throat. He's lying limply with one leg across hers, his knee pressed to her fur, her tongue toying with his ear. She will not entertain his apprehensions — has her mind on other voices — the Chief's pants down to his knees, her hands locked firmly to his staff, a just barely audible of someone whistling in the background.

> There was a lady who had no eyes
> She went abroad to view the skies;
> She saw a tree with an apple on it,
> She took no apples,
> Yet left no apples on it.
> (Traditional)

He thinks it has something to do with her 45th Street film operation, her latest venture into the business world, and regrets having thought of her, even in jest, as a cripple.

"You need a night on the town," Frazer tells her. "You've been holed up too long. You should get out and see the sights."

He pauses awkwardly.

"I mean, well, at least you could listen to the sights."

But there is more. Moments later, on the bedroom stage, she whispers, lips and legs parted properly, inviting.

"Oh, talk to me," she begs in her best deep-throated Dietrich intonation. "Tell me what you will do to me. Will you hurt me? It makes me feel alive.

"Oh, yes, and how much we will make? Oh, Ohhh. Yes, yes, Oh. Ohhhhooo."

But this is a quickie. The Captain's fountain flowing, gushing, spent. He too is over the hump and pulls up his pants. As if by plan, she takes his hand and promptly leads him to the door.

"We need luck on this one," the Captain says. "Good luck."

Our Lady of Glamourous Graft muses.

"But Captain, what good would that do? Even if we ask 'What is good?' would you not agree that what is good for you may not be good for me?"

Keener is stymied. It is not clear to him where the argument is going.

"Oh Captain! My Captain!" she says, "we'll have better days. I'll have something more substantial next time. Remember, we ride the victor ship. The prize we seek is one."

She listens wistfully as he goes down the hall.

"Next time will be better," she calls after him. "We'll get into the kinky stuff. Maybe gerbils and knotted ribbons. Be sure to bring your handcuffs. The kind without a key."

Yes, times will be better. Spring blooms in her bosom, the summer a watermark, a mirage on the leaves of her flimsy calendar. She knows enough to suspect that the rift between the Lieutenant and his exec-pro has widened.

"The schmuck," she says to herself with a wide, warm smile.

And herein lies the makings of an intrigue, a coupling diabolique. If she has her way, it will go off like a MRV. And along with the object of her inspection, her affair-haired boy, she'll extract a smattering of what has for centuries been considered virtue. The anomaly she has taken on as a quirk, an idiosyncratic preference, a character trait, indulged in and enjoyed by the world — the pleasure of revenge.

the in-house teevee
develops historical
prurient interests

In a stroke of wizardry, the in-house teevee at the 9th or 11th does a late season shift, cancels the remaining three episodes of the hit soap opera, *The Loves and Lusts of Catherine the Great,* a series of inventive ribald and raucous romances featuring the lives of powerful women in history who took pleasure wherever they could find it. Naturally, the boys-in-blue who have come to depend upon the in-house system to view the world (as it is) are astounded by a view of the world as it really is.

"Just watching the old broads fornicate with donkeys, I've been better able to understand the whores on my beat," one ground-pounder says. "Man, take away those shows and you take away the heart of American life."

Par usual, not everyone is happy. Complaints roll in. Sixty-nine precincts report. They don't like the changes.

"You'd expect this from NBC or ABC, but not from SAMIE. I mean, this really screws up my epistemic awareness," one complains. "I know it goes on, but how can we face the people who do not like cops when they know what we do?"

The problem, however, appears endemic. What is expected of the B's and C's, they are more than willing to provide. On orders from high, with a surreptitious nod from E.Erie™, Winslow Olson, an Emmy winner in 1976, in the best of the Joe Pyne tradition, leaps twelve steps from his usual patter and banter interviews with grunting faces, and adopts a strident, abusive format of sexual insinuations with which to intimidate his guests.

The first bosom to suffer his shtick is Sally Stack, the newest starlet-heroine of ABC's prime time sex comedy, *Stick It to Sally*.

With a somber but interested face Winslow offers a probing question.

"How much of your stardom and success do you owe to your big tits and all the network brass you've been screwing?"

The blonde and gutsy Ms. Stack smiles, an engaging, how-about-that smile, unbuttons her blouse and unharnesses her 38-D's, takes the now silent Winslow's hands in hers, presses his clammy fingers to her luscious, large russet nips and says, "What do you think Mr. Olson?"

Well, the audience loves it.

Sally loves it.

Winslow loves it, and there is a demand for more.

Two nights later, in keeping with the futuristic theme, adhering to the adage that duty is whatever catches and molds the eye of the beholder, the news programs on the three networks, in a clip of superbly fortunate footage, run and rerun at five, six, seven, ten, ten-thirty and eleven (with invitations to those with queasy constitutions to avert their eyes) the open air rape and strangulation of twelve-year-old Constantia Magelenda on a fifth floor fire escape of a south Bronx tenement by a band of somewhat disenfranchised minority youth.

come back,
   Telly, Telly,
come back

Still, *Kojak* is leaving The City.

Fatso gets a few lines on page three of *The Daily News*, repeating the obvious.

"You can't buy the stuff you have here in The City for all the wonga in the world. How are you going to fake the Fulton Fish Market or steaming sewer caps and the hustle and bustle?" he boasts.

In a telegram to Telly, Patrolman's Benevolent Ass. Pres. Sam Inella notes that "We need a teevee Lieutenant in The City. Your performance, in its authentic portrayal of a City cop, has received the appreciation of The City's finest. Stay here, Telly. We need you."

In 1974 Savalas received a plaque from PC Garfield for his efforts on behalf of The City Police Department and was honored the same year by the Society of Professional Investigators. At a police demonstration at W. 52nd Street and 7th Avenue in September of 1976, he was hoisted to the shoulders of protesting off duty cops and paraded around.

"Television always needs a cop show, that's for sure," Telly says. "And this is an interesting cop, a real cop from the The City streets. I come from a tough neighborhood. I used to be a 'Dirty Greek.' But my father always said to me, 'When you grow up and realize what your heritage means, then they'll need a permit to speak to you.'"

Cops on the street do not necessarily agree with either of them.

"I don't give a damn what Lohmann does," one homicide detective says. "They cram a month's investigation into an hour — or fifty-four minutes. It can't be viewed as realistic. Now *Barney Miller*, that's another story. We have every one of those guys in our squad."

But *Barney Miller* is filmed on the West Coast — and *Barnaby Jones*?

Walter Wood, the movie producer who heads The City's movie and television office, insists that economics is not the reason for moving *Kojak*. More than that, he promises The City will do three hundred million nuggets of movie and television business this season. Among the planned productions is a three-hour Frank Sinatra film for NBC entitled *Contact on Cherry Street*, the story of a detective and the Italian-Jewish-Greek Syndie in which someone absentmindedly remembers *From Here to Eternity*.

It's a sensitive cop-on-the-street beat who truly loves his fellow man, except those he blows away with a shotgun in a moment of rage for having dissembled someone else he truly loved. A loving story of crazy cops and sane gangsters, a lower East Side drama set on the waves of unhinged minds warring over the take.

"A twenty-five-million-dollar production of *Superman* is to be filmed in The City," Wood shouts off-mic as the camera dollies away.

the PC is paranoid - or is he?

As with most things in The City, it's easy come easy go. Within the year *Kojak* will be cancelled and Garfield suspects his act, likewise, will be scrubbed. He talks about it, now, talks about little else, this, and his PR campaign: what might be done, what has not worked.

"When the media is misbehaving," he says, "it is very difficult to get to our audience. It's like sending a messenger through enemy lines. Only 10 percent of the truth makes it. Of course people believe what we want them to believe, but we have to get our message through.

"Following a Soap wedding, the studio fills with wedding gifts. How many time is Allison MacKenzie assaulted in the parking lot or the grocery store because the bitch in *Payton Place* is mistreating her lover. The old ladies think she's Mia Farrow.

"People talk to their teevees. Sometimes they yell. 'That's not true. You're fucking lying.' But they still believe what they hear and see. I mean, we're dealing with the bottom 90 percent. And in the real world that's not much to shoot at."

Twice in recent weeks, supported by E.Erie™'s assurances, Garfield has gone on radio, the one avenue, he believes, still open. He bought time slots

Psyaint David

with dollars from Police One's slush fund, only to find that he's out of synch.

A program, in his best voice, something of John Huston's gravel, wizened, wheezing whisper, on which he applauds the Beame regime, his (Garfield's) office, the efforts of the police to apprehend the shapeshifter, as well as a multitude of other unimpressive administrative personages, when aired, in a rather bold, heartless display of bubbling duplicity, sounds pretentious, withered, maniacal, and suspiciously untrustworthy.

The matters of which he speaks, the actual words on the air, are not only not what he had in mind, but trite and redundant explanations of his mundane posturing. The context, text, and texture, is scattered and incoherent. A smarter man might understand the significance of the betrayal. But not The Garfield. His is a special kind of paranoia.

"What we say is misunderstood," he whines. "The words just don't mean the same thing to different people."

And he has the uncomfortable premonition, as all politicals do, that the specter, the phantom in the mist, the murky somewhere, is not only out to get him, but will get him.

Hans-David asks Sam
to quiet the dogs

Still, times are slow. Spring shows signs of sauntering into the sweltering sweat and soot-stained suns of summer with Peter-David approaching his desert days. It is time for contemplation, a bottle of Perrier (Bernard Villemot, *La femme noire*, 1977)

> Femme nue, femme noire
> Je chante ta beauté
> qui passe, forme
> que je fixe dans l'Eternel
> Avant que le destin jaloux ne te
> réduise en cendres pour nourrir
> les racines de la vie.
> (Léopold Sédar Senghor)

Debbie Harry (*Blondie*) is booked at Hilly Kristal's former biker bar, the Punk Rock, New Wave venue, CBGB. The best thing about CBGB is the music from the psycho-side where nobody can sing, nobody can play, but everybody can weird. The dive/bar is a cavern of red and yellow and green and black and blue fliers, stickers, and graffiti holding up the walls.

Harry is to appear in the flesh and promises to perform with aplomb. Which is more than likely. Even when she's obnoxious and spaced-out, she offers an amusing, but not condescending wink with a zombie's voice — seductive and wooden at the same time.

Darlin' darlin' darlin'
I can't wait to hear you
Remembering your love
Is nothing without you in the flesh

Went walking one day
On the Lower East Side
Met you with a girlfriend
You were so divine

Ooh, warm and soft
In the flesh
Ooh, close and hot
In the flesh
Ooh

> (Stewart, et al.)

Tonight for those captivated by romantic memories, old music at the Café Carlyle offers a pleasant way to drift into the past of Sammy Davis, Jr. and Joey Bishop sipping blithely from martinis and crooning old jazz standards while tuxedoed waiters light the cigarettes of starlets Dixie Virginia Carter, Elaine Stritch, Judy Collins, Barbara Cook or Eartha Kitt.

Although the club originally attracted young Upper East Side swells, today songs like "I Get a Kick Out of You" and "Body and Soul" are for older out-of-towners who show up as they might for a Broadway show, giving the old John F. Kennedy hangout an aura of nostalgia.

Beneath the colorful music-themed murals of French artist Marcel Vertés cabaret singer Bobby Short is at the piano to make it an "I've Got You on My Mind" evening. Bobby croons,

My story is much too sad to be told
But practically everything
Leaves me totally cold
The only exception I know is the case
When I'm out on a quiet spree
Fighting vainly the old ennui
And I suddenly turn and see
Your fabulous face

I get no kick from champagne
Mere alcohol doesn't thrill me at all
So tell me why should it be true
That I get a kick out of you
I get a kick every time I see
You standing there before me

Psyaint David

> I get a kick though it's clear to see
> You obviously do not adore me
> (Porter)

Beyond old-time entertainment, however, there's a drift for retuning, for a restructuring of plot. It is time for those who must to philosophize, to consider their fate, rue the day without a way out. Yes, and a time for penitence. But not the sack-cloth-and-ashes variety. No pained-pounding of the chest or harsh mea culpa here. This is a nobler variety, still, a heart sorrowed and laden with the eternal burden, a madness driving the Psyaint to a slow but certain martyrdom.

For the first time in weeks David rests comfortably, encouraged, prepared to push on with the plan. He pulls a chair to the window looking out over the Hudson, and with pencil and paper takes to authorship — prepared to embellish the story with a newly ordained apostolic narrative.

the Second Epistle
of Psyaint David
to Sam Carr

David, the Son of Sam, and prisoner
of his most revered word, to Samuel Carr
the voice by which he lives:
life be with you, as in death.
2 We give thanks to Sam and seek inspiration
in his name, and brought to remind you
that I have charged you to quiet the voices
3 which you possess. Again I must encourage you
if we are to have peace and rest.
4 I have asked you kindly to stop the dog
from howling all day long, yet it continues
to do so. I have pleaded with you.
5 I told you that it is destroying my family —
we have no peace and rest.
6 Of course, now I know what kind of a person
you are, and what kind of a family you are.
7 You are cruel and inconsiderate,
you have no love for any other human being.
8 You are selfish Mr. Carr. My life is destroyed now.
I have nothing to lose anymore.
I can see there shall be no peace
9 in my life or in my family's life until I end yours.
You wicked evil man — child of the devil!
10 I curse you and your family forever.

11 I pray to god that he takes your whole family
off the face of this earth. People like you
11 should not be allowed to live on this planet.
12 Peace be with you and love from the darkness.

Satisfied with its tone, the details, the delicacies of written communication, he reads it aloud, twice, three times, listens to the words echoing
in the empty apartment, in the canyons.

Still, it sounds convincing, the murmurings beneath the words, things
left unsaid. Certainly, nothing is simple, not Sam's advice, nor satisfaction,
not even escape. He folds the letter and places it in an envelope, ready for
another face with a smear of red above one eye that is now an open wound.

confidence restored
David seeks a new venue

*And so, at last, at last, they piece together fragments, leavings, evidence,
establish task force O-Mega, prepare to gather resources and take pursuit.
The hunter, now, the hunted, tracked and driven, as yet unknown and
faceless, invisible, a phantom riding the wind, to blow, to float freely among
them, to appear again, by whim, circling The City — the numinous laughing
as they pass on the street, the hiding they go seek, who does not reveal his
name, his nature, leaves no clues, no pattern or plan, who taunts them with
a harsh dog's bark then disappears into the night.*

*And now they wait for me, Sam's protégé, to make my first mistake, to
hand my life to them, as others have. Their footsteps fall beyond my door,
the face of night etched on the walls, a dim sun, the single eye of madness,
their hot breath, until it is time to take flight, and give them what they seek.*

*O-Mega men beware, in flight the Psyaint sees with night eyes,
sharpened, alerted for every detail, recorded, set in memory, and may yet,
in the hunted and haunted invent another escape, an avoidance of
extinction's needle — teeth clamped tightly on the spinal cord, the neck —
massive jaws shaking the prey until the bone snaps and pain courses
through the brain into the eyes in bright and blinding blossoms of red and
white. Or he may not, and choose to stand firmly, a flame in Death's eye,
arrogant, prepared to defy my despair and theirs.*

Sam recalls his quests
  as celebrated
  in *Paradise Lost*
and *Fleurs du Mal*

Art is, however, always art, and Sam drops in at Columbia University for
a bit of psycho-quibbling, "The Personification of Evil in *Paradise Lost* and
Les Fleurs du mal" with literary scholar and Columbia Professor Travis

Psyaint David

Berman.

The audience is small, colleagues, friends, fellows, students. A quiet gathering with chit-chat before the lecture: observations, esotery laced with literary allusions — reverence for the esteemed and honorable Dr. Berman. Most have read *Paradise Lost* and *Fleurs du mal* years before, several times, then again, with an article or two, the critical appraisal of Barker, C. S. Lewis and various French writers on Baudelaire.

At his appointed time, Professor Berman, a burly man with a great moustache and bulldog countenance, a tuff of grey hair above either ear, a bright dome shining in the light, mounts the podium, spreads copious notes upon the lectern, clicks his teeth, and begins.

"It is a rare occasion, indeed, when the genius of an entire century is located in the talent of one man, not once but twice. And as unlikely as that may seem, it is not too early to proclaim those men as John Milton and Charles Baudelaire. For the genius of the seventeenth century in England is, in fact, Milton's genius. His life spanned the middle part of those one hundred years, beginning a literary career in 1629 and culminating in 1674."

Sam enters unnoticed, finds a seat near the door, relaxes and pulls a cigarette from the air. It's comforting to know men such as Dr. Berman are at the gate, the caretakers.

"And the same can be said of Baudelaire," Professor Berman continues. "He lived from 1821 to 1867. The political events and social upheaval of those years in France have been voluminously documented.

"What," Dr. Berman queries, "of their centuries did these two geniuses see to personify Satan? Surely not the benevolence of authority — the need and the ability of man to rebel? Well, maybe so. But what especially of rebellion?

"To better understand we need look more closely at religious Europe — the concept of Divine Right, the plan of God for man as Europeans saw it and how, in revolutionary times, a subject of the monarchy might fit or not fit into the scheme of things."

A pleasant, inauspicious introduction which a moment later takes a seditious turn.

Berman approaches Augustine for a beginning.

"'The human race is the Devil's fruit tree, his own property, from which he may pick his fruit. It is a plaything of demons. Evil is nothing, since God makes everything that is, and God did not make evil.'"

So there's no evil? Does this make sense?

Sam is pleased, then annoyed.

"Have all the years, the centuries been for naught?" he whines.

Indeed, Berman sounds a discordant note, pinches a nerve. Sam squirms in the yoke of old arguments — Augustinian bogus banterings upon which the religions of the West rest. Another bleeding wart. Sam's face contorts, an expression he wears for centuries. Some wounds never heal.

He mumbles, piqued by the inventions. Augustine's thought god could not help but create good. So he could not have created evil. Why not tell the truth? Am I coeval with the good? Or am I also the good?

The smoke is thick.

A gaunt and nervous female settles on the seat at his side, liberates a True from its blue box, pinches off the filter to get to the nitty-gritty, lights up and with the aid of a seven-inch holder, puffs a noxious cloud into the air.

Sam's eyes dim, irritated with the affront, the maledictions men heap on him. He didn't come here to hear monarchs and gods praised. He stands, hand in the air, prepared to correct the record, and discovers, of a habit acquired in a time long lost, that at the moment words fail him, syllables will not form. He drops to his seat, into his abyss of discontent and loathing. Too easily he is reminded these days of the failures; the frauds and falsehoods, the malice of revenge he has not yet properly contrived — the deceits and lies, his stock and trade to serve a sorry end.

His eyes are clouded with a gray film, barely visible.

"I'll last as long as man," he tells the woman puffing Trues.

She isn't listening.

"When humans disappear I will still be here. When they return I will be here to greet them. I am the imperfection of the amalgamation of matter and consciousness," Sam says.

The Professor continues, skims over a spate of theories, observations.

"We find Satan first in Milton,

> So stretched out huge in length the arch-fiend lay,
> Chained on the burning lake; nor ever thence
> Had risen or heaved his head, but that the will
> And high permission of all-ruling Heaven
> Left him at large to his own dark designs,
> That with reiterated crimes he might
> Heap on himself damnation, while he sought
> Evil to others.

Sam guffaws. The True woman squirms. Berman consults Baudelaire.

"In the poem 'Au lecteur' ('To the Reader') that prefaces *Les Fleurs du mal*, Baudelaire accuses his readers of hypocrisy of being as guilty of sins and lies as the poet.

> ...If rape or arson, poison or the knife
> Has wove no pleasing patterns in the stuff
> Of this drab canvas we accept as life —
> It is because we are not bold enough!

Psyaint David

Sam's mumbling.

"But Baudelaire also said that 'It would be difficult for me not to conclude that the most perfect type of masculine beauty is Satan, as portrayed by Milton.'"

Then a few lines from "Les Litanies de Satan" to support the point and assure the audience that he (Berman) has done his homework.

> Ô toi, le plus savant et le plus beau des Anges,
> Dieu trahi par le sort et privéde louanges,
> Ô Prince de l'exil, à qui l'on a fait tort
> Et qui, vaincu, toujours te redressesplus fort,
> Toi qui, pour consoler l'homme frêle qui souffre,
> Nous appris à mêler le salpêtre et le soufre.

Perspiring, baldhead aglow, Berman rambles on for an hour in and out of literary theories, psychological anomalies, then concludes, with another passage from *Paradise Lost.*

> Of four infernal rivers that disgorge
> Into the burning Lake their baleful streams;
> Abhorred Styx the flood of deadly hate,
> Sad Acheron of sorrow, black and deep;
> Cocytus, nam'd of lamentation loud
> Heard on the rueful stream; fierce Phlegethon
> Whose waves of torrent fire inflame with rage.
> Far off from these a slow and silent stream,
> Lethe the River of Oblivion rolls
> Her wat'ry Labyrinth whereof who drinks,
> Forthwith his former state and being forgets,
> Forgets both joy and grief, pleasure and pain.

Berman receives a warm round of applause and pronounces, "I will entertain questions."

But Sam is not appeased. He squirms, waits his turn, a lull, a dying moment in the conversation when Berman is about to thank those in the audience for their kind response.

"To my mind," Sam says, standing, demanding, with a basket of words in the haze. "Several points should be clarified — certain matters you seem to ignore.

"I cannot speak for a hypocrite like Milton, but for myself, the attitudes he attributes to me, if I may take the liberty, are, at times, a mockery, mere sketches. The reasons for this are many, but at the source it has to do with the idiosyncratic twist of the Christian mind.

"I do not betray anyone. I make the obvious, obvious. God does not have anything to do with it. Man will destroy himself with or without god. I cannot help him."

But the lights have dimmed, Professor Berman collects his notes, steps down.

The audience stands, migrates slowly to the ends of the rows, gathers in groups of two's and three's, a few quiet remarks, handshakes, small talk and soft laughter. Quietly, slowly the room clears. The professor exits with friends, a student or two, and the room is silent — almost.

Sam's holding up a battered and scarred 1777 Robert Bell copy of *Paradise Lost.*

Over a century after the first publication of Paradise Lost in London, the Philadelphia printer Robert Bell, perhaps inspired by the Revolution, ignored British copyright and published this two-volume edition of Milton's work. This is the extremely rare first American edition, in contemporary sheep binding with a frontispiece portrait engraving by John Norman, to which a previous owner has added a moustache in ink. Milton had long enjoyed a high reputation in this country.

Sam is reciting.

> With what delight could I have walked thee round,
> If I could joy in ought–sweet interchange,
> Of hill and valley, rivers, woods, and plains.
> Now land, now sea, and shores and forests crowned,
> Rocks, dens and caves! But I'm none of these
> Fine places of refuge; and the more I see
> Pleasure about me, so much more I feel
> Torment within me, as from the hateful siege
> Of contraries; all good to me becomes
> Bane, and in Heaven much worse would be my state.

Sam chortles. Just helping humans adjust to heaven turning into hell — pleasure for despair.

"From the beginning it has been beyond the Christian mind to imagine or appreciate a world without warring factions. It is in the metaphor of armies, they form, spawn and spew their visions. The Christian mind does not understand that evil is not an invention, but a discovery, not a creation damned to what I am, without power to create, and cannot disarm the contradiction of omnipotence, the figure of a godhead limited to what it is and what it cannot be.

"Conveniently, to avoid contraries, Christians call one mystery, the other nonsense. It is to them that two creators might exist coevally a nonsense, but reducing the number to one, a mystery.

"Whether one, the other, or both are before creation is not impossible to comprehend. Still, thinking creates its opposite, spinning nonsense out of mystery."

His eyes glow.

"That's the mystery of nonsense.

"Augustine believed before he thought, despite the tenor of his life. His belief was the nonsense of one uncreated all-good being creating another that is not. Doesn't a flaw in creation signify a flaw in the creator? Two bits of nonsense in one. That good, in deficiency of the Christian mind, might spawn evil — as if a serpent in its own absence might copulate with a Wyvern and bring forth a hybrid offspring that was neither serpent nor Wyvern."

The audience files out and drifts away. Students depart, the nervous, gaunt female with the extended cigarette holder connects with Dr. Berman in the hall. The janitors push in, take up the folding chairs and stack them on carts. One carries a broom, a radio on his belt. The sounds of an all-night rock-station echo in the room.

"A misconception," Sam says, "about what I am, over the centuries, my place, my position today. Once I would have accepted nonbeing, rather than serve, or so Milton thought, when in truth, it is ennui, I would say, that carries — that enlivens me. I do not see death as virtue, nor as salvation."

He pauses, patient still, as the janitors push the carts into the hall. In the distance a siren wails.

"Milton's arguments, the words he attributes to me, served their time well, but are now, specious at best — and, then, again, absurd. Imagine with me, once more, that good comes of evil. That torture of the soul, an excessive demand for pleasure: lust, greed, pride and envy produce art, leaders of nations — discoveries by which the world profits. Yes, he gives me words, and yet does me more benefit than harm. My reputation is advanced, my honor enlarged. My legions grow as humankind comes to love itself and what it cannot but be."

The last janitor out snaps off the lights, closes the door. The key turns in the lock, and for a long moment in the silent sense, the imminent presence of the netherworld, of not quite quieted despair, the bright end of a cigarette glowing, a microscopic sun in a vast nothing of deep, cold vacuum remains — and two small flames waver with contemplative, eternal discontent and discomfort.

how little girls are made

An eye for an eye, the rude reckoning of impulse to correct and rectify by recompense or punishment, acts that threaten honor, name, and order.

I am watching Sam's house for movement. The fiends want girls. Sugar and spice and everything nice. That's one of Sam's favorite sayings. Then they begin to yell.

"Get them! Get them!"

the last great commandment

Newly created for the evening, Hans-David rides the elevator down, comes out into the cool air. The weather is nearly perfect, a positive sign ending the Psyaint's long winter, the sleet and snow of doubt. The Palisades are tinted green, the seed germinating, sprung loose, hull split, embryo swollen. The earth is warm, moist, steaming, sap running in the heartwood.

He feels strong, relaxed, alert, and confident. He knows what he must do, prepared to spread himself into The City. The great commandment: Love Thyself Above All Else. Self-love is true debauchery, (Camus).

the Psyaint stumbles
into a domestic dispute

Below Pine Street the Hudson is swollen. To the North the sky opens, laced with stars. It is cooler in the early evening. Cars pass on Glenwood Avenue and a block from Pineview Towers David stops to listen as Alsea Alburton, with the strum und drang of a praecō in Nero's Rome, announces from her front porch, that weekend frivolities may now commence.

Alsea is a large woman with puffed red eyes and frizzed red hair. Since early afternoon she has been parading about her small house in an oversized faded red-cotton-print housedress and pink bunny bedroom slippers, while sipping a concoction of cheap wine and vodka. She has been roaming the rooms fanning the fumes of her feud with the city of Yonkers. She believes, despite the city's disclaimers, that the water coming into her house is contaminated. All of her house plants have died and her kitchen wares — pots and pans — have developed a hardened crust on the edges and handles that she has been unable to remove.

Frustrated and infuriated with trying to combat the corrosion, as a demonstration, offering evidence to the court, she hauls a box of her corrupted pans and deceased plants into the city manager's office, drops them on his desk and announces that "This is the result of using the Yonkers' piss you put in my pipes."

The manager, a large black-haired man with a pulp nose and glasses, chewing the butt of a sodden cigar, observes the box and its contents. After a long moment, he takes one of the wilted bronze stems in his thick fingers.

"What did the autopsy show?" he asks, and then tells Alsea that if she does not promptly vacate the premises he will toss her "ass into the street," and if it bounces twice he will arrest her for littering and loitering.

The following month she refuses to pay her water bill and the city shuts off her water. She retaliates by tossing her garbage and stool into the street. A week later the neighbors swear out a warrant against her.

Tonight she is drunk, the tinder of malevolence kindled anew, her contempt and fury focused on the personage of her husband, Orlando, who she believes has sided with the city.

She drifts down the steps to the walk beneath a street light, a shotgun cradled in the crook of her arm. Hans-David watches from a short distance, listens to her command, demand from back of the stage, that the man come out of the house as she says, and "face the music."

An old tune it is, her voice wailing in the footlights of night, in vaulting of the trees, floats out over the audience and drops on the river.

In a moment of austere silence, the ultimatum echoes and dies, the screen door immobile, reluctant to surrender its contents.

"Your time is up," she shouts. "It's time you answer for your crimes, you chicken-fucker."

Again she shouts, "Orlando, you goddam turd, get out here in the street with the rest of the shit." She smiles as David passes, whispers a soft, pleasant maternal, "Hello."

Tonight her face is caked with a white powder-paste, her red eyes painted with circles of orange blush.

twas slithy and the brillig groves
did gimble and gyre in the wabe
all bimsy were the borotoves

The night is calm. A balmy 64, wind out of the northwest at 7, barometer 29.99 and rising. David points the Galaxie south, circles slowly, cruises The City, the sights, sounds, the smells of a night of fun and games.

The lights are on, blazing from the marquees. *Jabberwocky* is on at Cinema 1, a pleasant story from the kingdom of Bruno the Questionable which is being ravaged by a monster who must be slain before law and disorder can prevail. And Saint Dennis-the-cooper's son, a fumbling St. George of the impotent variety, slops his way to victory (of a sort) through a swamp of human waste.

The Beast is loose and playing, if play it is, along the streets, the byways of The City. It is a sleazy fairytale, a fantasy of Freudian foolishness, a flabby, perverted priest plants a soggy kiss on the lips of a passive, doleful-eyed adolescent, pops a sweet into the boy's mouth, his hand going into the boy's pants, and greedily kisses him again.

Otherwise, a season of prurient pursuits presents a Hardon Inc feature frenzy of copulation, rampant, roiling sex between Our Lady of the Wasted Womb playing a dreamy blonde and her furry masturbatory fancy, the beast of her imagination.

Recently she has become the darling of the O-mega Unit (for obvious reasons), which she refers to as Mega-O United. Here it would seem a fourth woman is born and mated to whatever else one might hope for in *3 Women*. Millie, Pinky, Sissie, Shelly, Willie, Janice — the outer edge of

Dodge City, in all their dour dance-weight, coming down, from the goddess in Norwegian farm girls to the back-breaking whores of Wichita. The wraith lives in *Woman's Day, McCall's*, where Polly and Peggy, the twins of vitality and disease, merge into a nymphet, a woman to become the ghost of failing flesh, haunted by the least differentiated cells of corporeal reality, the nightmare reproduction that will no longer produce.

Tonight is still April, acclaimed, renowned for soft showers, fragrant flowers, the gush and growth of life, and Mephisto. And balmy as the weather, Margherita lies in a dismal cell on a pallet of straw, condemned to die, awaiting execution. She is incoherent, her mind in a state of confusion, her thoughts wondering.

"L'altra notte in fondo al mare."

She has been imprisoned for poisoning her mother with the sleeping draught supplied by Faust, and for drowning the baby she had borne him. Faust begs Mefistofele to help them escape together. They enter the cell and at first Margareta does not recognize her rescuers. When she sees Sam at the door she is horrified. Here is the visage of her despair. Her joy at being reunited with Faust turns to desolation, her face a portraiture of doom. However, she refuses to succumb to further evil and falls to her knees begging divine forgiveness. Of course god answers her prayers, as he does the prayers of all those in despair. Relieved, she collapses to the cell floor as a celestial choir proclaims her redemption.

Picasso's goat

Down the street *The Rite of Spring* feeds new life into a virginal dance, the rising, falling, the pulse and beat, and menses flow of sacrifice — the fifth day of the Cerealia, the Fordicidia, and a somber resignation that without an alchemy of species, like will bring forth like.

To appease Tellus, the wonder of growth and birth insured, blood must flow. A Lolita vessel, a container, wherein unseen, deep in the cavity of human hope, seeds of generations germinate, is offered up in a dance breeding life, the full female torso lifting from the stage floor, twisted in the passionate, dull purple light to encourage motion into life.

The air pulses, life pushing into the fabric, imposing itself, a reminder of other times, in other places, before The City, before iron or industry, before the green of greed.

In the spring of millennia past, women who gave birth in winter, wrenching life from pain, in love, and not necessarily with love, on a night ordained by lunar cycles and solstice, their heads and arms garlanded with leaves and flowers, made their way into freshly planted fields.

Beneath the soft pale light of a full or crescent moon, they linked arms and danced beneath the giant Oak. They spread into the deep fields and buried grain kept from the previous year's harvest, then kneeled and with maternal care stroked the warm earth, and fell forward, faces pressed to the black, fertile loam, to milk their swollen breasts into the soil.

Their husbands, and later other men, who had followed at a respectful distance, came to them and lifted their frocks over their elevated, extended buttocks, unsheathed their phalluses and with throbbing thrusts, emptied their sacks of seed.

Year after year, planted and encouraged, the grain grew until the evidence suggested that sacrifice would, if added to the gifts of milk and sperm, further please the gods and encourage even better fortune. In extended rituals, a newborn kid or lamb, and later a child, was given up, offered to enhance the fertility and yield of the field.

Added to the gospel, the quest for redemption and blessings, goats (scapegoats) were utilized. On an assigned day (Goat Friday?) a goat would be saddled with sacks of rocks representing man's trespasses, (maybe a rock per million sin), a scarlet ribbon tied to one horn, and led into the desert to wander and ultimately to die.

Sam winches, rubs his hand over his scarred ass.

He is in Brooklyn modeling for Pablo, Diego, José, Francisco de Paula, Juan Nepomuceno, Maria de los Remedios, Cipriano de la Santisima Trinidad, Picasso, of 1133 Fulton Street. Pablo is doing an oil, water-based paint, and crayon on canvas cubist self-portrait, Je ne suis pas qui je suis, that he will sell to The Metropolitan for seventeen thousand dollars. Pablo is arrested several times, not for stealing from the Louvre, but, since forgeries sell better than originals, for forging his own work. He remains, however, undeterred by the repeated inconvenience of spending a month or two in jail.

"Why," he asks, on the way back to his studio after being bailed out for the seventh time, "is it a crime to fool the experts with paintings so many enjoy? So some arrogant fool blows a fortune on something no one can judge with any certainty — and even if they could, what difference would it make? You never get what you see or see what you get anyway. So what? You gonna arrest me for that?"

These days (and nights) his son Pablo, Diego, José, Francisco de Paula, Juan Nepomuceno, Maria de los Remedios, Picasso works at the other end of the studio, forging Pablo, Diego, José, Francisco de Paula, Juan Nepomuceno, Maria de los Remedios, Cipriano de la Santisima Trinidad, Picasso's originals.

"After all, art is illusion, artifact," a Picasso says. "We are all abstract three dimensional objects in multiple layer/planes of geometric shapes giving an illusion of depth, a 3-dimensional appearance of a person from different views. Remember, a copy is an original until the original becomes a copy. We are all copies or copying someone. There is no such thing as an original. Not in man or art. Life is like art, a series of imitations, copies. Even if it is just style."

the men in the cave
tighten their shackles

By nine o'clock The City is a whirl, a carousel of flying flags, lights, horses, riders, and music. Distractions, a dime a dozen, stretch long the midway, through the Bronx to Brooklyn. The Ferris wheel spins wantonly, faster and faster to a new and dizzying magnitude, greater sensations.

By midnight the sideshows sell out. The Fat Lady giggles — Champagne tickles her nose. Vasserot the armless ambidextrian wipes his nose with his toes. The Tattooed Man is blue — with a tint of red, sorry he has no uncharted skin upon which to again experience the needle's pleasant sting.

Beneath the big top the dwarfs make the most it. They go about doubled up on one another's shoulders, draped in long coats, careful to stay away from the third ring where The East Side Gourmet Club has settled in for a new day repast. The club, as it is known, is celebrating a Mass of fine wine and organs and limbs supplied by a member who recently infiltrated the cleanup crew at The City Morgue.

In another part of The City, David wheels through traffic, the Galaxie, circling Manhattan to Queens.

our forensic wonder
wonders
at the murkiness of it all

After a late dinner uptown, the Lieutenant appears briefly on Channel 2. His wife, who is suing for divorce, is away on a guest gig visiting her mother in *The Guiding Light,* and he's uncomfortable and alone in the studio. The clock above the dressing room door gold star, chimes the hour, midnight, and he snaps on the studio set, Channel 11, in time to catch the beginnings of *Crimes of Passion.* He slips out of his shoes, pops the tab off a can of Old Bulldog (a Bronx brewery), and tries to relax.

It's been a long week. He wonders when Keener's going to knock on Our Lady's door to ask what the hell? Clearly, the task force hasn't been up to the task. It needs new lines, a few gags, a pun or two. Yes, when will Our Lady of the Puissant Passion have something? He will ask Keener. Nothing seems to be coming together — fifty men looking for the proverbial needle.

He flips another tab, pages through the Sunday *Times*, world news, national events, The City — special departments. A new theory on Son of Sam. A cleric — a minister from a prestigious metro church. What else? Ads for the United Lodge of Theosophy, featuring a lecture, 7:00, "Suffering's Cause and Cure." The Church of the Truth and Dr. John Lee Baughman to elaborate on "The Ticking package." Eric Butterworth at Avery Fischer Hall on "How to Break the Ten Commandments."

The redundancy is numbing, even for mumming.

Psyaint David

in which Hans-Peter
confronts an image
that may be Hans-David

You can't go home again, but you can try. The rooms of 7E are saturated with ill-will, the shadows of his latest hits. And voices, voices, a distant repetition of syllables, Peter-David in conversation with himself, and the discussion in a mirror on the disposition of his odyssey, his resolve, the bitter taste of The City, bring only a modicum of hope. He suspects the persona in the mirror is not a reflection of what he thought he is or might be, but instead a spy hired (no doubt created, instructed, inspired?) by Sam. Indeed, he suspects it is Sam's plan. The room behind the voice, the mirror, the porthole through which the missives fly and he touches life (and death) is designed to reflect the room.

In a swift retreat to the kitchen he sulks, out of sight, surrounded by empty soup cans, dirty dishes, the trash of another day. He waits for a face to appear on the wall. Later, the fit quelled, relieved to be alone, he hangs a blanket over the bland wound of white glass. Then, in the night, unable to sleep, he crawls from the bed, along the wall and pulls back the blanket to peer into another room where he finds an imposter leering at him.

Aware, now, of the blemish on his pelt, he thinks maybe it isn't Sam after all. The imposter speaks when he (Hans-David) does not and he hears him (the other David) behind the blanket, conversing with himself. Once he (Hans-Peter) smells cigarette smoke. Another time the other is entertaining a lady (Donna Lauria?). He listens to their animal sighs. He listens, the sounds growing louder, until, gun in hand, he sidles up and in a flurry strips the blanket from the glass, leaps in well-formed military style into the center of the room, the .44 held firmly in both hands, pointed at the glass, out across the Hudson to the Palisades.

herein lies the legend
of Sam and his son Sam

So they catch on, raise hue and cry, and the proverbial voice of the wronged lifts with anguish, a whimper against the odds, echoing from the cave, along the streets, through the alleys, seeking assistance, assurances to prop up public confidence, and organize a manhunt, as

I knew they would. They call me Son of Sam, stamp me with a lyrical verity and legitimacy, convinced, now, that

I am real, here to be hunted, my tracks inspected, defined in their search. And so it is

I am free, adrift, meant to wander at the edge of discovery.

I am remade, no longer animal or plant, who does not breath or defecate, and may not fall onto soft breasts, the warm nest of a human encounter.

I am the son of my father Sam

I am sterile, sterilized, cleansed of human connections,
I am made pure, a sinner, saint, martyr, cannot cry or hope, but live in the details, the flimsy facts and gatherings of unrelated clues the investigation strings together. Those who hope to expose me by search and imitation, who walk as
I walk, eat, sleep and drink with me, to know my habits, my mind, peer through a single peep-hole, squint-eyed, discover the visage, for a moment, of grim fate, to replicate the hunter-hunted, an inclusive inner self of desire and bondage.

we are all
Sons of Sam

We evolve into a colored glossy, full-page Mad Ave print, and contemplate, nervously at first, a contrivance of deceit, duplicity, and cunning in which cynicism serves as the maxim.
We cast our eyes away at talk of honor, avert our gaze, avoid the awkward, the innocent beliefs of children, and, in the tinker's shop of an alert, somewhat intelligent mind, temper the single, simple code, greed-driven, for power, wealth, fame, privilege, or whatever carries the day.
We take pleasure where
We find it, pleased with power, belittle the misfortunes of others, reduce the present to memory, see as historians see the faceless horde of the deceased and frozen painted in numbers on a wind-blown winter hill of the Grande Armée's retreat from Moscow.

you are all
Sam's Sons

You intuitively focus your energies to become sanguine.
You collect literature on destruction, read far into the night the cryptic, laconic coded prose of *The Murdering Mind* and *A Revolutionary's Diary,* noting the ease with which weapons are acquired and stockpiled, explosives made, and delight in the soft tone of the narrator's voice.
You clip news stories of bombings, murder, and imagine a nefarious world of plots and schemes wound about
You like the strands of an enormous web to contain, capture, and hold even the smallest atrocity.
You take a Pretty Boy Floyd stance before the mirror, in profile, and revolve slowly, noticing the soft chin, long nose, the distortions police mugshots make. You recline in the barber's chair, eyes closed, draped with a pinstripe barber's cape-shroud, face lathered, as white as a ghost. A pair of

heavies are posted at the door, armed and ready. Then a black limo careens around the corner machine guns rattling and spitting, the slugs slamming through the glass front, the bottles of barber tonics and salts disintegrating like a bar-backed mirror in a John Wayne western. The barber stands over

You, hangs motionless over

You, his face serene and quizzical, as

You open your eyes, one-fourth of the top of his head missing, before he topples forward to the floor splattering your white beard with cerise splotches. His dead man hand drags the razor across your face opening a gash on your cheek and

You roll out of the chair to the floor as a second car speeds by raking the shop with automatic rifle fire. The heavies are quickly dispatched. One with three rounds in his chest from an AR-18:

Weight: 6.7 lb (3.0kg) (empty)
7.18 lb (3.3kg) (loaded w/20rd. magazine).
Length: 38 in (970mm).
Barrel length: 18.25 in (464 mm) (6groove rifling).
Cartridge: 5.56x45mm NATO.
Action: Short-stroke piston, rotating bolt.
Rate of fire: 750 rounds/min.
Muzzle velocity: 3,250 ft/s (991 m/s).
Feed system: 20, 30, 40-round detachable box magazine.
Sights: Iron sights or removable 3x scope,

The other is quieted with a well-placed single .38 Smith & Wesson slug in the top of his head. He was looking down. What was he looking at? What was he looking for?

You scramble to the backdoor, wipe away the pink lather with the clean edge of the apron, and gun ready, crouching, creep into the alley, over a low fence, remembering how, two nights before, head held high, erect, dapper in a thousand-dollar suit

You walked into the 596 Club, the music playing, the crowd mesmerized by

You, by your presence, as

You now creep through a vacant basement and reappear two streets over, walking unhurriedly, pulling your sport coat over your stained shirt, a handkerchief held to the cut on your face, the first seeds of revenge simmering, festering into a clear and apparent plan.

You make it to the restroom of a small out of the way Italian restaurant with a sign on the door for Genoa Salami Calzones to wash up before having lunch. The following day

You discover yourself made hero, set against the proponents of order, the middle-class, bureaucratic governmental intractability, who admire

You tacitly, made hero by the press and eulogized, the pale, cold flesh of your being bathed, powdered and dressed in fine linens, once again the lace of panegyrics scented with the latest colognes. Revered as a necessary rebel, without tribe or family, set free, voyager, who stands boldly upright against the wrath of the masses, who dares defy, who steps beyond a non-animal-plant being, offered up to be devoured,

You become the all-powerful night-stalker fantasy-warrior of Broadway.

You are acclaimed in the chorus chant amid the fest of candles, midsummer's eve, a full and fertilizing moon, the night-eye of heaven lit with sacred fire, phallus unsheathed, a hieros gamos, the will of the gods, Attis, cleansed, Cybele's statue christened with the fluid of the severed organs of the Galli.

The City wakes to atrocity,
then
expediently goes its way

The morning papers headline the Suraini shootings. Undaunted, undismayed by the inability, unwillingness of another of his stars to follow orders, St. Juan Lamiae offers calm, if somewhat ambiguous advice.

"We need to wait out the Blood Moon," he says

"Where does that leave us? Up shit creek," Aigilas tells Mathias. "I told you we couldn't trust him. He hasn't the haziest notion of going along with the program. The bastard's goofy. Jesus! Now he's taken to writing his own press releases."

"So," Mathias says, "nothing's lost. Nothing's changed. Nobody is going to touch this until we throw in what they need to hook it up. Until then, they do a wooden horse on a carousel routine — with the calliope piping. As long as we go on as usual, no one's going to say anything. Shows can always be salvaged or saved at the last minute. This is no different. Then they vanish like disappearing ink. Let the psychologists and social historians guess at what happened. Not that it makes a difference. They always come up with the same rap.

"Marcelo, you've been in the business long enough to know that. Son David's still in the old story. We've have a deal. He'll stay with it. Hey, we were the ones who made the changes, not him."

"That's easy to say," Aigilas the director says. "You sit up here a couple miles off the street. We're down on the concrete. I mean, no way to know who he'll turn on next. Christ, that kook gets his rocks off blowing people away. That gun is his dick and I'll be damned if he's gonna stick me."

"Girls, he's after girls. Anyway, you never get hit with the one you see."

"And that's not all. The silly S.O.B has taken to writing his own press releases."

"So he has a flare for publicity. Don't worry. It's not all bad.

"Have you seen Theo today?"

"No," they shake their heads. "He was on Channel 31 a little while ago. That's another thing, Matt. He's been jumping around. Before too much longer, he's gonna become a problem. He's chewing cactus buttons, talking about going cable — more outlets, less interference. He's taking this thing personally. I mean, he actually believes he's a cop on a case.

"And morose. I told him he needs a shrink. But just between you and me, I don't think a shrink would help. It's those new fucking writers — that's the problem. A bunch of goddam naïve kids and their psychological crap. Everything has to be soul-searching. Have a redeeming grace. Self-flagellation with whimpering and moralizing at the end."

"Well, he can feel any way he wants," Mathias says, "It's not going to change. We have a schedule and I intend to meet it."

He lights a cigar, blows the smoke toward the ceiling.

"Did you get any footage of Suraini and Esau before they were shot?"

"No luck. We were set up for next week. Then little Lord Fauntleroy . . .."

"Okay, okay. I heard it. So we made the mistake," Mathias says, more than a little irritated.

But he's considering the reality of the schedule. It may be worse than he thought.

"We'll put in a little sugar. We're still on budget. Currently, anyway. You know how big this is?"

"So it's big." Aigilas says. "You were right the first time."

Mathias is calculating.

"If you took two hundred million chess boards and arranged them in a square and then began playing not only the game on each board, the boards as Pawns and Rooks in the game where Knight and King could turn to Castle and Queen, depending on where the board was moved or placed in conjunction with every other board — and you finally came to check, you'd be where we are now."

"Okay. Spare me the details."

"The least of it all is the actors. They're a dime a dozen. This town is crawling with riffraff who'd give their lives to be on teevee. They'd die happily for stardom.

"A couple years ago someone asked a bunch of Olympic athletes if they'd use drugs to help win their event if they knew for certain they would win, but also knew for certain that the drugs would kill them — say a year or two down the road. They all said they'd take the drugs. To the last one, they said they'd take the drugs.

"Hell, most of the nit-wits in this city live with the possibility of snuff without acclaim. If they knew for certain they'd make the front page of *The Times* or they'd get an obituary in *Variety* — well, that's better than going to heaven. I mean, life is short and heaven doesn't exist. Do something notable, get a pat on the back, and check out. What's the difference?

"Anyway, we're on the old schedule, and this time it's going to come off. Hans-Peter is on this — we can't undo that. I've had four calls within the last week wanting to know what we're doing. If we have to sweeten the pie for the Lou, we will. What's a detective's salary? Remember the frame? When was that? Little over a year ago. A few thou extra here or there has a nice way of bringing folks around. Hell, he'll take the money. Give him command of O-Mega."

"Who's calling you?" Aigilas queries.

"Who? What? When? I don't know."

"You don't know? Bullshit, you don't know. You know. If god called you'd say, 'I don't know.'"

"Even if I did know, even if I had names, which I don't, it wouldn't matter. You have to understand. When someone calls, he's calling for someone else. It doesn't matter who. It all depends on interpretation, not on who. Just think of it as THEY. Jacob fucking with his angel. Sisyphus with his rock."

"The big Why, then."

"Yeah, we all get plugged in. The only choice we have is to go along with it or not. If you get out, nobody cares. You go back to Plainfield, another anonymous face in the crowd and rationalize the rest of your life, make believe you're a better person for having made the choice. But nobody gives a shit. Other imposters are plugged in and the parade goes on. As it turns out, quitting didn't make you a cent, and you find, in the end, you really didn't give a shit about it all, anyway. So why not stay in the business and take the money?"

"You must have heard something," Aigilas says. "I mean about the un-clean spirits in the swine and a couple hundred chased into the sea."

"I heard it. You want a verbatim report? Would it make a difference? Listen, in this business we could have a planning session with the holy ghost and it wouldn't change anything. Hear that sputtering way off in the distance? An absurd, mindless sputtering. You hear that? This place is a New Year's Eve backroom bar in Poorsville and god is a standup comic with sore feet and a hangover who's wondering how in the hell he got into the business in the first place. Which means there's nothing beyond survival — and that's the purpose that gives order.

"As it stands, the mistake is not that Suraini and Esau were shot, but that we failed to get a roll on it. And if we let on that we screwed up — some invidious little prick in a penthouse office, some place in The City, is thinking we are at fault. That it's going to cost him or one of his keepers money.

"That means that friggin duck Drake will be in here flapping his feathers, squawking, hissing threats, and ultimatums, ringing the Liberty Bell."

He's looking north to the Empire State Building.

"Juan, check the newsrooms. See if their camera crews made it to the scene. Location shots. We'll run a batch of studio stuff with it. Maybe we'll be lucky. We can still give 'em what they want."

it would appear
The City of the Gods
is without prospects

Captain Keener-McNeil, for his part, doesn't know what they want, or what to give them. The difficulty with the media is seriously hampering SAMIE's effectiveness. He decides to call a press conference, a mini-conference, to slip in unnoticed, with only minimal distortions.

"We have tips and possibilities," he tells a handful of reporters. "But no person of interest. The murders and shootings occur at night, and only five witnesses have gotten a glimpse of him."

"The Commissioner said you knew the identity of the killer."

"We do. The detectives in Queens have consulted with psychiatrists and psychologists and have a profile of this person.

"We have a variety of opinions from varying portraits. Yes, I know profiling is discouraged. But we do it well. And what choice do we have? I mean, we know the killer as well as we know anyone."

"Word has it that the Mayor is disturbed and wants something like action."

"The Mayor does not pick up the phone and tell the police 'I want action or else.' It doesn't work that way."

"Is this a plan to expand citizen termination to reduce city welfare rolls?" a reporter says. "If enough press conferences are held, enough words spill into the media, the slayings will become euphemized and the words 'murder' and 'killing' made 'nonoperational.' The shootings will become 'dispatchings' or 'send-offs,' or maybe 'reduction-events.' Then the media might report that those subject to the 'reduction-event' as 'Having cheerfully resigned their souls to god,' or 'Taking comfort from their youthful flight,' or were merely 'Called forth too early.'"

"Would you talk about this?"

Keener lays his hand on top of the teevee on his desk.

"I'm going to put my best man on this case, put him in charge."

He turns on the set, then stands back, wondering what Lamiae and Aigilas have in mind for Loko in this episode.

"This is our most experienced homicide supervisor," Keener says.

The Lieutenant tries to smile, to project a confident and cheerful demeanor. He stares at the camera.

"I thought he was already on the case."

"Actually, every cop in The City is on the case," Keener says. "But technically, someone has to head up the task force. From this day forward,

Superable-Sleuth LoKoJakMan will be in charge of O-Mega."

"What did Dowd say about being replaced?"

"Who's Dowd?"

"He's the Detective leading O-Mega."

"Under Inspector Dowd's direction, detectives patrolled the Bronx and Queens in unmarked cars, and female police officers with long, dark hair sat in cars outside discos and singles bars. Inspector Dowd and other police officials described the hunt as a needle-in-a-haystack endeavor.

"At one point, the Police Department set out to trace all .44-caliber weapons ever made of the type used by the killer. There were an estimated 28,000 of them."

"What's he say about it?"

"Not much. Of course he doesn't like it. He says 'This case is particularly complicated because there is no apparent motive. When you can't establish why someone is killing, it's difficult to predict who he is or where he will strike again.' Inspector Dowd thinks we need 'to be prepared to be lucky.'

"All he says, otherwise, is that he would prefer Columbo. Lulled by Columbo's rumpled raincoat, ever-present cigar, bumbling demeanor, Holmesian powers of deduction, and good manners, most cunning murderers make a fatal, irrevocable mistake. They underestimate Columbo's investigative genius. And that's important.

"Dowd thinks Falk, though not as polite as Columbo, does have a better system. Untidy and appearing distracted, Columbo pokes around in a practical but random fashion, always stumbling in the direction of a solution. More realistic. I mean, isn't that how most crimes are solved? Luck? We come across some small clue and it becomes the key and the whole ball of wax unwinds. The universe is six parts rote and four parts random and four parts luck.

"But, then, Columbo's in LA, so what are you going to do?"

A news man suggests that to get a better view of what Kojak might do as head of O-Mega, they transfer the visual to the large screen in the corner.

Keener objects.

"A lot is lost in transition and translation. The *Blow Up* effect is real."

When the Lou appears on the Sony he goes right to the point.

"You'll have to take me the way I am, sweetheart. I'll do the best I can. The Chief has let me pick my own bosses and I know they are trustworthy. My job is to do all the things that should be done in cases like this. Then, if I get lucky . . .."

He hesitates, briefly contemplating blind luck.

"But if I don't do all the basic things, then I can't get lucky."

And for the moment, Keener-McNeil's luck appears to have improved. Despite the fact that the Lou's *Chinatown* nose is still sore (the wound from the splinter refuses treatment, the infection threatening to spread), it seems that they may indeed be onto something. This could be a superbug.

Psyaint David

a rambling dialogue
by which the Loo
confronts mortality

The press conference appears on the Channel 2 early news with only slight interference, a surprise that draws nothing more than a hunch-shouldered-so-what from E.Erie™. The Lou parades out of the office with a .357 Magnum on his hip and the manhunt swings in behind him or the skirts of Lady Luck, hung on coincidence, an unnoticed twist of plot.

Then, following a brief message from a new sponsor, at 8:00 the Lieu-tenant lurches by a protesting, babbling Mrs. Blasberg, onto the set in Teivel's office.

"But you can't, Mr. LoKo . . ..

"Mr. Teivel does not . . ..

"Appointments are . . .."

Before anyone can intervene, the Lou's on in closeup, Mathias standing behind his desk, arms folded.

"It took you long enough to show up," Teivel says.

"We had a press conference. I've been put in charge of the task force."

Mathias turns slowly, the glare breaking over the long folds of his charcoal robe, his full white afro (a wig) his face scarred with paint and powder or maybe a Thalia/Melpomene mask.

"Have a seat, Bogie."

The camera dollies to the divan, a coffee table, and Kojak eases down in mid-shot, a Dutch angle, lights a cigarillo, fully aware of the misconception that man will seek the good simply because he finds it and that the FCC is prepared to ban smoking on teevee.

"What do you see when you look out that window?"

"Déjà vu. A giant aquarium," Mathias says, raising his arms. "A giant pool of squid and sharks."

"Nicely put," The Telly says. "You have a way with words. But what are you going to do about it? Don't you think it's time we put a little order and sanity into the fish tank?"

"That's what you want? You want to clean it up and set the record straight?"

He nods as if he might see the sense in it all.

"Admirable. Indeed, a noble proposal."

His voice shifts abruptly to business as usual.

"I had a long talk with Marcelo and Lukema," Mathias says. "As you know, or should know, things have gotten a little sticky. Like flypaper."

"And you're gonna try to stick that on me."

"Well, you have to admit, you were out of line. You've been a cop long enough to know that you don't put your business on the street. Go back to the frame. It's easy for people to misinterpret what you say and do."

"Because I wanted to make a few bucks more off the shoot?"

"Because it didn't work. You did nothing. You mess up the shooting schedule. And for what?

"Theo, this may not be your fault at all. What I mean is, maybe you're just doing what you have to do. Maybe you can't help yourself — like other teevee heroes. We talked it over and everyone agrees. It is a matter of ego."

"I didn't come here to talk about me. I'll play me the way I need to be played. There's nothing wrong with what I'm doing. There's nothing wrong with who I am. What we need is a new plot. We need to change — get away from the whodunit — a new story line, new themes. New writers."

"We're in this for the long haul," Mathias says. "We can't change it. I can't change it. And you're into the part wrong or maybe into the wrong part. The story's been the same for years. It'll be the same years from now. Just like over the water, adversaries walking around saying 'We gotta get rid of Kojak. I want Kojak dead.' Yeah, there's a killer hunting for you."

"And I'm out to get him. It's who gets to the gun first."

"Yeah. The character's wrong. Holmes makes money because he solves puzzles, not crimes."

"So what else is new?"

"More than that, you're a human who thinks he's an actor, an actor who thinks he's a cop, a cop who thinks he's human. The only thing right about any of this is that everybody is wrong."

"An actor who plays a cop. A cop who wants to solve the big Why. People are dying all over The City and only a few at the top are cashing in on it. Somebody has to do something."

"So how did changes in the shooting help that? What good did it do?"

"Well, you can't win 'em all. That should have worked. Some things just don't make sense."

"Okay. But you're just another white shirt. It's the spirit of the hunt that counts. The myth of crime detection, keeping the ball rolling, so to speak, so the audience can hope and continue to believe. Do you have an idea how many of the cons in the pen are innocent? Most of them. Just ask. They'll tell you. They're not all lying.

"You owe your existence to Emily Hoffert and Janice Wyle — unless you want to get into the theology of the hunt, the psychology of chasing yourself around the block."

"You mean Marcus-Nelson, don't you?"

"No. Hoffert and Wylie. And any complaints you have — you know what will happen if we try to change the plot? I'll tell you. Pffffft! Did you hear that? Pffffft! Just like that, you vanish. Did you ever hear of Buford Pusser? He tried to change the plot, then got caught up in it. Check it out sometime. It doesn't work. Right now, right now a number of would-be sponsors are sitting around a big table in an obscure room thinking maybe you should be cancelled. Okay. We can keep you alive. But tamper with the plot and the show dies, you're dead. This is a group project. The story line stays."

The Lieutenant is pensive. He squints and grimaces through the cigarillo smoke.

"You know," he says at long last, "every murder is a milestone. How people die is as important as how they live — and why. Every time a consciousness disappears, it sets off marks the road mankind is on."

"And it is not our business to mess with that."

"What you're saying, or at least implying, is that we should read road signs and travel accordingly."

"But even so, it doesn't solve our problem. What we're faced with is footlight fatigue. Your psyche is drifting. Last year, six months ago, you would never have said something like that. Regrettable as that is, it may be nothing more than over exposure — but your personality has termites."

"You think I need a psyche tune-up."

"Remember that psycho from out of the shadows?' What was his name? Sylk, Villers — anyway, it doesn't matter. You were talking to him in the end. He says something about 'I was just fighting back. Sometimes it gets so heavy, the pressure, the failures, the frustrations. You don't know who to strike out at.' You tell him he's not a killer and you'll prove it. Then when Crocker lands the killer, the perp lying dead on the sidewalk in a scattering of shattered glass, you ask Villers 'Do you know this man?'

"'It's me,' he says.

"You say 'No. But it could be. I suppose it could be a lot of us.'"

"Yeah. I know. The body fell in a tow away zone."

"Actually, it would be a painless way to go. All you have to do is check in with Abby Mann. He can cook up a few new personality twists — a line here, a gesture there. Give you a tainted life. A tattoo on your scrotum, a scar on your cheek. I mean, a big nose and a left jaw mole aren't enough. Not anymore. Audiences are getting smart, more sophisticated. Hell, your history is full of it. How about Feto Gomez or Pontius Pilate. The little things that make a difference. You'd be surprised what it would do for your attitude. Shit. Better than EST.

"The way things are going we'll need all the help we can get. Opportunity doesn't knock anymore — we can't wait."

Well, okay. But what about Sam? Surely he's in the area, somewhere. Maybe he has something to say about reconstructing the human psyche, about the fate of man, of humans.

the PC and Sam Inella
spend
an afternoon assigning guilt

Meanwhile, amid the construction hammering and sawing, E.Erie™ prepares to move a line of mainframe computers and sophisticated lightwave surveillance equipment, on loan from the Bell Laboratories, into Police Plaza One.

Not to be outdone, Garfield pushes forward with his smoke-and-mirrors campaign. Buoyed in recent days by the success of Captain Keener-Frazer's mini-conference, he suspects that TCPD's snooping and E.Erie™'s aura have intimidated or wounded the audio-video fiend.

Today he's out to spread the word at St. Elizabeth's Catholic Church at Atlantic Avenue and 84th Street in Woodhaven, Queens for the funeral of twenty-eight-year-old police officer Robert Mandel who was shot by an ex-con out on bail.

Officer Robert Mandel and his partner, in plainclothes, respond to a call of drug possession and drug sales inside 762 Franklin Avenue, Brooklyn. They arrest one suspect and turn him over to two uniformed officers. When a second man tells the officers he has information for them they exit the location. Once outside, the second man gains control of the service weapon of Officer Mandel's partner. He opens fire, striking Officer Mandel in the face, and his partner in the torso.

Officer Mandel and his partner are taken to Brooklyn Jewish Hospital, where Officer Mandel dies from his wounds. His partner makes a full recovery. The suspect is arrested later in the day at his home and charged with attempted murder and murder.

Officer Mendel served The City Police Department for five years and was assigned to the 77th Precinct Anti-Crime Unit. He is survived by his wife.

Garfield appears at the church trailed by a battalion of mourning cops. However, in keeping with the spirit of the ceremony, hoping to take advantage of the Little Taylor possibilities of boys-in-blue bunched on the church steps, someone phones in a bomb threat. The ceremony is postponed and the church searched by the Bomb Squad.

When the press asks for statements, Garfield takes his place on the top step and blasts the courts for their leniency with criminals.

"I think people need to speak out very clearly and very loudly to their courts and their legislatures," he says. "There's definitely a valid place for the death penalty in the case of one person destroying another."

Yes. That's the death penalty — one person destroying another.

Samuel, Sam Inella, promises "We are going to find out who the judge was who let this man out on bail and demand his removal. The judge is as guilty as the man who pulled the trigger, in my eyes."

Clearly, the ball is in their court. And Sam (Inella) has a lot of "I's." His newest manual, "The Law According to Sam," was rejected by twenty-two publishers. The content was good, the ghost writing satisfactory, but no one could find a printer with enough uppercase "I's" in stock to print it.

After the ceremony, in an attempt to finish the month, use up the remaining days so that waste shall not create want, Garfield and Sam Inella go trucking off to the Junior League of Brooklyn "Underground Society

Bash." It is rumored they are looking for the guilty judge, etc., etc., among the 750 odd (very) partygoers who ride a special subway train from 57th Street and The Avenue of the Americas to the Old Court Street Station in Brooklyn.

For many of the hoity-toity, the high- born, the pale and wan of flesh, of superior taste and, of course, wealth, it is a chance to mingle with the hoi polloi. Some admit they do not ride the subway — one claims he cannot remember the last time he descended to street level, much less below.

the Lou makes
an appeal
to a killer

In keeping with his duties, the obligation as taskmaster of O-Mega Force hoping to provide something substantial in the way of investigatory results, the Loo issues an ecumenical response to "The Epistle of Psyaint David to Captain Joseph Borrelli."

"We know you are not a woman hater — and we know how you have suffered," the message reads, in the implied monotone of stoic indifference. "We wish to help you, and it is not too late.

"Please let us help you. Call Captain Borrelli or Inspector LoKo at 844-0999 or write them in care of the 9th or 11th Precinct"

The communiqué raises a number of eyebrows.

"How do you know he's not a woman hater?"

"Why have all his victims been women?"

"That's something we would like to ask him."

"Who in the hell is Sam?"

"Uncle Sam? Or Samson?"

"Yeah. Maybe."

"Well, Samson didn't need a .44. Do you have a motive?"

"We believe he is reaching out. He's suffering. He's had serious pain in his life. We want to find him before something tragic happens."

"Before he kills three or four women?"

"Have you tried Sigma Alpha Mu at CCTC?"

"How about the Society of American Magicians?"

"We're going on the assumption that he will strike again. He doesn't want to, but he's acting under a compulsion."

"Oh yeah? Why didn't I think of that?"

the *Daily News*
appeals to a killer

Within a few days the dust and strain of inquiry and response settles and the manhunt drifts into lassitude and languor. Now it's a matter of phone calls and guesses, interviews and stakeouts — the minutiae of unrelated facts, which when discovered and revealed can give cause and flutter to flags of circumstance, the pennants of logic flapping on the wind to facilitate a further understanding of the scheme, the mind of the design.

Still, other possibilities, the turns of fantasy, the webbed hand on the sill, a shadowed face smeared on the warped glass, lie somewhat beyond the pale of reason. The night is unusually warm, humid, a bit of thunder on the dead air. Dogs whine, cowering, heads down, tails lowered. David pages through the *Daily News*, rereading the reviews, the police report, a public plea.

> The *News* is appealing to the killer of Valentina Suriani and Alexander Esau to give himself up before he commits any more crimes or is killed or wounded himself. If he has any reservations about turning himself in to the police or other authorities, we urge him to surrender to the *News*. We will undertake to deliver him safely to the police. If he wishes to contact the *News*, he may reach us at (212) 949-3648.
>
> > (*Daily News*, April 17, 1977)

Peter-David turns the pages, stacks words, letters, tilted forms, toppled type into new realities of lines, designs, the signs and sentences of a New Jerusalem. He's annoyed, nervous about his "Epistle to Captain Joseph Borrelli." What was it? The police said? "Rambling — incoherent." Now the newspaper. "... give up before ... more ... killed or wounded himself." No. He hasn't been seen, much less shot at. He is someone other than David Berkowitz. They'll have to do better than that. "... surrender to the *News*." Give yourself to god. "... undertake to deliver ... safely ...."

Not too late? For what? Five life sentences? One hundred thirty-five years in the Hall of the Mountain King — cloistered, beaten, sodomized, starved, throat cut — fill in the blank?

Who knows? You may come up with a pen pal, a friend for life, to develop and expiate your guilt. You might be born-again, à la Chuck Colson. And if not, we can still provide you with our all new, super, once in a lifetime Loony-of-the-Year award for 1977.

"No thank you," Hans-Peter says.

And, of course, that is the way of it. Our boy may be a zealot in pursuit of mayhem, as he sees it, but nothing, at this moment suggests his mind has failed. His standing as splendid citizen may have been degraded, but nothing in the story thus far suggests he has fallen from the graces of survival instincts into believing the police will actually help him.

"... undertake to deliver ... safely ...."

Yes. That's it. He'd prefer deliverance. Oh, lord, salvation in the heart of the benevolent god of all — washed in the clan of the canine. He would like to be clean as a hound's tooth. Yes, he would. But . . ..

**a killer sets out
  on a rectifying
adventure**

The following week, however, offers a temporary peace, a serenity. Sam's been absent for several days and Hans-Peter of god's likeness, prowls with a new zeal, the magic of numbers and names, messages on the air. He whistles softly to himself, washes his hands, and carries the .44 in a brown paper bag. The bolt set free, the door swinging in, beyond the sunlight that fills the hall, shadows in the door frames, a shade darts out of sight, vanishing into the wall. The lock clicks and he clicks back the hammer on the .44 to be sold later at auction as "Charter Arms Bulldog .44 Special 3 Inch Son Of Sam Gun."

Alsea Alberton has, the night before, obliterated Orlando's personage with two blasts from her 20-gauge and the police have the street cordoned off. To avoid their stares, King Wicker circles the parking lot, along the retaining wall to a secluded spot with a view of Sam Carr's house. He cradles the Bulldog in the crib of both hands, the black canid of Sam's shadow — Garmr, Brimo, Yama — eyes shining — Cerberus at the gate.

> But the poor dog, in life the firmest friend,
> The first to welcome, foremost to defend,
> Whose honest heart is still his master's own,
> Who labors, fights, lives, breathes for him alone,
> Unhonored falls, unnoticed all his worth,
> Denied in heaven the soul he held on earth –
> While man, vain insect! hopes to be forgiven,
> And claims himself a sole exclusive heaven.
>
> (Byron)

This, however, is not Cerberus, but the doublet, a two-headed Orthrus, of smaller mythological fame, to be struck down by Heracles in his Tenth Labor while stealing Geryon's Red Cattle in the Hesperides.

One shot, the gun jumps, barks, the howls and whining complaints of the demon lift in a puff of yellow smoke, the fetor of brimstone drifting toward the Hudson. Two police officers in the parking lot pause, listen, scan the horizon, shrug. They heard something. A car backfiring. Maybe a kid with a firecracker. A gun shot? Who would fire a gun in Yonkers? Beside a crazy woman who killed her crazy husband? They go about their business — whatever it is, today.

SoS T-shirts
go on sale

April fades into the budding tranquility of May. For a week or so after the Suraini-Esau shootings, business is off throughout The City. Kevin Margruder's ice cream shop suffers with the rest.

"Every time that nut strikes business goes to hell. People won't come out at night. An ice cream cone ain't worth getting your brains blown out. Ten days, two weeks later, it's back to normal — but The City is scared."

So scared that Son of Sam tee shirts go on sale in Central Park. A police sketch, a composite, nose, ears, eyes, a mouth, hair, an oval shape stenciled on the white, red, blue cloth. "Son of Sam: Get Him Before He Gets You."

You have to believe Our Lady is in on this.

the Balls & All
offers a diversion
and gets into the hunt

In an attempt to upgrade business, dislodge some of the hot bodies and cold cash from neighboring discos, Salvador Carnese, owner of the Balls & All bar at 280 East 53rd Street announces a Son of Sam Wet T-shirt contest. Salvador is already nationally recognized as director of the Toad Licker Friends, a group of psychedelic seekers who gather on Saturdays to chase toads. When a toad is captured, hoping to open Huxley's doors of perception, to recast hell as heaven, the members lick its skin, ingest the poison, then stumble around in a psychedelic trance banging into trees. Of course Salvador denies that anyone in the Friends has ever chased or licked a toad.

"We buy toads from local pet shops and crystalize and smoke the stuff," he says. "The only toad that's 5-MeO-DMT active, the stuff we use, is the Bufo Alvaris or Colorado River Toad, a large, squat animal with smooth, leathery, greenish-grey skin and a tan belly. It has glands above the ears and where the hind legs meet the body. In order to get smokable stuff, we put the toad in a glass dish and rub it behind the eyes. This pisses the toad off, and it secretes 5-MeO-DMT. Once we have enough we let it dry to a crystal. After it's dry, we scrape it off, put it in a glass pipe and smoke it.

"Man, then the elephant-toad sits on you. I mean it comes in, sets its fat rump right on your head, like this really heavy weight or something. For fifteen or twenty minutes. Sometimes longer. It's good stuff. Heavy but good."

Harmless entertainment, wasting time. But nothing of Sam here.

Today, however, Salvador has wet T-shirt plans. Ten females, ages eighteen (eleven) to twenty (fifteen) pay ten dollars apiece to enter with the hope of being crowned Queen of the wet SOS-T.

Psyaint David

The Balls & All provides the SOS T-shirts as well as black plastic made to order imitation .44 Charter Arms Bulldog Special water guns for the all-male, forty-four, by one count, at twenty dollars a head, salivating, already drunk audience.

The barroom tables, supplied each with a two-gallon container of ammunition (East River water) are pushed against the walls forming a narrow corridor down which the contestants must (not run, not trot, not even prance, but . . .) walk, slowly, twice, as if they are prisoners with their hands on top of their heads.

At 9:00 festivities commence.

Shouts! Jeers! Cat-calls!

"Look at the tits on that!"

"I hit her right on the nips!"

"Nips hell, shoot her in the snatch."

"My god, I've gone to heaven."

"Hey baby, how do you like my .44 fun gun?"

The event is, however, well managed. None of the contestants, and only two of the audience became inappropriately unruly. One, a middle-aged, balding gentleman with a large flat nose, drinks too much, and unable to control himself, in the excitement, wets his pants. The other, a harelip with one ear, forgetting the propriety of place and time, and caught in the wonder of the full, firm female flesh, unlashes his cock and points it at one of the girls, pumping ecstatically and shouting, "Bang! Bang! Bang!"

At 11:00 the last contestant strolls the gauntlet, and amid the frenzied hooting Carnese crowns the winner, thirteen-year-old Sally Hollis, Queen of the wet SOS-T, lady of mammary excellence — and presents her with the first place trophy, a hand-carved, wooden dildo replica of a Charter Arms Bulldog Special with a large pink muzzle (to show that it is not real), and a cash reward of forty-four two-dollar bills.

Carnese calls the contest a success.

"The idea," he explains, "is not to popularize SGV. I was working with the police on this. We thought the maniacal misanthrope would show up. Then we'd have him."

"You notified the police?"

"We invited them. I personally put in a request for a dozen officers and a couple plainclothesmen."

"Where are they?"

"They declined. The Police Department refused to send anyone. So we hired four security guards on our own. If anything had happened, I mean, if the sex fiend had been here, we would have apprehended him."

Other saints will have to wait for other days. Truly, Hans-Peter is their boy, belongs to The City, now, as the spirit belongs to the chase. His is the beloved shadow of fear, the best of hatred, a sense of oblivion, the pleasure of pain, and no one's about to abandon the romance.

in a practice what you preach
dalliance
Our Lady entertains the Captain

Back from the Balls & All with contest highlights securely imprinted on two rolls of Hardon Inc film, Our Lady of the Well-felt Frame has her transistors piping. It's a child's song. She tells cop Keener,

> Three blind mice, see how they run.
> They all ran after Babbitt's wife.
> She cut off their dongs with a carving knife.
> Did you ever see such a sight in your life,
> As a trio of dingy-dongless mice?
> (Thomas Ravenscroft)

"What does it mean?" Keener probes, one hand on the head of the Grey Wolf Lupanar, the other on his service revolver. "So? I mean, why are they blind and just who the hell is Bobbitt's wife?"

"Oh, just a little prophecy. More about it later," she says. "Right now we have other things to do."

This week she's into strapless dresses and bareback halters, unbuttoned blouses that slide off the shoulder, giving her a city-cool appearance. She has an array of brightly colored blindfolds, one for each day of the week.

The bearing is definitely bare.

She unbuttons her unbuttoned blouse and draws him toward her, pressing her hand to the bulge in his pants.

"It's been three months," Frazer says, "and we still don't have a clue. We don't even have a make on him."

"You are unhappy," she says.

"As a matter of fact I am."

She has his pants open, sitting astraddle him on the couch, breathing heavily on his neck. She emanates a touch of Country Girl.

"Oh, Capeetan, be happy. I have never been happier. That's our purpose. Be happy with me. We should live life freely and be happy."

"I wish to hell I knew what you are talking about."

He stares at her blindfold.

"You sure you can't see?"

"Yes, it is human to be happy, and to find pleasure wherever we can. Even in politics. And of all things, this is a political matter," she gasps. "A question of who has the power, the money, the insight, the timing — of, of, I, of, oh, oh, oooooooohhhh."

Indeed, her visions have improved.

She's on a fully programmed channel computing the applause, the dollars and sense of prime time and sales, the ecstasy of multiple monetary orgasms.

Psyaint David

whereby the antagonist
  of this tale
takes on another face

And now ladies and gentlemen, your attention please.

One morning in May, one morning in May, the fantasy of let us go, you and I, and Hans-David, Làszlô Löewenstein the Great, prepares a new role, examines himself in the mirror, profile, straight on, grotesque faces, spreads his lips and lifts his eyebrows with his fingers. Today he will play the magician, a chief, a king, Deus David, beloved child. He leans closer, now, into the light falling from the mirror, vanishes, reappears, here, then again, a new costume, makeup, the powder and paint and grease of chiaroscuro and anonymity.

He sees himself walking with a familiar stride and infamous posture, his voice sharp, belittling. Now he's the great sleuth Telly, set loose on The City, his large lover's lips locked on the round hard firm form of a lollipop. And face to face with his counterpart minutes later he's slick-pated, naked, and exposed.

"By god," he whispers, "if Kojak can do it, so can I."

His great pate shining, Moto the Inscrutable joins the hunt for the ever allusive, shifting delineation of Hans, David, Peter. And though he is yet a step from the *Recruit of Ingolstadt*, the fame of *Moreder Unter Uns*, his true self lies somewhere beyond rival Sydney Greenstreet.

Secluded in a pair of reflecting sun glasses, he's off to Queens and the 109th in Flushing. Crossing Union Street, he pauses, checks the rearview mirror to catch his reflection, the broad nose, demonic mouth, one eye brow cocked in the glass. He is pleased. Truly a demon.

He wheels the Galaxie into a parking slot, exits and mounts the Station steps. Two cops lounging in the foyer turn to watch, then turn away. He finds the on duty Sergeant hunched over behind his desk of papers ashtrays and at least one smoldering cigarette.

"I have information that will lead to the arrest and conviction of Son of Sam," he tells the Sergeant at the desk in the best of beastly whines.

"You know where we can find Son of Sam?"

"Yes."

"Who is it? Your mother?"

"I have talked with him."

"What did he say? Go down to one-0-nine and tell them where I am?"

"I can tell you about Son of Sam."

"Yes. You and every other kook in The City. Here. The phone number is 844-0999."

"You don't understand."

"I understand all right. I understand you're going to get locked up for impersonating an officer. Running around with a bald head?"

The City of the Gods prepares
to export additional
detritus to the hinterlands

Well, it was a nice try. The Mobro 4000 and The Break of Dawn are still ten years away, and he'll do better next time. Undaunted still by threats and rejections, Maximus Personae departs the station house and scampers off to CBS, 6th Avenue, the Blackrock, for an afternoon in the lobby watching crowds, familiar faces, the stars and pros as they come and go. It's home week, seeking favors, introductions, a pat on the back, a pleasant "Oh? Who are you?" Business makes playmates. Of course, he's been here before. *Playhouse 90, Rawhide, Checkmate, Kraft Suspense Theater, Climax.*

Then someone complains.

"Who's the baldheaded dude with the pop-eyes and crooked mouth?"

"I thought they cancelled that."

"Well, they did, but some fictions die hard."

"They keep coming back?"

"Yeah. Even when there's nothing left."

They hustle our boy to the street, send him stumbling, Harold Lloyd, heart and hat in hand, sun glasses smudged, fingerprints, head cracked, a cut from the scuffle.

But that's pretty much the sense of showbiz, the wheel of fortune as he's come to know it. Fortuna with a finger on the Rota Fortunae, at the ready. One day a star, the next out on the street without a friend.

"Who're you looking for?"

"Success."

"Yeah? Well, she just left a few minutes ago with another poseur. That's one fickle broad. Another arbitrary, blind female."

"Time does get away."

"You can only go on so long."

"Un huh. Like eating soup with a fork. Or getting blown away by a marauding crazy."

An hour later the 111th in Bayside receives a phone call.

"This is the Son of Sam. Next week I'm going to hit Bayside."

A pause, then sputtering on the line.

"Yes, but, I mean . . . you can't do that. It's not fair."

Otherwise the big wheel spins. The Big Apple summer shimmers. Sun on concrete, asphalt — pollution. Noise. Traffic. More pollution. Residents go out less often — for good reason — move quickly and disappear just as quickly behind locked doors. The season of improbable claims dawns and rumors sweep the canyons, echo along the sidewalks and avenues. What else can you do in the hiatus?

"Son of Sam is dead."

"He's left town. Moved on to greener fields."

"Any field."
"How do you know?"
"It's true. He's gone."
"What does it mean?"

The Times laments
   the possible fading
of Sam's lucrative presence

In a never-ending commitment to expose crime *The Times Magazine* carries a full-page bold-print-photo-cover of Harlem millionaire drug king Nicky Barnes and an article titled "'Mister Untouchable': This is Nicky Barnes. The Police Say He May Be Harlem's Biggest Drug Dealer. But Can They Prove it?"

As it turns out, they don't have to. The unnecessary publicity for routine accomplishments gets Drake Duck's attention. He flaps about the pond whistling, cooing, yodeling, and grunting, insinuating his displeasure. This is a diving variety of duck (as opposed to dabbling) and seven months later Barnes will be escorted from the feeding trough to a federal lockup (for life) leaving his multi-million dollar industry and his Mercedes-Benz, Bentley, Citroën SM, Maserati, several Thunderbirds, Lincoln Continentals, Cadillacs, a yellow Volvo and one GMC vintage, WWII DUKW (DUCK) named "Drake," (a six-wheel drive cabover GMC AFKWX powered by a 270 cu in GMC straight six, with a .50 caliber Browning heavy machine gun in a ring mount), to his heroin distribution Council members — who were not featured in *The Times.*

The Barnes photo-shoot stimulates a lower East Side citizens' committee, fearful of slipping from national attention, to convene an investigation of the rumors of Sam's demise. Attentive to all possibilities, the next day, along with a report of the Citizens' Committee convocation, *The Times* carries a plea. "Say it ain't so Sam. Say you're still among us."

Rightfully so, everyone is worried. E.Erie™'s SWAT team is up and running, monitoring the environment with a bank of high-powered main-frames, electronic rifles tracking disturbances, watching for renewed video-virus infections and deceit. Beame goes on the air. Delivers his message supporting Mayoral and police competence.

But conspiracy theories grace the rumor winds.

"It's an election gimmick."

"Beame has impounded Sam — has him locked away with John Kennedy and Elvis."

"He'll announce the capture a couple hours before the polls open."

Beame is content, however, to deny the accusations (and therefore support police incompetence) that they have captured Sam. He assures the nattering ninnies and nervous nellies that he is not manufacturing a coup.

And unlike the host of corporations and other ingrates who have forgotten what The City has done for them, and loaded up and moved out, lock, stock and dollar, Sam will be with them for a long time.

"This is his town. He loves it here. He lives here. He has roots here."

But rumors persist.

"Get a writ of habeas corpus."

"Deliver up the corpus delicti."

"My brother-in-law says Sam's been mugged in Brooklyn. Two ten-year-olds with a baseball bat and a curtain rod. Took his gun — undressed the bastard and beat him nearly to death. Threw him in the river."

"Sorry Sam. So long Sam."

Possible?

quite by accident David
    misses the dog,
quite by accident

Yes, criança prodígio's marksmanship leaves a little to be desired. Sam is not dead or even missing, but shuffling about with a slug in his leg. It's a painful wound, the .5291 oz. (15 g) of lead lodged between the muscle and the bone, the entry hole torn and black.

Sam's pissed.

"Okay. Okay. So he's lollygagging in Sam Carr's backyard — minding his own business — but who told him to shoot the dog? I sure as hell didn't."

The scene simmers. Sam's eyes flare, his breath parched and toxic. The skin on his arms burns, rumpled and red, a blazing rash, small blackened scales flaking off like dirty, baked dandruff.

"What kind of a cheap stunt was that?"

David scrambles for the kitchen and sets the table between them.

"You're a demon," he shouts to keep his voice from shaking. "You deserve to die. You and all the rest. You and Jack Cosmos."

"So what else is new, you imbecile. I've half a notion to kick your ass."

"You can't do that."

"I can't do that? You want to see what I can't do?"

He spins and points to the opposite wall, above the desk, a low-angle shot of 42nd Street, the sidewalk crowded, the late afternoon work crowd, shoppers headed home. Then the picture settles, steadies into an over-the-crowd shot of a brown, beaten, and battered '72 Oldsmobile as it careens out of traffic, leaps the curb severing a fireplug and burrows into the crowd, tumbling bodies to either side.

A human body struck by an automobile can take to the air like a whirligig, a horizontal cartwheel, spinning for a hundred feet or more. After launching a few additional whirlygigs the car slams into a storefront. People scream, anticipating another, and attempt to get away, trampling the fallen. The street is a carnival of confusion and carnage.

"You want to see the rest?" Sam says. "Since you're an authority on what I can and can't do."

His voice is belligerent, vicious.

"Have you ever tried to walk with a goddam bullet in your leg? Even if you have four legs, it's a bitch. In my case it's a son of a bitch, and that's embarrassing to a dog."

"That wasn't supposed to happen," David whines. "He won't let me stop until he gets his fill of blood.

"And what about the fires? All the fires I set in the last two years?"

"Nothing," Sam says. "You think I need fires? But that's another story, for another time.

"You think you're Reggie Jackson? You have the market cornered? You believe you can do anything you want? And that shit about, 'It wasn't supposed to happen.' What did you expect?"

"I, well, maybe, I, I don't know." David's voice falters.

"What did you expect? You don't know. Well, I'll tell you. You thought maybe, maybe you'd get help if you did something courageous. You really expected somebody, and not just anybody, but somebody to rescue you. Maybe an arm with a flaming sword to come through the wall and finish the job."

"Yes. I want to die. I sit on the fire escape and want to throw myself down. I want to jump. When I think about dying, I think about being transported into a world of bliss and happiness."

"You silly asshole. And that letter. 'I have asked you kindly to stop that dog from howling.'

"You got it wrong. You take a shot at me with nothing more than the hope that some ridiculous creature of your fantasy will help you."

Sam limps across the floor dragging his bad leg, riding a wave, not just the indignation, righteous or otherwise, but the intensity of his presence, solidified, made whole by the Psyaint's doubt and lack of resolution, determined to drive home his point.

"That's incredible," he snarls, points menacingly. "For centuries I've dealt with mad men, deranged sadists, hopped up homicidal deadbeats, rapists, and most actually believed some fantasy deity would help them."

hereby it becomes apparent
    that the best
of psyaints are psychos

And then in the failing of a saint's mind, his rationale for existence, the absence of motivation, buried in faith, be it in Sam or otherwise, Hans-Peter does not remind Sam that others have failed before, dampened the torch, disappeared in the river, fallen from the battlements. Or how explain

Sam's scars, the tattered hide on his ass?

Providing for another day, with advantage to be gained in mind, when confrontation demands, Sam will claim he too is reasonable, and admit that the seas he sails are calm and safe. He, too, has been deceived, and cheated (for isn't that what he is mostly about — to deceive and be deceived? Isn't that what creation is all about?). As the stories go, in the trials and incidents of their wanderings, deities are mostly irrational and angry, less than kind, less than perfect, unless malevolence is in-and-of-itself a quest for perfection.

"At least they had some sense of destiny," Sam says, in the bluff of bravado, twisting his way into whatever the Duke of Death might want to believe.

"Intelligence alone should eviscerate the joke of salvation. Whoever proposes it offers you nothing. I'm all you have. You are at least the Son of Sam. Otherwise? A sad, gruesome, comic nothing, going through the motions of living with no direction, or connections, no reason to be alive, and even less to die. You said it yourself. 'Now the void is filled.' That's what I am. He-Who-Fills-The-Void. Christ, I should have been a fuckin' Indian."

"But they're out to get me."

"So, you expected to live forever?"

"Yes."

"You were dead the day before you were born. Or have you forgotten. Yes. That's what they do. They forget to remember that they are dead. Ignore the truth the inevitable, hoping, fantasizing that they will live forever.

"The only reason you're alive today is because someone on the street or in the woods hasn't found a way to turn your ghost to their advantage. When they do, you're gone."

David shrinks, curls up on the bed. Lashed with anguish, certain Sam, too, has abandoned him, he sobs softly.

"What do I do now?" he whispers through the tears.

"We have two more sorties — letters to write."

"But the job at the Post Office is killing me."

"You have only begun?"

"I can't go on."

"A few months in the scheme of time. You have only a few months left."

"I can't. Those names. All those names of people I don't know."

"But they will know your name. Every one of them. Stay with it until the end of July."

"And then?"

"Donna is alive."

"Where?"

"The end of July."

Psyaint David

**Sam applauds
the recognition
of the terrorist industry**

Sam pauses in the plaza to extract a morning edition of *The Times* from a kiosk. The carbuncles and boils on his face, the swollen and red pustules leak, fluids dripping, falling and striking the sidewalk in small puffs of smoke.

He's headed for the American Psychiatric Association breakfast at Windows on the World. This is a special event. He seldom gets a free ride to the top. Ascent is always a heady experience. It is again this morning, and after a moment to adjust to the altitude, he locates a table with his name.

Still he rasps. Small wisps of steam puff from his eyes as they alternately tear and flare. It is the altitude. The rarified air. He pauses at the window, unsteady: vertigo, acrophobia. He finds his place at the table, opens the paper, folds it at page B2 — waits, reads, chortles.

This morning Dr. Leo Stole, director of the Midtown Manhattan Study, proclaims (at the American Psychiatric Association's annual meeting) that urban mental health is superior to rural mental health.

"The data stand in total refutation of the prejudgment continuously pressed since the eighteenth century that urban mental health is on a one-way downward spiral.

"Urban life does an awful lot of good through the cultural and other resources it provides, that many city dwellers thrive on."

Ignored for the most by the other seventy or so attendees, Sam checks the menu, orders Frittata of Chipolata, Potato, and Spinach. A Soy Grilled Baby Eggplant — good for an old goat's digestion.

Listening to Stoles patter in the background, he gazes off nostalgically over the Manhattan skyline, the Empire State Building, a plethora of memories — yeah, Sam reminiscing. This is the place. Saturday, July 28, 1945 is the time.

Another foggy morning. Suitable for Sam. Lieutenant Colonel William Franklin Smith, Jr., pilots a B-25D Mitchell (named Sneezy) from Bedford Army Air Field to Newark Airport, asking the tower at Newark for clearance to land. Visibility is zero. Smith is refused permission. Riding co-pilot that day, Sam encourages Smith to proceed. Disoriented by the fog, after passing the Chrysler Building, per Sam's instructions, the B-25D banks right instead of left.

At 9:40, still at zero-visibility, the bomber punches into the Empire State Building's north side seventy-eighth floor. The plane hits the building like a dart, and sticks.

One engine shoots through the south side opposite the impact and flies on into the next block, dropping nine hundred feet to land on the roof of a nearby building and setting a penthouse on fire. The other engine, and part of the landing gear, tumble down an elevator shaft.

Fourteen people die: Smith and two others aboard the plane — Staff Sergeant Christopher Domitrovich and Albert Perna, a Navy aviation machinist's mate who was hitching a ride. Perna's body rifles into an elevator shaft and falls to the bottom. They don't find it for two days.

Eleven people in the seventy-eighth floor offices of the National Catholic Welfare council also die. Betty Lou Oliver, an elevator operator, gets to ride a free-falling elevator to the bottom of the shaft and survives the ride.

"A goddam hit," Sam says in a low, melodious voice. "Good enter-tainment. Something to talk about — a cherished memory. The kind of excitement pop culture thrives on. Something to write a song about."

He hacks up a chunk of toxic phosphorescent phlegm and splatters the thermopane. It sticks and glows like a marker.

Dr. Stole leans over the podium, suggests, "The City's super mental health derives from the masses of psychiatrists located here who seem to be thriving better than their rural counterparts. Perhaps 'symptoms of psychological distress' need to be rethought. Perhaps difficulty sleeping, the feeling that everyone is against me, and worries that get me down physically, are signs of superior health, of minds tuned in on reality."

A follow-up presentation focuses on Village inhabitants. Dr. Hermes Cosmos amplifies Dr. Stole's findings.

"The vast majority of Village dwellers are more than reasonably satisfied with their lives. From the testing done it is evident that Village residents are healthier than the residents of the four rural communities used in the study. Even those suffering disabling effects of environmentally related diseases believe it was worth the sacrifice just to be in The City."

"Can you give us a sampling of the questions used in the survey?"

"Certainly," Dr. Cosmos says. "We asked three questions.

"One, would you leave The City to go to a remote sea-island — even if the volcanoes were inactive?

"Two, are you bothered by the presence or activity of the sharks in The City Bay?

"And three, has concern with either of the above questions caused you physical distress such as pimples, hives, shingles, impotency or frigidity?

"Now, these questions may seem nebulous, but it is a recognized Freudian fact that neurotic concerns with sea-islands and sharks are the first symptoms of those under severe emotional stress caused by their environment.

"The results imply that The City residents under stress who are likely to dream of respites or vacations on remote sea-islands surrounded by sharks are also more fearful of being abandoned (thus, the remote island) and of being eaten alive than they are of staying in The City — as healthy or unhealthy as that may be."

Psyaint David

Dr. Cosmos is reminded that less than 5 percent of urbanites use the "substantial cultural resources" of their cities. Most are content to sit indoors, comatose, waiting and watching the pale blue teevee campfire light shift in the center ring.

"Pretense," Sam says. "Even if they do not participate, they're delighted to hear they're at the center of something. Pleasure by association, the APA, and fantasy."

Sam stands, stretches, runs an open hand over the wall, the shattered glass and scorched plasterboard walls already stained with the rolls of the dead and maimed.

the prospects of sales are further
  enhanced by the images
of executive felonious memories

Let me have your attention, please. Now, ladies and gentlemen, Syndicast Service presents David Frost playing to a massive audience as reported by Nielsen and Arbitron, in The City, Chicago, and Los Angeles (the major markets) interviewing that wizard of illusion, the grandmaster of fabrication, the once and former king of the bingo game, Richard Nixon.

In anything but a spectacular performance, with his little-boy attentiveness and awe, Frost wheedles his guest, the ultimate egoist, (best known as "Would you buy a used car from this man?" and symbolized as a member of a fanciful trio of losers: A knocked up whore, driving an Edsel with a Nixon bumper sticker) through an hour of self-effacing reflections and admissions.

"I brought myself down. I gave 'em a sword. And they stuck it in, and they twisted it with relish. And I guess if I'd been in their position, I'd have done the same."

Sam fizzes.

"Boo! Hiss! Did the same thing," he says. "You were eager for whatever advice I could provide."

But others are watching, too. The program penetrates 150 markets and reaches 92 percent of the nation's households. Thirty-second commercial units sell for sixty-three thousand dollars each.

Bristol-Myers. Alpo. Calico.

For his part, Nixon receives two and a half-million to further substantiate the aged retributive legal adage that "no man should profit (too much) from his wrongdoing."

"That's what it's all about," Sam lectures instructively, chuckles. "Once you're in, no matter what, the money is guaranteed. The greater the crime, the richer the pot. And that's the way it is supposed to be. Otherwise, how else might the world run? What else?"

Sam is pleased with the show, the prospects. These are, indeed, good times. Nevertheless, he's staring into another mirror. He's developed a large yellow furuncle on his upper lip.

money at Blackrock
  with or without
money and/or genius

Understandably the Nixon fiasco foreshadows a realignment of the rivalry among the B's and C's. Teevee fare suffers a seasonal quiescence. With time on his mind, (his leg has improved, a mere bulge of bullet in the muscle) putting his instigations and encouragements aside, for the moment, Sam shakes a ticket out of his hat for the Thursday 7:30 preview of the Barbara Montgomery become Lady Macbeth (Edna Thomas), a La Mama Experimental Theatre Club revival of the WPA/Orson Welles "Voodoo Macbeth" from 1936. Sam has a deep regard for the "lady," believes she is truly lethal. He dresses old hat, Elizabethan garb, adopts his ear to the Caribbean dialect. Intrigue, suspicion, deceit, villainy, lust for power, serves an old devil almost as well in Haiti as in Scotland.

And in The City? Well, the war of the airwaves has not subsided. A deep and somber rumbling along the corridors of Blackrock, prophetic of St. Mathias' words, settles in a patina of corporate dust on the desks of Paley, Arledge, and Silverman.

"It's that cop persona that's ruining us," Wee Willie says. "We have to change it. Too goddam much *Kojak* and *Hawaii Five-0.* What we need are more of *Charlie's Angles* and *Police Woman.* And *Gunsmoke."*

"They're cops, too."

"Yeah, but that's different.

"Tits and ass. Tits and ass. Nobody cares about the plot.

"When a luscious cunt serves up a limp-fingered karate chop or a couple of pieces of lead from .38 Special, it is always justified. The men like it because she's a sweet piece of meat — a bit of pugnacity with life that fights back — and the women like it because she's a woman. Just as long as the camera gets an eye on enough skin — people would rather fuck and fight (which may be the same thing) than do anything else. We're losing our corporate ass."

"So what about *Gunsmoke*?"

"People like horses and frontier whores."

Well, some of them anyway.

"And what about the news?"

"I realize we don't have the control or influence over programming we once had, but from now on I want every news segment we produce laced with an accusation of inadequate cops. Police negligence, brutality, corruption — whatever you can find. We've been kind too long. And don't give me that crap about constitutional rights. We show cops doing it and the Constitution will take care of itself. This will go into effect immediately. And by all means, get rid of that goddam *Kojak*."

"That's going to screw up scheduling."

"That's going to cost us."

"*Kojak* is a money-maker. We need Kojak."

"Worry about the nickels and dimes we lose our ass. We're done."

Paley's in his office, standing arms folded, staring down the camera. Numerous CBS award trophies proliferate the background, along with glass microphones of various designs, and jade statues he has collected on his not infrequent trips to the Orient. Photos of Murrow and Benny hang on the far wall.

"We have to anticipate. Do away with a money-maker to beat everyone else to a bigger money-maker, and catch everybody flat. Get in before the others have the sense to get out."

"Hey, nothing's sacred. We can change it."

"But there's the contract with The Universe — until they catch the anta-gonist."

"So what? Bury the goddam thing. Find a dead slot and stick it in."

"We could have the Lieutenant apprehend Son of Sam in the next show."

"That wouldn't hold up in court. Our legal department believes that time and intent are the spirit of the agreement. The contract is specific. If The Universe wants to hold us to it."

"Maybe we could make a tradeoff — use a couple of their new shows."

"Maybe."

"By the way, what's Silvas Fredman planned for the fall?"

"Does it matter?"

"Yes, it matters. What about Antonowsky?"

"Fredmen. Antonowsky. C'mon. Who are they? They don't know any more than anyone else."

"I suppose that's why they're the world's greatest programmers. Because they don't know."

"It is called the Fredmen Effect — what follows when you get hired at a million a year to resurrect a sinking ship."

The acoustics reverberate with Sam's voice, Sam's grunts, Sam's words.

"Genius in teevee is ex post facto. Regardless of research, guesses, odds and/or mistakes, the system still works. Those at the top, in the right slots at the right time get the accolades. If it happens a couple years running, they swear their talent made the sun rise. But once you're in the captain's cabin, regardless, even if the ship sinks, you are then and forever after a million-dollar-a-year exec. You know that and I know that. In truth? Though nobody will admit it, we could program a whole week of two mutts humping in prime time and nothing would change. We'd still make a profit. Maybe more than we're making now.

"More than that, the narrative insists that mariners who pick up that kind of change do not sail into fog banks. But those misfits have all programmed a flock of turkeys. Enough to serve Thanksgiving dinner to everyone in The City — with two servings. But error is for mortals.

"Also, failure has a thousand rationales. Hell, the situation was too far gone. The first mate wouldn't listen. The weather was uncompromising — whatever, we are told it is not the million-dollar messiah's fault. From then on wherever he goes it is green — big green.

"Nobody in the business knows what the public wants. The public doesn't know what it wants. Shows are made, time sold, stars born. We know people watch, but we don't know why or even what they see. Ask the average teevee viewer to explain his fascination for *Hawaii Five-0*. Don't. He'll grunt and babble something about tempo. Sounds like the old *American Bandstand*. 'I don't know, but it's got a good beat.' Every shoot comes out of the box different.

"And now we've got the FCC dicking around. What's the name? E.Erie™? Yeah. That's it. E.Erie™. What or who the fuck is that thing, anyway? Where did it come from? And I mean, before that."

Well, he does get excited and go on sometimes.

"Then why not keep *Kojak*?"

"Because there may be something else that will make more. When the bean counters talk about profit they're only talking about how much more we made this year than last. Even if we make less than last year we're still making, big money, but losing money we might have made. So even when we lose, we are making money. It's just a matter of how much. And even taking a chance, we don't want to lose money."

E.Erie™ considers
changing his name
and crossing over

E.Erie™ is quandarized. His hard drives are sectioned and fragmented with the video malignancy. Rumors suggest the mainframes are main-lining, that their operating systems converted, crossed over, and are now working as double-agents.

The disorders he sought to control have not responded. In one week the C's and B's carry a barrage of:

> 1003 false ads
> 973 cases of fraud
> 83 assaults,
> 64 batteries,
> 57 attempted murders
> 16 rapes,
> 14 first degree murders,

14 kidnappings,
11 cases of brutality,
10 grand larcenies,
9 manslaughters,
9 breakings-and-enterings,
8 cases of sodomy
7 second degree murders,
7 indecent exposures,
6 false imprisonments,
5 suicides,
4 child molestations, and
3 blackmails.

Before courts of law the networks are culpable in excess of a thousand years in prison each for the compounded felonies of their offerings, and E.Erie™ is feeling the heat — his quandary? Felonies. How to eradicate the virus and better sell felonious products?

Of course business is at heart misdeed (at least teevee business), and reacting to Columbia's intention to give the cops a bad name, SAMIE launches a counterattack. Sirens wail, tires screech, moans and screams drift street ward from backstage alleys.

newly therapized
the Loo regains his mojo

Suddenly there are no clear lines of demarcation. Who's working for whom? Nobody knows. Even fewer care.

Pursuit becomes the word of the moment, and casting caution and civil rights to hell, in a seven-day binge of retaliation, retribution, vengeance and revenge, teevee cops set out to rid the screen of all criminal elements. Informers, suspects, anyone and everyone in the way is stepped on. Here swings the powerful swift sword, here the trampling out of sour grapes and Lieutenant LoKo is at the front, leading the lord's jack attack, intent on rubbing one out. Prime time audiences cheer the heroes and hiss the villains.

"It worked," the Lou tells Crocker who signed in at the studio door as Kevin Dobson. "The Saint was right. I needed a tuneup. I feel better already."

They're in closeup, black and white, an old round 11" Zenith, currently on Channel 2 wheeling through lower East Side traffic. The renowned squad car interior is set in deep-claustrophobic-focus, the shadows and closed spaces insinuating the tension and strain of what is to come.

"I don't worry as much as I used to," the Loo says. "I'm more laid back. Better self-awareness — got my own space."

Crocker agrees. He's noticed the change, a shift in demeanor and attitude in his boss. He's grateful.

"You don't yell as much," Crocker says. "At least not at me. What did they do?"

"I got new lines — a different way to talk. A better self-concept. I come on more in black and white. More absolutes, less distortion, avoid distractions of bright colors. A lot to do with word order, syntax, intonation, emphasis. Even picked up some highbrow literature stuff. Ezra Pound things. 'Give me language and I'll control the country.' The mot jus. You gotta get the right word in the right place. Brings out my true self — I mean, I got the language."

Simple Sidekick sympathizes.

"You can get lost in this job. It is easy to forget who you are. We're not like other schmucks."

"We're unique," Kojak-Holmes says. "That's why we hunt. We're different. Remember, good people are not predators. We are not predators. Therefore, we are not exterminators."

"So they lifted your suspension."

"What'd you hear about that?"

"Well, they had to do something. I know it was eight years ago, but there's no statute of limitations on murder."

"He may have killed the wrong mark, but it wasn't murder."

"Suspensions are routine when you kill somebody."

"You mean the Hans Commission."

"Ah, yeah. I guess."

"I didn't kill the wrong guy. They suspended the wrong cop. It happens all the time. Remember, that was the summer of '69: part 1."

"But this isn't part 2. We still have six months or so."

Marlowe's eyes are wide, set on the light at the end of the street, when they hear the voice of an ominous dark angel. The radio sputters another invitation.

"That's it," the Lieutenant says. "Let's go."

"But what is it? A homicide?"

"Yeah. That's for us. D'you hear that? D'you get the description?"

"No. Did you?"

"No."

The intonation on the radio, reminiscent of the narrator's voice on the in-house teevee, of necessity reiterates the location and description.

"Just what we need," the Lou says. "Four shots. Screams. A horn blowing. A dead female. A hole where the bullet went in. A wounded boyfriend. No clues. No witnesses."

"How do you know?"

"Oh, I know. This is more than likely another Son of Sam exposé."

"But what about your suspension?"

"I'm no longer suspended. Self-awareness has set me free."

"But what if it's a warning of things to come."

"Yeah. Well, everybody knows I'm a renegade. A little hanky-panky will improve my image. I am a mild-mannered good-hearted schmooze. If they ground me, lock me in the Captain's office, the audience will be on the edge, curious to see what I'll do next — how much I drink, what females visit me.

"Three, four hours, three times a week I'll show up, hang around, kid with the people on the set, collect my pay. But I'll bring the crowd along. It's good business. The women love it. Meanwhile, I'll psych-out the killer's presence, where he intends to strike next. The Clever Hans Effect. Every killer displays unintentional clues — to communicate with the police. I'll devise a trap for him. There's still time. We have six months or so."

"Maybe this is the killer."

"Yes, it's Son of Sam again."

"Where?"

"Assault & Battery Park this time. Where else?"

"What about Queens?"

"He's moved across the river. It's a condition in homicidal psychology known as the Death Drift. The locations of murder scenes mark the area of concentration by the presence of decay to a degree of uncertainty directly in proportion to the square of the distance between the bodies. Having developed the arena of its concentration, but unable to contain itself in an established area, extinction must of necessity push beyond the perimeters of its own boundaries. This is the first wave of the invasion."

Crocker is amazed. "Wow!" is all he can say.

time for a Schlitz commercial

Break in the action.

Fade out.

Fade in on a small sailboat south of Battery Park, tacking and veering with the Staten Island Ferry in the background. The music rises, gently, lively, then a somber but upbeat voice over.

"When it's the finer things in life you are seeking, you don't take a chance on second best."

Cut to a low-angle three-shot of the Ferry, the sailboat and the Statue of Liberty tilting in the distance. The camera closes on the faces in the boat.

Cut to a full-shot as the massive hulk of the Ferry grows larger, dwarfing the sailboat.

"Just being alive is sometimes reward enough, to say 'We did it.' When you want to savor the wonder of life . . .."

The sailboat crew turns to face the camera, smiling grim, weathered macho smiles of endurance and steadfastness, either unaware of the looming Ferry, or too drunk to care.

The voice continues.

"When you want to remember the real things, the guts it took to do the job, only one beer will do, and that's Schlitz."

The sailboat captain stands in mid-shot, holds up a bottle of Schlitz.

A crew member waves and shouts (silently, of course), "Hi Mom," then stumbles over a hemp line and falls face down on the deck. The other two laugh.

The captain leaves the wheel and takes another Schlitz from the cooler and holds up a bottle in either hand while the boat spins sharply in the wind, dumping a crew member overboard. The Ferry rams the sailboat, snapping its mast and shattering its hull.

Cut to the capsized, broken hull of the sailboat and Schlitz cooler bobbing and spinning slowly in the Ferry's wake, the Statue of Liberty in the background, the crew nowhere in sight.

Voice over.

"For those days in your life that really count, it's Schlitz."

now back to the action

The commercial fades.

Covering what will be listed as a random homicide the camera swings in, silhouettes the Inspector Lieutenant among the rotating red and blue lights of police cruisers.

A crowd of passersby watches the action as a police officer squats on the sidewalk beside a dead woman later identified as Victoria Weisberg of 17 Linden Court in Roslyn Heights. Her face is badly discolored.

"She's dead," the officer says.

The Loo surveys the crowd, disparagement on his lips, disdain, detestation of the foul-filth who would do something like this paining his heart.

"She's dead," the cop repeats.

"Yeah, she's dead," he says. "What did you expect? A pellet gun?"

The Lou turns and walks toward the crowd.

MET diva Linda Levan Cordell of 815 5th Avenue, from Songs to Raise Women, a branch of Enabling Women to Stand, steps out of the crowd to add her soprano to the gathering with a stirring rendition of "Des Knaben Wunderhorn" from Mahler's "Resurrection," 2nd Symphony.

> O Röschen roth!
> Der Mensch liegt in größter Noth!
> Der Mensch liegt in größter Pein!
> Je lieber mocht' ich in Himmel sein!
> Da kam ich auf einen breiten Weg:
> Da kem ein Engelein und woilt' mich abweisen.
> (Traditional German)

Psyaint David

The crowd gives her a standing-by ovation. She is pleased. The Lou is not. He doesn't like Germans or Jews.

"Did anyone see the specter?" the Inspector wants to know.

"No," someone says, "we ain't seen it happen."

The ever resourceful Inspector approaches a man in the front row.

"Sir, what'd you see?"

"Nothing."

"That's amazing," the Lou says. "How is it you see nothing? I suspect you saw something. But don't want to talk about it. Or maybe what you saw isn't relevant to this case. Maybe you would feel better telling what you know to the DA? You are an accessory after the fact."

The man shrinks back, shakes his head.

"I don't even live here. I'm just a tourist. I thought this was a tourist attraction. Street theatre. Like over in Brooklyn at the beginning of the story."

A thin blonde in skintight levis and high heels comes forward.

"You must be the fierce Lieutenant we have heard so much about."

The Lieutenant pauses, trying to figure what's what, before answering.

"What did you see?"

His voice is shaky and uncertain again, the ambivalence in his disposition now seemingly in charge. Of course that's what therapy does to you, sometimes.

The blonde with the wasp waist pushes (his/her boobs) closer to the camera.

"I think you're the most wonderful and exciting man I've ever seen. Oh, and so violent. I absolutely adore violent men. Do you swear? I once knew a sailor who could swear like a sailor. My god! It was wonderful. Did you ever hear a sailor swear? I love men with hair on their chests. Men with horsepower. Rummm! Rummm!"'

"What did you see?" the Lou whines, squirming away.

The blonde smiles an enchanting, vibrant smile.

"Oh, my! What do you see? You should know as well as anyone that things are seldom what they appear to be."

"I can arrest you for not seeing and interfering with a police investigation," the Lieutenant says, his voice fraught with anxiety.

The blonde squeals with delight.

"Oh, would you. Would you do it personally? Would you put me in handcuffs and drag me off, brutally and without regard for my safety, beat me mercilessly with your fists, without the least thought of either my wellbeing or your reputation? My god. Do you have an Electric Stick? Would you poke me with your fun gun?"

The Lieutenant smiles meekly at the camera.

"I suppose that's all you want. A little action. A few bruises, a broken bone or two."

"Oh, no. You poor, poor man. I didn't mean it that way. I want you. I'll do anything for you. Anything."

Obviously the romance is going nowhere, at least not for the moment. The blonde drops back into the crowd, dejected, wounded by the Lou's inactivity, the failure of soul-mates to link up.

The Lieutenant, severely tainted by his inability to maintain his composure in face of an all-out assault on the values he has long represented, regroups. Moments later he is ready to regain lost ground.

"What about the rest of you? Every crime has a witness, and this one's no different. Is there anyone who saw anything?"

His lips tremble as he stares at the crowd, about to begin again, when Detective Rizzo's voice springs out of the shadows of the park.

"Here she is. I found her."

"Rizzo? What the hell is Rizzo doing here?" LoKo wants to know. "I thought he was redacted. He's supposed to be on special assignment."

"Maybe they used disappearing ink."

The crowd turns as of a single mind and divides as Rizzo comes through pushing an old woman in front of him.

"I found her in a trash can taking pictures," he says. "She's seen the whole thing."

The woman gives her vitals as seventy-five-year-old Martha Farnsworth (who has aged significantly since her last appearance) of 3324 Chapel Hill Drive in Brentwood. In the interim she is suffering from Photo Progeria, a variety of the Mary Tyler Moore Premature Aging Syndrome. And though middle-age, and fame and fortune as a photographer have eluded her, she is still taking pictures.

Shamus smiles an appreciative son smile. She reminds him of his mother.

"How about that? Mom, what do you know about this? And what were you doing in that trash can?"

There are no easy answers. But, clearly, all is not well. The old woman hawks and spits at the Lieutenant, lands a wad on his ruffled white satin poet shirt and lifts her cane. She lashes at the air. Kojak-Hammer steps back and swiftly frees his Bodyguard service weapon.

Now, the Bodyguard is valued by undercover police officers who need to carry a highly reliable weapon clandestinely, and need the option of single or double action in a firearm that will not jam inside a pocket when fired from one. Its compact frame, shrouded hammer, and light weight make it easy to hide. The Bodyguard has a five-round capacity.

The small J-frame revolver is available in either .38 Special or .357 Magnum. This one appears to be a .38 and given to instinct, the Loo brings the weapon down and across in a slashing motion against the woman's cheekbone.

The crowd recoils, gasps, then edges forward chanting, "Replay! Replay!"

In slow-motion this time, the old woman, back bent beneath the crippling hump of age, arthritic, palsied, and weakened by fast food and exhaustion, tries to make a point by poking at the air with her cane.

Even before she raises the cane in the replay, the Lieutenant lifts his revolver and brings it down in a looping, graceful motion, the cold blue steel shimmering in the dim light, slamming against her face in a crimson splash of splatter cinema at its best. Her head snaps to one side, her eyes wide, glazed, her broken jaw quivering.

Again she tries to speak and again the gun thumps her face.

The blonde swoons and falls to the ground writhing in ecstasy.

"I was," the old woman tries to say, "I was just passing. . ." her words lost beneath the crowds rising chant.

"Kill! Kill! Kill!"

"You shouldn't lie to me," the Lieutenant says and takes her by the throat with his free hand.

"Mom, you're as guilty as sin."

He raises the gun again, but before he can deliver the blow, Frank grabs his arm.

"Hey, hold it, we're on camera."

Momentarily Martha recovers something of her senses and swings her Canon AE-1, a 35 mm single-lens reflex camera on its lanyard in a circling trajectory landing a punishing blow to Kojak's forehead.

Tracy recoils from the strike and smashes Martha again. Her head snaps to one side (as it did the first time and again on the replay), eyes rolled back, her face a mass of bruises and lacerations.

"She'll talk," he whimpers. "You'll talk, won't you Mom? I want answers, now. Truthful answers. I want you to tell me why you treated your son the way you did."

The old woman gurgles. Pink bubbles pop from her mouth. Her head falls forward and Tracy pushes it back.

"She knows when she's had it," he says. "Mothers always do."

Crocker's face is red, tense. He steps between Byrd and the camera, glances at Kesil.

"Shut that thing off."

The crowd presses in, chanting, "Hit her! Hit her!"

"That's our tax dollar at work."

"We're gonna get bad press from this," Crocker says. "Police brutality. Unnecessary force. Mother's Day is just around the corner. We'll get blamed for all kinds of things. The CCRB will cut our balls off. We can use force but it must be done artistically. I mean, used to support realistic themes and settings. It must have socially redeeming value. Otherwise, the do-gooders are gonna bust our cookies."

Kenner-McNeil (Frank) watches from the periphery. So this is what the PC wanted. Well, why not?

The argument continues but does little to convince the Lou.

"The woman has to carry her weight," he says. "This is teevee. A lot of people are making a living off this. That's what keeps the economy going. These are my fans, my people. They like what I do. It's a respectable show."

"You shouldn't have hit the old lady," Frazer says, finally. "It's a bad example. You know what's gonna happen? Some kid will see that and go out and knock off an old broad and we'll get blamed. I can see it now. Prolonged intense, involuntary, subliminal television intoxication.

We have to be careful about the effect on our viewers. Things like the Neurological Effect, Mean World Syndrome, Teaching No Nonviolent Solutions, the Aggressive Effect, Desensitization Effect and Imitation.

On average there are more than five violent scenes in an hour of prime-time, and five murders a night. There are twenty-five violent acts an hour in Saturday morning cartoons, and 2,605 acts of violence on teevee every day. American kids witness more than 8,000 murders and 100,000 other violent acts on teevee by the time they leave elementary school or 40,000 murders and 200,000 other violent acts by the age of eighteen. Don't tell me they don't like it. If they don't like it, why are they watching it?

Remember Ronnie Zamora. They say teevee warped his mental and emotional process, diseased his mind, and impaired his medial prefrontal cortex."

"Well, what'd you expect a kid to do with the old broad? Kiss her? Anyway, confronting a delinquent parent can be socially redeeming. I mean, where's her children?"

We've heard that before.

He towers over Martha, who has dropped to her knees. She's bent, crying, head down, drooling.

"Okay. Take her away. Book her."

Crocker has his hand over the camera lens.

"We are gonna get burned. The Universe'll get sued for this."

"Oh, Kevin, you worry too much. They don't have a case. We're covered. You have never heard before that this is a free country?"

"Yeah, but . . .."

"Well, we have freedom of expression. Or why rioters in the street? *Mothers with their kids. They're free. We make their lives livable.*"

"But you didn't have to hit that old woman."

"Oh, that was without intent. Something just came over me, a madness, an urge, a duty. And without intent there is no crime. Anyway, how can a fictional what's-it have intent? I mean, any intent I might have had would be fictional. Also, the attempt to shift responsibility for criminal acts away from the individual and into the media is dangerous."

"But that woman didn't harm the girl."

"You might be surprised. You don't know that old lady's sins. She's trained half the prostitutes in this town and she's got enough cash to keep her tracks covered. She sells little boys to quirks . . .."

"Quirks? Quirks?"

"Well, we can't call them queers anymore. You got a better word? Anyway quirk sounds better than queer.

"Anyway the quirks use the kids, then dispose of them. Disposable kids.

"You worry too much. Nobody cares about beating up old women. Or young women, for that matter. Remember, we are the word. The logos. And the logos is."

"So who's the girl?'

"Some chippie caught in the wrong lane."

"Somebody wacked her."

"Yeah. It's a shame. She got nailed to the cross. And that's not the first. But once a chick is dead, what can the cops do? Oh, a few quick photos, statements for the press — so they know we're on the job. That's what counts. We can blame it all on Son of Sam. A little carnage — our Nielsen will go up."

"Who's the old woman?"

"No matter. Rizzo tossed her purse down a manhole. It was all an act, okay? To keep the crowd interested. Halfway to the station he'll dump her off in an alley. She'll wander around for three or four days. Snap up a couple rolls of film. By the time she finds her way home everybody'll have forgotten the whole thing."

Crocker seems apprehensive, if relieved.

"I suppose you're right."

"Of course I'm right. Time's like that. And this is my town. I know these people. Wonderful people, and it's our job to take care of them."

Now the crowd has quieted and the blonde, after a severe fit, is once again regained her composure. She is seated on a park bench shaking her head, mumbling to herself.

EMS paramedics load the body into a van while the film crew gathers up the cables, cameras, lights, shotgun mics, tripod dollies, monitors, and various and sundry equipment.

The Lieutenant pulls his ever trusty sidekick to one side, off camera, a boom mic dropped in for the conversation.

"Confidence and secrecy are the two most valuable items in the police lexicon. No matter what, we stick to our story. You may want to include a story within the story, maybe even two, but remember if we lose the story line we're done. I mean, the gig's canceled. We have to trust our partners. That's the way it's always been."

does E.Erie™ hold the key to the mystery?

In room 224, 109th in Flushing, the Captain dawdles and diddles, swaddled in time, leaning back in a captain's chair, feet up, hands behind his head. These are the long days of inactivity and boredom polished down to a dull gloss. To pass time he spends the morning poking through the black bags of trash the Lieutenant has gathered form the crime scene. A broken roller skate, two pair of cracked sun glasses, four used condoms, a can of hair spray, a Boy Scout badge, and several hundred other items that he hopes will somehow define the miscreant. His attempt to rehash the old, the obvious patterns and small details, has failed, and he turns the mirror to another angle, affects a shift in shadow, a glimmer of light, a line, then prepares to move it again.

But beyond the collectable odds and ends of the Lieutenant's gatherings, he has nothing. No theories, no guesses. To further complicate matters Our Lady of the Pulsating Passions has kept him on ice, now, for nearly two weeks without so much as a whimper or a sniff. He wonders if she is real.

When the phone rings he breaks into his disconsolate reverie, cradles the receiver on his shoulder and listens to the weary voice on the line.

"John, this is the Commissioner."

Keener shuffles through the folders on his desk. He's expecting the call.

"Yes, Commissioner?"

A cough and, "Yes."

"How can I help?"

"John, it's our baldheaded wonder. Now before you say anything, I want you to know that I am aware of what he's done for The City. Hell, what he's done for the country. But it seems to me he's becoming an embarrassment to the department. I'm sure you know what I mean."

"Yes, I do," Keener says.

"I have been informed that he's still under suspension. What's he doing at the scene of a crime?

"As you know, this is an election year and our campaign does not include a story about police brutality. I have a report here on my desk that I know you've seen. If this gets out, heads are going to roll. Understand?'

"Yes," Keener says.

"Also, I'd like you to pay closer attention to the in-house teevee. In the last few days E.Erie™ has pointed out certain revealing details that may provide what we need to solve this Son of Sam thing."

What has E.Erie™ detected? Kenner suspects it has to do with Disorder Media Theory and entropy. The teevee malady might be an irreversible type. Of course, there's always Norio Taniguchi and the possibility of nano-technical mites building nano-nests in the transmitters. At least that's what E.Erie™'s humming and whirring implies.

well, maybe not

The Captain replaces the phone, a hairball in his stomach. Calls from the top are hard to digest. Sometimes he can forget, let it go, sometimes not.

He lights a cigarette and wonders where the old days have gone. Police work today is too goddam complicated. Not only do you have to accept SAMIE's edicts, you have to understand why. Everything's circuitry. Banks of gas chromatograph-mass spectrometers, laser scanners, and now this goddam self-righteous auto-directing, arrogant in-house teevee — not to mention E.Erie™'s blinking and buzzing tubes and displays.

Where are the good old days? A horse, a saddle, a Winchester and a star — a mean S.O.B to track down. Corner the splay-footed sob, shoot his scaly skinned ass and haul him back to town in time to get a drink before sundown. Hell, even if the bastard wasn't guilty, so what? No one to ask questions, and the corpse to serve as a symbol of evil and decaying flesh that Americans love. Shit. Justice. Pure and simple.

Still the Captain is hopeful. It may all work out for the better. Within a year the police in The City, Chicago and L.A. will be hooked into the same communications set up. And then? Bigger and better electronic games of cops and robbers. Satellites to track smugglers. A whiff of breath and the bastards know your old man's name, chromosomal structure, and whether or not you have fallen arches.

In the west, Chicago wants a piece of the pie. Entertainment, expanding markets, showbiz, murder-for-hire, gang wars, feuds. Drag the specter kicking and thrashing, into the public square for the audience to stare at, to shrink away — then conjure a dynamic campaign to sell the freak, the deformed oddity. No family is complete without one.

Keener flips on the set, settles back. Nothing to do but watch, contemplate the Commissioners orders and wait — and wonder. What's the plan?

still, it appears the affliction has spread

Waiting for the evening news, the Captain catches the end of a commercial and a deep resonant voice in a Texas accent, imperative and condescending with moralistic insinuations, speaking over a cut of Pathé WW I newsreel.

"Plans have been completed for the Arch Duke Ferdinand's trip to Serbia and his forthcoming assassination. Czar Nicholas II's control over his Generals has diminished sufficiently to make the Arch Duke's trip both feasible and advisable. Kaiser Wilhelm could not be reached for comment, but it was learned from sources inside the Wertheimer Government that the unrecognized British plan for Germany to cultivate freely and openly a thorough and ongoing anti-Semitic spirit will be given serious consideration.

"Gavrilo Princip from Sarajevo was not available for comment, and will not be available for some time."

"In other news, a special team was dispatched today to cover a late breaking story on Israeli Prime Minister-to-be Menachem Begin. Before dawn today Mr. Begin, on the advice of his staff, chauffeured to the far side of town to a séance with a middle-aged medium, a woman whose name has not been released. It is said, however, in a moment of inspirational preternatural maneuvering, she conjured up the scattered psychic remains of Adolf Hitler. After an undetermined period of frantic activity, enough of the Fuehrer's mind and heart were pasted together to give the illusion of a whole being and the two ghosts sat down to a strained but amicable discussion. Hegel, Kant and the God State were topics of conversation, and three hours later, Begin appeared outside his office, smiling and cheerful.

"The news of the Begin visit collected noisy support from Jewish organizations who claim Begin is finally softening to their demands that Palestinians be driven out of Palestine or interred in placement camps."

The Captain's reading the handwriting on the wall. Youth groups (street gangs?) — invasions of privacy. Power ripped from saner hands. Nuit et brouillard. This seems certain now. He wonders about the future of concentration camps. Nuremberg. The lessons learned. Never again will men forsake their moral obligations for political gain.

"It is reported another séance, a seating of four, will be held next week with Dyan and Himmler expected to join Hitler and Begin.

"Further, it is England's belief that nuclear unrest for the second half of the twentieth century might be encouraged by tying the United States and the Soviet Union into a Mideast conflict."

The Captain rubs his eyes.

"For this I need a teevee," he tells himself.

SAMIE

The idea finally trickles down through SAMIE, in all its whimdom, that the maintenance of a legal-illegal or extrajudicial adversary organization operating within The City, is both expensive and inefficient — allowing for an unnatural amount of freelancing and, therefore, waste. The not-so-petty burglaries, armed robberies, etc., outside of police and gang control, are depleting resources otherwise available for juice, prostitution, protection, gambling, drugs, kickbacks, bribes, etc.

In accordance with the USDJ edict, the words "mafia" and "costa nostra" are no longer operational for SAMIE. The word (directive) states that as soon as bureaucratically possible, SAMIE will "sit-down" with whatever it was once called and attempt to hammer out "an assimilation agreement." The idea seems to be that while still two in technique, the organizations are intended to become one in spirit — to further intertwine the immutability of egos and spirits.

Syndie members and associates are to be moved laterally into the SAMIE structure, given authority and duties commensurate with those previously enjoyed. Hitmen, hustlers, patrolmen, cops on the beat will work side by side. Decisions of command will be shared, and a new code developed for retirement and benefits.

"It make sense," Garfield reiterates. "Our philosophies aren't that diffe-rent. We can carry on just as well working together, concocting giant mock games of cops and syndicators. Albeit we will need a few dead and wounded to make sure it is not mistaken for what it is not. We can orchestrate an outcome to suit the issue and situation (casuistry), without the expenses we have now, and rake off substantial profits."

The reasons for the merge are obvious. SAMIE may have superior num-bers, but for several years morale and dedication have been low, and the Syndie comes one-up in discipline.

"This will provide the intraorganizational competition necessary to improve productivity and profits," Garfield confides. "The laws of The City and gang will supplement each other. We'll revise the *Patrol Guide* to include a chapter called 'Street Wise Success.' No one will tell from what."

"As it is," a deputy commissioner confides, "you need a scorecard to identify the players. A scorecard and uniforms."

"Do you know how much time the average cop spends in court each year? We can use the Syndie's extralegal expertise. Utilize their savvy to avoid court and keep our men on the street turning a profit."

Garfield is optimistically Garfielding.

"This may very well solve The City's crime problem. Now, no matter what happens, whatever, it will be police business, an activity of the arm. We should be able to decrease felonies by 80 or 90 percent. Just don't report them — or list them as police business."

Plaza One and the Syndie
arrange a get-together

The mayor's Committee to Dissolve Crime dumps its final report on Garfield's desk advising that Garfield get the ball rolling. He is especially mindful of Galante's offer at the beginning of the Son of Sam thing, and since it is still several months before the Czarmine is remanded to jail for parole violations (associating with known underworld characters?) a meeting is to be arranged at the Bareon Arms in a suite SAMIE has reserved for covert activities.

Within the hour word seeps out of Puzzle Palace One. Unable to resist the temptation, with nothing of interest to do, and rankled by not being invited to the pow-wow, Gambino leaders convene, confer, and plot an ambush. This, they say, will even the score and open the market.

"Should we hit 'em both?"

"Just Galante. Make the cops look bad without givin' 'em sympathy."

For three days preceding the summit, deputy commissioners and under-world lieutenants stage sit-downs to discuss ground rules and otherwise work out preliminaries for negotiating sessions. Cigar smoking is permitted. Meals are to be catered by a Syndie contact — hijacked beef, a fresh load of purloined broccoli and tomatoes. SAMIE will provide security. All items of the merger and incorporation agreed upon will be committed to writing, printed, and initialed, but not distributed or published.

By early afternoon Friday, Frank "Delicious" Indelicnoseo and a rank of associates from the Carvense Family join the Gambino's to prepare the ambush — artillery at the ready — machineguns, grenades, enough hard-ware to kick off a small war. Three squads of four goons each are to sulk and slither onto the scene. It is assumed that when Galante arrives he will be accompanied by a couple of Zips. The Zips may or may not have gone over. Something like Schrödinger's Cat — dead and alive. No one knows the Cat's fate until the box is opened. So it is with the Zips.

Squad one, masked with a stoic chorus visage of menace, (to provide commentary on actions and events and create a deeper and more meaning-ful connection between the characters and the audience by controlling the atmosphere and expectations and preparing the reader for certain key moments in the storyline in building momentum or slowing the tempo) will wait until the quarry disembarks his limo and ambulates into the clearing of the wide sidewalk between the street and the revolving doors of 150 East 44th Street.

They will open fire from the east with shotguns.

Seconds later, giving Galante and the Zips time to assess their peril, and an additional second or two to plot a course — and a chance to regret their sins of the past, which is unlikely — but before they can fully implement a defense or escape, squad two will move in from the west with shotguns and finish the job.

If for some reason the assault should fail and Galante make a run for it, squad three, stationed down the block (it is a one-way street), in a well-staged, dramatic finale to a splendidly arranged and choreographed pro-duction of death in the late afternoon, will, with a couple sixty calibers on the back of a rented truck, obliterate the black Lincoln as it passes.

Kesil will have camera crews set up across from the initial assault venue and at the end of the street along the imagined escape route. And in accordance with the current methodology all moving objects are to be tracked within the field of view of an electronic camera system, which is illustratively composed of a fixed spotting camera and a movable tracking camera. Images are sequentially generated then stored at scan intervals.

in the planning

In spite of three days of preliminary sit-downs, hitches and blips develop that very nearly cancel the talks. As late as Thursday evening Pastel is waffling, saying he does not like SAMIE and that it is not the fashion and custom of the Foul Friar to be summoned, but instead for him to summon those he intends to malign. Something like a call to Orders or having a Vocation. After negotiations of several hours, however, in a ploy that requires the most sensitive, delicate fondling of the Capo's insensate psyche, an arrangement is worked out for him to place the call to PP One to initiate the conference, and for Garfield to humbly accept, and, thus, retain the sacrosanct smack of custom and protocol.

Aware of the complications, Garfield responds graciously, as agreed, with the second of a two-faced bureaucratic politeness, stressing the importance of Galante's position as warlord, self-declared head of the Bonanno family, etc., and the benefit the meeting will provide.

Later the same evening another snag develops when Garfield's henchmen and Czarmine's assistants arrive to prepare the conference site and Pastel's bodyguards attempt to erect a WWII surplus Browning Automatic on a stand on their side of the arena, as they say, "just for the hell of it."

Garfield is reminded that Galante's approach to negotiations is not talk, but extended periods of silence — and kill, kill, kill. Taking his staff's suggestion, Garfield refuses to sit and stare down the hollow, cold, steel eye of doom, manned by the erratic, itchy psycho-finger of a stone-lunatic who without remorse and/or for pleasure might pull the trigger.

"Czarmine lives on the edge," a capo confesses, "and is comfortable only when there's a chance, even a remote chance, of a big bang."

However, no obstacle is too great for the nebulous negotiations of the invincible SAMIE and the long suffering, persevering PC. With the soft-green soothing solace of promised fortune, SAMIE associates massage the galled-ass of Galante's greed, and relieve the insistence of his addiction to ordinance and the pleasant, titillating prospect of carnage. They agree to place several open boxes of live grenades beneath the conference table. Easy to grab and throw — or as the case may be, to roll.

With Galante satisfied, but not wanting to fall behind in the I-can-out-absurd-you department, Garfield insists with something akin to maniacal rigidity that they make certain they are not tailed and arrive separately.

Czarmine mumbles, "Rivelazione crea i problemi dell'uomo."

If he believes it or not is anybody's guess.

"As PC of The City of the Gods," Garfield says, "it is my duty to promote the infiltration of criminal organizations. So we need to keep this quiet. Not only would an open meeting attract adverse attention but it would destroy the confidence SAMIE has in its leaders to operate behind the scenes."

the probability
in Pastel's wager

At 2:00 Friday the lobby of 150 East 44th is cleared. Sometime after 2:15 the doorman finds a small roll of fifties in his hand, is asked (politely, of course) to go out for a cup of coffee and not return until the next morning.

He is reminded that he will hear nothing, see even less.

A replacement in a royal blue uniform frequently worn by busmen and ushers, with a .44 in his belt, takes his place at the door.

By 2:30 the street is deserted. A refugee Dingo with tan stripes, inspecting a garbage can in the alley, turns to watch, aware that he is being watched. He whines, uneasily, then sprinkles the garbage can with holy water.

At 2:40, wearing a one-piece mask consisting of horn-rimmed glasses, large plastic nose, a thick greasepaint mustache and bushy eyebrows, a homeless 1975 Bellevue reject with an exaggerated stooped posture — barefooted, in soiled, torn trousers — following his blunted instincts, fumbles along, off course and lost, into the lobby.

"You'll have to move," the doorman tells him and glances apprehensively to the Fellini fresco-faces shadowed in the doorways and alley across the street.

Momentarily the hand of god, guiding fools and children, is extended with a soft, warm smile in the deep black of priestly garb, a Roman collar, moustache and French beret. A Jesuit? Maybe a Franciscan.

"I will take care of this man," he tells the doorman in his best broken Italian dialect.

"Who are you?" the doorman says, fingering his .44.

"I'm Father Blazing Pastel."

The doorman stands with his hand inside his coat, eyes cast away from Fatuous Father.

"Thank you, Padre," he says. "May the saints and the Blessed Virgin reward you."

"I will take care him," Pastel says.

The doorman yields, the derelict agrees and bows his head as Pastel shuffles the wino onto the elevator.

"People no longer take care each other," Pastel says, gazing fondly on his newly discovered remnant of this the least of his brethren. "Some have trouble caring for themselves."

"I've been down on my luck of late, Father," the man says.

They ride silently to the seventeenth floor. When the car stops, the door opens, Pastel steps off.

"Here," he says, handing the man his card. "If I can help, give me a call."

The wino turns the card over, squints at it as the elevator elevates and then rocks to a stop (it's an old building). A kind gesture, he thinks and imagines he will call the good Father. On the nineteenth floor he finds apartment 19M, knocks lightly and is admitted.

The padre creeps along the wall, quickly to the stairs, then up two more floors. A moment later he appears at the door, and after a soft knock, he, too, enters.

"Don't get any funny ideas," he tells Garfield. Still in the uniform of the day, in a most unpriestly way, he reminds the PC that "This is business. Tutti gli aspetti della vita sono I calculi."

All of that said and done, the wino takes a seat, flanked by aids and advisors, his attaché case opened on the table.

"The first order of business is to thank you for coming," Garfield says. He removes the mask and wipes off the greasepaint.

"I realize how difficult it is for you, how out of kind it is for you to deal directly and forthrightly with anyone, much less with the police. This, no doubt, accounts in part for the lack of familiarity of your voice, the vague and menacing shadows of your face. Despite our differences, we have come here in a spirit of cooperation.

"I realize that the enmity of our organizations has at times been bitter, and I further realize that we cannot expect mayhem seekers and hitmen and other low-life, who get goofy when they sense a lack of respect for their transgressions, to behave as civilized human beings, even part of the time. Nevertheless, we believe that after you have considered our proposal, you will agree that what we offer is in your best interest."

"Who sent you?" Padre Pastel grumbles.

As if he has not heard the question, Garfield gazes something less than absentmindedly at an aid, a lovely brunette with bangs, large gray eyes and prosperous breasts draped in a revelatory see-thru blouse. He refreshes himself, finding renewal in recalling the delicious morsel of her warm sensuousness, those firm breasts, the open thighs on his office desk. Clearly, he appears unconcerned, maybe uncertain, about the deeper significance of Pastel's inquiry. He takes a multi-page memo from his attaché case, scans the missive for a name, then pushes it across the table.

"That doesn't merit consideration," Garfield says. "Perhaps we can share such information later. Suffice it to say the weight is heavy. Maybe genetic and generic."

"Big money, or is it political?"

"Both and neither," Garfield says. "Big money and politics are in every-thing — especially everything big or powerful. But eventually it doesn't mean anything, anyway.

"Now, I'd like to outline our proposal, taking care to enumerate, not the reason for this, since that rests eternally with its authors, who may or may not eventually divulge their motives, but the precepts I've been given — that I've brought with me from the mountain. My job, SAMIE's job, is to present it all as clearly and as concisely as possible, considering the limited aptitude and intelligence I must deal with."

Lilo leans back, takes a cigar from his pocket to chew on. He gives no indication of what he thinks or how he might respond to the proposals. Not known as a man of compromise, he's aware that if he agrees to the pro-posals, his possibilities for power and authority will be seriously dimin-ished.

On the other hand, profits will increase, which may, in and of itself, be enough to placate the unbending blind resolve of his ego.

At the moment he's making a cool million a day on the heroin trade, and could use a bit more.

"Umanesimo pagano," he observes. "Conviene crede in Dio."

Garfield trips through the major items of the proposal (edict), finishes, turns to an aid, as if waiting for Pastel's reply, then interjects in an aside, a minor item that, "If you do not agree, as of this AM your contract to do business in The City is cancelled and your Constitutional Rights are suspended. All known underworld figures, large and small, have been identified, located and tagged. And waiting only for an order from me, PC of The City, all will be executed summarily where they sit, stand or lie."

Lilo's face grows stern with these harsh words. He's seen *The Godfather* seven times. He looks around craftily with shifty eyes, feeling that he has been trapped. In unison, trigger fingers go beneath bulging jackets and a heavy tension permeates the air. Indeed, the Zips are nervous.

"You have no respect, no honor," Pastel tells Garfield.

But what to do? Does Garfield exist? Or is he a figment of someone's bizarre imagination. Even on the scene, sitting across from him it is hard to tell. Galante sequences the probabilities or possibilities.

If Garfield exists and I agree — no problem.

If Garfield doesn't exist and I agree — no problem.

If Garfield doesn't exist and I disagree — no problem.

But if Garfield exists and I disagree — PROBLEM.

That is, if Galante's assessment of Garfield's attitudes and inclinations is correct. Will Garfield carry out his threats? Can Garfield carry out his threats? Does it matter if he can or will?

But that is not all. The good Father has another card up his sleeve.

"P-One has more leaks than a silicon tit," he tells Garfield. "The PD is infiltrated with associates. Whatever is left is worthless anyway. When the purge is done, my men will be standing."

So it is coups are made, bargains struck. Garfield returns to his seat as pale and shaken as god when Adam, following his instincts, refused to leave the Garden.

"Yes," he says, with a great deal of consternation. "Yes."

a human fly goes up
the info, news,
entertainment wall

There is a fly on the wall, and existence, staying alive, is not high on the agenda these days. To avoid big city anonymity and other imposed urban deformities, to keep the crowd entertained until something else comes along, adding a bit of sauce to Phillippe Petit's 1974 World Trade Towers' high wire theatrics' pudding, at 6:30, using homemade clamps in the window-washer's tracks (the clamps are designed to lock in place when pulled down by his weight and to release when he raises them) George Willig heads up 2WTC, the third tallest building in the world.

Of course, there are no nets or safety harnesses, only the concrete street waiting 2, 10, 75, 100 stories below — waiting with unrelenting certitude. One mistake — one mistake leads to two and with irrevocable severity to the sidewalk. So as with Petit's funambule or promenade matinale skywalking, each decision must result in a near-perfect act, a well-placed grip and/or step.

Climbing toward the one hundred tenth floor (and *The Tonight Show Starring Johnny Carson, Good Morning America, The Merv Griffin Show,* ABC's *Wide World of Sports,* as well as toward jobs as a cascadeur for *Six Million Dollar Man, Trauma Center,* and *Hollywood Beat)* Willig is intercepted by two police officers, one a pre-suicide therapist, who are lowered in a window-washer's basket to meet and greet him. What the cops intend to do blowing around in the wind, is not clear.

Willig avoids the cops until they are sure he is not a threat, declines treatment, of course, then gives them his autograph with a note, "Best Wishes to my co-ascenders," though they descended.

By then the crowd of the three and a half hours it takes him to get to one-ten is in a frenzy. Some cheer in appreciation for the hutzpah of the stunt. Others encouraging gravity's demands, hope to tell their friends, and someday their grandchildren, that they saw Icarus descending from his encounter with the sun.

Still, it is acclaim from fellow stargazers that Willig craves. He turns a rabbit-ear to the cheering crowd. What does it profit a man to live a sane and moral life if no one notices? Yes, let there be acclaim: shouting and praise and encouragement — even for foolishness. But that's showbiz — accolades from the groundlings for someone, anyone rising, climbing out of their midst.

At the top at 10:05 police pull Willig inside through a small porthole and arrest him. Willig signs his name and date to a piece of metal on the observation deck of the South Tower, then is hauled off ceremoniously to be booked and lauded. Later in the day Mayor Beame elbows in on the publicity by fining Willig $1.10 for his stunt.

intermission: a brief
  respite from
the intense action

After a break, an intermission, a commercial and restroom jaunt, action resumes with Galante saying, "What do I care for the Constitution? I'm an American. The Constitution doesn't mean anything to me."

"Nevertheless," Garfield says, "no sense having too many heads roll. Think of the men we'd be wasting. Think of the cost of training new men."

"This contract with The City is no good," Czarmine says. "The contract with my people is good. Did you read the *Vallachi Papers*, see *The Godfather*? Americans love the family. You can't take our love."

"Everyone here would agree that you have a long established tradition," Garfield the diplomat says. "That as drug suppliers and peddlers you keep millions happy, I dare say, high and satisfied. You have handled the prostitution racket with acumen and provided gamblers throughout The City countless opportunities to exercise their pathologies, as well as giving those obsessed with neurotic guilt a new hold on life by victimizing them with the juice racket.

"This, however, and I say this along with the universe, does not constitute an obligation on our part (obviously he's been reading Stephen Crane — or remembering what someone told him about Crane). I might point out that it confirms, instead, how closely you are related to SAMIE and how this knowledge should serve to encourage you to accept our offer."

Galante calls for a caucus with his accountant, his lawyer, and two deputy capos. When they return a nervous hush falls over the room. A faint, thin mist of hydrogen sulfide infests the air. The right sleeve of his summer jacket is scarred with a still smoldering scorched black handprint. Will he consent, give agreement to the plan, or will all hell break loose?

Lilo returns to his seat, stares menacingly and thoughtfully across the table, shakes his head, thinks of several possibilities for dispatching Garfield and says, "No profit from a fight."

Of course this is all highly unlikely. And although he ran often to protect his ass, he never missed an opportunity to kill someone.

Nevertheless, the deed is done and the story goes on.

There has been a meeting of minds.

Now levity in the halls. A war has been averted. Comedy prevails.

Will there be a ticker-tape parade? Well, not quite.

But a Certificate of Incorporation is to be filed the following morning with the Department of State, Divisions of Corporations. The company will be known as the Society of Savants and Mystics and will absorb TCPD, SAMIE, and Syndie as they dissolve. The operation will run in *Pascal* and be kept in a hidden Bell System's memory bank dedicated solely to capturing (creating) maintaining and marketing Son of Sam.

Its principle places of business will be listed as One Police Plaza and 721 North West Street which houses Milo's Bar, Grill & Kosher Deli, with a warehouse in back to store hijacked contraband, house a still or two, run games of Baccarat — and manage Son of Sam's image, of course. Other locales and activities will be developed and utilized as business demands.

Article III lists the specific purpose of the corporation as "The cultivation, preservation and otherwise management of the Son of Sam name, and the development and delivery of Son of Sam visions and merchandise in their historical, scientific, educational, ecological, recreational, agricultural, scenic or open space opportunities, in the sole endeavor of money-making — as much as possible. The property of SoSaMy Inc is irrevocably dedicated to the subliminal, ritualistic subterfuge of profit-making, and the role the exploitation of mayhem and carnal desire have in merchandising, and no part of the net income or assets of the corporation shall ever inure to the benefit of anyone or anything beyond the principals of SoSaMy Inc and their heirs.

In the weeks to come further negotiations, long hours of sweat and heated tempers (and occasionally drawn guns with hammers cocked) hammer out the details — further terms of incorporation, holding companies, fiscal policy, etc. New vistas are charted. An agreement on rights to territory (including Montreal and Havana), rake-offs, a managerial flow-chart, and forty-four pages outlining the packaging and selling of Son of Sam merchandise, as well as the trendy sexual-violent possibilities connected to the Son of Sam insignia, are delineated.

For the first year Garfield and Galante will share CEO responsibility. They will report to the mayor (whomever) and to Joseph Bananno.

Then what? Everyone knows who the mayor reports to — who is that? To whom is the mayor responsible? Drake the Duck had something to do with it — but what?

Anyway, under closer inspection it becomes clear that nothing is clear. But that can wait. For the present, reports from City Hall (with the Bonnano Family approval) will lift in the political mist, onward, and outward into the ether. There are no gravitons here (a hypothetical particle that may or may not exist and about which we already know a great deal — see $1/r^2$). After that, anyone who wants to know more can get down on his knees — as humans do — and ask for the best.

Friar Pastel
as a marked man

Even as they affix their black marks to the founding document, newly enfranchised SoSaMy Inc soldiers emerging from the building are cheered by a crowd of five thousand (the police will estimate ten thousand) SoSaMy Inc fans carrying placards and flags.

And the meeting was supposed to be secret.

"Is this a rally, a protest or, just for the hell of it — a riot?"

No one knows.

"We needed another celebration," someone adds.

A slate of speakers parades to the mic to declare the end of crime in The Big Apple. No more worms, no more rotten spots. No more Blue Mold,

Mucor Rot or Sooty Blotch. No more Union Necrosis. The crowd cheers: hoots, howls, and whistles.

Then gunfire ripples the air. Fifty or so shots are fired, though miraculously no one is injured. And silly as it seems, the celebration actually stifles the ambush. There are simply too many people with guns for anyone to know who to shoot at, and the disgruntled soldiers of the anti-Pastel factions, frustrated and embarrassed, retreat to an alley to hide their shame and to wait out the demonstration. Surely it won't last that long. Nobody's interested in crime prevention — unless it's a money-maker.

Then, as might be expected, lolling about, amid garbage cans and stacks of trash, the trolleri of a crap game erupts among the hitmen. Quickly the ambush is forgotten and everyone's on his knees. Snake eyes (rolling two 6-sided dice 25 times gives a probability of 0.505532 that at least once, Snake eyes will appear) and box   cars. Seven Out, Fever-Five and "Make your point." If five is up, what's down?

Of course, there's talk, heavy talk. And in the abandon of desultory conversation, someone mentions a cartel of impending contracts and hits soon to be filled, listing names and prices. And like a turmoil of trolls the gamers relocate, haul out and revive, and then attempt to reconcile, festering grudges and perfidies. The game splits into OK Corral camps and more gunfire erupts. In minutes the alley is littered with bodies — seven dead, a dozen seriously wounded. Among the dead are Tony "Pinocchio" Saberese, Angelo "Guardian Angel" Orontono, and Narco "Big Fingers" Salamona.

An hour later the Support SoSaMy Inc demonstration dwindles, leaving the street, like the alley, cluttered with trash. And though no one seems interested in cleaning the street, even before the EMS arrives, the alley is tidied up, the wounded removed, the bodies of the dead ritualistically dismembered and stuffed into large electric-blue metal oil barrels (Syndie coffins) of sulfuric acid with TOXIC WASTE stenciled on them.

For half-an-hour or so the EMS wander about the alley, perplexed, wondering — ready for something. Then, because they do not belong to the ILA (Marine Freight and Warehousemen) Local 976, and therefore may not touch or transport the barrels, they return to their vehicles and depart.

When the truck arrives to transport the seven deadly elec-blue sins to a dock on the East River for disposal or shipping (something less repellant than the basement grinding rooms of Soylent Green Syndie butcher shops preparing loss-leader hamburger to sell the following day) Sam is seen hovering complacently near a fire-barrel in the far end of the alley, picking his teeth with a broken, grimy fingernail. When did a claw become a polished fingernail wrapped around the trigger of a .38 Special?

Still, Sam's sullen, brooding — though he'll take credit with no credit due. Today it's the lust for life in muted colors. He prefers black and white. Too often the élan vital dips into his handbag of mishaps. Pain, suffering, loss — destruction and human carnage — on occasion, arise by happenchance. So mayhem displaces misadventure. But what are you going to do?

"Well," he whimpers, "think what they will. Next time . . .."

On the other hand, it's been a good day — as most are for Sam — and as planned. Sam has a plethora of patience. Long ago he succumbed to the profits of forbearance. It has to do with his position in the queue. He's been called an aberrant genetic manifestation of the human collective unconscious. Indeed, he is present — persistently so. What goes around comes around as reliably as the hands of a clockwork orange. Monopsychism. He likes the definition. Especially the aberrant part. And the collective unconscious. The senescent hallucinating Swiss master had his finger on it. Yeah, he thinks, next time . . ..

The Times reports the gunfight in the alley as another chapter in the never ending struggle of gangster entrepreneurs to gain control of the heroin traffic in the Big Apple.

Still, there are rumors.

Galante used a disguise to make a meeting with Garfield to further solidify his power and cheat the families out of their fair share of sales. Yes, but that's not news. That's rumor.

"Disguise or no disguise," a displaced shootout survivor says, "We'll get the bastards. We been set up. Nobody crowds our ambush and lives."

That night, in a convulsive lurch, amplifying Sam's pledge, a reflexive response to having been outwitted — made the goat — orders drift into subterranean channels. In a rash of activity that cannot be seen as anything but a warning, the sword drops and a stool of informants who floated the word from Puzzle Palace Mountain are sacrificed, throats slashed and privates chopped off. It has all the markings of police retaliation. Vengeance lies in the conviction that someones somewhere will get the message. The message is, however, more of the same.

okay, so who owns Son of Sam?

Within the week CBS and The Universe Studios trail into Federal Court with twelve hundred pounds of documentation in seven wheelbarrows to file a thirty-three-million-dollar damage suit against SoSaMy Inc. In several days of pump and dump, working out of a storefront on McKenzie Avenue, SoSaMy pockets over three million dollars.

"It is the intent of SoSaMy Inc," the suit contends, "to produce and market Son of Sam posters, shirts, stamps, statues, books, guns, coins, commemorative (used cartridges), and other various and sundry apparatus and paraphernalia without granting due compensation to CBS and The Universe Studios who have Son of Sam under contract and possess exclusive rights to the profits of his creations. We petition the court to purge SoSaMy Inc bytes, to wipe them off the pages and screens — wherever that may be."

of course Son of Sam
  and the Lou
have a different view

And then another hitch.

"We have to locate Sam," Garfield tells the first meeting of the SoSaMy Inc Board of Directors. "Now we have to get the S.O.B in captivity. We do that and we'll have CBS by the balls. Remember, possession is twelve-minus-three-points of the law."

"We have other possibilities," an assistant tells him. "If we get nailed in court, we can create our own model. Get the PR luminaries to convince everyone that Sam's switched guns. He can use a .32 or maybe a .38. There'll be no way for CBS to interfere."

But it is easier said than done.

Even Mathias is losing confidence in his ability to keep Sam's creation on the straight and narrow — and find a new direction for the Loose Canon Lieutenant.

"We need a better way to make a buck," he tells Aigilas. "Nothing makes sense. Not that it ever did. But now it's worse."

"Well, two more programs and it will all be history."

"How do you do that?"

"Amnesia. Self-induced amnesia.

"Maybe forgetting's at the bottom of it. Maybe we had these problems before and solved them so well that we forgot that we ever had problems — and then also forgot the solutions."

"I wish," Mathias says. "Our chances aren't good."

He hands Aigilas a folder.

"Have you seen this?"

Marcelo shrugs. He hasn't.

"It's interesting reading. The tale of our baldheaded wonder's latest escapade."

An hour later Mathias has Abby Mann on the phone.

"I suppose you know why I called."

Mann admits to some knowledge of the problem.

"What happened when he came in for a tuneup?" Mathias asks.

"Well, it's not that simple," Mann tells him. "When I first came up with the idea of a police Lieutenant for *The Marcus-Nelson Murders*, I saw the character as a hardnosed, realistic cop. As you know, I took the idea come from Selwyn's book *Justice in the Back Room*.

Serialization and teevee adaption — too many other writers and directors — have caused drift, distortions. In the beginning he was a composite. Mostly based on T. J. Cavanagh, the slick from the Upper East Side 19th called "The Velvet Whip" because of the way he could damned-near get anyone to confess to anything. If you remember, he saved

Whitmore's life. Good detective work. D'ya ever come across Cavanagh?

"And there were a couple of others.

"Maybe we should have him come in for another sitting. I know a number of newspaper artists who would like a chance to make a few bucks. The SAMO© (Same old shit — Same old — Samo — SAMO©) graffiti writers could do a spray profile with a little personality.

"Well, you know what it's like. I can make suggestions, some softening touches. Humor, sympathy, maybe even a couple scenes at the cemetery — the loss of a buddy — a bereaved widow. But in the end words can only do so much.

"Matt, it's out of my hands. This is beyond our control — and theirs. The role's gone off on its own — a different personality. I wish I could help."

Mathias cradles the receiver, thinks maybe, just maybe the problem is in the writing. Maybe it's the young writers. He decides to send out a call. Then he shifts over, falls on the cold steel of the flip side, the second half and even larger problem of the Psyaint.

"Shit," he says.

His gout has not improved. His toe hurts. He's tired of crutches.

"I guess we are all just ideas, at that," he says — which seems, in hustle and bustle of recent events, more appropriate than ever.

Sam survives a game of bocce

Sam's become arrogant, sloppy, of late, careless, a poseur, perilous with success. In the twilight on East Houston Street, ahead of schedule, he joins a bocce game. He pulls a wounded rat out of his hat, an argument, resurrects an old country grudge of perfidies, sleights and imagined wrongs. The squabble heats up, someone swings, Sam's looking the other way, gets sucker punched, toppled asshole over split hooves — a flaming black eye, a split pustule on a swollen lip. Steel flashes, a slashed arm, a gun and the crowd scatters — shots echo in the brick canyons and a stiff is left in the doorway of a liquor store.

One dead, two wounded, threats buffet the air, to be honored later. Sam lifts himself out of the rubble in a vacant lot, wipes his mouth, a broken-toothed smile. Who cares? It's Syndie territory. Nobody's gonna talk about it. The cops look the other way.

Good entertainment, Sam thinks, no pain, no gain, settling into a private puanteur with a bottle of rum, a storm brewing, joyless clouds intimidating the night, laying a thick mist on the river. He's watching the teevee on the wall above the bed, the PD in-house system, the Dashing Darling of detectives rumbling over the Queensboro Bridge.

"This is what we've been waiting for," Strangeways tells Blount. "Tonight's the night — the payoff for all the blood, sweat and tears. Now it's time to collect."

a little prophecy
  from Fritz and Thea
in Berlin (1931)

A deserted street at night lit by a dim street light. A plainclothes policeman is assayed by a prostitute, but declines the assessment. Deeper into
the scene, beneath a street lamp, another woman talks with a client.

In a high-angle shot we see a dark street wet from recent rain. A couple
disappear beneath a single light bulb into a seedy hotel. A detective idles
beneath a street lamp, holding a portable teevee, the image rolling.

In wide-angle, the headlights of a car flash across the walls of the
buildings. Men leap from the car while it is still moving and quickly station
themselves in various doorways. Their footsteps echo over this and the
following shot.

Our hero appears on screen with Watson and Blount following. He
checks his watch and gestures to them. They move off camera.

Another high-angle shot. We see the street with the seedy hotel. Three
detectives come out of a nearby doorway. The officer with the teevee turns
up the volume. The Lieutenant gives a signal: a whistle blows.

Two vans filled with men drive up and skid to a stop. Policemen jump
from the vans. Motorcycle cops wait on their machines near the doorway
of the small, sleazy nightclub at 333 West 34th Street. In the distance a
group of plainclothesmen arrive, followed by uniformed men.

A young woman, Carol, possibly a symbolic Vestal Virgin, the girl Sam
conjures, the prototype of the Psyaint's desires, rushes down a spiral
staircase leading from the street into a basement bar, a hangout for petty
thieves — pickpockets, burglars, jack-rollers, bunco artists, paper hangers,
and prostitutes. A large stuffed rat hangs from the ceiling, an old piano is
propped up in one corner. The scene reeks of sweat and cheap wine.

Carol: Cops!

Instantaneously the clients, patrons — criminals and prostitutes — rush for
the exit, scrambling over tables and chairs.

Seen from the exit, the landlady lowers a grating which cages her behind
the bar. Everyone rushes for the stairs. All is chaos and confusion, seen in
a high-angle shot down the empty staircase. Carol appears first, followed
by a thief who gives a sudden start and, furious, turns back. Others pass
him and are turned back.

Police whistles. Several policemen, advancing steadily, push the fleeing
crowd down into the room.

Psyaint David

Cut to the street: two plainclothesmen lead a prostitute to a police van.

Policeman's voice: Police. Get back.

Carol: (among others) Let me go, you motherfucker. Let me go, you baldheaded jackoff. Let me go.

The detective carrying the teevee descends the stairs. The picture is clear, cleanly focused, with the Lieutenant descending the stairs with Carol in his arms. The camera tracks them and stops at the bottom of the stairs, beneath the Romanesque proscenium arch. The symbolism is obvious — the concept, ideation, pattern of passage, a travelling trooping of man in and out of the festering nether world of Homo sapiens' aberrations and revulsion.

Carol: Let me go, you sleazy, baldheaded prick!

Thief: Let the girl alone.

General noise, shouting, a crescendo.

Lieutenant: All right, quiet down.

The officer sets the teevee at the top of the stairs so everyone can see the screen.

The Crowd: Ah, ha. Head-honcho cop. Badass. Ouuuuuuuu!

Head-honcho Badass: (from the teevee) Quiet!

A Voice: Don't nobody talk during . . ..

The camera tilts down the stairs to a dimly lit basement with the crowd of thieves and prostitutes in the background; in the foreground, the paste-up of sidekick Bobby Crocker.

Crocker: Police orders. Nobody leaves this place. Get your identification ready. We want to know who you are.

A Voice: So do we! (They all laugh).

Cries of protest and whistles rise around the room. Crocker stands in the entrance flanked by police. Brother George comes down the stairs with one of his men.

Badass: (Cheerfully from the teevee) Come on now children. Let's not do anything silly.

A Voice: Turn up the volume. I can't hear.

A Thief (Raising his hat) Who wants to hear this bullshit? Three cheers for baldy Badass.

A Voice: (With others, chanting) Badass, Badass, Badass, Ouuuuuuu!

Another Voice: The greatest cop of them all. The noble, honorable, loveable, Badass the Great.

Several shake their fists in the air.

Everyone: Long live Baddy!

Sam, Our Lady, and the Wasp

The scene shifts to the hermitage, Pineview Towers, a seven-story fortress, the hall of mist and panic, of bad dreams, old faces and names, ghosts, a silent, somber procession — young females — the deaf and mute, a conspiracy of spirits.

Startled by a noise, David wakes, his head pounds, a Terrier's howl mingles with sirens. An hour later, the hammering unabated, cowering in a corner, he hears a voice in the mirror, prowling behind the blanket. In the Hour of the wolf he sees himself imposed on the city-scape, the country-side, a reverse image. He sees a second world, another domain, and then a third and/or fourth realm, etc. — alive and violent and as beautiful and enticing as any one might smell or touch. A macabre aubade lingers, grips the sill with long charred fingers.

Sam pours a jigger of rum, hunkers down in his corner, perusing *The Times*, chuckles, picks his nose.

He's into reading obituaries, police reports. A little smoke on the water, spit in the eye. And there's plenty.

In the Bronx, by way of a collapsed windpipe, with the aid of person or persons unknown, sixty-seven-year-old Estelle Tucker of 110 Bond Street, Apartment 2D in Brooklyn, is shuffled off. Not far away, not too far over polluted waters, on Staten Island, seventy-five-year-old Jeanette Mae Laughlin of 115 Albion Place, Port Richmond, in an argument with a male friend over who should ask a neighbor to turn down his hi-fi set, is, with the aid of a seven-inch blade, swiftly dispatched and sent unprepared to her maker.

"Good copy," Sam says. "Indeed."

Page two news carries a report that a new conversation between Alice and the Wasp has surfaced. Out of the galleys and into the open, a suppressed episode springs from the original manuscript of *Through the Looking Glass.*

The episode features Our Lady Alice as she concludes her romp with the White Knight and sets off to explore the Looking Glass countryside. For her bucolic sortie she wears a low-cut (with a plunge bra for a bit more décolletage) pale blue knee-length rumpled crushed full taffeta dress with a white-outlined-in-red pinafore overtop and red and white stripped stockings. Her blonde hair is held back with a wide blue ribbon. Thus attired, she happens upon a hoary, whimpering Wasp, tiresome beneath a tree.

All though Our Lady of Invidious Invidia is curious and kind, the Wasp is feeble and querulous and after a few whining words admits to Our Lady that his life has been ruined by his tousled blonde wig, which he covers with a yellow handkerchief. In his youth, he says, he had been advised to shave his ringlets and now he is mocked by all.

"And still, wherever I appear," he intones, "they hoot at me and call me 'pig!' And that is why they do it, dear, because I wear a yellow wig."

"I'm very sorry for you," Our Lady says heartily, "and I think if your wig fitted a little better, they wouldn't tease you quite as much."

"Your wig fits very well," the Wasp murmurs, with admiration. "It's the shape of your head as does it. Your boobs ain't well shaped, though — I should think you could do better. Maybe a little plastic and silicone?"

Our Lady of O-Cuntillation yips with laughter (or laughting, in a written marginal afterthought) which she turns into a cough as well as she can. At last she manages to say gravely, "I have already done that."

"But with a mouth the size of mine," the Wasp persists, "I should want something more. I mean, if we was to go to fucking, I would need something more to hold on to."

Alice blinks coquettishly and tickles the Wasp's large purple abdomen. "Oh, Wasp. I'm afraid not. Who's interested in holding on while you're fucking?"

"Well, I am," the Wasp says. "However, the top of your head is nice and round."

Our Lady giggles and runs her tongue over her moist, full lips. "Certainly, Wasp. Is yours nice and round?"

Page two, third column. Sam chuckles. The plan according to Sam is developing nicely, evenly — the temperature a balmy 65, soft breezes out of the southwest and The City of the Gods prepared for yet another celebration.

Six o'clock and light showers, which clear away two hours later. The City, or at least some of The City, ambles into an inverted Parentalia, the laying on of flowers that the sacred-to-memory dead, for whatever reasons, might rise into the upper world.

Right-to-lifers, Connie Patterson of 6222 West Seldon, Bronx, and Judith

Priven of 7345 South Merkel, Brooklyn, lead an assemblage pulling five miniature Landau Funeral Carriages with intricately carved flowers, doves and scrolls, and heavy velvet draperies. They parade into 2ⁿᵈ Avenue Marble Cemetery to place a teething-ring wreath on a shoebox sized green-plastic portable grave of the Unknown Ungrown Fetus, and to call for legislation to stop the slaughter.

Across The City, about the same time, forming scattered ranks of hundreds, the glorified who consecrated themselves to their country, to be beaten, baptized, and beatified (and later canonized) as martyrs for right, a battery of military veterans, led by fifty-eight-year-old John Morohan of the American Legion, falls-in for Manhattan's Memorial Festivity march up Riverside Drive from 72ⁿᵈ Street to the Soldiers and Sailors Monument at 89ᵗʰ Street.

Morohan, a WWII vet, as a twenty-three-year-old Corporal in 1943, survived the Bataan Death March, and claims that his survival and arrival at Camp O'Donnell, the terminus etrĕmĭtãs of the march, was assured by the talisman (a small American flag) that hung with his Dog Tags over his heart. While a bit shorter, the march up 89ᵗʰ Street reminds him of Bataan.

However, in spite of whatever else he might remember, when the troops arrive at the monument he discovers that while the stragglers have a flag pole, they have no flag. The Parks Department turned down a request to supply one. For the last several years, as part of the patriotic fervor it represented, following the ceremony, the flag disappeared.

"Next year we'll bring our own flag — I guarantee it," Morohan says — thus completing the cyclical celebration of death slightly before life to life slightly before death.

Laudemus viris bellatoribus.

Otherwise, Our Lady is having difficulty. After her tête-à-tête with the Wasp, she feels spiritual and connected, her pipes primed and prepared to receive, but still somewhat off-channel. In the afternoon she picks up the crowd noise of NBC's *Game of the Week*, the Yankees at Fenway. She taps her right temple with an index finger, shakes her head. She would like to turn down the teevee, if she could find it. But it's not likely. In matters of the material world she's as ephemeral as a late June batting slump.

The din is more of the same. This time a near brawl in the Yankee dugout. Somebody Martin, somebody else Jackson, minor, mostly worthless players in her drama, to say the least, threaten each other. Her head vibrates. Will I not be freed of this noise?

And still more.

A grumble erupts on pier 40, off Houston Street. Singing and shouting, cursing and threats where the hulk of the U.S.S Bellows sulks at dock with two-thirds of her 292-member crew on liberty.

"A lot of the crew have had a fun time — some have been robbed, three or four mugged and beaten — one was rushed to the hospital in critical condition," Fire Control Technician Third Class Oscar Bennettee says, in what sounds like a news broadcast. "They are truly enjoying their frolic with the natives. After all sailors are warriors."

Our Lady of Salacious Superbia listens closely.

"That's more like it."

Sam lays the newspaper to one side.

a night-stalker addresses the authorities

Again, Hans-Peter, as ministerial envoy, attentive to Sam's design, ruminates. It is a time for remonstrations, for righting wrongs, and setting straight the record. The world must be told, the mission of pandemonium clarified, epistles written, etc. A minor salutation in face of small annoyances — Sam's dissatisfaction, reprimands, the little doubts that plague the lonely. Hunched over whistling the melody from *Peer Gynt*, a stub of pencil, the paper divided by a shadow, he sets to composing.

> Since the police haven't published my first letter, I am writing today straight to the newspaper. Keep up your investigation. Everything will happen just as I have predicted. But I haven't yet finished my work.
>
> Mr. Breslin, sir, don't think that because you haven't heard from me for a while that I went to sleep. No, rather, I am still here. Like a spirit roaming the night, thirsty, hungry, seldom stopping to rest; anxious to please Sam. I love my work. Now, the void has been filled.

Sam keeps an eye on his protégé. His black eye is clouded over, his lip puffed, still. He watches closely — suspicious, jealous lest deeds undone remain to . . .. Today the spin is extensive, more complex. Indeed, life scratches like a bitch with a batch of fleas, an irritating skin disease.

Of course, as always somebody wants in. Scam artists — politicians, clergy, economic nobility — to preempt his act. Occasionally a devious enterprising peasant fashions a personal memorial day of sorts.

The numbers rumble down the centuries. In the late seventeen hundreds south of Padua, just for the hell of it, he tormented, encouraged a farmer into burying his parents alive and selling off their herd. The progeny, a dim-witted, one-eyed blackguard, was not so dim that he couldn't figure out who Sam is, or that the clergy would pay handsomely for a testimonial of Diablo's misfortune. One night, after a round of drinking and whoring in a roadhouse, he turned coat and attempted to further pad his coffers at Sam's expense.

"Pinned my ass to the stable door with a pitchfork," Sam recalls. "Ruined a favorite coat. Lucky to get away from the bastard."

Myth and fantasy pinned to the hardwood of reality by the tines of time and space.

Sam glances askance. Sure of himself again.

"If god can get his ass nailed to a cross, I suppose it's not stretching it too far to understand what that dimwit with the pitchfork was trying to do to me."

The village priest appreciates the scam, declares the man a Defender of the Faith and helps suppress what everyone suspects but no one can prove about the disappearance of one-eye's clan. The charred door becomes a shrine of sorts, (an inspiration for Bergman's cupboard in the *Devil's Eye*). The innkeeper, the priest, and one-eye consecrate the stable as a shrine and share the revenue (donations) from pilgrims who want to witness the blackened door, the scorched memento of Satan's presence in their midst.

But now? Sam's thinking of the SoSaMy Inc specter and Father Pastel.

"Since we can't find the S.O.B" Pastel mutters, (Sam winces. You really have to keep your eye on the Sam when he gets his tail between his legs) "we'll create our own."

Forty-eight hours later in a smattering of gunfire in Greenbourgh Town of Westchester County, echoing the plan, three young women — within two hours and two miles — are dead, with a handful of .32 slugs as evidence. And the question, for the moment, is if — and if not, then who?

A convincing demonstration. The production comes in off the road with the promise of a long and prosperous run. SoSaMy Inc announces a complete Son of Sam line. Stalking apparel — sneakers for running on concrete — stencils for assembling anonymous messages, brown paper bags, getaway cars, a variety of Son of Sam weapons: dart guns, air rifles, BB guns, pistols, automatic rifles, slingshots, crossbows.

The Wall Street Journal carries the story.

SoSaMy Inc stock gains, built on confidence in new product contracts which are reportedly long term and include plans for expansion.

Hans-Peter revels in the publicity.

"How Many Sons of Sam Are There?"

Sales are booming, and profits. Viacom Enterprises wants to do a film, *The Son of Sam Story*. Negotiations are slated to begin the following week, if they can find the rightful owner of the Son of Sam image. The grapevine, smart money, conventional wisdom, has Hardon Inc on the inside track for rights to the story.

the gnomes hear voices

The gnomes assemble nervously for a working dinner at Larre's on West 56th Street, poking over duck (not Drake) with orange sauce and a favorable Bordeaux (1964).

"Oh Jesus," Lamiae says. His hands are shaking. "It was a mistake," he'll tell them. "It is entirely possible that we cast the wrong killer. I mean, not the killer, but the aspect."

He'll pauses pensively. The signs are undeniable, irrefutable. A chill coursing along the spine. The spin of double-dealing is afoot. Old wounds of ambiguity and fear leave deep scars. A pastiche of doubt, fear and more fear.

"Too many composites. It's just like the Whitmore case. We have the wrong picture. This could be a frightening mess."

Aigilas, Marcelo, will shrug his shoulders.

"There's never any way to be sure. We have useable footage — a few shots of the Esau/Suriani affair."

"Not just that," Juan must say. "We've been seriously misled. Mathias, we have been listening to the wrong voices. Looking at the wrong pictures.

"I have this archetype of the killer. And it is not like anything I have seen before. Did you know that Aphrodite was black, fat, and old, and Adonis a midget with a two-inch penis? But Adonis didn't care and Aphrodite, oh, she was circumspect. She accepted the proposition — what little there was of it."

As with most of Juan's statements, this one sounds as if it has been rehearsed.

"I have a picture."

"In mind?" Mathias says.

"No. A really, truly to life image."

"Of what?"

"Of the killer."

"But you saw him at the Tio Asesino. You know his face. Why do you need a portrait"?

"Tio Asesino? Dear Mathias, I have never heard of Tio Asesino. I don't know whose uncle it was, but I have never been there. Was it on one of the shows? Where is that?"

Mathias is silent.

"Do you know the uncle?" Lamiae asks Marcelo.

"Oh, one evening several years ago. If I'm thinking about the same one. Not much to it."

"What channel?" Juan asks Mathias.

"I don't know. I dropped the set while I getting in the car."

"So you were talking to the teevee again. Now all we have is memory?"

"It's real. Comes down to viewers not seeing what they intended to see. What they interpret, what they think they see, is not what they should see. The Great Grey Gap.

"Oh! Where have we gone wrong?"

Aigilas will screw up his face.

"You sound like you've been to the oracle."

"Yes he does," Mathias should say. "Well, the best we've got are the signs — which under the circumstances seemed pretty clear — and in conjunction with voices — anonymous, but nevertheless very real and very powerful voices — shouts, phone calls in the night from — hell, Tokyo, Rome, Damascus. Have you watched Cronkite lately? Have you ever had people talking to you in your sleep, all night? And people dying — people who are very much alike, dying in very similar ways. Patterns in the sand, predictable twists in the grain — that's all we have as a guide."

Aigilas needs to say, "We have two shows in the can. Don't get cold feet. Let's not throw away a good thing. I mean the shows are worth most of the tea in China."

Mathias might respond with, "Marcelo, it's not the money. The sales for the *Daily News* with the Breslin letter and article are over the top. They sold 1.1 million copies. No telling what the *Post* sold.

"Hell, you did your job. I did mine. I'll have to tell you we were chosen — we are the chosen people. Okay. We did that. But now it . . . well, like we're no longer needed. Others will follow. This isn't important, though it's not over just yet."

And Marcelo could possibly question this.

"Who?"

"They are who they will be. Who they are."

"And that," Marcelo will have said, "is double talk."

"Diablo talk, "Juan should say, holding out his fingernails for examination.

"Not really. But it's not important. What will be important is that we have read the signs correctly. The schedule calls for two more events. And even that's not important. In the end, it'll be the plot that counts — and the fact that we know when to get out.

"We are already echoes."

Aigilas chuckles.

"We were reruns."

So it goes. The summer solstice (8:13:41) in conjunction with the waxing crescent moon falls into a sorcery of dissipation. The day will endure for 14 hours, 53 minutes and 56 seconds.

Mathias will nod and say, "It's amazing a machine can read our minds. That goddam in-house system knows our plans even before we do. It's a real pain in the ass."

"It wants to plug the gap," Juan says.

Kesil tries to remember what he did with his ticket for *Tosca* at Van Cortlandt Park. He is especially looking forward to seeing Gilda Cruz-Romo and Giuseppi Giacomini (as the painter revolutionary Cavaradossi) and others thread their way through Pucini's fast paced operatic thriller.

"By the way," Mathias says, "what odds are they giving on Seattle Slew?

Should be pretty good."

Aigilas shrugs.

"Right now 2-5. If the track's dry, he shouldn't have any trouble."

"You want tickets?" Teivel asks. "How many you need?"

the Green Lady speaks
of the unknown
and discovers amour

For others the scheme seems less amazing, remains something of a formality, and Our Lady of the Vaunted Visions with another brainteaser.

> Diddle me, diddle me right,
> Guess where I was Friday night?
> The bone was hard, my heart did quake,
> When I saw the wolf, my fur did shake.

But the somber and gloomy Captain Keener doesn't feel up to her hey-diddle-diddle mood.

"We're paying you good money," he tells her, "and you spend your time in Central Park weaving daisy chains and skipping around singing absurd ditties."

She smiles into his thoughts, offers a carefree, confident toss of her head, as if to say, "Oh, Captain, if only you knew."

"We need results," Keener says. "We need something definite or . . .. Look. This case . . .. This is an election year."

She has the buttons on his baggies undone, prepared to do him palpitating pleasure, his voice a distant whisper of non-assertiveness. Her tongue toys with his knob, her warm breath coursing down the firm length of his candy stick melting it into a vibrant flow of thrusting groans and sighs.

When she finishes, he sags onto the couch, pale and wasted, the exhaustion and toil of the hunt showing on his face. And despite the Chief's intentions, his sincerity, loyalty, etc., the time for them has parted.

"It was so nice of you," she chides in her amber voice. "I'm so glad you asked for help. But, truthfully, we've gone as far as we can. And I know what you're thinking. I've seen it before."

So it's up to date. She helps him to his feet and leads him to the door and politely shuffles him out, dismisses the brave Chief, sends him off hat in hand on unsteady legs, head bowed, a touch of anguish and regret in his voice.

"What will you do now," he moans?

"It was an impossible task," she answers.

And that's about all she needs to say. For nearly five months she's stalked

Son David, searched, always searched, probing for clues, tightening her circle of intent and desire. Now she has a clear channel to Yonkers, a vibrato of the killer's condition, Sam's loathsome, odious proclivities, affection blooming in her bosom — with chaos in mind.

And what will you have Child-David?

And, where, oh where is my blue-eyed boy tonight?

Yes. Little Boy Blue come, let me blow your horn.

And again distant, barely audible mumblings, familiar sounds, congealing words — *Darling David*, the pleasing lilt of a female invitation in the gloom, the sensuous maternal syllables breathed and fading. And then again, the voice stronger, more insistent — and, as always, a soft tapping at the door.

David pulls on the bridegroom's wig, crosses the room and pauses ruefully before the mirror. No reflection now, only the dull light of loss in the silver backing, the dead kingdom of memory in the depths of has been. Yes, the tapping is always there, the small sounds at the edge of recognition, and he wonders what strange land this might be.

"Yes?" he says, in a voice that seems unlikely to be heard, his wide white clown-eyes set on the chain dangling from the bolt. And here it is boy-wonder opens the door to the Hall of the Mountain King to the murmuring of the woman in rags, her hoary and wrinkled green face, once lovely in the pink of youth and fantasy — imagination, steeped in the idealism of personification — now aged and wrinkled, aged and beaten, a tattered, battered abandoned goddess, exposed by the bright hall lights. She grasps his arm with soiled hands and sinks her splintered nails into his wrist.

Gripped by a still larger and stronger hand, his senses are filled with the musk of her breath, the insinuating discord of her voice.

Scene Five

Green Woman: (with a matted Fetid Fur lined blindfold) You are the king's son?

Hans-David: Yes.

GW: My father, too, is a king. He has his castle in the mountains.

HD: My mother has a larger one.

GW: Do you know my father? His name is King Stygian.

HD: Do you know my mother? She is the Queen of Fear.

GW: The mountains wither and turn black when my father's angry.

HD: When my mother screams, the streams run red with her screams.

GW: My father can shake the skies.

HD: My mother can dim the stars.

GW: (She is still holding to his arm. She runs her hand over his chest.) Have you any clothing besides these rags?

HD: Oh, I have a wardrobe filled with fine suits.

Psyaint David

GW: My clothes are gold and silver.

HD: They look like sacks and weeds.

GW: Yes. But remember, double shapes. So when you come to my father's palace you may think it a mere heap of ugly stones and rubbish.

HD: Yes. It is the same with me. You may think my goodness is evil, my lucidity irrational.

GW: Black is white and kind is mean.

HD: Big is little and filth is clean.

GW: Love is hate and death is life.

HD: Peace is war and calm is strife.

GW: Happy is sad and wrong is right.

HD: Morning is evening and day is night.

GW: Failure thrives and honor shames.

HD: Greed shares and praise blames.

GW: Money is paucity and compassion lust.

HD: Sam is god and fear is trust.

GW: The City is heaven and sick is well.

HD: Wisdom is foolish and harmony hell.

GW: Whisper is scream and thought is act.

HD: Freedom is slavery and fantasy fact.

GW: Strike is caress and pleasure pain.

HD: Self is other and sun is rain.

GW: Oh, David, we are perfectly inequitable.

HD: Yes, certainly.

GW: Well, let us go! (They proceed to the elevator and minutes later appear on the street) My coach! My coach!

A gigantic dog (St Bernard? Newfoundland?) with a rope for a halter trots up pulling a large packing crate on wheels, a SoSaMy Inc sergeant with a blue medallion pinned to his coat leading it.

HD: We will ride together to your father's palace.

GW: (Tenderly) And to think I was feeling sad and lonely — one can never tell what will happen.

HD: (Whipping the dog as they ride off down the street) Great people are known by the style of their carriages.

GW: (Sighs) At last I've found you — after all these months. We are together at last.

HD: (Concentrating on steering the dog) Yes. It has been a long time. A lonely time. But the void is filled.

Scene Six

A garbage dump in Brooklyn.

The Williamsburg Bridge hovers in the background.

Across the East River the Empire State Building rises like a giant phallus.

A dozen or so young boys investigate the smoldering refuse, picking through the debris.

Our Hero and The Green Lady rattle into the dump in their canid coach with several hundred Whole Earth peasants following them. Paparazzi from *The Times* and the *Daily News* scramble through the crowd documenting the dog procession. The crowd chants "Hans-Peter! Hans-David!" The boys stop to watch and one turns toward the crowd to urinate.

GW: My father's palace. (She stands and spreads her arms.) This is his kingdom — as far as you can see. (She crosses herself.) Pray for us St. Mauvais, in this our hour of need. May our enemies be vanquished.

And so it is, Our Lady of Lithesome Lust appears, inexplicit and indifferent, dressed in the Sherwood Green and gaiety of spring holding her child-lover's hand. It has been a winding ordeal, a maze of theories, superstitions, the rumor and hearsay, the back alleys of logic scattered with the trash of facts, the rancor of publicity. Presently she will remove her blindfold, reveal her great apatite eyes to the world and confer upon her followers the evasive twists of her final riddle.

For now, however, she is content to mark time — it is time Our Lady of Ascetic Acedia peddles best — steeled with a new confidence, lover David at her side, zombie like, sheet-wrapped and draped, eyes glazed, somnambulist Cesare waiting to be activated, carrying an ancient curse on his lips.

SoSaMy Inc expands its fiduciary obligations

Encouraged and stimulated by the prospect-fantasy of mega-bucks in the art and craft of murder and mayhem the midsummer battle among the Bs and Cs takes on new dimensions. Recruits are drafted, reserves called up. SoSaMy Inc joins the scuffle with a pastiche of acrimonious accusations. Strategy sessions run far into the night among rumors, albeit reports, of reconnoitering and espionage.

Wilson Tribout, an ABC trainee, of 30-16 Melbourne Avenue, Staten Island, stations himself among the cables atop an elevator at Black Rock intending to surreptitiously record the conversations of CBS execs. Not only does Tribout's eavesdropping attempts fail (the execs have little to say about Son of Sam — and not much else either) but Wilson suffers severe disorientation from the constant up and down and whirring, loses his balance, his grip, and

loses two fingers when his hand slips into a four-inch cable-sheave.

Maureen Oldsky of 77-33 South Park Place, Queens, a mid-level development exec at NBC, secrets herself in an executive suite closet of The Universe Studios with a Minox spy camera hoping to get a reality shot of the Son of Sam icon, and a boost into an office two floors up with a view. As it is, Maureen hasn't yet discerned the camera's operation and after twelve hours in the closet, slips out on to the street with nothing more than half a dozen blurred closeups of her boobs and shoes.

In other action, CBS and SoSaMy Inc file a joint suit against The City and its in-house police precinct teevee system for appropriating Kojak, Marlowe, Bannion, etc. Nobody is happy. It is noted that more than likely before this is done, someone will get wasted. When the courts are remiss, gunfire usually follows.

"Public use," SoSaMy Inc lawyers claim. "Teevee detectives and killers, Holmes and Poirot, Jack the Ripper, Peter Kürten, Son of Sam, are the backbone of our campaign — a first step in making The City a haven for lucrative SoSaMy Inc investments.

"It is the plaintiff's contention that cops and robbers created for teevee, and therein through contracts with The Universe Studios, and others, are the exclusive property of those aforementioned studios and broadcasting companies, or the network corporations, and any attempt by the defendant to make-over said ethos as an honorable police officer is a violation of CBS et al's sole rights to the symbol and/or icon of the aforementioned cops and criminals, heart and soul."

The following day the U.S. Attorney General, under guidelines drawn up by "Duck" Drake, opens an investigation into the alleged illegal activities of SoSaMy Inc and its connection with Hardon Inc.

The government will argue SoSaMy Inc has with malice and muscle moved in on some twenty Medicare Clinics throughout The City, and claims, further, SoSaMy Inc has become a lucrative employment boondoggle for retired cops who, while unslung of their priestly law enforcement duties, have not yet successfully kicked the bribe, kickback, payola, payoff, on-the-take, sweetner, backhander, hush-money, grease, wet-my-beak habit. Justice believes rake-offs have proceeded without higher authority, giving the peons more than their fair share of the loot.

The "G" becomes interested when a psychiatrist who squeals to protect a very private segment of his person is "hit" in a less than vital part of his anatomy with a couple of purposefully directed .44 (SoSaMy Inc?) hit-squad slugs. After a few days of recuperation, he skips the country for pastures, if not greener, at least with grass tall and tangled enough to provide cover.

Connections for billing and payoff protection are traced from street level upward, deep into the Department of Social Services. The grapevine says CBS initiated the investigation, and with powerful argument, and even more powerful dollars, coerced *The Times* into joining the headhunt.

"Put the heat on," a CBS spokeswoman says, "and they (SoSaMy Inc) will be more easily persuaded to relinquish their claim to Son of Sam."

When asked about the lawsuit, Our Lady becomes hazy and increasingly abstracted. She has been captured as well as enamored by her hostage. In this her bonne heure et bonne nuit, pleased with the coup of her discovery, acquisition, with her reputation rising, she announces she will go into seclusion with her paramour.

however, the Lou
is still on the hunt

Fighting crime is not easy. Despite his efforts, the Lieutenant's ass burns from the rawhiding he received from the CCRB, Beame, Garfield, via Frazer, as well as from half a dozen teevee critics.

He's still chaffing under the summer of '69: Part 1 suspension. The Farnsworth episode Crocker called "feistiness in the park" has not yet cooled. Then there's the frame, and in off moments he wonders if maybe, just maybe he did take the three thousand dollars, the bribe Harry Dubin didn't offer. That's a lot of quick money for a cop, for anyone, he thinks. He doesn't believe he took the money, but he's not certain. Even if he didn't, it would have been nice of Dubin to offer it.

Now the Internal Affairs Division is breathing down his neck. He twists slowly in the wind onto Channel 2, at 9:00, a 19" Sony in a sleazy bar in the West Village. Even though the bar's empty and the waitress-barmaid is chewing gum and reading an old copy of *Silver Screen,* he's still intent on stamping out crime. He produces a new sack of clues: cigarette filters, broken dildoes, a ruptured diaphragm, rusted cans of vaginal foam, two discarded pussy pleasers, and other lovers' lane gimcracks and thingies.

Of course, the clues have nothing to do with the frame up. Of course, he's playing the Clown Prince of the good guys, made up in teevee paint, mask, bald dome, a curled lip. But prepared to make the most out of a bad situation, he meditates on the psychology of unadulterated homicide. He's considering taking Prince David's advice. What did he say? What did the letter say?

"Here are the names to help you along. Forward these to the Inspector for use by the NCIC."

> The Duke of Death
> The Wicked King Wicker
> The Twenty-Two Disciples of Hell
> John Wheaties
> Rapist and Suffocater
> Fornicator of Young Girls

"Will the real Son of Sam please stand?"
"And you, sir, what do you do?"
"I am His Excellency, Azrael."
"Will you remove your hat so our audience can see your eyes?"

Psyaint David

The Lieutenant is perplexed.

"How many?"

"Hard to say, Inspector. It may be a clan, a tribe. We had a list of possibilities at the beginning. What does the NCIC say?"

"It's a gut feeling," he tells Crocker. "But seems like we've been through this before. I know we don't have much to go on, but we'll have that S.O.B. within the month."

The loyal sidekick wonders, now, just who his boss is, and from whence this optimism emanates. Nothing indicates a break in the case, nothing suggests dedicated police work will solve the crime. If the scramble for commendations, promotions of officers, and officials involved in the hunt have anything to say, times are going to be tough.

And there's more, always more. Because of brutality and excessive teevee carnage, the Lieutenant pistol whipping the old lady, the SoSaMy Inc is coerced into signing a consent decree with the ACLU, providing that onlookers at police actions can take pictures, write down badge numbers of police officers and make comments without being subjected to harassment or arrest.

The agreement states that:

None of the following constitutes probable cause for arrest or detention of an onlooker unless the safety of the officers or other persons is directly endangered or the officers reasonably believe they are endangered or the law is otherwise violated.

Speech alone, even though crude and vulgar.

Requesting and making notes of shield numbers or names of officers.

Taking photographs.

Remaining in the vicinity of the stop or arrest.

"Fascism," the Lou snarls. "Worse than that. Big Brother. Why wasn't I allowed to testify — to give my side of their story? If those do-gooders want to stick their noses into police business they'd better be ready for a shot to the chops."

"You know," Dobson says, "that ain't so much different from what goes on now."

"It's a nice trade," says Deputy Police Commissioner Lorenzo Casanova when you can give them what they already got — even if it's for nothing. They go away happy, thinking something has happened.

"Nothing here that we're not already required by law to do. By law we cannot arrest someone just because he may call a cop a pig. Only thing new is that it is in writing — in the newspapers."

The Lou's eyes narrow. He knows the responsibility for the entire matter lies with him. However, the unexpected paranoid side effects of his psychic tuneup refuse to believe Casanova's explanation.

"Even pictures constitute a threat to an officer's safety," the Lou says. "Get your picture posted where the rots on the Lower East Side can see it and you'll get your head blown off."

"We'll have to wear disguises. Lose our anonymity and soon we won't know who we are."

The sound on the teevee goes off as the Lou takes a respond with Crocker riding shotgun. The barmaid leaves her magazine and changes the channel to *The Young and the Restless.* She's tired of cop shows, anyway.

But Sam knows the truth. Smart cops find the scent. Agreements, written documents are for losers, for the most part useless, unenforceable. A nimble verbal shuffle, a foot-dragging committee or two, a few files lost, will avoid the most carefully formulated stipulation, principle or rule.

"And anyway, screw the revolutionaries," Sam says. "They're part of The City, too. If they want action, hell, we'll have at it. Nothing like the viciousness of idealism gone sour to spice up the times, give history a dramatic human flare."

It's all enough to make the Telly mumble to himself.

"It's getting harder and harder to be a cop," he says — and, parenthetically, harder and harder to keep his habits straight.

"Where are we headed?" Watson bleats with a nearly born holy innocence.

"Across the screen to Queens. A report from the 102nd. Some guy's fifteen-year-old daughter is being followed by Son of Sam. They brought the girl in to view composites. She made him."

"Which one?"

"Which one?"

"Yeah. The Job has four sketches."

"All four, dummy. She said, 'That's him. That's him. That's the man. I know that's the man.'

"It's the Richmond Hill High School Annex on 114th Street."

"That's where Bujar and Klyop are headed."

"Who set this up?"

"I don't know. Probably Fortunato."

"Louie Fortunato? He's working as a dispatcher?"

"Yeah. He's been there a couple weeks now."

"Fortunato? No! I should've known."

The picture rolls, fades.

a time for various other images

Fortune and fame spin in the wheel of a goldeneye. This evening The City Theatre presents Rainer Fassbinder's *Gotter Der Prest* with Sam as guest celeb. In a rehash of Bogart and Cagney and Robinson and Raft, hero Franz (Harry Baer) becomes entangled with women and murder, women and drink, women and robbery, and gray skies and women. In a sequel to *Liebe ist kälter als der Tod* (Love is Colder Than Death *)*, drifting from woman to woman, and then implicated (wrongly) in his brother's murder, Franz resumes a relationship with a black hood named Gorilla (Gunther Kaufman) who actually murdered Franz's brother. Franz joins Gorilla in a supermarket heist to finance an escape to a paradise that may or may not be The City of the Gods. It's spam and eggs for Franz in a vision of the world that sees everyone doing time in limited space.

and considerations

"What's prison like?"
Hans-David waits, then, seemingly answering the suspended inquiry from an extended intuition, adumbrates his psyche in a reflection/observation that appears in the mirror as: "No worse than on the outside."

meanwhile

Channel 7 runs Garfield's commercial amid cat-calls and hisses. This is no laughing matter. The City is damaged, listing portside. The rats, scheduled to inherit the world, are going off in droves.

Then in yet another panic-a-tactic, with inspiration, hoping to answer "How can good come from evil?" Garfield is on the phone with Glen Robinson, the man who destroyed Los Angeles in *Earthquake*, blew up the Hindenburg, conjured the fog bank in *King Kong* and built the hydraulically powered forty-two foot Kong.

For *Earthquake* Robinson constructed a twenty-five foot "miniature" dam with five separate systems to destroy it. The flood waters came out of a giant Robinson-made flume with enough calculated force to break the dam. In case that didn't work, a network of miniature primer cord would blow it up. In case that didn't work, a giant cable with a pair of tongs would rip it apart. In case that didn't work, Robinson constructed a hydraulic ram to push it out. In case that didn't work, a final cable system with a winch would pull it to bits. Redundancy is the name of the game. However, none of the extra four systems were necessary. The force of the water broke the dam, as Robinson knew it would. Yea, I say unto you, god may mumble and fumble, but though Robinson's dam fails, Robinson never does.

"He can build you a little cloud and it'll stay right there while you film it," a co-worker says. "He can set you on fire and put you right out again. He can blow you up and it won't hurt. MGM canned him a little while ago because he was too old."

"How old is he?"

"Oh, it's said that he's as old as god and twice as tired. But they had to keep hiring him back because god wasn't available. He is the only one who knows what he's doing."

"So he was there?"

"Yes, he was there."

"There? Where?"

"I mean, like the first illusion, 'Let there be light. The greater light to rule the day and the lesser light to rule the night.'"

"You mean he created the moon?"

"Yeah. And got paid for it. Even god couldn't do that. He had to wait around for some kind of earth-catastrophe."

The Commissioner is going futuristic. He is aware of anthropologists' claims that Homo sapiens sapiens' extinction is not only certain, but certain in a foreseeable few millennium, and that the planet earth will be overrun by rats, very large, Indian elephant-sized rats. Yes, echoing Juan Lamiae, it would appear that brother rat is definitely the future.

Hoping to be remembered as a visionary, Mayor Beame initiates Rodent Relief Regulations to subsidize rats, although the program is hampered by a number of groups, such as The Ryders Alley Trencher Society (R.A.T.S.), dog owners who take their dogs on night-time excursions to allow them to do what they do best: hunt and kill vermin.

R.A.T.S. state that they convene at the request of a state park superintendent whose guests at the park are being besieged by giant (three-foot) hungry rats figuring to make an easy score.

However, dedicated, R.A.T.S. is not expected to have much of an impact on the rodent program, or the rats. Experts estimate the rat community in The City is already nearly half of its 8.4 million people.

"Tell him this is the Police Commissioner," Garfield declares to someone who claims to be Robinson's agent. "Tell him I have an offer he can't pass up. This will make King Kong look like a whimpering chimp. I want a seventy-foot hydraulic sewer rat with seven-foot teeth and a twelve-foot dong. That's right. Even if the picture is distorted, they'll get the message."

"Of course! Of course!" Professor Marshal Message from CCTC shouts.

"It's not at all puzzling. It's a medium blue-screen summer and no matter the message the massage will be there. The special-effects movies with giant insects and green men and larger than life rats reflect the way ordinary people feel about the new, non-human environment.

"Every time we get on the phone, every time we listen to the radio, we leave our bodies, and without bodies we are free to roam other worlds, to dredge up terror. It's not necessarily bad, you know. Horror gives us a lift. If we can respond to the sound of angry bees or pigs or females being slaughtered, we're still alive, and that's terrorific. So why not a few rats? A few large rats?"

"People do not respond to people annihilated by other people," Garfield says. "Fantasy be damned. I want a sewer big enough to hold the rat, a marauding, damned-near T-Rex-sized rat. The City is just the place for it."

Psyaint David

"But a Godzilla rat's not very imaginative."

When news of the Commissioner's plan leaks the Wall Street Rat Market responds. Not only does the price of rat meat shoot up, but the demand for rat-market prognosticators proliferates. Office of Pest Control Services, Aston DaLuna, dispatches a troupe of ratologists to the Pulitzer Fountain near Central Park to survey the rat population available for harvest.

With SoSaMy Inc subsidies, consultants, and ad writers, a scheme is hastily devised and a rat commercial taped and distributed, with E.Erie™'s now confident assurances that equilibrium has been established within the media kingdom.

Garfield's spot, featuring Garfield, appears on teevee screens across The City, five times a day, slinks into focus and grows majestically, a dum-de-dum-dum beat of the old Jack Webb–Joe Friday *Dragnet* shamble laced with shards of the theme from *Peter Gun.*

Ah, yes, and, now, at center screen-ring-stage of Times Square the barker steps forward, his black stovepipe hat in one hand, the mic in the other.

"Ladies and gentlemen, a face carefully selected to suggest the average, and avoid the risks of sales resistance, the magnificent, splendid, superbly sculptured features of the Police Commissioner of all of The City."

The shadow of Garfield's visage appears superimposed on a low level shot of a bustling Times Square evening.

In a splash of flash and color a man with an afro and a gun leaps from the Commissioner's left ear, a brain child, fire flying from his weapon, as if he's about to blast his way from the confinement of law enforcement's cerebral cortex into the freedom of light waves zipping away into the universe. His gun flames while behind him in trailing white lines of afterimages, for a brief second, a row of bodies set out like stepping stones of a garden path stretch into the depths of the tube revolving slowly to the left to the ends of the earth—and beyond.

Then again an explosion of light from the shadow of the Commissioner's enlarged eyebrow. A youth gang with luminescent purple clubs and orange knives swells in a tumult of activity into an undistinguishable blur of blows. The blotch struggles en masse beneath the glass to the picture's frame and out onto the wall.

The pulse and throb of music accentuates the guns' brilliant blaze, the swing and surge of bodies locked in combat. From somewhen in the visual recesses of the Commissioner's frontal lobe one of The City's Finest boys-in-blue frisks an up-against-the-wall-motherfucker, as the sonorous voice of a celestial narrator observing that, "The integrity of Police Commissioner Michael 'S. F.' Garfield and the men and women of the TCPD are all that stands between residents of The City and (total?) chaos."

Well, maybe. And the rat? Where's the rat?

"The rat symbolizes all that is cunning in The City — low-life forms that by a combination of perverse instincts, guile, ruthlessness, and innovation, feed on the innocent and unwary."

In other words, business as usual.

But then, the Comissaire is contrite. Yeah. Easy come, easy go.

"After all, we decided not to use the rat. The metaphor could be misleading. With a little thought, it is easy to advance the implication that all of The City is a sewer."

So. Three hundred forty-five feet of tape and sixty thousand dollars of good entertainment go down the tube.

The Year of the Rat (1982 — first of Chinese zodiac signs because it has spirit, wit, alertness, delicacy, flexibility and vitality) will have to wait. The truth is, however, that advertising fees were just too much to allow a sustained campaign. Rates for commercial spots stand at a cool one hundred thousand dollars a minute — six million dollars an hour.

"And this is the year of the jugular," says Irwin Segelstein.

"No network can bear the disgrace of running third," says Frederick Pierce.

"It's going to be a confusing season," says Robert Willussler.

The consensus is solid — the fare about the same: serial adaptions of novels, two-part historical, biographical or non-fiction movies, dramatic specials, variety specials, movies and sports specials (with doping). This is the latest. An important cog in the sales scheme.

Drugs to augment performance in sports have been used since the Olympic Games in 776 BC. The word 'doping' comes from the Dutch word 'doop,' a viscous opium juice, the drug of choice of ancient Greeks.

Moreover, the ancient Olympians were professionals who competed for large cash prizes as well as olive wreaths. And most of what is today considered cheating was perfectly okay with the Goldens, save game-fixing. They gorged themselves on meat — not a normal dietary staple of the Greeks — and experimented with herbal medications in an effort to enhance performance. They drank wine potions, used hallucinogens, and ate animal hearts or testicles to increase potency.

"Also, it has to be set in The City, Washington or Paris," Willussler continues. "It's either politics or fashion. If it doesn't come from The City the zombies in the hinterlands will not accept it. We are America's ideal of fortune and fame — sophistication. Our intellectual and social standards are the bias for measuring the inadequacies of the country."

And what else might the gods have in mind? What's on the trading-bloc — what goods exported and what asked? What lies closest to the American heart? An agglomeration of Watergate and assassinations. The names are legend; Oswald, Ehrlichman, James Earl Ray. Thomas Thompson's *Blood and Money*, *The Godfather*.

Segelstein pontificates, voice over.

"Every week will be a separate ratings race. This translates into fewer news programs in prime time. No one will want to give away a single time period to the competition. Actually, it represents a vast improvement over what we have now. Our research indicates viewers do not need news programs. They do better with soaps and other high fantasy deliveries."

So? Who needs spirit, wit, alertness, delicacy, flexibility and vitality? And though the idea was a bit too innovative for the moment, it's a sure bet the Year of the Rat will come. Yes, it will.

a gathering of the holy family

After the mid-summer celebration as paterfamilias of the Holy Family Sam relegates Hans-Peter to Our Lady's capable, albeit stained hands, and fabricates a coup (of sorts), a symposium with David Rockefeller, exploring the haunts of high finance, big league plotting and scheming, the excitement of mega billions. Comfortably lodged at the Schwezerhoef Hotel on the east side of the Station Square, he collects his notes, composes an address for the Bank for International Settlements' free Monday luncheon. Sam's a grin in the mirror. He limps in on a torn hoof. It feels good. Not exactly avant-garde, but he likes the view. All is copacetic.

Dressed more conservatively now, thirty-five pounds heavier and balding (he never had much hair, and still has one broken horn), he reflects on his task.

These are serious matters, mega-bucks, a nation's entire gold reserve held as collateral for its debt, giant loans, and criticism of the way governments of the world are running their economies, swaps and other kinds of international credit, set up to support member banks.

A hush falls on the room. Deals are made in whispers as bespeaks the solemnity of sacrosanct transactions. Financial stability, the status quo in a gold plaque on the vault wall, is the byword of the convocation. Change must come slowly, the priests whisper, reciting their office. Only then can money grow and markets expand safely and god be comfortable in heaven.

Jelle Zylstra, the Archbishop of the Dutch Central Bank and chairman of the BIS College of Cardinals, notes that the organization has seventeen billion dollars in deposits, and after decades, during which politicians tried to hamper and hinder the BIS, it is again coming to power.

"Central banks are more influential because governments now recognize that money has a lot to do with inflation," says His Eminence Cardinal Dr. Otmar Emunnger, Bishop of the Bundesbank. "We must enthusiastically incentivize seamless channels while authoritatively targeting resource sucking innovation."

When he finishes, Sam steps to the rostrum, the scent of incense on the air to obviate the mephitis. He has an annoying case of foot-rot, in addition to the bullet in his leg, and thus the limp. (Do goats get hoof and mouth disease?) He stares the soft whispers and mumbles down to silence. He will follow a fearful priority, a solemn protocol, elaborate on BIS success in extracting, in these hard times for shareholders, a substantial profit from the storm-tossed seas of international monetary embezzling.

"Virtue," Sam says. "And genius. We must continually negotiate premium value while monotonectally cloudifying parallel process improvements."

In a splattering of historical comparisons, he paints a dim picture of Roman senatorial splendor, the Guardians of Plato's *Republic*, the gods of Olympus. These are, he believes, the Michelangelo's and Da Vinci's of their time. Once, when religion held sway, art was god. With supporting quotes from Goethe, Shakespeare, Dante, he comes full circle.

"Duty," he tells them, "and survival, command you to take from the world what you can. Objectively incubate performance based applications. Dominion by domination, subjecting the world to your compulsions, you will force human evolution into a new framework, assure its failure to adapt and encourage the genetic mutations that brought mankind (and not so kind) down out of the trees. Fail at your task gentlemen, allow the world, mankind, to luxuriate in splendor, spectacle, and comfort and you sound the death knell for the advancement of life as it has been — the death of catastrophic, cataclysmic capitalism as we know it."

Sam pauses a moment to check the negatives, receives a standing ovation, a solid round of applause, and a muffled, under-the-breath approval from the conventioneers.

Yes, great they are and subtle the arguments of their aspirations.

Sam's eyes flare, then leap with a new, clean intensity.

Petro dollars and debts for oil. Nations drained, bankrupt, and then the empty coffers and imports no longer forthcoming, to discourage meaning-ful revolution and clear the way for speculation, incite the natives to riot, to civil (class) warfare. And when they are decimated by war and disease, they will encourage survivors to systematically slaughter one another.

Sam, always alert for another Psyaint, shakes David Rockefeller's hand, receives a warm thank you, an invitation to lunch, "To discuss certain, uh, financial considerations, a spot of speculation, maybe the Bowery. Does Sam have an interest in Lower Manhattan?

"You know, there's money to be made. A waiver from Port Authority for cheap construction. Well, not exactly cheap, but affordable. No more than four hundred million. Like we did with the Towers. What do you think?""

A splendid holiday, and Mephitis comes away better wrapped in the woof and warp, the design in the rug. He has not underestimated the banking community's intentions and resolve. He is revitalized with a new determination to support Our Lady's growing commercial aspirations.

a menagerie of discontents

With a wave of a finger the picture on the in-house teevee rolls, flips, heats up three hundred thousand phosphorescent dots, and focuses on a

Psyaint David

Queen's street corner where, in the phase of the new moon, seventy-times-seven women materialize, claiming their husbands have been mistreating them and they are no longer misses to be treated but misses (Mrs.) to be obeyed. They are prepared to march into court with a suit against City policemen and Family Court personnel for unlawfully denying them assistance after they reported incorrigible husbands.

The 362-page document (a page per-diem for the next year with a day off for Mothers' Day, Christmas, and New Year's) alleges that at the hands of their husbands the plaintiffs did suffer grievously, innumerable contusions, split lips, and broken ribs — not to mention fractured fingers and sprained backs, wounded egos and bruised psyches. The men have not yet responded to the extent of their wounds and afflictions.

So George and Martha are again taking their wits for a walk, exercising the god-given right to escalate bantering into the world of sticks and stones.

Of course, SoSaMy Inc is ready with an answer. Reading from a prepared statement Garfield speaks with the authority vested in him by his newly gained teevee status — as two-dimensional as that may be.

"It is not enough," Garfield says, "that brutality of this sort be confined to the home and family — that husbands go about indiscriminately and viciously assaulting their wives. Cruelty of this type must be confined in our schools and on street corners, to the subways, bars or wherever else victims go in search of safety and security. Under the present trying circumstances, with a troop of uncivilized and undisciplined misanthropes running loose, the Police Department is doing a commendable job.

"What we need is more manpower," Garfield explains, and before the syllables are off his tongue, Lilo is on the phone with a suggestion for SoSaMy Inc involvement in the project.

"We'll send the Black Spots, our youth group hit-squad. We're gonna keep 'em on the street — you know, street kids need work. Give 'em a chance."

Garfield consents.

"We'll sign them on as "Constabulary Initiates."

The kids, it is agreed, will operate as Defenders Armed For Fortune to lend SoSaMy Inc a certain filial class it as yet doesn't have.

The DAFF is given orders, and an afternoon two days later, beneath mostly fair skies and a few twisted rays of sunshine, at Samuel Gompers Vocational-Technical High School in the South Bronx, thirty-four-year-old good housekeeping teacher Hilda Gore finds herself surrounded by a spot of youth wearing stockings over their heads who threaten to "... mess her up if she doesn't cook them a batch of electric brownies."

When asked about DAFF and his chances of surviving a mano a mano with the troops in his classroom, English teacher Hank Crystal says, "It's turned into a war zone. They show up with complaints, armed and threatening, in packs, packing the latest semi-automatic hardware."

Later in the day Hank crawls along a back hall, his senses somewhat dimmed, his lips split, three incisors missing from a rap in the teeth with a lead pipe delivered by a hooded DAFF hit-youth.

When informed of the classroom disruptions and Crystal's missing teeth, Principal Cecil Benjamin disagrees with the teachers' assessments. He believes reports of student savagery are "totally erroneous."

"They was just practicing. And Henry ain't got no use for them teeth what's missing. He don't never use them. Anyway, crawling is good exercise," Benjamin says.

Appropriately DAFF takes heart and proclaims its right to self-expression, self-realization and with the help of an order from District Court Judge Herman Schelling wiggles in under the protective umbrella of the First Amendment. Leaders are quick to point out that Americans have never been very fond of education, even less so of teachers, and now is the time to tell it like it is.

"It ain't got nothing to do with not likin' ed-ju-ca-ton," says DAFF spokesman David Trillo. "We know learning. The school just ain't teached us right."

Thus it seems authorities are made, tribal gurus chosen, as rival groups elbow their way into the clearing d. c. stage in an attempt to get on camera. Answering the male establishment plot of DAFF, NOW spearheads a move for a recall election of Judge Archie E. Simmon for his refusal to sentence a DAFF fifteen-year-old youth to jail for his part in a rape.

"Should we punish a fifteen or sixteen-year-old boy who reacts normally to a sexually permissive society?" simple Simmon says and wags his head.

"If he had issued an immediate apology, even a half-baked apology, the case would have blown over," says Anne Gaylor, a NOW associate. "But he later told women to quit teasing men, which was just as controversial as his original statement. I mean, women are not going to stop teasing men. It is our right to do it. Our god-given obligation to keep the species alive – on our terms. Men just don't know what is like being a woman and having no one look at you. This displays Simmon's abysmal ignorance of what rape is and what it means to women."

"Rape is sacred, special to women," a second NOW body says. "It is our one advantage. We have always used it as an advantage. Sexual attacks are a possibility for every woman, a rallying point for true rage. I mean, without rape (violence) where is the mating conflict? No excitement at all.

"Do you know what would happen if there was no resistance to mating? Well, the world would be over populated. Then where would we be?

"We must keep this alive and not let hammer-headed judges dilute or temper the contest. It is more important today than ever before.

"We'd prefer *The Virgin Spring.* 'I hear what I want and see what I want. I hear what people whisper in secret and see what they think no one sees.

You can hear for yourself, if you will like me, just listen!' etc. Three cheers for Max von Sydow. This is a battle of Christianity and paganism. You can't stop rape without mutilating someone."

However, when informed that her sixteen-year-old son Alex is accused of swinging the pipe that rapped Hank Crystal in the teeth, Gaylor is outraged.

"My child was just practicing with his Chinese Health Wand (Jian Gan) and Crystal got in the way. The classroom belongs to the students, not the teachers. Hank Crystal should be arrested for interfering with students' education. We can always get another teacher."

someone is in this bed
is breathing - and . . .

I feel her breathing in bed beside me, now, she who
I love, must love, the source of pain
I cannot undo, from the beginning, cannot live without, alone, Maya and Durga, her blindfold in place while she sleeps.
I too am blinded to what is not only not me, but not other, in me, condemned to live with what
I am, cannot be. She sleeps at peace and
I lie ill-awake and listen to the soft, maternal, sensual sounds, that, too, from a beginning remembered before perception, then first in touch, and the female fragrance, the aura surrounding her, speaking before she speaks, before she touches me as moon, earth, and water, whose elements command do, not why, but do, right or wrong, good or bad, to guide me, hand in hand, but do, finding me lost in the jungle, my refuge, Nemesis,
I must hear, may not ignore, must hate and nurture, love and destroy. She has come, old woman, child-bride and crone, nubile and withered, receptive, rife with rejections, elusive and demanding, to vanish in desire, an apparition to disappear beneath my touch, to reappear in a secrecy of dread, succubus, her voice enchanting, the lyre of Orpheus, Eurydice dead, the Furies quieted for the moment. So
I am Tantalus, arms extended, Sisyphus at rest upon his stone. She is huntress and whore, warrior-mistress, spiteful, pulsing with deceit, Clytemnestra wronged, abandoned, bent on revenge, Venus enraged with jealousy, Psyche at last, alone, left on her nuptial hill, mourning wrapped, waiting a demon dragon lover she cannot see, to be borne away.
I am her sheaves of wheat, poppy and millet, the shining fleece, a dram of black water from the River, and finally an inspiration, a companion, for her silent passage seeking Persephone, the giver of the charm kept safely, who will refresh and make her goddess-like in her beauty. And she, Pandora, the agony she hopes to heal, regret and fear, a Sibyl, avaricious and wise in one, Our Green and Virginal Lady, Eve, searching her vast, lost

paradise for another Adam, a new consort, to fall abed, or carry on a ritualistic mating in-the-flesh-dance. And Adam, who did not choose Eve any more than he chose first to breathe, Adam without mother, did not create woman, and, cannot, now, not give consent, but also animus, or no, finds in himself an anguish greater than any power he might take as amour, finds that the air stirs first with the spirits of Tituba in her coven, and spells, transforming rivals to cats, others becoming animal-like braying, soiling themselves, her enemies blinded, broken, reduced to madness. Or, Joan d'Arc wielding a double-edged sword of mysticism, she, too, condemned, at last, sentenced and burned, a holy virgin — warrior, anima, and mother.

now you see it
  now you don't
now you might

Sam's in the squad room of the 111th Bayside monitoring the manhunt. He, too, will be working from a revised edition, an edited copy. He checks the time, the phone jingles in the background and a voice rasps out a routine inquiry, complaint. Our Lady has kept her word. Right on time. Sam gloats. But then, she always does. And another jingle, another voice.
"Hello, one-eleven."
"Hello. This is Son of Sam. I just want you to know that next week I'm going to hit Bayside."
The camera tracks along Northern Boulevard to the glittering high relief facade of the Elephas Disco, the moon halved by a black cloud (again), the shadow of a man along the sidewalk foliage angled toward the camera. And, yes, and the soft, haunting sound of someone whistling the theme from *The Peer Gynt Suite* as the lens creeps in and closes on the face of a blind man.

Blindman: I've heard that before.

He has. On several occasions he heard the refrain, wisp like, elusive and smelled the astringent decay. He walks, tapping his stick.

Blindman: Hey, hey, Henry!

A young man in a cap pops up immediately. Medium closeup of them.

Henry: What is it?

Blindman: (Listens a moment) Hear that?

Henry: Yes.

Psyaint David

Blindman: Did you see him?

Henry: I can still see him. He's talking to a girl.

Blindman: What's he look like?

Henry: He has a long nose, small black eyes and ears that stand up.

Blindman: Don't let him get away.

Henry: But why?

Blindman: The night Chris Freund died . . ., a fellow whistled just like that.

Henry: Oh, Jesus!

Henry Hunter sprints to the end of the block while the music lifts into a drumroll, the insinuation of incest, guilt, and bestial desires hung on the air, posing the question of whether or not the noble hunter, the protective father, all that is logical and kind and good, will arrive in time to pluck the innocent, virginal daughter from the clutches of the wolf.

The camera follows him as he enters a quiet street, a beaten path, and tracks along to a light falling onto the walk from a small candy store. As Henry approaches, the camera cuts to a view through the window from above into the back of the store where a great gray Steppenwolf Lupanar and Rotkäppchen are waited on by an old woman.

The woman is familiar, haggard, her face lined with the worries and troubles of a life lived in solitude and loneliness. Later she will give the police her name as Rosie Gold. She frowns painfully at Rotkäppchen, as if she is about to speak.

Yes, it is Jack's mother. She's had the candy store since Jack traded the cow for the beans. And yes, she did throw out some of the beans out. Some. The rest, the largest part, she kept to accommodate her miserly and self-serving self. And though she seriously jeopardized the story (what if the beanstalk had failed to take root and grow?) after all, how many cannellini beans, magic beans, does it take to grow a beanstalk to the sky? Well, those who know beans claim one will do. And entrepreneur that she is, Mother Gold dipped the remaining beans in chocolate and then went looking for a candy store to sell them.

Of course, finding the right candy store vexed her a bit. But after a few days prowling the neighborhood she settled on the Midnight Rose at Saratoga and Livonia Avenues in Brownsville, east Brooklyn, an already prosperous establishment. When the owner refused to sell and implied that he was Syndie connected, she informed him of her magical prowess and that, contrary to folk belief, it wasn't her son who cut down the giant.

Two days later the owner showed up in the Emergency Room at Kings-brook Jewish Medical Center with a broken arm and a thromboembolism behind his left eye. Nobody is sure what he walked into. A week later Rosie took over the store.

Of course, with the harp and the goose (and shylocking out of the back room of the candy store) she needed no longer suffer the hazards of frugal living, but in keeping with her tightfisted nature, her time-locked, rock-ribbed intractability — purposes for which she was created, devised — she could not in good conscience allow even one bean to go to waste.

These days the store is furnished with the latest Brooklyn kitsch: a gold-framed mirror that doesn't reflect, a worn ornate accubita (often used by Our Lady of the Loose Libido) a Turkish hammock with a blue felt mattress, a mini softwood cellaret, two faded ottomans, and a beat up tile-inlaid chess table.

These days the store is stocked with racks of Musketeer, 100Grand, Butterfinger, Nut Goodie, Cherry Cocktail, and Smooth Sailin bars as well as various fruits (apples, blackcurrents, elderberries) and vegetables (cabbage, carrots, broccoli).

These days, the two hundred pound, five-one Momma Rosie is still a venomous kvetch. She ambles about the store complaining of syracuse veins, reminding everyone that she is a sick woman who is more than willing to share her illness with them.

Of course, son Jack (The Dapper) is no consolation. For the most part, and to her chagrin (though sometimes pride) he roams The City in a Jag XJ-S, 2-door coupe with RWD, automatic 3-speed gearbox, 5343 cm3 / 326 cui, 182 kW / 244 hp / 248 PS and 365 Nm/269 lb-ft torque. It has an outside length of 4883 mm / 192.25 in, a 2591 mm / 102 in wheel base, a base curb weight of 1785 kg / 3935 lbs, with a top speed of 215 km/h (134 mph) (theoretical). It accelerates 0-60 mph in 9.1 s; 0-100 km/h in 9.6 s, with 1/4-mile drag time (402 m) of 16.7 s (a-c simulation).

When not zipping about in his Jag, son Jack is fond of detaining and leaping succulent maidens, reiterating for them, at intimate climatic moments, the power of his beans and beanstalk.

The old woman hands Rotkäppchen a small sack of apples, lychees, per-simmons, mangosteens, and tamarillos for her basket. The girl thanks her, curtsies cutely, while the wolf hovers, tail twitching, casting furtive glances about the shop. The old woman approves of the wolf in ways she could never approve of Jack — even if he was a Jackal.

Is not this fine beast gentle and polite? Is he not patient, decent, the perfect symbol of civility?

The old woman wishes she was Rotkäppchen, that she had someone to buy her fruit. Yes. What a fine son this wolf would make — what a fine and wonderful . . ..

The camera shifts to a reverse shot of Henry Hunter. There is panic, then reckoning in his eyes. He hesitates momentarily. After one last look, he runs off to the right. The camera cuts to Henry Hunter lurking behind a tree.

The old gray one and Rotkäppchen come out of the shop. She hands him an apple from the sack. Tail flicking, he looks right and left. The street is empty. Slowly his hand disappears into his fur. The camera zooms in for a mid-shot. He withdraws a knife. The camera cuts to a closeup of huge glinting canine tooth, then back to the knife.

Quick cut to the noble and iron-jawed Henry Hunter, his soft steel-gray eyes locked on the wolf.

Return in closeup to the wolf's large, sparkling teeth — the blade peeling the apple.

The camera pans back to a full-shot of Henry Hunter searching his pockets. He takes out a piece of chalk. Possibly, he hopes to redraw the wolf. An extreme closeup of the palm of Henry Hunter's left hand that resembles a Palmist's sign and upon which he marks off his lifelines, then draws a large, soon to be iniquitous, W.

Slowly the camera creeps back to the wolf, facing Le Petit Chapeau Rouge (who has little hope of rebirth), his back to the camera. He finishes peeling the apple, throws the peelings on the ground, and looks about once more, furtively, embarrassed with loitering and littering.

Hurriedly, Henry Hunter approaches the wolf and bumps into him, as though by mistake. Surreptitiously Henry H. places his left hand on the wolf's haunches. Terrified at the touch, the wolf springs away, the hair on his neck bristling. My god, is HH a quirk? Is it proper for people like this to go around on the street fondling animal haunches? Is there no civility left in humanity?

The wolf drops the knife and freezes in place, feet apart, lips curled, teeth bared.

"Snarl, snarl, snarl," says the wolf.

The camera drops to a closeup of the knife on the ground. Le Petit Chapeau Rouge picks up the knife, examines the blade as if she might use it, then reconsiders and hands it to the wolf, smoothing out the wolf's bristling fur with her hand.

The camera circles until the wolf and LRRH are framed in profile. Rotkäppchen leans over and kisses the wolf on the head. She is always mixing with wasps and wolves, and so, even in dangerous situations, portrays a mature (though some might say, naïve) elegance. The wolf takes the knife as the camera continues to circle, showing his back and the W outlined in chalk on his swarthy fur.

Almost accidently the wolf sees the W. His bright eyes bug out, his jaw drops, and he spins frantically, chasing his tail, trying to lick the W off. Faster and faster he spins, until he is exhausted, panting, eyes glazed, tongue lolling. Little Red Cap tries to dust the W off, but as she does, the motif becomes even more pronounced, takes on an eerie glow. It would seem the wolf is forever stained, and then not stained, but branded. The night air carries the scent of sulfre and seared hair — maybe from the wolf chasing his tail.

where art precedes life,
life precedes art

On the morrow, however, it is still l'art pour l'art. Sam's moving in wider circles now, the ripple effect, with big money, power, maneuvering at the top. In a genteel mold, exploiting the traditional synthetic scramble of money, power, art, and politics, he finagles (forges) an invitation for The City Ballet Guild's spring gala. For one hundred dollars a plate revelers eat, drink, dance, and make merry.

Sam's stylishly late, white gloves and tails, debonair, tall, svelte, split-hoofed, hovering, his eyes crisp, and pointed. And a fine time it is in Vulturesburg, scavenging with a superfluity of heads bobbing and wings flapping. Of course, Sam's mellow, as mellow does, courting dollars and clout — prestige and reputations in the finely decorated entertainment haze of delusion — the magic of circus and magician, sleight-of-hand, of high-theatrics with a touch of mirth and myth — diversions to use up time, alleviate boredom, keep the mind busy, adrift, off the morbidity of oblivion.

It's a preview performance of Balanchivadze's mirrored marvel Vienna Waltzes, the audience watching itself watching itself, then dancing beneath the watchful eyes of the gigantic *Circus Women* and *Two Nudes,* to the music of Lester Lanin's orchestra on the Promenade of the State Theatre at Lincoln Center.

The Promenade features an 18K gold leaf ceiling and two gigantic Elie Nadelman sculptures. The twins, carved from an Italian virgin vein of Carrara marble, are replicas of smaller (4-foot) versions of plaster and paper that Nadelman stuck together decades before. The name of the Italian sculptor, who actually did the chisel work, is lost to history.

Overhearing construction workmen remarking on the naked "goils," (Lincoln) Kirstein arranged to have the immense artworks brought into the Theater just before the fourth and final wall was closed up and before the Lincoln Center leadership could order their removal, which, in fact they did; but the statues could no longer be removed. And so they are still there today.

Tonight the dancers wheel in and out among the mirrors, and beneath the music Sam drops in on the soft chit-chat, unobtrusive, but within earshot.

"Have you seen *The Goodbye Girl?*"

"Yes. No wonder there's so much controversy over the Beaubourg."

"I hear that Hilton Kramer does not care for the 'Recent Acquisition' at the Museum for Modern Art."

"So? Who's Hilton Kramer?"

Snickers.

"Marcia Haydee is magnificent in *Requiem*."

"My god! Bart Cook has a broken nose. He was mugged, you know, after the Saturday night performance."

"Maybe they should have done it before."

Henry Kissinger is flanked by Patricia McBride, the dancer, and Jacquine Lockman, the recent bride of Charles Lockman, who is the L in Revlon.

What was it in *The Observer of London*, Henry? Two million for your memoirs?

"I think one has to consider that I was deeply in debt when I left office as a result of public service. Even now, a considerable amount of my income has to go for providing personal security for myself, which doesn't affect my life style."

"But Henry, surely you don't need security. What have you done?"

"There is talk of prosecution for war crimes. My, my, you naughty boy."

"Henry, do you think Begin is in control in Israel?"

"Yes. I would say so. The Liberal block can command somewhere around 61 votes."

"Did you hear that Edwina Sandy has become engaged?"

"Yeees. And Robina Lund's got out her book on J. Paul Getty. *Getty: The Stately Gnome*."

"And it's true, J. Paul thought he was the reincarnated spirit of the Roman Emperor Hadrian."

"Why that sounds magnificent. I've a deep affinity with Cleopatra."

"And I with Ann Boleyn."

"Henry, darling, are you sure you're not Wolsey or Metternich?"

"Teehee. How about Nijinsky?"

"Oh no. A spirit must be dispossessed of matter at least a hundred years before it can occupy another form."

"Do you think a spirit might infest several bodies at once? Or several thousand at one time?"

"My goodness! What a deliciously promiscuous idea."

"Yes. And have you heard? The Whitney is expanding."

"They plan to emphasize their permanent collection."

"Will you be in Kassel for *Documentia VI*?"

What's that?

Well, *Documenta VI* formulates an independent, new definition of the concept of the thematic exhibition following the extensive, encyclopedic concept the preceding documenta adopted. The media concept of d6 created by artistic director Manfred Schneckenburger, attempts to rephrase the question about the position of art in the media society, and to do justice to the concept of art as an independent area nevertheless rooted in society, and responsible towards it.

"And by the way, who did cut off Cock Robin's cock?"

"Palace Punishment. I'll bet that Greek wench got him. The one from *The Lustful Turk.*"

"Which one?"

"Viva la Emily and Sylvia."

"Yes. I'll take the wine glass."

Shortly before midnight Governor Hugh Cary and Kitty Carlisle Hart join Sam at a prime location table already occupied by Felix G. Rohatyn, Elizabeth Vagliano and Frederick Melhado and Robert Marschik, the Counsel General of Austria.

so it's time for Our Lady
to take
Child-David in hand

In Yonkers, Our Lady of Avenging Ardor is also holding court. Hers is, however, a clear, untainted vision, vibrations pulsing along the cerebral paths, poking into the thickets of memory and imagination.

She has regrouped to take on the pretenders. The imposters intend to rob her, snatch up the fruits of her labor, or so she believes. SoSaMy Inc has unveiled a neo-David model of a dartgun sniper and allocated funds to commission an eighteen-foot sculpture of David to accompany the Wall Street Bull. By god, if Michelangelo can do it, so can we.

The Universe and CBS are preparing a faded and shaded light-show compilation of all episodes, Hans-David sculpted in celluloid with a Veronican imprint of dirt and sweat staining a towel, a wound in the side clearly marked by a spot of paint on the shroud. In addition, SoSaMy Inc's in-house teevee has serialized the pilot of "Henry Hunter and the Wolf" into a four-part mini-series — a taunting, confused blend of Henry's relation with Little Red Riding Hood with the Wolf as pedophile and pimp.

Adding a splash of crime to the gumbo of turmoil and deceit, the composite sketches of the Son of Sam pinned to station bulletin boards have been doodled over, teeth blackened, moustache penciled in, large black horn-rims circling the improbable eyes. The enhancements are gleaned from cloak-and-dagger fantasies, the car coat and Bulldog Special trappings of Garfield, Keener and LoKo — a construct of the bits and pieces forensic and criminal behavioral psychology have provided.

"Presumptuous assholes," Our Lady of Wanton Wrath proclaims. "Presuming pigs poking about in the muck."

Her voice carries a lilting, lethal tone, a promise. She alone knows who will have Robin's cock (Why is a hard man so good to find?) and knows well, why and when again he'll take to the streets. She alone holds the Child-David hand. To protect her interest, she is prepared to snap on a complication, diddle the dandies — their uninventive imaginings, greed, and aggression. Already she has the Lieutenant off in Queens on a mild, loose case.

Indeed, if she rests comfortably, satisfied, and it appears, now, that she does on occasion, this, too, is a shadow of her lasting motif. Her search ended, she concocts a plan, a scheme, so to speak, for handling SoSaMy Inc and CBS. To date their tampering has been a minor annoyance, but she knows well, Hardon Inc could be jeopardized.

Quietly she settles into the snuggery at 35 Pineview Towers, amid the reek and teevee voices: Sam belching and coughing, his profuse, noxious proliferation, abscesses dripping. The apartment is not what she expected, but she makes herself at home, relieved to have at last attached, of needs be, both appendage like, of a part, and independent, to the Child's soulful image. Maybe, she thinks, a "contingent relationship."

For this is Child-David, the enfant terrible lover who strikes in the night, randomly, and without remorse. And she, Our Lady of the Blindfold, Scales, and Sword, mother and waif to this twisted and convoluted mélange, sprung from his rib in a new paradise, now follows him as she leads. The enraptured vapors of her fragrant wrath bubble softly, the infatuation of the flirtation still new enough to command civility.

By now the plot has come full circle. She passes the evening reviewing spec-scripts for a new shoot-em-up (syringe) series at Hardon Inc. The proposal, entitled *Psyaint David,* features a serial killer taking on the police and the mafia (a word, as we have been told, no longer extant in political-press vernacular) to wring heroin profits out of chaos (for a time) and re-establish The City of the Gods as the Catastrophic Capitalist Center of the world. Just as it is claimed Rome converted from a political capital to a spiritual mecca, so shall it be acclaimed that The City of entertainment has become the ultra CCC with a base code of SVGSVGSVGGSVGSVGSVVGSV-GSVGS. This will be Our Lady's legacy. The Neo-City of Capitalist Gods.

She commissions an opera, *Psyaint David,* advanced on a leitmotif of mayhem (SVGSVGSVGGSVGSVGSVVGSVGSVGS) in pursuit of virtue. Some-thing like fucking for chastity or fighting for peace. She has production specs on a cult fashion line featuring crimson stained blazers and levies torn with bullet holes, as well as a Son of Sam collection of coffins and caskets with retractable lids for the victim-to-be to use as a bed in which to sleep comfortably in preparation for the ultimate non-experience. The coffin and casket line will include a variety of shapes, sizes, and colors — and themes — for fading into the unknown. One is modeled on a .44 projectile; another has satin-crimson padding cut into the cushioned contours of an open wound.

SOS coffee is available for those who need stimulation while stressing over the probability of being shot. She has a wine label in mind — two in fact — Psyaint Devil Red and Psyaint Shocked White. Of course, there is more.

Within days, however, the soft edge worn thin, the peace of new love at 35 Pineview settles into the torments and tribulations of everyday psychic aberrations. In the erotic light of a glowing dawn, to get the show on the road she coaxes her conceit abed, lures Child-David to her with promises. She paints his mind with the wonders of her offerings, the pure fantasy of receptive flesh opening like the Red Sea. She stretches the bounds of imagination to a bursting point, before turning away, petulant, pouting, evasive, elusive, out of finger's reach, and touch. She has come full circle.

And Sam is there. He passes the days flipping through Avicenna, Roger Bacon, Moses Maimonides, the *Summa Theologiae*, reviewing the loopholes in Tommaso "Doctor Angelicus" d'Aquino's arguments. Aristotle's true son, TA lists women as inferior beings. Our Lady has her nose in the air and her legs spread, as if to say "We'll see about that.".

The vivid, exhilarating folly, still hangs at the edge of Sam's dissident memory, the lamp brightly lit, of tavern nights, listening to Tommy's overwrought weak-kneed leaps in logic. Lord, lord, but the centuries steal away — highlighted by nights of whoring and drinking on the road to the second Council of Lyons, the Saint's demise at the hands of a jealous husband.

"Intent," Sam says, suspects, festers at the heart of the argument like a hank of rank pork. "Maybe that's what he's talking about, after all. Reason slipping his hand beneath Faith's dress and into her fickle drawers."

Sam as watchful patriarch watches, inspired by Our Lady's muliebrity.

"Inferior?" Sam asks, glancing askance at Our Lady. "Inferior, maybe, but still potent enough to bring the motley monk down in a frenzy of carnal ecstasy. The feminine touch," he notes, "or the promise of it can be deadly."

He smirks at the humor of torment, knowing well the course she has charted to encourage the knight-errant, the Psyaint. She has taken him up side-streets and byways that even he (Sam) may not expedite.

"Women contribute their share to the chronicle," Sam tells Our Lady of the Big O. "They have been most accommodating. They have supplied us with killers and thieves, deceivers, charletons, better than we could have asked for. And done it willingly, albeit, often intentionally. I find nothing inferior in this.

"Who would have thought procreation could bring such havoc?"

More than that, Our Lady of Obstinate Obscenities speculates — paces the room like a rumpled cat — ruminates on the advent of her ill-faring — Medea's cheeks smeared with scars, and tears, and excrement.

in a moment of reverie
Our Lady ruminates

So I am brought finally to this, and what, now, bereft of grandsire, father, brothers, no husband, childless, of choice of course, but barren nonetheless, circumscribed by circumstance, and time, stripped of promise, of virginity, of the gifted womb bearing gifts, with no prospect for Eternal Motherhood, temptress, strumpet, harlot, a field to be ploughed, an unending furrow to swell about the rutting tool, where too soon and times too many the male seed will fall, though not to incubate and flourish.

Blind, unrelenting biology enslaved, soul-chained, and held its concubine, and what I taste or see, all that I perceive, am forced to do, reduced to this — now, legs open to the impulse of spawning generations, or bent, splay-legged and spraddled on the bark's aft rail, or any other, all positions the human figure might allow, at first reduced to this, but always.

Made blind to my own needs by the incessant prayer of a holy-order-of-must-be, what am I to do but lie awake until silence blankets deceit with a treacherous affection, and if he sleeps, remove my loathsome stiletto from hatred's sheath, rusted in sorrow from tears, and plunge the pitted blade into his heart? Or, holding my rancor, cutthroat revenge, stroke my vengeance, playfully, into a pleasure mask and tease his soul to madness, agony, mounting his pain with mine until temptress and Son are one?

Should I play the barking-bitch and soil the floors, the air with the heat of my promiscuous cunning? I could cuddle him, hold his head to my bosom, the child I never had, and tell him he is forgiven, the beating of my heart speaking, comforting him, until . . . and then . . ..

Well, the arrogance may be the same, but there are no Niobids here, so unlike Niobe there will be no tears.

temporary difficulty
 on the network,
please stand by

Lohmann's ulcers are kicking up — his heart erratic.

"Don't talk to me about help from the general public. It disgusts me just to hear it. Sorry, but that is the truth. Good god! Has help from the public brought in one useful clue? Just a thousand calls of the most incredible accusations. Calls to the police when a garbage man steps on their lawn. But when we want really accurate information they can't remember, they've seen nothing."

In answer to the Loo's complaint/observation, Abigail [of 5175 Crescent Street in Queens calls in with the "accurate information" (from her observations) that her husband Orin is the Son of Sam. Abigail has already been heralded as the only woman to have an application for State Executioner on file — should an opening ever arise.

"One of these days Orin is going to kill somebody and get the death penalty," she says, when asked about the app. "And when that happens, I want to pull the switch. I've been reading up on it."

"You said he is the Son of Sam. So he has already killed someone."

"Well, I mean, when he gets caught. When the police get off their dead asses and actually figure out he is the killer."

She waves a copy of *The Assassin and Executioner Handbook* she purchased at the Hardon Inc adult store on Broadway.

Of course, other buttons wait to be pushed, pages turned.

When the word gets out that Our Lady has Son of Sam in hand, Galante is pissed — smells a double-cross. After all, she worked for TCPD. As a well-schooled paranoid he suspects, knows, Garfield is in on it and takes out a contract on his SoSaMy Inc co-CEO.

**thank you for your patience
we now rejoin the network**

"See that?" Blount says. "That yellow Galaxie, across from the school."

Wolfe pulls in down the block in long-shot behind the unmarked car.

"Un huh," he says, "a two-thousand-pound canary waiting for a cat."

"But Lieutenant, that's not all. Lookie. Lookie. We're on camera."

"Col. Primrose, we're always on camera."

"But I haven't seen the playbook."

"Hey, baby, it doesn't matter. Use your street smarts. It's all the same."

"Are they from The Universe?"

"Of course. Teivel probably set it up."

"That car has press-plates."

"Well, well, what do you say to that?"

"Maybe it's SoSaMy Inc or Hardon Inc."

Wimsey shuts off the ignition.

"C'mon. This is ours. Hey, this is the "me" generation. If they want a face on the camera, it might as well be me."

He hesitates, not exactly introspectively.

"And you know? Goddam, I feel it in my bones. We'll have Sam by the balls in another two hours."

Thus it is in The City of the Gods generates a mini-festival. An extemporaneous celebration in face of adversity, develops.

A collective of randy youth gathers to follow the director, following the cameraman, following the reporter, interviewing the undercover officers, no longer undercover, following Son of Sam.

"I'm going to be on the news! I'm going to be on the news!" a boy shouts as he dashes in front of the camera.

Fifty extras gather at ten bucks a head and Nero swaggers into the crowd to be spontaneously recognized.

"Hey, Lou, how about an autograph?"

"Anybody here got a lollipop? A thin cigar?"

"When you gonna catch Son of Sam, the Chubby Behemoth who holds The City in the grip of fear?"

"How long you been bald? My uncle's got a cure for baldness."

"Is that so?"

"Yeah. Creosote, whole-wheat flour, and a shot of scotch. Drink the creosote and rub the scotch on your head."

"What's wheat flour for?"

"For baking bread, dummy?"

The reporters pick up the beat.

"Lieutenant, do you expect Son of Sam to appear?"

Super Sleuth smiles his Colgate (Kyle Rote, Jr.) best for the camera.

"Why else are we here?"

"We've been told Sam enjoys a good show. If he is here, do you think he could be talked into an interview or a joint press conference?"

"Maybe we could bring him on as a mystery guest. The world wants to know who he is."

"Is it true that Sam has invaded our high schools — schools like this one?"

"Yeah, Sam could be a high school student. An unhappy dude with poor grades, a bad complexion, and nobody to love him."

"You say 'dude.' Could Sam be a girl? Could it be the Daughter of Samantha? Maybe the Son of Samantha. Or the Kópn or File or Hija or Tochter or Filia of Sam? There's bound to be a woman in this someplace. I mean other than getting killed."

Moments later they're still gabbing when assistant principal Luciano Ascerra appears with a quizzical smirk.

"The .44 Caliber here at Richmond?" he says, "Oh, no, that cannot be."

When the crowd defects to a diner across the street to discuss and marvel at what they have just seen, Ascerra continues with the interview.

"Maybe I'm paranoid," he says, "but I should tell the cops . . .."

His words drift into the vacant schoolyard, unheard, as unobtrusive as the click of the hammer faling on a firing pin.

the Pullysnit Players
set out to rescue
the Lou's fading image

"It's an assignment," Keener tells the Lou. "An assignment, like any other, and anyway, we don't have many alternatives."

"Let me see if I got this. I'm on loan for the next couple weeks to a troupe of street theatre looneys run by a misfit name Ontolo Bennett. Even though I'm supposed to be the boss of O-Mega? So we're back to carnival."

"Yeah. You can wear whatever mask you want. You're right. Though that's not all they do."

"So you think the ghoul might get loose in the drama, may be a singularity surfaces in one of their skits, and you need someone to make the collar."

"That's part of it. But it'll add class to your act. Get you off the traditional stage. It won't hurt to spice up your delivery. New worlds, a new face, new words. You know, dramatic elocution and all that."

"What do you know about this bird, Bennett?"

"He has a substantial reputation in psychodrama. That's why our psychiatrists chose him."

"You mean he has a long history of psychotic behavior."

"Well, he may not know what he's doing, but he does it anyway. He has street smarts to go with his flair for melodrama. Honestly, Theo if anyone can help get you straight, he can.

"Along with his troupe, the Pullysnit Players, he was the overwhelming choice for The City Drama Critics Award, 'The Best of The City.' They were chosen to take The City's best talent to the outback with their rendition of, some say confrontation with, Shakespeare — the bard's *Othello*. Take it from me, this is a golden opportunity."

In his own words Bennett professes to be less a director in the traditional sense and more a group leader in a nontraditional sense.

"It is an attempt to educate the country — the parts we will play. Since we are from The City — since we live here — and have experienced the very best, our presence alone brings the play to life. We are the play and Shakespeare's words, anyone's words, the play itself, are just a form within which we move. As you know, it's not the shoe that counts, but the foot that makes the peddle go.

"We will be ourselves. We dress as we do in our own dives. We have no presence portrayal, as such. Willie Henson will be Iago. Willie Henson is Iago. A jive nigger, out to rip off the fat-cat Othello, also a nigger — no racism here. Marie Daggott is Desdemona.

"In all my life I've never known a more laid back, innocent chick. Despite a couple rounds with heroin, a dozen or so prostitution raps — she has not understood one thing. She's untouched, unsullied, you might say. A perfect Desdemona."

And Othello?

"Frank Carcidio. Let me tell you about Frank Carcidio."

I'm not sure . . ..

"You got to hear about Frank Carcidio."

I'd rather . . ..

"Well, despite his humble beginnings, his trivial mind, deep inside Frank is this fat-cat — this big exec-type. It's in everything he does. The way he walks — his vocabulary. He walks bent over and stumbles a lot because he's so powerful inside. That's a heavy load to carry.

"First of all, he doesn't have to demonstrate his power — he's what you might say, comfortable with it. He's a true General.

"Second, he's trying to keep it under control. One thing you'll learn about Frank is that if he ever lets his power loose — I mean, like, wow! It's all tied in a knot. If it ever explodes . . . like, WOW!

"Then he's got a mojo with language. It's awesome. You gotta hear . . .."

I'd rather . . .. Maybe . . ..

"You know why he uses monosyllabic words? Let me tell you. It's for effect. To break down the assumptions of polysyllabic words. Sometimes, like, he goes right off the scale and grunts — once he even relocated the sound emanating from the deepest part of his soul — The City center of his being.

"Iago comes in and wails, 'Hey, wha da fuck, man, ya know, wha ya wan me ta do?' and Frank farted the answer. I mean, like wow. He just let off a Command Fart. And Iago knew exactly what he was supposed to do. He ran off stage holding his nose.

"It was the best part of the play. The audience went crazy. Before the play ended chicks were coming up to Frank and offering themselves to him for a Tickle or Orgasmic Fart. I mean, gastharsis."

By the way, where did this tragedy come from?

Why did it come at all? Why is there anything at all?

Sam returns
to Americana '77
or paradise lost

In a festive mood, the following day, Mayor Beame announces plans for a gigantic street fair to be held on 52nd Street between the East River and 9th Avenue. The live entertainment includes the cast from the Broadway musical *Grease*, bringing the metaphor to metaphor, once again, to the avenging avenues.

Sam surveys the crowd, thumbs a pinch of Skoal under his upper lip and strolls up 52nd Street.

"A lost paradise," Sam says, amused with the mini meanderings. "A hype to live and love and believe in."

He has aged significantly, is a bit subtler now. From the back he might be anyone, except for the legs. Small blue blazes flare, and smoke puffs, where his hoofs touch the street, leaving a faint fetor.

Anyway, the flags are up for Americana '77, along 52nd Street from First to 9th Avenue. A million revelers turn out for His Honor Lord Mayor Beame's "biggest block party in the world," with a smattering of the ancient, but nevertheless viable vecchia religione. Along the thoroughfares wares are hawked: trinkets, foods, philters and charms — Al Smith buttons and Mickey Mouse salt and pepper shakers. For nursing mothers, to keep the milk flowing, small bronze statues of Gilles de Rais. Near 8th Avenue Franklin Melnick is selling plastic and steel pyramids, guaranteed, he says, to exude "free energy." His sign claims that "Seeds sprout sooner, makes coffee less bitter, mummifies, and sharpens knives." Around the corner, performers from *Grease* and *I Love My Wife*, entertain an ebullient crowd, while the Big Apple Circus opens at 52nd Street and Broadway.

Within the hour, following a troupe of Antonioni *Blow Up* mimes, a crowd gathers at 52nd and 6th Avenue and twenty-year-old Patricia Dentuso of the Center for Environmental Dance at 6668 Termnale Avenue presents the festival featured, "Romancing the Snake." She is accompanied by a sallow sunken-eyed youth with two dumbbells, a bearded kazoo player, a bucket drummer — all baldheaded and in white robes. A Sapuakela snake charmer wearing a red dastar, churidars, and a light ivory sherwani, sits cross-legged in the street fingering a flute.

In an act that will gain a modicum of notoriety, dressed scantily for the occasion, her waist length red hair flying, Patricia twists and circles her improvised street stage taunting the now gathering crowd.

The second time around she picks up a drum beat, hands clapping, rising to the moment, and flush faced, in glass-eyed ecstasy, loins heaving, breasts heavy, bends back slowly, stretching over a fur covered packing crate into a back-breaking, arching pose, unsnaps the bottom of her frayed Levi shorts, and lifts the flap, her white thighs gleaming in the sun.

The drum roll mellows, and the wafting airy notes of the charmer's flute caress the air. She begins a soft Padmatola and within a few seconds, to the astonishment of the crowd, a three-foot rattlesnake waves and weaves from the portal of her labia majora.

Gasps, moans, shouts of derision rise from the crowd. Weak smiles cross the faces of the men — women clutch their skirts.

Moses' staff?

Where is St. Patrick when you need him?

"It's a fake," someone yells.

"Could be real," another swears.

"It came out of the box."

A woman in the front row retches, covers her mouth with her hand and, turning, launches a rancid yellow torrent onto the man next to her.

Patricia is up, then, twirling, holding the snake overhead. She spins and leaps, and, to insure the illusion of a true chunker, two passes later drops again to the box and deftly, with an ease of penetrating, pleasurable place-ment, maneuvers the snake back into its nest.

The audience is silent. A murmur spreads through the crowd, a titter, dipping into groans of ecstasy and disgust.

Wet with perspiration, whence the snake has since disappeared, tail first, one scale at a time, Patricia extracts a live, writhing Hump-nosed Pit Viper (Crotalinae).

The Sapuakela's flute weaves and wavers with the snake.

The crowd recoils.

Mothers grab their children.

Not that they need to. The kids are having fun. Isn't this the way the world is supposed to be — the way they are told it is?

Up again, the snake, tongue lashing, coiled about her arm, Patricia pauses on either side of the stage, exhibits the venomous reptile to the now hysterical, cheering crowd, a beginning cherry-trickle staining her inner thigh, dripping over her knee into a small pool at her feet.

"It was the snake bit her," an old woman screams, tears in her eyes. "Jesus, here we go again. She'll die."

A wino stumbles onto the scene, a cigarette butt between an index finger and thumb (right hand) and a half bottle of Diego Red under his arm (left) and says, "For Christ sake lady, this ain't the Garden of Eden."

The woman crosses herself and bows her head.

Again the cadence, rhythm of clapping picks up as Patricia uncoils the snake, takes it firmly by the neck, and lowering it to the platform, places her bare foot on its head. A round of scattered, appreciative applause ripples through the crowd. Father's hoist young children to their shoulders. Now everyone is chanting. Especially the kids.

"Kill-Kill-Kill-Kill-Kill-Kill!"

In a genteel gesture of admiration, a dapper gentleman, suntanned, white hair, with blue flaming eyes, lays a bouquet of pansies and a stack of twenty-dollar bills at Patricia's feet.

The crowd is silent, again expectant, shuffling, uncomfortable, as Patricia, misty eyed, thighs smeared and streaked, legs spread, nurses the snake, tongue and fangs, back into the pit.

With the snake in place she rises on weak legs, bows, steadies herself with one hand, face pale, drained, exhausted, stomach heaving, then lies back on the box and from the matted fur of her nest, with a sudden convulsive thrust of her hips expels the original snake. Piercing fangs flashing, the snake explodes into a puff of newly formed bud and bloomed blossom of a very red rose.

Spent, Patricia lies, head back, while the crowd exhausts itself screaming in a foot stomping, hand clapping approval of "Snake-Snake-Snake-Snake!"

Vendors move into the crowd with souvenir plastic and rubber snakes.

"After a performance like that, sales skyrocket," Jerry Wingate, a huckster from 1593 Sterling Place in Queens says.

"People want to know if the snakes are real. I tell them they are, but the girl is a fake. She's bionic. The snakes are trained to vibrate. The girl has an elastic/plastic womb lined with motion sensors. The sack stretches as the sensors pick up the snake's vibrations. You know how it goes. Lorca said 'American women's wombs are filled with gold.' Yeah. I like that. And swords and snakes."

Workers from SOS Inc., a subsidiary of Hardon Inc, set up stands to peddle imitation .44 slugs, Barbie dolls with pieces of their heads missing, that bleed and cry "Help me" — statues of a night-stalker with a blank face, life memberships in the Son of Sam Fan Club. Lottery tickets to his promised appearance on *The Tonight Show Starring Johnny Carson,* when he's captured, are hawked for five dollars each, three for ten.

Within the hour Mayor and Mrs. Beame lead a four block parade, shaking hands with everyone, while Bella Abzug plays the fiddle. It's Rais, the Prince, the crowd shouting.

"Where is he?"

"Who's that?"

And then word spreads that Son of Sam is in the crowd, was seen munching a hamburger — that he is come to greet his followers, to, to . . ..

Actually, he prefers cheeseburgers with lettuce, tomato, and mayonnaise.

The crowd pushes up the street in a viewing frenzy. People are trampled — nothing serious — a couple fractured skulls, six broken arms, and three sprained ankles. Shortly, however, the rumors dissipate, the Son of Sam possibilities drift away, breeze-like, lost in the crowd. Yes, all is well. In other festive sections of the concrete canyons, better than real.

Disappointed with not seeing Son of Sam, intent upon placating their privation with the delight of haute cuisine, the multitude advances and descends on the booths along Literary Walk.

In spite of the threat of Chocolate éclair laced with LSD, as part of the Americana '77 celebrations the Central Park food festival offers "A Taste of the Big Apple." For the remainder of the afternoon, among the busts and bodies of the most-often-not-so-literary-greats — best represented by the bronze Fitz-Greene Halleck sitting cross-legged in his cloak, pen and pad at the ready, staring off into nothingness — the hoi polloi rub elbows and raise a cultured pinky with the hoity-toity. Mussels marinara, crepes suzette, chicken bouquet and, to the sweetest sounds of jazz, a frozen banana daiquiri or two.

Sam mingles with the milling mob, personable, trying to decide if the epinards in the Quiche Florentine are fresh, savoring, for a moment, the lingering afterglow, a touch of lemon thyme — trying now the Pâté of veal, now the Miniosa cocktail, and his favorite, Bouernbacker. Gastronomical delights are sautéed to tickle the taste buds, grace the palate, and substantially enliven the activity of the most dormant ulcer. Sam muses over the fare, surveys the kingdom of his latest innovation, issues his stamp of approval for the forty or so booths of new synthetic foods, chemical additives, artificial colorings and flavors, extenders, and emulsifiers.

Emissaries from Archer Daniels Midland join him, dishing out samples of fabricated fish fillets blended with Haarman Reimer's flavor 94,750, Ardex 700 F, textured vegetable protein and minced fish.

Fries and Fries serves frankfurter pretzels, seasoned with liquid frankfurter flavoring. R.W. Freck (We make your life more delicious) presents its new powdered seasoning for potato chips.

Amaco Foods, a division of Petro Amaco (Whatever helps your car will help you) introduces a low calorie (high octane, summer and winter) creamy garlic dressing made with Torutien-50 (10w40), which it claims, "Mimics fat mouth feel."

So how is your engine these days? Is your exhaust pipe dripping?

The Fideo subsidiary of Nestle Company tenders Great Pretender — artificial mushrooms (the non-sacred variety) ham and bacon essence, to give meat and broth a roast-meat flavor.

"This is more like it," Sam says. "Hail to thee, King Alchemy."

Sleight-of-chemical, -hand, and -slogan abound.

"Hocus Pocus, a new food magnum opus."

For the lower links of the chain, Globe Extracts Incorporated provides a series of artificially flavored pet foods. A taste of bacon, beef, chicken, garlic, ham, hamburger, lamb chops, and cheese. When asked why the flavor, spokesman Leanord Weiner replies that, "It's the only way to get pets to eat the garbage they put in the food."

Sam's stomach growls. He's interested in the prospects, the possibilities for a new line of puppy chow as a tax dodge. He listens as Bob Dole, the crafty American singles senator from Kansas, regales festive revelers making hay in the Big Apple by stiff-arming James Carter's proposed consumer protection agency.

"If Americans are given adequate information about the products they buy and the food they eat, they are intelligent enough to act sensibly without the intrusion of more bureaucrats operating as advocates."

Sam's playing chess on the Periodic Table, marvels at the combinations, compounds, reactions, aye, the possible side effects. Indeed, a new enterprise, mischief well-aligned in days of yore, and he's onto it — searching, contriving, unveiling the familiar Faustian possibilities. An atomic cocktail: weights, valences, charges. A dash-of-bitters, a peel-of-lemon.

Indeed, is there a doctor in the house?

Our Lady offers a prediction - provides a prophecy?

Other voices are, however, more encouraging. Hans-David's head hums with Our Lady's exhortations. He listens attentively, his eyes gray-blue lobo slits reflecting the dim of the Yonkers' sky.

Exhortations and admonitions. Her sensors throb. She drums her fingers on the table, the machinations of retribution circling slowly, setting in place the canons of her infamous batteries. She's detected a failing of nerve, a buffeting confusion at CBS about why they cannot help but make money, and promises silently that she will see the malaise of doubt spread. For his part Friar Pastel is not yet in a betting mood, although on the day he is, she will be there.

Today she settles for a reminder, a calling card dropped on the desk, a short message from Western Union, to let them know she has not forgotten. Both Galante and Garfield (the G-CEO duo of SoSaMy Inc) are fearful (pathologically so) of cats, especially common black alley cats. For devilment, (she has a playful streak) and to send a message, the following night she slips a Persian longhair into Galante's Lincoln. Galante finds the cat, realizes that someone is toying with him (the gods?) and suspects Garfield has a hand in it. He instructs his driver, his eighteen-year-old nephew, to remove the feline from the Lincoln and to spread its entrails on the walk in front of his high-rise at 155 East 38th Street — the only way to override the spell. He then makes a hasty retreat up the block and locks himself in the sanctuary of the Church of Our Savior.

Later, the storm warning lifted, watching the street sweepers scrub the sidewalk, Galante dismisses his flight to Our Savior's as a planned escape to avoid detection. He blessed himself apply with holly water, left a C-note in the poor-box, and said three Our Fathers and three Hail Marys, just in case. This time he didn't fall off the truck.

"In due time," Our Lady of Envy promises, "they will be brought forth SoSaMy Inc, CBS — and E.Erie™. Yes, they will."

Yes, E.Erie™ too. She puzzles over E.Erie™'s Clark Kent demeanor, and the oil slick of bureaucratic malaise spread around him. In the afternoon at Plaza One, waiting to confer with the Garfield and Keener, Our Lady has a bit of luck. Not that she needs it.

Here's the skinny. Left in an anteroom to cool her heels, she tunes in on an overseas transmission coming from the E.Erie™ barrios. It takes a few conniving moments to determine the Hz and crack the code, but finally it makes sense.

As ordered, E.Erie™ purges felon records from the SoSaMy Inc's files, but instead of obliterating the evidence, shutting down the machines and allowing the information to dissolve into the cosmos, he closets the data in an IBM 360 Model 67 mainframe in South Africa. Why did he do this?

The SoSaMy Inc files were purged in compliance with the new policy of no longer recognizing traditional categories such as "Mafia" and "Mob." It makes sense. Why not?

Later, quizzing Garfield, in her inimitable way, she wheedles an oblique confession, of sorts. She leaves the meeting, determined, promising that in time each would receive his due. Indeed, there will be time for . . ..

Hans-Peter recites
the tall-tale
of his next escapade

However, tonight Our Lady is out on the town, riding shotgun, a divertissement, with the deferential Hans-David, rumbling along the Bronx River Parkway to Bayside. He is chuckling, mumbling to himself, tongue lolling, saliva dripping — his mise-en-scène prepared.

Psyaint David

Music in the background, a disco beat. The scene fades to the shadow of Henry Hunter in the front seat of a late model red Cadillac with Le Petit Chapeau Rouge as the wolf stealthes the neighborhood, house to house, yard to yard, tree to tree, his eyes large white circles, his mouth open, the strange, desolate moon of his great wolf-face hung on the night.

> Walking into Bayside Park
> Under the cover of dark,
> A loving couple I spied
> In their auto side by side.
> You should hear my Bulldog bark.

It is easy. Too easy. He is invisible, unknown in the nocturnal overlay of anonymity. A tingle ripples his spine, his crotch, excitement, reckoning with chance, opportunity. Arriving from a hidden world, striking a distant land, sending small speedy missives into the physical ambit, between and beyond. Destiny taken in hand (Telly calls him "a killer of opportunity"), then a quick retreat to the privacy of cloister and namelessness.

> I see her long hair.
> I look. The street is deserted.
> I approach, keeping to the shadows. When
> I reach the car
> I stop to get the gun out.
> I step onto the curb and take a few steps, which brings me directly in front of the passenger's side.
> I can see them in the front seat. They aren't looking in my direction.
> I do not intend to shoot the guy, the driver.
> I crouch to bring myself eye to eye with the girl.

He pauses, absorbs the silence of 3:20, the silent and unmoving, the Cadillac, the Goose Girl waiting, Joan d'Arc at Rouen.

He has a .44 Charter Arms Bulldog Special in one hand, the W glowing on his coat, and suddenly, out of the night and into the light, he lifts the weapon.
He raises the .44, levels the sights

(I squeeze the trigger) ONE! TWO! THREE!
(I have the demons to protect me) and then, and then Aaron's rod blooming
(I have nothing to fear from the police) the cold flash without-fire, of no-car, no-people, the signs, the houses floating mirage-like.
It is raining.

Someone screams.
Someone yells. "Oh fuck!"

"My god! All of a sudden I hear echoing in the car. There isn't any pain, just ringing in my ears. I look at Sal, and his eyes are open wide, just like his mouth. There are no screams. I do not know why I do not scream. I never know why. I just do not.

All the windows are closed. I cannot understand what this pounding noise is. After that, I feel disoriented, dazed.

What is happening? What is happening?

and then
   what appears
   to be a replay -
though not instant

They are on a Televideon Mod. TEE112 — a 12" portable b/w with 8 programs keyboard preselection with potentiometric tuning system, parked on Bayside Expressway, near a playground, beneath a streetlight, using the rearview mirrors, watching the street. They have been staked-out for thirty minutes or so when an intermittent pit, pit, pit — water dripping — accompanied by a soft rustling, breaks the silent hum (of the universe? Pranava?).

"What's that?" the Lou queries. "Do you hear what I hear? Did you hear that?"

Crocker cocks his head, listens.

"What is it?"

"In the back seat."

He turns.

"I don't see anything. There's nothing there."

"There. Near the fence. What do you see?" Fearless asks. "That shadow near the fence?"

They wait. A tremor of breeze absorbs the pitting. The trees are motion-less.

Still, the illusion persists in the breathing of a shrill voice mingling words, humming, then chanting in the park, in the trees, in the night, mixed with the distance, faint rumble of a disco beat.

"723?" comes over the radio.

"Yeah, this is 723."

"A disturbance in Bayside, Queens. Units responding report a bulldog ate a little girl. A couple shots — a few screams. Sounds like somebody shot the dog."

Lieutenant Inspector LoKoJakMan and his sidekick take flight along Northern Avenue to 211th Street. Running in light traffic it is easy to find.

Psyaint David

The scene is classic detective noir — what one would expect — a dark, rainy night, a street shadowed by a canopy of large trees, a car shattered by gunfire. The crowd on the sidewalk in front of the Elephas disco mills about (witnesses, audience, devotees) sullen, mumbling in the rain.

The Lieutenant pushes through the crowd in his command mode, demanding attention. Crowd control at its best.

Down the block, up the block a wolf pulls on his red hood, cowers behind a large elm. The white W on his haunches glows in the muted light. He's scratching tonight, patches of hair missing, red skin, scabies (sarcoptes scabiei canis), discomfort. So, there is no need to ask where Sam is tonight, though it might be worthwhile to note that the W has burned into his hide and to speculate on his frame of mind and/or his inclinations for the future.

Otherwise, the scene is cropped and blocked, the camera focused on an isolated, bare sidewalk square of an endless street where someone, the right side of her face a bright crimson, should be lying. Is it Petit Chaperon Rough we are missing?

"Where's the victim?" The Lou wants to know.

"Sorry, Lieutenant. We haven't been able to locate one," the officer says. "So what's the crime? Why are all these people milling about? Who are these people?"

"Over here," another officer says. "Here. Look at this. Red gooey stuff. What do you make of that?"

The Lieutenant is perplexed, but understanding.

"What we have here is a wolf eating a little girl. Did you ever hear of a wolf eating a little girl without leaving a spot or two of gooey stuff?"

"Wolf? I thought it was a bulldog."

"But that's not how the story goes. He's supposed to swallow her whole. And you left out the grandmother. Maybe the old lady was in the kitchen cooking red gooey stuff."

"Well, by morning the rain will have washed it away."

On cue the rain intensifies. Rivulets drip from the Lou's hat and nose.

"Okay, let's get the mess cleaned up," he says. "We ain't got nothing 'til we get something. Hearsay, rumor, imagination, fantasy, gossip won't stand up. We need a corpus delicti. I want a door-to-door for six blocks. See if anyone took LRRH in. And since you got the hots for the grandmother, see if you can find her. Maybe she's got the wolf in her backyard. Keeping it as a pet. I hear they make good pets for old women."

"That's gonna be tough," another officer says. "It used to be clues solved crimes and led us to perps. But not these days. Clues don't do nothing. Just lead to more clues. The more clues, the less we know.

"The streets don't have names and the buildings ain't numbered. When you walk under 'em the street lights go off. I mean, you know how fairy tales are. Just the forest and the trees. How will we know where we are? Even if we uncover something, how will we find our way back?"

"Follow the trail of goo or crumbs or something," the Loo advises.
Clearly he is perturbed.

"Make it up as you go. Out of whole cloth.

"We need a body. If the wolf did it, he'll surface. Sooner or later he'll have to come out of the weeds — indigestion or something."

"Will we have to cut open the wolf to get the girl out?"

"Of course."

"Okay. That sounds right," Crocker says. "But you sure this ain't a back-lot for some fly-by-night studio?"

"That's no way to talk. Kids might be watching. What will they think?"
Anyway, it's time for a commercial. The batteries on the 12" are low.
And it's still raining.

reverse angle

Freeze frame.
Everyone stares.
Rewind.

Jimmy Yu is mixing it tonight for a dance floor of hustlers at the Elephas. Fronting the bump and screech of El Coco's "Let's Get It Together" bouncers Kasim Dubur (aka Crazy Ninja Dude or World Class Karater Middle Weight Champion Kick Boxer) and Angelo Vasti (aka Angel, specs unknown), are working the door.

Sometime after 3:00 Sal Lupo and Judy Placido step out for a cigarette and a quiet talk. Lupo and Dubur are friends and it's raining, so they use Dubur's Cadillac.

The rain streaked windows shroud the car's interior. They're talking about, of all things, Son of Sam, the news of the town.

Meanwhile, seven cars up a shadow, a mist, a shape moves slowly, silently on the crepe soles of webbed canine feet, stirs the uniformity of the night.

It drifts along the walk, approaches the car, license 524-XSY, a red deVille with a rectangular grille set deep in the front bumper, giving the car a road-hugging appearance. Two massive front bumper guards with rub strips flank the recessed license plate. The crosshatch grille emphasizes horizontal textures topped by a chrome header-bar that frames the grille on both side, from the bumper up. The headlamps are widely spaced and have their own individual chrome bezels. The parking and front turn signal lights are located between the widely spaced headlamps. At the moment they are not on.

The rain-streaked windows shroud the car's interior and a gun lifted with both hands points to the car.

Predictably, the thump of a muffled report buffets the soddened air.

Three or four feet from the closed passenger-side window, loosed with a muzzle velocity of 1000 feet per second a Blazer 200-grain (13g) Gold Dot paints an exquisite rose pattern on the car window. The kinetic energy of the Gold Dot melts a white opaque halo in the tempered glass surrounded by a starburst web of spiked needle lancets and overlapping concentric arc radials leaving a gapping small black eyehole at the center.

The Gold Dot tears through Lupo's right wrist (with no stippling — the window blocked the tattooing) and penetrates Judith's neck. The round frags and lodges near her spinal column.

It is still raining.

Another thump.

The window shatters. A second Gold Dot strikes Judith near the right temple, a tangential/graze entry leaving an abrasion and torn skin tags.

A third thump.

A Gold Dot opens a furrowed entry wound in Judith's right shoulder and mushrooms deeper into the tissue.

Chaos!

The interior of the Cadillac is ringing, singing, humming. Judith slumps to the floor, unaware that she has been shot. Holding his shattered wrist, Sal hurriedly exits the car to get help. She hears a thumping in her head, wondering "What's this? What's this?" and manages to push open the car door, screaming, "Help me! Somebody, please! Help me!" before collapsing.

Dubur and Vasti do not hear the shots, but see Lupo standing in the street. They rush to the Cadillac. After all, it's Kasim's car that is shot up and he's had experience with shootings. A year or two down the road in a parking lot at Ripples on the Water, a disco under the Throgs Neck Bridge, he'll go down, shotgunned by a Brooklyn con he bounced the night before. Or something like that.

But tonight it's Lupo and Placido at center stage, though once out of the car Placido's role in the spectacle becomes difficult to verify. The bouncers attempt to locate the source of the calls — the reason for the screams. They walk around the vehicle several times, peering inside, but find nothing. By now Lupo is sitting on the curb holding his wrist.

Word spreads to the disco, the lights come on, and a call goes out to the police. Dancers stumble out onto the sidewalk. Within moments, its sirens blazing on glistening streets, a unit arrives — tailed by a clack of reporters. The Lou will be here soon (that's to be expected), but in the confusion and rush, indeed, in the mysteries of the night, the body or at least their expertise in locating a body on a rainy night goes missing.

"What happened? Who is it?"

Everyone's perplexed, wandering about in the soft mist.

"Where is it? Who is it?"

Finally, the Lou makes the scene, prepared to direct his investigative forces, and the search begins for real, both for the perp and the victim.

An hour later, Geraldo Rivera is set up across the street beneath a huge umbrella. A makeup technician waxes Geraldo's moustache. Rivera is preparing for his life's work, or at least the next forty years of it. He stands in front of the Good Morning America cameras, holding up a broken toy plastic gun he claims belongs to the killer. Likely? Who knows? Geraldo is always making claims — hoping for the best.

Hours later, near dawn, after a thorough search, the police still have not located the body. Seeking an explanation of the probable cause of such an unusual event, reporters press the harassed, troubled, but unflappable, Captain Keener.

"Who took the body?" one asks.

Another is more accusative. "You're hiding it."

"Did you see the killer?"

"Did you hear the shots?"

"Were there shots?"

"Was there a shooting?"

"We've checked the cars in the neighborhood," the Captain says, "to see if he carried her off and ducked into one. But we didn't find anything. No one's been killed yet.

"We tried to get the license number of every car within six blocks. But somebody took all the props — all the paint, all the words and sounds — the license plates are missing or unreadable.

"Look at that."

He points to Kasim's Cadillac.

"The license plate. What happened? The letters were there a minute ago."

Indeed, the plates are tableaux blanc.

"What we have here is une table rase, un nouveau monde for murder."

"You gotta do better than that," a Post reporter yells. "We're gonna need a Weegee or two for the afternoon edition."

Keener approaches the crowd of extras lined up on the sidewalk.

"Any of you ladies want to volunteer? Get your picture in the paper? Come over here and lay down in the gooey stuff."

Hands go up.

"If you get some on you, you can always sell the clothes as memorabilia. Let 'em know you were here."

But beyond bartering the good chief is exasperated.

"Where is the EMS?" he asks. "Did anyone call them?"

"They were here earlier. Got out, walked around. Took the kid . . . what's his name? Lupus? Lupiêo? Lupido? Lupino? Virlupo?"

"No. Lupo"

"Lupus in fâbulâ?"

"Yeah, they took him to the hospital."

"Did they take the body?"

"I don't think so. Maybe, but I doubt it. Course, anything's possible. I didn't see 'em load a body. Just worked on the kid. Bandaged him up and took off."

Indeed. How do you explain this? He lights a cigarillo. He doesn't usually smoke on duty, but now is the time.

"We are left with only three possibilities," Kenner says as the flash bulbs pop. "Either he gives himself up, we catch him fumbling a kill or we do our investigative work. That's the only way this thing will get solved."

"But right now it doesn't seem likely."

For the moment the wolf crouches in a neighboring yard, behind a low white-picket-fence, accommodating his mange. He's interested. His eyes are bright red, about the color of Kasim's Cadillac, but no one notices.

Keener faces the camera, a shadow on his face. He's trying to remember.

"I mean, locating the perp is difficult, but we don't even have a victim."

"All right, wrap it up," Aigilas calls. "We got what we need."

The boom-mic swings away. The grips dissemble the scenery. The extras are paid five dollars each and told to go home, or wherever they go at 5:30 in the morning.

"By the way, where's the Lieutenant?" the Chief wants to know.

"He left half an hour ago. Said something about a bad script. He wasn't feeling too good. The batteries on the teevee were low. Distorting his image. Said he'd be back at the office in the afternoon,"

a customary rending
   of garments and
gnashing of teeth

The spectacle receives rave reviews in the evening papers, with large photos of the car, the police, and the Elephas. The grandmother is interrogated, asked why she didn't suspect the wolf was masquerading as a wolf. The old woman, somewhat hysterical over the turn of events, admits she often loses sight of the real world, longs for a finely furred son, and is always taken in by the wolf she takes in.

Two days later, a cub reporter digging in the old woman's backyard discovers that "The Grandmother" is an alias. In other precincts, she goes by Goldy Rose, which may or may not be her real name. The reporter suspects she is Helen Hayes, aka Madelon Claudet of Victoria Regina fame.

But there is more pain than fame. The City is rife with anger, fear, guilt, hate, sorrow — anguish. It is clear the females, young females, at least those out late at night, are in jeopardy. And within the ineffectualness of their hopes and demands, in lieu of staying home, they concoct intended life-preserving schemes and move about with apprehension and trepidation.

"Most of my friends are wearing their hair up," says Debbie Pannuillo of 5532 Salsnick Place, Bronx. "My boyfriend wants me to dye mine. It's so scary. I have to go out, I try not to come home late. Maybe I'll shave my head. It works for Kojak. He never gets shot."

In Bayside, (which is just down/up the keyboard, the slip side of the bay, one letter from Batside) Robin Striar recently of the National Academy Museum and School of Fine Arts at 1083 5th Avenue, laments her misfortune. With hair too short to put up, she notes, "You can't do much but worry, when it hits close to home. I'll think twice before I park."

To meet public demand a SOS Retreat, a private youth organization, opens a twenty-two-client house at 7199 Ambrose in Queens, and another at 84-99 Coleman Place in the Bronx, advertised as "A safe house for young adults to pursue their carnal desires for a few hours, free from the possibilities of attack." However, no dancing, card playing or alcohol allowed.

Henry McDevitt

Early afternoon, a burglary-in-progress is reported at 3706 Anthony Avenue. Forty-three-year-old Detective Henry "Pappy" McDevitt and his partner Richard J. Melville of the 48th take the call. When they arrive, the landlord is on the street waiting for them.

While Melville guards the front door McDevitt secures a ladder and attempts to climb in the apartment window. Teetering on the top rung McDevitt loses his balance and ". . . whosoever of you are justified by the law; ye are fallen from grace" (Galatians 5:4) topples to the ground shattering his right knee. When Melville comes to his partner's aid, the perp absquatulates with the booty.

Several weeks later, following surgery on his knee, McDevitt develops an arterial occlusion (a clot) and dies.

Edward E. Mitchell

At the other end of the island (Manhattan) Officer Edward E. Mitchell and his partner Willis Longtree from the 34th answer a call at 3809 10th Avenue and arrest a suspect they believe has robbed the Soup Bowl luncheonette.

Longtree secures one of the perp's arms while Mitchell attempts to hold onto the suspect's free arm. The perp, however, takes exception to the collar and struggles violently to free himself, throwing Karate chops and kicking and saying nasty things about the officers. Longtree grabs the suspect in a headlock and attempts to force him to the ground. As they grapple, the suspect removes Longtree's gun from its holster and fires three times, striking Mitchell in the chest.

Civilian bystanders rush to Mitchell's aid and encourage Longtree to pick up the gun the robber has dropped and join an off-duty police officer who has arrived on the scene to chase the suspect on foot.

After a brief pursuit, they locate the perp (a block away) as he attempts to carjack a vehicle. Both Officers fire at the suspect, killing him.

Mitchell is taken to Columbia Presbyterian Hospital where he dies from his injuries.

Fellow officers remembered Mitchell as a kind, hopeful, courageous, prudent, and fair police officer. He is survived by his wife Mae and a son, and is carried to South Carolina for burial.

otherwise it's business as usual

Otherwise it's business as usual, the Loo on stakeout with a decoy squad from the Pullysnit Players, waiting for a little Son of Sam street theatre. Tonight the ever present Crocker and Stravos are not present. Officers played by Stephanie De Stacio, James Monohan and Tim Hurly are in the car with him.

It is 7:30.

"He'll be here," LoKo says. "He'll be along soon."

"What are we looking for?" De Stacio says. "Yeah, I know. Son of Sam. But what are we looking for?"

They are at the corner of 10th Avenue and 43rd Street sipping coffee from Styrofoam cups and discussing how they will go about choreographing the capture when James Monohan discovers another role ebbing from within his deepest City person, and suddenly yells.

"Purse snatch! Throw your coffee out the window."

The car lurches into action, chasing two young men, light, fey newcomers to the Pullysnit troupe, as they run up the block.

"Freeze or I'll blow your fucking brains out!" Monohan shouts, reading from the script he has taken from inside his leather police waistcoat, while clinging to the wheel of the radio car.

De Stacio and Hurly jump from the car, guns drawn and tackle one of the youths. Monohan speeds into oncoming traffic, breaks his car on the sidewalk, and Petrosino-like leaps out, covering the second youth and immediately handcuffing him.

The two "perpetrators," as police call them, are shoved into the backseat, pouting. A crowd gathers. Small boys shoot toy guns into the air and an ashen faced cab driver tells Monohan, "I made a sign of the cross when I saw you coming. You want me to call a backup?"

"I'm fifteen," one of the boys playing purse-snatcher tells the audience. "Are they allowed to hit me? What do you get for purse-snatching? One to three?"

"Do you belong to DAFF?"

"He knows more about acting than we do," De Stacio says with a decidedly exasperated feminine sigh.

The boys fidget.

"Just be cool, my man," she tells one, laying a warm un-police-womanly hand on his thigh.

"I don't like to run."

From the sidewalk, seven-year-old Jose Michaels stares at her.

"You got a .38, right? You an undercover cop?"

She's smiling.

"She don't look famous," he reports to his friends. "Shit. She don't look nothing like Kojak at all."

Sam reconsiders
taking up the serpent

And all of that done, it seems a decent and fitting time to make an end to another month of playtime in The City. Other events could be recorded, some nearly forgotten, some pried from memory, players dragged onto the stage or to a Police lockup. But suffice it to say the thought of a psychopath stalking random victims and eluding detection — like the Spirit of Sam — has long terrified and fascinated mankind, although today it seems both fact and fiction.

Five are dead, six wounded by vidunderbarn, with the counsel of Sam and Our Lady of the Luscious Labia — the Archduke and Queen of humdrum doom, crown and scepter, holding court in the twilight and gloom of their kingdom, deep in the fabled and fashionable passages of The City of the Gods.

In the ensuing days, with little discourse or discussion, Our Lady of the Organic Orgasm and Sam come easily to a meeting of minds.

"We will do this once more," she says, "then call it quits."

But instead of respite, argument presses the air. In the humid swelter of summer, Sam's nemesis, the poison-tipped thorns of pomp and the rational, the misdirection of Augustine's assumption prick the old goat's hide.

The reviews on the last caper are less than remarkable. What happened? Chance, misdirection, an intervention of what? The rain, the night, the site?

Still Sam's dealing from a shaved deck. He's a pack of flea bitten curs sniffing assholes and pissing on fire plugs. In a moment, an inspiration, just for the hell-of-it, to relieve anxiety, gain a modicum of reassurance, keep holy the Sabbath, he's out running with three bone-thin white hounds with "a taste only for living flesh." They're perusing a vacant lot garbage dump in the south Bronx when they come upon two six-year-old girls. The girls are also hungry, but take time to pet the dogs. The dogs retaliate, in kind. They snuff and partially devour one of the girls, and savage the other, severely. Meat is meat, regardless, and it is amazing what a little pain, a few screams can do to relieve tension.

Après-dîner   Sam's better, his bib stained with gore. He's in the kitchen looking for a toothpick — relaxed, melancholic, nostalgic, reliving the glory of old tricks, the affection of friends who take interest in his ventures.

And tomorrow is a new game: arson for hire, human guinea pigs for experimentation, mass suicides, and insurance frauds to exploit man's everlasting lust for security.

Still, something of the old zest is missing.

Even though recruiting has gone well — adding names, innovating programs developed to promote disorder and enliven the vulgar, de mauvais goût, activate base instincts, puff up the respectability of double-dealing, selling trash, pandering vice as virtue, he's mindful of the times, the necessity of change, familiar faces fading, two or three at a time.

Paging through *The Times*, his eyes dim to small, faint fires, he knows it's not just a matter of the times — but after all, friendship, yes, friendship and heart, an instinct for the insidious preying of the species upon itself.

Most, he knows, have short memories, little of reason, and in Homo sapiens' insatiable appetite for self-deception, events that should promote outrage and a deadly swift sure-fire scorched retaliation, are dismissed or endured. The surest way to peace is lethargy.

Of course, a few demonstrate felicity, creativity in pursuit of perdition, but to enliven the vast unmoved majority to vengeance, the scene must be carefully set, the pot stirred, spikes struck firmly into flesh and timber.

Page five, Sam's eyes the headlines, the paper singed, small swirls of grey smoke rise from beneath his fingers.

"Justice Irving H. Saypol, 71 Dies; Rosenberg Spy-trial Prosecutor."

This may be as close as Sam gets to sadness — Saypol's slither into the ephemeral — losing a real world warrior, a seasoned veteran. Theirs was an extended alliance, a history in a heyday of legal insanity, the letter of the law fulfilled, the last gram of retribution extracted. Together they traveled the littered byways of logic and precedent, conviction to condemnation. Hiss, Chambers, Coplon, and then Rosenberg, Rosenberg and Sobell.

Roy Cohn and Saypol made the case, Sam at the stead fanning the conflagration with promises of fame, prestige, the approval and appreciation of the swaying, frothing hordes. Success and the good times, gloating victory, the jury in, bowing, honoring the warped construction of another legal, logical abstraction, fiction. Faust collecting his reward. A large canid whining with anticipation.

"It's not possible for a great nation to be free from traitors," Saypol contends. "But this case illustrates that it is possible to reach them and ultimately bring them to the bar for punishment."

"An eye for an eye," Sam says. "Send the MF home blind."

Punishment and vengeance, and how they laughed at those simple-minded idealistic fools, seeking a utopia, a ticket to paradise, and how easy it was to expose their childish schemes.

A framed editorial, a cartoon of a snake entwined with a Soviet hammer and sickle which says: "Hissss," commending Saypol for the Rosenberg conviction hangs on the wall of his office. The snake is pissed, pierced with a pitchfork labeled "American Justice." Nearby two cowering figures cower, stamped as "fellow travelers" and "innocents."

"Not so," Sam says, searching for a resemblance in the snake. "No, that's not it. The eyes, yes, the eyes — they are too large and clear, the curve of the mouth pliant, too soft. The expression on the snake's face is not surprise, but shock. No, this snake is from another part of the jungle. It may be an uncle, a garden-variety snake, not really a serpent."

Sam hangs over the room in a blue-gray haze, a moment of silence to speed along a worthy to its festering repose.

The Ballad of Shark Bone Sam

And then a new day, the methodical Heliacal Rising of Dog Star Sirius, the primitive, compulsive, reflexive reflection in ritual's mirror of a mini-mid-summer function, Harbor Festival '77 and the national emotional hemorrhage of piety and patriotism of another July 4th weekend.

Saturday morning the Hudson fills with a flotilla of six Caribbean bound ocean liners led by the Oceanic. In procession at fifteen minute intervals the Doric, the Rotterdam, the Kazakhstan, the Cunard, and the Statendam.

Sunday the Parade of Sail sets off from the Throg's Neck Bridge, down the East River. Character ships they're called: schooners, sloops, brigantines and barkentines — antique vessels and yachts. One hundred in all, through Hell Gate, down the East River past Gracie Mansion, Roosevelt Island, past the reviewing stand on the terrace of the United Nations, through Buttermilk Channel, around Governor's Island, Liberty Island, Ellis Island, past Battery Park, and up the Hudson to the George Washington Bridge.

There's the Canadian barkentine Barba Negra; the Pride of Baltimore, the Black Pearl, a two-masted or "hermaphrodite" brig; the Clearwater and the gaff schooner, Pioneer.

For landlubbers there's the Parade of Nations and the People's Parade, the reading of the three main areas of the Declaration of Independence (When in the Course of human events . . . let Facts be submitted to a candid world . . .. We . . . solemnly publish and declare . . .) and numerous ethnic festivals on the lower East Side.

And Sam's up for it, in a holiday mood, costume and paint, swaggering, swashbuckler of the fo'c's'l of the *Goddam*, leaning, mocking, Buster Keaton, poker-faced into the wind, pistol, dagger in belt, cutlass sparkling, boarding ax, bottle of rum in hand, menacing and delightful privateer extraordinaire.

Aye, the good ship *Goddam*, Sam's command, 64 cannons, swivel guns, crew of 431 spooks beneath the Jolly Dodger, the scourge of the seas, the pride of the main. The *Goddam* comes around 10 degrees, cannons primed.

Psyaint David

Sam's into his own celebration, riding above the voices, shouts, spectral chants drifting onto the water. Teach, Kidd, Bonnet, Rackham, memories of drunken fêtes, dalliances (rapes — both men and women).

The voices carry into the sails. Nothing of the Greeks here, as yet, just the mania of the rolling over the water, a chorus mixture of sopranists, altos (falsetto or countertenor), and basso profundos.

It's "A Pirate's Life for Me."

> Yo ho, yo ho, a pirate's life for me.
> We pillage, we plunder, we rifle, and loot,
> Drink up, me 'earties, yo ho.

Jugs of rum circulate with a few verses from the "Drunken Sailor."

> What do you do with a drunken sailor,
> What do you do with a drunken sailor,
> Earl-eye in the morning!
>
> Put him in the hold with the Captain's daughter,
> Put him in the hold with the Captain's daughter,
> Earl-eye in the morning!
>> (Traditional British)

Then a chanson balladée — Sam's favorite, the "Ballad of Shark Bone Sam" — Sam's version of "The Whiffenpoof Song."

> It is on July four, in the harbor of Gore
> At the end of a slip called Scud,
> In the dark of the moon, in the Whale Prong Saloon
> And the whores are dealing stud.
>> The whores are dealing stud.
>
> There's smiling Sal, one helluva gal,
> And a beat up wench named Sue,
> A scaly twister with a fucked up kisser,
> And a black mermaid called Blue.
>> Oh Blue, oh Blue, oh Blue.
>
> There's Betty Ann Jones, known as bones,
> Who can ride a sea snake to hell.
> And across the table, next to Mable,
> The infamous strumpet Nell.
>> Ah, do tell, do tell,
>> The infamous strumpet Nell.

Well Sal draws a straight, Sue holds an eight
And Blue takes an ace from her pants,
Betty Ann Jones, the girl known as bones,
Says she knows she don't have a chance.

Amid scratching and bluffing, belching and puffing,
Mable has to fold.
Sal raises her three for a chance to see
If Blue has an ace in the hole.
       Yes, the ace Blue keeps in the hole.

Aye, deuces are wild and Blue smiles,
And Mable stands up to fart.
Yeah, Queens are high and Jacks don't lie,
And Nell catches a four of hearts.

Yet when the betting is done, Nell is the one
Who famously rakes in the honey.
Blue shakes her head, "It's hard," she says,
"For a whore to fuck a whore out of money."

Well the girls think they might, in the dim lamp light
Play another round or two,
For time hangs hard, and other than cards,
There isn't much to do.
       To do, to do, to do,

Yes, the lights are low and business is slow,
And the clock in the Whale Prong Saloon
Is ticking its way toward the end of the day
In the ominous dark of the moon.

And then in the night, as if recoiling with fright,
The door blows in with a blast,
And the Whale Prong air is filled with the terror
Of all the demons of the past.

Sal, she groans, and Blue, she moans,
And Sue lets off a shriek.
Mable faints beneath the table,
And Nell gets to her feet.
       Yes, brave Nell gets to her feet.

Psyaint David

It's the Pride of the Seas, the myth of the main,
Just in from the good ship *Goddam*,
A sonofabitch with a terrible twitch,
And his name is Shark Bone Sam.
        His name is Shark Bone Sam.

Well his eyes are fire and his hair is like wire,
His teeth are broken and black.
He's just come in from humping a squid,
And he has no shirt on his back.

He is terrible and mean, his skin is sea green,
His face all scarred and beat.
He stands in the door, and dangling to the floor,
His forty-four pounds of meat.

Oh, the girls' eyes are wide, and their hearts tied
To the fear of instant death,
To the death-rattle fright and to old Sam's might,
And the dead-fish stench of his breath.

Yes, fixed in their chairs, held by his stare,
They wait for him to speak,
As he stands in the door, eyeing the whores
For what seems to them a week.

Then with a bellow, in a voice from Hell, oh,
With a snarl and a rotting curse,
He offers ten sous for a bottle of booze,
And the better part of his purse,

To the pussy, the wench, the cunt, the whore
Who will tackle his dangling meat.
To the lowdown, beat up, no good whore
Who can fuck him down to defeat.

Well, the girls' eyes roll up in surprise
With the thought of money to spend,
When suddenly they see, with less than glee,
Sam isn't poking fun at them.

Now they fume and fuss and bitch and cuss,
And decide that for their part,
If the money's the same, and the bastard half tame,
They'd just as soon fuck a shark.
        Yes, they'd just as soon jump a shark.

But when the talking is done, there is only one,
To handle old Shark Bone Sam.
The one who has lived by the guile of her wits,
By the down of her snatch and the nips of her tits,
  The infamous, humping strumpet, Nell.
  That infamous strumping humpet Nell.

Her legend is grand, for by tongue and by hand,
Reputedly one afternoon,
Without breaking a sweat, on a five-dollar bet,
She wacked-off half the saloon.

In the fondest way, they remember the day,
Nell took on a two-headed dog.
And another time, in the town of Slime,
She went on stage with a hog.

"A trick for a buck, a lick or a fuck,"
She is often heard to repeat.
"It'll cost you a lot, all the money you got,"
She said eyeing Sam's throbbing meat.
  Staring hard at Sam's terrible meat.

Sam thought he'd allow, that they'd get it on now,
For his five-pound sack of gold,
They'd go no-holds-barred, an inch to the yard,
Until one or the other would fold.
  For one or the other would fold.

You see poker's fine, but fucking's divine,
And a much superior game,
If blood is your taste, or someone to waste,
Or merely someone to maim.

The contest is set and the money is bet
as the sun rises over the street.
Nell powders her snatch and prepares for the match,
To meet the meat she would meet.

With his dangling part, just for a start,
Sam bangs it against a pole,
"Soon's it's awake, it'll start to shake,
And then look for an available hole."

Psyaint David

Well, they begin at the door, and circle the floor,
And Nell gives a leap and a moan.
And then with a cry, spreading her thighs,
Throws a lock on old Sam's bone.

Yes, he struggles and shakes and thrashes and takes
A mighty leap of his own,
Then his balls turn blue, his prong a green hue,
But still she clings to his bone.
         She clings to old Sam's bone.

With her claws in his neck, she rides him to the deck
And Sam seems all but through.
In that first hard round it is clear Nell has found
A pot for to cook old Sam's stew.
         Oh, Nell is cooking Sam's stew.

For a moment it seems, and all the girls scream,
That Sam has met his match,
But with alertness and style, and a bit of a smile,
Sam shows why they call him Old Scratch.

He thrusts with might and the girls scream in fright,
At the awesome power there,
And the dim room is filled with the sight of blood spilled
And the smoke of Nell's singed pubic hair.
         Oh, smoke fills the air.

So around again once, they go in a bunch,
Then tumble into the street,
A humping and flailing, cussing and wailing,
A yelling and slinging meat.

It's round and around, both up and down,
A low slung gaff-prattle ride,
A high wind mainer and a surfside gainer,
Rocking from side to side.
         Oh, sliding from side to side.

A humping and swearing, a scratching and tearing,
Sam's tool grows harder and longer.
A whimpering and groaning, a shouting and moaning,
Nell's cunt grows tighter and stronger.

they go then and around they go again,
Down the alley and into the park,
A fucking and kicking, a sucking and licking,
Until it is almost dark.
       Yeah, fucking the day into dark.

It is a helluva shame, and no one's to blame,
But somebody has to lose.
About eight that night, in the fading dim light,
In the dark of the North Star moon,

Nell lets out a cry, a death-rattle sigh,
And grabs for her suffering part.
Then she curses the day, in a terrible way,
And puts another on old Sam's heart.

She curses his soul and her damaged hole
For failing this final feat.
She curses her fate, her black luck of late,
And those forty-four pounds of meat.
       Yes, those forty-four pounds of meat.

When at last she dies, with a sigh Sam pries
His prong from the clasp of that whore
Who had fucked him so well, the infamous Nell,
And makes his way to the door.

Then shaking his head, he smiles and says,
Wiping the sweat from his beat-up meat,
"She was a great fuck, and with a little luck
She might still be on her feet."
       Oh, Nell could still be on her feet.

Still there is nothing to say for Nell that day,
For she died as all whores must,
But the tale will be told of her love for gold,
And of Sam's indomitable lust.

The burial is brief, because of the grief
Of the girls for their lost Nell.
And as for old Sam and his good ship *Goddam*,
They sail straightaway for hell.
       They followed the stars straight to hell.

Psyaint David

It is quiet for days, and no one can say
The terrible cost of the ruin;
How they cleaned up the blood on the slip called Scud,
In the old port town of Doom. Doom!
        Yes, in the old port town of Doom.

But still to this day, they have on display,
In the shrine of the Whale Prong Saloon,
High on the door, the hide of that whore
Who died in the dark of the moon.
        Here's to Nell, in the dark of the moon.

Sam salutes Lady Liberty

Fun and games.
Reputations gained, respect, the authority of mythic personae.
Sam laughs, cackles, his true fondness for Nell, the spirit of contest.
He's drunk, raises his bottle.
"Here's to ye, me lads."
The *Goddam* eases into the East River, the west channel, behind a flotilla of Naval Academy yawls. Cutlass flashing, he staggers, misses a step, stumbles on the deck, rum splashing, stove-pipe hat, red and white stripes (blood on snow) yelling.

"Tell 'em who we are," Sam shouts. "Let 'em know we're coming. We'll blow her to hell — tits, ass, and hair."

And it's punk to powder and a roar of gray smoke and shot flying, the recoil rocking the galleon, the thunder announcing the quest, the High American Holy Day.

Indeed, the old boy's in fine fettle, good spirits, offers the bottle to Our Lady of Supercilious Sins. She accepts — Ann Boney, Rachel Wall, Grace O'Malley, Mary Read, naviatrix along for the ride, a Black & Blue Eye Mask, sensors, mind's eye, sonar, fathometer ticking, keeping a close imprint on Sam.

Hans-Peter of the Holy Family, Das wunderkind, in a new and expanded role of mindful reminiscence, waits on the quarterdeck with the twenty-two disciples of hell.

At Dock Street Sam is on his feet, spyglass up, focused on the pleasure craft *Airma* adrift without power near the East River Ferry.

"Drop a ball on her bow," he commands, filled with malicious mischief, mischievous malice, the cheers of the crowd gathered on the U.N. Terrace rising on the breeze.

"Rigging cutters, chain and bars."

Again the *Goddam*'s cannons roar, echoing. Water sprays dance above fallen shot. An errant ball tears into the stern of the *Airma*. An explosion rocks the air.

Cheers go up — insults shouted at the damaged craft, ridicule for the fools. Post haste a Coast Guard 41-foot UTB with a displacement of 28,500 lbs., 2 Cummings diesels engines and navigation radar, arrives to snatch the survivors from the water.

Francesco Huerta, owner of the *Airma*, suffers minor injuries and Julia Diaz and her son of two years, Mike, are severely burned.

"*Airma* la deuce," Sam shouts as the boat burn down to the waterline.

"Sometimes," he says in pointless reflection, "shit happens. It's old American fun — all for a show, no harm done. The best of America."

Below Governors Island the procession swings out into Upper City Bay. The blue hulled Naval Academy Yawls *Intrepid, Swift, Alert,* and *Vigilant,* the exigencies of minuteman mentality (eternally on watch for treachery) native intuition, guile (New World Yankee self-esteem and pride, prepared to gain a toehold, make hay while you can, be the early bird) maneuver into and out of the wind, cut toward Liberty Island followed by the frigate *Goddam* with Sam weaving along the deck, rubber-legged, shouting, rum bottle raised in a salute.

"Mistress of the possible. Liberty, libertine."

He stumbles, catches himself on the rigging, and the *Goddam* pulling 5 knots, swings toward Liberty Island, tacks to the south as the yawls drop their spinnakers in unison in a salute which brings a round of cheers from the shoreline.

At the wheel now, Sam guides the *Goddam* in, brings her about broadside, shouts, "On command," cutlass raised, then drops the blade.

The roar of seven cannons hammering number nine shot beats the air. Smoke discharges puff and drift down wind. A well-directed ball tears into Liberty's hollow head, copper flying, smoke rising in a black cloud.

Cheers go up — congratulations all around. And then reports that two, possibly three balls, found the mark. The left eye and part of the nose are gone. A chunk of the left ear falls to the pedestal maiming forty-one-year-old Walter Williams from Twin Falls, Idaho and twenty-two-year-old Alfred Wiggins from New Orleans. They are spirited off to the hospital in serious but stable condition, or so it is reported.

But this is spectacle. An extraordinary beginning — at least Carl Werth from Johannesburg thinks so.

"This is so impressive," he says. "I've never seen anything like it. I wasn't here last year, but this is a good show."

"What an ingenious idea," Della Hampton of 6771 Barthod Dr. says. "I never did like that statue. Maybe now they'll put up something reasonable that people can use. The last time we were on the island there wasn't even a place to get a hotdog or hamburger. They could use a McDonalds. Anyway, if The City would scrap all that copper maybe it could pay its bills."

It's a July 4 celebration. The remainder of the day is a flood of opinions, explanations, and educated guesses about human fascination with fire.

"Man is the only animal who is afraid of the dark, because into the emptiness of the nighttime are projected all the demons which haunt the human imagination and appear in dreams," Professor Joel Kovel of Albert Einstein College of Medicine says in an Elizabethan attempt at understanding symbols.

"In the display of fireworks these imaginary qualities are suddenly made lucid under human control and almost as suddenly disappear. The experience is both a realization of what is repressed and a triumph over it."

Indeed. Double, double toil and trouble.

A more general interpretation of the role of power in the appeal of fireworks is offered by Dr. Nolan D. C. Lewis former director of the Psychiatric and Pyrotechnic Institute and professor of psychiatry at the Columbia-Presbyterian Medical Center.

"It is a substitution in a way for the general interest humans have in fires — fire represents power, and it represents destructive power, of course. It's very much like the excitement and pleasure that a lot of people get out of watching a prize fight: the tougher and bloodier it is the more enjoyment they get."

Dr. David Abrahamsen, the psychoanalyst and author of *Nixon vs. Nixon, Our Violent Society*, and *The Murdering Mind*, suggests that "It could be very closely related to a sexual experience, not on the conscious level, unconsciously, you understand."

Certainly.

the forces of goodness
  are out
to stamp out smut

Hans-David is excited by the cheers, catastrophe as celebration, the water lapping the *Goddam's* battered hull. Of late the signs have not been encouraging. He's not had a hit in ten weeks. No cheers. Tells himself that's why they cancelled the show.

"They knew I'd miss."

A lump of regret, a knot of failure in his throat.

"I didn't want to hurt them. I only wanted to kill them."

The ministry wans, dwindles, now, even at times like this, Sam's essence dimmed to a pale glow. He's felt it before, a sense of doom, the world, his world spinning unevenly about the little man in the red and white stripes and flashing eyes, and the Lady, Our Grand Dame of the Liberated Libido, with her Brown Leather Padded Eye Mask, classic Bloodstone eyes, and wet crotch.

Murmuring emanates from the second circle. Stamp out smut — smudged fingerprints on the wall near the elevator — circles with twisted

Ss inside — Stamp Out Sam.

Then in a moment of invention, as yet no ripples of repentance, remorse, nothing of the sorry slings of guilt, he pulls on another mask, a new face. He's trying to remember what Teivel said — something about "... boy you have the gift, the knack, a viable sense of nasty."

He will keep a closer watch, take count of who he talks to, how often, not only the words but a tone that might betray intent.

He avoids eating on consecutive days in the same restaurant, carefully varying what he orders — pizza, fried chicken. Ask for the same food in the same restaurant at the same hour of the day from the same waitress and she knows, yes, she knows ... ..

"You will betray your gifts."

Who said that? He will not remember the oddities, peculiarities, the coincidence of ... ..

Not to be forgotten, the incomparable, rampaging, ever hopeful, searching Lieutenant, blazing a trail along the byways of The City, leaving no forensic manhole cover unturned. He wonders how much the police really know, what the Lieutenant is up to, and decides on an investigation of his own. Kojak has missed something.

"We don't have a clue," he has said, "but we know who he is."

That sounds like the Lou. A fount of knowledge, without evidence — the Platonic gleaning of form from intuition, divination, the true heart of man activated in one grand mystical leap. He knows the someone — even before there is another someone .... Then it's simple — wait for the deed, step in and with flashbulbs popping, snatch the perp.

If the Lieutenant has missed something, a small clue — heat prints, the voices of shades left hanging, the restless shift of air, the dead searching for retribution, peace — how then to track it? What else from which to deduce and impute? The bare-bone bleached moldering in the grave? Age, sex, race, stature — the cause of the spirit's exit, and approximate time — residing in the shadowed folds of the small but violent reptilian brain.

The City provides
street games
to keep devotees occupied

Returning to the ritualistic beyond July 4 celebrations, Herodotus, trial by combat to condemn the false virgins, incorporating the best of Americana — the spirit of independence represented by The City — the fields of play as well as the national game are evolving — another twist in the odyssey appears, attempting to keep its juices flowing with something of entertainment.

"Implicit in the idea of fun is the belief that street games aren't invented, do not spring from books, but spontaneously evolve," thirty-seven-year-old Drucilla Richmond, self-proclaimed street game guru of 721 Warren Street in Brooklyn says. "Kids in the suburbs have such games, but they often are not as inventive as those where sidewalks, curbs, stoops, gutters, and alleys dictate style, content, and rules."

Skelsy, Mickey, Bury the Weiner, Johnny-on-a-pony, Homicide, Tickets, Fatty Box, Fat Butt, Patsy, Snake-on-a-pin: products for export to the outback, no doubt, in the growing movement to medievalize the hinterlands.

"In a game like Denice the Menace," Richmond contends, "you get a bunch of players and one of them is it. She's the Denice. But she doesn't hide her eyes and count like you would. She hides and the other players try to find her. OK? But when one finds her she's not caught. The two hide together, OK? It goes like that until everybody's hiding and only one player is left, so she's it. Then we knock the piss out of her."

On a baseball field at 174th Street and Sheridan Expressway in the Hunt's Point section of Bronx, twenty-five-year-old Mary Bancey joins Richmond's "street games" and is raped and robbed and left on a bench with her throat cut.

Across the street, hoping to expropriate death as a salvation commodity, several thousand Hasidic and Orthodox Jews gather at the corner of 51st Street and 13th Avenue in Borough Park for a rally in support of the state's death penalty bill and a return to Old Testament Law.

Dov Hikind, a possible State assemblyman from the 48th Assembly District in Brooklyn, often described as a racist-tribal-chieftain for hire, on his way up the greased religious-ethnic-political pole, addresses the crowd and notes that, "Nice people, good people, smart people are for the death penalty."

A Grey Panther in a Jewish home for the elderly announces that indeed she will vote for the Dov.

"To be safe, we need the death penalty," she says.

When reminded that Israel does not have the death penalty, she claims, "They don't have schartzer there either."

Conservative Party candidate for mayor, radio talk-interviewer Barry Farber resurfaces to support Hikind.

"The murderer must know he can no longer exchange seven years of his life for the elimination of one of us," he shouts.

Having come to the stark, raving (raging) fear of the absence of rationality and beauty, Renaissance man attempted to think and paint and scribble his way through the maze. To placate the fear of losing what little he understands of the past, modern man shouts into the maze, hoping to find direction in the echo.

Anyway, Farber has the diagram, the rules, of a new game in hand. It's a real-life fight-club of hipsters, marines, millionaires, and models (and anyone else who wants in). It's called Maim Sam, whereby players gather for impromptu matches of pummeling one another into insensibility, mutilating one another in preparation for encountering Son of Sam. The belief is that when they find Son of Sam they will know what to do and instinctively do it. After all, practice makes perfect. Farber expects to market the game among the seventeen-to-twenty-five crowd.

the Lou heads out
to Temple Court
to see what he can see

The Loo agrees.

"What doth it profit a man if someone bloweth his ass away? I mean if you're cancelled, where are you? So get the bastard fore he gets you."

He's passing the afternoon on Channel 2, black and white, 15" Sony Tabletop set on an imitation Ox Art teak coffee table in the living room of a two bedroom flat at 96-22 Albright Street, Apart 7E in the Bronx. He's on screen along the Avenue of the Americas with Stavros and Crocker in tow.

Single Mama of three, Ruth Messenek, the tenant of 96-22 Apartment 7E, is in the kitchen taking a break from child rearing, having a Full Flavor Kool (mentholated) Filter King and a cup of Maxwell House (Good to the last drop) coffee. She takes a puff then a sip, flipping through an old *Mad* magazine she found in the closet. At the moment she is wondering if Alferd E. Newman really does have anything to worry about, and how in the hell she got where she is.

Her kids, one, three, and five or possibly two, four, and six, (baby Ruth, Jr., Lester, and Lulu) are watching *Kojak,* throwing Silly Putty at the screen. They've seen it before — or think they have. Something is familiar.

But not to worry, too much. The morning is young. She still has half a pot of coffee, another pack of Kools, and a copy of *Zap Comix #3* (For Adult Intellectuals Only) she purloined from a used book store down the block. This particular *Zap* records the historic battle between Captain Pissgums and his Pervert Pirates and his nemesis, Captain Fatima.

Coincidentally, the Lou and Crocker are searching for Fatima, the Captain of the Quivering Thigh, a rogue lesbian pirate ship that often frequents the Upper Bay.

"I conjure thee by Rosaline's bright eyes, By her high forehead and scarlet lip, By her fine foot, straight leg, and quivering thigh" (Shakespeare).

Conspiracy theory has linked Fatima with Sam and therefore with Son of Sam.

So why look for the Captain of a pirate ship on Avenue of the Americas? Well, beyond the obvious of the number of bandit corporations operating there, rumor has it Fatima is fencing contraband she appropriated from a number of pleasure crafts on her way into the upper Bay.

Of course, Fatima will not be found on the Avenue of the Americas. At least not today. This morning she's indulging herself in self-indulgence, prepared to harass her nemeses the ungodly Pissgums and his homo but not yet gay band of indolent cutthroats. She's steering the Quivering Thigh into the Upper Bay in pursuit of Pissgums' un-ship-shape friggin frigate the Homo Hund, about to berate, castigate, emasculate, excoriate and/or castrate the prideful Captain — if she can.

scene 4 – on deck

The story opens with Captain Pissgums and Tony stretched on the deck nude, soaking in the sun.

GEORGE: It's the Dyke Pirates off the starboard bow!!!

(Quick cut aft)
The Quivering Thigh bolts into the Upper Bay, sails flapping, into view.

Suddenly a cannon ball crashes through the Homo Hund's foremast.

(Cut to the Quivering Thigh)
FATIMA: I'm willing to bet the tip of my red-hot tongue that ol' Captain Pissgums is shitting in his boots about now! Give 'em another round, Ruth my tart!

RUTH: Very good, sir!!
Baby Ruth, Jr. launches another glob of Silly Putty at the screen. The missile hits Felix in the balls.

(Back on the Homo Hund)
FELIX: Jesusfuckingchristalmighty!!!

(Cut to the Quivering Thigh)
FATIMA: Try these shots on for size, Captain Pissgums, you bitty ol' shit.

Another round, this time an entire volley, Lulu joins Baby Ruth, Jr. in launching a barrage of Silly Putty at the screen.

(Cut to the Homo Hund)
The volley nearly destroying Pissgums' ship. Some of the Silly Putty sticks to the screen. Then quiet.

CAPTAIN: They're a bunch of nasty ones, George. I lost my new hat and everything Better get the men together! That bitch, Fatima, will be over here like a shot, to fight us hand to hand. Long day ahead!

(Cut to the Quivering Thigh)
Lulu tosses another ball of Silly Putty at the screen.

(Back on the Homo Hund)
The ball hits Lester, who is in closeup, in the eye and bounces off.

LESTER: (Resigned to this unforeseen injury, Lester remains mostly unmoved, holding his right hand over his right eye) Can't see jack-shit out of this eye.

CAPTAIN: Alright, mates, grab a sword or club or some damn thing! Those dykes'll be over here in about a minute. And on us like stink on shit! Break out the arms, Master George!

GEORGE: Alright, mates, grab a cutlass.

Meanwhile on The Quivering Thigh:

FATIMA: Alright, girls, get your cunts a crackin'. Later on today old Pissgums will be beggin' for mercy! Let's let 'em have it!

LULU: (Reaching for another ball of Silly Putty) Have what, sir?

The ships are off in the distance rocking side by side at a distance.

CAPTAIN: HERE COMES THE DYKES!

The cry is taken up by all the men and then also by all the women.

ALL: HERE COMES THE DYKES!
     HERE COMES THE DYKES! (etc.)

Fatima's crew boards the Homo Hund. A gigantic fight ensues.

FELIX: I ain't used to fightin' women, not even dykes. How could I dare touch that nice tit with a weapon? I can't ….

Ruth, Jr. hits him with a board.

RUTH: I ain't interested in your sex life, mate!

CAPTAIN: Fight 'em, men! Remember they're dykes anyway!

LESTER: The Captain's right! These women just ball each other, . . . so let's fight their ass!

LULU: You snag-nut smelly bilge rat!

RUTH: You ugly mother, get your teeth off my titty!

TONY: Let go of my tool!

FATIMA: Where's ol' Captain Pissgums? I'm gonna fix his little wagon for him, by God!

Pissgums rushes on to the deck with a dead fish and smacks Fatima in the mouth with it.

CAPTAIN: Try this out, toots!

TONY: Smack 'er good, Cap!

Psyaint David

Fatima, maddened, rips off Pissgums' pants, bites his cock, and they go rolling down into the hatch.

Meanwhile the fighting between the perverts and the dykes has slowed down.

FELIX: Whew! This fightin's too much like work . . .. Let's fuck instead, mate.

RUTH: You're right, mate.

GEORGE: Nice jugs.

RUTH: You've got a nice touch, for a man. Hold my twat.

LULU: (Rushing in) Listen, everybody! I just discovered that this ship is SINKIN' FAST!

RUTH: We can all go aboard our ship, The Quivering Thigh, and have some fun! Pull ourselves together, and even though we're dykes, we can use you men cuzz you're all hung so nice . . .. Exceptions can be made. So let's go have ourselves a fat orgy!

LULU: You men are perverts and we're dykes? Hmmmm, we can work it out.

Both crews leave the ship to sink, forgetting to inform Captain Pissgums and Fatima who are about to cum.

CAPTAIN: Hmmmmgh . . . umpfff, Fatima . . .. Fatima, oh yer so fuckin' hairy, mmmm

FATIMA: Captain Pissy, I am yours forever! Please . . . eat out my clit.

CAPTAIN: Fatima, I love you, smmmmghk . . ..

As the pirate ship sinks into the water, both crews shout.

ALL: MAKE LOVE NOT WAR!
    MAKE LOVE NOT WAR!

    GLURK . . ..
      Gurk . . ..
        Blub . . ..
          Burble . . .. (S. Clay Wilson).

Mama Ruth stuffs out her cigarette, pours another cup of good-to-the-last-drop and goes back to the beginning. She admires Fatima. Chasing pirates (even if she is a pirate) and chasing men. Ruth would like to chase men. There's a chap down the hall that looks like Pissgums. She wonders. Hmmmmm!! Is he a pirate? Does he have a hidden treasure?

However, for his part the Lou is not deterred. Amid the coffee, smoke and jokes, the fighting and fucking, the plock, plock of Silly Putty hitting the screen, he is not pleased with the script and having been betrayed and upstaged by Pissgums and Fatima. He redirects his course, moves off up the Avenue.

"To Temple Court," he orders.

The camera zooms in.

"The rules are simple," he says, in a spur of the moment decision. "Mount a counterattack — take hostages. We'll ransom our way back on the air."

Crocker is skeptical, turns to face his boss, setting up a two-shot.

"You sure you want to do this?"

"If it doesn't our days are numbered."

Crocker agrees.

"Yeah."

He's negotiating a gig of his own with CBS, playing Mike Hammer. It's still a bit down the road, but the prospects are encouraging.

"Your days," Crocker says, "your days."

"Did you see what happened to Frazier last night?"

"I don't understand that. One minute he's himself — then suddenly . . .."

"Look at it this way, Bobby. We get canceled and we'll be in the same boat — stuck in old scripts, roles we've already played. We'll be condemned to reruns — seven nights a week, all hours, matinees, stuck somewhere between *As The World Turns* and *The Edge Of Night* with nothing in the audience but two-year-olds and the family dog. We'll be miming lines — we'll be ponies on the carousel."

"I don't know," Stavros says. "You had Ma Wonderly fooled. She thought she was talking to a real live detective, one that was dead. She thought you were the real thing."

"We'll be farts in an elevator shaft," the Loo says, "museum pieces, stuck away in the can for fifty or sixty or two hundred years until some pain in the ass hotshot comes along and dissects everything we've done for a study on how significant we were in our time — which will miss the point. Nothing about who we really are. Nothing to say about what we were inside. And you know why? Because there is nothing to say.

"This is back-fence gossip. We're idling. Whatever we do — it doesn't mean anything. No different than the genius explaining how the universe works. I mean, whatever universe you're in, it really doesn't give a shit. This is for naught. All we can do is get by and wait for the end."

Kojak frowns. Peers curiously at Crocker.

"Have you listened to your voice lately? And your face. Have you checked the mirror? If we're not careful we'll have to go back to acting — and you know what that means."

A pensive mask clouds Crocker's face — an intimation of his heart and soul moldering in a can in a damp forgotten warehouse on the waterfront. Which is only a little better than moldering in a barrel of glue in a damp forgotten warehouse on the waterfront.

"Do you know what moisture does to magnetic tape? Now I don't know about you, but I'm hungry for words, new words — and I don't give a diddly-fuck about the ideas. I want lines and paragraphs, speeches, whole pages, dialogue, and quick answers, Nora retorts. Whatever it takes to get to the end of the story."

"I thought you wanted more adlib."

"I do. But it's not that easy."

"But what about duty and crime? What about the fifth show? What happens if the specter is never apprehended — the crime never solved?"

"Crime? What crime? Oh, yeah. Yeah. The crime."

"And you're out of character."

"I'll get better. When the words are right I'm headed for NBC. Got a contract lined up with Evolving Planets Studio and NBC."

"Just like that?"

"Yeah. There's always another story. The bigger things in life. A more intense manhunt."

"Manhunt? Who?"

"I don't know — but whatever it is they'll find it at NBC."

"So you're gone, too?"

"You bet your sweet cookies. This is the big-one-time."

"But, well, I don't, we . . .."

"You don't have to," Kojak says. "This will make *Dog Day Afternoon* look like a game of prisoner's base. We'll go over to NBC, cross the Rubicon."

He pauses, smiles his ever-loving, knowledgeable smile and turns to Demosthenes.

"Your job is to get into Teivel's desk. The second drawer has unused scripts — six or seven. We've been penciled-in. If we get those we can keep going for a while. Before this is done I want the last Son of Sam draft of the Brooklyn Moskowitz story. After that we'll find folks who understand what we are doing."

Mathias and Aigilas
discuss the possibilities
of discovering why

Teivel's eyes fasten on the far wall, small scratchings, hieroglyphics, symbols, broken lines, intimations by way of suggestions left by salvage crews and vandals. Short time, less time, no time at all, he thinks, or sometime similar to an arrow $-$ > pointing to a termite eaten production board.

"This has to do with Son of Sam," he tells Aigilas, his voice rueful, weary. "The old days are gone. We should never have agreed to five shoots in six months. Especially five like this. Programs, projects like this need more lead time."

Marcelo agrees.

"And now Super Snooper wants to change the plot. Did you ever read *Basic Plots For Teevee Stories* by Max Master? All the stories are the same.

A few twists here and there — but basically the same. I think they're all here. Especially the hunt, street boy makes good, facing the madman, running for your life. Now Stooper Snooper is running out on us. Or at least wants to."

"Yeah," Mathias says. "He wants out. Says he's lined up another gig."

"What are you going to do about it?"

"Nothing."

"No lawsuits? No contract compliance?"

"No. Hell, fops are a dime a dozen. We'll plug somebody else in."

"But it won't be the same if Spade or Marlowe close the case."

"It never is."

"So what's the new gig?"

"It's the great "why.""

"Why?"

"Yeah. Something like Charley Whytorski the old outfielder for the Red Sox. Remember Charlie? He played leftfield, hit .321 in 1952, or maybe .322 in 1951. Changed his name, like Al Simmons. Simmons' name was Szymanski. He thought fans would like him better with an American name. He saw a sign advertising a hardware store — Simmons Hardware — so changed his name."

"Like NINA or INRI?"

"Whytorski changed his name to Charley Whye. Great hitter, but a short arm. A little slow. A very mysterious player.

"There were a couple others. Cleveland first baseman Walter 'Big Hare' Hoozo changed his name to Walter Hou and Philadelphia (Athletics) second baseman Zelous 'Rip' Watsinsky changed his name to Zelous Watt."

"Okay. So Charley Whye anything? But Walter doesn't know it?"

"He doesn't know Zealous or Charley. I suspect not. They played on different teams in different eras."

"So what?"

"And especially why. I don't know. I mean, he's asking 'Whye is there anything?'"

"He could check the record books."

"Yeah. But that's a little beyond. I don't care."

"Okay. So when Kojak shows up he can have the new scripts. I mean, we know what he wants."

"You expect him?"

"I'd say he'll be here in the next ten minutes or so," Aigilas says. "I had the kidnapping episode rewritten."

"How bad is it?"

"Well, hell, depends on your point of view. A couple schmucks get iced, two or three more injured. I've asked your secretary, Nettie to come in for the shooting."

Mathias smiles weakly.

"That's a shame."

"Well, c'mon, Matt, who then?"

"Oh no, it's alright. I was just thinking."

"I know. But somebody has to do it. We can pick the rest of the cast off the street — some will be on the bus."

"Bus? You've already written the bus in?"

"Yeah. We need a chase scene. Vehicular action. Kojak commandeers the bus, takes hostages, and orders the driver to go to Kennedy where he demands six million dollars from CBS as reparation for having his act cancelled. Then he orders a plane."

"But he's scared of flying."

"We re-did it. A new perspective."

"Why does he need a plane?"

"He wants to go to NBC."

"NBC? The National Broadcasting Company?"

"Yeah. Thinks he will get a better deal there."

"So he wants a plane. To go across town? Not even across town."

Aigilas laughs.

"That way he can avoid Hell's Kitchen and the theatre district."

"Why not a taxi?"

"Not dramatic enough. Actually, his celebrity requires more. We're still trying to sell this."

"So you put him on a bus?"

"Yeah. Let him hijack the bus. Then the police can take him away."

He hands Mathias a stack of scripts.

"Here. Put these in your desk. They'll be easy to find.

"Anyway, he never makes it. NBC doesn't want him. It's just another of his fantasies. The series is kaput. Good while it lasted, but done. We were hoping for a new life with Son of Sam, but it's not going to happen. Not this time."

"You're sure this will work? The bus business."

"Yeah. He has to follow the bouncing ball. What else can he do? Fritz has agreed to help. He's been overseeing the setup."

Mathias glances at the clock above the door.

"How long do you think it will take?"

"If we do it in real time, I'd say ten hours, maybe the afternoon and the better part of the evening. Of course, natural time has a way of spilling over into the psychological and you know how tedious that can be. We could be here for a week. Let's hope not."

"Why not have an off-duty cop stumble onto the scene and terminate him before he gets on the bus? You know, the tragedy and disappointment of an honest cop gone bad having to be put away. Hell, that's one of Master's plots. I think it's the deliverance."

"Well, then there's no drama. No real suspense for a surprise ending.

Also, we want to preserve the image. Heathcliff and Crocker, okay. They'll be gone as soon as they hit the street. They're written out. Shakespeare had to get rid of Mercutio and Falstaff. Some characters are expendable. But he kept Richard III around for as long as he could. And for good reason."

He points to the window.

"E.Erie™'s Insouciant Chronic Evaporators replaced SWAT. They're in the trees and on the roof across the street prepared for recoding, ready to make adjustments as they are needed. E.Erie™ will realign TCPD software to pick off Fatso and Crocker.

"We'll put him away at King's County. A storage facility — maybe in the basement, put him on ice, say we are waiting for a re-evaluation, a magnetic tape autopsy, a CAT scan. We may want to bring him back someday. One of his nine lives. Of course, nobody can spring him as long as we hold the copyright. We'll keep him on salt — defunct teevee personalities have a way of reviving.

"Hell, Matt, who knows, ten, twelve years and we'll break him out, get some new writers, a gimmick or two, a little makeup, a new name, a few electronic additions, and start over. He's money in the bank. You know how many redoes Mike Hammer has gone through?"

So it is. An onionskin masterplan, a scenario for freezing the Lieutenant, keeping the dollars and cents of the icon in escrow. A savings account of sorts. Escrow. But a shift of fortune, a reversal for Crocker and Brother George — for Frazier, Demosthenes and Telly. It looks as if the Son of Sam case, the hunt for and apprehension of the killer, will proceed without them.

"The timing is important," Aigilas says. "Everything has to go on schedule. The bus needs to arrive at precisely the right moment — to be in synch — so don't do anything to hold us up. Go along with whatever happens. The first rule in dealing with crazed gunmen, whether he's a terrorist or a kook, is 'Do what he says.' Let him believe he's succeeded and keep him thinking of the next thing. When he's thinking he's harmless. He's busy. It's the gaps between when he might do something silly. Like Yogi when told he had to think about what he was doing at the plate. He said, 'How can I think and hit at the same time?' You can't. Confront a crazy and interfere with his plan and more than likely he'll do what he planned to do — kill you."

"You think he'll be armed?"

Aigilas checks his watch.

"Okay. 1:20."

He reaches over and snaps on the 18" Color Tabletop Emerson.

"Have you ever heard of a City cop without a gun?"

He points to the monitor and Kojak's faded, washed-out face in a misty medium closeup on an elevator with Stavros and Crocker. He's waving his gun at the security camera.

Mathias squints into the bright light.

"What's wrong with the set?"

"It's not the set," Marcelo explains. "It's him. His videocentric aura's about as thin as air on the moon. He's eroding, fading out. He's in worse shape than I thought. Probably hasn't got more than a scene or two left."

"Yeah," Mathias says, "even the light on the off button is brighter than he is."

the delirious deleterious
   delicate detective
   appears a mere glimmer
of his once magnificent self

The service elevator grinds to a stop at the seventh floor and Kojak weak-knees into the hall, wobbling toward Mathias' office.

"This has to be fast," he says, his voice spongy and slurred, a smeared echo. "If they sound an alarm the place will turn into Hamburger Hill. That will take time, and we don't have time."

He coughs, the delicate, dry cough of desiccated and softening vocal cords.

Eyes glazed, he is, indeed, drifting.

"One autumn, my most memorable, involved just such a case as this. I had been dejected for some months over a small but salient financial misfortune, the type of irritant that lingers . . . ."

The voice is familiar. But who? Wimsey? Cannon? Bannion? Maybe Spade. Crocker thinks he sounds like Spade. Maybe so. The Loo has been communing with Sam — Sam Spade. They crossed paths a number of times in bars, in saunas, at the race track, once at Studio 54. That night Spade was with Marlowe. In the haze of smoke and heated bodies they appeared strangely similar — anemic, worn down twins, (that had a lot to do with Bogie already dying of lung cancer) pale, sad, nearly broken.

"That's what time is," Marlowe says. "Away from the screen, without an audience, no story."

Sam (Spade that is) understands all too well.

"You take a beating," he says. "It won't hold up forever. The eternal manhunt saga. Stress. Wanting answers. Only small successes. Then you gotta do it all over again in a week or month. A year."

Kojak is silent, listening to the music. Their face is his face. But he has never had much to say in the presence of celebrity has-beens.

He stumbles, takes a deep breath.

"I'm almost out of words."

He pauses at the door, waits for Crocker and Demosthenes to find their places. Then with an awkward, feeble kick tries to knock the door open.

Again, he raises his foot and swings at the door with a potbellied soccer style kick, misses and spins off camera.

"Jesus," Aigilas says. "Pelé he is not. You'd better help him. Otherwise we'll be here all day. You never know. He could hurt himself."

"And it's not just his failure with words," Mathias says. "He's been drinking a good bit — both on and off The Job."

Mathias returns to the door and pulls it open. Kojak, caught in mid-kick, tumbles into the room, wheezing. Gently, with a certain respect for the delicate delirious deleterious detective's declining greatness, Mathias helps him to his feet. He staggers, swaggering away to the far side of the room and with a fierce, plaintiff cast to his eyes, attempts to collect the remains of his personality, his bearing, countenance, contemptuous behind the putty beige no-features of a blank face.

"Get the scripts," he groans, his next to last line, and for emphasis, his last line a desperate, whispered, "Get the scripts."

In a brief moment, a swift flash of the imperative, Heathcliff locates a stack of folders and piles them on the desk.

Kojak drops to his knees beside the desk and fumbles with the folders, gasping for air.

"Now I know how Superman feels when he gets too close to Kryptonite," Crocker says.

The Lou flips through the pages, as if something is missing. Tries to focus on the print.

"Rizzo?" is all he can say.

"Not today," Crocker says. "Remember?"

Fatso places a large, plump, supportive hand on his brother's shoulder.

"You want I should read you the story?"

Kojak waves him off.

"Okay, okay. So I don't know from what," Brother George says and pulls a folder from the pile. "Here's a fat one. It's called a day of infamy."

Kojak raises his head, reaches for the folder, then drops it.

"Here," Crocker says, "here, I'll hold it for you."

His voice barely audible, tears in his, the Loo lip-syncs an ancient refrain. "One autumn, my most memorable . . .."

But that is not what is on the page. Perusing the lines as brief as they may be has activated his memory. Flakes of dried skin, dandruff, peel off his forehead and float to the floor. His face muscles contract, his skull visible through the flaking skin.

"What's the storyline?" Crocker says.

"Piss on the story," Kojak mumbles. "Just give me words."

His hands are shaking, he's drooling.

"... just such a case. I had been dejected . . .."

He tries to remember ". . . a small but salient misfortune, the type . . .."

"But those are old words," Crocker says.

The Lou pauses to consider the observation.

". . . I rang not once, but twice, without thinking . . . the wrong place, a building . . . only similar to the one I sought, a woman I had never . . . not only by the unexpected face, but by a beautiful and enchanting . . ..

"Okay, okay. The rest will come later."

And just when he appears he is about to expire, Stavros turns the page and Kojak reads, "Okay, swizzle stick what's this about, etc., etc., etc.," a broad smile of guile and glee opens on the putty-soft features of his face.

Mathias nods to Aigilas.

"Are we on time?" Mathias says.

Aigilas thinks so.

"That's enough of the lollygagging," Kojak says, now following the script closely, rejuvenated and gaining strength. "We don't have time for babble."

He consults his watch.

"Alright. Let's go. You two are going with us."

"That was quicker than I thought," Aigilas says.

"Should I turn off the teevee?" Mathias says. Then to Aigilas, "Did you write this?"

"Yes, I did. Talking to myself (like Kesil) as I am not. Imitating myself as you are. The Chinese believe that there are only so many words in a lifetime. When your words are used up, you're dead. Turn it off."

"Kidnapping won't work, with or without the teevee" Teivel says. "The dialogue won't make sense. The dialogue doesn't make sense. It never does when you're talking to yourself."

"So?" the Loo says, with a dark-sun cast to his eyes. "It will when we understand Why."

Aigilas, Teivel, and Kojak
    develop the mandatory
    chase scene (sort of)
in antiquated space and time

1:31. The clock over the door shows the customary one minute after the official departure time, and following orders Norman Bozick trundles the bus out of the lower level of the Bus Terminal, negotiates the cumbersome forty-seven foot vehicle through a construction mess and turns north. A few passengers and a dozen or so extras settle in for the ride, waiting for the action.

1:33. This is a Transit bus, a GMC over-the-road air-spring New Look with an airplane-like stressed-skin construction in which an aluminum riveted skin supports the weight of the bus. The wooden floor keeps the bus' shape. The engine cradle is hung off the back of the roof, and as a result the GM New Look weighs significantly less than older buses.

The New Look has a unique "Angle-drive" configuration with a transverse mounted engine and a transmission set at a forty-five-or-so degree angle to connect to the rear axle. The engine is canted backwards for maintenance access. The engine-transmission-radiator assembly is mounted on a cradle that can be quickly removed and replaced, allowing the bus to return to service with minimal delay when the powertrain requires major maintenance. The only parts not accessible from outside the bus are the right exhaust manifold and the starter.

1:35. The New Look is powered by a two-cycle Diesel 6V71, the exception being the 29-foot [8.84 m] TDH-3301, which is powered by the GMC DH-478 Toroflow four-stroke V6, and has a more conventional T-drive transmission. The New Look features the Allison Automatic VH hydraulic transmission, a one-speed automatic which drives the wheels through a torque converter. At sufficient speed a clutch bypasses the torque converter and the engine drives the rear wheels directly.

All New Looks features forward-facing seats on slightly raised platforms to give the appearance of a dropped center aisle, a NB Miata steering wheel, and an 18" Sony teevee hung from the ceiling just to the right of the driver's head (for passenger satisfaction). At the moment *Night Visions* is showing.

1:38. Detective Bobby Crocker is last seen standing in the doorway at 5 Beekman Street. In a well-placed barrage by E.Erie™'s well-placed micro-assassins the back half of Crocker's aura antiseptically dissipates. All that remains of him is a cardboard cut-out where he dissolves on the sidewalk with chalk body outlines around it to aid the forensic investigation.

1:40. Demosthenes also falls victim to ICE's penetrating stare. He fades somewhat less hygienically, however. Descending the stairs to meet the bus his heart falls out and he expires slowly, exsanguinating, his teevee life draining away from the gapping chest wound — and a lack of form, of dimension.

1:43. The New Look, without a recordable destination (maybe seeking guidance) makes its way along Beekman. A volley of blips erupts and several men interrupt *Night Visions* to run across the screen from Temple Court. Unexplainably traffic jams up and the bus rolls to a stop.

Moments later a man pushes two men onto the bus, prodding them up the steps with a .38 Police Special.

1:46. The man with the gun is tentatively identified as a fictional teevee personage, a hassled and frustrated police detective. However, this may or may not be the case. Those in the know say that he operates under a variety of aliases, so at the moment positive identification is not possible.

He waves his gun, reading from what may or may not be a screenplay. He walks to the back of the bus, turns to give the bus driver orders.

"Take me to Kennedy Airport," he commands and the thrilling saga of a day of infamy begins, leaving the remains of Heathcliff and Crocker sprawled in the slick of their sudden demise — the vanishing features of a bit part — supporting actors who could have hardly expected anyone to remember, anyone to care, anyway.

1:47. The bus rumbles toward Kennedy and the credits roll.

1:49. At the intersection of Beekman Street and Williams Street, the bus is halted. Forty-year-old pedestrian Anthony Hodgson of 3742 Eliot Avenue, Queens is struck by a car. The uninjured Hodgson gingerly rights himself to the greetings of three witnesses who offer their testimonial services should he decide to sue the driver. The price for their eye-witness offer is fifty dollars. After a brief negotiation he agrees and is advised to lie down in front of the car and pretend he is hurt. Hodgson follows the suggestion and resumes his position on the street in front of the car. Then with his advisors watching, carelessly the idling car slips into gear, leaps forward, and crushes Hodgson's head. No one is sure if the advice was well intended or not.

1:54. The bus is stopped by the traffic jam. Quickly orders go out to ICE to cease sniping lest pedestrians or extras be unprofitably vanished.

1:58. But the deed is done. With Aigilas and Teivel as creating hostages, taken by what they have produced and directed, the good detective prepares to detour a pleasant tour into a horror trip. He has in hand a ten hour drama (shooting time) which will end finally in the gloom of night next to an out-of-the-way hangar at Kennedy International Airport. In the end there are four dead, three wounded, more than a score of hostages (extras) terrorized, and the operation of a major airport snarled for hours.

2:10. Informed of the hijacking and anticipating the lawless carnage about to ensue, Mayor Beame comes out of hiding.

"I have doubts about capital punishment as a deterrent," the mayor says. "But I have changed my mind.

"If we are to operate in a society where punishment fits the crime, sentences should eliminate the possibility of turning our prison doors into turnstiles, which return dangerous criminals into society long before the sentences are served."

Then he goes back into hiding. He's still trying to determine the name, address, and pedigree, as well as the span of the horns and exact weight of the testicles of the magic Bronx Bison that has saved the western buffalo from extinction.

back to the back of the bus

2:13. An extra, Andre Terhune, seated in the back of the bus takes his guitar from the case and pretends to tune it. He's bored with the activities thus far and has a few songs to work on for a gig scheduled the following week at Jalopy Theatre.

The guitar is a 1975 D-35 Martin Dreadnought he won in a poker game with a hoosier from Queens. He's working on, "I Ain't Marching Any More."

He only knows two verses. But that should be enough.

For I flew the final mission in the Japanese sky
Set off the mighty mushroom roar
When I saw the cities burning
I knew that I was learning
That I ain't marchin' anymore

Now the labor leader's screamin'
when they close the missile plants,
United fruit screams at the Cuban shore,
Call it "peace" or call it "treason,"
Call it "love" or call it "reason,"
But I ain't marchin' anymore.

(Phil Ochs)

2:15. At 2:15, bored with the marching song, Teivel asks LoKoJakMan, somewhat sarcastically, "Have you read the script?"

He says he has and thinks he knows it well enough.

Aigilas points to an elderly man seated near the middle of the bus. He too is bored with the inaction.

"By the way," he says, "that's John McGaven," (which appears not to be an alias).

McGaven is a fifty-year-old librarian from Hartford, and it is not clear how Aigilas knows him or if he has frequented McGaven's library. Some think they were DU fraternity brothers at Tufts.

2:18. FIRST SHOTS FIRED — To set up the key sound effects (FXs), motifs and mood.

1. (FX bus engine growling.)
2. (FX underscoring music — '*Kojak* theme from Cacavas.' Establish music theme and fade out under heavy breathing, sounds of a man in distress. Sudden cut.)
3. Narrator: Kojak points the gun at Mr. McGaven and fires. Why does he do this? No one knows. But it does not seem unusual or unexpected considering the circumstances.
4. (FX interior, muffled gunshot. High piercing scream of a small girl.)
5. McGaven: He looks like he wants to get me in the face.
6. Narrator: But the bullet goes through the side of his neck.
7. McGavin: It hurts like the devil.
8. A Woman: You beast!
9. (FX man moaning. Women crying. Kojak growling, mumbling.)
10. Kojak: Any of you want the same? Just ask.
11. (FX a shuffling, scuffle. A struggle of men moving in the bus. Teevee dialogue chatters in the background.)
12. Narrator: He pulls McGaven from his seat and pushes him up the aisle. His hand is on McGaven's neck. He turns to the bus driver.

13. Kojak: Alright, step on it. Get this thing moving.
14. (FX bus engine growling and the rattle of worn and loose bus windows — underscore the theme from *Kojak*.)
15. Narrator: He looks at McGavin.
16. Kojak: If you live 'til we get to Kennedy, you can go.
17. Narrator: He directs McGaven to lie on the first row of seats and divides the other passengers according to their heads and noses. Baldheads and Rumpole noses to the right side, shags and snub noses to the other. What to do about shags and Rumpole noses, he doesn't say.
18. (FX air swooshing of a speeding vehicle, people grumbling, whining — bus theme.)
19. Anonymous voice: What about baldheads and snub noses?
20. (FX Kojak theme from the teevee.)
21. (FX thump of bus door opening.)
22. Narrator: He leans out of the bus and shouts that he has been "mistreated" by The Universe and CBS.
23. Kojak: *Kojak* is a favorite. I am popular with the law enforcement officers because they identify with the approach Kojak takes to The Job. Kojak has a neighborhood approach. He's not quick with a gun and he's not violent. He has dedication and a loneliness."

2:43. A Port Authority police patrol car at Kennedy radios that a bus has crashed through a metal gate next to the police headquarters building and that it is out in the area near the longest runway, which runs 14,000 feet next to Jamaica Bay.

2:50. Shots are fired from the bus at the police car. The wounded man, Mr. McGaven, is dumped out of the moving bus. Shouts are heard.

"Kojak operates on instinct and decency."

Yes, this is the buzz.

2:54. Officer Al Itkin drives a bright yellow semi-armored, dual-range, ten-speed, four-wheel-drive, Tonka Mighty Modified Port Authority police vehicle toward the bus which has gotten into the area at the western end of the runway near Hangar 12 of Trans World Airlines. A shot shatters the windshield and Mr. Itkin is heard to utter a dramatic and thoroughly convincing, "Holy shit."

2:59. Port Authority police notify The City police, the Federal Bureau of Investigation, and the Certified Interrogator's Association. They also put out a call for doctors.

3:02. Someone quickly questions Mr. McGaven. He claims the man inside the bus, a man with a large nose and baldhead, has a gun and a bag of ammunition. The police hostage team, a seventy-three member multi-logistical unit trained to translate, negotiate, and mediate with kidnappers is called.

Mr. McGaven says that the man has a familiar face and reminds him of someone he has read about or maybe seen on teevee.

3:07. With a siege on one runway and no way of knowing when it might shift elsewhere, the police close the airport.

3:08. A howl ripples from the bus.

"It's the same drunk Kojak who turns in at night and comes back the next morning to borrow a buck. If he kicks a kid who has knocked down an old lady while stealing her purse — and then kicked her while she's down — it's because Kojak doesn't understand that dimension of cruelty."

3:10. Two youngsters — twelve-year-old Lester Rumms and ten-year-old Ronald Zateau, both of Miami, Ohio — are sent from the bus into the waiting arms of the policemen. Rumms carries a handwritten note with directions for camera angles and costume suggestions. It demands an airplane (with a range of 3,000 miles) and six million dollars. It will likely need fuel, also.

3:12 There is a brief, violent, and confusing fight. Nettie Blasberg 57, originally of St. Louis, Missouri, Mathias Teivel's secretary for seven years (she signed on as an extra) is shot and her body tumbled out the bus door. She had a City address of 93-47 Taylor in Brooklyn.

Inside, Army specialist, twenty-two-year-old Susan Bruso of Houston, Texas, who is sitting in a front seat, tries to fell the gunman with a karate chop and severely sprains her right hand. Mr. Bozick, the bus driver, lunges toward the gunman, too.

Mr. Bozick is shot and he, too, is toppled out the door.

With Mrs. Blasberg is her husband, David, who operates a newsstand and lunch counter in the courthouse in Clayton, Missouri. They have two children, six grandchildren, two cats, and a Schnauzer named Schnoz. No one has yet explained how or why the Blasberg's are together on the bus or by what strange arrangements they lived their lives.

Kojak orders Mr. Blasberg to operate the bus.

"I can't drive. I'm legally blind," Mr. Blasberg replies.

Kojak runs to the back of the bus to consult the script.

Marcelo turns to Mathias.

"Christ, will we ever get him off the book? And he wanted to adlib more. Auteur, my ass."

3:14. Several pages are out of sequence, and in the confusion Mr. Blasberg escapes, along with Miss Bruso and Leon Nesbett of Mosca, Colorado. They are last seen holding hands, skipping (there may be a typo here — slipping instead of skipping) off toward Jamaica Bay.

Somewhere along the way — either in the confusion after the shooting or immediately after the freeing of the first two hostages — twenty-six-year-old Robert Fernandez of Venezuela and nineteen-year-old Israel Maldonado of Mexico also escape.

3:17. Two Port Authority police officers, Robert Arnold and Drew John, dash out from the safety of their vehicles and drag Mrs. Blasberg and Mr. Bozick out of the line of fire.

3:19. Using a bullhorn the police try to talk to Lieutenant Kojak. Don't be nervous. Follow the plot.

Detective Lee Fowler and Lieutenant Stone shout, "Remember, this is your city. You've done more for The City than anyone. The hell with politicians and media moguls. Paley and Beame can't hold a candle to your ass. Just stay with what you're doing. No harm has been done yet."

3:21. A high, shrill voice sends out a reply from the bus.

"I'm not talking about police brutality. It's a cautionary kick. A kick in the ass is better for a kid than being shut up in a juvenile hall somewhere. That's what Kojak stands for."

3:25. When police officers reach her, it is determined Mrs. Blasberg is dead. Still no harm done.

3:26. A break in the action. Two of The Universe Studio's portable video recording units are malfunctioning. Director of Photography Lukema Kesil signals for everyone to remain calm and stay in place. The technicians claim it will only take a few minutes to correct the mauvais functionnement.

3:28. The PD emergency service personnel arrive in total darkness.

3:29. Seven members of the police hostage negotiating team, headed by its commander, Lieutenant Frank Bolz, arrive.

"They are eleventh hour additions," Juan Lamiae says. "We called them in to give the story sophistication, make it more believable."

3:31. A seventy-two member band from a primary school in Queens is diverted from Main Stage 1 Plaza, to Hanger 12 to entertain the police officers and early arrivals. There is an overflow crowd waiting at the gate.

3:33. Angelo Palmer, president of The City Actors Guild appears and threatens to shut down the operation if the officers of the police hostage negotiating team do not become paid-in-full, card-carrying members of the Guild.

3:38. Palmer, Lamiae, Bolz and Detective Fowler hold a brief but heated meeting in a corner of Hanger 12.

3:42. The first wave of workers from the New Old Women and Technological High-End Neophytes arrive with coffee urns and boxes of sandwiches. They set up a stand near the back of the hanger, out of the line of fire. Coffee is fifty cents a cup and Opulent Girl sandwiches are three dollars each.

4:09 CBS issues an official communiqué via satellite to the rest of the world that Mr. McGaven, regardless of his condition, is a liar.

"There is no truth to Mr. McGaven's hysterical remarks about the identity of the gunman or the gunman's alleged association with CBS."

4:10. Norman Bozick, the driver (former) of the bus is DOA at Jamaica Hospital.

4:20. With the drama apparently limited to one set, the police permit the airport to be reopened for service again.

4:26. The first spectators with General Admission tickets file into the grandstand around Hanger 12.

4:28. Reps from the Collective Unit of Nubile Tuchees, the Association of Sad Sisters, the Syndicated National Association of Tangentially Concerned Hedonists, and the Prurient Ungulate Society of Seasonal Yearning arrive on the scene. They accuse the police of contributing to Sister Blasberg's demise.

"If they had women on the negotiating team Sister Blasberg would be alive and well," Rosie Rosenblume shouts. "It is well known, but ignored by the police, that deranged men respond to the female voice — no matter how strident or shrill if might be."

4:31. Palmer, Lamiae, Bolz and Detective Fowler emerge from Hanger 12 scowling but agreed that the negotiating team members who deliver lines on camera will be required to join the Guild.

4:33 Catherine Baalasan of 210 Union Street in Brooklyn introduces herself to the police and informs them that she is there to corroborate police brutality. It is, she claims, her god-given right as a mother and citizen to witness and record broken arms and battered skulls for posterity.

"Without my words, who will know?" she tells reporters. "I mean, who will know what these brave men have done?"

4:35. Lieutenant Bolz throws a quarter-inch rope toward the bus. It lands about twenty feet away. Over the bullhorn the police tell LoKoJakMan that the line is attached to a telephone. The door opens and a woman hostage walks nervously over to the line and drags it to the bus. The telephone is pulled in and the Lieutenant begins to talk to the police team.

4:39 "We try to resolve the problem through lay psychology," Lieutenant Bolz says.

He grew up in Garden City and has a B.A. in psychology from Columbia University.

"We tell Kojak we are here to help you. What is your problem? We have all kinds of programs. TA, EST, DRAD, XOB, you name it. We get very little from him except that he wants six million dollars and a plane to take him to NBC."

4:40. A fistfight breaks out at the back of Hanger 12 between the New Old Women and Technological High-End Neophytes.

4:41. Police equipment converge. A motorcade with lights flashing atop squad cars escorts a flatbed trailer carrying a big yellow armored Tonka Mighty Personnel Carrier that is used to approach armed assailants.

4:48. Officers with bullhorns announce the official attendance at twenty-three thousand. Paid admission is twenty-one thousand six hundred ninety-six, with one hundred ten no-shows.

4:49. A thunderous ovation goes up from the crowd.

5:18. Two girls with baldheads and large, wide noses — one seven-year-old and one eight — run from the bus into the arms of waiting policemen. The police announce that Kojak has let them go. He claims he could not shoot children who look like that.

5:35. The brawl at the back of the hanger subsides with only minimal damage — a few loose teeth, a couple of bruises, a broken finger, and a few smeared egos. Curses are flung.

6:48. A single shot is heard from the bus.

6:50. A single shout is heard from the bus.

"Do you hear me? The law enforcement officer in my neighborhood would kick me if I was doing something wrong."

6:55. The crowd is growing restless, milling about, threatening to become nasty if the action doesn't pick up.

7:18. Another shot is heard from the bus. Cheers go up. A man in a rubber mask, that resembles Mayor Beame, giving vent to his natural leadership and enthusiasm comes out of the stands and leads the crowd in cheers.

7:18:37. During one or the other of the shooting incidents a passenger, Zak Lo, is wounded. Kojak says "Shut up." Mr. Lo thinks he says "Stand up." He does and Kojak shoots him in the right shoulder.

7:19. The passenger door of the bus folds open and the inscrutable Mr. Lo slithers out. Clutching his shoulder, he runs to the line of police cars and falls to the ground behind the yellow semi-armored vehicle.

7:20. The crowd gives Mr. Lo a sound ovation. They appreciate what he has done for them.

7:42. An ambulance rushes Mr. Lo to Queens General Hospital where he dies without fanfare.

9:18. Without warning the bus lurches into motion. Bruse De Boers, a seventeen-year-old high school student from East Hartford, who has never driven a bus, is ordered by Kojak to drive.

The police vehicles, led by the battered yellow semi-armored dual-range, ten-speed, four-wheel-drive Tonka Mighty Modified Port Authority police vehicle, trail the bus, trying to crowd it away from the central terminal and into one of the back areas to the north.

Uncertain of where it will halt, the police again order air traffic suspended.

9:18:41. Without warning, following the bus, the CBS tracking vehicle with a camera mounted on the hood leaps into motion, spilling two of the camera crew onto the concrete runway.

9:24. The bus comes to rest near the old North Passenger Terminal, facing the DC-8 that has been offered as a getaway plane, about forty feet away. Kojak does not know it, but the plane has no fuel and no crew.

"Our policy — nobody gets free air time," a policeman explains. "Zero tolerance. Once you're cancelled, that's it."

9:30. The crowd swarms down out of the stands and follows the bus and the police chanting "Ko-Jak, Ko-Jak."

9:35. NOW and THEN, with the aid of CUNT, move their concession in behind the DC-8.

9:45. The two toppled members of the CBS camera crew are identified as Marcel Trotter, twenty-nine, of 7337 Winona in Queens and Rafael Durkam, twenty-three, of 1919 Wellington Place, Bronx. Trotter has a fractured skull and broken right arm, Durkam a broken ankle and badly lacerated right cheek. They are taken by ambulance to St. John's Hospital in Elmhurst.

9:47. Another shout comes from the bus.

"Our basic purpose, after all, is to entertain, but the attitudes and the accent of these shows are accurate."

9:58. A note floats out of the bus informing the police that the passengers, those uninjured on the bus, have been watching the show on the 18" Sony added to the bus several months ago for passenger satisfaction.

10:00. Using a bullhorn, Lieutenant Bolz continues to try to reason with Kojak. In response, an occasional shout, a loud snort or belch, emanates from the bus.

10:30. The police are becoming increasingly nervous about the nervousness of the crowd. The crowd watches the action across the tarmac with varying degrees of humor for the spirit of the chase, though if the scene is again shifted the crowd threatens to become violent. The police decide not to let the bus move and the armored vehicle rolls up and squeezes against the front of the bus on the driver's side.

10:45. The signal lights on the bus begin to blink. No one knows why. Some guess that the bus wants to make a right turn. Others contend that Bruse De Boers, the seventeen-year-old high school student from East Hartford is bored and playing with the levers and buttons on the bus. But that is only speculation.

10:46. The bus lurches forward, scraping against the police vehicle, breaking loose, then driving off at a speed police say reaches 75 mph.

10:58. Helicopters equipped with television cameras and floodlights hover overhead so the crowd can follow the action on the monitors set up in the hanger and in the terminal.

11:02. Someone from Jim McMullen's arrives with additional mix for Manhattans.

11:06. Police officer Paddy DeBeneditto, now the chauffeur of the Port Authority semi-armored, yellow, ten-speed, four-wheel-drive, dual-range, Tonka Mighty Modified police vehicle tries to cut off the bus. Suddenly, unexpectedly, without warning, David Modiano, twenty, of 838 Dean Street, Brooklyn, tumbles from the passenger's door, out into the vehicle's path. Kojak has apparently shoved him. Officer DeBeneditto's vehicle careens sharply to avoid hitting the hostage who is now no longer a hostage but a former hostage with a broken arm and severe lacerations and contusions about the head.

11:07. A cheer goes up and the crowd shouts for more.

11:11. Near Hanger 6, at the north end of the field, officer DeBeneditto finally succeeds in ramming his car against the bus. A police wagon squeezes in front. The bus is trapped.

11:12. Someone shouts that the floodlights from the helicopters that bath the area in a daytime glow — exposing the pursuers — should be doused. An E.Erie™ darkness falls on the scene. Lieutenant Bolz continues to talk over the bullhorn. The crowd is agitated.

11:14. Shouts of disparagement emanate from the crowd — demands for refunds — accusations of false advertising — threats of lawsuits and/or gunfire.

11:15. Shouts rise from the crypt of the bus.

"You can't ask an actor to talk about constitutional law. Kojak represents the rules, and the public wants rules."

11:23. The madding crowd (estimated by police at six thousand) surges onto the runway and enters into a mano a mano with a maverick Beechcraft King Air attempting to cook up enough power to get rolling. The struggle goes on for a full minute as the craft inches forward, then the crowd stops it or the pilot stops it or the invisible hand of the market stops it. But someone or something stops it. Again the engines whine — again its forward progress is impeded.

11:25. The airport is closed again.

11:26. The remaining passengers spill from the bus into the arms of policemen who hurry them behind cars.

"We know he is still in there," Lieutenant Stone says. "The ghost in the machine."

The hostages sob and shout.

11:27. Without light Kojak strikes a match against the obscure, tries to read between the lines. He curses over the last few lines, turns to the door of the bus and yells at Lieutenant Bolz.

"Kojak is public relations for law enforcement."

Bolz agrees.

11:28. Holding a match too close to the script, Kojak sets the pages on fire. He throws the conflagration onto the bus floor and stomps on it vigorously. But to no avail. The pages are burned or scarred beyond recognition.

He stands for a moment in the bus doorway.

11:31 The crowd, now estimated at thirty-three thousand by Research Estimate Associates, a Madison Avenue counting firm, begins dissecting the King Air for souvenirs. Some have broken away from the main group and build bonfires on either side of the plane about to become skeletal remains.

11:33. Theostotle Kojak, an aging, baldheaded badass from the TCPD, detective extraordinaire, steps out of the bus with his rectitude tarnished but rejuvenated and intact, and his hands up.

"I'm Kojak," he says. "That's Ko as in low and jak as in off."

And that's where the script ends. The burnt script. A roar goes up from the crowd.

11:34: The in-bus teevee meant for passenger satisfaction is blank.

11:35. Dancers prepared for a Runway Festival, form circles about the fires, strip down, and cast their clothing onto the flames.

11:39. Spectator Harold Razmik of 24 Oakland Avenue, Statin Island is appreciative of the action-drama of the evening.

"I was headed for my neighborhood bar to get a beer when I heard the program on the police scanner. Thought I'd come over and see what was happening. It was worth the trip — and the money. Good show. Dramatic, and fulfilling to watch."

11:42. Mathias Teivel and Marcelo Aigilas, from The Universe Studios, leave the bus and move into the shadows, unnoticed, then into the crowd. Mathias is without crutches, but still limping with a sore toe, walking on the side of his foot.

"That went well," Teivel says. "I hope Lukema got the crane-shots."

11:52. They are in a cocktail lounge in the main terminal drinking Manhattans watching the police lead Kojak across the screen into the recesses of late night teevee. A well dressed, small man sidles into the lounge trailing a heavy scent of Fabergé Brut over basic stench.

"I know him," Mathias says. "Yes," he says softly.

They laugh and lift their glasses.

"We have been overcome," Mathias says. "We have succumbed. Sălutăre!"

"Okay. But what about the fifth show? We've lost our leading lady."

'We'll figure it out. Or someone else will. These things never heal, are never set to rest. If we don't do it someone else will."

The lights dim over the wounded hulk of the New Look and the skeleton of the King Air abandoned near the hanger at the far end of the field. The soft vibes of Andre Terhune's Martin cover the soft words of

> Call it "peace" or call it "treason,"
> Call it "love" or call it "reason,"
> But I ain't marchin' anymore.
> (Phil Ochs)

Padre Pastel gets himself a real deal

Though times are questionable, Pastel, too, has his betting blinders on. He's on the phone to Garfield.

"The CBS suit against SoSaMy Inc will go to the Supreme Court," Galante says. "Could cost a lot of money. I have people interested in the stock. They'll go 50 percent of market. We can talk them into 70."

Garfield scratches his ass. It's the loan shark in Galante that gives him pause.

"I'll need time," he says. "There are considerations."

Not the least of which is his tainted image. Never deal from a position of weakness. Probably pump and dump. Next week 74 percent, then, . . . well, hell, no telling. Street buzz has a contract on Galante's head.

"I'll need time," Garfield says.

"We will not have a chance better than today, Galante says, verifying the veracity of phenomena. As bosses of SoSaMy Inc we have a duty to turn a profit. We are certain of today — tomorrow, who knows? Weigh a certainty against a doubt."

If he could think at all, he'd lay out the arguments — to see what life is like, and to believe what you see. To hell with pretense — explain away original sin if you can — if not, embrace your faith in man's depravity. This is The City of the Gods, after all.

Garfield puzzles over the observation.

What might SoSaMy Inc export to the hinterlands? What enterprise strike?

A lengthy, pregnant pause at the end of the line, then a chuckle, a laugh.

How about the law of the jungle, the KKK, KGB, SS, FBI, CIA, Minutemen. Develop and sell fringe theories. Psychiatry and medicine clothed in the respectability of new approaches to mental health. Build and market kits for contamination, a potion to keep offensive neighbors at bay — bone-pointing.

Then, too, Garfield has exposé in mind. Yes, by god. What if SoSaMy Inc was exposed? What if the pseudo-PD was to infiltrate and break a crime network based in The City? A network exporting murder (Murder Inc), arson (for hire), dope, prostitutes, graft, and the other cotton candy, rollercoaster rides of pleasure and profit mankind lives by? Would not the people of The City turn their fickle fancy attention again to the Honorable Lord Mayor and his associates? And might, then, not he, Garfield the Commissioner, change or trade his distorted persona for a new and respectable reflection?

He tells Galante, "Yes," he will consider the offer — check the tea leaves, see if the times are right, but Galante must also include a reduction in his frontline troops.

Of course, there's a kicker, an ace in the hole. Don Galante carries a price on his head. Garfield knows Pastel will be in prison by March for alleged parole violations — associating with known felons — Garfield already has the papers on his desk. And then — and then — one day in Little Italy — one day they will find him, as predictably as the sun setting — it will not be a white shotgun or lupara bianca affair, except as Sam has a hand in it. But the Frequent Friar will not avoid the appointment, either.

Why not? Yes. If the price is right and the times are fair. In the forbidden lies profit. Garfield knows. And with Galante's star waning Garfield expects he can bargain, reclaim the wounded operation at whatever price he wishes.

"Ingenious," he tells himself. "All of it taken quietly. No shattered glass. Not even a shout."

Psyaint David

He drives, watching the pedestrians, counting the dogs and the number of faces on the block, watching the dogs squatting, lifting their hind legs.

He's driving, hoping for customers, for one to invite him in so

He will go in and up a stairway to a large room where people are drinking and having fun. "Hey, man," they'll shout, shake his hand and ask him where

He's been and what's new and how

He likes The City and if

He's been to Washington Square on Saturday night, and what

He wants to buy. What's

He got to sell? "You can get it here," they'll say. Someone takes him by the hand, someone beautiful, a Cybil Shepherd or Jodie Foster or Faye Dunaway look-a-like and they go off alone and she undresses for him, slowly, and all the time she smiles and

He wonders when it's going to get hard, disgusted with himself for watching her undress, wanting to tell her she doesn't have to do this. With a slow sick feeling in his stomach

He stands and excuses himself and runs to the bathroom.

He vomits on the floor, then starts crying because they shouted and shook his hand and he wanted someone to say, "Yeah, I know him."

He drives, perusing the crowds, listening to the old man on the radio talking about the things that can happen in a cab — about the lesbian circuit, the humping and groaning — about the dumb old men and little girls — Elsie Beckmann — the little girls in the back seat of parked cars all over The City — mostly about the little girls who regard him as a freak and screw up their faces when

He speaks, even though

He is just talking and not asking them, not asking them or expecting them to say "yes."

He drives through The City, considering the lights, waiting for someone to tell him what to do when

He sees a young (mid-twenties) man wearing a leather sports jacket.

He pulls up and the man gets in. **Passenger:** 417 Central Park West.

He drives off. Later

Psyaint David

He slows down in the 400 block of Central Park West, checking apartment numbers. **Passenger:** Just pull over to the curb a moment.

He turns the wheel. **Passenger:** Yeah. That's fine. Just set here.

He waits impassively as the meter ticks. After a long pause the passenger speaks. **Passenger:** Ya see that light up there on the seventh floor. Three windows from the side of the building. Ya see that woman? That's my wife. But it ain't my apartment. A nigger lives there. She left me two weeks ago. It took me this long to find out where she went. I'm gonna kill her. What do you think of that? Huh? What do you think of that? Huh? I'm gonna kill her with a .44 Bulldog. Did you ever see what it can do to a woman's pussy? I'm gonna put it right up to her. Right in her. You must think I'm real sick, huh?

A real pervert. Sitting here and talking about a woman's pussy and a .44, huh?

He is driving through The City studying the pimps and the whores, when a woman waves from the corner — a woman with white hair and a dog, a large black, slick-haired dog. They are dressed in matching outfits — identical colors with a foul smell — and she waves and opens the door and gets in with the dog and says, "I want to go to the deceased part of town."

He smiles and says "Yeah," and inhales her poison vapors. "Just see that you get me there on time," she says. "You are all alike."

He floats into traffic. On 43rd Street a fop in drag crosses against the light.

He swears under his breath and hammers on the horn. "Young man," the woman says. "Young man, stop the car. Stop right here."

She hands him a ten and

He smiles at her good fortune, the .44 in his belt, nuzzling his crotch.

He plans to turn into the next alley where it is written in large white letters on the brick wall above a row of garbage cans that Death Is Nature's Way Of Telling You To Slow Down. Of telling you what? Nature's way of evening old scores — of healing old sores.

He smiles at her good fortune that a nigger, a tall, thin light-skinned nigger with a large hat, lipstick, a tight skirt and platform heels went shaking his/her derrière across the green light.

He intends to pull into the alley, step out and hold the door open for the lady. "Pardon, Madam, but this is your destination."

He will nuzzle the .44 in her lap and blow and breathe heavily on her. And then, to her surprise,

He will pull the trigger. "Madam, allow me. You have been tickled by Sam's hot tongue. This is his town." And the woman opens her mouth to scream but cannot. The dog smiles, his eyes glowing, opaque marbles, then small fires, jumping brightly in the night.

He is a Mohawk brave on the trail, chest and thighs painted, gliding gracefully through the forest.

He knows who she is even before her pimp confronts him.

He says, "Your name is Jeremy McCoy," and the pimp glares at him. "Ah, yeah, man."

He knows it is the same girl. Now

He can see into the green eyes and feel the touch of her soft, warm skin. A knot forms in his stomach and

He thinks about another gun — a big black weapon to wipe out the pimps and cops and con men.

He wants a gun that does not need to be reloaded, that can be fired by thinking — fired at Juliet.

Beame and Garfield assure

the citizenry that they

have the situation under control

Which hand, no one knows. Is it off hand? Or the other hand? Or, this is my hand, and on the other hand, this is my other hand? But so ends another pleasant, drifting night on the Big Town.

The following day the beaming Mannequin of Brussels takes to the streets, calls the press to the 109th in Flushing. The news conference is, as he says, "To assure the public that everything possible is being done on probably one of the most troublesome problems affecting the feeling of safety of people.

"I have directed Police Commissioner Garfield to spare no expense, use any resource of the department to get at a solution," the Mayor adds.

Garfield reports that outside experts in hypnotism have been consulted and have assisted in some of the questioning. Specialists have been employed to elicit recollections from survivors of the shootings.

"We're asking the gunman to come in to get the help he obviously needs.

"There have been very productive results from public cooperation, public participation. There is somewhere out there in the possession of some citizen, some information which, if it were in our possession, could lead to productive results."

It is by oblique admission that the PC sometimes gives himself away.

"Do you want Son of Sam for personal reasons?" a reporter queries.

"Of course," Garfield responds. "All police work is personal. It is very important personally to me that the stalker be apprehended. I can't sleep at night. My hair is falling out with worry."

"Commissioner," a *Post* stringer queries, "reports claim that because of the suit against CBS and SoSaMy Inc and the suit against SoSaMy Inc by CBS, that you will profit from capturing Sam. How much do you stand to make?"

Garfield acquiesces.

"Yes," he says, "it would appear to bear that interpretation. But catching the perpetrator is more important than my reputation and money."

Before he can answer Beame steps forward and reading from a prepared statement, apologizing for the Kojak affair.

"We have determined," the Mayor reads, "that the shouts coming from the fifth floor at Kings County in Brooklyn, are, in fact, those of Theostotle Kojak. We feel now that he is confined, the people of The City are safe, and the investigation can proceed."

"Do you think Kojak will resurface, maybe under an alias?"

"That is not necessarily so," the Mayor says.

"But it could happen."

It is believed, however, that Kojak is only part of the problem. The authority on criminal behavior, Dr. David Abrahamson, suggests that the psycho is a "very lonely, a very secretive man, who fantasizes possession of women" by his ability to shoot at will. Dr. Abrahamson says that "Killing has not solved his inner conflicts," and expresses concern that he might increase the frequency of his attacks.

"Then it will occur again?"

"The etiology of the psychopathic serial killers suggests that they kill after undergoing some sort of stressful event, are of average intelligence, are socially competent, are apt to plan the offends, wish to revisit their victims and bring a weapon to commit the murder and take it with him when he leaves the crime scene.

The story always repeats itself.

OurLadydetermines
  thatifsexandviolence
  aretobeturnedtoprofit
nowisthetimetodoit

It will occur again.

But more importantly, someone stands to make a buck, and Our Lady of the Magnificent Mammaries intends to be that someone.

"No limp-dick is going to harvest my vines," she tells Sam. "I gave birth to this baby and I'm going to reap the fruit of my womb."

Sam agrees. She'll no doubt have her way. When Our Lady of Gluttonous Gold shakes her money-maker judges and politicians squirm — the Gross National Product (unusually gross) has been known to shuffle a point or two.

But the struggle is heating up.

Others join the fray.

Monday morning Delores Thebeau of 285 Arlington Avenue, Spuyten Duyvil in the Bronx obtains an 8 x 11 of the Son of Sam composite from the 50th Precinct. She tapes it to her living room window, facing outward. She does this, she explains to a *Post* reporter, "To let everyone in the neighborhood know what Son of Sam looks like. I think after all it might help catch him."

But then, she explains further, "When I raise up the blind and stand back I can see the face through the paper and after a short time I get this urge to draw some hair and a moustache with a beard on the face."

What happens next seems to be the basis for Delores' travail.

"When I finish, it is like the picture turns around and instead of looking out to the street it stares at me. I mean, I can't hardly get my breath. My knees shake and my heart is racing. Those two eyes pierce my heart like white-hot daggers. My head is spinning. I just collapse on the rug right there in front of the window like I been shot.

"When I come to I'm white as a ghost. It was the holy ghost what descended on me in love and saved my life. It was a visitation. And I'm shaking bad. I mean palsied-like. Still am to this day.

"Here. See this?"

She holds out her hand.

"I can't hold it still.

"Then I realize what they done. It comes tom just out of the blue. The face is that of my savior, the lord Jesus Christ. He is just there staring at me with those burning eyes. The police used Jesus for their drawing. Just so they could catch a killer.

"And it was Jesus, alright. I'd know that face anywhere. I've seen it in a thousand places.

"So I decides, right then and there, I'm going to get to the bottom of this. I find a lawyer and talk to him about my constitutional rights to freedom of religion being violate. But you know how lawyers are. It costs me a hundred dollars and he lies to me for half an hour, then says I ain't got a case."

She does not say if anyone else saw Jesus that morning — or Son of Sam, for that matter. But she plans to submit the picture (with her embell-ishments) as evidence.

"That's why I come to the court house. To defend myself. I'm gonna find the judge and tell him what they done and collect my damages for the police using my savior's picture — just to catch a thug. And then violate my constitutional rights to freedom of religion."

She plans to petition the court for five million dollars — though she doesn't know what she will do with the money — when they pay. She thinks she might give some of it to her three-year-old granddaughter who "needs a new pair of shoes." Or she might use it to fix the porch railing on her house, which is broken and which her husband refuses to get off his dead-ass to repair.

"Every time you get married," Madame Thebeau says, (she has been married four times) "you think you are marrying Jesus and you get some lazy shit what never done nothing worthwhile in his life."

The following day, true to her word, Our Lady of Invariant Invidia joins Ms. Thebeau in Federal Court and files for a Preventive Injunction to keep

CBS and SoSaMy Inc from using Son of Sam logo for purposes of profit, to be followed by a trademark infringement suit.

A preventive injunction is an injunction commanding a party or parties, to refrain from doing an act. In general, injunction is a preventive remedy. However, if necessary, to meet the exigencies of a particular situation, the injunctive decree may be both preventive and mandatory.

Certainly, concerning the exigencies, liabilities, and circumstances of the situation Our Lady would prefer the injunction to be mandatory and eventually permanent.

United States District Court

_____X

Hardon INC, Vibrant Veritas, Son of Sam, Psyaint David,   :
Our Lady, et al.

    :

Plaintiffs,

    :

-against-

    :

CBS, SoSaMy Inc, SAMIE, TCPD, The Universe Studios,
E.ERIE™, Abraham Beame, William. S. Paley, Carmine   :
Galante, Father Pastel, PC Garfield, Kojak (and all aliases),
Samuel, Sam Inella, Aristotle Savalas, et al   :

Defendants   :

_____X

COMPLAINT FOR TRADEMARK INFRINGEMENT

Plaintiffs, by their attorneys, for their complaint against Defendant, allege:
JURISDICTION AND VENUE

1. This is a civil action seeking damages and injunctive relief for infringement of trademark laws of the United States (17 U.S.C. § 101 et seq.).
2. This court has jurisdiction under 17 U.S.C. §101 et seq.; 28 U.S.C. §1331 (federal question); and 28 U.S.C. §1338(a) (trademark).
3. This court has personal jurisdiction over the Defendants, etc.

The uproar is general. Paley, Garfield, Beame, Galante come out crying free enterprise and First Amendment. A distant shout is heard from Kings Hospital, and a whine from Temple Court.

The courts, they protest, have a responsibility not to undermine the American right of free enterprise. They claim their constitutional rights are being violated.

"This is an integral part of the Commerce Clause," Paley contends. "Limiting the use of Son of Sam impressions is un-American and a breach of a fantasy contract with the American people — it is a blow limiting those who might capitalize on their talents."

"Where would the police be," Garfield queries, "if they could not create working profiles, psychological sketches or posters with accusative captions? Just as J. Edgar Hoover worked with Dillinger and Baby Face Nelson, to build the FBI, we need Son of Sam. The threat of a passionate psychopath roaming The City, looking for a victim, is our lifeline to funds, to kick-backs, pay-offs, and the other important aspects of a modern law and order society."

Father Pastel nods. It is the second time he has agreed with someone else's idea.

Garfield continues.

"Take away the fierce outrage and hatred for the criminal that bubbles in the heart of every police officer when Jack the Ripper strikes, take away the our-team-their-team concept and the right to throw darts at the image of a killer and you take away the spirit of the hunt, you will destroy the morale of the entire department. Take away Sam and you take away the nuts and guts of police work."

Beame echoes the sentiment.

"We live on images — they're our bread and butter. Without them we are lost. Phantasmagorias are at the bottom of what is great about The City and the American Dream. Take away our god given right to fulminate and hallucinate about Sam and you will break the hearts of those the world over who want to see someone who has succeeded."

Paley is vehement.

"For twenty-five years we have fed the public a diet they have come to expect. Examine our teevee fare and you will find that we have exported the best of The City. We have given our audiences what they needed, what they would eventually appreciate, and they have developed an insatiable appetite for it.

"We contracted with The Universe for *Kojak* because we know viewers want Kojak and we intend to use Son of Sam because he is what they need."

Galante is more philosophical.

"Obviously the kid ain't got it as a hitman — too erotic or exotic or esoteric or anorexic or anagogic. Anyhow, he don't follow orders. Got style, a flair for getting' attention. He's good for the Syndie — keep's everybody's mind off the usual — makes the hum-drums happy for safe business like hookers and gambling and shakedowns."

SoSaMy, Inc lawyers ready a multiple-perspective appeal to overturn Our Lady's Injunction.

Judge Theodore Lambosio promises to take the case under careful

Psyaint David

judicial consideration.

"I shall review all aspects with the utmost care and thoroughness. The case has all the complexities and intricacies of a game of 'drop the hand-kerchief' or 'button, button, who has the button,' and I intend to give it a lengthy and correct reading.

"I shall consider the strength of the mark, the proximity of the goods, the similarity of the mark, evidence of actual confusion, marketing channels used, type of goods and the degree of care likely to be exercised by the purchaser, defendant's intent in selecting the mark, and the likelihood of the expansion of the product lines."

with fond remembrance
Hans-David attempts
to visit an early victim

Hans-Peter makes ghoulish faces, admires his reflection in storefront windows and turns quickly to catch the flit of a shade, a shadow. He is certain the Duke of Darkness will be found and his identity discovered. He trots off, nose in the air, into Roseland Cemetery, heart pounding, face flushed, the scent of newly turned earth, the embalming fluids of spring.

He's been hanging around Sam too long — stops to piss on a grey stone, the yellow streaked marble, and stumbles over a large white cardboard vase of plastic flowers. He walks on searching for Donna Lauria's grave and when he cannot find it settles for the first fresh heap available.

The earth is yellow-gray damp from the rain, shielded by the endless row on row of small Stonehenge monuments: stones, statues and vaults. He stretches out, abandoned, arms spread on the grave of Margarita Marconi, formerly of 1735 Harold drive in the Bronx who two weeks earlier, took the sting of the assassin's needle, a stiletto in an unseen hand.

Margarita it is said, possessed a creation theory, or was possessed by it, and in the heat of a fit, in the clarity of certitude one night drove at an excessive rate of speed in her Honda Centurion to Central Park to find, to examine once again the circumstances and scene of her exile. It is further said the theory came to her from a thought, a guess, a hope, and she believed that on the mythic creation day long ago god set down Adam and Eve by the lake at Manhattan's Center.

Some say she dreamed on matters such as these and claimed that when she found the sacred ground she would conjure again the serpent to undo what had in that prehistoric time been done.

Yes, she was a pious girl, intent of mind and purpose, and in the park that night, pausing for a moment, a mental lapse all agree, (she stooped to pet a dog that lay beneath a tree) she met her doom — although some believe the second before she knew it was too late, when she saw the flaming eyes and smelled the rancid odor, she suffered to enjoy the satisfaction of knowing she had found the garden.

Then she died without a whimper in a mini struggle with a bloated, ruddy, purplish, night-stalker clad in a grimed linen shroud (no doubt the dog's master) with only a left eye, his teeth, hair, and nails grown long, blood seeping from his mouth and nose. She died without fanfare from two small wounds on her throat.

"No actor stands alone," Our Lady warns.

She is there watching over son David, feeling, transient and ephemeral, her aspect spread thin — as thin as Margarita's.

"Farewell Margarita Marconi of 3997 Salzar Drive. Fondly remembered. We will miss you."

but it's time to move on
   and Sam's ready
to call in the dogs

And Sam's there too, the lights low, the fist-head of his giant, gallant horse-cock shines beneath his stretched black silk tights. To his left, Hans-David rests on the grave, the glow of a small blue beam illuminating his still figure. Sam steps forward, a murmur washes over the audience — then a prolonged silence caressed by Sam's hot breath.

"One day you will be forced to recant, withdraw. Denials and repudiation lead to doubt — self-doubt," Sam warns. "A denouement," Sam whispers, "to what began long ago. She lies in the cage — condemned."

He turns between the granite and marble vaults, the slant, bevel, ledger, dome and Gothic Tablet stones. History, the weight of desire, a sense of vision must accompany the spoken line. Without the assumption of belief, actions are frozen, bas-relief in soft stone — even for a homicidal maniac.

"This is the Garden of Eden, what man purchases for wisdom.

"Yes, the will to know, to do, to be, to search the heavens and understand — to comprehend."

He pauses, his long shadow falling across the Psyaint. Sam looks down. His canine incisors grown longer.

"And then this. Biology — enzymes, hormones, a delicate balance to harness the genius of thought and feeling: to keep it to a narrow way — and then this. An unbridled mind, a willing Faust, Hamlet or Lear . . .. And then.

"Man dependent on biology — survival, the dance, the female stamping her feet, yelling defiance, feigning indifference, contemptuous, resisting overtures, invitations . . . thrashing . . . rake-a-cheek fury . . . shrieks and, to override rules of the dance, a codebook, a new two-step, and . . . the shout of shots and a new mating.

"Pain! Ecstasy!"

The house lights rise. The applause is moderate.

And then this.

Psyaint David

The impulse to do,
"Jugie! Indeed, "Sam says. "No angels here. No one borne to heaven on eagles wings. And despite the magnificence of their pretense, locked as they are, one to the other, they continue to toil without relief."
The stage is painted with a redshift — distant, and dull, and silent. Sam pulls a cigarette from the air.

however, there's still time
for a bit of mischief

At street level the skirmish-line shifts to 228-232 West 42nd Street (in the commercial sex district) where Sam orchestrates a coup d'état to re-install the owners of the defunct Crossroads (Adult) Bookstore. The building, next door to the Amsterdam Theater, is the former home of Hubert's Dime Museum (1925-1969) and Professor Heckler's Flea Circus (in the basement) with real fleas attached to very thin wires racing miniature chariots on a teeny, tiny track.
One of Hubert's sideshows features the bearded lady (Jane Barnell) known variously as Princess Olda, Madame Olga or Lady Olga Roderick, who claims to be the half-sister of a French duke and to be from a castle in Potsdam (not Ohio) Germany, though she is from South Carolina. When not out on a circus tour, Olga is often in residence at Hubert's with Susie the Elephant Skin Girl, sword swallower Lady Estelline, Princess Sahloo a voodoo jungle snake dancer, Prince Randion a human caterpillar, Zip the Pinhead, and street preacher James Jefferson Davis Hall, who believes god has given him the ability to read between the lines of the Bible and so goes through the streets day and night announcing damnation and ruin. A time or two over the years, sponsored by Our Lady of Adventurous Avaritia, the Serbian Gypsy Volga Adams (Mary Miller) a fortune teller who scams vulnerable women out of money in what she called *hokkano baro* — the big trick — often appears among the aberrations at Hubert's.
When Hubert's closes the building morphs into an aviary for "Chicken Hawks," and is eventually ceded to Crossroads. Several months before, after a two-year fight to evict Crossroads, the police open a traveler's information center on the premises.
In opening the info center streetwise Mayor Beame takes to the sidewalk and, in another beaming manifesto, announces to an audience of amused drug-pushers, passersby, and prostitutes, amid their daily chores and scores that "The City's grimiest is to be replaced by The City's finest.
"Let's not stop until the 'street of dreams' blossoms again," Beame says.
But today the police are relocated, by court order — something about forging a lease and fixing parking tickets — and the bookstore is again in business.
A little farther into the dream, the same day, Battan, Burton, Dewstine

and Osborn advertising of Madison Avenue release their "Report on Daytime Network Television 1977."

After thirty years soap operas are the prime daytime network television fare. The woes of unrequited love, infidelity, abortion, divorce, rape, drug addiction, and other stumbling blocks on the road to the good life, account for 52 percent of network teevee from 10:00 to 4:30.

It's a long way up from 1947 and *A Woman to Remember.* The long years of tedium in the trivia of personal intrigue have brought thirty-second ad slots into the fifteen to thirty thousand dollar range.

"Why not?" Paley says. "This is the best of the best."

He points to another report that Kenner Products division of General Mills has decided to get their cut of the Barbie Doll action. Prodded by research that claims at twenty-years-of-age Barbie has a grander life style than most American females, and has done better than Love, Peace, and Soul, and Leggy, Kenner plans to bring out Charlie's Angels dolls.

The PR people are concerned, however, that a program airing at 10:00 will not reach the prime audience of girls from four-to-ten-years-of-age, and Our Lady of Cunny Collusion is called in as consultant — what to do?

"It's easy to see," she says without seeing. "If you can't change the product, the schedule, then change the audience. Start a campaign for girls from four to ten as little ladies of the night. If you're going to sell flesh, then sell it. Don't pussy around. How about Campfire Hookers or Strumpet Scouts? Sponsor a national beauty contest and have regional winners appear on *Charley's Angels* with an opportunity to join Flesh Peddlers International and make some real money off their pre-pregnable bodies. Hire mothers as advisors. They will be more than happy to help. They know what sells. When it comes to cold hard cash (and a promise of fame) mothers have never been hesitant to sell their daughters."

In another corner of the B's and C's the series *Soap* is readied for airtime. Echoing Our Lady's wise and not too whimsical counsel the first episode features a tennis pro who provides sexual services for a mother and her daughter, a black servant who becomes a clearing house for racial slurs, and a homosexual youth who is partial to wearing his adoring mother's clothes.

Sam, and others, prepare
for The Dog Days of Darkness

Still, all is well with the big Turmanga.

John Carrey reports in *The Times* that "By any objective standard we are going kaput, which means down the drain, and out the tube, and into terminal discomfort. Even the Department of Sanitation is saying that some of our streets are filthy, while the Fire Department freely admits that it must be so judicious in answering alarms that some of the alarms don't get answered at all. The taxis no longer have springs and come 8:00 the storekeepers along Madison and Lexington Avenues bolt the doors, drop the grates, and get the hell home before the Huns swarm in under the cover of darkness.

"However, as The City's children we are accustomed to disasters, neither welcoming nor condoning, but instead just accepting them. We are acclimated to horror."

Well, what else? The Dog Days have long been noted for excessive heat, the boiling of the seas — wine souring and mad dogs — not to mention fevers, the phrensies of hysteria.

Beneath the grates and locks of evening, WNBC-TV unveils *Coast To Coast*, an electronic compendium of short essays built on the blurb concept. Twenty-two minutes of air time are stuffed with trendy non-features followed by the *Coast to Coast Players,* introducing a woman surgeon, Areola Benaticto, who specializes in castrating men (for ontological clarification) and in her spare time, operates a clinic dedicated to aborting male fetuses. She also speaks Hindi, has a working knowledge of the Son of Sam reviews, and is determined to balance the ledger.

"You never know when aborting a male fetus will eliminate a serial killer," she says.

and Sam?
well, Sam's . . .

And Sam?

Well, Sam's wallowing in perennial discomfort, lying in wait, preparing for Con Ed's midsummer Dog Days of Darkness. Orion's hunters, in a yearly celebration set up in opposition to and as a denial of the directive "Let there be light," will demonstrate what it is, indeed, that modern technology can offer.

By 9:20, the evening of Wednesday, July 13th, all appears ready and Mayor Beame dials up Con-Ed President Seymour Lusk to officially begin the celebration. In the past Beame has been reluctant to credit Con Ed for its part in the festivities. Complaints from the mayor's office claim that in 1965 Con Ed breached its contract with the boroughs by restoring service in record time.

"If the residents of The City are to discover the true nature of our mission," Beame says, "then the management of Con Ed must honor its contractual obligations and remain shut down during the Dog Days."

This year Con-Ed's massive generator, Big Allis, is designated as the fail-fail contrivance. Located on the shore of the East River in Queens on Vernon Boulevard, in a neighborhood known as Ravenswood in Long Island City, to set the celebration in motion, at a prescribed time, Big A's tortured windings will knot up in convulsive spasms, dropping nine million into the abyss of the solemn night of Maniacal Mayhem. As it is, Sam's star glows with temperatures in the high nineties. He wraps his fingers around Big Allis' windings, prepared, at a moment's notice, to squeeze.

Yet it goes deeper. It's a matter of convenience, a means to an obvious end. No Luddite, Sam often socializes self-indulgence. And most of the world accepts one of his best kept secrets. Only a few live better than the deprived, and many more suffer. Sam isn't apologetic. Indeed. Things are just the way they are supposed to be and at 9:36 Beame gives the word. Sam squeezes, the lights go out, and the Dog Days of Darkness descend upon The City.

As usual, opening activities are sluggish. The hours before midnight are reserved for adaptation and perpetration, though reports of muggings, pocketbook snatchings, petnapping, and break-ins do tickle police precinct phone lines.

The adage holds that if you are pissed at someone, viciously so, or even just a little bit, and have not had the guts to do anything about it in the bright light of day, this is, indeed, the time for reckoning.

Patrol cars, crawling along the streets, are pummeled with bricks and bottles, and an occasional round of small caliber gunfire.

Sometime around 10:30, Sam decides to enliven the mix. He opens the gates at Rikers and a dozen inmates escape — under the cover of darkness.

An hour later, however, the celebration takes on new dimensions. Certain by then that the Stygian haze is for real, crowds gather and systematically and strategically lay siege to store fronts in a potlatch of removing merchandise from shops that three hundred sixty-three days a year practice the good and approved business of extracting usury rates from customers for shoddy products.

Early in the celebration Brooklyn mom, Angelina Modiscci, of 56-21 Orlando Street, plugs in the family's newly acquired air conditioner and gets nothing but hot air blowing in from the darkened street. She pushes the unit out the window and, as it clatters to the sidewalk two floors below, yells at her son to get out and come back with functioning merchandise next time.

Otherwise, gunfire crackles in the neighborhoods. The police report they are taking sniper fire. A desk officer at the 24th Precinct on Manhattan's West Side, confirms that "Quite a few shots are being fired around the West Side."

At 138th Street, between Brook and Cypress Avenues in the South Bronx, police try to clear looters from stores and are assaulted with sticks and stones. The boys-in-blue eventually close the street to traffic and rout the vandals.

Otherwise, the police go lightly on celebrants and merry-makers. They are outmanned, seriously, and aware that there are a proportionately absurd number of hand guns floating around The City. It is in no one's interest to have an O. K. Corral over a cheap (possibly non-functional) air-conditioner or a rack of not-so-fashionable threads.

Then, too, there is no way of identifying fellow card-carrying members of SoSaMy Inc. The Galante, Garfield, Sam Inella merger has truly shuffled the deck.

An hour later, to show that the police really care, Commissioner Garfield issues a clarion, ritualistic call for ten thousand off-duty police officers who are not sick or on leave to return to duty. And following the dictates of festival custom, the officers refuse to heed the call. Of course many of them are already on the street, celebrating.

"Turnabout is fair play," says Sam Inella, somewhat whimsically. "In the old days, somewhere about the beginning, when police power was first placed in public hands, off-duty officers were in the habit of responding to emergencies. That was when citizens still believed in the police and believed that using force was an acceptable and viable way to celebrate the Days of Darkness, and encourage 'Let there be light.' But all the good times are past and gone. Police salaries in the last years have sagged under the weight of the Consumer Price Index. Extra duty unfairly penalizes the underpaid officers, who need their fair share of the loot just to make ends meet — though certainly not meat. Many officers work private security jobs. Since the Police Benevolent Association formed, officers refuse the call to extra duty. It is a matter of duty or booty.

"But they're still in the spirit of the celebration," Inella says. "This is a midsummer Saturnalia, except what's that got to do with servant and master? It's economic. Our way of putting overpriced mostly worthless stock into circulation with a minimum of overhead, formality, and red tape."

A woman in her fifties, carrying shopping bags, steps through a smashed storefront and while filling her bags, echoes Inella's words.

"Shopping with no money, no money required," she says with a smirk.

By midnight the celebration has escalated. Sam guides a battalion of five hundred teens and preteen disciples along Fulton Street in Brooklyn taking down doors and smashing windows of stores. At each as yet unmolested store they pause for a moment chanting, "Let's do it! Let's do it! Let's do it!" Then someone throws a brick through the window and the youths swarm in locust-like, knocking out the remaining glass, and picking the shelves and storeroom clean.

At 2:00 Mayor Beame proclaims the "Hour of Self-help," officially opened, a festival special scheduled at Ace Pontiac Showroom, 1921 Jerome Avenue in the University section of the Bronx. Carl Newfield, the owner, who cannot help himself, watches as a steel door and showroom window are smashed and twenty new automobiles valued at two hundred-fifty thousand dollars taillight-off into the night to be disassembled for parts and sold to further fund disadvantaged youth.

"Easy" Ed Mathewson of 9791 W. Conley Street in the Bronx commandeers a new red and white Chevrolet C10 Silverado from the showcase of
Lordurso Chevrolet and drives three blocks through the mayhem to the
Claradon Furniture store. He knocks out the front window, drags a 72"
Black Chesterfield 3 Seated Leather Buttoned Back sofa to the street and
attempts to load it into his new truck. A passerby pauses to watch Ed at
work. The couch is bulky and heavy, and difficult to handle. Ed solicits the
stranger's aid. The man declines. After several attempts, Ed succeeds in
loading the couch and prepares to leave. The stranger takes a Smith &
Wesson 19 2.5 from his back pocket, levels Ed with two shots, lifts the keys
from "Easy Come, Easy Go" Ed's hand and drives away.

In an attempt to discourage the gods of the nighttime-noon hundreds of
ceremonial blazes are set. Dutifully sounding the call to arms against the
fire gods (the breath of Hephaestus — the reason Prometheus gave man
fire) twenty-two thousand, four hundred twenty-two alarms are turned in
to report nine hundred fires. For the next hours the clang and wail of the
Anti-pyro Association rattles unremittingly through the streets.

"The primary reason for the rush to the firebox," anthropologist Herman
Klinkowitz of Queens College explains, "is that people have historically
while reacting to the gods of the palpably obscure suddenly become
frightened that the fires they set could possibly engulf the world.
Something like J. Robert Oppenheimer's trepidation that the first nuclear
explosion might set off a chain-reaction in the atmosphere and blow up the
entire planet. So as soon as the ceremonial flames flare, a call goes out to
the rain god, in this case represented by TCFD in black boots and helmets
and black and yellow fire-retardant suits, to quench the flames. It is sort of
a shock reaction to the magnificent burst of light breaking the hold of
tenebrosity on the heart of mankind."

Already a major ceremonial blaze has taken life at Stone Avenue and
Somers Street in the Ocean Hill section of Brooklyn. A sprite touches
(torches?) a looted factory warehouse and within an hour the fire leaps the
street and destroys four tenements, before spreading to two houses
behind the warehouse. Twenty-five-year-old Andrea Kentowski of 105
Somers and her three children, Mark (5), Diana (4), and Rosemary (2) are
cremated in their pajamas. Two of their three cats, a Sphynx named Spinks
and an Abyssinian named Ramses are also fried in the conflagration. A
third feline, a Silver Tabby named Sylvester escapes through a bedroom
window with a couple of patches of singed hair and his tail blazing like a
blowtorch.

"It was the hand of god on the switch," Con Ed reports in a ritualistic
denial, meant to fool no one, but necessary all the same.

God was messing with Big Allis. Sam's eyes sparkle.

"Big Allis, the biggest generator in our system shut down. These things
are beyond human control. This is Providence. Part of god's plan."

The following two days, three thousand three hundred looters and celebrants are arrested and The City reopens the Tombs prison in Manhattan.

"They couldn't understand why we were arresting them," officer Gary Parlefsky says. "They were angry with us. They said 'I'm on welfare (echoing Wall Street). I'm taking what I need (echoing Wall Street). What are you bothering us for (echoing Wall Street)? What is this, government regulations (echoing Wall Street)?'"

Deride Carmody reports in *The Times,* for all the world to believe, that "It's The City's real badge of pride — not the little red apple lapel pins — that whatever else can be said about them, one truth is undeniable: our residents know how to cope when trouble strikes."

City Council President Paul O'Dwyer admits that, "I don't know what caused this, but I can tell you I have it from a source very high up that god had nothing to do with it."

Of course, the streets are rife with cries and accusations.

"Infidel! Heretic!"

"But if not, who then?" says the Mayor. "God? Well, my name may be Abraham, but before . . .."

Complaining of the lack of police gunfire (though there was some) during the night, the following morning the *Post* chides Garfield's ". . . absurd order to go slowly . . . as the mobs ran wild."

Two days later the fête grinds to an exhausted somewhat extinguished finish — with a few smoking embers. The sun also rises on the third morning — Sirius appears a bit later — and Con Ed puts a binding on Big Allis' buns while the celebration cools. Still, the soot of anxiety drifts over the streets, and a cynocephalic figure at the end of Hull Street sits on a pile of smoldering debris watching — watching.

In the ensuing cleanup, behind a sporting-goods store on Broadway, among the mutilated pale and brown arms and legs and heads of mannequins, a rookie cop discovers a cardboard cutout of Garfield with three small bullet holes behind the left ear.

A *Times'* sports writer wonders, "Czarmine? Where were you last night?"

Of course, he has an alibi.

but back to the hunt

It has been twenty-one days since Son of Sam fired four shots to wound his tenth and eleventh victims, and on this particular evening six teams of detectives are dispatched to the search. They'll continue to scour the neighborhoods while the one who could help them, the one who has seen his face and could provide an accurate description of mortality's grim bearing, the great and honorable Kojak, rants and raves amid the storm-blown fury of terminal madness in a security cell at Kings. Is this tragedy? Probably not. But who is the killer, anyway? And why?

"Everyone knows someone who matches the composite," O-Mega stalwart Detective Sgt. Edward Dahler says. "The problem is the different composites since last March. But you've got to check out each lead, each clue. You'd hate to let the right one pass you by."

At 8:30 detective Gerald Shevlin and Frank Pergola take to the street in their white, late model unmarked used car to check on leads that have come in during the day. Tonight it's job number 1007.

"Last night," Shevlin says, "we rush over to the 108th Precinct because we heard some guy had shot his wife. He put fourteen rounds into her. It was an incredible sight, but it wasn't Sam. His name was Orin Grovier. Maybe Sam was on the scene. I mean, we couldn't say for sure. But we didn't get him."

"Tonight, who knows what we got?" Pergola says. "You can only hope that in this maze of job sheets you can find something to work on, something or someone who heard something or who knows something. So far we haven't been too lucky."

"But tonight," Shevlin adds. "Frankie, maybe we'll get lucky. It's so frustrating after all these months. When I go home, I can't sleep. I'm still chasing Sam. I dream of him. I'd give thirty days' pay to get him tonight. I hope our luck is running."

Sam picks his ass. Fat chance. He's hunkered down at the end of the hall. The detectives come up the stairs and knock on the door of apartment 7E. Shevlin holds out his badge and Pergola steps into the background while a voice from behind the door shouts, "Coming."

Then a long pause, a quiet moment, after the door opens, with Shevlin and Pergola pondering whether the man in mid-twenties standing in dungaree shorts in the doorway is the Son of Sam.

"We got an anonymous tip that you fit the .44 killer's profile," Shevlin says. "Mind if we come in?"

"Sure."

The man, Richard Kowaler, turns and the detectives follow him into the narrow living room. The Met's game is on television and the man turns off the sound but leaves the picture on.

Shevlin's voice is soft, almost apologetic. He talks with his arms folded in front of him. Pergola takes notes. Neither of them notices the eyes watching from the bedroom door.

"Saturday, June twenty-six, were you with anyone?"

"Yes," Kowaler says, thinking back, his eyes focused on his feet.

"Would it be too much of an inconvenience if we checked with this person?"

Richard shakes his head, meaning "yes," and then pauses to consider.

"Yeah, there's a woman you can check with. She was here until 3:00.

Only trouble is she drinks a lot and she was drunk that night, so she might not remember anything. I mean, she's blind too. Wears a blindfold all the time. Had a Black Rose one on that night. She has hallucinations. Claims to see things. No telling what she might say. She goes around sometimes with a large Grey Wolf.

"Okay," the man says, "I know why you're here. It was my wife who told you I'm the .44 killer. You see, we're getting a divorce."

"Do you think she'd really say that about you?"

"She does a lot of crazy things. I got a week's vacation once and first day I was away from the office she sent a letter of resignation to my boss. Another time she had my furniture moved to a vacant lot."

"Well, do us one last favor," Shevlin says. "Would you write out the alphabet and the numbers one to ten for us?"

In the car Shevlin tells Pergola, "When I meet Son of Sam, I'll know right away. When I walk into a room and Sam's there, I'll know. How will I know? Right away my gut will tell me. I'll know it in the gut."

a brief return to Papa Fatorium

Sam burps a blue vapor, a sour taste, and settles in for the night, Channel 4 and *The Hunchback of Notre Dame*. Our Lady of the Grand Garter approves. And, yes, she does have a Black Rose Blindfold — though it is not clear, if she was there, or why she would be in Richard Kowaler's 7E apartment that night.

Anyway, tonight's a bash of fond memories in the ebb and flow, the festering fissures of Hugo's old Paris.

"The early eighteen-forties," she absentmindedly reminds Sam.

It's a media rerun. A wistful wisp clouds Sam's eyes — a heyday among the corrupt and brutal politics of torture and dismemberment, consorting with a clergy openly pursuing their vices. Dinner and fine wine with the Cardinal (played by Terrance Boyle, who bears a pleasing resemblance to Fulton J. Sheen) entertaining himself by pawing young female prostitutes or popping sweets into the innocent mouths of even younger boys.

A prepared for teevee saga of the "Feast of Fools" with Quasimodo the "Pope of Fools" crowned by the gypsy girl Esmerelda who has been for convenience married off to Pierre the poet — the virgin girl coveted by the archdeacon, loved by Quasimodo, and scorned by the ambitious Captain Theobus, the one man she wants. Sam's eyes are bright, an amber glint of delight, possibility, a melodrama of misplaced emotions crushed beneath the weight and madness of the Fates and Fortūna.

At 10:00 a news special carries a detailed tale of Father Senam Mentiri of St. Benedict the Moor Catholic Church on West 53rd Street. The good Father is under investigation (reluctantly) by the Archdiocese for using the confessional to supplement the insufficiency of his vows by locating available women (Bless me Father for I have sinned . . .) and to blackmail burglars and pickpockets, with little hope of reducing their deviant habits and bringing them to their knees for Christ. It appears Friar Mentiri, a native of Ghana, has quite skillfully translated the spoken word and images of repentance into penitential sexual pastimes for his bed and a bit of sharking (sharing of dollars for Christ) for his pockets.

The investigation seeks to uncover how much (possibly) the good father withheld for his own use and to determine how the Archdiocese might detect and therefore avoid future skimming.

When located for a statement, Father Mentiri is in the church courtyard at sundown pouring alcoholic libations on the ground to energize his ancestors, while sticking pins in a voodoo doll of the Archbishop.

Then at midnight, in what supposed to be the quiet of night, pudgy Oswald Cobblepot of 7410 Ridge Blvd in Brooklyn skulks into Central Park in a tux, carrying a net disguised as an umbrella and two five-gallon buckets of sodium cyanide solution (NaCN). He is followed by a large black Lab, trotting along aimlessly, or so it seems, pausing now and then to pee on trees. As the credits run the lab pauses at a bench with two lovers embracing (who do not see him), lifts his leg and pisses on the girl's foot. She gives off a muffled scream and the dog trots away.

Oswald is no longer satisfied with poisoning pigeons in the park, a practice he twice served time for, but this night intends to kill off a bucket or two of fish in Central Park Pond to supplement his diet. Why NaCN? Well it is quieter than dynamite and attracts a lot less attention.

It appears, however, that Oswald is mostly on his own in the venture, that Sam has not gotten wind of the little man's intentions, or really doesn't care, assuming that whatever gets done will be icing on the cake.

The dog has no connection, physically, spiritually or metaphorically to Sam. At least not tonight. It's just a large black, warm-hearted, happy-go-lucky pooch Oswald brought along to retrieve dead and stunned fish.

However, as nonchalant and unobtrusive as the activity may be, all is not well with Cobblepot's enterprise. As he is about to empty the buckets into the Pond, two Emergency Officers step out of the bushes and take him by the arms. In the ensuing ruffle Oswald tries to throw the buckets and umbrella into the Pond, then claims he was framed and threatens to file a complaint with the police commission and take the officers to court.

When informed that while cyanide fishing works in salt water, it does not work as well in freshwater, Oswald says, "You're shitting me. This isn't fresh water."

Of course, among the important and knowable things Oswald doesn't know, he does know he needs food.

When pressed, he admits he's not a "mumbler" but confesses to several months of pigeon poaching in the park, a pedestrian land-based version of pirate-fishing. With a collapsible (for convenient transport) rod and reel concealed in the handle of his umbrella, and a small sack of crushed corn Oswald collects pigeons. He drops a small pile of corn in the middle of the walk, then retreats ten feet or so. When the pigeons gather to war over the corn, Oswald casts into the cluster, hooks one, and reels in the flapping bird.

Occasionally the practice brings him into conflict with pigeon owners and trainers whose bird or birds happen to be in the park and stop for a bit of Oswald's corn and get the hook.

Over the months, however, the feral pigeons wise up and boycott Oswald's offerings. He has no choice but to turn to fishing. This is unfortunate. He alleges to have thirty-three recipes for pigeon soup.

"I'm hungry," Oswald tells the arresting officers. "Since I lost the store with all my birds, I am always hungry. And this shit-hole called The City never provides enough food for us.

"If I'd known cops were waiting for me in the brush, I would never have done this," Oswald whines. "I been framed."

another of Pastel's wagers

But time is short. It is only a matter of weeks until the last hot days of July and the anniversary of the first (or what TCPD claim to be the first) Son of Sam shooting. Our Lady of Gleeful Gula is despondent, restless, feeling dismal and ephemeral. Her battle with SoSaMy Inc and CBS has intensified. The powers in question ignored the court order and moved ahead with a plan to market Son of Sam metaphors and illusions. Kojak's incarceration has cluttered the path to a speedy settlement and Our Lady of Seismic Sexual Sensations has been toying with the possibility of springing the honorable detective from the loony bin.

"Vengeance is mine," sayeth the woman, as she sorts through the historical occasions of Star Chamber "trilemma" for a particularly pertinent precedent.

"Old hat," she tells Sam, holding her finger on the page, chapter and verse of a case in point. "Water under the bridge."

She has her feelers out monitoring the schism at SoSaMy Inc. She's been watching Sam, his penchant for brutality — thinks she might incorporate a bit of his shtick into her scheme. She invites Father Pastel to lunch and a carafe of wine.

Of course, Pastel is pleased with her attention, sees a chance for a hostile takeover — knows Garfield's been badly damaged, admits he's been ill-at-ease working with cops.

"It's not that I don't like 'em," he tells her majesty, "some of my best friends are cops. They make good neighbors (most of the time), keep the block safe, keep the trash out."

He smiles.

"They make loyal pets. But the wolf should not lie down with sheep. Let sheep find somebody else to lie with."

"I want to spring Kojak," she tells Pastel. "He understands what good means. We need him."

"What would you like? An execution squad? Take hostages, cut off the arms and legs, gouge out a few eyes? You know, dig 'em out with pocket knives. We can smuggle him out in a garbage can, a piece at a time. Create a new history, an alias."

Our Lady of the Bouncing Buns waves him off with a well-polished hand of fingernails, sniffles at his trifles.

"Heavy handed," she says, reconsidering. "You're no help at all. Mayhem is a waste. Give me a few hours. Belt buckles will jingle, doors will open."

That afternoon at a sparsely attended press conference she announces an agreement for Kojak's release. Speaking in a prepared voice and referring only obliquely to Son of Sam, after confirming her sole ownership of the Kojak image (she has become the darling detective's guardian) she tells the reporters she is no longer working for Keener and SoSaMy Inc.

"Still," she says, "I support liberty and justice. I mean, liberty and justice for all."

Okay. SoSaMy Inc has agreed, tentatively, in principle, since principles are always tentative and open to interpretation, to cease and desist from further commercial exploitation of the Son of Sam image without the express consent of The Universe and other parties directly involved.

The Lieutenant, slumped at Our Lady's side, babbles excitedly, his baldhead aglow, glazed eyes wide, a froth on his lips. When she finishes two attendants lead the Lou back to his padded cell. She thought for a moment of installing him in a bedroom in her apartment with Lupanar, but then decided against it. The wolf has a decided dislike for men. So she will keep Fabulous Fosdick in the psych ward for the time being.

So what is freedom if you are free to go but have nowhere to go?

When he hears the news, Garfield sees sacks of dollars falling into the river.

"I shouldn't have trusted that firkin skank," he says. "Who hired her, anyway?"

"You did," someone says.

"Well, goddammit fire her."

"She already quit."

"Well, shit. It's obvious," he tells his financial consultants, "if I sell my SoSaMy Inc stock, I'll lose my ass."

"It's obvious," they tell him, "if you don't, you'll lose your balls."

When they tell him about the cardboard cut-out with the mosquito bites behind the ear — Malaria, Dengue Fever, Yellow Fever, West Nile Virus, Encephalitis — he can only say, "What the fuck? Where was Pastel last night?"

Psyaint David

a good report
for
The City of the Gods

Sam is circumspect. The pulse and beat, once again the vital signs of The City, wobble into balance. Even when nature (human nature) appears to be tumbling toward extinction, Dicé and Eunomia have a way of restoring order.

Monday morning, echoing Sam's discontent, Jonathon Freedman, professor of social psychology at Columbia comes forward to bear witness and report that cities are not harmful to human health.

On cue Sam appears above the footlights.

"These worlds revolve slowly but the cycle is nearly complete," Sam tells us. "One day Kojak will again roam the streets attempting to purge madness, to convince himself that he, too, is honest, a proper man, despite the evidence and indications that, in his madness to preserve his tough cop reputation, he is a killer.

"And caught in the revolving doors of thou shalt not, the deed of wrong done and punishment and profit, the killer prepares for another sortie."

Or so Sam says. But here it is a time to make an end, bend the last month to its knees in a fashion of contempt and intrigue on the anniversary of a year of terror.

"What will you have for July twenty-ninth?" Das Wunderkind says.

"It's the ultimate test," detective William Martin claims.

"Sam holds the aces. We're sending out hundreds of men to comb The City, daring Sam to strike."

And then. And then.

"Nothing, again tonight," Keener says.

He misses the lady with the blindfold.

Through the evening, pairs of policemen pour out of the 109th to begin the search. The officers come from all the boroughs. Some are assigned and others volunteer, work their off-duty hours without pay to participate in one of the biggest manhunts in The City's history. After all, the atmosphere is festive, the hunt joyous, what most of the detectives have waited for, worked for, all their lives.

"This is something to tell our grandchildren," officer Pat Wilkins says. "Years from now someone'll say 'Do you remember . . .' and we'll be able to say 'I was out on the street that night.' It's better than the World Series. Yeah. Better than New Year's."

"It's important to get this guy — that's why I'm here on my own after putting in a full day," explains Sgt. Andrew Rosenzweig of the Manhattan District Attorney's office. He arrives at Flushing command headquarters with ten of his men, without saying anything about his wife being seriously pissed at his drinking and his penchant for not coming home at night, anyway. Truthfully, he's more interested in hunting deranged killers than he is in listening to her harping.

All hunters are given a rundown, a description of Sam (from the composites) and a warning — one of the certainties in the case — that the perp is armed and dangerous.

Disappointed with Our Lady's abdication, in his hour of grief, looking for solace, and something to do, McNeil calls the theatrical agents on his "to-do" list and notifies them that the clairvoyant position with O-Mega is now open.

And The City responds.

The following morning by 6:00 the phones at the 83rd are ringing. An hour later a host of mainstream paranormal peculiars crowd the hallways and McNeil crowds them — twenty or so — into a second floor conference room until the morning shift is on the street. Six Extra Sensory Perception wizards, four Astrologers, two Spiritualists, four Magicians (one claims he will "Pull Son of Sam out of a hat as if he were a rabbit"), one Numerologist, an Alchemist, and a Niggám master from Cameroon (who claims to be two people), sign the visitors register.

As expected, they carry a variety of theories and visual devices through which to locate the predator. There are zoetropes and thaumatropes (The Wheel of the Devil — The Wheel of Fortune) and kineographs.

One candidate huddles in the corner, absorbed in divinations, flipping her flipbook with the dexterity of a Vegas dealer. When asked how she thinks she can help, she claims her book contains all the known illustrations of the wraith, to date. She explains that the many different sketches (police and others) are the manifestations of the psychic perceptions the world has of the slayer. Melted together, that is, flipped together, they will contain the Truth, the true image. She sounds like an Oklahoma preacher, and it's her particular brand of Truth she's got in mind — the Truth, the whole Truth and nothing but the Truth, as she foresees it.

"I'll need a few days," she tells Keener, "to get the truth etched in my mind — and then I will know who you're looking for. I'll have the killer by the scruff."

She hesitates.

"Is that worth anything to you?"

"Is that the truth?" Keener says.

It appears to the Captain that at the moment it's the best story available. Yesterday it was another story — a tall tale — tomorrow it will be still another. But today it is the best available — and that, too, is the truth.

On the other side of the room the numerologist is counting his fingers, trying to get to ten. He's made it to seven, twice. Chances are, though, he won't make past eight.

Keener wonders if he is the only loony in the house. The case is driving him crazy. Already he has taken a psychic to the sites to see if . . ., or maybe?

Psyaint David

and of all things
Sam speaks of love

   Sam curls his lip, turns his back to the audience, takes a long beat, waves a hand in the purple haze, a now you see it now you don't Mandrake, Harry Houdini of camera angles and haze out of the bottle, Aladdin's Lamp, a young woman in a blue chemise standing head bowed, hands clasped.
   "Ah, ha," Sam says, "victim-lover."
   He chuckles.
   "And what are your desires? What fate assign this lovely creature?"
   He blows a puff of smoke into the crimson air out over the footlights.
   "And what will Our Lady of the Gyrating G-spot say? What complaint offer? To this dream? This apparition. Cagliari's Cesare?
   "Begot in love?" Sam says. "Or was the spark kindled in a predatory coupling? In the stinging pleasure of conquest, the demon's harpoon striking into the nest of a Dietrich Lola Lola to be pleased only by a maddened magic conjugation of taunt and tease and no-touch thin fingers on the nerves — the froth and fury of a flesh-splitting explosion?"

however, things are not
**   the same**
with the inspector

   Inspector LoKo whistles away the evening, lodged in the barred cave of his Kings' fifth floor office headquarters, his war room, from which he will deploy his imaginary troops. He plots the movement, shifts Lego units about on a large map, and monitors reports from a special police radio frequency assigned to the 0-Mega force.
   Occasionally he turns to Kojak and they stare at each other, their eyes deep mirrors, pools, reflecting the void.
   "You've been here before," he tells Kojak.
   "I've been here before," Kojak repeats in a dead staccato, nodding, his head bobbing mechanically. "I have been here before."
   His face is white, tense, a tremor on his lip.
   Throughout the evening, into the post-midnight hours he holds to his senses, keeps his wits, remains neatly dressed in a blue cord suit from Telly Apparel, his tie tightly and neatly knotted in place.

> With a bald spot in the middle of my hair —
> (They will say: "How his hair is growing thin!")
> My morning coat, my collar mounting firmly to the chin,
> My necktie rich and modest, but asserted by a simple pin —
> (They will say: "But how his arms and legs are thin!")
>   (Eliot)

The long hours are sometimes disrupted by radio reports.

12:08. "Shots fired at Queens Boulevard and 102nd Street."

"Who's got that sector?"

"Nothing here, Inspector. A couple of dogs nosing around in the street. One's got his nose poked in a brown paper bag."

12:17. "Shots fired at 126th Street and 95th Avenue."

"They're both workable locations," the inspector says in a calm tone. "The kind of neighborhood Sam might choose.

"We've done crime-profile-analysis of The City. With only one percent of the crimes on any one night reported we can tell where the next homicide is likely to take place. Once we had a homicidal cluster-fuck — twenty-two dead in a three block area. Maybe . . ., I don't know, a gang war? A couple casualties by arson. It was too close to call."

His eyes droop.

"Each of those nights Sam struck."

The inspector's eyes water with fond remembrance.

"It's times like that that you know you're needed. People running through the streets in panic, needing help, calling for the police."

He pauses.

"That's us. We're the police."

Kojak grunts, nudged by a weak impulse. He tries to stand, excited, wavering, pointing at the screen of his cell's (555) in-house set.

"That's him," Kojak mumbles. "I'd know him anywhere. I saw his picture on the corkboard at the station"

The picture flips, clears to a smiling face with blue eyes. Officer William Connally checks the set.

"That's not Sam. That's the Police Commissioner, Michael J. Garfield."

Kojak staggers, drops to his chair. "Oh. I thought . . . .. You see . . .."

it would be just like Sam to do this

It is a night of unconfirmed reports. A man waiting for half-an-hour in front of the 9th or 11th Precinct is apprehended, spread-eagled, and searched by a suspicious cop. He's carrying a concealed bus token and six dollars, a checkbook (legal), a ring of keys (legal), a pair of glasses, (without which he is legally blind), an extra pair of shoe strings (extra-legal), an uncertified quantity of an uncontrolled substance referred to as aspirin (Bayer or possibly St. Joseph — though it is in a bottle and in his pocket) and other small assorted but unspecified suspicious and possibly dangerous objects.

"Still, it could have been Sam. It would have been just like him to come right to our front door," a detective insists. "I know Sam. He is an arrogant, vicious, nasty person who enjoys making fun of people. He is spiteful and mean and very unkind. In fact, he used to come visit my mother-in-law. I got to know him pretty good.

"Yeah, I been to hell a couple of times."

As part of the hunt, the ritual, that night a patron of Willie Brown Hat Bar, 89-02 37th Avenue, Queens, is beaten and turned over to the police by an assailant who describes himself as a "cop's son" and his victim as Son of Sam or as someone "fucking just like Son of Sam."

Slowly, the word has gotten out. Precinct phones jingle. Calls buzz in from California, New Mexico. Callers want to talk to Son of Sam. Dozens lay claim to the name, confess that they are Son of Sam, leave their press agent's number with LoKoJakMan.

Our Lady of the Word and Image
appears at center stage

Indeed, indeed, Our Lady of Vibrator Vacuity taps her fingers, reading The City's tea leaves and pulse. Hanging her well-endowed frame with the latest summer fashions, she's mindful that at all times she wants to remain feminine, though not frilly, simplified, as clean and fresh as a newly laundered hankie. She is, today, pure white, or off-white or a dipped-in-tea beige, embellished a bit with the kind of detail found on heirloom linen: scallops, fagating, embroidery, drawnwork, tucking or narrow edging of crocheted lace. The time has come, she thinks, and declares, in a manifesto of one that she is prepared to advance, scepter and crown.

"My subjects are waiting. My Cuntry Queenydom is at hand and you are my Prince Charming," she tells David.

"Are you sure?" he tells her. "I have other things to do."

"You have no plans," she says. "Nothing beyond your rather twisted, hostile psychology."

"I'm anonymous."

Our Lady of Prurient Pursuits lifts her skirt a bit.

"So you are," she says with amusement. "You are a mythic creature. In another week or two you'll not only be anonymous, but once again condemned to the underworld searching for another identity."

To keep her word, that night she preempts the B & Cs' prime time slots insinuating her persona into a new Star-of-Jerusalem beam of glowing carnal delight.

Are you ready for this?

"And now, from The City of the Gods, in her finest appearance on national television, the lovely grand dame of fortune and fame, in her majestic role as First Lady of the Empire, Our Lady of the Fabricated Flesh."

Trumpets flare (although it may be blare, flaire, glare, despair of prayer — depending on the poet), the curtain parts, and lights flash. The cameras zoom in on the pale nude form of a woman draped over a Roman accubita. Tonight she is brooding, querulous, the cool soiled flag of manifest destiny and avarice painting her smile, her arms wrapped softly about the neck of her pet, Lupanar.

Viewers in Newark, Des Moines and Modesto are amazed, hypnotized, eyes wide with appreciation. Hefner in Chicago calls downstairs to check on unused photos in the archives. *Hustler, Penthouse, Oui, Time, Forbes* dispatch emissaries armed with lush contracts.

And there's more.

Slowly she rises, more slowly she turns and silhouetted on the backdrop of a cool Moon Illusion backdrop, prepares to speak. A heavy dumb-numb silence speeds westward onto the rivers and farms, over the salt flats and blackjack tables, into the mountains and on to the sea.

"The west must be won again," she says.

With something akin to panic the C's & B's correspondents are summoned and assembled. Following the broadcast they will materialize in froth and fumes to attempt to salvage something of the day with an in-depth analysis of the lady's words, her body language, the import of her enterprises.

"No one," they are told, "will say anything about how she got on the air. Right now we're trying to buy a little time."

For the next two hours she holds forth, mindfully undaunted by the signals leaking in from backstage, behind the scenes. Finally, with the world watching and waiting, now properly prepared, lights blazing on her finely feminine fashioned features, she presents her final riddle.

> In marble halls white as a sheet
> Lined with skin soft as wheat
> A golden apple doth appear
> And I found something good to eat.
> No doors there are to this stronghold
> Though it is neither flesh nor bone.
> Yet thieves break in and steal the gold;
> I shall keep it till it runs alone.
> (Traditional)

whereby Our Lady
  casts caution
to the wind and bares all

Punctuating the last line with a deft twist of the wrist, she pulls away the blindfold to reveal her lustrous Peridot eyes.

Pandemonium. Hosannas, hallucinations. The switchboards at the B's & C's light up like Christmas trees. Crowds in Bozo's Bar in Buffalo break into a chorus of "American the Beautiful," "The Star Spangled Banner." Street dances erupt in Atlanta, Houston, Spokane.

Times Square, gritty, dark and desperate (disparate?) as it may be, is ecstatic. Audiences from porn theatres spill into the street to join the hustlers and pimps and prostitutes and tourists. A merriment of thievery, pickpocketing, purse snatching and assault ensues. Nine rapes, six armed robberies, twelve assaults, and two murders are recorded the first hour.

Of course, her timing is impeccable, though it is suspected that the westward movement of her image and the spontaneous eruptions (beyond Times Square) had little to do with her late and great performance. The celebrations were calibrated and fueled by citizens' gratitude for the release of three congressmen (to be named later) from the Federal Prison (USP Marion), the success of the latest underground nuclear test in the Nevada desert, and a twenty point leap by the DOW.

"What's this about?" gossip columnists ask. "What does it mean?"

Rumors spread. Wild guesses and speculations are rampant. The marble goddess is not coming clean. Detractors are shouted down.

"It's another riddle."

"Two riddles in one. Nobody expected this."

"And what about her closing words? 'There will be more on a day when all is in readiness.'"

Cronkite and Rather nod solemnly.

"The Last Judgment," someone says.

"Yes," Leslie Stahl says from outside the White House. "It does appear to be, Walter."

Severide is more pessimistic.

"Doom," he forecasts, prophesies. "Doom and destruction."

could Yonkers be the Garden of Eden?

The following morning *The Times* compounds the chaos with large headlines, "Remains of Apple Discovered in Yonkers," accompanied by four front page stories with details and opinions.

"Not since Mary Leaky stumbled into Olduvai has such a discovery rocked the scientific community. In a brief joint statement, Dr. Seymour Woolsthrope and Benjamin Olsen of the pre-history, anthropology, and sociology departments at Columbia University claim that 'This is the beginning of a new era in our understanding of man and his environment.'

"The momentous discovery was made by Adam Maluski of 737 Union Blvd in Yonkers" *The Times* states. "Immediately following the find, in an attempt to limit thrill seekers and fortune hunters, police cordoned off the area. Mr. Maluski, who works part-time evenings and Saturdays at a fruit stand in the Bronx, was not immediately available for comment.

"Following the announcement of the discovery he was spirited away by the police and is being held in seclusion pending debriefing. Speculation grows, in his absence, as to what he was doing on the playground in Yonkers where the remains were located.

"It appears Adam did not eat the entire apple that Eve gave him. This then throws into question the severity of god banishing them from paradise and condemning their progeny to incomprehensible toil and trouble, all without parole, for eternity. By today's standards the sentence seems unduly harsh.

"Police Sergeant Anthony Brian said he could not say what part the discovery might play in solving the Son of Sam murders, although a reliable source high up at PP One, who wished to remain anonymous (but to still claim a piece of the action for The City PD), suggested it had to do with Lieutenant Detective Theo Kojak, the former television super-sleuth, and his link with CBS.

"During the afternoon Mayor Beame (to avoid embarrassment) was unavailable for comment. The Mayor and his wife Mary left for the Catskills after a lunch of cold cuts in the family dining room at Gracie Mansion. Earlier Mr. Beame had gone to one of the neighborhoods most severely enhanced by the looting and arson (destroyed, picked clean, and prepared for urban renewal) during the Days of Darkness, the Bushwick section of Broadway, where he officiated at the opening ceremonies for the Eden Project which will plant 2,000 apple trees in Brooklyn.

"Yonkers residents were shocked at the discovery. 'We figured The City is where it all began — you know, the fall and the toil and trouble stuff. Not in Yonkers,' a woman says who identifies herself as Evaline Kukulinski, a direct descendent of Mitochondrial Eve. 'It should'a been in Brooklyn.'

"David Berkowitz of 35 Pine Street, Yonkers, suspected the apple would be found there.

"'It makes sense,' Mr. Berkowitz says. 'If you think about it, it seems logical.'

"To prove his point Berkowitz quoted copiously from the Book of Genesis, '. . . and she took of the fruit there of, and did eat, and gave to her husband who did eat/And the eyes of them both were opened.'

"'Yes,' he adds, 'it makes sense.'

"On several occasions Mr. Berkowitz has allegedly tried to contact the Yonkers police about the apple. They admit they thought he was just a crackpot with a wacky theory.

"Craig Glassman, another resident of the area, seems not to share Berkowitz's certainty. 'Some nut dropped it,' Glassman, who is a part-time policeman, suggests. 'Some kid probably lifted it off a fruit wagon and dropped it when he got caught red-handed. It's probably a hoax. Maybe like Piltdown Man.'"

The evening news carries additional stories. In a redundancy of detail, authorities on apples, apple trees, fertilizers, insecticides, apple pies, apple butter, applesauce are introduced and interviewed. Bakers and fruiters find themselves on camera with theologians — Bible experts, anthropologists and historians, and a scam artist or two.

"What kind of an apple was it?"

"A Flower of Kent," Dr. Woolsthrope says.

"What color is it?"

"Green."

"You really mean it? You mean Malus Domestica?"

"Yes. Pyrus Malus."

"Where would an apple like this grow?"

"On a tree."

"You mean, on an apple tree."

"That's right."

"Are there other trees here in Yonkers that might produce such an apple?"

"Fruit?"

"Yeah."

"A Ginkgo Biloba."

"A Ginkgo produces fruit?"

"Sarcotesta. Yes."

"But could it serve as a link between earth and heaven? I mean like Jack's beanstalk. Apparently that's what this is."

"Possibly."

"Just think of it. And how long would it take? Say for a normal apple — or what did you call it? Ginkgo ...?

"Sarcotesta. The flesh part of the Ginkgo fruit."

"And that's what we could be talking about here since we have no indication from the authorities that the fruit they recovered was abnormal in any way whatsoever.

"So how long would it take?"

"Two months, give or take a week."

"So this apple or whatever it is, could have been around for a while. If say, it germinated and grew last spring?"

"Some of these trees last four or five hundred years. Germinated is not really the right word."

"What is then?"

"Bloom, flower. Something like that."

"But it has been around a couple months?"

"I didn't say that."

"What did you say?"

"I said we have no sure-fire way of dating it."

"None at all?"

"No. It could be of indefinite age."

"What about carbon dating?"

"The remains did not contain carbon traces. There was plenty of copper, iron, magnesium, manganese, phosphorus, potassium, selenium, sodium, zinc."

"I thought all living things have carbon in them."

"The apple is dead. No carbon. But a high concentration of diphenylamine."

"Which means?"

"It could be coeval with carbon or older. We don't know which came first."

"Oh. How old is carbon? What about inscriptions or marks on the skin?"

"Yes. We found two distinct sets of teeth marks."

"And these . . . ?"

"What you might expect. One is from a male and the other from a female."

"Is it possible that this . . . this object, could be from some other source?"

"Anything is possible."

"What else might it be?"

"Maybe it's the Golden Apple. Maybe Melanion dropped it and Atalanta didn't pick it up. Maybe it's a Golden Delicious. "

"But how could it be golden if it's green?

"Maybe it wasn't ripe."

"That would change the story. We've been advised to stick with the story. So it came from a snowman?"

"Yeah."

"A snowman with a golden apple for a heart?"

"Hmmmm. Could be. But probably not."

Indeed, the big town is in a quandary. CBS schedules a special, *In The Year Of The Big Apple — Day One,* to follow the late news.

"We are now sixteen hours into Anno Pyrus Malus (APM — Golden or not), day one and counting, and an expectant exhilaration has risen among the metropolitan tribes.

"Does the discovery herald the second coming, a Messiah? Moses descending the twin towers carrying a sack of golden apples? A Judas prophecy of 30 golden apples?"

The following morning, even before a transcript of the police debriefing of Maluski is released, Woolsthorpe and Olsen launch a campaign to establish The City as the official site of Isaac Newton's enlightenment, where resting under a tree, contemplating the probabilities of turning lead into gold, he was beaned with an apple — the green one, they contend, found in the snowman in Yonkers.

"Truly, Newton rubbed his head," Olsen explains, "and exclaimed:

> *Every point mass attracts every single other point mass by a force pointing along the line intersecting both points. The force is proportional to the product of the two masses and inversely proportional to the square of the distance between them.*

"It was time someone or something knocked some sense into the old man and split him off from moon gazing, comets, alchemy, and the occult."

Woolsthorpe and Olsen have located a tree in Brooklyn (Yes, they know a tree grows in Brooklyn — though that was a Tree of Heaven) and will ask that the site be made a National Trust. Of course there are always detractors, those who claim Newton never travelled to America and, therefore, could not have been hit on the head by an apple falling from a tree in Brooklyn. Woolsthorpe and Olsen see the objections as "sour grapes," or "a rotten apple spoils the barrel," or "conspiracy theory complaints" that have little to with reality.

"So Newton was beaned with a golden apple. I bet that scrambled his formulae."

"No, no. A green apple."

Psyaint David
narrates the hunt

Well, maybe. But The City has other matters to attend to at the moment.

And it's the usual fare — an *Oh! Calcutta* evening, garlanded with *Godspell, Grease,* and *The Why Files.* In a night of reruns the teevee line-up includes *Bride Of Dracula, Mask of Dijon,* and *It Happened In Brooklyn.* After midnight *Disco 77* and *The Wasp Woman* are available.

And there is always the night-stalker to worry about. At 9:00 David pulls on his midnight-meant-for-murder wig to emerge in a dead-darkness dream. Shivering among a pastiche of old movies that still have the power to panic, he pulls the blanket from the mirror and stands staring at the cavernous reflected interior of a room he has never seen before.

The dummy prods the ventriloquist, raises a loose-jointed arm and turns the man's head. The shapeshifter flits into the night — sin-eater, wraith, whispering to Our Lady.

"Is tonight the night?"

"Brooklyn," Our Lady of Seductive Salaams mutters. "Give the fools something to clamor about."

So.

I drive through Queens and out of Huntington, then back to the South Shore. When

I get to Bay Seventeenth,

I know

I have the right spot.

I park and walk away as a blue and white police car turns the corner.

I have the feeling they will go by my car. But

I am not in the car and it is visible.

I watch them write a ticket.

I wonder. A ticket to what?

I wait till they leave, then

I go back to my car and take the ticket and place it inside, on the dashboard.

I am not worried by the ticket. It doesn't matter.

I pay it, of course, in a couple days.

I walk south on 17th Street past a row of apartment buildings, find an opening between the buildings, then walk through. On the other side is the Bay 16th Street Park enclosed in a chain-link fence. There are handball courts on the right and a softball field directly ahead. A rectangle passageway opens in the fence and

I step through onto the ballfield.

I look ahead and see that the park is two blocks long with a pathway lined with trees and concrete and wooden benches on either side. At the north end of the lane an abandoned overturned car casts a long shadow from two lamps midway down the lane. Across the field is a fenced in children's play area with swings and teeter-totters and a bocce court.

I can see the indigo shadows of Bath Beach, in medium distance. A man on a swing rocks gently, pendulum swinging, time nodding in the spots of moonlight beneath the trees.

I stop and wait by the pedestrian bridge, then move on to the lineup of cars along the roadway. The sweet smell of marijuana drifts from a Volkswagen and

I stare at the couple inside. They do not know

I am watching them. Fifty feet ahead is a Corvette parked in the light of a streetlamp. My hand feels for the gun in my belt and

I grasp the handle. They are moving about inside and know

I am watching them.

I cross the street and see the girl's long brunette hair.

I begin to lift the gun from my belt.

I focus on their movements and

I notice them sit back suddenly. By now

I am at the right rear fender, my left hand running across its smooth surface toward the passenger side door. "Patience is a virtue,"

I hear Sam say.

I turn. He lifts a hind paw to scratch his ear, shaking his fur in the soft breeze blowing off Gravesend Bay, beneath the pale full moon, the grand necklace of bridge lights arching over the Narrows of The City Harbor from Fort Hamilton in Brooklyn to Staten Island. "A trysting spot for lovers," Sam whines. Suddenly the car starts. The engine spins alive, coughs, rumbles. The car inches forward, out of the circle of light of the street lamp.

I move away, swiftly, to the fence to wait. Immediately another car moves in. The plot is clear.

I watch David in the shadows of former quarries outlined on a teevee screen reflected into the face of a mirror,

I watch the park, a familiar park, identical to the one in which

Psyaint David

I am waiting, watching — credits rolling behind the polished glass, with a safe buffet of breeze, blowing over the humid night — whispering of thrills in a Clark Gable movie
I once saw, laced with the intrigue, passion, defiance of . . ..
I stop, frozen in place.
I am not sure they see me.
I don't move. So
I just wait for someone to scream at me. But nothing happens.
I turn away and walk up the street alongside the parkway. When
I stop, the sports car is about fifty feet farther away.
I don't know what to do. Should
I follow them or shouldn't
I?
I move into the black of the park to wait and think.
I find a swing at the far end opposite the overturned car. From time to time,
I glance back to the vacant spot under the street lamp, and stare at its emptiness.
I know they want me here.
I can't understand why they let that couple get away. Maybe
I am here to get someone else. But
I do not have long to wait. At 2:25 the spot is vacant, then a 1969 Buick pulls in. There are many other cars around but the only spot open on lover's lane is under the street lamp.
I watch the driver open the door. They get out and walk into the park.
I remain seated on the swing as they approach. She gazes at me with indigo eyes, but doesn't say anything, and they walk by. They turn left into the playground and
I position myself behind the abandoned car, keeping them in sight.
I have the cover of the car and move to the bordering fence. It is then she sees me for a second time. She points to me and
I sink into the shadows. Minutes later they walk back to the car and
I follow, staying close to the fence.
I stop, still inside the park and watch as he holds the door open for her, then runs to the other side and gets in. There are other cars in the street.
I quickly eye them. No one seems to be paying attention.
I step from the shadows to the sidewalk and then into the street.
I am now in the light from the streetlamp over the car.
I walk straight to the car. When
I get to the rear of it
I look around, then
I move right to the driver's side and pull the gun out. The voices begin again. They begin to howl.
I have to go through with it this time.

I do not care if anyone sees me. It does not matter,
I have to shoot.
I crouch and hold the pistol with both hands.
I point the barrel into the car at the heads of the couple and pull the trigger. At 2:48
I see a shadow move slowly from the park to the walk, near the rear of the car. The long glinting scarred shadow of Sam's hand beneath the streetlight lays out over the bumper, the trunk lid, crawling onto the glass. Then the tentacles of chance, in a macabre dance, the mirrors near the back of the cave, the open hand knotting into a lead fist, slamming the glass, ending time, abruptly, stopping the clock at 2:48.52, chiming the dead hours, Bang! Bang! Bang! Bang!
I shoot the last three times at both of them.
I am not sure why.
I mostly aim at the girl, more than anything.
I don't know why I shoot the guy. But they are so close together.
I step back and watch. Here is everything right in front of me, framed in the light of the streetlamp. Then silence, if only for an instance, that seems like forever. Time stops. It is like a movie, freeze frame, etching the finality on my mind.
I turn and walk away quickly toward the center walkway of the park. There are three people there who
I did not see. They must have come into the park after I got here. But they are not watching me. They have set up large cameras along the fence near the street.
I keep the gun in hand and run across the cobblestone walkway to the overturned car, turning right through the opening in the fence and onto the softball field.
I run along the fence that is the rightfield wall until
I reach the second opening.
I do not stop.
I continue directly across the bordering street and go between the apartment houses and out onto Bay 17th Street, and slow down.
I am out of breath and have to walk. The gun never leaves my hand.
I finally turn it upside down with the barrel in the sleeve of my jacket.
I reach the car and fall in.
I see the parking ticket on the dashboard.
I wait for five minutes to catch my breath. No sirens. No screams. No howls. Just a horn blowing, somewhere.
I cannot hear Sam's voice. At 2:58
I start the car and drive away.
I drive northwest on 18th Avenue as far as it goes. It is a pretty big street. There are only three cars on the street.
I can see that it goes pretty far.

Psyaint David

I follow 18ᵗʰ Avenue to Coney Island Avenue where it turns left.
I enter Prospect Park and drive around the park.

somewhat generic
  description
of murder after midnight

It is near midnight along a walk, in what appears to be a multi-purpose park. There is a softball field, four swings, and two bocce courts near a sign that reads Bath Beach. A lone man is sitting on a swing. It is a warm summer night and he is dress in a T-shirt and tan slacks and brown shoes. He holds a brown paper bag in one hand. His other hand gripes a chain supporting the swing. His blue T-shirt and trousers and shoes are dappled through the large trees by a waning day-old full moon and the light from a park lamp at the end of the walk. You cannot see his face. The swing set is for children. He seems overly large for it, moves gently to and fro, the spots of light appearing and disappearing, sliding over him almost at random.

Adjacent the park, Shore Parkway is lined on both sides with parked cars. The only vacant spot is beneath a streetlamp next to a chain-link fence. A car pulls into the vacant spot. The car might be a red Corvette. It is difficult to tell in the sodium-vapor light. It has a Big Block Hood and the large engine rumbles softly behind cutouts. When a car pulls away the Corvette moves from beneath the streetlight forward to the empty slot. Momentarily another car pulls into the hazy orange-yellow circle of light. This is not lovers' lane but a narrow patch of the Parkway that is used as lovers' lane. The car might be black as Gravesend Bay is black.

Of course, there is very little movement.

Then a dog appears. We see him a little at first, then more pronounced and defined in the vague vapor of after-midnight glow. He is not nosing the ground for food as a dog might, but stares across the street. Is he expecting someone? Is he waiting? What are his prospects?

He appears from behind the rear wheel of the car. No, that is too easy, a man near the park fence thinks. The dog does not just appear. He has been there for some time. No one else notices him. No one can say for sure how long he has been there.

The dog is a mixed black with a white face divided by a black stripe. He has rose ears, a saber tail, and dolichocephalic snout. The occiput is barely visible. The dog comes into view and fades and comes into view as randomly as the light spots on the man on the swing, which have now disappeared altogether. The dog inspects the license (674-CZG) of the Buick, and the sticker above the plate — Register Matches – Prevent Forest Fires — and seems satisfied. His tail wags, slightly.

A couple exits the black, silent car, and enters the park. They have just come from seeing *New York, New York*. She is medium height with what might be short blond hair. She is wearing a white A-line organza cocktail dress and white heels. He is somewhat taller, though not much. His hair and clothing are not important. They cross the street hand in hand and stroll into the park, along the walk, past the swings. It is clear that this is their first date. He holds her hand protectively. She is hesitant, but seems to appreciate his attention. She hums the theme from *New York, New York.*

"I want to wake up in a city that never sleeps and find I'm a number one, top of the list, King of the hill, a number one" (Ebb).

As they pass the swings, she notices the man and turns to look into the shadows. If she could see his face she might wonder about his quizzical smile. He looks a bit like the Joker. They walk several hundred feet to the end of the park. Background music drifts over from the tenements on 17th Court. They kiss. After a second kiss, they return slowly past the bocce courts and the swings.

The man has gone. The swing twists unevenly, buffeted by the soft release of his going. She wonders about the man.

There is no movement in the park.

A car passes on Shore Parkway.

The couple re-enters the Buick.

The night is warm but the car windows are up.

They sit for a moment as if waiting for something to happen.

A man near the fence moves out of the shadows. He has come from the park, but is not the man who was sitting on the swing. Or if he is, he has changed. He is shorter, though people often appear taller when they are seated. He seems not to care that he is alone or that the couples in cars near the streetlamp, occupied as they are, do not see him. The white flesh of a leg is visible through the rear passenger-side window of one car. Probably a female leg. He gravitates to the dull glow of the vapor streetlamp, steps between the cars, around a cameraman with an ARRI 35BL-II silent, reflex, dual-pin registered hand held camera capable of high speed photography up to 100fps, with a Zeiss Super Speed lense, an Angenieux 25-250mm T3.9 zoom, a bayonet lens mount, 180º fixed butterfly shutter, a digital analog tachometer, footage dual pin registration and four pull-down claws. He pauses near the rear of the Buick, his hand on the trunk. He does not have a brown paper bag in either hand. He is looking at the dog. The dull glint of what appears in the soft light to be a gun appears in the man's hand.

Four shots from a large caliber revolver pummel the night. Even as the muffled sounds dissipate, the man moves off into the park and disappears in the shadows of the large trees.

Sam watches from a canine p.o.v.

Sam stretches out on the floor near the window on a spread copy of the morning *Times,* pursuing the columns, reviewing the previous night's activity. *The Times* is circumspect, the narrative redundant.

In a *Times'* story the attacker creeps up to the Buick, fires four shots, and trots into the shadows of nearby Bath Beach Park. Severly wounded, Mr. Violante leans on the horn, trying to attract attention. The humid air, stirred by breezes from Gravesend Bay, spreads the sound of the horn. A bit later it suddenly begins to blare.

Awakened by the noise, a neighborhood resident named Dotti rushes out. She sees nothing strange in the strange light of the streetlamp, except that the Buick's brake lights are flashing and a black dog, leg lifted, pissing on the back tire. The dog seems not to be bothered by the horn blaring.

"It is this weird, long honking sound," recalls Stephanie Nuecie, fifteen-year-old, of 8867 Bay 16th Street, grimacing with fear, horror.

"Then I see the guy get out of the car; he has on a blue shirt and blue pants, and there is this big stain on his clothes," Dotti says later, hooking her hands tensely in her blue jeans. "He is screaming with pain, saying 'Help me!'"

"His voice is sort of high, like a little boy's voice and he is screaming 'Help me! Don't let me die!'" a thirty-two-year-old Brooklyn housewife recalls.

Dotti and her thirty-four-year-old husband, David, throw on clothes and race to the Buick. Mr. Violante, on his feet, lurches back toward the car, smearing its top with blood, and tottering into the lamppost.

The neighborhood quickly comes alive. Gently, one man gets Mr. Violante to lie down and wait for medical help. He lies, face up on the gritty sidewalk beside the stretch of lawn that adjoins the parkway's inland side.

"Now the wounded guy is screaming. 'Where is the ambulance, where is it?'" David says.

"Another neighbor brings out towels, Dotti recalls, and tries to staunch Miss Moscowitz's bleeding as the slim victim sags against the seat, her head still more or less erect.

"Mr. Violante seems to be having trouble breathing and a policeman helps turn him over, face down.

"You try to do what you can to help," says Dotti, a wiry woman with glasses and a strong face. "So I put a towel under his face so it won't get in the dirt and weeds. His face is all swollen by then."

"Meanwhile, bystanders help Miss Moscowitz out of the car and coax her onto a stretcher, though she wants to walk around, Dotti recalls. Within fifteen or twenty minutes the couple is carried off by ambulance to Coney Island Hospital. They are then transferred to King's County Hospital."

"Cut," Aigilas says. "That's good. Yeah, very good. We got what we need."

He lights a Cleopatra and stands for a moment shaking his head, pleased with the scene.

"Yeah, that was good."

The Times picks up the story.

"Maybe so, but for Dotti and David, and other residents of the quiet, tree-shaded reaches of southwest Brooklyn, neighborliness soon gives way to pangs of fear and dread. Then comes the criticism of the police, talk of forming vigilante squads, calls for vengeance.

"With first light dozens of policemen flood the area, perspiration pouring from their faces, as they search for bullets and other clues. One bullet is found in the car's steering column and two others in the victims' bodies. Several young men stare grimly while the police rake through the lawn beside the parkway, searching for the missing fourth bullet.

"By midday anxiety is running so high that Dotti and David insist on withholding their last name. Others worry, for fear the attacker might come back. The neighborhood, home to mostly Italian-Americans and Jewish families, is gripped with tension.

"Further north, along shady East 5th Street, neighbors watch the trim brick façade of the two-family building, 1740 East 5th, where Miss Moscowitz lives with her family.

"A few faces peer out through the green plastic curtaining behind the balcony. Then Miss Moscowitz's sixteen-year-old sister, Ricki, steps out flanked by a policeman. Her great dark eyes are impassive, but sad.

"'I really can't talk. I can't answer questions,' she says and disappears, as a second policeman peers out a small fanlight in the front door.

"'Son of Sam — I think he might make trouble in Brooklyn sometime, but never on this street. This is our home,' says Vincent Semonelli of 1770 East 5th Street.

"A burley telephone company worker, he is one of the neighbors keeping a vigil under the leafy trees.

"Another neighbor, Marcus Rubin, an art director, who lives at 1707 East 5th, says 'It's scary. This maniac striking, he's saying he can strike anywhere. I tell my wife to be careful. There's no way to protect yourself.'"

But then there never was.

Sam gloats.

caviar and scotch for breakfast

Our Lady of the Luxuriant Libido is nibbling caviar, tuned in on the rerun of the shooting.

"Did you imagine you were safe?" she hums rhetorically. "Silly, silly man. No one is ever safe."

Wrapped in a grey goatskin cloak — nothing else — she waits for the day to struggle to its feet. Her boy-wonder, the picture of innocence and peace, sleeps soundly. Indeed, it couldn't have gone better, quickly, search-and-destroy, punctuated by the Bulldog's hollow bark, and a well-executed retreat. For what do the police know? She has already advanced a scheme to get the video master of the action from The Universe.

And where does that leave SoSaMy Inc?

Psyaint David

the markets open with aggressive trading

The morning dawns August 1, 1977, dateline, Big Apple, Fun City, The City of the Gods. On Wall Street today in heavy trading Son of Sam stock shoots up .44 points. This will blow your mind. Forty-four thousand shares finished the day at .44. Is this possible? Is this the tonic business needed, the fire to breathe life into the decaying corpse? Catastrophic capitalism. The City is in a frenzy. Plastic statues of Son of Sam look-a-likes, .44 centimeters tall, are selling well in the parks and on Times Square, which gives rise to the observation that The City may yet be the center of the known universe — despite Disney Land.

"The City's attraction is its unique appearance," Eleanor Timberman, NBC's director of program development for the East Coast says. "Everything's the same in California. If you've seen one Californian, you've seen them all. But here, people are different. We have the market cornered on weird people and events. And they're all for sale – at the right price."

Our Lady as bon savant

The following morning Our Lady of Taunting Temptations is up and about early for breakfast with David Rockefeller. This not-too-early hour she's attired in a citified turnout by Beene Bag, a Futé cardigan, silk-and-wool-fishnet pullover, raw-silk-and-wool wrap-skirt, and a rhinestone tiara. It is lips and hips. She is vibrant, bon savant, a spring to her step and an air of gaiety riding the soft caress of her hands. She is totally reflective of a new ovarian confidence. Her eyebrows are penciled in, her Apple green Seraphinite eyes covered by a dark olive Butterfly Bat-woman Blindfold.

Things have gone well and she is pleased, intending to offer up her wares for a piece of the action, if the piece is large enough. Only yesterday she took control a multi-million-dollar bar business in midtown Manhattan. Riding shotgun with Mathew "Matty the Horse" Iannielo and his financial wizardry, she joined the topless and nude dancers in a shakedown of holding companies, talent agencies, as well as interior decorating, garbage-collecting, and vending machine companies.

"If you want to open a bar and grill or a sex establishment in midtown Manhattan but don't have the cash, or have some other problem, you go see Matty Iannielo," a Police Department Intelligence Division expert on Organized Crime says.

And Our Lady says, "Yes!"

It's Matty the Horse, Big 16, and Our Lady of the Finely Financially Flaunted Figure making it on the Big C. She sashays onto the Penthouse terrace at Blackrock and slips into a seat at the breakfast table between Mohammad Både-Talen, of Iraqi Enterprises, and the Iranian National Bank Minister Ali-Syed Shahid. The Drake "Duck" arrives early, squats across from her, nibbles a pile of cracked breakfast corn.

"Have you seen Mr. Rockefeller this morning?" Drake says.

The Belle of the Breakfast Bunch giggles, snickers.

"No, but I will. Before the day is done I'll tickle the old toad's testicles and have his loose change in my hand."

Duck is pleased.

"Oh, I know," he says. "These are such lucrative times. It's just wonderful knowing you are part of history. We are changing the face of humanity. The welfare of the world belongs to the congregants of this room.

"The tentacles of organized crime reach into legitimate business. They are so extensive and well-hidden that it is virtually impossible to delineate where criminally obtained money becomes legitimate business capital," Drake the Duck says.

He pauses, nostalgic with reverence for the thought, then ruffles a feather and wriggles down farther in his chair.

"Quack, quack. Do you realize we now know how to manufacture and market fear packaged in the illusions of safety and well-being."

He extends a mottled feathered wing across the table and pats her hand.

"Yes, my dear, the new capital of untapped markets with an infinity of possibilities. Think about it. Fear as entertainment. Fear as success. Fear as a way of life. We at Justice are prepared to do our part. It is our patriotic duty to overlook, shall we say, (quack, quack) episodes, events which while unusual, remain consistent with expanding the gross national product — as long as it is gross enough. Quack, quack."

is it time for the blind lady to sing?

Brooklyn. Heated talk of vengeance. Young men, enterprising lads seeking their share of the chaos, organize posses in Bensonhurst. Armed patrols tour the streets at night as in, "Looking for this guy."

Groups of women gather on street corners to discuss revenge.

"He should go to jail?" a fat woman says, "so they can say he's insane."

"Exactly!" two women on the outskirts of the group reiterate.

"He should be hung," the fat woman says.

"Hung by the balls."

"Lady," someone says, "if he has balls, he's already hung. You want him hanged by the balls. Yeah, that would be nice."

"They should let the people take care of him. It sounds terrible but then you see — there won't be no more murder."

"I don't hate nobody in Washington this bad. I'd rather have a pinko-yellow commie queer from Hanoi come and rub up against me."

At the Midnight Rose an outspoken round little man with bristles on his chin and bright eyes, that become larger as he grows excited, has visions of a punishment for the .44 caliber gunner.

"You know what I'd like to do with him?" he says in thick Brooklynese. "I'd cut both his legs off and say to the police, 'When you give me the reward, I'll bring the rest of the pieces in.'"

"We're starting a group, looking for the guy," a twenty-six-year-old laid-off, but not back, construction worker named Vincent says. "Tonight we're going to go looking. And if we catch him, I'll tie him to the car. All the parents are going to be able to do this thing to this guy, and then we'll tell the police."

Sam is pleased, mumbling, smirking, "Took the silly shits long enough. Maybe we'll have a lynching, after all. Maybe."

why me, god,
   why me?
well, why not?

Police are deluged with calls, letters — five thousand in four months. Everyone wants in on the act. Kojak advances a new plan to pump up his fading reputation. He is still the King at Kings incarcerated in a padded cell, hoping to resuscitate his career. Wistful on a 10" black and white, he remembers the days when he was clean and clear, in prime time high resolution and the investigation was his.

"What went wrong?" he asks. "Crocker and Stavros are gone."

Even Our Lady of Insidious Infidelity has abandoned him.

The following day his plan will be laid even lower by the president of The Universe Studios, Sane Scottie, with a rueful, but, nonetheless,

"Sorry. But when abandoned stars return, they come back in new skin. Have you thought of joining SoSaMy Inc? You got the makings of a hitman," Scottie says. "Try SoSaMy Inc. Yeah, Kojak reformed as a hit-man. That would make a helluva story. Take a year or two, then come and see me."

Indeed, there are numerous precedents. Hollywood has been recycling and casting has-beens ever since the "talkies" began. Audiences are always eager to see what the new edition of a worn out idea has to say.

a Son of Sam celebration

And there's more.

Shortly before noon thousands of workers pour out of their offices into the streets, causing traffic and pedestrian jams. Throngs gather in the rain, pushing against rope barriers in front of the Department of Defense offices at 342 Madison Avenue to witness the booming beginning of the early August Son of Sam celebration. Beame has billed it (by Mayoral Proclamation) as an extension of The Tournament of Ethnic Dominance with Son of Sam penciled in as a publicity booster. Of course Our Lady's latent motherly instincts are pulsating — incestuously — and she has no intention of allowing her inamorato to attend.

William Spiller, III, Chief Coordinator of the Defense Department's Canadian Liaison Division gives the keynote address and sets the tone for the frustration to come.

"It may seem strange that the Department of Defense should invest in a celebration named after a wanton like Son of Sam, but to the critics let me say that it is easy to criticize those in power — but damned difficult to get them out of power. We at Defense recognize the right of the public to complain — but we do not agree with treason."

To illustrate the point, Mr. Spiller turns and points up to the twenty-first floor and in a well-timed response (and you'd imagine Glen Robinson is in on this) clouds of smoke blast out the windows and a thunderous report with dust, debris, and black smoke descends on the crowd.

An hour later the festivities migrate to the Mobile Oil Building at 150 East 42nd Street. To entertain the crowd with additional fireworks, via a second explosion, one Charles S. Steinberg, twenty-six, of Viva Temporary (very temporary) Service employment agency makes a swift and exhilarating exit from a twenty-sixth floor window. Some think he was shot out of a canon.

When it is announced that Charles has, in fact, given the last full measure of devotion, a deafening roar goes up from the crowd. Revelers link arms and a block party ensues with vernacular dances, accompanied by shouts of "Excelsior! Excelsior! Excelsior!"

Of course the mayor is pissed. This is like throwing bricks and milk cans from three-story buildings. He fights his way through the crowd to a teevee camera and announces that, "It is my official duty to open and conduct City ceremonies and celebrations. This is an outrage and I will not take it lying down. People who do things like this should be put to death. Do you know how many millions of dollars are lost to business every time someone steps out of line and takes things into his own hands?"

Fuerzas Armadas de Liberación Nacional Puertorriqueña (FALN) agrees with the mayor and accepts responsibility for the fireworks.

"We are guilty and want to demonstrate by our actions that the Yankee Imperialist's attempt at assimilating and annihilating the Puerto Nation is not going to be taken sitting down by the liberation forces.

"Any attempt to suppress the Puerto Rican Liberation Movement by Imperialist Forces, the FBI, and the Carter administration, will be met with revolutionary violence."

the Mayor is appalled by the unwashed

By early afternoon a half dozen or so lunatic fringe groups contest FALN's claim. Beamed goes sputtering back to City Hall to convene a press conference (you have to know by now that he loves press conferences) to announce that he is still in charge. PC Garfield is beside him.

Dressed in a grey three-piece — with chalk-stripes to match his waning impression — propped up at a large mahogany desk, The Beame continues.

"Who do they think they are? Usurping the functions of an elected official? Not only have these groups not received a mandate from the populace, they don't even have the right to vote. They cannot read or write and come out of the jungle and take over the celebrations and festivals that mean so much to our people. When in Rome, do as the Romans do."

"But Mayor, that's what they are doing."

"Oh. Okay. But at least they could ask."

These are tough words, but you have to admit this is shocking and the mayor has a point. He also has a pale face and shaking hands, and is accompanied by a battery of Vices hovering just beyond the camera's eye, a heavy, ominous shadowed chorus crowding up as if it knows something the rest of the world should know.

"What we need is a resumption of the death penalty," Beame intones. "That would act as a deterrent to terrorism. I spoke with the FBI . . .."

His voice is subdued, drags into a lower range. His lips are moving in slow motion. He is lip synching his lips.

"My god," someone says, "it's happening again."

"It ain't again. Nothing ever happens again."

"Is this where the story begins?"

Garfield steps forward, surrounded by a crimson aura and tries to support the mayor, who is now a flat copy of quarter-inch cardboard, tottering life-sized, a distant cast to his opaque eyes. Garfield knows about cardboard cutouts. Thinks it must be something like sticking pins in a voodoo doll. If they have Beame and Garfield cutouts, they could easily have Beame and Garfield dolls, and a box or two of pins. He feels the pin-prick, jumps forward a small step, and rubs his ass.

"We have talked to the FBI," Garfield says, before the camera fails altogether and he too becomes a poster board, photo paste-up, locking the conference into freeze frame.

Methodically, aides move in and replace the Beame/Garfield cutouts with life size SoSaMy Inc posters as a voice over apologizes.

"Difficulties on the Network."

Then a sigh and a lull in the action.

"Good lord, will it never end?"

"Why should it? At least we have something interesting to write about."

with a small instigation from Sam
all hell breaks loose

That evening in the Sheepshead Bay section of Brooklyn the police disarm a man with a .38 caliber revolver and a .357 Magnum and a passerby runs into Captain Walter's bar at 2301 Emmons Avenue shouting that the police are arresting Son of Sam.

Bar patrons swarm into the street to attack the prisoner who is hustled into a patrol car and quickly driven away. The prisoner is one of two hundred out of work actors the SoSaMy Inc. has hired to walk the streets armed with revolvers so the police can make arrests and circulate rumors that TCPD is in fact on the job and closing in on Son of Sam. The spinoff of the program is a substantial increase in the arrest rate per officer on the beat. In fact, business on the Big Board is up and Beame, having shaken off his cardboard image, decides to rehire one hundred thirty-six policemen. Sam (Sam Inella) offers a personal word of thanks to Son of Sam.

"We need more men," Garfield tells Galante. "Now is the time to come to the aid of The City."

"I always support The City," Galante says. "And it supports me."

"We need another five thousand men to help find this goblin."

Galante agrees. He's in one of his pastoral, benevolent, Pastel moods.

"Peace my son. Ah! Goodness will prevail."

He's been praying for the souls of the eighty or so people he has wacked.

"The bigger the hunt, the more publicity and name recognition. The more PR, the more money.

"But what do you know about Kojak?" Galante snarls.

"Well, Philosophically, he's Schrödinger's Cat. Phenomenologically, he is the mystery he is trying to solve. Psychologically, he wanders along the Affective Disorder Spectrum. Personally, he is a schmuck."

"Where did he come from? I don't want that S.O.B in on this. Locals will believe the shit about honest cops, and they might even blame the Syndie."

"Not to worry," Garfield says. "Not to worry your head, Czarmine. He's been quarantined. We will take care of it. We'll work on the publicity."

Sam Inella agrees. He too would like to keep the wobbly dick off the case. He and Galante agree on this — that, and getting the lion's share of the cut.

"Five thousand men. What? You need an army?"

"We'll apprehend the real daemon and dump him in the river. Then our bogie will be the authentic Son of Sam."

"Bogie? How'd he get into this?"

"What's good for the bad guys is good for The City."

Garfield buttonholes Keener.

"These are trying times. We need to get our men back on the job."

Keener shrugs. He's less than enthusiastic. He holds his head.

"Damn. For just one old fashion thief. The psychos are driving me loony." The psychos and the reports, the phone calls and letters.

"Another thousand letters this morning," he is told. "That's what's driving this case. If those yahoos would lay off we could do our job. You know how much time it takes to read all those letters?"

"Here's a report you might want to read. An unusual case."

Psyaint David

A report? A scenario, a drama of frustration and failure, guilt, recrimination is scheduled to begin shortly before 7:00 the next morning.

yes, what should (uncle) Sam do?
or the season
of he-who-carries-the-badge

David spends the night with his head hung over the side of the bed, his ear to a glass placed against the floor.

"What would Sam do?" he poses. "What would the apostles do?"

The voice he hears belongs to Craig Glassman — the intruder.

"Another demon? Sam's enemy? Why didn't I think of that?"

He watches the light crawl over the wall, the ceiling, and prepares to do what he needs to do.

I am in the season of
> He-Who-Carries-The-Badge comes, is sent to where
I live, to wait in the trees for the right time when he will be joined by legions of
> Others-Who-Carry-The-Badge from other parts of The City for act one of the
> Claim-To-Establish-Rectitude. They will be led by
> He-Who-Leads-Many-With-Badges, who will, when his time is at hand, and the way has been prepared, descend from the
> High-Hall-Of-Force-Of-The-Many, where wise counsel has decreed that in due time boys must be separated from their mothers who love them and taken into captivity and given tests so they may step into the next world. And

I have seen the eyes of
> He-Who-Carries-The-Badge and heard his breathing at the door, waiting, watching me.

I find his scent and

I am ready to go, to resist, to go to my mother and cry to her asking for safety and then biting her hand when she tries to comfort me.

I will be called
> He-Who-Does-Not-Honor-The-Many or
> He-Whose-Mother-Cries. The season speaks with voices from the trees, and

I am sick with the full moon and the odor of their boiling pots cooking and steaming
> The-Brew-To-Make-Men-Of-Boys.

I have seen their faces in the fires of dreams, their eyes burning on me so

I may never again live without fear.

I hear them laughing and rejoicing, as if only they understand the joke.

Then they are quiet for a long time and the smell of the smoke and the boiling kettles fills the hall and seeps beneath the door until
I cannot breath and my eyes cloud up.
The-Day-Of-Total-Readiness they paint their faces and wear
Robes-For-Somber-Occasions and follow
He-Who-Leads-Many-With-Badges. They chant,
He-Whose-Mother-Cries.
He-Who-Does-Not-Honor-The-Many.
He-Who-Does-Evil. Then they are silent. They wait for
The-Great-Spirit-Of-The-Just-And-Virtuous to instruct them and give them courage for what they will do.
The-Great-Just-One will appear and say, "You have been given
The-Voices-Of-The-Many-To-Speak-As-One in a voice that no one may speak for himself. It is your duty and right to make men of boys, evil into good, and drive away the forces of the night." And Sam will be satisfied, and they will hammer on my door, banging, waving badges and guns to keep away the light of
The-Spirit-Who-Does-Not-Believe is in Sam's eyes. They say,
"You-Who-Have-No-Balls,
You-Who-Are-The-Shit-Of-The-Earth,
You-Who-Are-Gutless," and fall upon me in a horde with the smell of their
Brew-To-Make-Men-Of-Boys on their robes, their eyes dull and gray. They will beat me, which is the first test, and
I will resist becoming
He-Who-Remains-Unrepentant. They will shake their beards and say, "Naughty, naughty. You are bad, villainous, a wretched child, and not worthy of
The-Grand-Just-Spirit."
I will be called
The-Unrepentant-Manacled-One and taken from my sanctuary, along the Progression of Glorious Migration where crowds will gather for the annual
View-The-Demon-With-Revulsion celebration. They will say "There goes
He-Who-Defies-The-Many, who will be known henceforth and forever as
He-To-Whom-Our-Wrath-Will-Be-Done. They will chant
He-Who-Tortures-Our-Minds must die.
He-Who-Gives-Us-Fear must die.
He-Who-Tells-Us-Of-Our-Fears must die. They will have a tickertape parade up Wall Street, down Madison Avenue, with banners streaming. "Glory be to
He-Who-Brings-Us-Prosperity."

Psyaint David

I sleep among
  Those-Who-Do-Evil-Without-Remorse, and on the second day
I wake early, before the sun rises and purify myself for the ordeal of the
second great test to become in mind
  He-Who-Must-Love-Sam and
  Who-Lives-By-The-Impulse-Of-Man.
I anoint my limbs, my members, and paint my face with
  A-Smile-To-Answer-All-Questions, mold a shield to deflect
  Words-Designed-To-Assuage-The-Rejection-Of-The-Many who
can create an explanation of
  The-Deep-Pattern-Of-Mysterious-Motives that
I live. The morning light of Act II breaks with the same dull gray of
previous days and
I spend the hours staring down at the pieces of traffic cars make as they
speed by chasing one another.
I am concentrating, learning my lines for scene one, *Identification of the
Monstrous Villain.* At 10:00
  He-Who-Watches-Tirelessly-For-Evil stops outside my cage and
tells me to prepare for the journey into
  The-Tunnel-Of-No-Light, sacred passage to
  The-High-Halls-Of-Great-Force, with many of
  He-Who-Carries-The-Badge watching. Between dawn and dusk
they come with fetters and manacles and snap about me
  The Chains-Of-Chain.
I clink on the door, clink when it closes or opens. One is already my friend
and believes in the benevolence of man, the spirit of the holy ghost that
abides in us. He says, "Good morning," and enters politely. "Are you ready
to go?" The other does not care for his work. He says, "Okay, let's go,
they're waiting." We leave the cage-cell and
I wave good-bye, say "See you later," and my friend turns to whoever is
left behind to see if they will wave back, but no one does. They are
surveying the sky, listening to the planes from Kennedy soar off into the
distance.

model, scheme or notion,
 does anybody
have a hypothesis?

"This is no simple matter of footprints," Garfield says, "or the trail of a
hank-of-hair hung on bark. Werewolves can change themselves into
people. People can make themselves invisible."
He still has three red welts behind his left ear. Mosquitoes, he thinks.
Fucking mosquitoes.
"While we haven't had much success with clairvoyants," Kenner-O'Neil

tells the press, "we are definitely stepping up the use of mystics and numerologists — and an astrologist and psychologist or two."

Thomas Burke, coordinating psychologist of the College Accelerated Program for Police at the Institute of Institute Technology, teaches a course for police officers, some of whom are working with the .44 caliber case.

"We know he reads the paper and follows the case carefully," Professor Burke says, referring to the letter to Breslin. "One thing about the paranoid personality is that it tends to be very ego-involved. It also wants to be seen as doing a good job. To be thought of by observers as an exceptionally competent person.

"When we catch him we will find that he does have many friends, all of his relationships are superficial, and he is not married and does not have any children."

"The letter or calling card, is the unique, personal expression or ritual demonstrated by the offender. When a signature is left, so is an aspect of the offender's personality. What he is doing is playing a game with the police — Moriarty toying with Sherlock — or maybe the Joker taunting Batman," says a Burke colleague, a professor who does not want to be identified. "He's saying that he's more of a man than they can ever be."

The Times finally catches on, reports that "Hypnotists have been brought in to see if survivors of the Son of Sam attacks are subconsciously repressing valuable information. The seers, astrologers, and numerologists have worked out a number of theories to unravel the enigma."

"They give us ideas," says Kenner. "Believe me, we'll take all theories."

The frustrated inspector admits that "We now have an entire city to protect. Sam is telling us he will strike anywhere. At least that's our theory."

Sam wants to know
who killed the dog -
and the flies

With Our Lady of Lewd Longing as consort and adviser, the possibilities have multiplied. Sam's strutting on The Avenue of the Americas at West 3rd Street to the Waverly Theater to see Rainer Werner Fassbinder's sit-com, *Satan's Brew*.

It's the story of a beleaguered poet with a hefty wife who complains loudly about their nonexistent sex life and a brother whose hobbies are exposing himself and collecting dead flies.

The menagerie includes a duplicitous whore and a bug-eyed, warty mistress, and Stefan George, a German poet favored by the Nazis, who is writing a new opera, *No Ceremony for the Führer's Dead Dog*.

It is a wonderful drama about the relationship between sex and money:

a woman in kinky purple underwear has orgasms while writing checks (while her lover shoots her) and the brother who collects flies tries to use them as both erotic offerings (Spanish fly?) and as currency. One haunt, a masochist, has scrambled eggs splattered on her face and happily lets it dry there."

"After whom does thou pursue? After a dead dog, a flea," Sam wants to know. "Why should this dead dog curse me, lord the king?"

A fair feast for Sam's robust appetite. He's contemplating a return to old forms — unwashed habits of mind long left on the line, a salient sniff at the soiled underwear of gluttony and greed. He's hanging around the entry of the IRT subway at Lincoln Center, waiting for a diversion, someone, just anyone from the crowd and settles on thirty-four-year-old Claudia Curfernes Castellana of 560 Riverside Drive (near 125th Street), pushes an assailant out of the shadows, a slovenly scabbed and deranged misanthrope wielding a large folding knife with a black handle, and orchestrates the closing notes to the dirge. Mrs. Castellana is raped by three penetrating thrusts striking deep into flesh and bone.

At the conclusion she stumbles down the stairs at the 66th Street station, before collapsing between the token booth and turnstiles.

Sam's still into the Bible.

"Remember," he says, ". . . after Jehu kills King Jehoram, he confronts Jezebel in Jezreel and urges her eunuchs to kill her by throwing her from the parapet. They comply.

> And he said, Throw her down. So they
> threw her down: and some of her blood was
> sprinkled on the wall, and on the horses: and
> he trod her under foot.
> And when he was come in, he did eat and
> Drink, and said, Go, see now this cursed woman,
> And bury her: for she is a king's daughter.
> And they went to bury her: but they found
> no more of her than the skull, the feet,
> and the palms of her hands.
>
> (*2 Kings* 9 : 33-35)

Another card out of Sam's ruff sleeve. A fine story, a deuce of deceit, the magic of mirrors.

The IRT attacker vanishes among folds of humanity pressed into the northbound local that has pulled into the station.

Would be heroes of the moment, decent folks, pure hearts, and noble minds, vigilantes with vengeance, the dust of justice on their parched lips, give chase, and return breathless to tell their tale.

"He ((Jehu?) got away and we don't know whether it was the right man or not."

But you were chasing something?

"That's not a lonely, isolated station," a Transit Authority rep contends.

"We can't say it was robbery," a homicide detective says.

"What would convince you?"

Sam pokes about the scene, chatting with reporters and standers-by.

"The real thing," he guesses. "Chance is a wonderful game."

They agree. Why not? Stories built on happenchance sell. The thrill of walking the streets knowing it could happen to you.

"Yeah, it makes my crotch itch."

"Maybe you got crabs."

"Do you know what it is like to feel a six-inch shiv slide between your ribs into the chest cavity?"

Haven't we heard this before? What was his name? Melvin something.

"Oh, my god!! Do we have to go back to that?"

"There were plenty before him — and after."

However, across The City the speakers and listeners are in a cheery mood. The politicians get into it. Bella S. Abzug duck-waddles out framed in a mirror decorated with an Amazone on a warhorse, reads from a prepared statement. She promises that if she becomes mayor she will ". . . see to it that The City, like Hollywood, like London, is a film and TV capital of the world.

"I mean, can you picture King Kong falling off the Brown Derby?"

"We have a vast array of superstars right at our fingertips. We have Kojak, Sam Patch, Czarmine Galante, Our Lady of the Bodacious Boobs — and don't forget Son of Sam. Do you realize that of late there have been rumors that Sam is actually here in person?"

Edward Koch, who promotes himself as a crusading reformer, quietly promises plum city jobs to the political powerbrokers in the boroughs in exchange for their support. Cuomo runs on banning the death penalty. When that backfires with The City dwellers who are sick of crime, he goes negative with slogans like "Vote for Cuomo, Not the Homo." Koch backers accused Cuomo of anti-Semitism and pelt Cuomo-campaign cars with eggs

Sam agrees it is time
 for the curtain
to rise on the last act

Lo now, strength grows in his loins, the force of power is in the naval of his belly (*Job* 40:15).

"A new faith," Sam says, "which is the oldest faith of all."

Sam's prepared an evening of sex and spirits, arranged and catered in a delectable splendor, a vivid reminder that wickedness dines and fornicates conspicuously.

Psyaint David

Sam's playing host, mingling, Beau Geste, with an all-star cast, a trendy repast of fish, fowl and meats, fine breads and distinguished wines. The walls of 7E and the seventh floor hall of 35 Pine Street are lined with tables, the mensa domini of appetizing aphrodisiacs, goblets and tankards of ale and mulled cider, tall cylinders of Fourme D'ambert from Auvergne, wedges of Danish blu, Belle Bressane, chicken liver mousse, Polish dried mushroom caps, cochentrise, green parsley bread, imported Italian truffles, fettuccine and risotto, Gelye De Fysshe, Chardwarden, large bowls of St. John's rice and fruits.

A sax sextet tunes up at the far end of the hall — one in blackface, the others in Classic Clown whiteface (Frost pulling Alma from the waves, the cannons booming). The sextet is reminiscent of the Brown Brothers (Alec, Fred, Tom, Vern, William, and Harry Fink — Baritone, Alto, Alto, Bass, Tenor, and Baritone). The program includes *Peter Gink – One Step*, George L. Cobb's 1919 ragtime rendition of *Peer Gynt*, *Bohunkus – One Step*, based on a variety of themes from Dvořak, *Shivaree*, taken from Schubert's *Ave Maria*, as well as a number of extracted, purloined, and transformed themes from Moszkowski.

On the street a crowd of sightseers, celebrity watchers, gather. The area is cordoned off, the less notable held back. Teevee crews work the crowd with cameras and mics. Floodlights bath the sunken front entrance as the early "by invitation only" Divine 54 arrivals smile and wave to the cameras.

Broadway is closed for the night. The mayor has declared the day All Sam's Eve. When Sam calls, the world lines up. Tonight the casts from *Godspell*, *Grease*, and *Hair* are in attendance. Limos, a wagon train of Silver Clouds, creep up Pine Street.

Yul Brynner waltzes Constance Towers in from the Vries Theatre to a chorus of "Western People Funny." Howard Nimroy and Al Pacino follow them to the elevator. Upstairs the crowd spills down the hall. Jody "*Taxi Driver*" Foster (playing *The Little Girl Who Lives Down the Lane* — Bau Bau, nymphet and tomboy strumpet of the assness-blue-denim-thriller) chats with *La Grand Bourgeoisie*, Catherine Deneuve.

"We have a little time before festivities begin," Sam tells Jimmy Doyle (playing Robert De Niro). "Time to enjoy yourself, sample the fare."

His eyes are white-hot, his breath desiccated.

Hung from the ceiling in one corner, a teevee flickers. Marlowe, Spade, The Op (take your pick) come on the large screen, red-veined eyes as big as dinner plates. He's been hitting the sauce, waiting. He is still in residence at Kings, but Our Lady has pulled him to join the ceremony as a depleted guest of some honor.

"This is my day," he says, swinging a wooden flagon of ale over his head, splashing rivulets onto the camera. "Here's to Lady Justice," he slurs with an obscene gesture. "She's still the best lay in town."

"Here! Here!" the crowd shouts. "Bravissimo!"

Cries of jubilation ring a welcome. Our Lady shakes her well-cast derriere.

"Anything you say."

Indeed, she's up for it, willing, ready for action, for taunt and tease, and happy to please.

"The day we have waited for," Teivel says.

What is written has been written — and filmed. Within hours the specter in the mist will be apprehended, his development arrested, held in check, driven into yet another abyss of the underworld for yet another season. The masses will gather before the throne for the final judgment — the decree — sentences handed down, and those who have profited little will be condemned.

"But one day," Our Lady of Stuprum Inferre promises, "he will rise. He will be resurrected, an insurrection for the second coming (no pun intended)."

"The Commissioner will be here," LoKoJakMan says. "As soon as the arrest is made. The Mayor is with him. They have a press conference scheduled for some time after midnight."

"By invitation alone," Sam tells him, pleased with the politics of it, the attention and publicity.

"The Mayor has a prepared statement."

One ghost to another.

"What is curtain time?"

"Around 11:00, 11:30," Our Lady of Scurrilous Scams announces. "As soon as the yo-yos at Yonkers get off their duffs."

She's seated on the platform bed against the far wall, David's head cradled on the pad of her luscious thighs. Two, cute 38-24-34 entrées, dressed (nearly undressed) in bikinis and plastic German Shepard ears work large feather-fans over them. The 38-24-34s have been rented from Seduction, Inc. for the night to supplement the overloaded portable AC units Sam confiscated during the Dog Days of Darkness festivities. After all, this is not the Ritz — well, not yet, anyway.

Hans-Peter-David
recalls his anguish
in the human attic

It's August, the Dog Days, and faces are flushed, ties loosened. Across the room on the far side of the crowd, a facsimile of Hans-Beckert is already at the desk composing his final epistle, a summation for the jury. Peter Lorre glances over his shoulder. David has been silent, now, for several hours, pensive, aware that the end is at hand, the ordeal done, a bittersweet passage, a completion.

"Ends seldom speak of endings as well as they speak of beginnings," Sam says.

The shadows of *M* skulks onto the teevee. Hans-Peter-David bugs his eyes, looks about apprehensively.

"Ah know," he says, balefully, the small brush strokes of dopy dementia lighting his face.

The shadows and shapes merge, voices mingle. In the gloom of the attic he hides in a corner, alert, panicked, breathing heavily, listening to the door on the landing close and the key turn in the lock. Again he is trapped, as he has been, must be, and again begins his Sisyphus return (at least until the celluloid crumbles) to force the lock of the attic's main door with his knife. He swears in a low, hollow voice.

"Bloody hell!"

He removes a screw from the lock. When it does not come loose he rattles it furiously.

"Damn it!"

He examines the lock from beneath. The infamous W (M) shines on his haunches. He pushes the blade between the lock and the door, trying to pry it open. The blade snaps and he falls against the door, half standing, half leaning.

"Damn it!" he says and raises his arm prepared to throw the instrument away.

"Hell," he mutters, freezing abruptly, arm up and eyes rolled, playing again *The Recruits of Ingolstadt, Squaring the Circle, Mad Love, Crack Up, The Lost One, The Comedy of Terrors, Moerder unter Uns*.

Beyond the door the Everlasting Watchman passes, dressed in his dull black suit, pauses to reset a time-switch, and prepares to leave.

The camera holds a medium closeup of Peter-Hans-David trying to lever a nail out of one of the wooden attic props. The broken blade appears in closeup. The camera tracks back as he struggles to remove the nail. Finally, the nail comes out.

He squats behind the door, tapping on the nail, in extreme closeup, flattening one end of the nail with the handle of the knife.

"In the attic," a voice says. "He's in 7E. I hear him knocking."

"In the attic," another voice chants. "He's in the attic. He's in 7E."

By now, Hans-Peter has succeeded in bending the nail into a skeleton key. He puts the key into the keyhole and moves it around. He withdraws the nail. Crouched again, he hammers on the nail. On the floor, he studies the skeleton key.

"There," he says proudly.

He turns to the door, about to push the nail into the keyhole when the handle turns. He backs away, cowers against the wall, eyes bulging, staring at the door handle. He presses his ear to the door, then steps along the passage toward the camera.

Seized by one last fantasy, to be lost in the dark undiscovered, he turns back and switches off the light plunging the attic into darkness, with only a yellow slice of light at the bottom edge of the door. His shadow, his shape passes in front of the camera and moves out of sight.

A moment later the door opens and Henry Hunter appears in the frame as out of the woods in silhouette. Behind him the eyes of flashlights glare into the pitch black.

The camera cuts to Henry Hunter's prey cornered in a cage within a cage, weak with fear. A feeble glow from a skylight illuminates the terror forever sculpted on his wolf face.

"He's not here," a voice announces.

"He must be here," others proclaim.

Flashlight spots crisscross as they probe the slats and bars of the attic storage cages. Henry and his huntsmen trample forward, fall over furniture, banging into the timbers that support the roof.

Then, in a moment of panic, Hans-David-Peter leaps to his feet, spot-lit by a powerful force. His face twists with fear, his large canines glistening in the paltry grey light.

Backing away from the camera he stumbles into a grandfather clock.

"Here he is! Here he is! The bastard," a voice says.

"A rather ridiculous conversation," Sam says in a voice over. "They have him, as if that is definitive of a solution. Yes, they have him, but even that will not be enough.

"He is in custody — some kind of detention intended to demonstrate that as a callused freak he is weak and fearful. A coward. That he is the spirit, the anguish of their suspicion.

"But Hans-David is no coward. He's Sam's son and this by no means the saga of a timid soul. He will be resolute and ill-endure his trials, the ordeals and trepidations of doubt, of uncertainty, of non-existence.

"The Son is act, carved into time with a well forged blade. From here the debate will rage, the why — layer upon layer of speculative ash to settle and cover the question of doing, of having done, the small grimaces of the less resolute, with which the timid assure themselves that his condition is temporary, a mistaken manifestation which sometimes becomes act, and act is folly."

a bit of an epilogue

> Come listen to my tale of woe,
> it happened many years ago
> when cunts were wide and
> cocks hung low in hoary old Jerusalem.
> Hi, Ho Kafoozalum the harlot of Jerusalem;
> Hi, Ho Kafoozalum the daughter of the rabbi.

Psyaint David

Once on a time there lived a dame
who plied a trade of ancient fame
she was a girl of ill repute,
in fact she was a prostitute.

Kafoozalum was a wily witch
a filthy whore, a scurvy bitch
and she caused every dong to twitch
that dangled in Jerusalem.

(Traditional)

Our Lady as entrepreneur

Dining and dance, drink, wine spilled. Our Lady of the Fancy Figure is on the table doing the Can-Can, teasing the crowd's hardcore. Shouts are raised.

"Take it off. Take it off."

A fight breaks out. Tables are overturned, a broken wine bottle, flesh is split, blood spilt, someone falls and passes out.

Sam prods the dying man with a split hoof, turns the limp form over and rolls it into a corner.

"He'll be more comfortable," he says. "It's easier to die face down."

"You can't worry about the rest of the world," Our Lady of Irrevocable Ira tells him.

She's radiant, a peaches-and-cream glow, reveling in her celebrity, the enchanted haze of fame.

"Business has taught me that. I'm more aloft now. More matter of fact. I've found my own style.

"I'm more disciplined and directed in both my professional and personal life. That makes me feel feminine and safer about myself. I never go to sleep at night without knowing exactly what I'll wear the next day or even sometimes next week. I don't waste time browsing in my closet in the morning. I'm simply more comfortable when I know I am properly dressed, that my hair is in place and my accessories are coordinated."

Part of simplifying a complex life means knowing in advance what clothes will suit the day's activities. And Our Lady of the Cunning Caress knows exactly. For a tough day, an on-her-back-lunch-in-bed day, she wears a great shirt brightened up with a Missoni scarf. When the day is upscale by a chic business lunch after a hard morning of oral sex and self-manipulation, and mutilation, she wears a dress.

She has transformed thousands of years of lies and perfidies into propriety. She's cleaned up her act. And it's simply more than a change from old to new. Pants suits? Not on your life. No longer the steel-gray flannel suits of masculine muscle. Clumsy, too difficult to get out of. She prefers silken fabrics, fluid lines that fall softly over her mounds of pale flesh.

Instead of blazers, kilts and anoraks, she wears full dirndl skirts, big overblouses, loose, unlined shirt-jackets, frail sundresses, even flowers in her hair. Le coup d'oeil is bare, whether in a sexy strapless dress or sporty shorts. She dresses carefully, impeccably, watches her makeup.

"Why should I give up a low voice (she's been seeing a voice coach — affecting a Dietrich delivery) a soft smile and a pair of Hanes legs when that is part of me?"

"This year's fashions are just right for me. They're soft, feminine, womanly. The beige tones are warm, complementary to the skin — Scott Barrie calls it 'boneless'."

Clearly, if the word of the day is "legs," Our Lady of the Lascivious Loins is spreading the word, jambes en l'air, une jambe au-dessus. Of course, prurient interests are time consuming. Her schedule, a growing directory of clients (it's an 8:00 to 6:00 world of keeping sex interests alive and serviced) does not permit much time to shop.

"I scan the fashion magazines," she says. "I know what might be right for me, anything that designers whose lines I consistently admire, like Norell, Trigere, John Anthony, Calvin Klein. I then check to see where it is available."

"I love that classic Norell navy jersey, the one with the pussy cat bow. It makes me feel exceptional, especially if I'm going on for cocktails. But I wouldn't wear it to dinner. For me and my own sense of myself, it isn't enough of a statement for the evening."

Hans-Peter sips a glass of Demerara Rum, eyes glassy. A vestige of Kojak has slithered through the bars of the asylum, a shard, a phase, a phrase, to linger in a crevasse of the mind.

HPD sidles through the crowd to the teevee and wraps his arm around LoKo's electronic broken form. And for just a moment the hunted and the hunter stand arm in arm while Tracy tells of the difficulties of the case.

"Catching the wind is hard work," he says, modulating his bulb-nosed, square-jawed voice. "Not as dangerous as it used to be. Mostly hard work and chance. But I'm still gonna be sorry when it's over."

"It's never over," Hans advises. "You'll have another case. You have to keep the hunt going. Don't call in the dogs just yet."

The rum has gone to his head. He's unsteady, unsure of himself.

"It's difficult to see now."

"That's what I sometimes think," Telly says. "But in another way, it is over. Each case is a stepping stone, a record of who we are. The loyal opposition, advocate adversaries. Criminal investigations warp the soul. A search into the depths. You'd be amazed at what we find. It's a maddened mosaic."

"You've been at it too long," David tells him. "Too many dead ends. Eternal vigilance is hard on the nerves."

"You haven't had that trouble?"

"No. I mean, the cops and perps thing will go on forever. So do your part and get out. Nobody expects you to carry the ball all the time. That's my motto."

Loko is reluctant.

"I see what you mean. Icing your neighbor is natural. Yeah, wondering why is okay but it won't solve anything. Create an investigation — a forensic explanation of how, and pretend it will explain why."

The Lou would rather avoid the issue. It's become clear that he's treading water.

"You're right. I should enjoy the hunt."

"At least stop pretending. This isn't the real thing."

"No. See, that's when I get into trouble. If this isn't real . . .? That drunk female with the Variscite eyes? Is she real?"

"She's real," David says. "Real enough. I wouldn't be surprised if she instigated this whole thing."

The Loo hasn't considered the possibility. Women attacking women? Encouraging women to victimize women?

"Quid pro quo," Sam interjects. "And hard times. What do women get from violent males? Progeny — whether they want it or not. Genes passed along. They are immortalized — those who succumb, so to speak — in the biology of the species. And hard times. Stuck with off-springs to feed and house, male aggression, violent aggression becomes a tool, a force to harness and control."

They raise their glasses.

"The two go hand-in-hand," Sam adds. "Civilization is a fiction for prosperous times — rules to be observed so the weak can fill their coffers at the expense of the more aggressive and violent."

"And no guilt?" LoKoJakMan says.

"Do you?"

"No. I should have done more. Yeah. I could have done more."

"As a detective you haven't conned enough people? Haven't you beaten and maimed enough of the low-lives?"

"There could have been more bodies."

"What about the uniform?"

"But that's not me," LoKo says.

The accidental elements of the drama have worried him before — the inscrutability of the heart. Today he is only a shadow of his former self, his better two-thirds ranting and raving, babbling, pacing the hallowed halls at Kings.

"We are forever at the moment of realization, strung out, unable to go back to innocence or to purge ourselves with guilt and remorse. We are hung here, no way out," Sam says.

"Hamlet or Othello?" HD asks.

"Who's that?" Telly wants to know.

"You feel nothing about what you have done? I know it is show business, but you must feel something."

"I'll miss the excitement, the fun — raising hell and watching the no-names squirm," Telly reports.

He lights a cigarillo. The smoke caresses the air.

"But I'm new. I've learned new lines in my spare time. It's a reclusive, withdrawn, sullen part. I've been born again. I claim to be saved. It's the way to go. Some of it is easy — natural — I'm naturalized. The rest will require time and the patience to develop a believable self-hatred, to identify with exiles, the landless, the homeless, the misbegotten, etc., etc."

Then they are silent, pensive, wistful, overcome with the inexplicable camaraderie of melancholy, a longing for the old days of hunt and capture or kill.

"No one expects the species to go on forever," Sam reminds them. "We know that now. But consciousness will always be part of the universe, or some universe. And the imprint of the act will remain in some conscious-ness somewhere. That's immortality. Once an act has been committed, it is forever marked in consciousness always to be found and resurrected. It will always be there, somewhere. If not here with us, then with someone else, some other time in another place."

The images fade and, as if to placate nostalgia, to explicate their wonder-ings, the teevee takes up the conversation with a rerun of *M.*

more from Fritz and Thea

The burlesque pushes into the gloom of an abandoned workshop-court-room inside a factory. A staircase stands to the right. Inarticulate cries are heard in the distance, gradually drawing near. Two men come down the steps and disappear off camera.

Hans-Peter-David: *What do you want with me? Let me go . . . let me go!*

Man: *Go on . . . keep moving . . . go on.*

The two appear out of nowhere, the man pushing Hans up a short stairway on the far side of the room. He struggles furiously, although his jacket has been pulled over his head. At the top of the stairs a third man joins them.

H-P-D: *I've done nothing to you . . . Let me go you pig!*

At the top of the stairs an iron door opens and a foot appears.
H-P-D: *Let me go!*

Two men push him through the door and down the steps.

Psyaint David

H-P-D: *Bastards!*

He falls to the bottom of the stairs while the men watch from the doorway.

H-P-D: *Bunch of bastards!*

One of the men closes the door. He pulls off his coat.

H-P-D: *What do you want with me? Bastards. What do you want?*

He turns to stare into the depths of the room where assorted members of the SoSaMy Inc. are gathered, watching him. They are silent, motionless. At a large table in front of the crowd Father Czarmine Pastel is seated on a small wooden box, prepared to adjudicate the dispute. Zips in trench coats and hats are on either side of him.

H-P-D: *I want out. Help! Let me go.*

He retreats to the steps and Pastel waves his hand in the air, the stands.

Pastel: *You will not get out of here.*

H-P-D: *But gentlemen . . ..*

David's hair falls over his face, hides his eyes. He reconsiders and approaches the table, grinning his Joker grin.

H-P-D: *I don't know what you can want with me. You've made a mistake. I'm sure we can make a deal. Please.*

The crowd behind Pastel stirs, then parts as the King's Loyal Huntsman, Henry, strides out and lays his hand on H-P-D's shoulder. H-P-D cringes under the assault.

Henry Hunter: *There is no mistake.*

H-P-D: *What do you mean?*

Henry holds up a small red cap.

HH: *Do you recognize this?*

He holds up a photo of Christine Freund.

HH: *How about this?*

H-P-D: *I don't know her. I've never seen her.*

HH: *Oh, yes. That's right. Young women killed by a stranger. You didn't know her.*

Father Pastel opens a book on the table and removes several photos.

Pastel: *What about his one? And this one?*

H-P-D: *You have no right to treat me this way.*

Fists wave from the crowd. Voices are raised

Voices: *You don't have any rights. Kill him! Kill him!*

Pastel: *Quiet! Quiet!*

Voices: *Kill him! Kill him!*

Pastel: *Shut up!*

He stands and leans over the table, staring intently at Hans-Peter-David as if he might have an appreciation for the travail of a serial killer.

Pastel: *You'll get your rights. You will even get a lawyer. Everything will be done according to the rule of law, as it should be.*

H-P-D: *I don't need a lawyer. Who is accusing me? You?*

A large man in a rumpled suit which bears the wear of age, the creases of someone having slept in it (maybe on the church steps with a bottle of wine), steps forward and stands beside Henry Hunter.
Large Man: *Your career is at stake — a substantial segment of the human race. If I were you, sir, I'd keep quiet. Take the Fifth. Maybe the Eighth and the Fourteenth too.*

H-P-D: Who are you?

Large Man: *I have the dubious honor of being your defense counsel. It is my job to keep them from pirating your representation — from changing you into a grotesque logo* (Logos is a statement, sentence or argument to convince or persuade a viewer by employing reason or logic) *to be auctioned off to the highest bidder.*

Pastel raises his head from a whispered but animated conversation with the man on his right.

Psyaint David

Pastel: *We want you off the market. Do you understand? Nothing more serious than that. We have our own Son of Sam to sell. You might say we are engaged in the first principle of war and good business — elimination of the opposition.*

H-P-D: *But if you kill me it will be murder.*

Derisive laughter echoes through the room. The lawyer sighs and shrugs his shoulders.

H-P-D: *I demand that you hand me over to the police.*

The Reverend Father breathes deeply. Clearly his patience is being tried.

Pastel: *That would suit you. Then you could be put on ice, preserved in an institution. Eventually, your picture hung on the wall as a tribute a famous occupant/patient/noble personage. Maybe you could escape or maybe Our Lady could work a deal or you could get a pardon. Then where would we be?*
    Okay. Okay.

He waves his hand, rejecting the idea. Then he motions to the crowd and Garfield steps out and approaches H-P-D.

Pastel: *Here's the police. The Police Commissioner Michael "Soft Fin" Garfield.*

Garfield approaches H-P-D and stands over him shaking his head.

Garfield: *How can I help you?*

H-D-P's eyes roll wildly. Now he is doomed. He sags to his knees, covers his face with his hands.

H-P-D: *What do you know about it? What are you saying? If it comes to that, who are you? What right have you to speak? Who are you? All of you? Criminals! Perhaps you're even proud of yourselves? Are you proud of being able to break safes, to climb into buildings or cheat at cards, to take bribes? Things you could just as well not do? Would you need to do that if you had a proper trade or if you worked? If you weren't a bunch of lazy bastards?*

He clutches his chest.

H-P-D: *I can't help myself. I haven't any control over this thing inside me — the fire, the voices, the torment! Always, always, there's a force inside me.*

It's there all the time, driving me out to wander the streets following me, silently, but I can feel it there. It's me, pursuing myself, because . . ..
Pastel: *You mean you have to kill? I never thought of that.*

H-P-D: *I want to escape . . . to escape from myself. But*
    I can't.
    I can't escape.
    I have to obey.
    I have to run the streets, the endless streets.
    I am pursued by ghosts. Haunted by the faces of the dead. They never leave me. They are always there. Except when
    I do it, when
    I . . .. Then
    I can't remember anything, and afterwards
    I read the newspaper, watch the news on teevee,
    I see Kojak hunting for me and
    I ask, "Did
    I do that?"
    I can't remember. But who believes me? Who knows how
    I feel? How
    I am forced to act."

Czarmine turns to Henry Hunter, a serious twist of doubt on his face.

Pastel: *Have you ever come across a dement like this? Have you ever heard of such a thing? He does not want anyone to remember what he did. .*

HH: *A compulsive killer? That might be bad for business. We'll need some control over him, otherwise. . ..*

Pastel: *No, that won't work. This is big money. Money so big that proper management of your name is nearly a civic, patriotic duty. You, my friend, have been careless — reckless — totally unorganized, irresponsible. We'll have to clean this up, eliminate the image. How many illustrations of the specter are on the street now?*

Henry shrugs.

HH: *Officially? Maybe a dozen. Maybe two dozen.*

Voices: *Let the lawyer speak.*

Large Man: *Thank you.*

The lawyer stands and rubs his hands together.

Psyaint David

Large Man: *Father Pastel? You are an honest man. But what is your image? How many people have you killed? Aren't some of your best friends in the PD? This man is sick. He presents a sick society. You can't help but make money off him. Keep him alive.*

A roar goes up from the crowd.

Voices: *Ridiculous! Kill him! Kill him!*

eyeless in Gaza
   Sam(Son) says, yes,
eyeless in Gaza

But what now? Will Delilah clip Samson's hair? And what kind of shears will she use? Accusation, recrimination among the Philistines? Three hundred flaming foxes? A blue haze hangs over the proceedings. Sam's shifts into the shadows, among the guests, snaps off the teevee, whispers causally to David who seems lost in meditation.

"You are very old," Sam says, smiling, his gums black and rotted, his broken, yellow teeth dull in the dim light. "The pennants of justice ride a light breeze in the final fortune of your bargain. You move as old man moves. Pause now to think, to wait the last finger of fate to make you well. These are the praises they sing, for you have won. Night comes cheering your remains."

"There's more," David says, "thoughts, ideas driven like nails into my head."

"We have seen in vivid, living color," Sam says, "a reign of terror, madness, dementia scraped together, manufactured from shards of sanity. And even so, the curtain is about to fall, our job this time, our venture done, our fortune, our legacy we remand to contemplation, to the scribes, give leave to history to retell and again tell this tale.

"Truly we live in another time, another world where masses are moved by what they least expect — when folly speaks for intelligence and virtue is stupidity. Mankind is plagued with a Jungian collective of terminal despair — global warming and/nuclear war will destroy the species, possibly the planet. Still everyone gains from the ordeal, given short shrift — as gain they must — the dead, the maimed, even those aggrieved have come to stare over the footlights into the abyss and their lines laded with import — as if words might save the day — the audience chanting, 'Bravissimo! Bravissimo!' squirming beneath the pleasant sting of the sudden darts penetrating their visions."

"Of course he's right," Our Lady of the Variegated Visions says.

She's in an ebullient mood — nibbling a morsel of Fourme d'Ambert, delicately waving her Black Forest, Whisper light cigarette holder with a

Gold Tip Ariston as if it was a maestro's baton. She is dressed in smoke rings, a dreamy ballet of her well-endowed semblances dancing through the grey veils.

"We live with this, bent beneath the weight — scared by the stigma. You can name it. Distress, despair, the dispossessed, aliens, exiles, cut free to wander . . .," she smiles an alluring smile.

"Eyeless in Gaza," Sam says. "We have done more to nurture The City than Lindsay or Beame ever did. We are The City," he tells Our Lady.

He steps forward. The lights dim. A crimson spot shines on him from the right.

"But it is time," Sam says, "to make a satisfactory ending, a tidy closing to this farce. Already they have the area cordoned off, plainclothesmen hovering in the shadows up and down the block on both sides of the street. A half-dozen are stationed on the roof, assassin's eyes fixed on the rear fire-escape, as if they expect he might not go willingly or that the drama is not yet ended. How cautious they are. Small boys about to discover a secret passage, the Open Sesame that will lead them to where they began."

Opposite the seven story mountain, a crowd gathers, to watch, to witness. Up and down the street vendors appear with beer and hotdogs, Italian sweet sausages. A granita peddler pushes a cart of shaved ice and an organ grinder, his old and nearly hairless Merry Melodies' monkey on a characteristic chain, cranks out a familiar tune.

Of course, the usual names are there — curiosity seekers, those with a vested interest in the pageant. Admission is free, if the travail is not.

Olivia Brockmeyer, the fat lady of yore, settles in a yard across the street with her two-headed pet dog Orthrus Demikhov II.

Meta Canevari shows up with her son Gus.

Oswald Cobblepot of 7410 Ridge Blvd in Brooklyn, out on bail, slinks along the walk, umbrella in hand, cadging food. He's still hungry.

Douglass Dogger is there, as is Paula Verlinda.

Martha Farnsworth, an ugly red scar marking her left cheek and eye, is snapping pictures. She has a new camera and three rolls of film and has taken up police-brutality photography.

Agnes Grossman of the See Nothing Amiss Group, as usual, has decided not to look, looking at the great space between Venus and Mars. Myopically, she sees nothing.

Harvey Leer, on a meet-and-greet search-and-destroy mission, always alert for threats, prowls the neighborhood, mingling with the crowd. He heard Jimmy Coonan would be here. He hopes Jimmy Coonan will be here.

Sally Hollis is caught at the end of the block showing off her new T-shirt.

Adam Maluski hawks apples out of a basket. Two dollars for red, one for yellow. Fifty cents for green.

Anna Marcella mumbles obscenities about police brutality and hopes there will be some today — so her difficulty in getting here will not have been in vain.

Doris Masi holds up a photo of her daughter for the cameras. She has had the picture enlarged and mounted in an antique ornate gilt gold frame — for $214.21 — all the money she had on hand. And though the frame is garishly handsome, the picture has lost definition and color and appears strangely ghost-like.

Doris props the picture against a tree between small votive candles to encourage prayer and donations. She has begun a campaign for sainthood for her daughter and is searching for witnesses to confirm that her daughter (who was not very religious) did in fact perform at least two miracles. Doris is still mourning.

Helen McCarter wanders through the crowd, ill-kempt, seeking solace. She has recovered (physically) from her encounter with Sam, but may be psychologically scarred for life by the realization that Sam actually exists.

Sally Messenek has brought her kids along, as part of their citizenship training. She made them leave the Silly Putty in the car and the youngest is crying.

John Morohan displays a new "top of the line" cut-rate plastic flag he got from the Betsy Ross Foundation. The flag combines strength with additional richness and color, and is a favorite of flag users nationwide who need the extra durability that can be gained by using plastic.

"This is what makes America great," John says.

Stephanie Nuecie hides behind a large oak, her face still twisted with fear.

Alberto Rios, out of Elmira on parole, sits under a Linden tree reading his book on safe cracking, while waiting for the show to begin. Several months earlier, trying to blow a safe, he lost three fingers to an ill-timed detonation, and is having difficulty turning the pages. No doubt George Ramirez would be with him (they have been buddies since the first grade) but George was stabbed to death in a prison gang fight at Elmira.

Marcus Rubin's fear has the best of him. He does not agree with art for art's sake but came out to watch the shoot anyway. He, too, cowers behind a tree.

Vincent Semonelli keeps his eternal vigil under a burley, leafy oak. He's carrying a crowbar and an icepick.

Claude Sitton works the crowd, looking for loaded pockets to pick, hoping to get another handout from Sam.

Warren Valensky saunters down Pine Street astride his mule. He was told that there was a church at the end of Pine Street.

Heather "Bad Weather" Whitman, still dressed for the cold, is trying to find a ticket vendor (a scalper will do). She wants to buy a ticket, says she feels bad for not paying, even if admission is free.

They're all there, hoping to get a glimpse of the action, maybe even an autograph, watching, waiting as the police prepare for the pinch.

Hans-David at center stage

When the time is right, two plainclothesmen enter stage right from a service van parked behind the Galaxie, bumper to bumper. They walk away swiftly, to wait — the scene set for Hans-Peter's entrance. This is to be his grand and glorious finale, bubbling with forensic guesswork, the anomalies of legal fictions and political double-dealing.

On cue, the cameras roll — Marcelo assigned six units for the shoot.

Hans-Peter-David exits the Seven Story Mountain as a shadow, a shade, as he always does, gazing pensively up the street, as he has many times before, to Alsea Alburton's house. Alsea is out on parole and is seated on the porch watching the crowd, the ceremony. She waves over the heads of two plainclothes detectives, who linger, chatting quietly, unobtrusively with the crowd in the black beneath a large elm tree. He wonders why the crowd has gathered. What's the occasion, what's amiss?

When the POs see him they freeze, wordless, prepared (if he should run into the crowd), to leap, to give eternal chase.

A quick smile shines in the dull lamp glow on his pudgy boyish face — the glimmer of madness of someone too long kept in this place — the face of Faust going to his end believing he will see, at last, the world as he wishes it to be.

and so

Cautiously the police approach the car — one to the right and the rear, crouched, moving in the shadows near the van, carrying Kojak Style, another creeping up on the driver's side.

"Mr. Berkowitz?"

"You've got me," David says, smiling. "Hi. I'm the Son of Sam."

"Keep your hands in the air."

David, hands in the air, waves apprehensively to the crowd as if unsure of what he should do, how they might react. He feels that he has played his part well. What else could he have done?

So on a dog-day fit for broiling a Deacon on a spit, the police apprehend the Psyaint. The misanthrope is pushed against the white Galaxie, hand-cuffed and read his Miranda's with no police brutality. Anna Marcella is pissed.

So this is it. The magnum opus, to further polish the philosopher's stone. The crowd is transfixed, faces on a silent screen, freeze frame, bas-relief, electronic carvings.

The arresting officers are relieved. They breathe deeply, congratulate themselves. They, too, played their parts well. There are regrets that Kojak was not there. That's a shame. They like him. It would have been nice to have him in on the collar.

Psyaint David

After the arrest, others rush in, daresay, swarm in, to lay claim to the fame of their proximity to the action and get their picture in *The Times,* the *Post,* the *Daily News.* The crowd mills about.

Veronica Lueken is praying for Marcus Christ, as is Rev. Stanislaus Koral — four Our Fathers and six Hail Marys, and do this in . . .," etc. She is enumerating for Marcus the benefits of divine revelation and the true resurrection.

"We've seen history made," Evaline Kukulinski says. "Yes, we have."

And yet, in the now calm of Pine Street there's the sense that nothing has been undone or solved. Somewhat bored with the show, others shrug and drift away, move off to wait for another day, another entertainment.

Marcia Gonzales throws her sign

> 10,000 DECENT
> PEOPLE LIVE HERE.
> BUZZ OFF FILTH.

on the lawn at 32 Pine Street. She's tired of carrying it, and no one read the thing anyway.

Carmine Ramirez still has a basket of red raw eggs. She's looking for someone to drop them on, or throw them at or give them to.

"What's the statement in all of this?" Reinia Glotto asks.

"Nothing, I'd say," Sam says.

"Faust, too, was eyeless."

"Yes, but not quite."

"Ah ha. So we come to it. A claim for inner vision."

"I would have thought so."

"What Faust sought and couldn't have, was all he received.

"Only then."

"Salvation is failure. But what was his mistake?"

"And ours?"

"Believing this is not real."

"We'll have to change the name and number of this place."

Neil Morrow of 7221 Barker Avenue in Queens lounges on the grass next to the Fat Lady fingering the soft, melodious clarinet tristesse of Dmitri Capyrin's *Chanson d'autumne.*

> Et je m'en vais
> Au vent mauvais
> Qui m'emporte
> Deçà, delà,
> Pareil à la
> Feuille morte

Of course, The Universe gnomes are grumpy. The schedule did not go according to Hoyle — or anyone else for that matter. They will have to improvise, make do with what they have — but they are good at that.

Aigilas, waving a spec-script for new series, calls to "Wrap it up. That's the story — good or bad, for what it's worth."

He's ready to light up. Standing in front of a stone wall with a life-sized painting of Federico Felony, he asks a woman in the crowd if she has a Cleopatra. He'd like a Cleopatra.

"No luck," she says. "All I got is OPs."

Mathias nods, extracts a flask of Jura Prophecy (heavily peated with fresh cinnamon and spicy sea spray) from his pocket and takes a swill.

Kesil squints into the camera eyepiece, startled, trying to focus on the real world. He's certain he's got enough footage to do the fifth show. It's the environment that counts. Who gets killed or arrested doesn't matter. It's always the same.

He says "You know, I've been thinking . . .."

Upstairs in 7E, Juan is stoned, talking to the corpse Sam rolled into the corner. He's sure they met one night several years ago at The Anvil, under the most sensual circumstances. He's mumbling again.

"Such were the birds Herculean art subdued, and with loud tumults to the skies pursued; and such the Harpies the winged brothers chased from trembling Phineus' illusive feast. The heavens were startled at their clamorous flight, and backward seemed to roll in wild affright (Petronius).

"Yes," he says. "Yes."

But the sun is setting over the Palisades, a massive fade out.

When the police depart with their captive the remains of the crowd watch while film crews load their equipment. It has been a good show, a pleasant afternoon — even if there was no shootout.

The party is over, the apartment empty, save the potato chip bags, Coke cans, liquor bottles, newspaper clippings — yellowed reviews of shootings, police composites, and timelines for the hunt.

The Dog Days of '77 dissolve, draw down the curtain, a veil to shroud the actors, encase the drama. In the Hall of the Mountain King the all-star cast, the gnomes, the Duck, the Lieutenant, Garfield and the Mayor, Czarmine and E.Erie™ assemble in the Cyclopes' mind of the world — the narrow-channeled vision of the street activity below. They step forward in front of the curtain to bow — then, one by one, they too fade.

Sam's peruses the latest copy of *The Sun* sporting a new composite police sketch of the Son of Sam and the bold headline:

THIS IS THE NEW SON OF SAM

But it is time to move on. Sam extricates himself from the print, lifts unobtrusively into The City in the grey day's cloudcover over Broadway,

Psyaint David

Hell's Kitchen, to settle on the East River, making his way back to the *Goddam,* exciting a small waterspout, a spray of sludge and debris.

From the door of the Captain's cabin the scythe-striker on the bell, swung by a skeletal hooded keeper, rings eight bells ending the First Watch. The echo drops onto the infected water, crawling portentously, a small toxic cloud, toward shore to greet Sam.

Of course the gnomes are waiting for him in the Captain's cabin.

"Do you know, we're headed to the middle-ages?" Lamiae says. "People just sit and watch — somebody else provides the program. All they do is point and grunt, and go back to the last picture. Masturbation. It may be satisfying and fun, but you're not getting much done."

Eventually, to stave off the fits, Kesil continues to shun all discourse, to recuse conversation with himself, as well as with others. So in the end he doesn't have much to say. He accepts Juan's words and goes back to masticating a Marshmallow Peep (chick) from Just Born, Inc., while taking inventory of the fat, salt, and caffeine contents of his Orange Salesman Sample Case.

"Did you see the size of the rats when we came aboard? The rats are getting fat," Aigilas says. "Life's too easy. I mean, after all, this is the home of the trinity. I know they're good at fucking. That's why there's so many of them. But they need to feed themselves. So cross yourself."

"Otherwise," Teivel says, "a hundred years from now no one will remember us or even know we were here."

With everyone aboard, and Sam at the helm, the *Goddam* slips its moorings and slides into a brown fog bank. It, too, fades from view.

Of course, all has not vanished.

Our Lady of Leviathan Luxuria is peevish. At the moment she is the talk of the walk, but is also prepared to move on. She has shrouded her sensuous manifestations in a beige zippered jumpsuit and a green rayon wrap skirt and jersey with a neck scarf. Her shoes echo the 1940s — high-heeled lower-platform mules with a single leather strap over the ball of the foot. To add an intimation of the clandestine, she offers a redolence of Opium by Jean Amic and Jean-Louis Sieuzac of Roure. It is an oriental-spicy. The perfume is a mixture of fruit and spices with plum, mandarin orange.

She fingers the scrap of a clipping from an old killing, "Latest News . . .." Prophetically she hands Richard the wig stolen from the Wasp, then cradles his hand in hers.

The Son of Sam logo (designed by Our Lady of the Lego) flashes on the screen, then steadies with a pliant, sensual voice over.

(FX The elusive melody of Grieg's *Peer Gynt* caresses the air).

"Just think," she tells the Psyaint, "The night has only begun. And we're going digital. Put on your wig, Mr. Falco, we have a lot of spacetime to kill."